Also by John M. McNamara

A LIFE WITHOUT GRACE

HUNTER'S WAR, A NOVELLA, AND SELECTED SHORT STORIES

This is a work of fiction. Names, characters, and incidents either are the product of the author's imagination or are used fictitiously, and any resemblance to actual persons, living or dead, or events is entirely coincidental.

Copyright 2012 John M. McNamara
All rights reserved

ISBN-13: 978-1475079005
ISBN-10: 1475079001

Without limiting the rights of the author under copyright reserved above, no part of this publication may be reproduced, stored in or introduced into a retrieval system, or transmitted, in any form or by any means (electronic, mechanical, photocopying, recording or otherwise), without the prior written permission of the copyright owner.

The scanning, uploading, and distribution of this book via the Internet or via any other means without the written permission of the author is illegal and punishable by law.
Your support of the author's rights is appreciated.

All Photos Copyright 2012 Robin S. Tryloff
All rights reserved.

Michael —
Another book for you to read. Miss you!

[signature]
10-12-2012

A FINAL REFLECTION

For Robin

Prologue

To say that Tallie doesn't like the idea redefines understatement. When I told her of my plans, she argued, she cursed, she yelled, she wept, and she accused.

She accused me of excessive pride, of fleeing before my deterioration becomes pronounced, before my vigor diminishes and betrays the image of vitality I have cultivated.

Accused me of misdirected compassion, of sparing her the burden of caring for me as my disease progresses.

Accused me of selfishness, of depriving her of sharing with me those final moments, as though the experience was a prize I reserved solely for myself.

The issues, I explained during a days-long conversation, involved trust and timing. Stymied by my intransigence, she relented… but with conditions. I accepted each of her stipulations because I love her, which I assumed to her would have been obvious. There's a journey I need to start shortly and Tallie needs to trust that what I'm doing is necessary.

My diagnosis: a terminal illness. My prognosis: six to nine months, perhaps a year if extraordinary measures are applied toward the end.

My doctor, Janine, assures me that during the first month, I shouldn't notice many physical changes beyond the dull pain in my gut and back that sent me to her in the first place...perhaps a tendency to fatigue more quickly than usual, a possible loss of appetite and some jaundice. Her professional concerns focus more on my emotional stability, so she prescribed medication to ward off anxiety and depression. I've been taking it since a second opinion confirmed her diagnosis last week. I also have an ample supply of painkillers should they prove necessary.

The journey...so it begins; or, as a friend of mine once counseled...the journey continues.

Day One

This morning, after emerging from the garage in our building's basement, I turned onto Madison, heading west, away from the city. A glance in the rearview revealed Tallie standing in the street near the curb, both hands crossed over her heart. She was barefoot, in jeans and a black, long-sleeved t-shirt. At the stop sign by the corner I lifted my camera from the passenger seat, aimed it at the rearview mirror, and snapped a photo. After I took the photo of Tallie, I turned on my iPod and played the first of thirty playlists I created for this trip, one for each day. The Eagles' "Ol' '55" suffused me with calm resolution. I'm propped up in bed studying that photo now. Tallie, in the mirrored glass stands in sharp focus. Everything else is blurred. It's an analytical photo and when she sees it, she'll appreciate both its composition and its symbolism.

I've allotted myself thirty days for this journey, but don't expect a travelogue…I'm not cataloguing any passing scenery or tracking the number of miles logged. Every journey involves self-discovery, and mine will certainly involve elements of that, but the point of this exploration lies in others. I have mapped out a trek through the western U.S. to visit seven people who are or have been important to me at some point in my life. A coin flip determined the western states as opposed to those states east of Chicago, where we live. I determined the seven individuals less by chance.

They include friends, family, old lovers…and a stranger.

Once she had accepted the inevitability of my trip, Tallie helped me pack, selecting my clothing…sweaters, pants, and shirts…appropriate for the weather she anticipated I would encounter. She double-checked the telephone numbers and email addresses in both my cell phone and on my laptop. One of the conditions she specified: contact her at least once each day. Tallie may have relented about this trip, but that doesn't mean her fear of my leaving is any less strident. We have been married for more than thirty-five years, together exclusively for three years beyond that. Both faithful that entire time. More deeply devoted to one another and more passionately in love now than the year before, also true for the year before that. The two of us have grown…independently and together…with a harmony that others envy. I understand how our history might frighten her…at times it both amazes and frightens me, too. Our connection seems too flawless, so she can be forgiven for expecting the arcing pendulum to slice through that perfection, to counter our mass of good fortune with unbelievable sorrow. If she needs a bogeyman, isn't that the role of my diseased pancreas? Is this illness the consequence of decades of unwarranted good luck? Not likely. I don't believe in karma; I'm inclined to place my faith in chaos.

I checked into a motel on the outskirts of Minneapolis that offers free Wi-Fi and a continental breakfast with fresh waffles. The TV is on but I've muted the sound. It was dark and raining when I parked the Saab. I considered telephoning Tallie but elected to send her an email letting her know I had arrived safely. She would have preferred a call, but an impulse convinced me to establish a fragment of separation on this first night. My computer lays cradled in my lap as I begin the first entry in this, what…journal? Already I fear what to say. How much is too much? What is too little? How much background is enough to understand the indulgence I'm trying to satisfy? Who is my audience?

I'm sixty-four years old. My parents are both dead. I have no children with Tallie. That's the outline, as ordinary as so many others. The extraordinary, as in so many others as well, is quantified day-by-day in moments captured by memory. Some of those moments will dictate how I spend the next twenty-nine days, as the people I visit have been actors in many of the remembered scenes. I'm not so different from millions of other people, but like each individual, I am unique. And, of course, I am dying, which scares me. How people neutralize fear varies with their character. It's not in my character to accept this death sentence easily, but I don't tilt at windmills, either. On at least one emotional level, I have accepted that I am going to die. I simply need a bit more preparation. Hence the trip. Securing a leave of absence from my firm was not difficult…my name's on the letterhead. I laugh when I reflect on how fortunate I've been throughout my life. Dying may very well be the only hardship I ever face. Not many people, in my experience, can claim that.

The choice of who to see on this trip was mine, something I didn't share with Tallie. No point in compounding her anger over my trip by layering decision on top of decision like bricks in a wall. Keeping her in the dark led to another condition: when I return home I owe Tallie a debriefing. She'll get a complete report, perhaps in the form of this journal. On that I am ambivalent at the moment.

Tomorrow I'm having breakfast with Ellen Solomon…a former college lover…whom I haven't seen in more than twelve years. When we met in the early seventies, she was a dark-haired and dark-eyed girl, with an angular face that emphasized her edgy demeanor. She expressed inflexible opinions with a passionate personality. That passion carried over into the bedroom. I caught Ellen during the height of her rebellion against everything her middle-class parents cherished. For a short time we shared an off-campus apartment where we regularly fucked with the devotion of athletes in training.

Ellen joked about being the only Jewish child in North Dakota. Her parents farmed a small acreage outside of Hague, near the South Dakota border. As the valedictorian of her high school class, she garnered a scholarship to the University of Iowa, where she studied literature and film criticism, and practiced a highly-personalized variety of revolution designed to thwart the intrusion of any influence of her mother's values on her own. She purified her wit and insightfulness, later earned a master's degree in journalism from the University of Missouri, and moved to Minneapolis to work as a film and theatre critic. She married and later divorced. I saw her at the Chicago Film Festival, where she moderated a panel contrasting postwar films from World War II through the first Gulf War.

She retired from the Minneapolis *Star-Tribune* a year ago and now writes a blog about film, politics and women's issues. Ellen remains one of the most intelligent people I've ever met… astute, funny, acerbic and nuanced. We've corresponded over the years… she more than I…writing seemed to come easily to her. Watching Ellen channel her energy into articles, and now her blog, has been a pleasure. For the past twenty years we've mostly maintained an email relationship: lengthy periods of silence periodically shattered by a few days of frenzied volleying, as we dissected a current event. Ellen never filtered these discussions through our shared past…her vision always seemed focused on the horizon.

Tallie knows about Ellen….she and I long ago disclosed our romantic and sexual histories, enumerating the various partners. So Tallie knows of Ellen's existence, but not the extent to which I have continued the relationship. There's no infidelity, but Tallie's jealousy would never allow her to see my correspondence with Ellen as friendship, only as a threat. No reassurance could ever convince her otherwise, she's that insecure. So I have kept Ellen a secret.

I suppose I've revealed the first crack in the veneer of our perfection, haven't I?

Tallie and I met at a rooftop party weeks after I passed the bar exam. She lived across the hall from the woman who threw the party. Alison worked in my office, a serial monogamist with devastating taste in men, favoring assholes with flashy disguises to plainer men of substance. When Alison's lovers inevitably tired of her, Tallie comforted her neighbor with tissues, chocolate, a pint of ice cream, and a sympathetic shoulder, while Alison sniffled her way through another break-up.

That first night I spotted Tallie, her blond hair, always wild and unkempt, seemed aflame. She had a symmetrically round face, a delicate chin, and above a petite, but slightly crooked nose she wore granny glasses that magnified glacial blue eyes. She was stunning in faded corduroy pants, a cotton turtleneck and scuffed leather boots. The imperfection of her nose, that tiny bend of the bridge, tempered her beauty and made her seem approachable. She was drinking red wine, so I boosted an open bottle of Merlot from the serving table and crossed the deck to refill her glass. I've never been shy, but as I chatted with Tallie that night I felt my mind seizing up from time to time; I worried I would say something stupid enough to allow her to ignore or dismiss me and bestow her attention on someone else. Certain people in life you meet and the encounter seems less a meeting than a reunion, so immediately comfortable are you with one another. I sensed Tallie and me embodying such serenity that night.

I recall morsels of our conversation that night…we each regarded our jobs as good entry-level springboards; we agreed the view of the city from the rooftop deck was disappointing; and the fate of the Cubs was just that…their fate…but what impressed me as most extraordinary was how her eyes deepened to indigo as the sun set, how the candlelight teased her smile in the dark, and how the wine warmed us both when an evening chill rode the breeze. Sex was prominent in my imagination that night. I had already envisioned the contours of Tallie's body, the smoothness of her skin and the softness of her lips. Honestly, the physical attraction had been immediate and I fantasized about the two of us sleeping together from the first minute of our conversation. Spoiler alert: we didn't have sex that night, but we embraced one another's company throughout the rest of the party.

Years later, on an anniversary, each of us recounted for the other our impressions from that first night. Nostalgic honesty is required entertainment for a couple. Tallie had understood that sex constantly occupied men's consciousness, but years after the fact, I had stunned her by recounting the specifics of assessing the kind of fine fuck I thought she'd be. Yes, she had been attracted to me as well and had entertained the possibility of intimacy. But intimacy, she had explained, outshined the physical; it occasioned an emotional bond. Women and men, she had chuckled, approached these affairs from divergent positions, at which point I had made a coarse joke about positions. Tallie had rewarded me with an open palm slap to my ass. Did I mention we were in bed at the time?

We spent a lot of time having sex in our early years together, craving the sensation of skin next to skin, clasping one another so tightly, merging as closely to one being as we physically and emotionally dared. We exploited fucking as a language and relied on spontaneity to schedule it…anywhere and everywhere. Besides our apartments: after hours in our offices, an alley behind a bar in the Gold Coast, a parking garage in Old Town, along the lake shore bike path. The threat of discovery in public places intimidated us but never prevented us. Sex with Tallie is the most intense connection I've ever attained with another person. I remember the Sunday morning of my epiphany during our first summer together, a few weeks after that rooftop party, weeknights of slippery pleasure and weekends of sluggish tenderness. Tallie lay beneath me, her legs roped around my ass, as I slowly slid in and out of her. I propped myself on my elbows, gripped her face with both hands and searched her eyes…craving to recognize in her a sign that she reciprocated what I felt, that we were intended to be with one another. I distrust the impulse of fate but fixed on a romantic ideal: one woman would see me as no other would ever be able to see me. Had I found her? Was Tallie that woman? When I came I locked on her eyes…she stared at me and for an instant, an immeasurable pulse beat, they dilated and the arctic blue sparked with brilliant light. I know it was probably a projection, but that beam forged a link between us. Then her eyes softened, they visibly calmed as her face melted from a fierce expression into a smile more benevolent than anything I've ever seen. I identified with that moment more than in any previous moment in my life. It eclipsed romanticism and I knew it would devastate me if Tallie hadn't felt the same. I'm a far more cynical man now than when I was twenty-five, but I am and have always been a romantic. I needed Tallie or what Tallie represented…a matching puzzle piece, my complement…so that's what she became. If you strive for an ideal, should you be surprised when you find it? My God, that does sound cynical.

Tallie and I were the last people to leave the rooftop that night. I walked her downstairs where the party continued in Alison's apartment, but Tallie said she was tired, so we hugged and said good night at her door. I told her I wanted to see her again. She said she would like that. And history tells the rest of the story.

Driving today was more easygoing than I had expected. I wasn't certain how I'd react to sitting in the car for hours. I'm a bit sore; there's a stinging throb in my lower back, but Janine warned that could be a side effect of the cancer. I considered taking one of her pain killers, then decided against it. I worry about developing a reliance on them too quickly, not just on this trip, but in what time I have left. I don't know what I expected, but the moments when I dwell on the gravity of this disease and its death sentence erupt like ambushes; gooseflesh prickles along my skin and a chilly shiver surges from the base of my spine straight to my head. What an old-fashioned rush it is. I remember a sergeant in my platoon in the Marines, a veteran of both Korea and Vietnam, swearing that death was the ultimate rush. I suppose I'm primed to confirm that assertion.

Am I frightened? How could I not be scared. I'm months from death, and one thing I learned in Vietnam was you cannot defeat fear, but you can contain it, can prevent it from containing you. If you ask me have I accepted death…I don't know. I won't deny it, but the lack of denial doesn't constitute acceptance. This trip is evidence of at least partial acceptance.

I've always enjoyed my analytical mind.

I can be emotional but rarely sentimental.

Tallie and I have traveled. We've created some amazing adventures as well as humble moments. We've acknowledged our regrets and we've celebrated our triumphs.

I'm tired and I think it's causing me to ramble. I wanted this journal to be methodical and organized. But a linear storyline seems to have been blown out of the water already.

I'll try and get some sleep, although an Inspector Morse rerun just started on the TV. One of my guilty pleasures…BBC mysteries.

Day Two

Ellen asked me to meet her at a bistro in Uptown, walking distance from her home on Lake of the Isles. A waiter seated me at a table near the front window; tendrils of a hanging plant...some sort of fern...tickled my ear, so I scooted my chair away from them. I spied Ellen walking as she approached the restaurant. She's a tall woman...people notice her... and she now wears her hair quite short. Spiky and uncolored...the gray was striking. Ellen Solomon has always been a buoyant woman and her stride emphasized that quality.

She recognized me when she entered and dashed to the table, enveloping me in a forceful hug as I rose to greet her. The sunlight accentuated the golden flecks amid the softhearted brown in her eyes. Forgive me...I once loved this woman. I'm allowed a little contemplative license. Ellen transforms ordinary clothing into couture. She wore loose, but not baggy, jeans, and a starched blue Oxford shirt with the top three buttons undone, revealing a lacey ivory camisole.

"It's been too, too long," she whispered in my ear. I agreed.

Ellen sat across from me, clasped her hands together in front of her face and studied me. I smiled without parting my lips, hoping my facial expression conveyed the attachment I felt to her. She lowered her hands to the marble-topped table and returned the smile, her teeth bright against the olive tone of her skin. Her upper left incisor had grown in angled forward. Much like Tallie's crooked nose, it had tamed Ellen's loveliness when I met her. (My fixation, if that's what it is, on imperfections may demand some analysis later). Quiet seconds passed as I wondered how to start the conversation. Did my smile falter? Did doubt sweep over my face? Did my angst expose itself? Did my expression weaken for an instant? Ellen embraced my hands in hers and said "Oh my God. You're here to tell me goodbye."

I had assumed each situation would determine how much if anything I was going to reveal of the trip's purpose to Ellen and the other six. Very intuitive planning. While the seven are each quite different from one another, Ellen and at least two others can fathom me like a child's book.

The waiter approached the table with a pot of tea I had ordered before Ellen arrived. She lifted the lid and sniffed. "English Breakfast," she said. "You remembered."

"Yeah," I said. During the next half hour I unburdened myself with a thorough account of my plight; at the conclusion I felt amazed by how I had undervalued the catharsis of disclosing my illness to a confidant like Ellen. Her attentiveness as a listener strikes me as a peculiar complement to her strong-willed and opinionated nature. She has never relied on the volume of her voice to support a weak position in an argument. For engaging me during my monologue, for recognizing my need to expose it without interruption, Ellen will always have my immeasurable gratitude....or at least for another few months.

"You'll be fine," she said and I appreciated it was not a platitude about triumph over the disease. She understood that I'd get my head straight. "When you examine your life, there's so much beauty, even more to come."

"Maybe that's why you're the first I've told, besides Tallie," I said, realizing in that moment that I had known Ellen would not assail me with hopeful banalities.

"It does frighten me, Ellen."

"Naturally." She smiled again and took my hands in hers. "But is it dying or something else that scares you?"

"Like unfulfillment? Incompletion?"

"That. And regrets. I suspect you'll dwell on mislaid opportunities. You'll question your choices, of course. But I admire what you've chosen to do in the interval between learning of dying and death itself."

I nodded and acknowledged that I had already indulged in a life review.

"That will be some tale," Ellen said. "I'd be proud to co-star in one of the chapters."

"Prominently," I replied.

"I interviewed an artist last month," she said. "An older woman, a painter and the subject of a documentary by a Minneapolis filmmaker. She rendered landscapes that were recognizable for what they depicted." Ellen waved to the waiter and signaled for another pot of tea.

"In her fifties, she developed cataracts. She thought they'd be an artistic death sentence, but she continued to paint, reflecting what she saw onto the canvas. Her work grew increasingly abstract, but the woman resisted that label."

Unsure of where Ellen was going with this story, I asked if this was a parable.

"Patience," she cautioned. "The irony of what she first perceived as a tragedy was that her work began to sell. It gained not just popularity, but commercial success. Her paintings sold and she became quite well-off."

"It is a parable!" I laughed.

"I'm not finished yet. Last year she had the cataracts removed and her vision restored. You can guess what happened."

"Did she feel the surgery ruined her life?"

"From one perspective," Ellen said. "She never replicated the same technique in her painting, but she told me regaining her sight trumped the artistic loss."

"Ellen, is this the old adage: "When one door closes, another opens?"

"Locked doors never dissuaded you."

When Ellen met me in Iowa City, after the Marines, I ached to retreat into my surroundings, to remain inconspicuous…or from another perspective, to achieve more success at being less a target. Being Ellen Solomon's lover and fading into the background were incompatible. She demanded a partner, not an accessory. She challenged me, she inspired me and she motivated me to unearth my dreams. Profound in reflection, but accurate. She didn't pull me out of my postwar funk, but she threw me the rope that allowed me to pull myself out of it.

All that and extraordinary sex as well. Ellen trained me in oral sex, to make her come with my tongue on her clit and my index finger prodding her ass. When she came every muscle of her body stiffened, she'd scream and then try to push my head away as the pleasure approached pain. I'd slide up her body and often the initial thrust into her could trigger another orgasm. Ellen would pull my head down to her shoulder and whisper details of the fantasy she had enjoyed while I'd been eating her. The shameless vulgarity would arouse me as never before. That orgasmic intensity frightened me initially, but the realization of how I could give her pleasure was empowering. I remember my embarrassment when Ellen encountered my cunnilingual ineptitude and first instructed me how to use my tongue effectively, but she didn't belittle or mock me; instead she guided me, she mentored me. The results benefitted us both. She was as gracious a giver as she was a receiver.

The bistro crowd thinned and with it the din of conversations.

"I never liked doors, locked or otherwise," I said. "Such an irony…being locked out of rooms I don't really want to enter."

"So, how do imagine this trip of yours playing out?"

"I'm beginning to think maybe Tallie was right," I said. "Maybe I'm indulging a selfish inclination."

"How so?"

I gripped the table edge with both hands and leaned back in my chair. "I pictured a series of thoughtful conversations, chockfull of insightful reminiscences that unraveled wondrous epiphanies."

"How could that be considered selfish?" We both laughed.

"I wanted to say goodbye," I said delicately. "I wanted to say thank you for enriching my life."

"And hear that in return?"

"Maybe. But in truth I don't think it's what I primarily want." I paused. "Maybe all I want is discovery. Questioning the worth of it all."

"So we're back to regrets and an analysis of choices."

I nodded.

"You know what you mean to me or you wouldn't have put me on the list…first on the list, I might add," she said. "Have you ever had anesthesia?"

"Twice," I replied.

"When you sleep, you dream, and you're still left with the impression of time having passed. Anesthesia isn't like that. You count down from one hundred, your vision goes gray and then you're conscious again. There's no sense that time elapsed. That's how it is with us, you know."

"I do know."

"Years go by, we sit down like this and pick up where we left off. We don't reconnect, we resume."

Our bond possesses such strength that even when we ended the relationship in Iowa City, we both knew the familiarity would endure. We would always be friends.

"That's comforting and I'll miss it more than you can know."

"Thank you, Ellen."

"Do you still count?"

"Oh my God…yes."

Ellen is the only person who knows about my counting. I never told Tallie because it's not a big deal beyond being embarrassing. My unique, undiagnosed OCD…the counting. I'm not sure when it started but Ellen learned about it one night when we were watching TV in our apartment in Iowa City. A commercial for a local car dealership came on, crammed with lines of text, and I commented about the number of baselines on the screen…listing the exact number. She asked how I knew how many there were and that's when I explained to her that I "counted" things: lines of type on a bottle of moisturizer in my bathroom across from the toilet, players on the field for a football team (it's easier to count the offensive players than the defense, of course), actors onstage during any scene in a play, pieces of artwork hung on the wall of a restaurant in order from highest to lowest, and more creatively the areas of color within an image, "stepping stones" within my vision. The explanation of stepping stones drove her to label my habit an obsession. I will fix on one object then visually step to another object adjacent to it. The intent is to advance as far through the scene as possible by attaching your vision to each succeeding object. Like this motel room: the frame of the television overlaps the mirror that hangs above the dresser. I step from the TV to the mirror to the wall to the dresser, down to the carpeting and along the floor to one half of the drapes at the window, across the glass to the other half of the drapes, to the arm of the upholstered chair, then up the floor lamp to the painting beside the bed. There I'm marooned. The painting hangs on the wall with no egress beyond the lamp or the wall, and they've already been included in the path. I might begin again, not with the TV, but perhaps backtracking from the painting along a different path. There are always other routes.

"You know,' I continued, "I discovered a few years that I could abort it if I closed my eyes. It is a visual obsession, but it had never occurred to me to shut off, so to speak, my vision. Amazingly, in that moment immediately after I shut my eyes, there's an absence not only of light but of thought."

"Huh."

"It's almost teasingly brief. I've experimented with tracking my thoughts when I'm counting: is there an issue nagging me? Am I trying to avoid some unpleasantry?"

Ellen nodded. "And?"

"Nothing satisfying as far as identifying a theme, my thoughts seem totally random. But what is fascinating, is that when I close my eyes and abort the journey, the visual and mental stillness provide a moment of clarity."

"Sounds like meditation."

"Very much. And the clarity frequently offers me if not a solution to what had been worrying me, at least a fresh perspective."

"Have you tried using your obsession for that purpose rather than letting the obsession use you?"

"A few times," I admitted.

"How were the results?"

"Mixed. When it works, it's peaceful. But I still hate that I do it, that I can't control the onset. Such is the nature of obsession and compulsion."

We both fell silent then. Ellen regarded me solemnly as she stretched her arms across the table and enveloped my hands in hers, slowly rubbing her fingers in circles on my palms.

"It's intolerable that we'll never resume again," she whispered. "I've been trying to avoid becoming emotional."

"Me too, Ellen. I haven't learned yet what to say to people."

"I don't envy you that."

"You've been an incredible friend, which isn't surprising, because you're an incredible woman."

Ellen's face flushed. She released my hands and brushed at her eyes.

"Knowing you has enriched my life," I said. "I love the way your mind works and have always found your sarcastic humor fascinating."

Ellen and I stared at one another and this time I didn't have to wonder if my expression was conveying what I wanted it to. Our eyes filled with tears, which tracked down our cheeks. Neither of us moved to blot them.

"Why didn't you ever remarry?"

Ellen shrugged. "No need," she said.

"I understand, I think. Like why we broke up."

"I knew we could last as friends," she said. "The timing was critical. If I hadn't ended it when I did, we'd never been able to sit like this and have this conversation, or all the other conversations."

"I know that now. I didn't appreciate it at the time."

Ellen shrugged again. After a moment, she asked where I was off to next.

"Idaho. An old friend and a poet. She was at Iowa but I think you'd graduated by then, so you wouldn't know her." I paused. "As I think of it, none of you have ever met one another. Is that odd?"

"You're adept at compartmentalizing your life, and keeping those compartments isolated."

Ellen's observation intrigued me. "It's not something I've done consciously. Except maybe keeping you and Tallie separate."

"That was just common sense!" We laughed and each swiped away our tears. "She and I wouldn't have been very good friends, you know. Too much of a shared past."

"Not to mention that Tallie's the most jealous woman I've ever met."

"Mama lion," Ellen said.

"Oh, yeah."

"Let's say goodbye now."

"A photo first," I said. "Right where you are." I framed her with the ferns in the window draped behind her head, her hands resting on the table with her fingers interlocked, leaning back in her chair. Her eyes looked at me through the camera lens and I was reminded of something she had told me so long ago, that we find one another through our eyes. I snapped several shots and asked her if she wanted to see, but she declined. Then Ellen rounded the table and bear-hugged me. She inched back, took my face in both hands, leaned in and kissed me with a passion worthy of our days together in Iowa. "The mama lion can't possibly begrudge me that."

Today's playlist began with "Erotic City," by Prince, a way of paying tribute to both Ellen and Minneapolis. Ellen had shooed me out of the bistro, waving away my attempt to pay for breakfast. "Go," she said. "I'm going to sit for a while and nurse my tea." Seven hours later I arrived in Bismarck, North Dakota. There's an old, tasteless joke about North Dakota. Custer at the Little Big Horn, just before the Sioux annihilate his entire command, turns to the soldier next to him and says: "At least we don't have to go back to North Dakota."

The drive today entailed long stretches of farmland with occasional interruptions by towns. Many of the fields are green circles, from the irrigation. In the proper frame of mind the landscape could be considered barren…in another it's the landscape of opportunity. I took a photo of Stink Lake from the side of the highway. It captured my curiosity and I wanted to see if its odor lived up to its name. Not really. In what might have been unintended irony, the town just west of the lake is named Crystal Springs.

I checked into the Comfort Inn and ate dinner at the Gateway Mall…fast food Chinese in North Dakota was too tantalizing to for-go…and the homogenous collection of stores felt reassuring. Malls are the mother ship. After dinner I drove to Keelboat-Steamboat Park along the Missouri River, near Bismarck State College, and rested on the riverbank a few yards beyond the boat ramp as the sun set. A train of laden coal cars crossed over the river on a bridge south of me and I thought about Tallie.

When I called her this evening, she answered on the first ring and showered me with questions about where I was, how I was feeling, and did I miss her.

Bismarck, just fine, and horribly.

The call was brief and studded with silent pauses when I feared she might resurrect her misgivings about the trip. She chatted about her work. I assured her I was getting enough rest and not taxing myself with the driving. Tallie said the loft seemed exceptionally vacant with me gone. I almost said the motel room was probably lonelier, but checked myself. She didn't need to have her loneliness trumped.

More was left unsaid than said, but the notable things we might have said are understood. I told Tallie I loved and missed her and would call again the following day, probably from Billings, Montana.

Our loft occupies the top floor of a four-story building, east of Ogden Avenue and north of Skinner Park. Tallie's grandfather bequeathed it to us in 1989, along with a sizeable investment portfolio, before the neighborhood became gentrified. Her grandfather grew up in the panhandle of Nebraska just after the turn of the nineteenth century, claimed to have ridden his horse to a one-room schoolhouse, and after graduating from Chadron State College, disembarked from a train in the summer of 1926 to begin law school in Chicago. Land…property…represented wealth, he'd been taught by his father. The man had grown up on a farm and understood work from an early age. His savings didn't cover his law school expenses, so he worked…two part-time jobs…and he scrimped, saved, and invested. While in law school, he purchased a plot of land in the south Loop and converted it into a parking lot. The rent income more than covered his loan payments. By the end of his second year in law school, he had expanded to another three properties: two more parking lots and the three-flat near North and Leavitt where he was living. Among his fellow law students he was known as an empire-builder. By his third year he was clerking at a mid-sized law firm, on track to join the firm after graduation. He wasn't the top student in the class of 1929, but certainly one of the most ambitious.

He graduated, passed the Illinois bar on his first try, and then watched everything he'd built crash along with the stock market that year. The banks called all his loans, which he couldn't pay, and the law firm where he'd been clerking narrowly escaped its own bankruptcy. His job, his modest wealth, his home and his future all disappeared. His experience wasn't unique at the time, but the manner in which he responded to it was inspirational. If you listened to his stories of that day and the days that followed, you drew an impression of a young man still driven by his ambitions. He found work where he could, and when he couldn't find work (which was more often the situation), he created it. Hung out a shingle and accepted every client who approached him. Accepted barter in exchange for fees when there was nothing else the client had to pay him. Inside two years and taking advantage of depressed property values, he had re-acquired the south Loop property, an apartment building near Addison and Southport, and an office building west of the river off Grand and Milwaukee. He was lucky, but he believed you created your own luck. The building on Madison was a later purchase, after the war, for which, by the way, he volunteered at the age of forty-one, and during which he received a Purple Heart when he helped liberate Bastogne during the Battle of the Bulge with Patton's Third Army. The man was unconquerable, amassed a fortune, and had doted on Tallie since her childhood.

Tallie and I have prospered in our lives, but we could never have dreamed of living as we do today had it not been for her grandfather's generosity. I love what we've done with that building, especially our loft. More about that tomorrow. I'm sleepy.

Day Three

I spent the night chasing sleep, comparing my life to that of Tallie's grandfather and suspecting that the difficulties I've faced, and my accomplishments in spite of them, fall far short of the hardships he confronted and overcame during his lifetime, which spanned a period of history from the Wright brothers to Neil Armstrong. As a child Tallie spent many summer days at his home in Lake Bluff, a mid-century modern across from Sunrise Park. He bought it in 1947; he loved its isolation, nestled in the elbow of Mountain Road and Sunrise Avenue. Neighboring houses dwarfed it in size and extravagance, but he remained a simple man with easily satisfied needs. While some men rise from humble beginnings and flaunt their success, others, like Tallie's grandfather, understand that beginnings often reassert themselves, so they never abandon their humility.

Did I mention that Tallie was his only grandchild? One of the many things Tallie and I have in common: we're only children of only children. If you examine our branch of the family tree, you'll see the usual inverted funnel is right side up. Our branch is withering, ending with the two of us. How we each avoided being spoiled remains a mystery we discuss to this day. Tallie's grandfather came closest to anointing her a princess, but her parents grounded her, primarily with the values her grandfather instilled in her mother. Nonetheless, we both grew up privileged.

I entered Montana today…through Bighorn, Custer, Pompeys Pillar…and after crossing the Yellowstone River, stopped for the night in Billings. More hills here than in North Dakota, including some impressive bluffs on the east bank of the river when you drive into town, although they sit opposite a refinery. Before leaving North Dakota, I stopped near Medora and snapped a photo of the Little Missouri River and the surrounding hills in the Theodore Roosevelt National Memorial Park. I know I said this was not going to be a travelogue, but there are some vistas I want to show Tallie when I get home, so she can appreciate how the passage framed my reflections.

Staying at the Best Western tonight…steak and fries for dinner.

Tallie and I debated what to do about one of our tenants during our phone call tonight. Actually, it's Alison, the woman who worked in my office and threw the party where Tallie and I met. A few years later, when I struck out to establish my own firm, Alison accompanied me; she's been my assistant and a sisterly friend to Tallie all these decades. Our building on Madison houses shops and offices on the first floor, rental units on the second and third floors, and our loft on the entire fourth floor. Alison is our oldest tenant, both in terms of longevity and age. The age is the problem. She developed mild dementia two years ago but it's growing more severe and that concerns Tallie. Alison is a childless widow with no other family, on long-term disability from the firm. There was another incident today and Tallie believes it's time either to hire a live-in caretaker or shift Alison to an assisted-living facility.

"I'm sorry to burden you with this," she said. "You've got enough on your mind."

"Sounds like we can't postpone a decision much longer."

"No. I don't think we can."

"Take care of her, Tallie. Whatever you think best." When Alison comprehended her diagnosis, she requested Tallie accept power of attorney for all decisions about her medical treatment. Of course, she accepted.

In the time since, the cruelty of Alison not recognizing her has deflated Tallie. I've witnessed Alison's disintegration, the loss of memories they have shared and the love they nourished, decimate Tallie, and I've comforted her as she raged not only at her helplessness to halt the disease's progression, but at the bitterness it exacted. I could accept death more straightforwardly if I knew the two of them could comfort one another. Instead, I know Tallie will feel the loss of both a husband and her dearest friend. Digging for fairness in this quandary is unproductive.

I hate this. I hate the effect this isolation is having on my emotional balance.

Each of these women deserves better…they've earned it…and I'm powerless. Fuck chaos.

I'm going to shorten my driving day tomorrow and journey only as far as Missoula…maybe hike in the Clearwater National Forest. I have a choice of a northern route or a southern route to Moscow from there. The southern route would take me through the Nez Perce Indian Reservation, while the northern route cuts through the Coeur D'Alene Reservation. I'll probably flip a coin to decide.

Day Five

A couple of things…I neglected to mention my playlist from the other day. Leaving Bismarck I started with "In a Big Country" by Big Country…the version from the "Come Up Screaming" album…in the live version the music encircles me. I also skipped making a journal entry yesterday. When I arrived in Billings I was tired, from lack of sleep the previous night and the heaviness of my mood during that day's short drive. As for music, that morning I deviated from plan and searched my iPod for "Our House" by CSNY; I put it on repeat for half an hour, loudly singing along until my eyes watered up so much I was worried about seeing the road. Then I switched to an older compilation entitled "Melancholy." Immersion therapy for the self-pitying. One of the concessions I granted, both to Tallie and my doctor, was attending counseling, and eventually hospice, when this trip is concluded. Maybe seeing someone before I hit the road could have proved beneficial. Hindsight. At least the anti-anxiety medication helps trim the peaks and backfill the valleys.

Tallie and I spoke for about ten minutes last night. She's wavering about how to proceed, but I presumed from the tenor of our discussion that she's leaning toward assisted living, although that may be a selfish assumption: I doubt she'll want the responsibility of caring for Alison after I'm dead. That post-death narrative is a game I told myself I would not play. Envisioning how your death would affect other people's lives is petulance more suitable to a seven-year-old than a sixty-four-year-old, even if he is terminal. We have and will prepare, but I'm not going to construct dioramas of life without me.

Except for a meal, I spent my time in Missoula in my room, playing roulette with the TV remote control…three to four seconds of more than sixty channels…over and over. Early to bed and late to rise. Trying to erase the sleep deficit and use my dreams as an escape from the predominance of a single waking thought: dementia will cheat Alison of living an examined life, and let's face it, you should write your own history.

I chose the southern route to Moscow, Route 12, through the Clearwater National Forest, as verdant as anything I've ever seen, paralleling the Clearwater River, where I spotted several groups of rafters on the water and took a few more photos. The landscape hues began transforming from emerald to russet near Kooskia as the forest thinned, intensifying as I neared Spalding and followed Route 95. As I climbed north onto a plateau toward Moscow, patches of green appeared again like scabs.

I loathe listening to old men who describe every meal as though it might be their last (at least not yet), but tonight I enjoyed an excellent meal. At the Red Door Restaurant, I ate braised baby goat leg in Thai peanut sauce. Definitely a first.

My room at the Royal Motor Inn is walking distance from the University of Idaho campus, where Delores Calvin teaches in the creative writing MFA program. Delores, I knew her as Del back then, dated a friend of mine at the University of Iowa, where she studied at the Writer's Workshop. We're meeting tomorrow after one of her classes, a graduate poetry workshop. Our friendship has been atypical: a few months after I met Del, she broke up with my friend…he'd been cheating on her with another woman. That's not the atypical aspect, obviously. In an odd twist, after their breakup I grew more attached to Del than to my friend. We enjoyed commonalities in books and music, political theory, attitudes toward the destructive nature of religion, so that our friendship flourished. We banished the issue of whether or not a man and woman can be friends one night with a drunken, fumbling attempt at sex that ended in laughter and a resolve never to try it again…at least with each other.

Del, a short, thin woman, in those days wore her hair tied in a long ponytail that hung straight down her back and seemed never to sway, because Del moved deliberately, so cautiously. I attributed that to what I thought was her nature as a poet, or what a poet's nature ought to be: nothing rash or rushed, contemplative, introverted. Del's diminutive features reinforced an impression of fragility. I remember she often used a dessert fork to eat her meals, because a dinner fork held more food than she was comfortable eating in any one bite. She also hummed constantly…a song inspired by the splash of the water when she showered that morning, the tune that had last played on the car radio, or the soundtrack to a commercial on television. She did it unconsciously and explained when I questioned it that she couldn't imagine not having music playing in her mind…the rhythm of song reminded her of the meter of poetry.

Without seeming pretentious, Del could proclaim that life disappoints because it can't live up to literature and not appear inauthentic. She never embraced the persona of a self-centered artist. In a recent email, in response to my wishes for a happy sixty-first birthday, she told the old story of how when you're in your twenties, you worry all the time about what people think about you; in your forties you profess not to care what people think about you, and in your sixties you realize no one was ever thinking about you.

More than twenty years ago, during a visit to Chicago, she remarked on the Moscow-Chicago Hemingway connection. She didn't exactly complain, but noted how Hemingway-centric certain members of the writing faculty at the university were, implying that poetry received short shrift. There's a Hemingway Festival, the university sponsors *The Hemingway Review*, and the Hemingway/PEN Award recipient visits the campus to provide readings and meet with students and faculty. So one night during her visit, Del, Tallie and I concocted a scheme: we would endow a poetry journal, edited by Del, to showcase work by promising students at the university. You can imagine the type of evening from which this inspiration sprouted: the three of us lounging on our rooftop deck, wine in abundance, unshackled imaginations plotting poetic ascendance. We laughed a great deal, watched airplanes on their approach patterns to O'Hare and Midway, and went to bed in fine moods. In the morning, Tallie left for work and I sat at the breakfast bar with Del, mapping out the structure for a foundation to support the review, a publishing imprint to free it from the university's meddling, and safeguards for its future, should she ever leave the writing program. Del hadn't thought I was serious the night before, that we had merely indulged her vengeful fantasies about the "Hemingwayers." She sipped her coffee as I itemized my plan, slowly accepted the gravity of my resolve, and soon engaging as a co-conspirator. When auditioning names for the foundation and its publishing imprint, I chopped and combined Del's first and last names, settling on DelVin. DelCal ran a close second, but was rejected for sounding too similar to what a conglomerate might call itself. And she liked the play on words of DelVin sounding like delving, and its correlation to poetry. For more than two decades, the DelVin Foundation has continued to showcase young poets. The funding for the endeavor remains anonymous, and Del enjoys a reputation as a bit of a rainmaker for securing the money. Good for her.

She continues to write and to publish…not through the DelVin imprint I'm proud to say…and I own an autographed copy of each volume. I chuckled when I learned she lives across the street from a Catholic church…her antagonism toward religion has not diminished over the years… and that she regularly contributes to the church's food bank. Like most of us, she flirts with inconsistencies.

When I called home, Tallie said it was raining and that she was standing by the floor-to-ceiling windows at the eastern end of the loft. She described various shades of city gray and how the clouds scudded so low in the sky that the upper floors of the Sears Tower (I'll never call it the Willis Tower) were obscured. Listening to her prompted memories of the two of us lounging on pillows at those windows, cuddling one winter night in the warmth from the fireplace, surveying the skyline as furious winds powered the snow between buildings. The magnitude of the memory accrued from our sharing the occasion…the storm was unimportant…our witnessing it alone, in our home, holding one another, with no need for words to convey our feelings, insured its permanence. We'd communicated through touch, through contact, and my finest memories share that theme…instances with Tallie when the communication was tactile.

This journey has provoked associations and memories I'd forgotten or hadn't recalled in many years; they rocket into my consciousness while I'm driving. Ellen mentioned meditation and it strikes me that the murmuring of the Saab's tires on pavement, like a mantra, induces a state that inspires reminiscence. Worried that I'll forget them before I can write about them each night, I've begun using my cell phone as a recorder, dictating notes to myself when I'm driving for later inclusion in this journal.

One of the notes I transcribed this evening was this: "I feel small."

In the Clearwater Forest the topography contrasted with my Chicago neighborhood in a way that generated admiration and wonder. The mountains and the hills soared in contrast to the flatness of the city. At night the stars here wouldn't combat urban haze to make their light inspiring. At the pace nineteenth-century settlers traveled, the plains must have seemed eternal and the passes through the summits must have reinforced a conviction of one's insignificance. The contrast reminds me of the impression the Vietnamese highlands made on me when I arrived in 1968. Jungle, I learned, embodied some onomatopoeia: the struggle of patrolling dense, impenetrable foliage; grass taller than a man's head that was sharp enough to slice skin; and perpetual heat, humidity and grime. The alien nature of what became familiar amazed me. Staying alive in that setting coarsened me.

The landscape yesterday and today tweaked my perspective… disease drives focus inward, arranging the universe in rings with me at its center. But the scale of these mountains and plains, and the stretch of sky above them, belittles that viewpoint. It's difficult to feel more celebrated than a speck in this country. I don't feel as though I've pandered to the temptation of self-pity, but the finality of this trip accompanies every thought, even as I try to keep it from dominating them. When I waited in the bistro in Minneapolis for Ellen to arrive and debated whether to tell her I was dying or was simply taking a sabbatical from work, the notion of having embarked on a farewell tour struck me as amusing. Was it fair, I thought, to conceal that fact from her and all the others I planned to see? Ellen apprehended immediately, of course, but I don't expect my exchange with her to function as a template for the remaining conversations… the relationships all differ in critical aspects. My histories with these people comprise chapters that exist alone as well as overlap, but each began independently of one another (except of course for the one stranger I plan to meet). Imagine a three-dimensional venn diagram, substituting spheres for circles…a model resembling a molecule… flawed even as I describe it because I'm back to casting myself as the nucleus. Is it possible not to be the protagonist in your own biography? Perhaps it's an easier task when you're not dying.

I'll tell Del why I'm visiting, but I didn't design this journey as a vehicle for passing the collection plate, for stockpiling best wishes for the dying. It's greedy to expect to have it both ways: fulfilling my wish to see these folks before I die, and ignoring the betrayal they'll feel when they learn later that I was terminal as we chatted over coffee and scones. Selfishness versus honesty…when characterized that way, the decision becomes plainer. Some things can so easily be over-thought and others so glaringly under-thought, that the absence of consideration just seems stupid. Anyway, in my next destination, Coos Bay, Oregon, I'll be asking Carl Zimmer to do me a huge favor, so secrecy is moot.

 A recurring dream has visited my sleep since leaving Chicago. Not the identical dream each night, but events and people interacting within a large house that is not a phenomenon new to this trip: it's been the scene of previous dreams. A second story hallway lined with painted doors (interestingly, I haven't counted the doors in this hallway); a high-ceilinged basement made of cinder blocks, with a jagged hole in the rear wall that opens into an abandoned space cluttered with dusty furniture and empty shelves; a wide concrete expanse that leads to a cavernous tunnel beneath the front of the house, but which doesn't connect with the basement. Dreams: logic is a secondary consideration. As driving has prompted recollections and insights, sleeping in a succession of motel beds seems to have populated my dreams with characters both familiar and strange. Predictably, my parents, and especially my father, have appeared. Tallie's often there. Ellen, in an erotic episode the night I left Minneapolis. Two of the people I have yet to see on my trip. Associates from work. Old clients. Men with whom I served in Vietnam…dead and alive. Logic, as I said, rarely governs dreams, so these characters pop up in combinations that do not mirror history. Tallie only met one of the vets I know, but in one dream she hosted a reunion party for my squad in our loft. In one dream about the house behind a violet door on the second floor, a young and healthy Alison reclined in a hospital bed, while friends from my office read aloud to her from a children's book.

Tallie enjoys dream analysis...as entertainment...nothing approaching seriousness. I play along, fabricating outlandish interpretations derived from details she'll tell me. I've never relished the game as much as Tallie does; I appreciate the factors that can influence my dreams, but have never considered them messages or believed they deserved scrutiny. When a late-night slice of pizza exerts as much influence on your subconscious as surviving an automobile accident, how can you trust the insights you perceive from the ensuing dream? I wouldn't have thought to ask my doctor if the anti-anxiety medication could affect me in this way...maybe I'll email Janine to inquire. Still, I'm as inconsistent in my character as anyone, and the clarity of the details in the dreams that I recall in the morning, coupled with the recurrence of the house as a stage for many of them, have chipped away at my skepticism. At least the dreams have so far entertained me, not left me apprehensive about what they might portend.

More associations: scenes from my dreams remind me of slide shows, which inspires me to consider creating a compilation for Tallie of the photos I take on my journey. I could produce one in PowerPoint on the laptop, in addition to making a journal entry each night. But maybe not. The scenery has impressed me and shaped my thoughts, even enabling some insights, but the land isn't the story and I fear the photos might detract from the message in the journal. Which begs the question: who is the journal's audience? The experience of the trip is mine, but the record of it is Tallie's. Every notation is a message to her. I read some years ago that old men tell their lovers their fears, but tell their wives their doubts. Ponder that distinction: how does fear differ from doubt? Fear suggests certainty; doubt implies hesitation. Fear must be overpowered; doubt need only be dismissed. Banishing fear is a perfect bragging point for impressing a lover, while confiding your doubts involves trust that men more readily grant their wives than their lovers. Sad that honesty with one's wife might arise from the erosion of a need to impress her anymore. Another writer once called marriage a long, dull meal with the dessert served first. If your marriage fits that description, then you have my sympathy and my derision for remaining in a marriage where you can't reignite any passion. My marriage won't last nearly long enough; I'm being fleeced of its longevity. Besides being offensive, I find the analogy clumsy; but if I extend it, then this meal with Tallie has sustained me, and I've never found it problematic to push back the entrée and savor another spoonful of dessert.

 I'm not bashful about telling Tallie how much I love her. I want her to know. When she relates her fears and doubts, feeling loved shouldn't be among either of them.

Day Six

I was early for my meeting with Del this morning, and a writing department assistant in Brink Hall directed me to the classroom where she was conducting her workshop. In the hallway I glanced through the window and saw Professor Calvin sitting in the middle of one length of a rectangle formed by blond wooden tables. Her students occupied the other seats, their attention directed to a young man who sat reading from a sheaf of papers in his hand. The door muffled his voice, but the tone of his voice conveyed conviction in his words. I studied history and political science at Iowa and those subjects baited students into impassioned discussions. I had listened to Del on previous occasions describe how students castigated one another's work. The toughest lesson she taught, she believed, was convincing pupils that climbing the literary summit on the bloodied corpses of their peers wouldn't be tolerated in her class. "Civility in criticism," she preached. Ellen would like Del.

I lingered too long at the window, for Del spotted me, grinning and beckoning me to join the group. The young man reading, I noticed, appeared annoyed by the interruption my entrance caused. I quickly sat in an empty chair on a short end of the rectangle and indicated he should resume. The classroom faced a shadowed courtyard bisected by a diagonal walkway. I had passed the Natural Resources and Naval ROTC buildings as I walked to Brink Hall, and the gray roof of the ROTC building was visible through the windows. The sight of a few students in fatigues on the sidewalk before the ROTC building immediately reminded me of my service days.

The peeved poet finished and silence followed. Unsure if this was class protocol, I looked to Del, who nodded at the young man, then asked for comments, specifically what others would do if the poem had been theirs. I studied her, noting the suggestions of age in her face, the puffiness beneath her eyes and the lines spidering from their corners. No more ponytail: her hair was styled in more of a bob, and shot with gray. Round-lensed, gray-framed eyeglasses. A woman in her early thirties spoke, directing her comments to Del and not to the young man whose poem she was critiquing. "Tell Robert, Jennifer," Del interrupted. "Provide him with particulars, not merely impressions." She paused. "And I don't mean to denigrate impressions. We all know they're important, too." The students chuckled.

Jennifer continued but I paid little attention to what she said. I was jealous of the environment…of the safety of the cocoon and how it cultivated creative expression. It occurred to me then that my car, during the past few days, had served the same purpose: a shelter in which to let my mind scamper through my history. These students should be jealous of me…we each enjoyed imaginative freedom, but I drew on a wealth of material far in excess of what they had experienced in their young lives. My attention was pulled back to the discussion when I heard Robert defending rather than explaining the coupling of the words "autistic" and "wall." Soon Del brought the session to an end, but not before introducing me to her students, saying that I was one of those lucky people who had the soul of a poet but did not feel driven to attempt poetry.

Del linked her arm in mine as we walked to her office, catching the glances of a few students, some of whom smiled and greeted her by name. She waved or nodded to them as they passed, maintaining a flood of questions: How was Tallie? Had I seen any good films lately? What had I been reading? Isn't Idaho glorious this time of year? And finally, when we entered her office, What's with this road trip of yours? I took a seat in one of a pair of curved-back wooden chairs, crossing my left leg over the right. Del sat in the other, caught me grinning as I noticed her feet barely reaching the carpet, and then I told her. She closed her eyes for a moment, sitting unnervingly still.

"I suppose I'll have to write a poem about you then." Del wagged her head and explained the coincidence of her new collection. She said the poems were inspired by the death of a close friend, which remained an unstitched gash, and she loathed elevating this loss to the status of inspiration, but she was, after all, a poet. "I'd like to imagine I'm motivated by nobler notions," she said. As Del spoke I was step-stoning through the shelves of books in her office…rows of thin volumes interspersed with thick anthologies…counting them as I moved from one side of the room to the other.

She was curious about the disease, how quickly it had been detected and how far it had progressed, what sorts of effects I was feeling, and how my emotions were running. We sat in her office and talked about me, about Tallie…Del wept when I described how Tallie was coping with my compulsion to undertake this journey… until I asked about her friend who had died.

"A former student," she said. "Talented, sensitive, confident for a poet." At this she snorted. "His work was published in the review many years ago." I watched her rigid posture deflate as she talked about this man, and wondered if perhaps they had been lovers. "He lived in Spokane…honest to God in a suburb called Greenacres…and worked for an insurance company; actuarial, not sales. I sponsored him here as a visiting poet once and he had to take vacation from his job to come for a week." Del rose and retrieved a box of tissues from her desk. She plucked one and dabbed at her eyes as she sat down again in the chair.

"He had a massive stroke. To look at him you would never have suspected that would happen. He was fit. He appeared healthy. And he seemed far too young."

"I'm sorry, Del."

She grimaced, closed her eyes, and waved a tiny hand in front of her face. "We all come to know death through others."

We ate lunch at Bucer's Coffeehouse Pub…paninis and giant cookies for dessert…amid students sipping coffee. I asked Del if she was planning to retire soon. She said she was in discussion with the administration about accepting emeritus status, reducing her teaching load to one workshop every other semester, and grooming a successor to take the reins of the review.

"Then I could have the luxury of writing fulltime most of the year."

"That must be tempting."

"And frightening," she said. "A few of my colleagues, one or two of the long-in-the-tooth dogs with tenure, blame their lack of production on the rigors of teaching. They're different from the undergraduate students who are in love with being a writer, but not so much with writing itself. But if time ceases to be a restraint, I wonder if I'll use it wisely."

"Out, out, damned doubt."

"It's probably best you never attempted poetry!"

We laughed.

Del had never married and I asked her why. She said when she was younger she had lived with two men, "At separate times," she added with a smirk.

"Each started well, but eventually the men needed more of my time, or me, than I was willing to give. Or capable of giving. Poets imagine we're driven to write, to tunnel into our souls in a search of truth."

I chuckled.

"Hey, for the poet it's not hyperbole. It's nature. But I've come to believe the journey might be closer to avoidance than a search. You know the old joke about the Buddha…don't just do something, sit there!"

There were cookie crumbs on the sleeve of Del's blouse and I reached across the table and brushed them away.

"I'll sit for hours, literally hours, in a chair on my back porch, watching my bird bath as different species…flycatchers, warblers, kingbirds, nuthatches, cuckoos, so many varieties…visit to bathe. During the winter I'll snuggle in an overstuffed chair in my living before the fireplace, gazing at the flames. If I'm feeling housebound I'll drive out into the country…there are some regal forested areas northwest of the city. The point is…I'll ponder and muse, forge connections between disparate echoes, lay words on paper and then reorganize and reorder them, reject some and embrace others, and then study the final lines and absolutely despair at how imperfectly they express what it is I feel." Del gripped an immense coffee cup with her small hands. "Even with good poems, I've still felt ineffectual. Talking with other writers, not just poets, I don't feel I'm unique. It's not that there is always something more to say. It's that I haven't said it right yet, which begs the question of whether I can ever say it right. Not just if I can ever translate what I feel into words, but if the effort is a denial of knowing it's impossible. Admitting that, for a poet, would be horrifying."

I told Del how my farewell tour…she laughed at that…had been affording me insights.

"Free association," she said. "Very liberating."

I then told her about the journal and she grew animated, as though the fragrance of the coffee around us carried caffeine.

"What a truly wonderful idea!"

She questioned me about my writing: Did I write during the day? Did I pull off the road to make an entry? Did I wait until the end of the day? Was I concerned about forgetting the insights that came during the drive? Was I grounding my thoughts in the places in which they occurred?

"You're such a teacher," I said.

"Use nature to nurture."

I explained my routine to Del, as well as my idea of creating a slideshow of photos from my trip. She surprised me…the wordsmith thought the photo medley was an exceptional idea.

"Is that a commentary on my writing skills?" I teased. "Will I need illustrations to make my point?"

She ignored me and asked how difficult I found it to maintain a perspective on things.

I wasn't prepared for that question. "I'm doing it for Tallie, of course," I said. Then I hesitated. Trying to explain to Del how I hoped this journal would afford Tallie insight into areas of my life with which she wasn't already familiar echoed Del's own creative dilemma. I also worry that what I write won't express what I feel, but the disease has stripped me of the possibility of debating whether or not the effort is avoidance. Time constrains my options for deliberation.

"I'm trying not to censor what I write," I said. "Tallie deserves my honesty."

"Admirable and demanding, I imagine. I'm certain it'll be an enlightening and intimate read."

I sensed where Del was headed. "I'm not sure I want anyone but Tallie to read it."

Del nodded.

"And I've considered giving Tallie the option of allowing others I visit to read it." I thought of those I had yet to see. "But there are good reasons why Tallie should keep it confidential."

"I understand. It's your legacy; you should have some control over it."

I was thankful Del didn't push the issue, although I suspected she was dying to.

"Your friend who died…when you speak of him, Del, I get the impression he was tremendously important to you."

Del nodded. "His hands had such long, graceful fingers. I'd watch him grasp a pencil and think that no words he could write could be as beautiful as his hands.

"He was the most temperate man I've ever met…expecting to discover the best in people and never disappointed when something different was revealed."

The music which had been playing through the coffee house's sound system surged in volume and then as quickly returned to its previous level. A bearded man behind the counter raised his arm, a white towel waving in his hand, and apologized, provoking laughter from the crowd.

"We'd sit beside one another at a table in my back yard, in the shade near the koi pond, analyzing the drafts of our poems. He would settle on each word and knead it, evaluating why he chose it, why he purged other words, and probing whether another word might be more relevant. He was deliberate and oblivious of time. That made his death more agonizing."

Del waved away a server with a coffee pot who asked if she wanted her mug refreshed.

"I can't help but be envious of your journey. To wonder what he would do in the same circumstances. To lust for what he would write as his legacy."

"Of course."

"But he may simply have chuckled about it and moved on as he did every day. His poems…and they are superb poems…are his legacy. I have hand-written originals, with his edits. When I die, I'll leave them to the university library."

"They'll be appreciated."

"He was my Tallie…with a twenty year age difference that neither of us paid any attention to."

"I'm so sorry, Del."

"And now you. The two of you will make grade A grist for the lyrical mill."

"I better grow accustomed to my friends weeping and crying during these conversations."

Del removed her glasses and blotted her eyes with a napkin, camouflaging her tears with laughter. "This volume promises to be my zenith!"

"Speaking of legacies…I'm going to make a gift to the university to endow a chair in your name."

"That's unbelievably generous. Do you know how much leverage that's going to give me as I negotiate my emeritus status?" She slapped the table top with her small palm. "But do me one favor."

"What's that?"

"No anonymity this time. And I want to credit you and Tallie with the support you've given for the review. I want your names on it."

"No objections."

I walked Del back to her office, photographing her in front of the five-story façade of Brink Hall…air-conditioners jutted from four of the windows….and finally in her office, behind her desk but from an angle, so the bookshelves on the wall are in the frame. She hugged me, her hair tickling my chin, the side of her face nestled against my chest.

The playlist this afternoon began with "Idaho" by Josh Ritter. During the drive today, through arid country in eastern Washington and Oregon, I lowered the car windows to smell the air. It was dry and clean, and as I followed the Columbia River for a time on I-84, I thought of Del and wondered if the loneliness ever overwhelmed her. It reminded me of a time Tallie reproached me for constantly struggling to transform myself into whatever the next person might need. We'd returned from a party hosted by one of Tallie's work colleagues who lived in Lincoln Park. Half an hour into the affair, I was introduced to a young woman, merely a year into her job as a social worker at an agency that received funding from Tallie's organization. I sat with her and listened to her describe the rewards of working with at-risk, elementary school kids. It may be jaded of me to say that she had not yet been jaded by the magnitude of the problems she encountered every day, but her youth and her passion animated her speech. As the evening progressed and she committed the rookie mistake of drinking too much at a work function, her conversation drifted from the rewards of her work to a narrative of her personal life. The woman described finding herself at the confluence of a rush of disappointments: she had recently broken off a relationship with the man she had been certain she would marry; her job, while emotionally rewarding and which she totally, totally loved, paid her crap; and she lived in a hideous apartment in Rogers Park.

 I've trained myself to be an excellent listener, but that night in the taxi riding home, Tallie, instead of reviewing the characters and their conversations at the party, said nothing and stared out the window. Back in the loft when I asked what was troubling her, assuming it was something I'd done, she leveled the charge: "You can't bear others suffering, but you're oblivious to your own." At the time I stupidly side-stepped the issue of Tallie watching me spend an evening in a conversation with a young woman, and fixated instead on her notion of my suffering. I was baffled…I lived a privileged life…and I pressed the matter. Tallie harrumphed and prepared for bed in silence…a treatment that lasted through most of the following day. We never resolved the issue…it seemed to decay as we resumed our routines. Since thinking of Del had kicked off this association, I pulled a page from Del's handbook, and dissected the word epiphany, saying it aloud as I approached Hooper, Washington, surrounded by sand-colored buttes. I accentuated the "piff" within the word… eh-PIFF-ihnee…and envisioned awareness surging wildly upward until it speared my consciousness. I turned off the highway to follow a sign noting the Upper Falls in the Palouse River Canyon. Nothing on a scale like Niagara Falls or the Grand Canyon, the drop off of a few feet seemed more like rapids, but I still wouldn't have taken the plummet in either a canoe or a kayak. Taken in perspective, in its time and place, when I stood above the falls, counting the striations in the face of the buttes around me, marking how the bronzed landscape greened along the river's banks, the "piff" whooshed through me and I realized that what had distressed Tallie that night was how empathy for the young woman's plight could tempt me to leave Tallie to solve the woman's problems. Casting me as a serial savior seemed a laughable image but probably a fear-inducing prospect for Tallie. A trust issue…a knot braided with so much vulnerability that she had deflected any discussion of it that night by spinning like a nimble running back out of the grasp of a would-be tackler to a different subject, an obliviousness to my own suffering, which, had I considered it more carefully and less selfishly, would undoubtedly have presented a clue to what truly frightened her.

I questioned her about that tonight when we spoke, asking if after all these years she still worried about my leaving her.

"You are going to leave me," she said. "Just not in the fashion I always feared you would."

Those words hammered me, and I wondered if forcing her to give voice to the fear had been cruel.

"That's just a question of timing, Tallie. Do you know how often you've made me feel as though our marriage was a long, unbearable audition?" I strained to maintain a stable tenor in my voice… even as anger grew within me, I knew venting it was pointless and certainly detrimental at that moment.

"I do…and I'm sorry. I'm sorry. You know how complicated this is for me."

"I do know. But I also know I nailed this audition."

Tallie giggled, sounding like the young woman with whom I used to walk hand-in-hand along the lakeshore on our lunch hours, listening to the waves slap the seawall in Monroe Harbor as gulls cried overhead. We'd enter Grant Park at Balbo and stroll north to the river, west to State Street, and then split off to our offices: hers on Madison and mine on LaSalle. I'd labor at my desk through the sluggish afternoon, agonizing at how waiting to see her again that night was an eternity.

"Yes," she sighed, and I could visualize her closing her eyes and lowering her head. "You have. And I'm sorry…I'm so sorry. No one's ever earned my trust like you have."

I was sitting upright in the bed of my motel room, legs extended, bare feet crossed at the ankles, eyeing my reflection in the framed mirror above the dresser. Suddenly I experienced a sensation where staring at an image too intently renders it as a flickering doppelganger of its reality. My sense of balance faltered and although I understood that I wasn't shifting in the bed, I felt as though my body was floating and tilting to one side. I closed my eyes, hoping my technique for quashing the compulsion to step-stone through a scene might also serve to ground me in this instance.

"Hey," Tallie said. "Are you eating healthy?"

I opened my eyes, relieved that my doppelganger had fled, and erupted in laughter at Tallie's question, saying it didn't matter. Remembering the scene in "Meatballs" where Bill Murray leads the underdog campers in a chant of "It just doesn't matter," I whispered it into the phone, increasing the volume of the chant with each repetition. "It just doesn't matter! It just doesn't matter!"

Tallie merged her voice with mine in the chant and we repeated it until we collapsed into a spasm of laughter so wrenching that we couldn't speak. I slid down in the bed until I was prone, propping the phone on a pillow against my ear.

"I love you, Tallie."

"I love you, too."

"I'll call you tomorrow."

The laughter at continuing habits of good health sparked a thought: as those behaviors have been rendered irrelevant, what others of life's rules can I dismiss? Which can and might I ignore?

Day Seven

Last night after speaking with Tallie, I swam in the kidney-shaped pool at the Rodeway Inn in Boardman, Oregon. Approaching the town I passed expanses of farmland dotted with wheeled irrigation towers. I was curious to know what an aerial view of the landscape looked like, so I opened Google Earth on my laptop and zoomed in on my location…I viewed dozens of uniform-sized circles, each nearly two thousand feet across, in varying shades of green, arranged in orderly rows and columns. But something else had caught my attention as I drove toward Boardman yesterday afternoon: the Umatilla Army Depot. I looked it up on Wikipedia…Umatilla housed twelve percent of the nation's chemical weapons stockpile until last year; the Army has destroyed nearly four-thousand tons of sarin and nerve agents through high-temperature incineration. Holy Christ! It's only about a mile from the depot to the Columbia River, and the whole damned place is surrounded by irrigated farm land. If I had lived downstream from Umatilla, I would have become an activist. I hope to God the Army knows what it's doing. Fun facts from the farewell tour!

I departed Boardman late this morning; I slept in after staying up until well past midnight, thinking about my conversation with Tallie and mulling over apprehensions that arose from it.

I worried if over the years my demonstrations of how much I love Tallie have been enough for her. Have they been convincing? Isn't the sincerity obvious? Perspective again…our measurements are based on differing scales.

I wondered if there is any relationship that balances need, or if one of the two partners will always need more from the other… and does the giving partner ever tire of the dependence.

When I'm dead, how will Tallie cope in those moments she can't anticipate now, of unoccupied spaces…preparing a meal, enough food for two, sitting at the farmer's table in the kitchen with an empty chair beside her; watching TV in the corner of the sofa with no one to hog the pillows; lying in bed uncertain if she should center herself on the mattress or remain on the side that had been hers for nearly forty years. Intimacy is a horrible thing to do without.

Death, I've decided, is one more hole that hasn't enough dirt to be filled.

I'm amazed that I stole any sleep at all last night. I amassed questions and few answers.

The playlist I'd programmed didn't acknowledge the previous night's revelations, so I searched for and played "A Matter of Trust" by Billy Joel, and when he sang out "One, two, one, two, three, four!" I steered onto the I-84 ramp from Main Street, recklessly accelerating with the windows open, the air coursing around me, singing along in a shout: "But that can't happen to us, because it's always been a matter of trust!" In that moment, as in so many others during the trip, I realized I had forgotten about the disease…I had shoved it to the recesses of my thoughts. In a month's time, the cancer won't be so generous. Its deliberate insinuation will restrict the day-to-day activities I now take for granted. That realization leapfrogged me to a consideration of whether or not this trip has been fair to Tallie. I've stolen from her a period when I'm relatively unaffected, leaving her with weeks where my decline will be more pronounced. I actually considered turning back…driving toward Chicago until fatigue forced me to stop, rest, and continue. Is it a symptom of dying that I examined the trip as a what-if moment? What if I abandoned this trip, which I began with a purpose, and later, when I'm debilitated by this damned disease, regretted it more if I had continued it?

It was a day launched with doubt. But I continued west, electing to stop in Portland, instead of pushing on to Coos Bay. En route I deviated from the MapQuest-suggested path to circle south around Mt. Hood's snow-capped peak amid the green swath of its national forest. I slowed the Saab and photographed it through the windshield, framing it in a less than touristy perspective, and then in mid-afternoon arrived in Portland, crossing the Ross Island Bridge over the Columbia River. After checking into the Embassy Suites at Pine and Third, I had an early dinner at Mother's Bistro on Stark Street…great crab cakes…then wandered down to the waterfront bike trail. Walking south through the crowds of people along the river to the Marquam Bridge, I passed a water park and a marina, where I considered renting a kayak to explore the river… but wisely thought better of it. I turned around at the bridge and retraced my route, following the river north to the Broadway Bridge. I had stopped near Ankeny to buy a gelato and rest for a moment in a circular plaza, where I watched a young couple frolic with their toddler in a fountain. Each parent held an arm of the child, wearing only a diaper, and swung her in and out of the water stream that arced nearly ten feet across the sunken fountain. The child's dark, wet curls flattened against her scalp, she squealed with each swing as though it was as exciting as the first. I sat on the shallow concrete steps above the fountain, where it occurred to me in a not terribly original epiphany this time, that youth truly should be lauded, should be treasured, should be cherished. I hoped the young family understood the depth of their fortune, because being alone in the world can be devastating. I ached when I thought of how Tallie would feel after I'm dead.

Another thought occurred to me on the walk back to the hotel tonight: I've been casually noticing things I'm going to miss by dying. I almost wrote: "things I'll miss after I'm dead," which made me laugh out loud at its absurdity. During the driving, the monotony of the road…like a mantra…shuts out distractions, it frees my mind to associate and connect different thoughts. Or so I assumed. But isn't it just as feasible that the immense distances and range of scenery through which I've traveled…it has been anything but monotonous…is the inspiration for those insights and not merely a rolling background to fill the frame of my movie? I've driven more than two-thousand miles in a week. If I had a rigid itinerary, I suppose I'd have to say I was making good time, maybe even ahead of schedule. When the purpose of this trip doesn't bully my contemplations, I find myself enjoying the journey, like it's a rehearsal for retirement. It's one thing I'll miss…traveling…certainly again to Europe, and to China. I wanted to visit China. Another thing…sitting on the rooftop deck in summertime…from that vantage we can spot weekend fireworks at Navy Pier and even occasionally the display from Cellular Field on the South Side when the White Sox celebrate a home run. I'll miss that. And although I would never have lived long enough to learn the answer, I'm so curious about how this human experiment turns out. We are our own best spectator sport; we're such an idiosyncratic and absorbing species. Speaking of which, oh my God, Carl Zimmer is one of its oddest specimens.

Where to start in Carl's story. We met in Vietnam; both PFCs in the same squad. Our tours overlapped for around ten months in 1968, he rotated home before I did, and I lost touch. After I graduated from Iowa and began my first year at Northwestern Law, I read an article in the *Sun-Times* about a Metra train accident in Berwyn. It described an incident where a woman waiting at the crossing at Oak Park Avenue steered around the warning gates as an eastbound commuter express approached. She stopped her car on the tracks. The driver of a pickup also waiting at the crossing exited his vehicle and attempted to extract the woman, as well as an infant and a toddler from the car. But the doors of her car were locked and the man could not break the window glass. He leapt away from the woman's car moments before it was struck by the train. The woman and her children were killed; the man, a Vietnam veteran, was taken to Saint Anthony Hospital, where he was treated for cuts and bruises, and kept for observation. The man named in the article was Carl Zimmer.

Carl was from the Chicago area and the combination of the name and reporting he was a veteran seemed more than coincidence. After class that day, I drove out to Berwyn to visit Carl in the hospital. I parked on South Farrar Drive by Douglas Park and observed how Berwyn didn't resemble Evanston in the slightest. At the patient information desk a woman told me Carl Zimmer was no longer a patient, that he had been transferred to the VA Hospital on Taylor Street in Chicago. She gave me directions…it wasn't far…and eventually I located Carl. He'd been admitted to the psych ward at the VA hospital. No visitors I was told, but when I explained we'd served together I was directed to a staff physician…I still remember his name, Mitchum…who described how when Carl was brought in to the Saint Anthony emergency room, the staff there had quickly recognized that he'd experienced a psychotic break after his attempted rescue of the woman and children. Mitchum asked if I remembered any incident from Carl's service in Vietnam that might in some way seem analogous to the incident at the train crossing. That angered me. Post-traumatic stress wasn't well understood then; common wisdom focused more on when a Vietnam vet might go berserk, not if he would. Mitchum's probing struck me as abrupt and naïve. Was he asking me if Carl had killed children in Vietnam and was latent guilt the basis of his breakdown?

"When can I see him?" I demanded of Mitchum.

He regarded me calmly for a moment and then said Carl would have no visitors during the first twenty-four hours. I told him I'd be back the next day and then left the hospital in a fury, incensed in general by the prevalent attitude toward us as veterans, and toward Mitchum and the VA in particular for not being more sensitive about Carl's care.

I encountered Mitchum several times in the following weeks, and I changed my opinion of him. He helped Carl. Mitchum steered him toward an acknowledgment of not just what had happened to him, but also why, and fortified Carl with a structure for coping with it. I'd misjudged Mitchum, and on the day he released Carl I took him aside and told him so, apologizing for my attitude. He shook his head and simply whispered "Semper fi."

Carl had been working as a framing carpenter back then. He said he liked the idea of building instead of destroying something. That was easy to understand. As school allowed, we'd hang out… grab a beer and talk about old times and our futures…but as law school grew more demanding, we saw less of each other. One day during my third year, he called and said he was moving to Seattle, where a cousin had a construction company…he was tired of Chicago and its winters. We met for dinner at the Berghoff and in the wood-paneled dining room with the proper waiters in their starched white aprons, gliding among the tables, Carl told me that my being there for him meant more than he could express. I said something which has become a response Tallie has heard hundreds, maybe thousands of times when she seems amazed by how I support her: "Where else would you expect me to be?"

Seattle lasted a year or two; Carl bounced around the Northwest, but finally settled in Coos Bay about fifteen years ago. He bought a house out in the country east of town on the bank of the Coos River; he occasionally works as a handyman, still collects a VA disability, and got in and out of tech stocks with exquisite timing. Carl is "comfortable," as he describes it. The friendship we initiated in Vietnam and reinforced in Chicago has endured. We email, we speak on the phone a few times a year, and when he comes to Chicago to visit family, we get together. Two years ago we went back to the Berghoff, where we traded stories and sipped dark beers. As pedestrian as it sounds, Carl is the brother I never had.

I just received an email from Ellen…she and a bottle of vodka are commiserating over my bad luck and she's debating the wisdom of reaching out to Tallie at some point in the future. Oh boy.

The day I returned to the VA hospital, I visited Carl for a brief time. We hadn't seen each other in nearly six years and yet our appearances had followed parallel paths: hair hanging past our shoulders…mine in a ponytail, Carl's looking stringy and in need of a cleansing…and short, poorly-trimmed beards. Carl's features tended toward his Aryan roots…blond hair and ocean-blue eyes. He pushed himself to a sitting position in the narrow bed when I entered his room and muttered "Pretty FUBAR, huh?"

The sedatives, he said, put him in a lazy stupor, and because of them he thought he'd been dreaming when the doctor had told him that I had visited. "What are you doing here, man?"

I explained law school, reading the *Sun-Times* article, and underscoring the odds of the two of us reconnecting this way. Carl settled his head between two balusters of the bed's metal headboard. "That's some crazy shit."

We both laughed as the weightier meaning emerged. Carl tipped his head forward, resting his chin on his chest.

"You want to talk about it?" I asked him.

"No. But I don't think I'm getting out of here until I do." He raised his head and grinned.

"The story's still big news," I said. "The husband says she'd been depressed since the baby was born."

Carl grimaced and shook his head. "She looked at me when I banged on her window and she had that gaze…vacant and final.

Scared the shit out of me. There's an asshole on the ward who keeps asking me if I thought about just turning to greet the train myself."

"Want me to have a word with him?" We chuckled.

"I'm cracked, but I'm not a moron."

"Hey, Carl, sometimes we carry more than we can hump."

An orderly told me to wrap it up…my visit was over.

"I'll be back, Carl. You be well."

We slapped our fists together as we had in the past with our fingers overlapping our thumbs and pumped the grip up and down.

"Good to see you, man," Carl said. "I mean that."

I nodded and left.

In the coming weeks, Mitchum helped cleanse Carl of his terrors and encouraged me to visit as often as possible. During one visit Carl and I sat in the ward's dayroom and he remarked that the pajamas and robe he wore fitted him a bit too loosely. It sparked a memory of how we always wanted loose uniforms in the heat and humidity of the bush, and Carl said when he went clothes shopping with his mother when he was a child, she insisted on buying shirts and pants a size too large, claiming he should stop complaining of the fit, that he'd grow into them.

I'm making associations again. It occurs to me that I may have unconsciously intended this trip as a purifying endeavor…a way to cleanse myself of curses, baggage and burdens. I don't feel I've launched a quest for redemption, and I don't believe I'm clearing my conscience before I die. I haven't lived an exemplary life, and there's no one among the seven who could construe this journey as a pilgrimage of apology. But I'm cognizant of the law of unintended consequences, so nothing's off the table in this final negotiation.

I'm not sure what to make of this, but my bathroom here has a scale, which seems to me an odd accessory for a hotel room. I've lost four pounds since leaving Chicago. I was going to renew the healthy eating joke when I spoke with Tallie, but I got voicemail on both the home phone and her cell. I left a message that I'd be in Coos Bay the following day and would call her then. I noticed a lot of symmetry in my room: two beds with a table between them, wall-mounted swivel-arm lamps above that table, the TV bolted to the surface of a dresser flanked by two desks and identical armchairs. When we began designing and decorating our loft, Tallie chafed at my desire for symmetry. It's another annoying manifestation of my OCD, but I couldn't confess that to her, as we huddled with the architect and considered the floor plan for our home. You can imagine the contrast…you could have laid a grid over my plan, all right angles and straight walls. Tallie and the architect took a more organic approach…curving walls segmenting rather than dividing the space, preserving sightlines of the surrounding skyline throughout the interior. Tallie functions best in open areas; I was raised in a house with small rooms connected by narrow corridors. Our loft, as I've said, spans the entire upper floor of the building and it's embarrassing to say how many square feet it encompasses. Watching her renovate that expansive cavern into our haven, while contesting my goal of symmetry, rejuvenated me. We'd been married about twelve years at that time, and although I can't say the joy of our marriage had wilted, we had leveled ourselves with routines and grown contented if not stationary in our tendencies. The gift of the building and the challenges of refashioning it into a home recoupled us…renewed us. Tallie insisted I leap from my comfort zone into something more provoking. Her nudging has never slackened.

I was scouting routes from Portland to Coos Bay on MapQuest...I've chosen the ocean-view option down Highway 101...and noticed that my cumulative course has been saved as a squiggly blue line. I think I'll embed a copy of the completed map in my slideshow of photos.

My legs ache a little from all the walking today, so I'm going to treat myself to a hot bath...there's a jetted tub in the bathroom... and then go to bed.

Day Eight

My cell phone jolted me awake at two o'clock this morning; it was Tallie with news that Alison had fallen in her apartment and broken her arm. She'd only just returned home from the emergency room at Rush Memorial, and she had resigned herself to the inevitable, complaining that her procrastination had been trumped by events. I cajoled and mildly chided her that deliberation was far different from procrastination. Guilt and fatigue infused her words and I lay on my side, balancing the phone on my ear, listening, occasionally interjecting reassurances and hoping I didn't sound too patronizing. I knew from experience that what Tallie needed most was to talk herself out of this funk.

"I pulled so many strings tonight, I ought to have rope burns on my hands. You know me. I don't like asking for favors."

"Yeah. I know," I said.

"The kicker is that Alison won't even know how many favors I called in." Tallie paused and I heard her sigh. "My God…even thinking like that makes me feel bad."

"Honey…"

"I know!" We both fell silent for a moment.

"I'm sorry," Tallie whispered. "This is difficult for so many reasons, and I'm really trying not sound like a selfish bitch for having to deal with it alone. Jesus, there's no goddamned fairness in any of this."

"No rebuttal, your honor." I contemplated asking if she wanted me to come home, but feared either of the answers and the burdens they might impose down the road. Tallie sniffled and laughed, and I envisioned her in the open space of the loft, weeping as she held the phone with one hand and cupped her forehead in the palm of the other. That loft…people shape their environments to meet their needs; Tallie fashioned our loft to meet our needs, my needs, and the completed design amazed me, dumbfounded me actually, by how flawlessly it suited me, amazed me by how specifically Tallie intuited my needs…knowing me better in ways than I knew myself.

"They're keeping Alison overnight at the hospital. Tomorrow she'll be transported to a facility in Lincoln Park that specializes in seniors with dementia." Tallie's voice was lifeless.

"Are we seniors now, too?" I mused, recalling one particular Saturday morning shortly after Tallie and I became lovers. She'd ridden the El up to my apartment in Evanston Friday night after work, the same apartment I'd had as a law student. It was summer, the windows were open and we'd thrown back the bedcovers seeking relief from the heat. Anytime we touched, that point would immediately pool with sweat. Tallie lay on her back. She'd pulled her hair off her neck and fanned it on the pillow and I lay on my side facing her, tracing a fingertip along her stomach, skimming as closely to her skin as I could without actually touching. A flawed technique…when my fingertip grazed her skin, she shivered, gooseflesh rippling along her torso. Even in the heart the chill seemed at times too intense to endure, but she shunned my offers to stop, whispering throatily for me to go on. She had closed her eyes and at that moment I confessed to her that on the night we met at Alison's party, after the hours of easy conversation, when finally I'd left and gone back to this very apartment, I'd masturbated in the same bed thinking of her. When I told her that, she opened her eyes and steered my hand to her pussy. She gently manipulated our linked fingers until she climaxed, locking her gaze on me, and contorting her face in a soundless grimace. We fucked that morning, dripping sweat in the summer heat, drenching the sheets, slipping and sliding off one another like otters, and laughing feverishly. When hunger and dehydration eventually overtook us, we spoke of love for the first time.

"Seniors? I'm afraid so, my darling."

"I love you, Tallie. I'm worried you'll never understand how much I love you."

She was crying then, making no effort to hold back.

I listened to Tallie cry. When she wore down I reminded her of what a selfless friend she's always been for Alison. I reminded her I would be visiting Carl later that day. I reminded her again that I loved her and wanted to hear her say she'd try to get some rest. We ended the phone call and I readied myself for the rage I felt swelling in me. I wanted to hurl my cellphone at the TV, to rip the door off the mini-fridge, to shatter the lamps against the wall… largely to trash the room with all the finesse of a coked-up rock star. How many ways are there to shriek about unfairness, or to curse the arbitrariness of death? Why is it so difficult just to concede to it? What about me is so singular that I deserve more warning, deserve more time to prepare? I suppose the anger springs from the fact that the answer to that final question is obvious: there's nothing singular about me and even if there was, it wouldn't warrant more time. The scales I picture tipping in my favor with good works and thoughts are fictional, a veneer we apply to conceal the chaos that absolutely terrifies us. I've mocked people with faith, but I always grasped the utility of God, of an explanation of the irrationality of living. Without inventing a reason for existence and our awareness of that existence, there lies nothing but pointlessness. And terror. If sentience develops from genetic mutations on an evolutionary roller coaster ride, and not from the anointment of a divine hand, then chaos succeeds. We do want rules. We crave community; we survive better in tribes than we do alone.

In the hours after talking with Tallie, these are the thoughts that kept me awake. I sent Carl an email at around four-thirty telling him I'd arrive a day later than planned. I wanted to get a room in Coos Bay and crash rather than drive out to his home…I knew when we got together it would a late night and I needed sleep.

I was surprised when he quickly responded to my email.

Welcome mat's always out.

What are you doing up so early?

Had to get up and piss. Bitch relying on an old prostate. Why are you up?

Dealing with some home front glitches. Tell you about it tomorrow.

In the weeks after Carl left the VA hospital, he'd telephone me when he grew particularly frail, and I'd answer regardless of the time of day, but the calls tended to come as dawn neared. I'd listen and try to pilot him around whatever obstacle he'd confronted, waiting to hear the plaintive tone of his voice fade and a cooler, if not confident, tone emerge. The next time we'd get together after such a call, Carl would again thank me for being there, and I'd respond again "Where'd you expect me to be?"

I realize I'm looking forward to seeing Carl perhaps more than, if not differently, anyone else on my list. The origin and strength of my bond with Carl are different than with anyone else; and the duration…he's the person on the list I've known the longest.

I'm going to try and grab a few hours of sleep before I head down the highway to Coos Bay. It's a five-hour drive and I flirted with the idea of leaving now, but I want some time to enjoy the ocean on my flank. I'll preview the playlist: "Louie, Louie" by the Kingsmen, a Portland band, and a song whose unintelligible lyrics were rumored, in my high school and hundreds of others nationwide, to be so teasingly obscene that the FBI launched an investigation into the matter. When I finally learned the lyrics, I was amazed at how bland they were.

Day Nine

I'm planning to catch up on sleep tonight; maybe the ships' horns I hear from my room will play a lullaby. The Best Western Holiday…perhaps an unintended reflection on this trip…is in southern Coos Bay, at the corner of the Oregon Coast Highway and Market Street, a clamshell's throw from the river. Would it belabor the obvious to say this succession of motel rooms is melding into a single generic interior? Fried shrimp for dinner at the Kozy Kitchen…doesn't warrant a mention, but what the hell. The view from the bridge over the bay coming into town was spectacular, but Coos Bay itself contrasts poorly with the scenery I passed through coming down from Portland. I picked up 101 north of Lincoln City and near Glenden Beach it began to hug the coastline. For lazy stretches the ocean lay on my right and foothills on my left. I pulled into a wayside at Seal Rock State Park and snapped some photographs of the rock formations and the processions of white-capped waves. Amusingly…no seals! Farther down the coast near Florence, however, at the Sea Lion Caves, I saw dozens of them, stunning...fat and tawny, woofing and yelping while they lounged on the rocks and lunged through the surf. It ain't SeaWorld. North of Coos Bay miles of sand dunes ranged between the highway and the ocean...they reminded me of some stretches of beach near Chu Lai, south of DaNang.

In March 1968 I deployed to Vietnam...the same month Bobby Kennedy entered the presidential race and Lyndon Johnson announced he wouldn't run for re-election. During that year Martin Luther King was assassinated, Johnson signed the Civil Rights Act, "Hair" opened on Broadway, the Beatles formed Apple Records and released the White album, Bobby Kennedy was killed, Andy Warhol was shot by a radical feminist, the CIA started the Phoenix Program, Saddam Hussein joined a coup d'état in Iraq, Intel was founded, Nixon and Humphrey were nominated by their parties, George Wallace ran as a third party candidate, the Democratic Convention sparked police riots in Chicago, James Anderson, Jr. posthumously received the Medal of Honor (the first black Marine ever to receive the award), Hot Wheels toy cars were introduced, "60 Minutes" debuted on CBS, Detroit won the World Series, Led Zeppelin performed live for the first time, two black Americans raised their fists at the Olympic Games in Mexico City, Nixon won, Yale began admitting women, the Zodiac Killer continued killing, and astronauts on Apollo 8 became the first humans to see the far side of the moon and the Earth in a single frame...they read a passage from Genesis.

Amid all that upheaval forty-four years ago, I met Carl Zimmer. Memory is serpentine, not linear...recollections dance like water droplets in a hot skillet.

Sunset lingers, but I'm weary and sleepy.

Day Eleven

Carl and I talked through the night, lumbering from our chairs beside his fire pit near the river to the house this morning as dawn advanced. I had expected that… spending eighteen hours meandering through shared and individual memories. What I should have expected, but did not, and was therefore somewhat ambushed, was the swiftness with which Carl discarded pleasantries and drilled me with questions about matters I'd only perfunctorily considered or avoided entirely.

Breakfast yesterday was coffee and a muffin, and I drove the eight miles to Carl's house on the south fork of the Coos River in less than half an hour, listening to The Animals belt out "We Gotta Get Out of This Place." His house rests on the north bank of the river on a deep lot where woods frame the house like a V, the open end facing the road, and the angled tree lines telescoping as they approach the river. Carl's home, a wide, two-story, clapboard farm house, painted a dove gray with black accent trim and blood-red shutters, sits thirty yards back from the road. If you elevated it from its foundation, lowered it to a flatbed and trucked it to the Iowa prairie, it wouldn't raise an eyebrow, with two exceptions: there's no basement, and instead of a porch that spans the entire width of the house, the front door and the three steps leading to it are sheltered by a small overhang with a pitched roof. Along the river, porches are built on the rear of the house, not the front…the river supplies the money view, Carl told me.

I had Carl's house number but I didn't need it. As I drew close to his address, I saw a mailbox with half a dozen helium-filled balloons tied to it…all black…passersby probably thought someone was celebrating a fiftieth birthday. I turned into a sandy parking area and Carl rounded the corner of the house wearing a wide smile. His blond hair had gone frosty white, it was still thick, hadn't receded, and hung over his collar and the tops of his ears. The beard was gone, replaced by a bushy mustache. He appeared fit, the older version of the tall, rangy Carl I'd met in 1968. I had barely closed the Saab's door when he enveloped me in his arms and lifted me off the ground.

"Damn, man!" he said and we laughed. He lowered me, grasped both my arms in his hands and said, "Let's take a hike."

Without waiting for my answer, Carl draped an arm across my shoulders and guided me across the road. I followed him up a shaded ravine for about two hundred meters, until he veered west and climbed about two-thirds of the way up the hill. He deflected my questions about where we were going. The pace he set wasn't casual and it was obvious he'd walked this course many times before. Carl had been an excellent map reader and was often assigned to walk point when we were out on patrol. At the edge of a clearing no more than twenty feet square, we stopped. I hitched my hands on my hips and gulped for air as Carl waved an arm like a gracious host, indicating his parcel of nine pot plants arranged in a perfect square, three to a row, each plant nearly as tall as a man.

"Just a little resupply mission," he said. "To replace what we're gonna work our way through tonight."

I reached forward and stroked the leaves of the nearest plant and then rubbed my fingertips beneath my nose. That lush scent evoked well-defined memories of Carl, me and others passing a bong in a bunker on a hilltop artillery base west of Dong Ha. We'd come off an operation where we'd overrun an NVA regimental command post and were relieved and happy we'd been pulled back to provide security for the artillery company. Two guys in our squad had been killed.

Carl stripped leaves from several plants and stashed them in a plastic bag he removed from his jeans pocket.

"It's beautiful up here," I said, scanning the sky beyond the treetops, inhaling the piney fragrance of the forest around us.

"It's peaceful country."

On the relaxed stroll down the hill, Carl and I walked side by side. "So you're dying," he said.

"Correct."

"Tough break."

I nodded.

"And you're driving around the country, saying goodbye to people."

"Correct again."

"Why not just call or send an email?"

"Doesn't work for me. This is a face-to-face operation." I paused. "And I need a favor from you."

"Anything, man."

"I need a knife."

Carl stopped on the trail and turned to regard me for a moment. "How about a Kabar?"

"If you can part with it."

"Send it back when you're done with it if you can. It was my dad's." We resumed our trek back to the house.

Carl had designed the interior of his ground floor as an open, high-ceilinged space, completing most of the work himself. He explained that a friend who lived up the road had helped him install steel structural beams so they could safely remove the load-bearing walls. From inside the front door I gazed straight to the rear of the house, where glass folding doors opened to the porch. We walked to the kitchen area beneath ceiling fans that reminded me of aircraft propellers as they lazily churned the air, and I looked down a gentle slope to the river's edge, where a T-shaped cedar dock extended into the water, with an aluminum rowboat lashed to one of the posts. Across the river black-faced cattle grazed in a pasture and I unconsciously began counting them from left to right. I felt joy that Carl had crafted a comfortable home for himself.

"My compliments to the decorator," I said.

Carl crossed his arms and leaned his hip against the edge of the kitchen island, which was capped in stainless steel. "Most people walk in and just gawk. The inside of the house doesn't match the outside for them."

"Well, it works."

Carl spread the pot leaves on the island. "I'll hang these to dry later."

We sat on padded stools and sipped orange juice.

"Where to start," I said.

"Are you working through your bucket list?" Carl asked.

"Not exactly. And anyway, the bucket's full of holes…the list drained out a few weeks ago."

Carl traced a circle in the condensation on his juice glass. "You might have some trouble seeing this as uplifting, but customarily the future's uncertain. You don't know whether to plan for the best that could happen or the worst. Knowing the future is the gift that won't keep giving in your case, but you could still accept it as a gift."

"When did you get so metaphysical?"

"It's part of my new practice." He indicated the pot leaves. "Mary-Jane Buddhism. I've mellowed in my old age."

"You got your head on straight, is that what you're telling me?"

"I'm a river rock. I don't fight the current. I let the water wash over me and smooth out the rough edges."

We laughed and for a time shared the silence of close friends.

Finally, I asked Carl about his bookshelves. Three tall windows afforded a view of the woods on the east side of the property and Carl had framed them with bookshelves of honey-colored wood that spanned from the floor to the ceiling. I walked to a section and examined the titles…classic and contemporary fiction, philosophy, cookbooks, politics, science, travel, photography, history and even law.

"I started reading when I lived in Seattle. For a while it seemed my only possession was a library card and reading was cheap entertainment."

"I'm not even going to ask if you've read them all," I said, taking in the physical and substantive breadth of his collection.

"I grew out of escapism and started feeding my hunger for learning. When I renovated this house I only owned enough books to fill one of these bookcases."

I realized I'd gone ten days without reading a book, rare for me. I enjoy history and biography; Tallie loves fiction. With two or three volumes beside the bed, I alternate reading portions of each of them…it drives Tallie crazy.

"Looks like you may need to build more soon."

"C'mon," Carl said. "Let's sit on the porch for a while."

"There's nothing they can do?" Carl asked as we settled into Adirondack chairs on the porch, which felt cool in the mid-morning shade.

I shook my head. "Did you build these, too?" I tapped the arm of the chair. There were seven of them on the porch lined up and facing the river.

"Uh huh." He indicated a wooden shed tucked into the woods on the west side of the lot. "That's my workshop. Pushing on…rate your fear on a scale of one to ten."

Remembering how fear seemed ever-present to us in Vietnam, I explained that the certainty of dying generated a different class of fear. Back then the fear had a metallic taste to it, like iron. One Gunny we knew used to say that without fear, there would be no courage.

"I remember how scared you looked in the VA hospital," I told Carl, "and I imagine it's similar to that. Or maybe nothing like it at all. It's a unique experience."

I wagged my head.

"When I was driving the other day, I realized that at our age we should be bracing ourselves for loss. Parents get old and die, friends get sick and die. Loss has a familiar face. But I wasn't prepared for being the one who would be lost."

"Are you angry?" Carl asked.

I considered his question.

"On a scale of one to ten? I vacillate between four and eight." I wondered why Janine had warned me about anxiety but never once mentioned anger…perhaps she believed discussing it might induce it. I had wanted to use this trip to achieve a sense of peace, and, as I realized the other day, have it cleanse me in some fashion. But at times I can't escape the anger. Ellen and Del never bluntly addressed it, but Carl's a friend with no qualms about forcing me to explore something I might choose to ignore.

"I used to believe that anger was fuel," Carl said. "It powered my rage." He sipped from his orange juice and tugged at an ear lobe. "In truth, anger wastes fuel and robs you of power…it weakens you. It weakened me until I let it go."

"Let it go…" I waved my hand as though coaxing a bird into flight.

"I know," Carl laughed. "So much easier to say than to do. It took me years to accomplish it and the process took its toll."

"But I've got the gift of knowledge."

"Yes," Carl emphasized. "I was unwilling to accept how hating underlay so many of my problems when I came home from the war. I didn't want to stop hating, but I knew I had to if I was going to survive."

"I'm not going to…"

Carl cut me off. "I know…let me make my point!" He paused. "I made a mistake back then…I allowed my pride to prevent, or to delay, me from making a course correction and it cost me. I needed to put my life on another path, or I'd wind up like my father. He worked at the Western Electric plant in Cicero until it shut down in 1984, and then he became a drunk-in-residence at a bar in Bridgeport, where he bitched from his stool about Jews, Mexicans and blacks.

"I'm not trying to give you advice on how to spend the rest of your miserably short life," Carl said calmly. "I'm trying to thank you. You helped me when no one else would and that means more to me than I've ever told you."

I was speechless.

"I love living by this river. It reminds me that life doesn't behave like water…it doesn't seek the most direct route to lower ground. Life zigs and zags, it shoots up, slides down and skids sideways. It's messy and unpredictable. But you…you have been predictable and reliable and a friend." Carl reached over and gripped my hand. "Thank you."

Emotions were firing in my mind, like a string of firecrackers exploding in slow motion…Boom! a thought appeared…seconds later Boom! another insight…Boom! a memory surfaced. On and on. I recalled the night I had decided to ask Tallie to marry me…and the moment in my life when I realized I had ceased to be impetuous….and that I want to tell Tallie that I'll always be lurking somewhere inside her, that when she misses me she can reach down inside and pull up whatever part of me she needs…and that this last visit with Carl comes at a time when I am facing death and longing to feel that my life is truly unique…and that Carl seems to have accepted with serenity that his own life is far from unique and that experiences are common. I'd tried so many times on this trip to avoid having it devolve into a fruitless succession of daily judgments of how I have lived my life. Now I wondered if it was naïve of me to expect to reclaim memory without judging it. Boom! A memory of sitting with my father, drinking beer in the kitchen of our home in St. Louis.

"My father was an executive with Anheuser-Busch," I told Carl. "When I came back from the war and confessed some indecision about what I would do next with my life, he told me that he had worked, saving and investing, so he could eventually buy time and freedom when he was older. At the time I thought that was pathetic, but I came to understand him. And I appreciate how he taught me to set expectations."

"Our parents grow smarter as we grow older, right?"

I nodded and Carl released my hand. "Our fathers were different. Mine put in the minimum. Everything I've accomplished I did in spite of him…and perhaps to spite him. I understand your father's goal…I did the same thing. I worked and saved, got lucky with those tech investments and now I have money to buy me time and freedom."

"How'd you manage that? Some kind of insider information?"

"No, counselor." He chuckled. "Stalking that bubble was like spotting an ambush…you need to sense the perfect moment to act just before hell breaks loose."

"Now you're living your dream."

"No thanks to anything my father ever did for me. But then, some people aren't equipped to be good parents."

"No."

"Why didn't you and Tallie ever have kids?"

"Timing," I answered quickly. Tallie and I had weighed the subject of our childlessness many times before. "We made choices and catered to demands that resulted in lost opportunities."

"I'm not gonna beat you up about it, man" Carl said. "But when I turn on the TV or surf the net for news, I see all the wrong people breeding, hurling their flotsam and jetsam into the human genetic pool."

"You're sounding a tad elitist there, Carl."

"How else can the educated sound when they talk about know-nothings?"

"You have a point."

Carl twisted in his chair to face me. "I've never been good with authority, as you may remember." Carl's smile lifted his moustache at the corners of his mouth. "And while I've come a long way toward practicing a live-and-let-live philosophy, I still bristle when stupid people try to impose their belief systems on me."

"That's understandable."

"Let's get some lunch. You like salmon?"

Carl grilled salmon fillets and tossed a salad of baby spinach, cherry tomatoes, strawberries, blueberries and shaved fennel in balsamic vinaigrette. I joked that it seemed he had read the cookbooks in his library.

"I downloaded some tunes for us," he said. "The top one hundred songs of 1968."

"Outstanding," I said and then told Carl about how I began each day of the trip with a distinct playlist.

"That's a cool idea. But I think you're going to be surprised by how much crappy music was recorded in 1968. There are some gems, too, and it's funny, but the crap is just as evocative as the good stuff."

While Carl prepared lunch and the music played from recessed speakers in the ceiling, I sat at the island with a glass of iced tea and the two of us chatted about subjects unrelated to disease, death and war. I complimented him on the idyllic atmosphere of his home. He spoke of the tranquility he felt living beside the river…of how he would sit on his dock and watch weasels, skunks, white-tailed deer, raccoons, elk, and during one nocturnal, inebriated occasion a Sasquatch, congregate at the riverbank. In the winter he fished for steelhead trout, and the entire area was a bird-watcher's wet dream.

The ease of our conversation soothed me; it herded into an alcove of my mind the thoughts I'd been generating about how little time remained in my life. The effortlessness of being around Carl silenced the anger.

After lunch, Carl showed me to the guest room upstairs, which was dominated by a bed with a carved wooden headboard…irregular forms layered upon one another, swirls like waves breaking away from the center, the depth of the carving deepening toward the edges. I pointed to it and tilted my head at Carl.

"An early effort," he said. "That's why it's in the guest room." Carl grinned. "I've always enjoyed working with my hands. When I keep them busy, my mind is unbound."

I told Carl how the driving had a similar effect on me during the trip.

"I started working with wood as a way to make a living. Now I work with wood as a way to express life."

"I understand, Carl." I placed my bag on the bed and sighed. Framed black and white landscape photos hung on the wall and an Oriental carpet lay on the dark-stained hardwood floor. In the corner of the room an old Martin acoustic guitar rested on a stand. Carl lifted the instrument, sat on an armless chair by the window, and played a few chords. The strings over the sound hole had dulled with repetitive strumming, darkening from the original gleaming bronze color. "Time to change your strings."

"They're nicely broken in…just the tone I want!"

"I can't get over this place, Carl. It's beautiful here."

"It has appealing balance. Isolated, but not remote. People quiet, if you know what I'm trying to say, but filled with the noise of nature. I find that consoling."

Carl was right. Unlike Minneapolis or Moscow, this river valley sanctuary possessed a narcotic quality…it resembled a destination more than a way station on my trip. As Tallie and I had with her grandfather's building, Carl had performed domestic alchemy: he'd metamorphosed a house into a home. The impact on him was as conspicuous as the sculpting on the headboard. He radiated an implausibly purpose of belonging here. Every feature of his home appeared as though it had sprung from him, as though he had hand-rubbed every surface within the walls, scoring them with his character. I could envision dying here. If I telephoned Tallie and told her to fly our here, what would she say? I've visualized my death scene…I'm nestled in pillows and propped up in a hospital bed in the loft, facing east toward the Loop, fire smoldering and Tallie beside me holding my hand, gripping it lightly, gentle, fat snowflakes drifting down on a calm winter afternoon. Quite a spectacle and unbelievably romanticized. I'd bored into the Web doing research on what to expect as the disease progressed, and Janine had been unrestrained in her description of the toll this cancer will extort.

"When you asked earlier if I was afraid?" I said to Carl. "I'm scared of dying, but I suppose I'm more afraid of pain."

"They'll manage that for you, right?" Carl replaced the guitar on its stand.

I nodded and lowered myself onto the edge of the mattress. "Of course. I've got pain meds now if I need them, but I haven't taken any yet. It's bittersweet how during this trip I'm relatively symptom-free."

"Like I told you…a gift. It's good to see you're not squandering it."

"I'm worried Tallie doesn't see it that way." I explained my fear that Tallie would eventually resent my having robbed her of this time we could have shared together.

"I think you know her better than that," Carl said.

"I've lost my grip on certainty these days."

"That's a good thing. Certainty can lead to some awful decisions."

"True enough."

"Are you going to go into hospice after you get back to Chicago?"

"My doctor recommended it."

"I do, too," Carl said, leaning back into the bedside chair. "It really helped my sister and her family a great deal."

"Oh…"

"Lung cancer…a year ago. Lifelong smoker…and she inherited dad's liver." He grinned, compressing his lips in a thin line.

"Her husband and kids stayed with her night and day for more than a week, never knowing when she might slip into unconsciousness. It was heartbreaking watching them wonder each time they spoke to her if it was the last thing she'd hear. The morphine knocked her out at the end and she died quietly."

"God."

"Have you considered other options?"

"Other options?"

"Taking the timing into your own hands."

"Ah…no, I haven't."

"Some do. For them it's logical and viable."

"Tallie would kill me," I said reflexively, and Carl and I hesitated for a moment, eyeballing one another until we simultaneously erupted in howling laughter.

"Well," Carl struggled to say with tears in his eyes. "That's an option, too, I guess."

I fell back on the mattress and we continued laughing, savoring the gallows humor.

Later that afternoon, Carl took a painted metal box down from an upper shelf on one of the bookcases. For more than an hour we'd been lounging in leather club chairs, nursing beers, and listening to the progression of 1968's greatest hits wind down. Carl had been right…time had not been kind in its judgment of some of that year's pop "classics." He placed the box on the coffee table and removed the lid. I recognized what lay inside…tracings from the Wall, the Vietnam Memorial in Washington, D.C. Seeing them caused me to inhale sharply.

"Jesus," I whispered.

"All the names I could find of guys I knew."

"How many?"

"Thirteen."

"Fuck."

We lifted each tracing and recalled faces that had smiled and cried, and that had worn expressions of fear, fatigue, compassion, hate, pain and which eventually had gone blank.

"You've been?" Carl asked.

"Several times," I said. "Every time I go to the D.C. I visit."

"Ever left anything there?"

"Yeah. You?"

"A boot," Carl said.

"One boot?"

Carl nodded. "One boot. The other's upstairs in my closet."

"Some kind of symbolism? One foot planted in each place?"

"Not what I intended," Carl said. "But that's going to be my story from now on."

We laughed and a slight twinge in my jaw muscles reminded me that we had laughed a lot that day.

"What did you leave?" Carl asked.

"Bush hat."

That evening while Carl chopped mushrooms and onions for a sauce to top our steaks, I sat on the back porch and called Tallie.

"I miss you," I said when she answered the telephone.

"There's a lot of that going around, mister."

"How's Alison?"

"Hold on a minute," she said. I detected sounds I'd heard hundreds of times before and I visualized Tallie slipping her bag off her shoulder and dropping it to the floor, sandwiching the telephone receiver in the crook of her shoulder as she wrestled off her suit jacket, and the thud of her shoes hitting the floor as she kicked them off.

"All comfy now?" I teased.

"Bite me," she snorted, and I visualized the grin that always accompanied that quasi-slur.

"Come on. Fight fair. You taste too good."

"I miss you, too, honey." Tallie paused and I heard her take a deep breath and release it noisily. "Alison is better. She's up in Lincoln Park at the center. I met with some of the staff; they seem competent and compassionate."

"How are you holding up?"

"They threw some compassion my way, so I guess I'll add intuitive to their list of qualities."

"Sounds like a fine facility."

"It's bright…modern. Alison's room faces west, but she can see the park and the lake from some of the common areas. It's very professional and I like the people I met."

"Are you feeling more comfortable with your decision?"

"Gradually getting there."

Telling Tallie I was calling from Carl's home, I described the spectacle…the curving river, the flatland pasture and the encircling trees…and how the fusion of the setting and the atmosphere of Carl's house had relaxed me, fairly mesmerized me with its tranquility. I told her I'd taken some photos that I'd show her when I got home.

"We should have visited before," Tallie said.

"Hey," I cautioned. "This is the farewell tour, not the trail of regrets."

"So, how's Carl?"

"Fantastic. He seems healthy both above and below the neck." Tallie chuckled. "I'm going to stay here tonight."

"Say hello for me," Tallie said.

"I will."

"Is the trip living up to your expectations?"

Tallie hadn't asked me that before. "Yeah. So far, nothing even approaching disappointment. The visits…" I paused to consider my words carefully. "Everything has been, I don't know, more than fulfilling? But that doesn't describe it adequately. The pattern, Tallie, of conversations with these friends, and the stretches in between them…it's been thought-provoking, insightful, instructive. We'll sit down and talk about it when I get home. I'm sure now it was the right thing to do."

"I'm glad. But I do miss you."

Carl at that moment stepped onto the porch and warned me that dinner would be ready soon. "Hey, Tallie," he called.

"Hey, Carl," Tallie answered and I aimed the receiver at him.

"Time to go, honey," I said. "I'll call you tomorrow night."

"I love you."

"Love you, too," I said.

After dinner, Carl showed me his workshop, and then we collected logs from an adjacent woodpile and carried them to a fire pit beside a willow tree near the riverbank. Gray ash and scraps of charred timber lined the bottom of the sunken pit, which was ringed by a neat wall of mortared river stones about a foot tall and a foot thick…I unconsciously began counting the stones. A circle of chairs surrounded the pit, each chair identical to the Adirondacks on the porch, but without the matching footrests. We walked down to the boat dock and witnessed a spectacular moment when the sunset reflected on the river. The colors sequined the water's sparkling surface, stretching in a flame-colored band from the bend east of Carl's dock to another bend west of his property. It lasted a minute or two before the sun dropped below the tree line, the sky darkened to a deep blue, and the river dulled to a black ribbon.

"Once a year the sun reaches the perfect position to line up with the river for that display," Carl said. "Your timing is uncanny."

Carl built a fire, we settled into the chairs, and passed the first of three bottles of red wine back and forth, dispensing with the formality of glasses. As nighttime enveloped us, the quality of Carl's property shifted…the sky seemed immense, populated with millions of stars. When I marveled at the magnificence of the panorama, Carl said he'd always believed the space between the stars seemed more intriguing than the stars themselves. The river grew musical in its flow and the fire formed an insulated space in which honesty seemed not merely effortless, but compulsory. I experienced a sensation in the darkness…daylight, I grasped, by enabling vision, sometimes curbs imagination. We envision no farther than we see. By eliminating visual barriers, darkness unshackles our imagination.

"Do you get lonely out here, Carl?" I asked somewhere into the second bottle of wine.

"Not really," he said. "I've got a girlfriend." His voice sounded playful.

"What?"

Carl chuckled. "I wasn't trying to keep her a secret. She went up to Eugene to visit family so you and I could have some time together."

"Hey, I'd like to have met her."

"I thought about that. But it seemed more important for us to have some alone time."

"Well, I'm happy for you."

"Thank you. I am, too. Her name's Brianne and she's really a wonderful woman."

"How'd you two meet?"

"At a supermarket in town. She was behind me in the checkout line; some of her stuff fell across the separation bar on the conveyor belt and the kid rang it up as mine. Neither of us was paying attention and I was halfway to my truck when she came running after me, explaining what had happened. We had a laugh sorting through my bags and retrieving what was hers. There were only a couple of items and when I refused to let her pay for them, she insisted she buy me a coffee."

The firelight illuminated Carl's face, revealing a smile that encompassed the expanse from his mouth to his eyes.

"Coffee led to dinner, led to this and that, and now it's been more than four years we're together."

"You never said anything."

"I wasn't sure it was going anywhere."

Carl went on to tell me that Brianne taught math at a charter school in Coos Bay, was divorced with no children, and grew up on an organic dairy farm. Her mother had been an original Dead Head in the mid-sixties, claimed to have dropped acid with Ken Kesey, moved to an Oregon commune in 1969 where she met and fell in love with a young man who tended the dairy barn, married him and had three children, and when the commune disintegrated, partnered with him to start their own dairy. Brianne, who was fifteen years younger than Carl, spends most of her time at Carl's but maintains her own apartment in Coos Bay, and while they have discussed marriage, neither feels rushed to do it. She once told Carl that she was impressed that he seemed to feel no need to try and save her from her past.

What impressed me about Carl was not so much what he said as how his voice softened when he said it. His cadence slowed, the tones mellowed and when he spoke Brianne's name the infection sounded like a breathy accent. The happiness I felt for Carl at that moment warmed me more than the fire.

Shortly after Carl opened the third bottle of wine, he jolted from his chair, saying he couldn't believe he'd forgotten the bong. He stumbled over to his workshop and returned with a bong that reflected the flames on its red glass surface. After that, the night evened out and then devolved. We talked for hours; I laughed so hard that at one time I had to rise from my chair and stretch out a cramp in my side. Carl rose and staggered to the edge of the trees to pee and sprinted back, yelling that something with blazing eyes had skulked up on him. The night was noisy with non-human sounds. Occasionally the breeze shifted, wafting the odor of cow manure across the river, reminding me of Iowa City.

We nourished the fire with logs and tracked the smoke as it curled toward the sky. At some point I realized Carl had been silent for a while and I looked over to see him peacefully sleeping. I slouched down in my own chair and closed my eyes, thinking of Tallie. Carl woke me with a shake of my shoulder; he told me it was almost four in the morning, and we dragged ourselves to the house and our beds.

I showered mid-morning, packed my bag and reviewed some of the photos I'd taken of Carl around the fire pit. The combination of the intense light from the flash and the warm glow of the flames lent his features an engaging quality. Carl stood in the kitchen when I came downstairs and offered me coffee.

"Hell of a night," I said.

"Hell of a life," he answered.

Our goodbye, in contrast to what preceded it, seemed anticlimactic. We clutched each other tightly, I told Carl I loved him, and he said the same. I think neither of us wanted to prolong the process…we'd reiterated the same emotions the night before, in words and in the silences between the words, just like the darkness between the stars of which Carl was so fond. The last thing Carl did was hand me the Kabar, in its leather sheath, and a whetstone. I nodded.

I veered from my plan and replayed "We Gotta Get Out of This Place" as I drove south and east for six hours to Klamath Falls, Oregon, with a short rest detour and some photos at Crater Lake National Park. I checked into a Quality Inn across the street from Lake Ewauna, ate a nondescript meal and retired to my room early. Saying goodbye to Carl distressed me more than either parting with either Ellen or Del. Carl and I share more history between us, and that history is…more profound? More significant? More primitive? Its nature is fraternal rather than merely friend-based…when I said early on I would be visiting family, I had Carl in mind. I did secure one pledge from him last night…he agreed to speak at my funeral.

My next destination is Elko, Nevada. I have to return some letters.

Day Twelve

The hangover and the disillusionment hadn't yet fully thumped me when I left Carl's yesterday. I only drove about two-and-a-half hours today, to a town named Lakeview, right on the California border, where I checked into the Lakeview Lodge Motel shortly after noon.

During the drive to Klamath Falls yesterday, the weather was drab, with low gloomy clouds shrouding both the day and my mood. In a break from routine, I emailed Tallie from the motel rather than telephone her. Writing yesterday's journal entry took hours and when I reread it tonight, I remembered portions of conversation by the fire pit that I hadn't included. It forced me to examine if I'm censoring what I write here. Am I being honest with myself on this trip or am I subconsciously protecting Tallie by glossing over some of my emotions? And what's the point of that if I am? I know that months from now, when Tallie and I have face-to-face moments, there will be no question of being anything less than totally honest. As Carl would say, it's another instance of timing, with time, of course, being a commodity that's running out.

I'm depressed…I understand that…but for the first time since my diagnosis I'm apprehensive that depression may become a constant state of mind. When I got in the car this morning, I searched for Albinoni's "Adagio in G Minor for Strings and Organ" on my iPod. The haunting nature of that piece evoked emotions that coalesced poignantly with the melancholy weather. At its conclusion, I played several Doors albums; that music's association with Vietnam, and with the memories of Carl and the other men I knew there, definitely was a regretful choice…it cemented my mood into place like the mortar binding the river stones in Carl's fire pit. More alarming than the likelihood of persistent depression is a greater fear that I'll slink into emotional autopilot…neutralizing every discomforting feeling.

Sitting by the fire pit, staring at the array of stars, Carl and I considered how from primitive man forward through history, people had ogled these same heavenly lights and pondered the insignificance of their existence. Then we guffawed at the predictability of two stoned men sitting by a fire, staring at the night sky and dwelling on their own triviality. But we also remembered star-gazing, mind-numbing nights in Vietnam…and we speculated whether the seeds scattered during that terrifying period in our lives had germinated any wisdom that the old men huddled decades later beside a river in Oregon could exploit. Carl said he believed Vietnam was the fuse and the incident at the railroad tracks in Berwyn was the explosion that prompted him to evaluate what kind of life he needed to live. He likened the current that had buoyed him to his present condition to something his uncle often said about his service as a Marine, island-hopping in the Pacific during World War II…he wouldn't want to do it again, but he wouldn't want to have missed the lessons he learned either. "Everything comes at a cost," Carl had said. "Try not to overpay, of course, but nothing meaningful is free."

I vented my fury that night as I hadn't since I left Chicago… like I haven't since Janine confirmed this death sentence. Carl bellowed like a pep squad. At one point we stood on the boat dock and I shrieked curses about the inequity of it all, visualizing the words burning along the surface of the river, bursting out to sea and then rocketing skyward to carom around the galaxy like an interstellar pinball. I stomped on the cedar deck planks as I wept. I told Carl that listening to Tallie laugh was like being tickled…you were forced to laugh with her. I swore at death, demanding it go fuck itself. When Carl asked if I believed in God, I declared I could not, and when I asked "Do you?" he barked that he would relish believing in God, would delight in meeting him, so that he could fucking assassinate the holy bastard for how he tolerated religion and all the other evils in his creation. Our visceral conversation plunged us down the mineshaft of emotions we each thought we'd climbed out of so long before, requiring on Carl's part almost superhuman effort. The night offered catharsis, but not an absolute reprieve, as evidenced by today's disposition.

I walked south on G Street to the edge of town by the Land Management Bureau, then retraced my route, stopping for a sandwich, which I ate sitting on a concrete bench outside the Post Office. I squinted as I glanced at a church catty-corner across the intersection, counting the rows of shingles on the steeple, and it reminded me of an expression Tallie makes when she's confused or deliberating. Her face scrunches up, as though reacting to having smelled something fetid, and her cheeks bunch on either side of her nose, emphasizing the crooked imperfection in its bridge. Carl had asked me if I wanted to talk about why I needed the Kabar…and so I told him. He listened, nodded and then said payback was a motherfucker.

Among the thoughts that have occurred to me since leaving Coos Bay, wondering how my life would have been different had I had brothers or sisters seemed a natural outgrowth of visiting Carl. As I said before, Carl is the brother I never had. Even so, we only met when we were already grown. What did I miss by living a childhood without a brother, a sister, or both? Because Tallie and I are both only children, we've talked about this before. It's curious, but when we each imagine living in families with siblings, I always envision myself ruling as the first-born, as the oldest; Tallie concocts a childhood with an older sister or brother. She joined a sorority as a freshman at the University of Illinois and remains in contact with friends from that time in her life, many of whom live in Chicago now. Tallie shares similar intimate friendships with one or two of them as I have enjoyed with Carl. We discovered early in our relationship that when we were both in college, Tallie and some her sorority sisters…including some of those who now live in Chicago…and their frat boyfriends had driven from Champaign to Iowa City to attend an Illinois-Iowa football game. In comparing recollections of the game, we realized we had sat in adjacent sections, no more than twenty rows apart. Neither of us could remember which team had won the game…we had to look it up.

Our parents never offered us an explanation of why they never had more children beyond saying it wasn't a conscious choice by either couple, and we've thought about the factors that would attract two only children to each other. Commenting on the role of chance in successes like our own, we realize that while chaos determined that we'd meet, it couldn't insure compatibility. Something in our natures sustained us beyond physical attraction. When we met, I remember Tallie's candor impressed me. She possessed confidence and intelligence, but never used them as a bludgeon when late night discussions among our friends boiled over with passion. Just the opposite. When other voices swelled in volume, as though discordance equaled truth, Tallie lowered her voice and spoke unemotionally, coercing everyone around her to hush if they wanted to hear what she said. It's not a grand secret, good leaders have practiced that tactic for eons, but when you command attention, don't squander it…say something of substance. That's where Tallie exceled and impressed. She wielded exceptional intuition and planned like a chess master. While some men might shirk from a self-assured woman like Tallie, I circled her flame like a love-struck moth. Her streak of self-assurance and poise attracted me for its lack of haughtiness. Tallie was never arrogant, never condescending, never conceited. Again, just the opposite. She was unpretentious, deferential and sympathetic. She knew…knows…how to listen, how not to speak when silence serves her better.

I met and fell in love with Tallie when I was young, ambitious and determined to climb whatever mountain led to greatness. If I had to settle on the greatest gift Tallie has given me it's this: she never deterred me from striving for greatness, but helped me understand that it shouldn't be defined as a stature you achieve in the world at large. Greatness should be judged by how well you perform in the relationships you build and hold most dear…your prominence in life is determined by the affection and esteem of the people who love you. Striving for any other appearance of greatness is mere selfishness. Fortunately, by that standard, I feel I've touched greatness.

Among the tidbits of introspection this past week, our childlessness persists as a weighty regret. Carl let me brush off the subject, but I know that when men consider their life's accomplishments, they first point to their children. I'm watching this funk into which I've stooped steer me toward the drearier alternatives as I chew over my legacy. Regrets are unresolved fears. Like the Gunny said, there's no courage without fear. I know what scares me…that Tallie might ever feel that she hasn't gotten the best from me. I need to hear from her that I've been what she needs and what she wants. When I hear that from her, then I'll feel that I've not only touched greatness, but have held onto it.

Laura Deskins lived next door to our family in St. Louis and her older brother Chip was in my class in high school. She was Chip's little sister, encompassing everything that dynamic has always entailed…an unwanted hanger-on, a snickering inconvenience, and an untrustworthy stoolpigeon. In 1968, on leave shortly before I deployed to Vietnam, I visited my parents. Chip had enrolled at Washington University and still lived at home, so on several nights we sat in his basement, drank Buds, and discussed a lot of inconsequential subjects. One night when his parents were out, Laura joined us. She was sixteen years old, wore her auburn hair long and straight with bangs cut in a severe line across her forehead, and had admirably filled out the flannel shirt she'd appropriated from her father. Laura had grown into a pretty teenager who drank beer. She was now a desirable hanger-on, disqualified as a stoolpigeon by her underage drinking, and, sitting in shorts cross-legged on the other end of the sofa from me, far too convenient. She had a crush on me, made no attempt to disguise it, and only Chip seemed oblivious to it. At one point when he went upstairs to take a piss, Laura crawled toward me on the sofa and kissed me. I was drunk and reached out to cup her breast, but she swatted my hand away. She mashed her mouth against mine with fierce, teenaged urgency and continued thwarting my attempts to push beyond simple kissing. When she heard Chip on the stairs, she retreated to her corner like a boxer hearing the bell at the end of a round.

Nothing more happened that night, but we wrestled with one another a few more times before I left St. Louis. I convinced her to dial down the aggressiveness of her kissing, and thoroughly enjoyed her willingness to learn. Eventually she relented and I elicited chirps of pleasure from her as I played with her nipples…from outside her bra. I left for the war, certain I'd be no more than a temporary bragging point in her conversations with her girlfriends. But two weeks into my tour, the first letter from Laura arrived. I have to admit I was freaked out a bit when I saw her name in the return address. What did she assume our make-out sessions meant? My God, she was only sixteen and an ember of guilt smoldered inside me. I opened and read the letter and felt relief. One of the first things Laura wrote about was her boyfriend…a forward on the school basketball team. Three pages in a fluid, girly script, the letter was the first of many, almost a weekly routine, and the more I received, the more anxious I grew to read the next one. They entertained and distracted me in a way that letters from my parents…the only other people who wrote to me…did. I answered Laura as I could, usually on lined paper with a stubby pencil, and at first avoided telling her anything specific about Vietnam. But as months passed, so did my reluctance to portray with accuracy what my day-to-day existence was like. Laura's letters were an unexpected lifeline; they meant more to me than mine probably did to her. Which circles me back to that question: is there ever balance in the needs of the people in a relationship? Even in a friendship between a teenaged girl and her older brother's classmate fighting in Vietnam?

I kept them bound in a rubber band and would often reread them from the first to the last one I'd received as a diversion from the fear. The earliest letters detailed episodes from her life…in one she describes how after a visit to the dentist to have a cavity filled, she chewed on the tender inside of her cheek, which was still anesthetized by the Novocain, resulting in a painful sore when the numbness wore off, and which her tongue constantly probed for days until it healed. In another she described the regular customers at the restaurant where she waitressed on weekends, and the same meals they invariably ordered, which were good tippers, which ones leered at her, and how she was always embarrassed when friends from school came in to eat. Laura also wrote how she cried when Martin Luther King was killed, saddened as riots scorched so many cities, and watched the convention in Chicago with horror. From a distance I witnessed the gradual erosion of a measure of her innocence as she reacted to my later letters and to the events across the country. At the time, news from home reinforced the isolation most of us felt, how the war raged independently from the ordinary, unaffected lives of so many back home. It angered us that life continued back in the States for millions of people, when we wanted them to stop what they were doing and acknowledge the costs we were paying. Here's another odd association…I've found myself thinking the same thing on this trip. People go about their lives, oblivious to the fact that right beside them, I carry a death sentence.

When I came home and reunited with Laura, there was no doubt that we'd created an intimate friendship, but there was also no doubt that it was nothing more. That was forty-two years ago and I still have those letters. The rubber band frayed long ago, succeeded by a discarded ribbon from a birthday gift. Laura, now Laura Mattin, lives in Elko, with a husband of Basque descent, who works as a geologist for a gold mining company. Their three children, all girls, are married and have provided Laura with seven grandchildren. All this I learned during a phone conversation with Chip, who still lives in St. Louis, works for Monsanto as a biotechnologist, has been married twice, and as a life-long Cardinals fan, hates the Cubs and spent some time letting me know it. I love the Internet…find anything or anyone at any time.

So tomorrow, or the next day, who knows the way I'm feeling right now, I'll visit Laura and return her letters. I hope she wants them and will value them as I have.

I received another email from Ellen, and also one from Del. My first reaction was annoyance that no one respects a clean goodbye. Awfully selfish of me. Then I placed them in the context of my earlier thoughts about greatness, and I felt ashamed. If what each says is true, I haven't seen the last of them. They're threatening to come to Chicago and I don't know yet how I feel about that. When Tallie argued to dissuade me from this journey, one of her accusations was that I didn't want her to have to witness my decay. She supposed I wanted to crawl off like an obstinate bull elephant to a secluded graveyard to expire. Reassuring her otherwise took time and sincerity. When I envision those last days, I picture us alone together. Selfish again. That's what I want, but I haven't considered what Tallie will need...I haven't asked her. But I will. We'll have that conversation after I return home. I want to watch her face when we talk, especially her eyes, the grayish blue flecked with bolts of silvery-white, and hear the tenor of her voice as she tries to deflect any consideration of what she wants or needs. She'll persist in her unselfishness, but I'll wear her down. Time's on my side and so is love.

Why does the humblest epiphany deliver the greatest impact? Beauty lurks there somewhere.

Day Thirteen

The three-and-a-half hour drive this morning began with "Sands of Nevada" by Mark Knopfler. It dovetailed with my recent mood, even though I'd selected it before I left Chicago. Just another eccentric coincidence of lyrics and attitude on this trip. Another observation…I've climbed hills and descended into valleys emotionally and geographically during this trip, and today's drive, thankfully, was a long flat course in both senses. I'm in Winnemucca, Nevada, at a Best Western. I could have driven another two hours into Elko, but the name of the town, when I repeated it aloud in quick succession…WinnemuccaWinnemuccaWinnemucca…amused me, so I thought I'd stop. The information card in my room states the town rests at an elevation of more than five-thousand feet, but the arid peaks surrounding the town range even taller. This is high desert…the temperature is in the mid-sixties…and this is mining country. I also passed three casinos on my way here…I'm definitely in Nevada.

I think I surprised Tallie when I called her at her office. She'd returned from lunch minutes earlier and immediately upon hearing my voice asked if anything was wrong.

"I'm fine, honey." I told her where I was and that I'd decided to cut short the day's driving…that I was considering spending some time in a casino to unwind.

"Just don't bet the title to the car," she joked.

I asked about her day and as she related her impressions from an on-site visit to an employment training center for single mothers, it struck me how much I enjoy hearing her expound upon her work.

"The facilities are austere," she said. "They need so much, especially technology upgrades for the computer classes."

"How many women can they accommodate?"

"Forty if they squeeze them in. Expansion should be a priority." Her voice, which she can tonally flatten, expunging all traces of emotion, as when she strives for objectivity during grant reviews by the foundation staff, revealed her compassion and empathy, as well as her frustration at being unable to satisfy the group's every need, or at least do more to help them. Often the timbre of her voice when she talks about her work leaves a starker impression than the words themselves.

"It's been almost two weeks," she said. "How is the reality aligning with your expectations?"

I remembered my earlier observation of peaks and valleys. "There've been some surprises. Overall," I hesitated, "it's an A minus."

"That sounded a bit glum."

"I didn't mean for it to." Never try to deceive the co-author of your life. "But at times the finality of this just royally pisses me off." I spat the word "pisses" with a burst of air and spittle onto the mouthpiece of the room's phone.

"If it didn't affect you, you'd be a sociopath."

"True enough," I said. "Carl said I had received a gift that won't keep giving."

"The man may have his crazy side, but that's insightful."

"I was driving on a two-lane highway this morning, and on the edge of the pavement there were raised speed bumps, to warn you when you stray out of the lane."

"Uh huh."

"So I drifted to the right and listened to the sound of the tires on those bumps. It reminded me of pinning playing cards to the frame of my bike as a kid, so they'd flutter against the spokes."

"I think only boys did that," Tallie chuckled.

"I was listening to 'Cinnamon Girl,' and I adjusted the car's speed until that thudding matched the tempo of the song. Exactly forty-two miles an hour."

"That's creative." I heard her chortling.

"Eventually a guy overtook me in a pickup, blasting his horn in a long burst as he zoomed past me."

"Don't provoke any cowboy road rage, old man." We laughed together for a moment.

"It rained this morning," Tallie said.

"Big bright sky here."

"They've started blocking off streets for the Taste of Chicago. Grant Park will be a zoo this weekend."

A few years ago Tallie and I hooked up with a group of friends to attend the first day of the Taste. We rendezvoused at noon on the east end of the Jackson Boulevard bridge near the Art Institute, about eight of us from both our offices (Alison was with us), and strolled south on Columbus Drive among the food booths, sampling restaurant offerings, listening to music, crowd-watching, and sweating in the Chicago heat. The smells made the most lasting impression… cooking odors, the tang of spilled beer, and the dankness of too much human sweat in a compressed area. On a later night, Tallie, Alison and I spread our blankets on a tiny patch of grass near the Petrillo Music Shell, hemmed in by thousands of people, and listened to 10,000 Maniacs. The oppressiveness of the crowd, as well as reports the next day of a related shooting in the Loop, alarmed Alison… in retrospect, I wonder if we might have missed an early warning of what was to come…so we stopped attending. Since then we've watched the fireworks from our deck, with a group of friends.

"It's shorter this year, isn't it?"

"I think you're right."

"Anything new to report on Alison?"

"No. I saw her last night after work. So far she's adapted well, but I think it's just a matter of time before she'll get agitated."

Slumped in an armchair by the window in my room, my shoeless feet propped on the arm of a matching chair, I counted the rectangular and triangular forms within the green and gold wallpaper border that ringed the walls of the room just below the ceiling. I closed my eyes, arresting the counting, and when I reopened them, I surveyed the motel's pool outside the window, where even in what I felt was chilly air, two young children leapt into the water, climbed out shivering, and then leapt back in, squealing repeatedly, again and again, while a woman reading a magazine, their mother I assumed, sat in a white plastic chair, wearing jeans and a hooded sweatshirt.

"The staff knows what to do," I said, but immediately knew Tallie would not be consoled.

"You're right." Her exhalation substantiated everything I presumed.

"You did the right thing, Tallie."
"I know." She sighed again.
"What'd you have for lunch?"
"There was an empanada food truck outside. How about you?"
"I'll grab something at the casino."
"I love you."
"Ditto."

I did go to a casino, the Winners Casino, where I bypassed the slots and played Texas Hold'em for two hours. I placed third in a Sit-and-Go tournament, my two pair losing to a rivered inside straight. The dealer suggested I skip the food offered in the coffee shop and directed me to The Martin Hotel, where I dined on Solomo, a Basque dish of pork loin simmered in garlic and pimentos. The taste was exceptional and in a moment of whimsy, I bought a baseball cap in the gift shop, a faded rosy color, with the restaurant's name, location and date of establishment, 1898, stitched into the brim in golden yellow thread. I think it'll become my new, official driving hat. Walking around Winnemucca isn't taxing; the town is as flat as a board. I photographed a huge mural on a wall of the Convention Center…snow-capped peaks towering over an azure-colored lake. Also, walking back from the restaurant to my motel, I passed a stuccoed house on Melarkey Street (fantastic juxtapositioning) with an arched doorway; in the window hung a hand-lettered sign advertising a fortune teller. I considered visiting to test her veracity, but kept walking. Perhaps I should have stopped…when I get to Elko tomorrow, I'll need some luck.

Ellen, Del and Carl (now that's a champion name for a law firm) all knew I'd be coming to see them. I haven't contacted Laura…

the visit will be a cold call. Chip gave me her phone number and address, but I decided against telephoning her. I suppose part of me worried she'd say not to bother, that I could just dispose of the letters; but they meant so much to me that I wouldn't care to discover that they mean nothing to her now, even though I understand that by not scheduling my visit, I'm not guaranteeing the outcome I want. In other words, I've done nothing to insure success.

    This tiny town, straddling a narrow, snaking river and surrounded by treeless summits, like so many other places I've passed in the last two weeks, seems otherworldly…quite alien…compared to my "real" life. I'll add this observation to the list of farewell tour epiphanies. I think our building on Madison Street is taller than any building in Winnemucca, and every man, woman and child of the town's population could claim individual offices in the skyscraper on Wacker Drive where my firm is housed. These things are obvious, I know, but I would not have given them a second thought even two months ago. Hey Carl, I'm commenting on my cosmic view again and I'm not even stoned! An even more pertinent curiosity: I'm unexpectedly mindful of how mammoth an ego is required to recognize one's own insignificance.

    I wonder whether I'll be able to detect the features of a sixteen-year-old girl within the face of a sixty-year-old Laura. Four years difference in age figures crucially when you're a teenager, but far less so when you're middle-aged. Seeing Laura will be the oldest reunion I've ever had…forty-seven years, and inexplicably I realize I'm nervous about seeing her. Is it the prospect of disappointment that's making me anxious? I don't know. With Carl and the others, I was confident about the nature of our reunions…these friends, after all, aren't strangers…but Laura, she's unique among those I'm going to visit. Carl would advise that I'm overthinking this, that I should behave like the stones in his river.

I'm going to start tomorrow's drive with "Young Girl" by Gary Puckett and the Union Gap. There's some propriety in that choice.

God, it's early…only seven-thirty. I don't want to leave too early in the morning; it's only a two-hour drive to Elko. I picked up some brochures at the Convention Center, and I could take a tour of a working gold mine in Carlin, just west of Elko, before visiting Laura. I'm stalling, I know. I'll get up tomorrow morning, have some breakfast, drive to Elko and show up unannounced on Laura's doorstep. If the visit's a bust, then I'll politely leave and start the long drive to Phoenix. That's my destination after Elko.

Day Fourteen

Nothing invigorates your mood like winning at poker. I returned to the casino after making last night's journal entry, and entered another Hold'em tournament, for higher stakes…five hundred dollar buy-in. My opponents yesterday afternoon consisted of quiet, unflappable seniors like myself. The evening session, however, attracted a far different crowd. I learned most of the other players worked in neighboring mines. They drank methodically, brusquely aired their disgust at bad flops, and promptly pegged me as an outsider. While it wasn't exactly a cakewalk, I won that tournament, along with almost three-thousand dollars. As a show of goodwill, I bought drinks for the small crowd that had gathered to watch me go head-to-head with a wiry, bearded trucker in the final pairing.

I sauntered back to the motel in bright spirits…but didn't get to sleep until after midnight. The tournament victory had electrified me like a shot of espresso.

Lying in bed with the audio muted, I played a game: I'd try to step-stone through a scene on the television as quickly as possible before it changed. If I succeeded, then I could advance to the next channel, where I began step-stoning through that scene...playing roulette with the remote, Tallie calls it, although she believes I'm merely trying to watch everything on TV in two-second bursts. During the process my thoughts pogoed, just as they have during extended periods of driving. Three weeks into my relationship with Tallie, I was convinced that she was the woman I should be in love with...and was. We spent so much time together that first summer. I remember seeing the Rolling Stones at the old Chicago Stadium in July, the two of us clutching each other after the concert and giggling nervously about how sketchy the neighborhood seemed to us, while we tried to hail a cab back to Tallie's apartment. Now we live four blocks from the United Center and think nothing of walking home after dinner at Café Ciao. Back to Tallie...far more notable than the swiftness of our connection was my perception of its intensity, and close on the heels of that sensation was fear. Fear that my feelings raced along a one-way street. Every emboldened lover wrestles with that burden of panic: am I in this alone? Is this a foolish endeavor? Can she possibly love me as I love her? And, of course, the worst fear: if I declare my love, will she end it?

I did, although not immediately; she didn't, thankfully.

I cannot imagine a more fulfilling, stimulating, gratifying or passionate life than what I've lived with Tallie. If I once again begin to list the what-ifs of my life, examining unselected choices and where they might have led, Tallie's name will never appear. God I love her. I want to believe that every man experiences quiet, contemplative moments when he gazes at his lover and shivers with the joy of simply being near her. Dozens of times Tallie has caught me staring at her and asked me "What?" At first I'd try to explain how sometimes watching her, noticing the elegance of a gesture as common as turning a page in a book or tucking her untamed hair behind an ear, encompassed an indescribable beauty that made me catch my breath. She'd scoff. I'd persist. She'd ask me "Why do you love me?" I'd say "I can't tell you that." She'd laugh and call me crazy and over time when the situation repeated and she'd again ask: "What?" I'd say: "One of those moments." And we'd both knowingly smile.

Laura lives in a white, two-story Cape Cod on a street that borders the Ruby View Golf Course; in the front yard a dogwood blossomed and a cluster of three young birch trees flanked the driveway. I parked by the curb and then retrieved the bundle of letters from the trunk. Laura opened the door before I could knock.

"I've been expecting you." She grinned behind the screened door. "Chip said he talked to you."

My earlier curiosity about whether I would identify the girl within the woman crumbled. I would have recognized Laura even in a crowd. Although the long straight tresses had surrendered to a shorter, curlier cut, and the auburn color had partially grayed, her face…tight-lipped smile below a button nose, doe-brown eyes that I remembered enlivened by youth…shown through unmistakably, transporting me back to St. Louis afternoons after school, Chip and I playing pinball in a drug store a block from our high school, invariably tilting the machine as we competed for high score.

"And here I wanted to surprise you," I said.

"Oh, it's still a surprise. Come in." She swung open the screened door and stood aside.

Laura led me past the stairway to the rear of the house, where a kitchen and family room opened onto a shaded patio with beds of tulips and daffodils still in bloom. Beyond the yard a foursome of golfers braked their carts on a path beside a green.

"Would you like some lemonade?" Laura asked.

"Sure." She wasn't as thin as she had been as a teenager, but Laura evidently exercised. Her thighs and upper arms were well defined, no sagging, grandmotherly flesh, and I noted that her ass hadn't broadened or drooped. I was checking her out and wondered if she caught me would I blush.

"You're probably wondering what I'm doing here," I began, accepting the glass she offered. "It must seem peculiar after so many years."

"Yes," she said, leading me out to the patio. The golfers' voices floated toward us. "Chip had no idea."

I held out the ribbon-bound letters to her. "To return these."

Laura stared at the bundle, furrowing her brow in curiosity and then arching her eyebrows as she recognized the envelopes. "Oh my God," she gasped. "I can't believe it. Are those my letters to you?"

I nodded.

"You kept them?" she whispered as she traced the edges with her fingertips. "Why on earth did you keep them all these years?"

So I told Laura what I should have expressed to her in 1969 when I came home: her letters had anchored me to a reality I pined for and distracted me from the reality I abhorred.

She untied the ribbon and leafed through the pastel-colored envelopes, smiling at her youthful handwriting.

"They're chronological," she said, opening the first letter and unfolding the pages. She read silently and her eyes grew misty.

"I never thought you'd answer me," she said, swiping at a tear and looking up at me. "Never thought you'd bother replying to a silly teenaged girl. I was flabbergasted and so giddy when I got your first letter."

Suddenly it occurred to me…did Laura still have the letters I had written her? Did she think I'd come all this way just to try and retrieve them?

"I suppose I shouldn't admit that besides my parents, yours were the only letters I got over there."

Laura weighed the bundle in her hands, as though measuring the memories by their heft. "Reading these will be like traveling in a time machine," she said. "Wait…is there anything in here that's going to embarrass me?"

"I don't think so." I smiled. "They're breezy…and in retrospect really rather tender. You were only sixteen years old."

"I had *such* a crush on you." Laura wagged her head and a pink flush rose in her cheeks. "I bragged to my girlfriends about kissing you in my parents' basement. Do you remember that?"

I nodded and grinned.

"And sneaking around before you left for the war. Oh, that was thrilling!"

"I was worried Chip would find out, and that he'd tell your father."

Laura shrugged. "Chip had his own skeletons."

Another cream-colored golf cart approached the green behind Laura's house. Laura glanced in its direction and waved at the men who walked to the rear to retrieve their putters. They returned her wave.

"I can't wait to hear the tongues wagging," Laura smirked.

"Am I giving you a reputation?"

She chortled. "It would liven things up." Laura sipped from her lemonade. "I'm still amazed you kept these." She flipped randomly to a pale green envelope, a later letter in the series.

"I took greater care with them later in my tour," I said. Laura's first letters bore faded smudges, relics of the dirt and mud that seemed always to besiege us.

"I was surprised to get your first letter," I said. "And a little scared."

Laura laughed, holding the green envelope to her chest. "Did you think you'd started something you couldn't finish?"

"Well, you were younger than me."

"I hope I didn't come off as too clingy."

I paused. "You never did. Your letters were newsy and quaint. You probably didn't realize how all the chatter about school, your family, your job, and your friends held back the bullshit at times. Every time I read one of your letters, it was like going on a mini-vacation."

Laura sighed. "I never knew. Why didn't you tell me when you came home?"

"You seemed even younger than before I left. Can you understand that?"

"Are you saying I sounded older in the letters?"

"No, not at all. That's not what I'm saying. Your age wasn't a factor when I was enjoying your letters. But when I got home…I don't know."

Laura smiled as we watched the golfers drive to the next tee.

"Getting got out of the Marines marked the ending of something for me. My life shifted in a terribly momentous way. Suddenly not only did that age difference seem more critical…you were still in high school, I was twenty-one years old....but the teeth in our gears didn't mesh."

"How so?"

"I could only have been disruptive in your life. I'm sure your parents had a plan for you...finish high school, go to a good college. Career, family, everything. I had no idea what I was going to do. Go back to college, sure. But where and when? It was too soon to give it much thought."

"Did you want something more from me then?" Laura asked.

"I've thought about that off and on and honestly, I'm not sure. I was nervous around you, wondering if you felt as close to me as I'd grown to you. Scared that the dependence I'd developed could never be reciprocated. And I remember getting the impression that you didn't want more."

Laura laughed loudly. "I was nervous and young."

"Your letters were important to me. My parents, especially my father, supported Nixon in '68. When I came home from school one day wearing a Hubert Humphrey button, it really steamed my dad. Walter Cronkite may have brought the war into our living room, but your letters made it personal for me and helped give me the courage to defy my father."

"War on the home front."

"Only in this analogy, I suppose I was the Vietcong!" Laura crossed her ankles and leaned back into the chair cushion.

"That's turning a situation on its head."

"When you combine teenage rebellion, a liberal social studies teacher, knowing friends who were fighting over there, with watching the weekly body count reports...that's a recipe for a perfect storm in the Deskins house."

"Be sure to read what you wrote when King and Kennedy were killed."

Laura crossed her arms over her blouse. "When Nixon won the election, my father gloated and I punished him with the silent treatment. For weeks nothing my mom said could shake me. You got home when, March of '69?"

"Good memory."

"I was counting the days, as I'm sure you were."

I nodded.

"Chip came home at Christmas break, and the tension shocked him. He'd transferred to Wisconsin by then, and talked to me about how politicized the campus in Madison was about the war. The year before student protests had closed the university for a few days."

"I remember."

"I burned to get out of that house…to escape my parents. My chauvinist, overbearing father and a timid mother who trembled in his shadow. God, but absolutes are so painfully obvious when you're young, aren't they?"

"Never more clear."

The shadow of a patrolling hawk crossed the patio stones and we both looked up, silent for a moment. I then gazed down to the patio, a fieldstone pattern of squares and rectangles, and began stepstoning from those set at our feet toward the other end of the patio.

"I asked Chip if I could stay with him if I left home. A flat refusal. He took after my dad."

"I didn't know."

"I thought if I wrote you about my plans to run away, it'd freak you out."

"Hmm." I chuckled and wondered if I had been more perceptive at the time, would I have fathomed that what I had accepted as teenaged angst in her letters, in truth masked a more deep-seated anguish. "I never understood, I suppose. I knew you were unhappy, you were candid about that. But I never had a clue you were considering running away."

"That year was so tumultuous and I was so impressionable," Laura said. "If I trace the evolution of many of my values, that year marks the genesis. Challenging my father were my baby steps. Did I convey that in my letters?"

"The evidence that you were changing is definitely there, but perhaps not the awareness."

Laura's smile was more tight-lipped than before. "You need some distance before you can look back and judge, don't you?"

"I think that's true."

"Well, I've been circling around what I started out to tell you." She hesitated. "When you came home, if you'd asked, I would have run away with you. But at the same time I was terrified you wouldn't ask, that when we met again, you'd see nothing more than an immature, whiny girl, frantic for attention, and I was certain you'd dismiss me without a second thought. In my own pretzeled logic, I decided the best way to stay close to you was to play it cool and stay aloof."

"Invite interest through disinterest?"

"Universal teenaged reasoning. I may have been a recent feminist convert, but I thought waiting for you to make the first move was the best approach."

"I felt the same way," I said. "I was scared, too. If I'd come on too strong and been rejected...well, that would have been devastating, to say the least. I felt we'd grown so close through our letters, but I didn't know where I really stood with you. What I was to you."

"Oh, I know…and that's my fault," Laura admitted. "Making the first move and being spurned feels awful. Especially to a teenager."

"I didn't have that excuse."

"But I think you were being considerate, in a way."

"I don't think so."

"Of course you were. I remember the first time I saw you after you came home, at the party your parents threw for you."

"In their back yard."

"The day you came home, wasn't it?"

"Yes. I'd caught an early flight out of San Diego."

"A Thursday. Your dad grilled burgers. I came with my parents; I hugged you but so many people were there and we never had a chance to be alone to talk."

"They'd invited the whole neighborhood."

"And the whole neighborhood came!"

"My mom kept touching me, stroking my arm, rubbing my shoulder, cupping the back of my neck, and always staring at me…I knew if I said anything she'd burst into tears." I remember a conversation with her years later, when she confessed how she had locked up her fear in a distant recess of her mind the year I was in Vietnam. Had she surrendered to her fear, she told me, she would never have been able to function. I'd been oblivious, of course, to how petrified she and my father had been. In their letters, they had decided to omit any clue about how worried they were for my safety. She grew inconsolable when she watched the body bags and the stories of casualties on television and said my father eventually stopped watching TV news. He'd never told me that before he died.

"I'd envisioned a homecoming straight out of Hollywood," Laura said. "Well, two versions. In one of them, you and I snuck away one night and drove west into a perpetual sunset, to San Francisco, and hung out with the groovy people. In the morning, my parents woke up and discovered the note I'd left, detailing how they'd alienated me and what horrible parents they'd been."

"Didn't the Beatles write a song like that?"

"Side one, track six of 'Sgt. Pepper's.'"

"How do you remember that?" I marveled.

"That album was the soundtrack of my life for a while. Anyway, in the other version…and I liked this one better…you'd challenged my father in a heroic confrontation, reciting an award-winning monologue, berating him for how he'd mistreated me, regaling him with an account of my extraordinary virtues, and then you whisked me away while he stood by, speechless, helpless and defeated. Very Prince Charming."

"I'm stunned."

"I had a blockbuster imagination epic and you played a larger-than-life character." Laura paused for a moment and sipped from her lemonade. Her voice had grown hoarse. "But seeing you at the cookout was a reality check."

I tried to remember that day in detail. I'd boarded a plane in DaNang four days prior, having only choppered out of the bush the day before that. Transitioning from combat to the suburbs so rapidly, I was at best only partially aware at the time of what I was undergoing. My foundation had shifted, not disintegrated as Carl's would later, but the benchmarks by which I appraised my life had been altered.

"Was it obvious?" I asked Laura.

"You were guarded. Clearly nervous and fairly withdrawn."

"Over in Vietnam, we all thought of home as a sanctuary. But when I got back, it didn't seem like a refuge anymore."

"How could it?"

"I think my father understood that. But my mom either couldn't or wouldn't understand. I think she simply refused to acknowledge how things…how I…had changed."

Laura related my mother's intransigence to dealing with her own daughters. "There are moments when you function as a sponge for them, absorbing all the excess they can't handle. Other times you watch, no more than a sympathetic witness. But on certain occasions you totally shut down and ignore what's right in front of you, because the change you perceive is so unwelcome and overpowering."

"Or the relief, I suppose."

"I always feared that karma would repay me for my split with my father with something similarly traumatic with my girls. But their teenaged years seemed more tolerable than my own."

"I'm not a huge fan of karma." I told Laura I'd come to believe in chaos as the universal driving force. She chuckled.

"I can't say I disagree. That's certainly what would have happened if we'd played out either of my fantasies. When you left for college, I brooded about how I'd lost an opportunity. If only I'd said something…if only you'd said something."

I recalled a night when Laura and I had driven down to Cliff Cave County Park. I carried an old blanket from the trunk down to the bank of the Mississippi and the two of us reclined, upstream from a train of barges. More so that night than any other, decency persistently reminded me of the age difference between the two of us. But lust betrayed my mind and I persevered, ramming the hard-on in my jeans against Laura's thigh and repeatedly trying to slither my hand under her bra. Laura thwarted every effort, pushing my hand away. We'd resumed kissing and I started again from ground zero, as though I'd landed on a space in Monopoly that sent me back to Go, having collected nothing at all; there was no question of restarting from the furthest point I'd reached. The game reset and I began again, and again was stymied. Ultimately I gave up trying.

"Think about the life we would have created for ourselves," she said. "We were young and I at least needed to prove my independence and strength to my parents. If we'd run off, at some point we would have crashed and burned, and the only emotion that would have survived was resentment. Fate…or chaos…kept us on the proper paths. If it hadn't, we wouldn't find ourselves here, and I'd never get to read these letters."

I nodded my agreement. Laura had brought all this up so calmly. She sat in her chair appearing wistful, yes, but not regretful. The conviction with which she spoke made me believe this was not the first time she had weighed the cost of opportunity lost against the benefits of opportunities taken.

"So. I have a feeling you didn't drive all the way from Chicago to Elko, just to return some old letters."

I had to decide, quickly, what, if anything, I would tell Laura, and instantly elected to keep the facts a secret. I told her as I neared retirement, I wanted some time to consider my future. The road trip I viewed as a sabbatical to weigh some options.

"Like what?" she asked.

"I've practiced law for more than thirty-five years," I began, drawing on my talent for extemporizing. I told Laura I had tired of the contentiousness and now considered becoming a professional arbitrator. That assisting people to reach amicable agreements might be rewarding.

Laura seemed to accept my explanation and I wondered why among those I was visiting I chose her to leave in the dark about my situation.

I continued to wonder about that as our conversation strayed into smaller talk. Laura had met her husband Greg at a fraternity party the University of Colorado, where she majored in Communication.

"And yes, considering how I'd feuded with my father, that was an ironic choice of study," she'd said, laughing, and then coughing to clear her throat.

She'd pledged Kappa Kappa Gamma her freshman year, and we laughed at the coincidence that Tallie had pledged the same sorority at the University of Illinois. She frowned when I complained that I was not an admirer of fraternities and sororities. She and Greg had lived in Denver for a few years, both working until the birth of their first daughter, Beth.

Laura asked who else I was visiting on my trip…neither Ellen, Del or Carl had asked that, although Carl learned peripherally of one.

"Just a few old friends. I'm headed down to Phoenix next," I told her. "One of my law professors lives there now. Retired, of course."

The sun had risen high in the sky as the time neared noon.

"Can you stay until Greg gets home tonight? I'd love for you to meet him."

I didn't want to meet Laura's husband. I wanted our reunion to remain untainted, an event that encompassed only the two of us. My early expectations of what might happen when I saw Laura had never fully congealed, but our conversation had imbued me with a warmhearted feeling and I didn't want to allow anything to devalue that sentiment.

"I need to start the drive to Phoenix. My schedule is loose, but I am expected there soon."

Laura didn't argue or try to convince me to change my mind. She walked me out to my car, took both my hands in hers and told me she wished she had safeguarded my letters to her. "I truly don't remember throwing them away," she said. "But I know they didn't survive one of our moves over the years."

Laura hugged me for a long time and extracted a promise that we'd keep in touch. As I drove away, I glanced in my rearview mirror and saw her standing at the curb. The similarity to the photo I had taken of Tallie that first day rippled a shudder up my spine.

Tonight I'm in Ely, Nevada, at the Hotel Nevada and Gambling Hall. The collection of taxidermy in the lobby stopped me in my tracks and made me stare at the walls. There's even a stuffed mountain lion that was shot some years ago in the hotel's parking lot by a security guard! The place is kitschy but endearing…and I doubt I'll go out walking after dark tonight.

I spoke briefly with Tallie tonight, about a single theme: my certainty that the two of us were absolutely meant to be together, and that I cannot imagine any kind of happiness in a life that did not include her in it.

Day Fifteen

With Tallie commanding my thoughts this morning, I started my drive out of Ely with James Taylor, singing "You Can Close Your Eyes," a live version with Carole King, and to me the snug harmonies of their voices epitomized my life with Tallie.

Last night after talking to her, I lay in bed on my side and remembered one of the Saturdays we spent together during our first summer. We had woken up after a post-coital nap, and I rested my head on Tallie's chest. She teasingly accused me of being obsessed with her boobs, but I whispered that I only wanted to hear her heart beating. I admit it was cheesy…even if truthful…but I enjoyed that even so early in our relationship, I didn't feel the need to be careful about what I said to her. There was no need to play a role with Tallie, and that effortlessness with one another matured the longer we were together. When I started my own firm and I came home from the office some nights complaining of clients and young associates, Tallie listened, single-mindedly focused, and then delicately asked me questions, or commented on some aspect of a larger picture I had not considered. She often altered my perspective, channeling me toward an understanding of not only what irritated me, but why. And she accomplished it in a gentle manner; she was never derisive or demeaning. She's level-headed, intuitive and an incomparable listener.….not one of those impatient people you recognize are only partially listening, too quickly assuming what you're going to say rather than what you are saying, formulating what they're going to tell you and wishing you would shut up so they could blurt it out. With Tallie I am a best friend, a lover and a husband.

This morning, shortly after I left Ely, near Comins Lake, I passed a pickup. The windows were down and the young couple in the cab sang along with blaring music on the radio. They waved when they looked over at me and I smiled, nodded and touched two fingers to the brim of my Martin Hotel cap. Laura's words, about "Sgt. Pepper's" having been the soundtrack to a period in her life came back to me, and I thought of how music had impacted different times in my life. Growing up as a teen during the sixties, marrying the music of that era with my drive for independence and my hormonal imperatives, left me with songs imprinted so deeply on my memories, that when I hear them now, they evoke those times and my experiences with stinging clarity. As driven home by the songs Carl played, our war established its own anthems, and the songs from that year still arrest me when I listen to them. The faces of men in jungle fatigues flash by like a slide show, set to the music we shared. In college at Iowa, I favored softer, contemplative music, by singer-songwriters who idealized love and peace and the promise of better days. Tallie and I have devoured the music of our city, especially blues, folk and symphonic. I can't imagine this trip without music accompanying me, without lyrics conjuring memories and spawning observations.

When I was a child, my father insisted on a Sunday afternoon ritual of driving in the Missouri countryside…but he never turned on the radio. He and my mother sat in front and I leaned forward between them, kneeling on the back seat, commenting on the passing scenery, pointing excitedly whenever I spotted livestock in a field. As I grew older, the Sunday drives naturally seemed a pointless waste of my time. I sulked when forced to accompany my parents, until one Sunday after church, they finally relented and allowed me stay home while they perpetuated their ritual without me. One summer when Tallie and I visited my parents in St. Louis…my father had retired by then…I apologized to him for having acted so badly in refusing to join him and my mother on the drives. He waved away my apology. He knew they never could have represented to me what they had represented to him…freedom. During his childhood, he explained, the mobility automobiles afforded people had still been a novelty. His mother and father would never have toured the landscape in a car for pleasure, would never have indulged in such an extravagance. I remember watching his face during those meandering drives, a journey with no destination, and it seemed he always wore a smile. When I asked him why he never listened to music during those Sunday treks, he looked at me and tilted his head, saying music would have been a distraction. I wonder what my father would think of my farewell tour.

  Having cancer…knowing I'll never reprise this trip or any other…I think is affecting my perceptions physically, as well as emotionally. The landscape in this area of the country, as lackluster as it initially appears, surrenders its details to a patient observer. The textures appear more dramatic and the colors more saturated, all features seem sharper and more acute. I know…only my perceptions have changed, but it feels as though I'm transformed by a drug that amplifies cognizance, a brew of my own concoction…I think I'll call it HDH: Human Death Hormone. I've avoided wasting time by dwelling on morbidity, but I know that sensation will overtake me at some point. I had hoped it would remain submerged until I concluded this trip, but I felt it lurking today.

Twice today I pulled off the highway and wandered away from the road. North of Cathedral Gorge State Park, where the highway had been carved through squat bluffs, I climbed to the crest of a hill, winding around stubby trees, tufts of grasses and clumps of spiky bushes, which from the highway looked uniform in their dullness, but up close displayed an incredible variation of color. One waist-high bush in particular caught my eye and I photographed it. The bark was reddish brown at the base but nearly white near the top and it bore fuzzy seed pods. Even the soil…so uniformly plain when seen from the highway…held surprises. Shades of browns and reds, studded with gray and white rocks, and the textures ranging from hard-packed earth to yielding sand. I stood atop the hill and gazed at the vista in an arc. The clouds hovered in a flawless sky so electrifying blue that I could imagine it singing like a choir.

The second stop was near Snow Canyon State Park in Utah, where the hills rose higher, some with sheer faces, and their colors looked sun-bleached to shades of desert khaki. The vegetation crouched closer to the ground, hardy grasses and sparse shrubs. I walked to the base of a crag, atop a sloping pile of rock I assumed over time had eroded from the face of the cliff. I jumped when a lizard startled me as it scraped away from my advance. Across the highway a duo of bluffs baked in the sun, nearly white in color, and beyond them lay another range more russet and with flatter domes.

I'd cautioned that this journal would not grow into a travelogue, but aside from the unanticipated splendor of this terrain and the impact it's having on me, I'm struck by another observation. Driving each leg of this journey sustains that hypnotic momentum I mentioned a few days ago. The humming of the tires on pavement produces a cadence, supplying me not only with a frame of mind for introspection and perception, but a consciousness that I'm speeding toward a destination. Frankly, I'm torn between two opposites: avoiding that destination, knowing my arrival is irrevocable and final, and reuniting with Tallie as swiftly as possible. I miss her so much and I'm questioning whether I've allowed the selfish intention of this trip to overshadow her needs and her love for me.

I hunkered in a patch of shade at the foot of that bluff and again weighed the option of rushing through the remainder of this trip. Skipping Phoenix and what I've chosen to do there is not an option…but setting a course for Chicago immediately afterwards, although it would complicate my plans, is doable. When I spoke with Tallie last night, I asked, as I have during every call, about Alison. "She's fine," Tallie said, but something in the tone of her voice made me probe. "What is it?" I asked. "Alison's been absent for a long time, but now it feels like she's gone. I miss her." That succinct comment drove everything home with the precision and scorching heat of a laser. The day I received the diagnosis from Janine, hearing the cancer was terminal, inoperable and untreatable, Tallie took and delicately held my hand. She didn't squeeze or grip it tightly; she didn't apply pressure…she reinforced presence. I mention it because when Janine spoke to us about the test results, I recalled an incident as a child being told during a doctor's visit that I needed a shot. At that time my mother had taken my hand, not to reassure me, but to restrain me. How did she know my first impulse was to run away from the bad news? My child's logic told me that if I could get out of that examining room, then the nature of the news would change. Flee the room and negate the needle. But in Janine's office that day I entertained no urge to escape, and Tallie took my hand to tether me to her, not to the room. I'm halfway through this odyssey and I feel as though the riches I've gleaned from the first four visits might be enough. For more than two weeks, I've been absent from Tallie. Soon enough I'll be gone. Do I owe her more than what I'm going to give her? The answer to that is uncomplicated…I can't possibly give her enough, not in this abbreviated lifetime, not even in two or three or more complete ones.

Don't misinterpret. No relationship is perfect, certainly not Tallie's and mine. I dwell on us as idyllic partners as much because of our differences as for our compatibilities. During the first year of our marriage, we unleashed an argument that I worried was beyond resolution. It was at that moment during our time together the most brutal instance of Tallie's insurmountable lack of trust in any enduring relationship…and I remember the fear, the unyielding panic that we wouldn't survive the hostility of the fight. Hardly perfection. At one point Tallie tried to flee from the apartment as though she were being chased, and part of me bellowed to let her go, but I stopped her, wagering everything on trust. I told her she could sprint like a cheetah, but she'd never outrun her memories. I asked her to trust me, to trust in us, and to realize the importance that word held for me. "Trust is not something I give lightly," I said. "And neither is loyalty." I reiterated that appeal numerous times over a period of several hours, and I'm not certain if my persistence convinced her to believe me…or if she just grew tired of arguing and relented from exhaustion. Then, unlike now, the journey was less important than the destination. We achieved if not complete trust, then at least a foundation on which to build more of it. Yet for a very long time, I heard murmurs of doubt within her silences.

I'm in St. George, Utah, and it's my first time in Utah…but as they say: "I'm just passing through." Looking at the map, it appears I have to make a choice in routes between Las Vegas and the Grand Canyon. I've seen both, so it comes down to preference: a natural… or an unnatural wonder. The canyon route maintains the continuity. I think. Vegas would just be wrong. On this trip, I'm changing the catchphrase to reflect my personal sin city: "What Happens in Phoenix, Stays in Phoenix." Sin…all sin can be forgiven, given enough time. Forgetting takes far longer.

Day Sixteen

With "You Know I Love You" by Big Pete Pearson as my morning drive song, I pulled out of the Best Western Abbey Inn parking lot and steered toward the Veterans Memorial Highway. The sense of it hit me immediately when I was mapping my route last night: there are no bridges spanning the Grand Canyon…you drive around it. Because of the coiling nature of the highway, I crossed the Utah-Arizona border three times in two hours, so now I've been to Utah twice in two days. Hallelujah!

    I checked into the Grand Hotel in Tusayan just past lunch time and then boarded a shuttle bus for the south rim of the canyon. Near the head of the Bright Angel Trail I stood and watched a group of tourists on burros descending into the canyon. The striations of color in the rock formations and the breadth and depth of the canyon made them appear tiny and dull. Suddenly my chest constricted and I gasped for air, overwhelmed by the certainty I would soon pass out and tumble over the canyon wall. I lurched backward, dizzy, and braced myself against the coarse trunk of a pinion pine. I lowered myself to the earth and tucked my head between my knees, yearning for the sensation to pass. My heartbeat resonated, an insistent voice shouting that I was going to die. All I wanted to do was escape from the canyon to some place safe. But where? Where could I be safe? The fear ballooned…enveloping me and pressing me from every direction. I clenched my eyes shut and strained to regulate my breathing, to deepen its regularity, and also to rein in this panic, a reaction I hadn't experienced since my first weeks in Vietnam. To rebuff this terror that seized me, I thought: "So, this is what a panic attack feels like." Janine had cautioned me about panic attacks and I had relied on the medication to deter them. She had also coached me on how to deal with one if the medication didn't prevent an onset. "Don't fight it," she'd said. "Admit what's happening to you and give the fear time to pass. If you don't add frightening thoughts to your panic, it'll begin to fade."

I sat for a few more moments until I was relatively sure I would not faint, and then awkwardly rose and strode back to the Village Loop Drive. I sank onto a wooden bench in a covered bus shelter. The dizziness had waned but I was thirsty…I reasoned that after a nap at the hotel, I could regain my stability. The return bus ride helped calm me…perhaps it was the feeling of movement, of going somewhere other than where the panic had materialized, even if just back to a room I could claim as mine for a short time. I bought a bottle of water in the gift shop and gulped it with the craving of a nomad stumbling upon a desert oasis. In the restaurant I ordered a steak…I ate it so quickly I barely tasted the meat or the baked potato…and washed it all down with three glasses of Merlot. Later, I closed the drapes to darken my room, switched the television to a music station with the volume barely audible, and then lay on the bed, sheltering myself with the stiff bedspread. I soon fell asleep.

When I woke, where daylight had before leaked around the edges of the drapes, there was darkness. The digital clock on the bedside table read 9:12. I rolled onto my back and inhaled deeply, testing for constriction in my chest. None. I sat up…no dizziness. No panic. Despite the relief its absence brought, I remained wary. I buoyed myself with the confidence that I had conquered the panic, but understood it could resurface. As a trial, I willed the fear to return. I perched on the edge of the bed and challenged the fear to reappear. Nothing. But I'd experienced calm after a firefight, and knew that even when danger recedes, safety isn't necessarily what it leaves behind. In the morning, I would call Janine and ask her if I should increase the dosage of the medication she'd prescribed.

When I called Tallie, I considered shielding her from the news of what had happened to me. But I discovered that telling her about the incident helped minimize its impact. Talking to her, as it always seems to do, grounded me. I envisioned myself at home, watching her massage herbal lotion into her arms and legs before bed. That fragrance signals slumber to me. She doesn't obsess about the etched lines beneath her eyes, and those astride her nose that track to the corners of her mouth, although she nightly applies a cream to these areas. I suppose she does this to remain youthful and attractive to me…unnecessary…and I wonder if after I die, she'll shun even this small vanity, surrender to aging and disregard how she is seen by others. As Tallie has aged, her beauty has leached into her core. Any erosion of her outer beauty is eclipsed by the concentration of the loveliness within her.

We didn't chat for long. I could overhear fatigue in her voice.

Tomorrow I'll arrive in Phoenix, and I'll visit two people. The first is Samuel Wortham, a retired professor educated at Harvard, who taught me criminal law and criminal procedure at Northwestern. He's in his late seventies, lives with his wife near Mummy Mountain Park, and we've corresponded sporadically since his retirement ten years ago. The closest I had as a mentor in my law career, Sam was always a reliable source of unembroidered advice. He offered me the wisest counsel when I split off and started my own firm in the early eighties. It'll be good to call on him again. But the primary reason for my visit to Phoenix is Todd Sachshausen. He's an old boyfriend of Tallie's. We've never met, although I know a great deal about him, and at one point more than thirty years ago, we sat in the same stadium in Iowa City, watching an Illinois-Iowa football game.

Todd sells real estate in Scottsdale, no doubt a fallback career from some other endeavor at which he failed. In the photograph on the website for his agency, Todd's face looks pudgy, plump cheeks, pinched eyes framed by thick flesh, multiple chins. His head is nearly bald and I imagine he wears hats not only to protect his skin from the desert sun, but to disguise his baldness from potential home buyers. He's probably still a vain man, as well as divorced, bitter, convinced the world has allied against him and conspired to keep him down, and clueless as to why his life hasn't furnished him the same rewards he received so effortlessly in college. He's a spoiled boy in his sixties and he has a debt to pay.

For a short period Tallie dated Todd during her sophomore year in college. They met at a party at Todd's fraternity. His family lived in Hinsdale, an affluent suburb west of Chicago. While the Sachshausens weren't the richest family in the village, they were far from the poorest, and according to Tallie, Todd's mom insured he never lacked any accessory. He had seemed witty, handsome and, once he and Tallie became a couple, was soon considered an object of jealousy by Tallie's sorority sisters. Although he was sometimes overbearing, every boy Tallie and her girlfriends dated flaunted the same possessive tendencies.

I learned about Todd from Tallie on one of the first nights we spent in the loft when it was newly completed. After months of construction, consultations with the architect and the designer, and visits to check the progress of Tallie's vision unfolding for the space, we had moved in…but not yet settled in. As the two of us toured our new home, remarking on how beautifully everything had turned out, Tallie gripped my hand and raised it to her lips, kissing it. I looked at her face and saw tears glistening in her eyes. I was overwhelmed that she was so happy. But she began shaking her head slowly and weeping in a way that told me this was not joy. What she was feeling was something else entirely…and it frightened me. When I asked her what was the matter, Tallie only shook her head and raised her hands before her, palms facing me…they trembled. I led her to the sofa and sat her down, kneeling in front of her and trying to get her to look at me. She sniffled and her hair fell around her lowered head, leaving only a wedge of her face visible. She removed her glasses from her beautifully crooked nose and swiped at her eyes with the sleeve of her sweater.

"What is it?" I persisted.

And Tallie confessed. She had never trusted she would ever deserve a marriage as lasting as ours. Had never believed someone would love her enough to stay with her and not wound her. I held her hands in mine that night and listened to Tallie tell me how her relationship with Todd Sachshausen had ended. During spring break the year they were dating, Todd and some of his frat brothers flew to Mexico. Tallie stayed in Champaign, working on a paper that was due as soon as classes resumed. During the day she sequestered herself in the library with books and a growing stack of scribbled index cards. At night she sat at the desk in her room at the sorority house, organizing her research and typing her paper. On the evening Tallie closed the books and removed the final sheet of paper from her typewriter, she decided to go for a walk, maybe get some pizza and a beer, to celebrate. She walked across campus, past the flag football fields to Neil Street, then north, where she noticed a boy from her American Lit class coming out of the Jane Addams Book Shop. They chatted as they hiked back toward campus and together stopped for pizza at Monical's. That's where they were seen by one of Todd's frat brothers.

After Todd returned from spring break, he picked Tallie up in his Camaro Z/28 and drove her to Meadowbrook Park, where they strolled past the gardens and then veered off the path into a stand of trees. There he confronted Tallie, accusing her of cheating on him while he'd been in Mexico, where he had probably been whoring with his drunken frat brothers. She was startled by the accusation and assured Todd nothing had happened, that they'd just shared a pizza…but he told her she'd been seen. And then he beat her… blackened her eye, split her lip, chipped a tooth, and broke her nose. Her nose…which had never healed properly…and I understood how that imperfection I found so appealing only reminded Tallie of that day. Todd drove her back to the Kappa house, called her a slut, and cursed her for bleeding on his car seat.

Even now the memory of that night enrages me. I vacillated between a knee-jerk compulsion to retaliate for the beating, and then a slow-burn determination to punish Todd Sachshausen for the legacy of mistrust he implanted in Tallie that night. As Carl had said: "Payback is a motherfucker."

That night when Tallie rolled back the gauze that had been binding her vulnerability, it became a watershed moment in so many ways. We grew closer, of course, but it was weightier than that. We achieved naked intimacy. The two of us recognized we had crossed a covered bridge, and then turned to set it ablaze and watch it burn. That night in bed with Tallie, I felt as though we would sustain the passion we felt for one another, that it had coalesced through an instance of hopefulness.

Yes, sins can be forgiven…but as I said, they are not easily forgotten, and for more than twenty years, I've visited moments of hatred and revenge for Todd Sachshausen. I've imagined punishing him countless times, considered an appropriate revenge, and drew on loathsome experience from the war to exact vengeance I thought might befit his assault on Tallie. Before I was diagnosed, I believed beating him as he had beaten Tallie might suffice; at times perhaps something a little more severe. But every time I remembered moments when Tallie retreated behind an emotional wall, held back slightly in a vulnerable situation…or when I looked at her face and contemplated what he had done to her both bodily and spiritually…then only murder balanced the scales. I want finality and I seek equivalence. If I'm going to die, then Todd Sachshausen is also going to die. Not solely as an exchange, but as a gift to Tallie. She may find it reprehensible, but I'm banking on her identifying the motive more than she loathes the action. I'm employing a perverted canon and I condemn myself for it. But never underestimate the narcissism of taking a life with your own hands, of slaying someone not from a distance, but up close, where you feel their breath, sniff their sweat and hear them gasping and grunting, knowing that if you do not kill him, he will certainly kill you. Combine that with the righteousness, however contrived, of retribution, and the euphoria is overwhelming. One of war's foulest secrets: killing is exhilarating. No experience rivals the incomparability of human butchery. The carnage of battle simultaneously repels and captivates the soldier in a principled tug-of-war. Fury contests morality…decency combats depravity. Drawing on training from forty years ago, I'll savor grabbing Todd Sachshausen from behind, covering his mouth with my hand, whispering Tallie's name as I thrust Carl's Kabar into his throat and tearing down toward his heart, and then watching him bleed out. He won't be given the chance to cry out for help or to express his pain. I don't know where or when I'll do this. I'll stay in Phoenix as long as it takes to learn about where he lives and works, to observe him and identify his routines. Does he frequent the same bars and shops on certain days, and does he follow the same routes to and from work? Does he have a lover? Does he get together with colleagues and friends? I need to find a time and place when he will be alone and isolated, but still accessible.

 I consider myself an ethical man and accept the criminality of what I am planning to do. Todd Sachshausen's punishment has been deferred too long; he has experienced decades of freedom since he beat the crap out of Tallie, and while killing him may seem extreme, I've decided that he deserves to die for his miscalculation, now and at my hand. I'm not going to regret this…I told Carl as much when he gave me his knife. When we talked about it, I recounted for Carl who Todd was, what he had done and what I planned to do. As I said, Carl quietly nodded his affirmation. Some communication requires no words.

Day Seventeen

Tallie knows Sam Wortham; they met several times in Chicago before he retired. When she and I spoke this evening, she asked that I pass along her good wishes to him and his wife, and also to remind him that she envies how he now avoids Chicago winters. Sam displayed affection for Tallie, saying she reminded him of the first time he met his wife's (his current, second wife) grown children. He read the judgment in their eyes, as they stacked him up against their father, who was alive at the time but has since died. It was for Sam a difficult moment, but he worked through it, with patience, kindness and an aloofness he used to convince the children that he wasn't going to go out of his way to curry their favor…he loved their mother and they would need to meet him halfway on that matter. Tallie, he told me, rather than trying to earn Sam's approval when they first met, impressed him with her indifference about making an impression. There's a lyric in a Joni Mitchell song: "The times you impress me most are the times when you don't try."

Our conversation this evening was strange, and I can't tell if the strangeness came from me or from Tallie, or from Tallie reacting to me…conundrum. From the back of my mind, the purpose of my being here poked at me while we spoke. I told Tallie that being in Phoenix stood in contrast to the rural roads I'd been traveling recently. Ever since I left Portland, I've passed through so many small towns. Phoenix, although a major city, still can't erase my homesickness for Chicago, though. Here, people drive everywhere…it's not a walking city. I told her I couldn't wait to return home and just walk the neighborhood with her without feeling suspect or out of place… we'd stroll east on Madison out to the lake, down to the museum campus and out to the planetarium, the aquarium, and then follow the lake north to the river. I wanted for us to sit at an open-air café and watch the tour boat traffic.

Nothing new to report about Alison. Tallie visited her and she remains the same…no better and no worse. She's acclimating, according to the staff.

The office called, she said, just to check up and see how I was enjoying my sabbatical. I haven't written much about my colleagues at the firm. Work doesn't retain the same importance it did previously. These days it's a chapter in my history that's already been published and there doesn't seem much more to say about it. I don't regret the long hours and the sacrifices from the years when I was younger and painfully ambitious…when I was trying to prove something about myself. But now? Well, I suspect even if I had not been diagnosed, my career would have faded in significance compared to…well to the fulfillment I glean from my friends and Tallie. I know…can I really divorce my awareness of the diagnosis from the way I view things now? No. Should I? It would be interesting, even if only as an intellectual exercise, to gauge my adjustment to aging both including and excluding the effects of this cancer haze; or to weigh my individual experience against the commonality of similar human experiences, understanding that commonality need not denigrate the uniqueness of an individual experience, even though the experience is perceived by the individual and the similarity to common experience is recognized by that individual. It's like the old adage: what is the most important organ in the body? The brain… but look who's telling me that.

Of course, I didn't burden Tallie with any of this mindfuck. In fact the tenor of our conversation might have seemed strange because nothing about it appeared any different from a conversation we might have had during an ordinary day in Chicago, as if one of us had telephoned during a work day just to hear the other's voice, to discuss the happenings since we left home that morning. Our conversation tonight wasn't overshadowed by the foreboding that has characterized some of the conversations during the trip. It seemed curiously normal by comparison and that seemed in turn very reassuring and comforting. That's what made it peculiar.

And it caused me to reflect on something…during the entire time I've been gone, the only person I've asked Tallie about is Alison. I'm driving throughout the western U.S., visiting people who are important to me, yet I seem to have no one in Chicago other than Tallie who might hold equal importance. Curious. So I conducted a kind of "friend inventory." The results are intriguing but I don't think they're unusual. Over the years, it seems I've shed friends… and I mean genuine friends. This is tough to admit. From the days of neighborly rooftop parties when Tallie and I first met, through the obligatory socializing with colleagues and power brokers for career-building, to the board memberships of targeted charities…can it be true that the only relationship worthy of sustaining has been the one I share with Tallie? Yes…and I don't think it's unusual to say so. By the time you reach my age, you feel the fatigue sometimes of simply making the effort. You weary of the forced small talk, of the coerced structure of a social situation, of the shallowness of the dance. Tallie and I each autumn and each spring receive invitations to so many fundraising events, which when we were younger we loved attending. These days we check the box that indicates we will not attend but would like to contribute. It's cut down on our socializing, but in honesty it doesn't address the issue of friends…of close friends. The shrinking of our circles speaks volumes about Tallie and me. When I want a challenging conversation, no one competes with Tallie. She provides the companionship, the understanding, the critical intellect and the history I need. The history…yes, the all-important, overwhelming history. As the time you have already lived dwarfs the time you have left to live, relying on someone with whom you can shorthand things becomes indispensable. And I'm not just referring to the abbreviated time afforded me by my disease, nor am I restricting this to just Tallie and me. I think all couples as they age compress upon themselves. It reminds me of how a star collapses, its mass shrinking upon itself until it goes supernova. Going supernova…not a horrible analogy for dying. Anyway. The shedding of friends doesn't seem a conscious decision, something you add to your to-do list one day: "Pare friendships." It's an innate development, another life stage. We acquire possessions throughout our life, and then as we age and begin to understand our mortality, we slowly shed those trappings. Families have experienced a similar phenomenon…mom and dad grow older, they dispense little things at first when the kids visit. Photographs, bric-a-brac. Then later, furniture, artwork, heirlooms. We begin life in our smallest enclosure, our crib. Over decades, if we're fortunate, we expand into homes chock full of acquisitions fraught with value for their effect on us or for their ability to impress. A few we prize for the memories they provoke. We end our life having sloughed everything, as unconscious preparation for our final small enclosure, our deathbed. I think that process includes friends. I think as I have grown older, I find people less fascinating, less deserving of the effort. And that is natural. Time makes misanthropes of us all.

It was a relaxing drive this morning, one with a purpose quite different from all the other mornings on this journey. I started the music playlist with "Murder Incorporated" by Bruce Springsteen. I thought it might set the mood, but it had the opposite of my intended effect, making me feel as though I was a potential victim, rather than the murderer. The highway north of Phoenix flattened out as I neared the city, traffic grew more congested. I checked into the Scottsdale Plaza Resort; it's a short distance from Sam's home and also a few blocks from Todd's office on North Scottsdale Road. One of the reasons I chose this hotel is that it has no adjoining golf course, so I won't look too out-of-place by not being a golfer. It may sound insignificant, but I'm determined not to be careless in any detail, however minor. Tomorrow I'll begin tailing Todd, compiling a timeline of his daily activities. Once I establish his routine, I'll decide where and when to confront him. On the following day, I'll visit Sam and his wife.

One final note. The heat! Screw the old adage. Heat is heat, regardless of how dry it is. I'm going out to the pool to cool off before bed. But I have to decide which pool! The hotel has five swimming pools.

Day Eighteen

Surveillance resembles baseball…ten minutes of action crammed into two hours. Or war…lengthy intervals of boredom punctuated by moments of perilous excitement. Sachshausen's website listed his office hours as ten a.m. to six p.m. So at nine-thirty I left the hotel and drove south on North Scottsdale Road a few blocks to Valley View Road. I parked in one of the only shaded spaces and angled the rearview mirror to give me a view of the door and front window of his office in an upscale cluster of medical and professional offices. I sat in the passenger seat of the Saab…advice I'd gleaned from a private investigator I've used in Chicago over the years…people assume if you're sitting in the passenger seat that you're waiting for someone. You seem less suspicious that way. Todd arrived at his office shortly after ten o'clock in a black Cadillac Escalade. He appeared heavier than I would have guessed from his headshot on the website. Short sleeved, yellow camp shirt. Khakis. Tan loafers. Ray-Bans. Green canvas shoulder bag. The heat must truly torment him.

He worked in his office for nearly two hours. I started the Saab several times to run the air conditioner and dispel the heat, which was oppressive even with the windows opened. At noon he emerged. I thought he might be going to lunch, but he drove south several miles to a walled and gated condo development on West 8th Street. A showing no doubt. The two-story buildings painted in hues from a muted, desert palette. The pool visible beyond the gates. The entrance across the road from a golf course. There was no place to park without being totally conspicuous. Something I hadn't prepared for. I had to make a decision…to gamble whether or not Sachshausen would return to his office after the showing on the same route he took to the condo complex. Or had he scheduled another appointment? In another part of the city? I slowly circled the development, looking to spot Todd's Escalade, and found two more entrances, both also gated. Turning off South Price Road, I headed west on El Rio Salado Parkway, stopped for a sandwich at a Jimmy John's, and then parked behind the Sports Chalet in the Tempe Marketplace to eat lunch and watch the west-bound traffic. With any luck I would spy Todd's car and resume tailing him. If by two o'clock I didn't see him, I'd return to his office and wait there for him. I was amazed by how many black Escalades passed me, and since I had not bothered to jot down Todd's license plate number, I had no way of knowing if any of them were his. Eventually I drove back to Scottsdale and spotted his car in a space in front of his office. In a larger lot to the east of Todd's office sat several rows of covered parking. Not wanting to risk having the Saab identified by parking in the same space again, I eased into one of the covered spaces in the middle of the lot, facing the sidewalk in front of the realty office. From that vantage I could monitor Todd's comings and goings. I sat there the rest of the afternoon. Todd had no more showings. He left at six o'clock and I followed him to his home in another gated, golf course community in Ocotillo. I drove past the entrance, but there was no place to stop except a nearby grade school; parking beside a playground for an extended period of time seemed like a truly stupid thing to do. However, a bit farther south there was a shopping center, a cluster of salmon-colored buildings adjacent to an apartment building. I established a circuit: parking there for a short time and then driving past Sachshausen's gated entrance to another shopping center and parking there for a while. I shuttled back and forth on this route until after eight o'clock with no sign of Todd. I understood it was a longshot to expect to see him, and I wondered how long I would have to follow him before I identified a killing zone. His home and office were unsuitable…too much risk with either location. A single day's surveillance hadn't revealed any other locations he might haunt. My PI friend in Chicago, who was a retired detective, used to say that a stakeout required patience and a clinical outlook. Expectation, he counseled, was the enemy of results. Patience I have, as well as purpose.

My earlier assessment that Todd Sachshausen had undoubtedly failed in life needed adjustment. His home, his office and his car all indicated money, success. In a way, though, I'm happy to learn that he has something to lose. I don't want killing him in any way to seem like a release or an escape. When he panics at the pain of the Kabar tearing out his throat, I want him to anguish over what he'll miss. I hope it's true that your life passes before your eyes in those final moments, that when I clamp my hand over his mouth and whisper Tallie's name into his ear, and then stab the knife into the side of his neck, that he flashes on everything he will relinquish. If he doesn't feel regret for having beaten Tallie, I won't care. The act is gratifying even if he only remembers her as a bygone nuisance, as that slut that cheated on him. Perhaps even more rewarding would be if Todd Sachshausen doesn't remember Tallie at all. If as he felt the life emptying from him, he huffs to scream and finds no voice, wracking his memories to place that name, to dredge it from his history, thrashing to make sense of something that means nothing to him. When I saw Sachshausen emerge from his SUV this morning, I clenched my jaw, not with anger, I realized, but with resolve. Fuck him up. That's what I'm going to do.

I completely forgot to play any music this morning and in retrospect, that seems appropriate. More than any other day on this journey…or maybe differently from any other day…this one promised consequences. Differently. Yes. Come to think of it, I never even turned on the radio today. I'd prepared for the monotony with newspapers and magazines…the choppiness of their stories prevented me from becoming too engrossed and possibly missing Todd's comings and goings. Bottled water, bananas and granola bars…a colossal infringement of my usual "no food in the car" rule… Tallie would laugh. An open map of Phoenix…another PI tip: if you're questioned, claim your GPS is malfunctioning and you're trying to get your bearings. So much preparation for contingencies. And so much time just sitting and thinking. About Tallie, of course. Her quirks…like her habit of ambling through the loft, examining, almost as though reacquainting herself, with familiar items in our home. Gracefully reaching out and fingering a book, or the porcelain pottery resting in the sunlight on a window ledge, or the black metal frame of a print we bought at the Old Town Art Fair, or the hem of a curtain sheer. Tallie curled on pillows before the fireplace…she had insisted on a gas fireplace with sealed glass doors, and it throws out heat like a stove…reading a book and jotting notations in the margins, a tumbler of whiskey not far from her grasp. Tallie perched on a stool at the kitchen island, laughing so fiercely at a joke that she coughs violently and her face turns crimson…she waves a hand to signal that she is fine.

    During lunch today in the parking lot, I called Janine's office. When she called me back half an hour later, I described the panic attack at the Grand Canyon, how I had dealt with it and my doubts about the level of medication she had prescribed. Janine listened carefully and asked if recalling the incident made me feel anxious. She chuckled when I said it hadn't, but that her asking me if it had made me slightly more anxious, as though she expected another attack to strike. "You can double the dosage from ten milligrams to twenty. I can phone in another prescription for you if you like, or just take two pills each day instead of one." I told her I'd wait until I returned to Chicago for a new prescription, that I had enough pills to double up until then. "You're out of town?" she asked. "Visiting friends," I said. "Just for a few days." "I understand," she said and told me to call her again if I needed anything.

    Back at the hotel this evening I ate dinner outdoors at Remington's, under an arbor completely sheltered by a canopy of leaves from a woody vine. Then I went for a walk around the resort…my rear end was sore from a day of sitting. Before I called Tallie, I went out to the pool again and sat at a table under a turquoise umbrella, watching children splash in equally turquoise water. At one end of the pool a waterfall poured over a patterned wall of mosaic tiles and I started counting each section, step stoning from one end of the wall to the other. The contrast between these lavish accommodations and the wretched reason for being here alarmed me and I momentarily feared the onset of another panic attack. But it simply passed. Back at my room, I sat on the enclosed patio and called Tallie.

It was apparent immediately that she was upset.

"Honey, what's wrong?"

"It's stupid," she sniffled. "It's just stupid."

"I know, honey. But if you don't tell me I can't help you."

"You don't have to fix everything all the time," she snapped.

What compels men to be problem solvers? Jesus. I know better. I know enough to listen, to acknowledge what Tallie is trying to tell me…in her own time, not rushed by me with a hasty, inappropriate solution. Sometimes, I've learned, people don't want their problems solved. They serve a purpose…a crutch, a trigger, an inspiration, a reminder, even at times relief. When Tallie tells me a problem, she's not necessarily asking me to fix it for her. She's sharing…because she knows I love her, that I care about her, and she feels the same about me. I know this and yet I stupidly blurted out exactly what she did not want to hear. Old dog and old tricks?

"Sorry, Tallie. I'm really sorry."

"I finally changed the bed and washed the sheets."

I stayed silent and hoped that was the right thing to do.

"The bed doesn't smell like you anymore."

"Oh, Tallie." Decades ago when we alternated between apartments, Tallie once stripped my bed and demanded fresh sheets, saying the old ones reeked and felt tacky against her skin. She was openly angry until I told her that I loved smelling her on the sheets each night before I fell asleep. The solution to that problem, which we both sought then and tried not to avoid, was sleeping together every night.

"I tried for as long as I could," she said.

"Hey, we both love clean sheets."

"You have to promise me something."

"If I can."

"I want a shirt. I want you to wear a shirt for as long as it takes so that I can have your scent. I'll never wash it. I'll keep it forever."

"I can do that." I paused. "But…"

"But what?" she demanded, her voice insistent.

"Nothing big. I'll wear it, but it has to be before I start to stink. I don't want you to remember me with the stench of death on me."

"You're such an ass," she snickered.

"Not news, you know."

"I miss you," she whispered. I imagined her on the bed, sniffing the sheets and my pillow for my scent.

"Me, too."

I'm writing this journal for Tallie. Ever since leaving Elko, I've speculated that what I include here gets subconsciously edited. That I have been slanting entries in one direction or another…trying to influence how Tallie will remember me. Can the jottings over a few weeks have the power to repudiate knowledge she has amassed over decades? Let's be candid: are there crimes worse than murder you can confess to your wife? Unfaithfulness…betrayal of trust. They might elicit more pain. I've considered discontinuing the journal. Or postponing it until later, when I begin to feel the full effects of the disease, to see if a change in my perspective might loosen emotions I now leave submerged. There's an otherworldliness to this trip…physically I feel healthy. No symptoms of the cancer. The panic attack…managed. No pain. No fatigue. I can't feel the sword suspended over my head, although I can see its shadow. Would what

I write change considerably if the blade lowered ever so slightly and nicked the skin on my neck?

Maybe Tallie doesn't want me to capture my final time. Would prefer to remember me, in my own words, as a healthy man. Maybe in actuality, I don't have a choice. Whether it's written or not, Tallie will remember every detail of my death. That's the kind of woman she is. That's the woman I love. Maudlin of me…but no less truthful. Chaos, of which I am so fond, threw us at one another, and the conquest of the odds that we found each other at times disorientates me. I consider myself not a what-if person, constantly wondering about choices not made, paths abandoned in favor of others. I'm more of a what-next person. Accept your choices and move on to another challenge, to another task. Yet the disease props a giant mirror in your face and you naturally look backward. Hindsight, yes. But I can control whether or not I pander to revisionism. Cancer limits my what-nexts. Rather than torture myself about that, I'm going to embrace it, as Carl advised, as a gift. Limits as freedom? Counterintuitive…but empowering, like being granted three wishes by a genie and being told you cannot ask for unlimited wishes. A choice between dwelling on experiences I will miss and feeling I have been cheated out of those experiences. Make the most of opportunities… you can insert any other applicable clichés here.

The journey and the journal are conjoined. I'll continue both. And I won't document the final days.

Day Nineteen

I thought I'd blown it this morning. I parked in the same shaded spot outside Sachshausen's office (a mistake I now realize) as I had yesterday, and when he arrived, he walked around to the rear of his SUV, lifted the hatch to retrieve a stack of papers and then turned and looked directly at me. I thought I'd been made…do I watch too much TV? But I didn't panic…I flipped the page of my newspaper, studying him in my peripheral vision. He paused for just that nerve-wracking moment and then continued to his office. I waited fifteen minutes and started the Saab, backed out and exited the parking lot, being sure to drive past Todd's office. I slowly circled the block and entered the complex about fifty yards south of his office, nosing into a space from which I could observe his Escalade, if not his office door. No movement until lunch, when he drove two blocks…yes, two blocks…to a Mexican restaurant, En Fuego, at the Double Tree Resort. I parked far enough away that it would be unlikely he would recognize my car, and then sauntered past the restaurant. I couldn't see him inside so I returned to my car, and feasted on a banana and a power bar.

Todd had one showing that afternoon, east of his office off East MacDonald Road, and thankfully in an ungated neighborhood north of Agua Linda Park. I trailed him carefully, turning and immediately pulling to the curb when he turned onto East Berridge Lane. Following him on that quiet street would surely have given me away. He pulled into the driveway of a house halfway down the block and parked beside a black BMW. A couple emerged, greeted him and they all walked into the house. I waited two minutes and then drove past. The house had both a garage and a carport…that struck me as odd. Then I returned to Todd's office, parked in the covered lot and waited. But he never returned.

This surveillance wasn't progressing as I had expected. And I was growing frustrated, no closer to finding a suitable location. I'm not averse to risk, but I don't want to be overly rash either.

Around six o'clock I drove to Ocotillo and resumed my circuit between the two malls. At seven-thirty, as I was parked in a lot on the east edge of the shopping center…here's some irony - outside a realty office…I spotted Todd's Escalade. I'd jotted down the license number after yesterday's experience. I watched him turn off South Alma School Road, east onto West Ocotillo. I started the Saab and followed. Traffic was light. I kept my distance in a leisurely stalk. He didn't drive far, perhaps half a mile, and turned into the parking lot of a bar, with the ungodly name of Old Chicago…as Tallie's grandfather would say: "I shit you not." The bar occupied the corner of a vast complex of stores; after I assured myself that Sachshausen had entered the bar, I drove around the periphery, searching for a shop that might sell binoculars. No luck. So I parked beside a median planted with trees and low shrubs where I still had a view of Todd's SUV and settled in. Over the next two hours the lot filled and at sunset I gazed at an astonishing spectacle…from the flat earth to the massive sky the color shaded from sumptuous gold to sinister rust. I took a photo from my car window…a Jiffy Lube in the foreground.

I didn't wait for Todd to leave. I'd discovered my killing ground…not as isolated as I would have liked, but a crowded parking lot, especially in darkness, can provide me with the seclusion I need. Time will not be an issue. I've been an efficient killer before in my life and it won't require much time to kill Todd Sachshausen.

Enigmatic mood tonight. I'd felt wired all day, but now…a temperament of resolution…of commitment. It's calming and not unusual: making a choice alleviates the stress of indecision.

I closed the drapes in my room and slipped the Kabar from its sheath, then slowly honed it on the whetstone. The sound of the blade scraping the stone, a raspy scratch, percussive and rhythmic. Musical. I began to hum as I drew the blade back and forth across the stone, flipping the knife with each pull. Reacquainting myself with the imprint of the grip in my hand.

I'm kind of creeping myself out! Sounding maniacal is not my intent. Confirming my intent shouldn't sound maniacal. I'm primed …that's what I want to convey. I've prepared my "kit." The Kabar, a long-sleeved t-shirt and old jeans…no belt…latex gloves, and a pair of cheap rubber-soled, canvas shoes. When I leave Phoenix, I'll bury the clothes somewhere out in the desert. Mail the Kabar back to Carl. I'll visit Sam the morning after and leave the city that afternoon. Whatever day provides the opportunity. I'm going to follow Sachshausen every day until he returns to the bar. That will be his last day.

Tallie and I chatted briefly tonight. It was late in Chicago by the time I returned to the hotel and I didn't want to tire her. She was even-keeled tonight and our conversation was newsy and shallow. I wondered if she purposefully avoided anything more emotional because of our conversation yesterday. At one point I yearned to confess to her what I was planning. But she would have attempted to stop me. She won't view this as justice…and I don't either…it's vengeful retribution, completely out of scale with the crime. And you know something? I don't care. I do not give a shit.

It occurred to me that perhaps I'm transferring my death sentence onto Todd Sachshausen. An exchange, of sorts. Nothing rational about that. I know. I can't say there's nothing to the theory, but I intellectually understand his death won't change the inevitability of my own. It won't erase mine as though a debt has been paid. No. In examining my motives one stands out: I want to. I want to kill him because it'll make me feel better. It's that simple and that primitive. Killing Todd Sachshausen will be a pleasure.

Day Twenty

Shadowing Sachshausen today was a bust. He arrived at his office in the morning at the usual time. Left for lunch…driving again a short distance, the fat fuck… and returned. Went home at five and never came near the Old Chicago Bar.

On one hand I'm impatient…now that every aspect of the plan seems to be in place, I'm anxious for the confrontation. On the other hand, I can't rush the moment. He controls the timing and he doesn't even know it.

I'm concerned that Tallie might grow suspicious of why I'm killing so much time in Phoenix. (Yeah…I said it). Days now and I haven't talked about visiting Sam Wortham, or for that matter, discussed any details about what I've been doing here. She suffered this trip of mine because she accepted its objective. If I give her the impression I'm doing nothing more than lounging poolside in the Arizona sun when I could be spending this time with her…well, I'm not eager to face that anger. For nearly three weeks, Tallie has restrained her inquisitiveness. She's allowed me to choose what I talk about and has only mildly prodded me for particulars. The patience she has displayed is an offering. I owe it to her to express my gratitude.

Music this morning: "Revenge" by Patti Smith. Made me smile. I'm tired of this room. I'm tired of this city. I'm anxious to be moving again.

Day Twenty-One

I'm sure you've heard this before: Know how to make God laugh? Tell him your plans.

As I was preparing to leave the hotel for the short drive to Sachshausen's office this morning, I received a text on my phone: "Stay put. Carl." I gazed at the phone's screen for a moment, dumbfounded by the message. It lacked all context and absolutely confused me.

I quickly replied: "What?"

"Be there ASAP. Don't leave your room."

I admit to being thunderstruck. Carl was here? I perched on the padded bench at the foot of the bed, gripping my car key in my hand, unconsciously step-stoning through the geometric shapes in the pattern of the chocolate-colored carpet. Even in the cool of the air-conditioned room, droplets of sweat formed on my upper lip. When I heard the knock on the door it startled me; I was unsure how much time had elapsed.

Carl stood, a tight-lipped grin on his face. He wore sunglasses, a Diamondbacks baseball cap, black shorts, an untucked, white t-shirt and flip-flops.

"What the hell?" I said.

He stepped past me, told me to close the door and then sank into the sofa cushions. "Nice room," he said. "More like an apartment." He gestured to the corner, where a tepee of kindling stood in the raised kiva fireplace. "A fireplace?"

I gawked at Carl and he began to laugh, motioning for me to sit in one of the barrel side chairs near the sofa.

"Grab me a beer and I'll explain everything, grasshopper." Carl chuckled, slipped off his flip-flops and rested his feet on the coffee table, crossing his ankles.

I didn't move.

"You in shock?" he asked, tipping his head at an angle as he stared at me.

"Maybe," I said.

"Beer first. Then sit down," he said. "There's a lot of catching up you need to do."

I complied and watched Carl take a long swallow of beer. "It's nine-thirty in the morning," I said.

"It was a long night and I'm thirsty."

"You're not supposed to be here." I said.

"I'm exactly where I'm supposed to be," Carl said. He sipped once more from his beer. "Oh, and Todd Sachshausen died last night."

His words stunned me. I felt light-headed…in my vision the edges of the room began to quiver and undulate like a road rippling in highway heat.

Carl remained silent, the beer bottle in his right hand dripping condensation to the carpet. His expression was stern, he no longer smiled.

"I want my knife back, by the way," he finally said.

"I'm..." I stammered. "I'm not sure what to say."

"Don't say anything, man. The guy had a showing last night in a place called Western Heritage Estates, a tidy little ranch house on a quiet street just west of a feed lot. The smell wasn't too intense. There's a pool and an orchard...out in some of the last ranch and farm land, rustic, the driveway is still packed dirt. The neighbors on either side keep horses."

"Sachshausen's dead?"

"Broke his neck in an apparent fall. But that won't hold when the medical examiner takes a closer look." Carl drained the last of the beer. "I could use another."

As I retrieved another beer, I tried to grasp the entirety of what Carl had told me. He had killed Todd Sachshausen last night after meeting the man at one of his listings.

"Why?" I asked, and then hurriedly added: "Did anyone see you? Were you careful?"

"Relax, man. Everything's cool."

"All right, Carl. Start at the beginning." He grinned again and rested his head on the sofa back.

"Fair enough."

Carl had arrived in the city two days before I had. He'd flown to Tucson, rented a car, booked a room in a motel near the airport, and then driven into Phoenix.

"I'm going to omit some specifics...thought you might appreciate some plausible deniability," he said.

Todd's website gave Carl everything he needed: a photo so he would recognize Sachshausen, and the man's listings, so he could find a fairly remote property for sale. Carl checked out the listing, found it suitable and then waited.

"I waited for you to get into town," he told me.

"Why?"

"Can I get a wit-ne-eh-ess," he crooned, raising his arms, tilting his head back and wagging it from side to side like a gospel singer arrested by the spirit. He looked to me for a reaction. "Sorry, man. I've been up all night and I'm pretty punch drunk right now."

I nodded.

When Carl spotted me tailing Sachshausen, he telephoned and scheduled a showing of the property he'd selected. Todd believed he was a California businessman who'd grown up outside of Phoenix and was considering moving back.

"I embellished the story a bit for my own amusement," Carl said. "But again, nothing specific you need to know."

When Sachshausen questioned the late hour for the showing, Carl had pleaded business meetings, a dinner appointment and an early return flight to Los Angeles the following morning.

"The fucker agreed to meet me at eight-thirty. He wanted that sale."

Sachshausen showed Carl through the house, pointing out the usual details of moldings, hardwood and tile flooring, kitchen cabinets, closets, the pool and the orchard…the complete circuit of the house and its rooms. When they returned to the entryway, Carl pointed to the pool and asked about its upkeep. When Sachshausen turned away from Carl, in the direction of the sliding doors to the pool deck, Carl quickly advanced on the man, circled Todd's neck with his right arm, positioned his left hand on the back of

Sachshausen's head, and then twisted and pushed with all his force. In less than two seconds, his neck was snapped.

"He went limp. I dropped him to the floor and checked for a pulse," Carl said. "I closed the drapes on the sliders, locked the door from the inside and left."

I began thinking rationally. "Finger prints?"

"I followed him through the house. He opened and closed every door…I never touched anything, and I wiped the front door handle when I left."

"Did he get your plate number?"

"I arrived after him. It was dark. And, false name, false city, nothing at his office can link me to him."

"Phone?"

"Burner cell. I've been careful."

I paused, noiselessly tapping my fingers on the chair arms. "I can't believe this, Carl. Why'd you do it?"

"You wanted him dead."

"Yeah."

"Was it important that you kill him or just that he die?"

That question caught me off guard and I grimaced as I considered it.

Carl continued. "I know you think you needed to set things right here…to get payback. But you don't."

I still wasn't sure how I to answer Carl's earlier question.

"You don't need to hump that kind of weight around for the rest of your short life." Carl tilted the bottle neck toward me. "There was no way in hell I was gonna allow you to carry that kind of guilt. And regardless of how you justified it…and I don't question that… you'd feel guilty eventually. You're a good man. The best I know."

Carl's voice cracked. He lifted his legs to the carpet and rested his forearms on his knees. "A man who does good things. I trust you and believe it's good that fucker is dead. And I know it's good that you didn't kill him."

I had no words for Carl. I had too many words for Carl. There's no other person in my life, aside from Tallie, with whom I could be so uncensored. No one in Chicago…hell no one in the world… even approaches the intimacy I share with this man. People throw around the phrase "There's nothing I wouldn't do…" But Carl… yeah, Carl. I had told God my plans, and God turned out to be Carl.

"I'm bushed," Carl said. "Been driving back and forth between here and Tucson every night."

"My God. I never…" So many thoughts swamped my mind.

"All I need is a thank-you and a place to crash for a few hours," Carl said. "My flight to Portland leaves Tucson at nine tonight."

"Thank you?" I asked. "How can thank you ever be enough, Carl?"

He shrugged.

"Thank you. You are an unconditional friend and the most honorable man I know."

Carl stared at me. "Semper fi," he said, and then yawned. He finished his beer and slumped back in the sofa cushions.

"Take the bed," I said.

"What are you gonna do?"

"I'll be on the patio. You need anything, call me."

Carl stood and we smiled, regarding one another in silence. As in music, sometimes the most profound sounds lie in the silences between the notes. Carl extended his hand. I gripped it in mine and we shook slowly.

So I'm sitting at the table on the patio with my laptop. The "Do Not Disturb" sign hangs on the door knob. Carl is asleep on top of the unmade bed, still fully clothed, and I'm making an atypical, mid-day entry in the journal.

I spent perhaps half an hour simply sitting here in the shade, leaning back in this chair with my hands laced and resting on my stomach, tapping the pads of my thumbs against each other in a pattern: one, two…one, two three, repeating that over and over. My iPod rests on the table. I had thought perhaps some music might set a mood conducive to contemplating all that Carl had revealed. But I scanned my music library and nothing jumped out at me. I imagine somewhere rests a fragment of wisdom about how the manner in which we deal with the unexpected defines our character. My character as well as Carl's. Our interaction over the past thirty years has been sporadic, but each successive instance seems contiguously linked to the previous. The gaps are insignificant, unlike the recesses between musical notes. Carl is a confidant. Our friendship evolved from the madness of experiences we survived…and it endures. It's a thought-provoking observation that our friendship has been bookended with death and killing…of saving one another's lives while ravaging others'. I'm drifting into that ridiculous construction again…I will miss Carl. More decisively, Carl will miss me…this is knowledge I revere and in which I take pride.

While resting earlier on the patio, I also grappled with a reticence to divulge the fullness of my emotions. Such a stereotypical male peculiarity. My astonishment at what Carl has done underscores my love for the man. The moment when we regarded each other in silence and then shook hands exemplified a classic dichotomy: so much was communicated with the strength of the look…and yet so many words could have described what the look entailed, and what emotions were conveyed. We understood each other and chose not to elaborate that understanding with words, chose not to taint it with spoken language. Or…we feared elaboration would concede vulnerability. Men don't do that…especially with one another…and frustratingly all too often with women, as well. Wasted time. Wasted, wasted time. Why do we squander opportunities for intimacy because of discomfort? Strong and silent isn't superior to strong and expressive. If anything, the risk inherent in expression, because of the sincerity it exposes, argues that the unrestrained man is the stronger man. Jeopardy walks hand-in-hand with revelation. I'd rather define the strength of a friendship by the openness displayed between the friends. I'm angry with myself for not telling Carl how thankful I am for what he's done. For what the enormity of the deed says about him and what it means to me. No more wasted time…there's simply not enough of it left. I ought to know better…this entire journey has been about time. Tallie considers it time appropriated from her. Carl regards it as a gift I should enjoy unfettered by self-reproach. And I vacillate. This farewell tour can't revolve around regret. How will I feel if when I return home to Chicago, I violate my nature and ask even one time: "What if?" No what-ifs or even what-nexts… only what-nows.

 I understand how my annoyance at not having expressed sufficient gratitude to a friend for killing a man I had intended killing might present a challenge to my preaching from any moral high ground. It's a valid challenge…but I don't care. I'm rationalizing the murder of Todd Sachshausen as defensible retribution; and I know that despite what Carl intended, my culpability in the man's death hasn't been minimized. Even within my gratitude I crave to bear responsibility...I aspired to be the cause of that man's death. I needed, I believe so completely, to be the cause of his death...to be able to tell Tallie that I avenged that unforgotten crime. I cannot save myself...so I must save her. I've betrayed much of what I believe these past three days. That betrayal must possess significance. What I had hoped killing Sachshausen would express to Tallie, Carl has expressed to me. From without...it cannot be justified; and from within...I've dismissed trying to justify it. As heinous as it is, as counter to my principles as it is, as reminiscent of that period Carl and I have struggled for years to forget and reconcile it is...I do not repent it. Fuck Todd Sachshausen and the malevolence he represented...even if only to Tallie, to me and to Carl. If I have any regret...it is this: I wanted Todd Sachshausen to understand in that final breath the reason he was forfeiting his life.

I'm hungry; it's past lunch time, but I'm not going to move until Carl stirs. While on the subject of confessions, here's one more ...weeks ago, when I first planned this trip, I told Tallie the decision of whether to travel east or west had been decided by a coin flip. I lied. I never flipped a coin; I simply couldn't tell her what coming to Phoenix was going to mean. It was an artifice...a deception to make the route seem unintentional. Perhaps I understood that had I told Tallie what I intended to do, she might have tried to dissuade me. Todd Sachshausen never really was a recurrent topic in our conversations. Maybe I'd embellished over the years the effects of what he'd done to Tallie, adapting them to complement my reality. The entirety of a moment can never be accurately reflected in memory...time repeatedly varnishes memory, one layer upon another. The more far-flung the memory, the more plentiful and opaque the layers...and, by extension, the distortions. Doubt in this situation seems normal. Not questioning my decisions would be cause for far more distress than the guilt I bear as an accessory to murder. In a perverted sense, I am buoyed by the acceptance that I have committed a crime… even a crime I may rationalize as justified…it means my compass still functions properly. If I truly believed nothing was wrong with killing Todd Sachshausen, I would be lost. With the abbreviated time I have left, I cannot afford to lose my way.

I've got to leave this alone. Sachshausen is dead; I had intended to kill him. Carl killed him so that I wouldn't have to carry what he imagined was a burden. But the burden persists and now I have to determine if that weight will bow my back and crush me, or if I can shoulder it.

I hear Carl…he's in the bathroom.

Our conversation after Carl woke mirrored my conversation with myself while he slept.

"I'm not going to say you shouldn't have, Carl," I began. "But part of me wishes you hadn't."

"I expected you'd say that," he said. I nodded.

We both sat at the patio table. Carl sipped from a bottle of water.

"But we don't always know what's best for ourselves," Carl continued. "You're the man you are and I'm the man I am. And the man I am could never allow you to…"

"I know why you did it. I just don't…"

Carl slammed an open palm on the table and I stopped talking. "No you don't!" He hissed. "Let me finish." He paused and breathed deeply several times. "You think I did it for you. Okay. In part, yes.

But my motives are also selfish. I did this for me, too. You wanted revenge; I understand that. You think I tried to spare you the hardship of taking murder to your grave. I understand that, too. But I also needed some way to pay tribute to you, to make you comprehend what you did for me so long ago.

"I was fragile, so fucking breakable, after that train suicide. My only thoughts in the VA hospital were how to convince the doctors I was level-headed enough to be discharged, so I could get out of there and drive my own car onto the tracks. The last person in the world I expected to see was you, and the last thing in the world I expected was to have your visits affect me in the way that they did." He sniffled. "You saved me. You…saved…me. Three simple words charged with so much implication."

I swallowed to disguise a sob.

"The gesture you made. The example you set. You never recognized how they changed me. I came to understand that I was ashamed of being weak for needing help."

"Talk about coincidence. I was actually thinking about that while you were asleep," I said.

"The motto of the Corps, remember? Semper Fidelis. Those austere words encompass so much and I reminded myself that it wasn't Semper Firmus…always strong and reliable…or Semper Valens…always strong and healthy. You were faithful and I latched onto that allegiance like salvation itself. So don't ever suppose this was done solely for you, that it was a straightforward attempt to unburden you. Killing that man was my emancipation, too. A pair of debts were repaid last night. Now perhaps we can each go to our graves a tad more appeased."

"So that you don't think me completely clueless," I said. "I always knew how you felt, just not how deeply."

"Consider this another gift besides time. Part of that debt I owed you is honesty, honesty even in the face of embarrassment. I mean if I can't embarrass myself in front of you, then…"

"Yeah, but it's not really embarrassment, Carl. It's fear…fear of admitting frailty, of admitting imperfection. Those admissions can be frightening."

"Well, then we're both heroes. That's all heroism is, we both know, acting in spite of your fear."

"I've been playing a game with myself. A ridiculous game of listing all the things I'm going to miss when I'm dead."

Carl chuckled. "You'll be dead."

"That's what makes the game ridiculous, of course. But I am really gonna miss you when I'm dead, Carl."

"Yeah, you will."

Carl and I ate an early dinner and then he left for his flight out of Tucson. I waved to him as he drove out of the parking lot and then belly-laughed as I turned the thought over in my head that I truly was going to miss him.

When I called Tallie tonight I asked her to plan a trip for when I got back. A week anywhere she wanted to go. I told her not to decide right away, but to think about it and let me know in a day or two. She sounded pleased over the phone and although I sensed she wanted to talk about something, she refrained. We said we loved one another and then hung up.

The other call I made tonight was to Sam Wortham. I'll be stopping by his home in the morning and then continuing on to Austin, Texas to visit the last person on the list. He's an exceptional bass and guitar player who once lived in our building, across and down the hall from Alison.

When I started my own firm, there were days I'd call Sam Wortham and present him with a dilemma, asking him for advice about what I should do. Sam would calmly ask me a series of questions: what was I inclined to do? What did I want to do? (I often didn't realize that inclination and desire were separate influences). What was the best thing to do? And, what was the worst thing that could be done? Sam's advice was always priceless, because the old fox never gave me any…he generously guided me through the process of choosing my own decision and insuring I'd be comfortable with its consequences. That was a more profound gift than advice from which I might learn nothing except dependence. He taught me that alternatives always exist, but that most people limit their options to what's easy and obvious. Few people ever take the time to explore more difficult and indistinct choices, even though they might in the end bring even loftier rewards. I wonder what Sam would have counseled about my plans for Todd Sachshausen. What questions would he have asked me? He once likened being an attorney and dealing with clients to a particular scene from the film "The Last Emperor." In the scene, the child emperor defecates into a brass bowl and one of his royal retainers examines his stool, swirling it in the bowl and sniffing it. He scrutinizes the odor and consistency, and then turns to another retainer and advises that the emperor needs more chicken in his diet. "That's what attorneys are like sometimes," Sam had said. "We examine our clients' shit and make recommendations that will change their lives." Sam displayed a cynical streak once in a while.

Something just occurred to me: if my conversation with Carl didn't initiate a panic attack, then I'm at a loss for what might precipitate another. Maybe I'm past that now.

Also, since talking with Carl, I realize I've altered my frame of mind. Leaving Phoenix tomorrow for Austin seems less a continuation of my journey than the beginning of my trip home.

Day Twenty-Two

Sam Wortham greeted me on the hard-packed earthen driveway of his home on East Cheney Drive in Mummy Mountain Park. The single-story house tinted the lusterless shade of adobe seemed modest in comparison to some of his neighbors' compounds. We shook hands…Sam's not a hugger… and he guided me on a short tour of his property. He wore leather sandals, a sky-blue pocket t-shirt, and white cotton drawstring pants. Sam looked calm and, truthfully, very happy. His demeanor had always tended toward even-tempered, but the easygoing way with which he indicated the carefully-tended native plants, an adobe wall outside the bedrooms enclosing one courtyard ("Keeps the snakes and scorpions out," he said), another wall encircling the raised pool deck, and a patch of lush grass and an outdoor kitchen ("I love the desert," he'd said, "but I need to rub my toes in grass once in a while"), while leisurely strolling with his left hand in the pocket of his pants and an indulgent smile on his face…it all put me at ease. His tranquil mood seemed infectious and the temperament I'd been in since arriving in Phoenix melted away, as though Sam was the sun above us and I was a bar of chocolate on the asphalt of his street.

"There are more than a dozen species of cacti here," Sam said. We had settled into chairs in his living room. Outside a set of folding doors, the disturbances on the pool rippled the morning sun as an automated cleaner with a long white hose crawled along its bottom. "And I'm trying my hand at cultivating some olive trees in the western courtyard. I'm not sure they're going to survive, though."

"It's a beautiful home, Sam."

"It suits us."

"Where's Maddie?" I asked. Sam's wife, also a professor emeritus at Northwestern, had taught in the theater department.

"Yoga class. She'll be back in time for lunch…you're staying, by the way. She insisted your attendance was not optional."

"Of course." In matters of business, Sam could be swift and direct. But in social situations, he preferred a meandering course, like a sluggish river tracing its own way through a landscape. My usual urgency of time was inappropriate with him. The tempo here was his.

"Yoga…admirable. What keeps you busy?" I asked.

Sam waved a hand, not dismissively, but as though to encompass a multitude of interests. "So much," he said. "I read…I've focused on biographies lately. Maddie suspects I'm comparing my life to those of the people I read about. She believes I can't bear not to measure up against them." He chuckled. "She always had a solid grasp on the extent of my ego."

"She must have big hands."

Sam laughed. "Strong, too." He paused. "I write a bit. I'm working on a text about legal ethics, but I'm not certain my heart is in it. It was a publisher's idea."

"That's a compliment, though."

"Aach. Lawyers are more contemptuous of the law than anyone else. Byproduct of familiarity, you know. They dodge and dance with the law because for the most part they write the law."

I couldn't disagree…especially considering Carl's and my activities of the past few days.

"Preaching to them about ethics is probably a waste of time. The few who need it will either ignore it or rationalize their behavior. The others will pat themselves on the back."

"Write for yourself. Not for them."

"You sound like that woman who has a firm grip on my ego," he said.

"Great minds?"

"If that floats your boat!" He rose and walked toward the kitchen. "Iced tea?"

"Yes, thanks."

I had deliberated last night and on the short drive to visit Sam this morning about how much I would tell him of my situation… the cancer, the murder. Telling him of the cancer seemed fine…I'd convinced myself Sam would want to know. But revealing to him the murder of Todd Sachshausen, knowing how it would alter his opinion of me, complicated the role I'd cast for Sam Wortham: confessor. Any hope of absolution from him was preposterous. Sam was my friend, my mentor, the father figure in my professional life… but he was an archetype of ethics and could never condone what I had done. I didn't want to devalue myself in his eyes. I didn't want to disappoint this man for whom I held such regard, and who I hoped respected me in return. When I contrast these feelings with the love I feel for Carl…my accomplice…the difference, I mused, is like that between fathers and sons, and between brothers. We never stop seeking approval from our parents, real or figurative, but siblings, whether actual or symbolic, are co-conspirators for life.

I contemplated my dilemma…honesty or selfishness? Complicating my decision: would Sam feel obligated to notify the police? It would be in his power to end my journey in a way that would destroy Tallie. Why was the urge within me to tell him what I'd done so strong? Did I still feel a need to justify my actions? Is this what Carl had tried to spare me? I considered a scenario in which I confessed to Sam and he in turn pardoned me by relating an episode from his past of questionable ethical behavior…a tit for tat on the scales of wrongdoing. Perhaps it was naïve to assume that Sam's closet lacked any skeletons, that he had never made a regretful judgment. Perhaps it was foolish of me to assume that even if in Sam's past there lurked a similar transgression, that he would choose to admit it as a gesture to assuage my guilt.

Sam returned with a tray…two glasses of iced tea and some crackers.

"I'm not sure what Maddie has planned for lunch," he said. "I imagine she'll pick something up on the way home from yoga."

"Yoga. I forgot to say earlier how impressive that is."

"She likes it. Keeps her limber…calms her. And the friends keep her young."

"You seem fit, too, Sam."

"I do a lot of hiking…and I still enjoy orienteering."

"I remember," I said. Sam and Maddie had invited Tallie and me to join them one spring Saturday morning for orienteering in Waterfall Glen in Darien, southwest of Chicago. Tallie had no conception of what orienteering involved, but I harkened back to map-reading in the Marines. Sam relished it…both the exercise and the problem-solving aspects of the activity. He explained to Tallie that several courses were set out in the forest preserve, some quite simple for beginners, and others more difficult for experts. Beginner courses followed trails and paths which led to the authenticating stations…usually nine to ten of them…where you punched a card to verify you'd located the correct spot on the course map. More advanced courses crisscrossed the landscape, ignoring those same trails and paths, instead using compass headings and remote landmarks as guides; the authenticating stations often rested in shallow depressions, halfway up the side of a ridge, or at the end of a rootstock. Serious orienteers sought not merely completion of the course, but documented their time in competition with others. Sam was a competitor. He wore skintight Lycra pants and shirts, shoes designed for running in the diverse terrain, and was masterful with a compass. At the registration table that Saturday, he elected for the expert course; Maddie took Tallie and me on the beginner's track. Tallie thought the maps and the authenticating stations spoiled an otherwise good walk. "It's like golf in the woods," she'd joked.

"At least you're not carrying clubs," Maddie had said.

At lunch later that day, Sam elaborated on his love for the sport. Orienteering provided him with an engaging correlation: veering from established trails rewarded him in both his life and in the practice of law. Problem solving by plotting your own path suited his nature. Of course, he had counseled, the risk of cutting corners always presented itself, but if you skipped an authentication station, you forfeited your victory. Rules, he had said, also intrigued him. "You chart the quickest and most efficient route through a regulated puzzle…it requires skills of navigation, patience, and vision. It makes me a better advocate, a better teacher, and a better person."

"Of course, the desert isn't like a forest preserve," Sam said. "And I'm not so fixated on my course times any more. I enjoy the exercise and the scenery."

"Well, you look fit," I said.

"I feel fit…as fit as an eighty-four-year-old man has a right to feel I suppose. And you? How are you and how is your wife?"

"Tallie's fine. She sends her love. Me? I recently received some bad news."

I told Sam about my cancer diagnosis, about the purpose of my trip, about my journal. He nodded his head deliberately as I spoke and I recalled that same gesture from years ago in his class. He'd nod then as well while a student expounded upon the particulars of a case, signaling a misleading sense of agreement with the speaker, so that when Sam then dispassionately critiqued the summation and conclusions, he often stunned the student with an opinion contrary to his or her own. The lesson learned included not only how to assess the facts of a case and extract accurate conclusions, but to recognize the danger of assumptions.

"So you're dying," Sam said. "That's unfortunate, my friend."

I'm not sure why, but Sam's choice of words gladdened me. I was so grateful he had not said he was sorry.

"I think of death at least once a day, every day," he said. "One of the perks of reaching my age."

"I understand…if a bit prematurely."

"Has it altered how you think and what you think about?"

"It has, but not as much as I had expected. I'm sure the effects will be more pronounced later." I told Sam the absence of physical symptoms diminished the influence of the disease. "Knowledge and perception are in conflict," I said. "There ought to be pain… physical pain."

Sam nodded in his familiar, deliberate manner.

"Instead, there's anxiety and I even suffered a panic attack a few days ago. At the Grand Canyon."

Sam closed his eyes and smiled. "Did your physician prescribe anything?"

I nodded.

"Working?"

"For the most part. When I described the attack to her, she said I could double the dosage if I wanted."

"Good." Sam massaged his right knee. "Tell me about the people you've visited."

I told Sam about my visits with Ellen, Del, Carl, Laura…skirting the subject of Todd Sachshausen…and also about then Micah, the last person on my list; I spoke of how each of them had engaged me during my life, their influential roles and the magnitude of their friendship and love. He listened patiently, occasionally scratching his cheek, or clearing his throat.

"You've placed me in gracious company," he said finally.

"Deservedly so, Sam."

"Have you come seeking advice again? If you have, then I can offer some."

"This might be the first time I don't need advice, but I'll never turn my back on it." Sitting with Sam relaxed me; his home and his presence inspired comfort.

"I saw *The Wizard of Oz* in a theater in downtown Chicago when it was first released. It amazed me of course…the fantasy, the Technicolor. I must have watched it dozens of times since, with my children, even alone. Did you know it was a box office flop at the time?"

I shook my head.

"Irrelevant, but interesting. My point is this: that film has pampered generations of movie-watchers. They all envision an omnipotent wizard behind the curtain, yanking levers, pushing buttons, manipulating fire and fury. If you draw back the curtain, however, there's no wizard…there's only a mirror.

"Intellectually, we accept that wizards don't exist, yet subliminally we desire…we yearn…to surrender control, to relinquish our accountability. It's not my fault! Don't blame me!" Sam's voice had grown shrill but his face belied any stridency. In contrast to his tone, he smiled…his lips compressed together in a threadlike line, his eyes alertly mirthful, folds in the skin at the corners of those gray eyes deepening as he looked at me, transporting me back to a classroom for a flickering moment.

"So…if you intended this visit as a quest for guidance, as a crusade for advice about what I'd do…then here it is: die."

I was stunned and the expression on my face must have betrayed me. Sam guffawed, patting his hands on his pants legs. "So, what you need to do is die," he continued. "Let your memories die; let your attitudes die; let time die. Kill it all…kill anything that inhibits making the last months of your life fulfilling." He paused. "The concept of your trip fascinates me, but I'm sure Tallie was less than pleased."

"Uh huh. Not pleased at all, Sam. She didn't want me to go, but eventually she relented. Then she argued for coming with me, but I was adamant about doing it alone. Finally she gave up."

"I can imagine that woman relenting, but never giving up," Sam said. "More likely she's just acceding to what you wanted, regardless of how wrong-headed she finds it."

Tallie cried more at the pronouncement of my plans for this trip than she did when we received my diagnosis, I recalled. So again, I considered how I'd robbed her. Time is our currency…the coin of our withering realm…and I've stolen a lump of it. Perhaps in her view, I've squandered it as well. Did my determination to embark on this farewell tour blind me to how passionately she detested my leaving her? Could I have been so impervious to her feelings that in my selfishness I trampled on what Tallie needs so that I could pursue what I want? Of all the emotions Tallie and I have shared, we've never been lonely together. But I left her alone in Chicago probably suffering more loneliness than she's ever experienced in her life.

"Don't beat yourself up," Sam whispered. "She may deem it wrong-headed, but that doesn't mean it is. You have your reasons and this is your life. I think taking some time to reflect, to visit old friends and be assured that you won't be forgotten, is a fine endeavor. Not many people get that opportunity."

"Carl, the fellow I visited in Oregon, said the diagnosis and the brief time it afforded me were a gift."

"I agree with him," Sam said. "We all want to live long, full lives. But there's a toll in outliving your friends." Sam fell silent for a moment. "That sounds childishly self-indulgent. Strike that. Just remember this: I admire what you're doing. I'm also flattered to be on your list."

"You're welcome, Sam."

I snapped a few photographs of Sam and Maddie on their pool deck, lounging on side-by-side chaises in the shade of a velvet mesquite tree. The Arizona sky shone brilliant blue, cloudless. If a perfect day had to be catalogued, it included today. They held hands across the gap between the chairs and grinned as broadly as I've ever seen them smile. Maddie had stopped at a local deli and brought home pasta salad and antipasti. We ate at a farmer's table Maddie said had been constructed from reclaimed boards from an English barn. I feel like describing her as bird-like, not because of her size; she's not a slight woman…taller than average, lean but not thin, starkly white hair cut short (much like Ellen's in Minneapolis). Her luminous blue eyes shone in her tanned face, constantly darting from one point to another. She fluttered about energetically…that's what made her seem bird-like… eternally in motion, not randomly, but with intent. Maddie had always seemed like a woman with an endless "to-do" list, self-deprecatingly aware of the impossibility of ever crossing off all her tasks as having been completed. She joked that three lifetimes would never be sufficient to accomplish all her goals.

She cast an aura of youthfulness. And it affected Sam. I watched him smile as Maddie moved around the kitchen, opening cabinets, drawers and the refrigerator while maintaining an attentive conversation with the two of us, never once losing the drift of what was being said or the goal of what she was doing. Sam unmistakably loved his wife…it materialized in the expressions on his face during lunch, where Maddie interrogated me about Tallie, about new plays in Chicago we might have seen, and then declared her joy at seeing me again. Like Sam, her reaction to the news of my diagnosis lacked any reference to the word sorry. "That just sucks," she said, and then listened to me recount some of the highlights of the farewell tour. She too wondered why Tallie had not accompanied me, and "tsked" me, shaking her head at the conclusion of my explanation. "You owe that woman. You know that don't you?"

I assured Maddie I more than knew what I owed Tallie…that word "knowing" fell horribly short of expressing the faithfulness she'd shown in me and of estimating the indebtedness I had incurred.

After lunch as I prepared to leave, Maddie took my face in her hands and quietly said "I will miss you." The she hugged me and wandered to the back of the house while Sam walked me out to my car.

"Forget what I said about killing memory," he said. "You really can't. But you understand what I was trying to say."

"I do, Sam."

"When you initially called me, my first thought was that you were driving around the country indulging a belated mid-life crisis," he said. "Now I understand it's neither mid-life, nor a crisis." We both chuckled.

"I will not forget you," he said, embracing me, patting my back.

"Nor I you," I replied.

I drove as far as Willcox in southeastern Arizona this afternoon…interstate all the way…and checked into a Holiday Inn Express. I ate dinner and I called Tallie. The drive's playlist began with "Better Days" by Graham Nash, buttressing what I'd fleetingly experienced the other day after talking with Carl: the trip's emphasis has shifted. My mindfulness now focuses on returning home to Tallie. I was worried this pivot in my viewpoint would affect the visits with Sam and Micah. Would an obvious impatience bleed into our meetings? Would those two receive less honesty and candor from me than Ellen, Del, Carl and Laura had? I wondered again: had I conceived of this trip as a pursuit of assurance that people would miss me? That my life had made an impression? Was I seeking validation? Did I *need* validation? Each friend I'd visited fulfilled those longings, but I'd persuaded myself when I undertook the trek that self-indulgence wasn't my goal. Am I so concerned with being honest with others that I've been dishonest with myself? I wouldn't put it past me…I doubt Tallie would either.

When we spoke this evening, we discussed Alison. Tallie drove directly to the facility from her office after work. Northbound traffic on Lake Short Drive was heavy, she told me, at one point nearly halted between Navy Pier and the sharp curve near the Drake Hotel. The combination of fatigue, impatience and the congestion had sullied her mood. By the time she arrived and located Alison in her room, Tallie's tolerance for people had wilted…she was irritable and short-tempered and intended a short visit with Alison, long enough just to check on her condition. Alison, however, beguiled Tallie with an upbeat attitude, smiling when she spied my wife, hurrying toward her and linking her unbroken arm in Tallie's. Alison led her along the corridors, introducing her to staff and other residents. Tallie told me it was the most lucid she'd seen Alison in months. The woman seemed to be flourishing in her new environment, and Tallie, whether out of shame or the cheerful influence of Alison's temperament, sensed the day's tensions slough away, as though she'd submerged herself in a whirlpool and allowed the swirling, heated water to loosen every muscle in her body.

"While I was stuck in traffic, I realized this is the longest we've been apart since we were married" she told me.

"Oh." I hadn't realized.

"It crossed my mind that maybe that's what you had intended all along. Helping me acclimate to life without you. I was in a funk; it was easy to be pissy."

"Sorry, honey." I told her Sam and Maddie sent their best wishes.

"I regret I couldn't see them," she said, and I wondered if I detected sullenness in her voice or had imagined it. "Did they say if they'd come up for the funeral?" I hadn't imagined it, I suppose. "It was heartwarming to see Alison so animated today, but sometimes I think it would be comforting not to remember everything all the time. Not so much bliss from ignorance, but bliss from unawareness. Every so often, I'd enjoy being oblivious."

"I've been thinking, Tallie, that taking this trip wasn't fair to you."

"Would you have stayed here if I'd insisted?"

"I don't know. When I planned it, I felt it was something I needed to do. But now? Now I just want to come home as quickly as possible."

"When I left Alison, I was in a really good mood. But on the drive home all I could concentrate on was the fact that you wouldn't be here when I opened the door, and that at least for now, that's a choice you made. It made me angry…really angry."

I breathed into the phone, understanding there was nothing to say; this was an instance when listening was the correct option.

"I don't enjoy being angry," she said. "Being angry only makes me more angry!"

I stifled a laugh.

"I hate being illogical."

"I know, Tallie."

"And I hate that you're not here."

"I know that, too."

"Every night I come home to this empty place, I can't help it, but I start…"

"Thinking of regrets?" I interrupted.

"Don't finish my sentences! You know I can't stand it when you do that!"

"Sorry. Go on."

Tallie paused for a moment, for emphasis, I assumed…she wanted her admonition to settle over me.

"Regrets, yes. But also unfairness, inequity, injustice and fury." She uttered those words in rapid succession, like accusations.

"That's quite a list," I whispered, hoping she would identify contriteness in my tone.

"And that's just off the top of my head. I don't think I'm ready to start thinking about grief, or sorrow, or loneliness."

Again, silence seemed the prudent option. Any words said to Tallie should be said while I held her, or lay beside her. I was sitting in the chair by the wall-mounted desk in my room and my OCD kicked in…furiously I step-stoned through the objects on the opposite wall: bedside table to bed cover, to headboard, to wallpaper, to generic, framed landscape. Then dead-ended…uncannily emblematic.

"There's no good way to end this conversation," Tallie said, and I could visualize her, the receiver to her left ear, her right hand supporting her head as she hunched over the kitchen island with her elbows propped on the surface.

"A week. That's all that's left, honey."

"Don't talk to me about what's left. Don't you dare say that! There will never be enough left. Not enough days. Not enough goddamned minutes. Not enough memories." Tallie was crying now. "Oh, Jesus! I don't want to be alone…I don't want you to die."

What could I say? Even shortening the trip would be a useless gesture. If I abandoned the Saab and flew home as soon as possible, I could never change the inevitability of my dying and Tallie being alone. I felt numb. I closed my eyes with the phone at my ear and just felt nothing. Not nothingness. Just nothing.

Tallie continued crying…the only sound between us. I imagined her head bowed, tears sliding down her face, the bump in her nose…that avenged imperfection…diverting the path ever so slightly.

"I think I'm going to hate you for a while…for dying," she said.

"I hate myself for dying now."

"You should, you bastard," Tallie said, a tender laugh riding her words.

"I'm not sure the trip has helped me accept it all any better," I admitted. "I'm not sure I expected it to."

"What did you expect, then?"

"Maybe some insight? My conversation with Sam made me wonder if I simply wanted to hear people say they'd miss me."

"You silly old fool," she said.

"Silly old fool is either the most respectable kind or the most pathetic kind." I paused. "Lately I've been assuming the pathetic kind."

"Probably right."

"I'm so sorry, Tallie, for everything…not just for leaving you alone while I'm on this trip. But for how I'm going to need you, to be so dependent on you. For the anguish and the misery, for that being the last memory you may have of me."

Tallie told me she didn't want to talk about what Janine said we could expect. "Not now. I don't want to talk about any of that until you're home."

I conceded and noted how this evening's conversation, in comparison to all the others since I'd left Chicago, had transformed the focus of the trip. I'm counting down the remaining days, not counting forward to the next destination.

Day Twenty-Three

I forgot to mention yesterday that as I drove away from Phoenix, before I plugged in my iPod and started the playlist, I heard a news broadcast on the car radio…a local realtor had been found dead in a house for sale in southwest Phoenix. I wouldn't describe my reaction as pleasure…more like contentment.

The playlist this morning: "Coming Home" by John Legend. Not one I had planned…a spontaneous choice I hoped would resolve the residual unevenness after last night's conversation with Tallie. Uneven, because after I slid into bed and launched into another examination of whether I've been dismissing everyone's point of view but my own, that reproach triggered a backlash, so to speak. If I've been behaving selfishly, so what? Show me someone more entitled to bathe in self-absorption than a dying man! It left me feeling slightly irritated with Tallie…but that passed quickly. This isn't how I ever imagined I would die; cancer would never have been a consideration. Old age, heart attack, perhaps in an accident. But I'd kept all impressions of illness at bay. Not unusual, I suppose.

Emails from Ellen and Del slept in my inbox during the time I was in Phoenix. I didn't feel in the mood to answer them while I was stalking Sachshausen, but I will respond tonight. I'm beginning to understand that I'd assumed my visits with them would invoke a finality, that there would be no more communication between us, no more contact. The ending I had envisioned is more tidy than reality...but then everything is.

Driving through El Paso this morning, I thought of Alison... imprisoned in her dementia. From there I step-stoned back to the circumstances in which I had ever imagined dying and judged that feebleness, if it included cheerful unawareness, might not be such a horrible fate. A blissful state of mind, accompanied only by memories. Cinematic. Nothing real. By that I mean such a notion would only occur in a film or in imagination...not in life.

I drove more than eight hours today...a work day in the Saab... and stopped only for food and fuel. I'm worn-out, spent, but that's all right...it's a function of the new emphasis on going home. Pecos County, Texas...Fort Stockton...Hampton Inn immediately off I-10. The airport must be nearby...one or two planes landed...but since then the only noises I've heard are trucks humming by on the interstate. Dinner nearby at a place called Stockton's Entertainment...beer and hot wings, which I ate while I viewed a group of teenagers bowling.

My conversation with Tallie tonight was abbreviated, but not contentious. Each of us seemed careful not to stray into areas that might still be tender from last night's exchange. During all our time together, we've never allowed a quarrel to fester. We've been direct, not hurtfully assertive, but open. I'm not saying we haven't passionately argued or provoked one another to anger, but we've never escalated it to wordless fury. We're not a perfect couple, but we understand that we're as close to perfection for one another as we'll ever find. And that's worth preserving.

So we spoke carefully, each of us silently mindful of not reenacting last night's conversation.

Micah Streets. My final stop-off.

We met Micah twenty years ago at the Old Town School of Folk Music during a benefactor's reception prior to a concert by Taj Mahal. Tallie had mistaken him for a member of Mahal's trio; Micah was flattered by the error and explained that he offered instruction in bass guitar at the school. His father, an auto worker from Michigan, had met Micah's mother, a nurse originally from Jamaica, at a Motown concert…talk about destiny…in Detroit in 1965. They married in 1967…an interracial marriage and a gutsy undertaking. According to Micah, both families disowned the couple for many years, despite the birth of their grandchild, Micah, in 1973. Micah's appearance made a striking impression: short and sinewy; caramel skinned; curly, sandy hair; copper eyes as dazzling as newly-minted pennies; and a narrow, oval face dominated by an expansive smile packed with white, even teeth. When he smiled, the edges of his mouth arched up rapidly two or three times. It seemed more like a nervous twitch than a planned expression. The incongruity of seeing him strap on an electric bass…it dwarfed him…or watching him stand beside an up-right bass bordered on the comical. Until you heard him play. Masterful…and that was when we first met him. His abilities have multiplied since then.

Micah shared a one-bedroom apartment in Wicker Park with another instructor from the school when we first met him, and his landlord (who lived on the ground floor of the three-flat) persistently grumbled about the noise…aka music…Micah made, regularly threatening him with eviction. We had a vacancy in our building. Kismet. He moved in a week later, across and down the hall from Alison, who developed an immediate, maternal crush on him. I remember one night years after Micah had moved in, I had arrived home from the office and encountered Alison in the garage; she'd returned from grocery shopping at Jewel, and I helped her carry the bags to her apartment. As we passed Micah's door, I heard an acoustic guitar being strummed and a voice singing lyrics to an unfamiliar song in a throaty tone. I paused a moment and then caught up with Alison.

"Micah practicing with a friend?" I asked.

"No," she said matter-of-factly. "That's him."

I hadn't realized he played acoustic guitar as well as bass. And I mean as skillfully as he played bass, not merely in addition to the instrument. The most thrilling evening of watching Micah was a Wednesday open mic night at a bar way out in LaGrange. He played a three-song set of his own tunes…ballads, love songs…that evoked common themes of loss, heartbreak, hope and expectations. The audience stood at the conclusion of his set and the bar owner asked Micah for one more song. Micah twitched his toothy smile for them and then strummed some introductory chords, all minors and major sevenths, whispering into the microphone that this new song was dedicated to his landlords. Tallie and I quickly looked at each other with a questioning glance. "It's called, 'Loving You'," Micah continued, and then sang a song he later confessed he'd written, inspired by watching Tallie and me, in a voice intriguing for its raw emotion and lack of self-consciousness. Tallie grew misty-eyed, gripping my hand throughout the performance. Later, when Micah joined the three of us at our table (Alison always accompanied us whenever we went to see Micah perform), the two women fawned over him mercilessly and I clapped him on the back, uncharacteristically wordless about my feelings for him and the song. At Christmas that year, Micah presented us with a framed copy of the autographed lyrics he had hand-written on simple, lined notebook paper. It still hangs in our bedroom. Here they are:

Loving You
By Micah Streets

It's not the time to think about
What I would have lived without loving you
When I'm alone I contemplate
All the ways I celebrate loving you

My days are rich because you're mine
Giving me a love I never thought I'd find
Your eyes peer deep inside of me
But I cannot imagine what it is you see, when you look at me

I've spent my life amazed and thrilled
Thankful every day was filled loving you
I see within your quiet smile
The reason I've been happy while loving you

The song, Micah said, was his way of thanking Tallie and me for befriending him. I always thought he was more grateful to us for providing him with a surrogate mother in the person of Alison, than for anything we ever did for him. For several summers, when we'd spontaneously gather on the rooftop on a Friday night, winding down at the end of a demanding week, when Micah didn't have a gig he would uncase his Martin D-28 and entertain, sometimes just strumming, other times picking rhythms, and when in the mood, singing songs he had written, but always concluding with sing-alongs where everyone joined in. He supplied the soundtrack for many of those gatherings, but the extent of his friendship was more far-reaching. Micah was an excellent teacher, both at the Old Town School, and during our informal sit-downs. Mind you I never picked up an instrument…my education entailed listening to Micah articulate his creative process, detail his aspirations for mastering not only his instruments, but his approach to music and what he could achieve through it. He likened playing music to achieving a meditative or out-of-body state. "I'm not talking astral projection here," he'd said. "But I want to know what it feels like to synchronize my internal rhythm with the rhythm of my music. That would be totally cool."

Micah was never what anyone would describe as a "struggling musician;" he regularly played in a jazz trio as well as a pop band. He's one of the most musically innovative and versatile, not to mention, good-natured people I've ever met, but in his quest for distinction, he routinely wrestled with his aspirations. Once during a break in a set when he was playing with the jazz trio in a bar on Rush Street, Micah told me he struggled at times with sadness in his pursuit of excellence. The chase, he'd said, frustrated him constantly and although he accepted the wisdom of the value of the journey versus the destination, he wished the self-actualization could be permanent. I asked him if the occasional moments of serenity were not more rewarding for their infrequency. He admitted I had a point and we wondered how long it would take for anyone to tire of a diet of relentless delight. Performance, he said that night, loomed as large in the pursuit of an elevated sense of peacefulness as the creation of the music itself. For him to grasp a fragment of spirituality, Micah needed an engaged audience to elevate the intensity of his performance in a quest for absolute joy. Audience feedback helped transport him nearer to the achievement of unequalled contentment.

Our discussion made such an impression that for weeks I attended every one of Micah's performances, to lessen the possibility of missing one of those moments of nirvana. During that period he vacillated in how he regarded my continual presence…at times as a compliment to his musicianship and at other times as an impediment to his ascent to the summit of contentment. I redeemed myself somewhat when I secured the services of an old law school friend, an intellectual property attorney, who helped Micah protect the copyrights of his songs and compositions.

Four years ago Micah told us he was moving to Austin. At a dinner in our loft for him and his girlfriend Ciara, and of course Alison, he recalled how he had moved to Chicago years before for the musical opportunities. Austin, he said, seemed the logical move now. Earlier in the year he had accompanied a friend to the city to help him record an album, playing bass on the tracks. Impressed with Micah's talent and versatility, the recording producer tempted him with assurances of lucrative session work. The combination of live performance opportunities and the milder climate convinced him to make the move. He'd be leaving in a month.

Alison took it hardest of all. Tallie insists she never got over it and marks her decline from that time.

According to his email this morning, Micah and Ciara live on Landon Lane north of the University of Texas campus, near enough to the stadium, he says, that when the crowd cheers, he can hear it on his back deck. He converted the loft above his garage into a recording and rehearsal space; he also mounted solar panels on the roof of the garage and the house…now at off-peak hours he sells electricity back to the grid. He's anxious to see me and wondered if I wanted to sit in the control booth the day after tomorrow during a recording session at a place called the Flying Carpet Recording Studio. I wrote back that it sounded like fun.

Day Twenty-Four

Shivering and sweating so exceedingly that I'd soaked the bed sheets, I woke in the middle of the night, sped to the bathroom and vomited into the toilet with such violence that I alarmed myself. My throat burned, my eyes watered, and my panic gushed. Competing thoughts wrestled in my consciousness: was the vomiting the result of bad food or was it a symptom of the disease? The odor in the bathroom repulsed me and I flushed the toilet, squatting on the cold tile floor with my back against the edge of the tub. More abdominal cramping forced me to lower my head again into the bowl and wretch. My stomach throbbed and my vision blurred as I strove to convince myself that the wings I'd eaten for dinner had been a horrible choice. I endured a few more spasms, producing nothing more than bitter strands of saliva, and then lay on the bathroom floor, waiting for my breathing to calm from stuttered gulping for air to a deeper, more even cadence. The panic I'd felt when I had lurched for the bathroom from my bed had ebbed, replaced by an excruciating pulsing in my temples. Sitting up against the tub wall, I extended my legs before me and rubbed a hand slowly across my belly, inhaling a deep breath and expelling it slowly. Those abdominal muscles ached. Despite myself, I stared at the opposite wall and began step-stoning through the tiled arrangement. Disgusted, I shut my eyes and hung my head until my chin rested on my chest. I pictured myself from above, a sixty-four-year old man, sprawled naked and shivering on the tiled floor of a motel room in Fort Stockton, Texas, furious about the domination of OCD on his consciousness, gut thudding, throat burning and mouth glazed with a corrosive tang. A pitiful, weak, dying man.

I thought: is this the blueprint for how it will happen? As my time winds down, will bitterness thrive like mint in a garden, overcrowding and smothering all other emotions? One comment by a cancer survivor I'd read came to mind: receiving a cancer diagnosis means your life will never again be the same. That woman survived, for years as I recall, and although I won't, I can't deny the truth of her statement. Cancer has changed my life; this journey has changed my life, but not always as I had anticipated. I expected self-discovery. I expected reunions charged with emotional flashes. I expected tears and laughter and anger. And I expected to kill a man and rationalize it as justice. What I did not expect, and I alluded to this earlier, was that each visit would not represent a conclusion, an ending. Perception is a remarkably biased and unreliable amalgam of the senses. Even to a man trained to remain objective and consider all sides of an argument or a conflict. With my time abbreviated, the polite conventions which would have held sway in my conversations with my friends vanished. We got to the point quickly, offering and receiving candor in record time. I expected finality but have been startled and rewarded with continuity. I had in mind saying "goodbye" and my friends are saying "see you later." I suppose if they had said anything else they would not be the people I love…and I do love them.

Intriguing what will occur to you when you collapse on the floor of a commonplace bathroom after discharging your guts into a toilet bowl.

I brushed my teeth and rinsed my mouth before returning to bed. The sweat had dried on my skin but the sheets clung to me, damp and clammy, so I scooted to the far edge of the bed and curled into a fetal position with the bedspread pulled to my chin. I slept until after eleven this morning, checking out close to noon, stopping at a grocery store for some Gatorade and a carton of saltines, and ruining my plan to drive straight through to Austin. I rejected any preset playlists and listened for a while to the Brad Mehldau trio from the "Live in Marciac" album. I needed something calming this morning.

I only drove for about three hours today, stopping for the night in Junction, Texas. I'm trying not to read too much into the town's name…another crossroads for me? Not everything you encounter necessitates a choice, or does it? I texted Micah to let him know the delay in my schedule. He replied quickly that one day wouldn't make a difference, he would still be in the studio and the invitation stood. I checked into the Rodeway Inn, bought some chicken noodle soup at the Super S Foods deli, and retreated to my room for the evening.

Even considering the panic attack at the Grand Canyon, this is the lowest I've felt on this trip. When I called Tallie this evening, I neglected to mention the nausea. There's nothing to be gained by worrying her excessively. She visited Alison and said the "sundowning" effect…where people with dementia fare badly later in the day…seemed pronounced today, an absolute contrast to the other day. Alison did not respond to Tallie when she spoke to her, avoided looking at her and waved her casted arm in front of her face as though to fend her off. Tallie confessed that those moments hurt the most. The nurse tried to cheer her but also admitted that there is little chance Alison's episodes will improve. It's the curse of the condition.

When I told Tallie I would be witnessing a recording session tomorrow, she expressed jealousy and asked me to tell Micah and Ciara hello for her.

"I want to go to Montreal after you come home," she then said.

As soon as she mentioned the city's name, it made sense…visiting Montreal has been a fascination of Tallie's for years. She deserves to have it indulged. I had proposed some years ago spending Christmas in Montreal, but Tallie said no…she immerses herself in the holiday, over-decorating every window of the loft with garland and strings of lights, and insisting on an enormous tree ablaze with white lights and dozens of handmade ornaments she has collected over the years on our travels. Alison always joined us for Christmas dinner, accompanied each year by a collection of holiday orphans: friends, colleagues and co-workers Tallie collected from work who for various reasons, often financial, could not find their way home for the holiday. She'd buy presents for each of them and snuggle the gift-wrapped boxes under our tree, reveling in their surprise as they opened them to find minor extravagances that they would never have bought for themselves. One year Micah and Ciara joined us when flights from O'Hare were canceled because of a blizzard. Tallie turned off all the lights except for the Christmas illuminations; we ate and drank by candlelight at our dining table while squall-like conditions raged outside. The gathering seemed magical. Micah sang several original songs and Ciara softly harmonized on one or two of them in a warmhearted voice. Later in bed, as Tallie clung to me beneath the comforter and we watched the city lights blinking through the storm, she whispered to me that she felt as though for a brief time that evening we had molded a family from those people most dear to us. The notion delighted me…to imagine Micah and Ciara as our children and Alison as their doting aunt.

So Montreal.

"That sounds wonderful," I said.

"Why don't we leave the week after you return?"

"Okay."

"I'll book it!" Tallie giggled and for a moment I pictured her eyes, their blue-gray steeliness penetrating me with vitality and warmth.

Soon after that, Tallie cut the call short and I chuckled at the idea that having wrenched an agreement from me for the Montreal trip, she sought to forestall any opportunity for me to change my mind. With time withering, I wonder what other passions of hers, and mine, I should indulge. Travel, obviously, but the where of us is not as crucial as the who of us…the mainstay is being together… whether in Montreal or in the West Loop. In the middle of my thoughts I realized talking with Tallie, however briefly, had brightened my mood. I love her thoughtfulness and her intellect and her passion…and her knack, even unknowingly, to pluck me from downheartedness.

While I spoke with Tallie, I step-stoned again, parading through the checkered sections of the patterned drapes, annoyed by the compulsion, picturing myself months from now, step-stoning through memories. Plotting out a course of passageways, not unlike the corridors of rooms in the house that occupies my dreams, and skipping ceaselessly from childhood to the present. Orienteering through my life, Sam would say. He'd be correct…right down to the target of completing that course in the fastest time.

Which memories, I wonder, will define the course? Perhaps another list to compile, like things I'll miss when I'm gone? I could anchor them by locations. St. Louis: my first Cardinals game at the old Busch Stadium with my father. He bought me a cap that swallowed my head…I wonder if that's why I bought the Martin Hotel cap. Watching the construction of the Gateway Arch as a senior in high school…surprisingly I've never ridden the tram to the top. Vietnam: far too many individual faces and days to remember… except for Carl. Iowa City and Evanston: using learning to wilt those faces and days from Vietnam. Chicago: meeting Tallie. Tallie: in her eyes, in her heart and between her legs…there's a concise outline of what I hope I'll dwell upon when trekking through memories becomes my final option. I hope I have the awareness to flesh out those recollections, to adorn them with specifics, and I hope that the memories of Tallie outnumber all the others, dwarfing them with the minutiae I recall…every feature, every aspect, and every facet of our life together.

Tallie…never forget your memories either.

I need to be remembered…that's perhaps the most unforeseen insight I've gleaned on this trip. I'm a selfish man…at least partially… and each of the people I've visited has in varying fashion catered to that selfishness, reflexively, without being asked. Or maybe I'm blind to the reality that they recognized my visit for what it was…an appeal not to be forgotten…but requested without desperation, I hope.

I'm feeling peaceful, both physically and emotionally. I'll get an early start tomorrow and meet Micah at the studio. It's only a few blocks from the Hilton Garden Inn where I'll be staying. Micah didn't say if he would be playing with his blues band or simply sitting in as a session bassist…it doesn't matter, it'll be uplifting to see him again.

Day Twenty-Six

I haven't skipped a day...well, technically I have, but only because it's past two o'clock in the morning and I only just arrived back at my hotel after enjoying a day with Micah and Ciara.

Let's dispense with the customary housekeeping...I left Junction at eight this morning and checked into the Hilton before noon, launching my musical day with "Villanova Junction Blues" by Arlen Roth, his contribution to a tribute album to Jimi Hendrix. Some truly appetizing guitar work.

I'll never forget the recording studio experience and the evening that followed....ha ha...for as long as I live! When I arrived at the address Micah had given me, I thought perhaps I'd written it down incorrectly...the one-story building looked decrepit and had no signage other than the door numbers. If a bystander had told me it was abandoned, I would've believed him...but when I knocked on the heavy wooden door, Micah answered. He'd shaved his head and grown a beard...a ring of coarse stubble the color of dried pine needles sheltered his face, the only gray visible in a patch on his chin.

"Look at you," I said, reaching out a hand but then pausing. "Go ahead," Micah said. "Everybody does."

I rubbed his glossy dome and immediately grinned. Then we embraced. Micah smelled like citrus and cinnamon…familiar and evocative. Greeting him reminded me of home. We stepped back and Micah beckoned me inside. He led me back to a lounge where he'd been eating lunch and introduced me to a woman named TJ. Micah warmly twitched his smile at me until TJ steered me to a control room and he retreated to an adjacent studio. I'd never before been in a recording studio…my first impression of the room was that I'd go insane if my OCD kicked in, trying to step-stone through the clutter of equipment and memorabilia. Head-high racks of electronic gear flanked the console, and the walls told the history of the studio: business cards, autographed photos of musicians, CDs of bands I assumed had recorded there, take-out menus, performance posters, a couple of cymbals…a flamboyant, uncurated museum. TJ scooted a chair up to the console beside hers and slipped on a pair of headphones, indicating a set I could wear. I looked into the studio and saw Micah perched on a wooden stool, cradling his Martin on his knee. An Oriental carpet covered the floor and two upholstered panels behind him angled to form a V, nestling Micah in the center. Cables, mic and guitar stands, amplifiers and speakers…all pushed back against the walls, upon which hung posters, flyers, and many years of more memorabilia. A pair of microphones fronted the guitar and another hung before Micah. Quickly I realized …Micah wasn't playing with the blues band or backing another artist: he was recording himself.

Micah strummed the guitar and the flawlessness of the sound relayed through my headphones startled me. When he spoke to TJ, his vocal tones seemed hyper-real.

"Wow," I whispered.

"Cool shit, huh?" TJ asked. I nodded.

The two experimented with numerous sound levels from the microphones until both men nodded, assured, and then TJ counted him in. Micah strummed the Martin and sang. I recognized the song as one he'd written in Chicago. We'd discussed his song-writing approach many times. He frequently invented characters for his songs, free-falling them into emotional predicaments and then depicting how they reacted. As Micah sang, TJ handed me a sheaf of papers… the song-list for today's recording session and printouts of the chords and lyrics for each song. I studied Micah, his face partially obscured by the vocal microphone. He leisurely closed and then reopened his eyes as he sang, rarely looking at where he placed his left hand on the fret board. I followed the lyrics on the sheet. Micah had written about a sad man, whose girlfriend had walked out on him.

A Change of Heart
By Micah Streets

The final candle flickers, dripping wax upon the table
An empty bottle lies on its side upon the floor
The windows are all shaded and the music's turned down low
There are footsteps in the hallway, but no knock upon the door

My eyes are heavy lidded and my back's against the wall
My throat is raw from pleading, and there's nothing more to say

I'm past the point of caring if I ever fall asleep
I can't believe I couldn't find the words to make you stay

And I'm silently praying that you have a change of heart
I'm wordlessly hoping that you have a change of heart

My mind is running overtime, the images are frightening
I'm dreading the dawning of another day alone
Trapped inside a prison of discarded hopes and dreams
Mutely staring across the room at a mocking telephone

I don't know how to tell you what you mean to me
And I don't know how you could leave me so easily

Sunlight frames the window shades as I blow out the candle
I'd cry again but what's the point, there's no one here to see
Everything I thought I knew is turned around, it's upside down
The life I hoped to live is now a loveless fantasy

And I'm silently praying that you have a change of heart
I'm wordlessly hoping that you have a change of heart

The yearning in Micah's voice spawned a brooding atmosphere and I also closed my eyes, shrouded in the richness of his music. Its authenticity remained, although the years had ripened his voice, refining the primitiveness; his singing imparted substance, experience, even wisdom. Midway through the second chorus, Micah stopped abruptly and apologized, complaining he'd been off key on a note and wanted to begin again. TJ nodded as though she'd heard the error, although I hadn't detected anything amiss, and they restarted the process. Studio work is meticulous...Micah played "A Change of Heart" four times before he and TJ were satisfied. I imagine most people would balk at the patience it takes to perfect a song in a studio, and I came to this conclusion just watching Micah perform by himself. Compounding the process with four, five or more band members...well, it requires a tolerance for repetition I don't possess. Even so, I was amazed at how quickly the time passed. Throughout the session, people wandered in and out of the control room, standing behind TJ or reclining on the striped sofa on the wall opposite the console, occasionally tapping TJ on her shoulder and leaning in to say something. None stayed long.

Micah had chosen to record songs of longing and abandonment...four of them by the time he and TJ concluded the session. Throughout the stuttering of the recording process, I empathized with the characters Micah rendered with his lyrics and melodies. Love defeated, dreams truncated, afflictions prevailing...but always, hopefulness enduring. Irony, of course, frolics here: neither Micah nor I can assert the melancholy of his narrators in our lives. Each of us has enjoyed astonishing rewards...we live with and love two beautiful women. What do we know of sorrow so crippling that it paralyzes? Ah, but I shouldn't pitch impulsively into the noose of discounting Micah's inventiveness...his facility to unearth and capture expressions of despair and mourning, conveying them through his lyrics and his music, has always astonished me and provoked both admiration and tinges of envy. He'd caution me not to unleash such a comparison; I should acknowledge our differences without fingering any inadequacy within myself. Sensible advice...even for a short-timer like myself. After five hours of listening to Micah's glum yet inspiring ballads, I felt shockingly upbeat. Micah's music had a cathartic effect on me...that and being near him. His calm acceptance of talent mesmerizes me...maybe it can inspire me in my final days.

After Micah, TJ and I listened to the "keeper" tracks, we emerged onto Trinity Street and the nearby rustling of traffic on East 7th Street. Micah, rather than appearing tired, seemed energized by his session.

"Ciara's waiting for us down the street. How's Tex-Mex for dinner?" he asked.

"Perfect." As we strolled the short distance to the Iron Cactus Mexican Grill and Margarita Bar, I told Micah how impressive the recording session had been. He clapped me on the back but just grinned and said nothing. As we approached Trinity and Sixth, we heard the hissing of tires on the bricks and cobblestones in the intersection and met Ciara outside the restaurant; she rushed into my arms and hugged me with more strength than I would have believed. Over her shoulder I spied a street sign designating a restricted zone for the loading and unloading of musicians. Very cool feature of the city.

Ciara, much like Tallie, remains strikingly attractive. She wears her hair long and straight, past her shoulders with a few streaks of gray mingling in the dark brown; she'd gathered and secured it with a plastic clip. She's slim like Micah but three inches taller; she wore cut-off jeans shorts and a black T-shirt advertising her jewelry business: Copper Connections. From her ears a pair of her creations dangled...hammered copper moons adorned with crimson beads and golden feathers. She leaned in to kiss Micah and the bracelet on her wrist, a band of burnished copper studded with bits of green glass, connected with Micah's eyes. She stepped between the two of us, linked her arms in ours, and marched us into the crowded restaurant, where the hostess greeted them by name. As we threaded our way through the tables, several people waved to Micah, who nodded and smiled back at them. He said they probably assumed I was a fellow musician, perhaps an old jazz or blues man. "Cause you don't look country," he said.

We were seated at a second-floor outdoor table that overlooked Sixth Street with a panoramic view of the happy hour crowd congregating below us. We ordered drinks and then I leaned against the wrought iron railing beside my chair, resting my chin on my forearm, and allowed a blissful mood to sweep over me. Ciara rested a hand on my back as I began to step-stone through the procession of people walking below me. I turned to face her and Micah.

"I've missed you both so much." I felt flushed with joyfulness, grasping one of their hands in each of mine.

They quizzed me about Tallie, Alison and the trip. Why wasn't Tallie with me? How long would I be able to stay in Austin? In an instant I sprinted through several thoughts: Junction…was that town's name prophetic after all? Carl had told me to accept knowledge, however harsh, as a gift. Sam recommended I figuratively die and then rise Phoenix-like and never look behind me. Austin was my last rendezvous…had I traveled all this distance only to make a choice so near to the end? I decided to push the awareness of dying out of my consciousness and I wanted Micah's and Ciara's assistance to do that.

I provided straightforward answers…confessing the pancreatic cancer and the discouraging prognosis, how I had conceived of the trip and why Tallie had not accompanied me, detailing Alison's deterioration and her move to the care facility…all in an unemotional voice and never once letting go of their hands.

Micah clenched his jaw, the corners of his mouth twitching without smiling, and glanced away, struggling, I could see, not to cry as he coped with my announcement. Ciara wept openly, drawing concerned looks from neighboring tables. I strengthened my grip on their hands. To those seated around us it might have appeared as though we were absorbed in prayer…although the margarita pitcher might have complicated that conclusion.

"Listen…we'll cry later," I said. "Buckets of tears. But not tonight. Tonight we get a preview of my wake. A kind of 'pre-wake.'" I laughed. "I want to drink and laugh. I want to wade through old memories and forge a few new ones with both of you. Let's not waste this."

My attitude surprised even me. Up and down Sixth Street the stirrings of live music drifted, melding with traffic reverberations and crowd echoes into an atmosphere of festivity. I recalled neighborhood carnivals and Chicago street fairs, block parties during my childhood in St. Louis, bars on a stretch of South Dubuque Street in Iowa City after a home football victory.

Micah released my hand and raised his margarita glass. He gazed at me with his gleaming copper eyes, his lips compressed into a wide, thin line. "I understand," he said. "There's no point in passing a death sentence on yourself. No wallowing."

I nodded as Ciara clinked her glass against Micah's and lingered for me to complete the circle with my own. "No commiserating…tonight" she stated, wiping tears from her cheeks.

"It's our pact for tonight," I said. We touched our glasses cautiously, the tinkling of the rims against one another certifying the declaration.

After the second pitcher of margaritas, Micah stopped drinking, saying someone should remain sober…as a "voice of reason," he said…to shepherd our party through the balance of the night. He wouldn't let me pay for dinner and after a brief call on his cell phone, he announced we were crossing the street to Maggie Mae's. Micah and Ciara once again were recognized. Hugs and introductions were dispensed and we followed a woman upstairs to the Gibson Room, where we sat at a high-top table in the rear of the room near the sound booth. We sat on padded stools by a window that looked down on Trinity Street. I immediately liked the bar…it had a high, wooden ceiling with crown molding; brick columns spaced along the exterior wall; bead board wainscoting; framed photos of past performers, paintings of Gibson guitar legends, some of their instruments mounted around the room; Oriental carpets and leather Ottomans; and an ornately carved bar…the space was furnished like a comforting lounge, not like a commonplace tavern.

Micah said live music wouldn't begin until nine o'clock. Ciara and I switched to beers…Lone Star longnecks…and settled in to talk.

While enjoying the buzz from the margaritas, we bounced our conversation from one subject to another, but eventually focused on Ciara's fascination with my trip.

"What made you think of it?" she wondered.

I shrugged but answered quickly. "When I started, it was all about saying goodbye to people who'd been important in my life."

I paused. "But in the past few days I've been questioning if that's a sham, if it's only been an effort to reassure myself that my life was important to those people."

"Why would you doubt that?" she asked.

"It's easy to doubt something if you try hard enough," I said. Micah grinned, his hands encircling his glass of Diet Coke.

"Okay," she said. "But you know, don't you?"

"Yes, Ciara. Up here I know," as I tapped my forehead. "And I believe it here, too." I rested my chest above my heart. "But reassurance has it rewards."

"Hmm."

"Have you gotten what you need?" Micah asked.

"Yes," I answered. "And much more."

"Tell me," Ciara breathed.

Our waitress placed a bottle of beer before each of us; Micah thanked her by name, but Ciara kept her eyes on me, never once glancing at the woman.

"I never thought of myself as a needy man," I told Ciara. "The impulse of dropping in on people and begging for validation…truthfully, it offends me. Although…perhaps that's what I was seeking, or at least part of what I've been pursuing. I'm not convinced the entire trip was a subconscious, self-serving reflex. I'll admit I had selfish motives…I wanted to see all of you and tell you what you've meant to me and how I feel about you. But the outpouring from everyone, their tender responses…they've made me second guess my intentions."

"Self-enlightenment," Micah said. Ciara nodded.

"I expected that and even wrote about it early in my journal. Somehow, I was convinced, I should be able to anticipate the course of my self-discovery."

"How's that working out for you?" Ciara smiled and sipped from her beer bottle.

"Peachy." I tracked a young man dressed in jeans, a Western shirt and a cowboy hat walk the length of the bar and then pause, hands on hips, in front of the stage in the far corner.

"Which is more shameful: stupidity or needfulness?" I asked, gripping my beer and draining a healthy swallow.

"Fuck shame," Ciara spat and we all laughed. "I figure when you're handed a death sentence, you should start to ignore all of the stupid shit. Fuck shame and embarrassment. And fuck the fear of asking for what you want, for what you need. Life provides you with balance, and when you snatch time from one side of the scale, something has to come off the other side."

"I love this woman," Micah said, lifting and kissing Ciara's hand.

"Time's not on your side," she continued. "You better wring everything from it that you can."

"I'm trying," I said.

"Don't ever stop trying," Ciara said, training a finger on me.

"I read a story online about a woman diagnosed with cancer who had exceeded her doctor's expectations," I said, "living two years longer than anyone believed possible. It petrified her. She'd accepted a calculation of a mythical date when she was supposed to die. She regarded every day beyond that not as a gift…" I thought of Carl "…but as a liability. She refused to plan anything…dinners, visits with friends and family…she dreaded the possibility of not being able to attend them. She died but the quality of her last days suffered. I've wondered how I'd react in similar circumstances."

"Better than her, I hope," Ciara said and then quickly turned to Micah, her gathered hair flipping and slapping her face, causing her to scrunch up her features. "We need to schedule a trip back to Chicago."

Micah smiled, his mouth corners rising and falling. "Okay, honey."

"That's another thing!" I said, beginning to feel the influence of the beer and the margaritas. "I thought there'd be more finality to saying goodbye."

"A crazy assumption," Micah said.

"Absolutely," Ciara concurred.

"My friend in Idaho, a poet, sent me an email…she's going to write a poem that she'll recite at my funeral. Woman in Minneapolis sends an email almost every other day checking up on me." I thought of Carl and the shock of seeing him in Phoenix.

"They're telling you what you wanted to hear, aren't they?" Ciara asked.

I nodded. "Yeah, they are. Loud and clear."

"The only clean break is a fracture," Ciara said, "and if you think you can fracture the way people feel about you, then the cancer may have spread to your brain."

"You never heard of a compound fracture?" Micah teased.

The flippancy of the reference to my cancer made me laugh, a barking eruption that astonished me with how it conquered the room. Slightly embarrassed, I stopped laughing, but the thunder continued rumbling and I swiveled on my stool toward the stage, where the young man in the cowboy hat I'd seen earlier, flanked by a young woman in a tank top and tight jeans, addressed a microphone, tapping it with his middle finger.

"Testing." The power of coincidence made me laugh again.

Micah chuckled, his mouth tweaking rapidly. "I know these two, Tinder," he said. "They harmonize beautifully. I think you'll enjoy them."

Micah was right. Tinder performed cover songs…pop, folk and a smattering of country…interspersing them with original compositions; their voices were tightly entwined. Micah was spot on with his assessment of their harmonies.

"Beautiful guitars," I said.

"Yes. Taylor GS-8s," Micah told me. "Exceptional tone."

When the woman leaned into her microphone and announced they were taking a short break, Micah rapped his fist on the table and excused himself.

"Musician's code," Ciara said. "Always meet and greet."

"He seems to know everyone," I said to her.

"Austin is really a small town, and the music crowd is a small town within that small town. Talent gets recognized fairly quickly."

"He's always had that."

"Hey folks," the male half of 'Tinder' said into the mic. "We've got a little treat for you tonight. A good friend of ours is going to grace us with a song. One of his. Let's give it up for Micah Streets!"

The room filled with applause as Micah perched on a stool before the microphone, holding one of the Taylors. The spotlights on the ceiling cleansed him in white light, in contrast to the buttery pools that washed the walls and the tables. With one foot on the stage platform and the other hiked up on the lower rung of the chrome stool, Micah strummed the guitar and leaned into the microphone.

"Years ago I wrote this song for some very dear friends in Chicago," he said. Ciara gripped my hand. "One of them is here tonight, and it goes out to him."

Micah sang "Loving You" with more expression than I'd ever heard him inject into the song before. He slowed the tempo and sustained some of the words, his phrasing lingering and meaningful. The lyrics have become so familiar to me over the years, but when Micah sang it this time, I sensed he focused it less on his feelings about Tallie and me as a couple, and aimed it more as a testimonial about me alone. I didn't ask him later, when he returned to the table, if that's what he had intended…if he hadn't, I didn't want to know. Even if in ignorant bliss, I chose to encapsulate that moment in my memory with a selfish interpretation.

The room rewarded Micah's performance with waves of applause. He descended from the stage and strolled past the bar, fist-bumping the male half of Tinder, pecking the cheek of the young woman, and then, nodding and high-fiving people, returned to our table. Ciara rose as he approached and swamped him in a hug. Over her shoulder we made eye contact and he smiled, not his predictable shuddering grin, but a fixed, expansive smile that infectiously produced one on my face as well.

We listened to Tinder perform two more sets, Ciara and I slowing our beer intake, but only marginally. After midnight, I texted Tallie that I was still out with Micah and Ciara and would call her the following night. She replied with a smiley face which I showed to Ciara, who found it far too amusing. I glanced at Micah who bobbed his head.

"Maybe we should call it a night," I suggested.

I expected Ciara to object, but she didn't. Instead she stated that they would walk me back to my hotel. In the cool evening Ciara gripped both my hand and Micah's, wizard-walking us down Sixth Street toward the Hilton, people grinning and scooting to either edge of the sidewalk to afford us a wide path; she chanted over and over: "Because, because, because, because…because, because, because, because." We arrived at the hotel before I had settled on which character I identified with more: the Scarecrow or the Tin Man. In the lobby, I approached the registration desk and extended my reservation for another day. I didn't want to start the drive home while half-drunk or half-asleep. I reasoned that resting through the morning and probably most of the afternoon would be a wise choice. I could afford the time…I had three days to reach Chicago. Ciara complained that she needed to use the toilet, so we took the elevator to my room…Micah and I sat in the chairs by the window, which afforded us a view of Lady Bird Lake and the Austin Convention Center.

I asked about Micah's parents. He said they were enjoying retirement…still living in Detroit…and during one of his last conversations with them, his father had joked that the two of them had outlived all the members of their families who had ostracized them when they'd gotten married. "It was never a goal, you know, something they had intended to do," Micah said, "outliving all that hate. Now that they and their cousins are the older generation in the family, everything's fine. They'd always been the most accepting but kept it on the down-low while all the parents were alive."

"It's almost too sad to be funny," I said.

"My Dad always asks about you," Micah said. "I've told him what a special person you are to me." Micah paused as Ciara emerged from the bathroom; she stopped and studied the two of us sitting in the chairs, and then smiled and crawled onto the bed, curling onto her side. "He's grateful for that, especially when he considers how his relationship with his father collapsed after he married Mom.

"He never found what I found in you," Micah said. "Not only a surrogate father, but a cherished friend who I love and respect so much."

"I love you, too, Micah."

"Missing you is going to hurt."

We sat quietly for a few moments, contented in one another's presence, listening to the swooshing of the air conditioner fan and the muffled thrumming of truck traffic below us on I-35. If there's a soundtrack to this trip, it's traffic noise.

"Tell me about your band," I said.

"'Bluesed Egos'…they're a good group, We're all over forty and creatively we're all in sync…like people who get married late in their thirties: the personalities are already molded, so if they get along well with each other, there's a strong probability they'll always get along."

"That's a special way of looking at it," I said.

"We're each passionate about the music and patient with one another. Accomplished, too. When we play, we challenge each other… it brings out the best in us."

I recalled how vital that was to Micah.

"Has it changed you? Knowing?"

"It doesn't seem totally real yet," I said. "I feel like I'm gliding through limbo right now. I haven't felt any onerous symptoms…

nothing that isn't easily controlled at this point. The awareness isn't like an intimidating presence I have to navigate around each morning. It's fog-like, indistinct, something there but insubstantial." I told Micah about the panic attack, the painkillers and anti-anxiety medication.

"I know what's coming. My doctor has spelled it out for me. As the disease progresses and this fogginess…" I paused. "I'm sure my frame of mind will change.

"I've spoken of my Marine buddy, Carl?"

Micah nodded.

"He told me this entire trip is a gift. Each day, each mile, lets me dwell on good moments and memories. When the time comes that the pain is so intense that it drives me to my deathbed, I worry that I'll grow embittered and only reflect on unpleasant moments and memories. I'm going to need Tallie so much then, but I'm terrified that she'll suffer being in the company of an acrimonious, dying man."

Micah glanced at Ciara on the bed. "Don't worry about that woman…Tallie's stronger than you know."

I nodded. "Yeah. I suppose doubt is one of the first symptoms."

Micah scratched his beard. "Ciara and I have never felt the need to get married," he said. "We recognize that we'll always be together." The tone of his voice made it clear there was a "but" coming.

"We met in Chicago…fell in love in Chicago…cried together when we left Chicago. Maybe we should get married in Chicago."

"Where's this coming from?"

"Ciara's impulse to take a trip to Chicago feels right. Maybe when we're there, we should get married…and you can give away the bride."

"I thought tonight you were supposed to be the 'voice of reason.'"

"Sometimes impulses are the most reasonable decisions," he said. "I know it seems rash…you probably think I'm overreacting to your news." I did. "But I hate the idea of letting go of you. Earlier you said you wanted to make some new memories. Well, so do I."

I reached over and patted Micah's knee. Ciara stirred on the bed, and we both turned toward her as she murmured something unintelligible.

"Where do you go from here?" Micah asked.

"Home. Chicago." I paused for a second. "With a stop in St. Louis."

"Visiting another friend?" he asked.

"No. Family." It occurred to me, during Micah's and my discussion of fathers, mothers and families, that I ought to visit my parents' graves. It would mean detouring slightly from the most direct route to Chicago…but it suddenly seemed necessary, and even with the extended stay-over in Austin, I had the time.

Micah held me tightly and sniffled into my shoulder as we said goodbye. Ciara stood by the door, leaning on its frame, instinctively giving us some space. She had already hugged me, kissed my forehead and whispered "I love you" in my ear. She'd smelled like beer and honeysuckle.

After they left I sat at the desk and began this entry and now I am so tired and really hoping that my mind won't drone like a hornet's nest and that I'll easily slip into sleep.

It's thirteen hours later and I'm at another Hilton, this time in Norman, Oklahoma. I slept through most of the day, although restlessly, and woke late in the afternoon. As I checked out in Austin, a clerk informed me that my bill had been settled and then she handed me a note. Micah had paid my hotel charges. Writing that he and Ciara would never forget the "pre-wake," he asked permission to compose a song to perform at my funeral. I thanked the clerk, pocketed the note before she could see my ears brimming with tears, and then I left Austin.

The evening's playlist began with "Piece of My Heart" by Keri Noble as I merged with the rush-hour traffic on I-35 and sped north. Darkness had settled by the time I drove through Fort Worth. I think my only goal for the day was to escape Texas.

Hearing Tallie's voice tonight struck me like a jolt from cardiac paddles in an emergency room. The first words out of my mouth were that I loved her. She chuckled and said she loved me, too. Without prompting I recapped my visit with Micah and Ciara. In a rush of words I described events beginning with the recording session, then dinner, drinks and music at Maggie Mae's, and then my time alone with Micah at the hotel. I tried to relay the emotions I felt after they'd left my room…love, of course, but also pride, fulfillment, happiness…and sustenance. Like so many times before during this trip, explaining to Tallie what I'd experienced guided me to a clearer understanding of what I'd felt…what I was feeling. When you tell a story, I realized, your choice of what details to include and how you describe them reveals as much about the storyteller as the tale itself.

Tallie said Sam and Maddie had called to ask if there was anything, anything at all, they could do for her. I reflected on the nature of family and remembered a story about an old country doctor and what he charged to deliver a baby. If when the doctor emerged from the delivery room the new father asked about his baby, the doctor charged him $200. If the new father asked about his wife, the doctor charged him $100. Families are assembled, they're not born or created by blood alone. Faithfulness emerges from choice and warrants respect. I told Tallie the trip felt at that moment like a procession of family reunions.

"Hmm," she purred.

"You're tired…I can hear it," I whispered.

"I am, yes."

"I'm on my way home."

"That makes me happy."

"Me, too."

Day Twenty-Seven

The route from Austin to St. Louis followed a protracted stretch of interstate highways…I-35 to I-44…past ranches, forest and farmland, but the scenery held little interest for me anymore. Playlist: "St. Louis Blues" by Louis Armstrong. I drove for seven hours and reached St. James, Missouri before I just grew too tired. Four weeks of sitting in the Saab has punished my body and spirit. I'm weary of the driving now that I'm headed home.

Two hours from St. Louis. Two hours from my parents' graves in Valhalla Cemetery on St. Charles Road. I haven't visited in several years…I don't travel to St. Louis unless business takes me there. When I looked at the area on Google Maps, I laughed: there are seven cemeteries and two golf courses within the same square mile. Oh, and a children's psychiatric hospital as well. A bizarre nexus. Also, I don't remember if in my grade school state history classes, the nuns explained why there are so many streets, towns and cities named after saints. It seems like the nuns would have taken pride in that fact and that I've simply forgotten or blocked it out. I'm staying at a Days Inn and followed the clerk's recommendation for dinner:

chicken and dumplings at Diana's Diner.

    I've been trying to recall memories of my parents from my childhood, since I'll be visiting their graves tomorrow. But I'm stymied. Several recollections have surfaced, but nothing I'd consider formative…that's curious to me. Episodes I judge to be seminal in my life seem to have evolved from Vietnam, college, and loving Tallie. Their correlation to the present makes them easier to remember in detail, and all the people I've visited on this trip have underscored the significance of those events. The choice of who to visit, when I consider it, points to the influence adult experiences have shaped as opposed to any childhood events. Have the time and distance from my childhood diluted any consequential memories? Do they even exist? Maybe I'm overly tired or trying too hard. Are only traumatic childhoods memorable? I had a happy upbringing. Perhaps the contrast between that innocent, suburban youth and the turbulence of the culture I encountered away from home amplified the intensity of the aftershocks from the war and everything that followed it. If I'm searching for something about my parents for which I can thank them, maybe I thank them for insulating me as tightly as they did from unpleasantry. I admire the love and the nobility behind the intent, and it's not their fault that I've been taught the folly of believing that impenetrable shelters could possibly exist.

Day Twenty-Eight

Beneath the shadow cast by trees near my parents' graves, the ground molted droplets of dew onto my shoes. I woke early this morning and drove to the cemetery in two hours, starting the odyssey with "Yesterday" by the Beatles. After the difficulties of memory last night, I surprised myself, parking the Saab and walking directly to their adjoining plots, marked by twin slabs of gray granite upright in a row of similar stones amid trimmed grass. I stood before them and removed my Martin Hotel cap, battling a disconnect. For a moment their deaths seemed as artificial to me as my disease, and what I seemed incapable of doing the night before came to me easily…memories, charging like rapids, and me, a mid-stream boulder, drenched by the surging torrent. I dropped my cap and put my hands to my mouth, breathing warmth into my palms, and then intertwined my fingers and rested my chin on my hands. My father, chuckling, saying "Whoa, boy!" as his young son crashed into him at the front door when he returned home from the office, a scuffed leather briefcase clutched high in one hand as that son's arms encircled his legs in the sheer joy of seeing him again. Lying beside him on Saturday afternoons in the faded canvas hammock strung between two maples in our backyard; he'd mown the grass and smelled like springtime as we tracked clouds, and I tried to out-imagine him with increasingly outlandish creatures discovered in the ballooning formations. Clumsily hiding cookies or candy beneath other items at the bottom of the grocery cart when shopping with my mother, certain she would not find the contraband until we unbagged them at home. A single candy bar or package of cookies would survive…she'd react with surprise in our kitchen when she found it…and I never caught her removing the others from the cart. Sitting cross-legged on the floor of our dining room as my mother ironed my father's work shirts…sparkling white, starched until rigid…humming along to music playing on the tinny transistor radio on the kitchen counter.

I trust the instincts that excavated such memories. They reflect what my parents intended me to believe were simpler times. I can't fault them for that reflex: with their experiences…deprivation and bleakness during a depression, battling and surviving a world war… they ached to believe the rhetoric that their future would embrace a measure of peace and prosperity, despite what their experiences had taught them. So they encircled me in a bubble and safeguarded me from grubby reality. As I said last night…the intent was noble and spawned by love.

Every child judges his parents. My judgment is benevolent and dappled with gratitude.

When my parents married they bought a small house in Maplewood. When I was six they moved west to Olivette. The bulk of my childhood unfolded in that unassuming brick house on Green Oaks Drive. I crept past it in the Saab but didn't stop. There'd be nothing to be gained from staying very long. Downtown I parked near the stadium, bought a Reuben sandwich from the Local Deli on South 4th Street and ate it while I walked east to the Gateway Arch. After the tram ride to the top, I walked through the observation deck and leaned into the rectangular window and gazed west along Market Street. Saying goodbye to my hometown from that height evoked very little sentimentality. I crossed to the opposite windows and stared to the northeast, beyond East St. Louis, step-stoning along I-55 and visualizing its approach to Chicago. I snapped a photo. I took no photos of Micah and Ciara, or of my parents' graves. It was not an oversight…it was a decision. I don't have a good reason…I simply didn't.

I'm in Normal, Illinois tonight for the first and certainly the last time in my life, dabbling in manifestations of the town's name. I could have driven home non-stop and arrived around Tallie's bedtime…two days ahead of schedule…but something occurred to me as I raced along the interstate after leaving St. Louis: when I finish this trip, the cancer within me becomes more unambiguous. It generated a fear…and irrational fear I know…that I hadn't anticipated. When I told Carl, Micah and others that the disease didn't seem real to me because I wasn't yet feeling any symptoms… well, the notion seeded itself today that if I don't go home, I stall the cancer. I don't die. I tell myself these cerebral maneuvers are normal…as normal as death, as normal as desperately not wanting to die. The finality I had hoped to achieve during my visits on this trip feels like a joke; it has doubled back to overpower me as I near Chicago. Having presumed my homecoming as a reunion, I now envision it as a reckoning. So many emotions have churned within me during the past four weeks…Tallie deserves an accounting of them all when I get home, but the only way she'll get one is to read this journal.

When we talked this evening, Tallie said she'd booked our flights and hotel reservations for the vacation in Montreal. Vacation…a trip with no purpose beyond enjoyment. We leave in three days. Our conversation was stunted…I'll be home tomorrow and it seemed as though she believed talking tonight might jinx that. Odd, but that's the sense I got. She asked one question before we said good night, and I'd been expecting: had the trip been worth it? I was ready to answer when she told me there was plenty of time to discuss it when I got home. Time.

So I'm contemplating…what was I looking for? What did I want? Did the revelations on the journey vindicate its purpose? For answers, I asked myself the questions others had asked me about knowing I was going to die. Was I searching for something on this journey? If so, did I discover it, or did I gain something else?

I wanted to say goodbye. No one would let me.

I wanted to mete out revenge. Carl wouldn't let me.

Whatever it was I was looking for, in the process I unearthed remembrance, loyalty and love, and I retrieved family.

Despite its obviousness, I find I want more time…but I can't have it. So I'll reconcile that unsatisfied longing through Tallie…my talisman, my totem, and yes, I was wrong, my impenetrable shelter. When I'm with her, I am well. Going home to die is made easier knowing I will not die alone.

I just checked my email…responses from Ellen and Del and from Micah. He and Ciara talked…they are going to get married when they come to Chicago. They're crazy. Oh, and he drafted the song he promised. Dear God, it's beautiful.

Day Twenty-Nine

Began the day with Ingrid Michaelson's "The Way I Am." Traffic crept on I-55 as I approached the south side. The cityscape reared against the brown haze of the sky, familiar and appealing. I rode out to the Drive and steered north, past McCormick Place, the "UFO" renewal of Soldier Field and the Museum Campus. Sailboats bobbed in the windy harbor, their white masts rising and dipping, swaying and rocking…maritime hypnotism; joggers and cyclists slipped along the lake shore while in Grant Park workers in green uniforms on riding mowers slalomed around beds of blooming flowers and rows of shade trees.

Thomas Hardy said "You can't go home again." That's true for me, because home is always with me. And I am home, "deskbound" behind the wheel of the Saab in the garage beneath our building. I've lowered the car windows; the air here is cool. Tallie's space is empty…I assume she's at her office. I always prided myself on being early for appointments, and I've finished my trip with a day to spare. I've given myself another day to spend with Tallie.

On the laptop I opened the slideshow of photos I'd created for Tallie. The first is the photo that I took of her the day I began my farewell tour. Her pose and expression as she watched me leave that day appear to me now as a greeting. She's saying "welcome home."

I have always placed faith in Tallie. Damn, how I love her. I cannot imagine never having loved her. And I am certain she will remember me always…will never forget me.

About the Author

John M. McNamara was born in New York City, and now lives in a suburb of Chicago. In the summer of 1999, he was selected to receive a professional artist residency at the Ox Bow Summer Arts Program for the School of the Art Institute of Chicago in Saugatuck, Michigan. He is the author of the novel **A Life Without Grace** and **Hunter's War, A Novella, and Selected Short Stories.**

Made in the USA
Charleston, SC
03 August 2012

Prentice Hall
The Reader's Journey

STUDENT EDITION
GRADE EIGHT

HARVEY DANIELS
GRANT WIGGINS

Upper Saddle River, New Jersey • Boston, Massachusetts • Chandler, Arizona • Glenview, Illinois

Acknowledgments appear on page 551, which constitutes an extension of this copyright page.

Cover Design: Judith Krimski, Judith Krimski Design, Inc.

Copyright ©2013 Pearson Education, Inc., or its affiliates. All Rights Reserved. Printed in the United States of America. This publication is protected by copyright, and permission should be obtained from the publisher prior to any prohibited reproduction, storage in a retrieval system, or transmission in any form or by any means, electronic, mechanical, photocopying, recording, or likewise. For information regarding permissions, write to Rights Management & Contracts, One Lake Street, Upper Saddle River, New Jersey 07458.

Pearson, Prentice Hall, and Pearson Prentice Hall are trademarks, in the U.S. and/or other countries, of Pearson Education, Inc., or its affiliates

ISBN-13: 978-0-13-322858-8
ISBN-10: 0-13-322858-4
11 17

PEARSON

Contributing Authors

The contributing authors guided the direction and philosophy of Prentice Hall *The Reader's Journey*. Their work helped to inform the pedagogical integrity of the program and to ensure its relevance for today's teachers and students.

Harvey Daniels has been a classroom teacher, writing project director, author, and university professor. Also known as "Smokey," Daniels serves as an international consultant to schools, districts, and educational agencies. Daniels is known for his work on student-led book clubs, as recounted in *Literature Circles: Voice and Choice in Book Clubs and Reading Groups* and his newer title, *Mini-lessons for Literature Circles*. He has authored or co-authored eleven other books. Recent works include *Subjects Matter: Every Teacher's Guide to Content-Area Reading* and *Content Area Writing: Every Teacher's Guide*. Daniels is on the faculty of National-Louis University in Chicago, and is Founding Director of the Walloon Institute.

Grant Wiggins is the President of Authentic Education in Hopewell, New Jersey. He earned his Ed.D. from Harvard University and his B.A. from St. John's College in Annapolis. Grant consults with schools, districts, and state education departments on a variety of reform matters; organizes conferences and workshops; and develops print materials and Web resources on curricular change. He is the co-author, with Jay McTighe, of *Understanding By Design* and *The Understanding By Design Handbook*, the award-winning and highly successful materials on curriculum published by ASCD. His work has been supported by the Pew Charitable Trusts, the Geraldine R. Dodge Foundation, and the National Science Foundation.

Program Advisory Board

The following educators helped shape the program from the very beginning. As classroom practitioners and advocates of a novel-based approach to the teaching of the language arts, they helped to conceptualize the program, lending their advice to the Student Work Text, the Teacher's Guide, and the Anchor Book library alike.

Linda Banas
Department of Learning
and Instruction at SUNY Buffalo
Buffalo, New York

Diane Boni
Director of Language Arts
Greece Central School District
Rochester, New York

Heidi Driscoll
English Language Arts
Curriculum Supervisor, 7-12
Taunton Public Schools
Taunton, Massachusetts

Laurie Herriges
Language Arts Instructor
Morgan Butler Middle School
Waukesha, Wisconsin

Sharon Hiller, Ed.D.
Director of Curriculum and
Educational Services
Richmond Community Schools
Richmond, Michigan

Darlene Groves Musso
English Department Chairperson
Broward County School District
Plantation, Florida

Deborah Nevill
Language Arts Instructor
Granite Valley Middle School
Monson, Massachusetts

Helen Shiffer
English Department chairperson
Carmel School District
Carmel, Indiana

Ginny White
Language Arts Instructor
Fernandina Beach Middle School
Fernandina Beach, Florida

Teacher Reviewers

The program reviewers provided ongoing input throughout the development of *The Reader's Journey*. Their valuable insights ensure that the perspectives of the teachers throughout the country are represented within this language arts series.

Ella Briand
Humanities Field Coordinator
Syracuse City Schools
Syracuse, New York

Julia A. Delahunty
English Department Head
Edison Township Public Schools
Edison, New Jersey

Sharon S. Hoff
Language Arts Instructor
Desert Sands Unified School District
La Quinta, California

Marilyn Kline
Senior Research Associate
David C. Anchin Center
University of South Florida
Tampa, Florida

Kathleen Oropallo, Ph.D.
National Educational Consultant
Zephyrhills, Florida

Elizabeth Primas, Ed.D.
Director of Literacy
District of Columbia Public Schools
Washington, D.C.

Ellin Rossberg
Language Arts Consultant
Westchester County
New York, New York

Helen Turner
English-Language Arts Teacher
Bancroft Middle School
San Leandro, California

Charles Youngs
Language Arts Curriculum Facilitator
Bethel Park High School
Bethel Park, Pennsylvania

A Novel Way to Learn!

Learning Through Reading Books
This program is like no other you have studied from. You will get to read lots of interesting books of all sorts, from novels to nonfiction. In each unit, your teacher will assign a book for you to read (your **Anchor Book**). Later in the unit you get to choose another book on your own (your **Free-Choice Book**).

How Does The Program Work?
You start in the Student Work Text.

Before Reading Your Anchor Book
You will learn reading strategies and how to set up your **Reader's Journal**.

While Reading Your Anchor Book
Along the way you will learn lots of other skills that will help you too.

From time to time you will get to talk about your Anchor Book and your ideas in special **Literature Circles**.

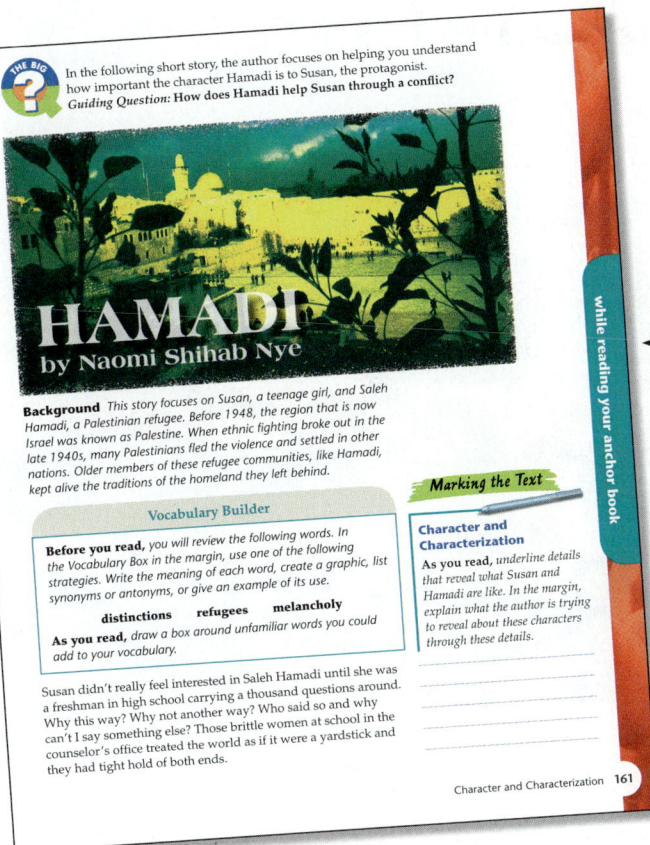

Learn to Mark Texts Too!
Here is what is really cool about this Work Text. It's *yours*. You will get to interact with the text by marking passages while you read—underlining important phrases, marking vocabulary words, and making notes in the margins.

Now It's Your Turn to Choose
In the middle of the unit you will get to pick a Free-Choice Book. How does it compare to your Anchor Book?

After Reading Your Anchor Book
You will get to do some fun projects based on your Anchor Book. Which project you choose is up to you.

So are you ready for The Reader's Journey?

Unit 1 Is *truth* the same for everyone?

Genre Focus: Fiction and Nonfiction

Unit Book Choices
With this unit you will read a book (your Anchor Book) as you learn unit skills. Here are six books that complement the unit well.
- Cut From the Same Cloth
- An Island Like You
- Uncommon Champions
- The House of Dies Drear
- Robot Dreams
- To Be a Slave

Free-Choice Book
Enrich and extend your learning with a free-choice book.

Before Reading Your Anchor Book

1-1	Understanding the Big Question		4
	Introduction to Fiction and Nonfiction		6
1-2	Making Predictions	Reading Skills	8
	"A Changing Society"	Informational Text	
	"Always to Remember: The Vision of Maya Ying Lin" by Brent Ashabranner	Informational Text	
1-3	Prefixes and Suffixes	Vocabulary Building Strategy	16

While Reading Your Anchor Book

1-4	Reader's Journal: Introduction	Anchor Book Activities	18
1-5	Analyzing an Informational Text	Reading Skills	20
	"The Greenhouse Effect"	Informational Text	
1-6	Narrative Texts	Literary Analysis	22
	from "Water Man Comics" by Dav Pilkey	Memoir	
	"Occupation: Conductorette" from *I Know Why the Caged Bird Sings* by Maya Angelou	Autobiography	

viii

| 1-7 | Conflict . . . . Literary Analysis . . . . .34 |
| | from *"Tears of Autumn"* by Yoshiko Uchida | Short Story |

Understanding Plot 36
 "The Attic" by Alvin Schwartz — Folk Tale
 "Amigo Brothers" by Piri Thomas — Short Story

1-8 The Writing Rules; Common and Proper Nouns;
 Concrete, Abstract, and Possessive Nouns;
 Spelling Plural Nouns . . . . Language Coach 50

1-9 Description: Descriptive Essay . . . . Writer's Workshop 54

1-10 📕 Literature Circles: Introduction . . . . .Anchor Book Activities 58

 ✓ **Monitoring Your Progress:** Timed Writing 60

1-11 Author's Purpose . . . . Reading Skills 62
 E-mail — Informational Text
 Memo — Informational Text

 📘 **Ready for a Free-Choice Book?**

1-12 Setting and Mood . . . . Literary Analysis 66
 from *The Land I Lost* by Huynh Quang Nhuong — Memoir
 from *"The Day It Rained Cockroaches"* by Paul Zindel — Memoir

1-13 Theme . . . . Comparing Literary Works 74
 "The Ant and the Dove" by Leo Tolstoy — Fable
 from *"The Grass Harp"* by Truman Capote — Novel
 from *"Child of the Owl"* by Laurence Yep — Novel

1-14 Personal Pronouns, Reflexive Pronouns,
 Pronoun Agreement, Spelling Tricky or Difficult Words . . . . Language Coach 88

1-15 Narration: Personal Narrative . . . . Writer's Workshop 92

After Reading Your Anchor Book

1-16 📕 Anchor Book Projects, Free-Choice
 Book Reflection . . . . .Anchor Book Activities 96

 ✓ **Unit Review** 98

Unit 2 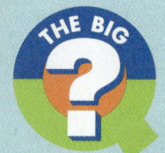 Can all *conflicts* be resolved?

Genre Focus: The Novel

 Unit Book Choices
With this unit you will read a book (your Anchor Book) as you learn unit skills. Here are six books that complement the unit well.
- Al Capone Does My Shirts
- The Schwa Was Here
- Code Talker
- Annie John
- Roll of Thunder, Hear My Cry
- Obasan

 Free-Choice Book
Enrich and extend your learning with a free-choice book.

Before Reading Your Anchor Book

2-1	Understanding the Big Question		106
	Introduction to the Novel		108
2-2	Making Inferences	Reading Skills	110
	"**Grandma Ling**" by Amy Ling	Poem	
	"**Animals Among Us**"	Informational Text	
2-3	Word Origins	Vocabulary Building Strategies	116

While Reading Your Anchor Book

2-4	Reader's Journal	Anchor Book Activities	118
	from **Bad Boy: A Memoir** by Walter Dean Myers	Memoir	
	from **The Giver** by Lois Lowry	Novel	
2-5	Flashback, Foreshadowing	Literary Analysis	120
	from **The Land** by Mildred D. Taylor	Novel	
	from "**The Birds**" by Daphne du Maurier	Short Story	
	"**The Scarlet Ibis**" by James Hurst	Short Story	

2-6	Action and Linking Verbs, Principal Parts of Regular Verbs, Irregular Verbs, Subject/Verb Agreement	Language Coach	138
2-7	Narration: Short Story	Writer's Workshop	142
2-8	Literature Circles: Subplots	Anchor Book Activities	146

✓ **Monitoring Your Progress:** Timed Writing 148

2-9	Compare and Contrast	Reading Skills	150
	"Weighing Your Options: Plasma or LCD TV"	Informational Text	
	"Extreme Weather: Hurricanes and Tornadoes"	Informational Text	

📘 Ready for a Free-Choice Book?

2-10	Character	Literary Analysis	156
	from "Raymond's Run" by Toni Cade Bambara	Short Story	
	Characterization		158
	from *Jim the Boy* by Tony Earley	Novel	
	"Hamadi" by Naomi Shihab Nye	Short Story	
2-11	Point of View and Irony	Literary Analysis	172
	from "Beauty Lessons" by Judith Ortiz Cofer	Short Story	
	"The Tell-Tale Heart" by Edgar Allan Poe	Short Story	
2-12	Oral Interpretation of Literature	Listening and Speaking Workshop	184
2-13	Verbs—Simple and Perfect Tenses, Vowel Sounds in Unstressed Syllables, Choosing the Right Word	Language Coach	186
2-14	Exposition: Compare-and-Contrast Essay	Writer's Workshop	190
2-15	Literature Circles: Power and Conflict	Anchor Book Activities	196

After Reading Your Anchor Book

2-16	Anchor Book Projects, Free-Choice Book Reflection	Anchor Book Activities	198

✓ **Unit Review** 200

Unit 3 How much *information* is enough?

Genre Focus: Nonfiction

Unit Book Choices
With this unit you will read a book (your Anchor Book) as you learn unit skills. Here are six books that complement the unit well.
- Anne Frank: The Diary of a Young Girl
- Open Your Eyes
- We Just Want to Live Here
- They Had a Dream
- Escape From Earth
- Phineas Gage

Free-Choice Book
Enrich and extend your learning with a free-choice book.

Before Reading Your Anchor Book

3-1	Understanding the Big Question	208
	Introduction to Nonfiction	210
3-2	Identifying Main Ideas and Supporting Details .... Reading Skills	212
	"Local Kids Clean Up Playground"	Informational Text
	"What Makes a Car Run?"	Informational Text
3-3	Synonyms and Antonyms .... Vocabulary Building Strategies	218

While Reading Your Anchor Book

3-4	Expository Writing .... Literary Analysis	220
	"The World of the Forensic Scientist"	Informational Text
3-5	Persuasive Writing .... Literary Analysis	228
	"Interview" by Sara Henderson Hay	Poem
	"The Trouble with Television" by Robert MacNeil	Editorial

| 3-6 | Delivering a Persuasive Speech | Listening and Speaking Workshop | 238 |

| 3-7 | Adjectives, Articles, and Adverbs; Comparative and Superlative Forms; Modifiers; Prepositions and Prepositional Phrases | Language Coach | 240 |

| 3-8 | Exposition: Cause-and-Effect Essay | Writer's Workshop | 244 |

| 3-9 | Literature Circles: Cause and Effect | Anchor Book Activities | 248 |

✓ **Monitoring Your Progress:** Timed Writing 250

3-10	Differentiating Between Fact and Opinion	Reading Skills	252
	"Women's Suffrage"	Essay	
	"America the Not-So-Beautiful" by Andrew A. Rooney	Editorial	

Ready for a Free-Choice Book?

3-11	Biography and Autobiography	Literary Analysis	258
	"Harriet Beecher Stowe"	Biography	
	Author's Perspective		260
	from *Narrative of The Life of Frederick Douglass* by Frederick Douglass	Autobiography	

| 3-12 | Author's Style | Comparing Literary Works | 266 |
| | "Volar: To Fly" by Judith Ortiz Cofer | Memoir | |

| 3-13 | Combining Sentences With Conjunctions, Spelling Homophones | Language Coach | 272 |

| 3-14 | Persuasion: Persuasive Essay | Writer's Workshop | 274 |

After Reading Your Anchor Book

| 3-15 | Anchor Book Projects, Free-Choice Book Reflection | Anchor Book Activities | 278 |

✓ **Unit Review** 280

Unit 4  What is the secret to *reaching someone* with words?

Genre Focus: Prose and Poetry

 Unit Book Choices
With this unit you will read a book (your Anchor Book) as you learn unit skills. Here are six books that complement the unit well.
- A Dime a Dozen
- The Devil's Arithmetic
- Maus I: A Survivor's Tale
- The Saga of Lewis & Clark
- The Watsons Go to Birmingham—1963
- Under the Baseball Moon

 Free-Choice Book
Enrich and extend your learning with a free-choice book.

Before Reading Your Anchor Book

4-1	Understanding the Big Question	288
	Introduction to Prose and Poetry	290
4-2	Paraphrasing .... Reading Skills	292
	from **Rumblefish** by S.E. Hinton	Novel
	"**For Some, Pain Is Orange**" by Susan Hornik	Informational Text
4-3	Word Origins and Roots .... Vocabulary Building Strategies	298

While Reading Your Anchor Book

4-4	Imagery .... Literary Analysis	300
	"**At First, It Is True, I Thought There Were Only Peaches & Wild Grapes**" by Alice Walker	Poem
	"**Alabanza: In Praise of Local 100**" by Martín Espada	Poem
4-5	Symbolism .... Literary Analysis	306
	"**Fire and Ice**" by Robert Frost	Poem
	"**Kim**" by Paul Fleischman	Memoir
	"**The Road Not Taken**" by Robert Frost	Poem

4-6	**Figurative Language**	*Comparing Literary Works*	 312
	"Ode to Enchanted Night" by Pablo Neruda	Poem	
	"'Hope' is the thing with feathers" by Emily Dickinson	Poem	
	"Dreams" by Langston Hughes	Poem	
	"The City Is So Big" by Richard García	Poem	

4-7 **Active and Passive Voice, Spelling Words With Suffixes** . . . . *Language Coach* 318

4-8 **Response to Literature: Critical Review** . . . . *Writer's Workshop* 320

4-9 **Literature Circles: Cultural Context** . . . . *Anchor Book Activities* 324

✓ **Monitoring Your Progress: Timed Writing** 326

4-10 **Using Context to Determine Meaning** . . . . *Reading Skills* 328
   "Short-Sided Soccer" — Informational Text
   "The Rhythms of Rap" by Kathiann M. Kowalski — Informational Text

Ready for a Free-Choice Book?

4-11 **Sound Devices** . . . . *Literary Analysis* 334
   "Onomatopoeia" by Eve Merriam

   Rhythm and Meter
   "I Hear America Singing" by Walt Whitman — Poem
   "The Gettysburg Address" by Abraham Lincoln — Speech
   "Slam, Dunk, & Hook" by Yusef Komunyakaa — Poem
   "The Eagle" by Alfred, Lord Tennyson — Poem

4-12 **Reading Poetry Aloud** . . . . *Listening and Speaking Workshop* 344

4-13 **Forms of Poetry** . . . . *Literary Analysis* 346
   Haiku by Bashō, Chiyojo — Poem
   "I, Too" by Langston Hughes — Poem
   "Fences" by Pat Mora — Poem
   "The New Colossus" by Emma Lazarus — Poem
   "Forsythia" by Mary Ellen Solt — Poem

4-14 **Sentence Structure, Revising to Vary Sentence Patterns** . . . . *Lan...*

4-15 **Exposition: Writing for Assessment** . . . . *Writ...*

After Reading Your Anchor Book

4-16 **Anchor Book Projects, Free-Choice Book Reflection** . . . . *Anchor...*

✓ **Unit Review** . . . .

Unit 5 Is it our *differences* or our *similarities* that matter most?

Genre Focus: Drama

 Unit Book Choices
With this unit you will read a book (your Anchor Book) as you learn unit skills. Here are six books that complement the unit well.

- A Raisin in the Sun
- The Effect of Gamma Rays on Man-in-the-Moon Marigolds
- The Diary of Anne Frank
- Nerdlandia
- The Miracle Worker
- Monster

 Free-Choice Book
Enrich and extend your learning with a free-choice book.

Before Reading Your Anchor Book

5-1	Understanding the Big Question 370	
	Introduction to Drama 372	
5-2	Cause and Effect . . . . Reading Skills 374	
	"Moving Plates of Rock"	Informational Text
	"The Red Tail Angels"	Informational Text
5-3	Using a Dictionary . . . . Vocabulary Building Strategies 382	

While Reading Your Anchor Book

5-4	Dialogue and Stage Directions. . . . . Literary Analysis. . . . 384	
	from **Let Me Hear You Whisper** by Paul Zindel	Drama
	Character Motivation 386	
	from **Pygmalion** by George Bernard Shaw	Drama
	"Thank You, M'am" by Langston Hughes	Short Story

5-5	Participles and Participial Phrases, Sentence Combining with Gerunds and Participles	Language Coach	394
5-6	Exposition: Manual	Writer's Workshop	396

✓ **Monitoring Your Progress: Timed Writing** 400

5-7	Drawing Conclusions	Reading Skills	402
	"*Golden Years*" by Joel Achenbach	Informational Text	

📘 **Ready for a Free-Choice Book?**

5-8	Suspense	Literary Analysis	408
	from ***The Diary of Anne Frank*** by Frances Goodrich and Albert Hackett	Drama	
	from ***Hatchet*** by Gary Paulsen	Novel	
5-9	Staging	Literary Analysis	416
	from ***The Dancers*** by Horton Foote	Drama	
	"*Coyote Steals the Sun and Moon*" retold by Richard Erdoes and Alfonso Ortiz	Myth	
5-10	Dramatic Speeches	Comparing Literary Works	424
	from ***FOB*** by David Henry Hwang	Drama	
	from ***The Piano Lesson*** by August Wilson	Drama	
	from ***A Raisin in the Sun*** by Lorraine Hansberry	Drama	
	"*Harlem*" by Langston Hughes	Poem	
5-11	Reading Drama Aloud	Listening and Speaking Workshop	434
5-12	Independent and Subordinate Clauses, Sentence Combining with Subordinate Clauses	Language Coach	436
5-13	Workplace Writing: Business Letter	Writer's Workshop	438
5-14	📕 Literature Circles: Asking Questions	Anchor Book Activities	442

After Reading Your Anchor Book

5-15	📕 Anchor Book Projects, Free-Choice Book Reflection	Anchor Book Activities	444

✓ **Unit Review** 446

Unit 6 Are yesterday's *heroes* and *events* important today?

Genre Focus: The Research Process

Unit Book Choices
With this unit you will read a book (your Anchor Book) as you learn unit skills. Here are six books that complement the unit well.
- Famous Hispanic Americans
- Ultimate Robot
- Baseball's Biggest Bloopers
- Cool Stuff and How It Works
- Crime Busters
- Amos Fortune

Free-Choice Book
Enrich and extend your learning with a free-choice book.

Before Reading Your Anchor Book

6-1	Understanding the Big Question		454
	Introduction to the Research Process		456
6-2	Setting a Purpose for Reading	Reading Skills	458
	Recording Your Announcement	Informational Text	
	Employment Agreement	Informational Text	
	from *The World Book Encyclopedia*	Informational Text	
6-3	Words from Mythology and Borrowed Words	Vocabulary Building Strategies	464

While Reading Your Anchor Book

6-4	Choosing Your Topic, Narrowing Your Topic	The Research Process	466
6-5	Finding Reliable Sources, Avoiding Plagiarism, Taking Notes	The Research Process	472
	"Flying to Fame"	Informational Text	
6-6	Primary and Secondary Sources	Reading Skills	480
	"A Great and Honorable Leader"	Informational Text	
	from "A Visit to Washington, D.C., 1879" by Chief Joseph	Speech	
	from "The Surrender in the Bear Paw Mountains" by Chief Joseph	Speech	

xviii

6-7	Analyzing an Informational Text	Reading Skills	486
	"Stephen King: His Books, His Life, His Wife"	Interview	
6-8	Revising Run-on Sentences and Sentence Fragments, Revising to Use Quotation Marks and Block Quotes	Language Coach	490
6-9	Research: Interview Report	Writer's Workshop	492

✓ **Monitoring Your Progress: Timed Writing** 496

6-10	Summarizing	Reading Skills	498
	Bicycle Warranty	Informational Text	
	from *"Kids on the Bus: The Overlooked Role of Teenagers in the Civil-Rights Era"* by Jeffrey Zaslow	Informational Text	

📖 **Ready for a Free-Choice Book?**

6-11	Thesis Statement, Organizing Your Ideas, Creating an Outline, Writing Your Rough Draft	The Research Process	504
6-12	Revising Your Research Report	The Research Process	510
	"Alexander the Great" by James Barraclough	Rough Draft	
6-13	Sources and Publishing	The Research Process	514
	"Alexander the Great" by James Barraclough	Final Draft	
6-14	Analyzing Media Messages	Listening and Speaking Workshop	520
6-15	Capitalization; Commas, Semicolons, and Colons	Language Coach	522
6-16	Research: Multimedia Presentation	Writer's Workshop	524

After Reading Your Anchor Book

6-17	Anchor Book Projects, Free-Choice Book Reflection	Anchor Book Activities	530

✓ **Unit Review** 532

THE BIG ?

Is *truth* the same for everyone?

Unit 1 Genre focus:
Fiction and Nonfiction

Your Anchor Book
There are many good books that would work well to support both the Big Question and the genre focus of this unit. In this unit you will read one of these books as your Anchor Book. Your teacher will introduce the book you will be reading.

Free-Choice Reading
Later in this unit you will be given the opportunity to choose another book to read. This is called your free-choice book.

Thinking About What You Already Know

In this unit, you will read a variety of fiction and nonfiction and learn how authors use the same tools to write both genres.

Group Activity

The following excerpts are from some of the selections you will read in this unit. Using what you already know, read the selections and think about whether they are fiction or nonfiction (or whether they could be either). Then, discuss your conclusions with a partner.

from "Amigo Brothers" by Piri Thomas

Antonio helped. "It's about our fight, right?"

"Yeah, right." Felix's eyes squinted at the rising orange sun.

I've been thinking about it too, panín. In fact, since we found out it was going to be me and you, I've been awake at night, pulling punches on you, trying not to hurt you."

"Same here. It ain't natural not to think about the fight. I mean, we both are cheverote fighters and we both want to win. But only one of us can win. There ain't no draws in the eliminations."

Felix tapped Antonio gently on the shoulder. "I don't mean to sound like I'm bragging, bro. But I wanna win, fair and square."

Antonio nodded quietly. Yeah. We both know that in the ring the better man wins. Friend or no friend, brother or no…"

from "The Day It Rained Cockroaches" by Paul Zindel

Tarantulas I like. Scorpions I can live with. But ever since I was three years old and my mother took me to a World's Fair, I have had nightmares about cockroaches. Most people remember an exciting water ride this fair had called Shoot-the-Chutes, but emblazoned on my brain is the display the fair featured of giant, live African cockroaches, which look like American cockroaches except they're six inches long, have furry legs, and can pinch flesh. In my nightmares about them, I'm usually lying on a bed in a dark room and I notice a bevy of giant cockroaches heading for me.

from "Always to Remember: The Vision of Maya Ying Lin" by Brent Ashabranner

In the 1960s and 1970s, the United States was involved in a war in Vietnam. Because many people opposed the war, Vietnam veterans were not honored as veterans of other wars had been. Jan Scruggs, a Vietnam veteran, thought that the 58,000 U.S. servicemen and women killed or reported missing in Vietnam should be honored with a memorial. With the help of lawyers Robert Doubek and John Wheeler, Scruggs worked to gain support for his idea.

from "Child of the Owl" by Laurence Yep

Phil adjusted his tie uneasily and growled, "What're you looking at?"

I looked ahead, keeping my eyes on the glove compartment. Barney and me had never talked much about stuff like this. I knew more about race horses than I knew about myself – I mean myself as a Chinese. I looked at my hands again, thinking they couldn't be my hands, and then I closed my eyes and felt their outline, noticing the tiny fold of flesh at the corners. Maybe it was because I thought of myself as an American and all Americans were supposed to be white like on TV or in books or in movies, but now I felt like some mad scientist had switched bodies on me like in all those monster movies, so that I had woken up in the wrong one.

Which passage(s) did you and your partner think could be either fiction or nonfiction? Explain what led you to this conclusion.

_____
_____
_____
_____
_____

1-1 Understanding the Big Question
Is truth the same for everyone?

Fiction and nonfiction are two kinds of writing that are frequently seen as opposites. However, both fiction and nonfiction share the purpose of communicating some truth about how we live.

The struggle to find the truth exists in all content areas. Nonfiction deals only with real people, events, or ideas. Fiction can be based entirely on the imagination, but it can also be inspired by fact. Have you ever described a piece of fiction as being "real" or "believable"? Although the characters, plot, and setting in a piece of fiction may all be imagined, fiction must reflect some truth for us to keep reading.

Directions To help you start thinking about this unit's big question, let's consider the idea of "truth."

- With a partner, first brainstorm for a list of words and phrases you associate with the word "truth."
- Next, identify one truth from the subject areas listed below.
- Finally, consider whether the ideas you listed below would be considered by everyone as truth.

Truth

Brainstorm:

Examples from:

a. Science

b. Social Studies

c. Math

d. Art-Music

Partner Activity Choose one example you have identified. With a partner, talk about how this idea influences another subject area.

Lesson 1-1

Directions With your partner, read and answer the questions in the chart that follows. Then, add at least two more questions of your own.

Questions About Truth	My Thoughts
Why is truth important to people?	
How can the truth for one person be different from the truth for another?	
How can stories that are untrue help me understand the truth about life?	

In this book, you will see questions labeled "The Big Question." These questions appear at the end of certain lessons. As you read, remember that although nonfiction is about real people, events, or ideas, it may not always be entirely accurate or objective. Also, remember that there is always some truth in the invented stories and characters of fiction.

Understanding the Big Question 5

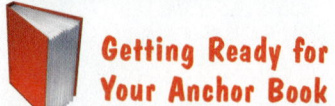

Getting Ready for Your Anchor Book You will start reading your Anchor Book soon. The next few pages in this book give you some background information plus a reading skill.

Introduction to Fiction and Nonfiction

Now that you have started to think about fiction and nonfiction, let's see how they are alike and different.

Elements of Fiction

Fiction began as oral storytelling. It was how people entertained one another. It was also the way a culture shared its history, beliefs, and values. All works of fiction share certain basic elements.

- Fictional works can include make-believe people or animals, called characters. A character faces a problem, or **conflict,** that must be overcome. The made-up series of events that describe how the conflict progresses is called the **plot**.

- The **setting** is where and when the story takes place. Details of setting—particularly, descriptive words and images—help establish the mood. **Mood** is the overall feeling that a literary work conveys to the reader.

- A speaker, called the **narrator**, tells the story. The narrator tells the story from a certain perspective, or **point of view**. **First-person point of view** is the perspective of a character in the story. **Third-person point of view** is the perspective of a narrator outside the action of the story.

- All the elements of fiction work together to help communicate the work's **theme**, which is its central message.

Types of Fiction	
Short stories are brief works of fiction. They usually focus on one main plot structured around one main conflict and can be read in one sitting. **Novels** are longer works of fiction. In addition to its main plot, a novel may contain subplots, or related stories.	**Novellas** are works of fiction that are shorter than novels but longer than short stories. **Historical fiction** is literature that draws in part on real people and events to tell invented stories.

Lesson 1-1

Nonfiction

Nonfiction is writing about real people, places, or events that explains ideas. Nonfiction must be true.

Types of Nonfiction	
Biographies tell the story of someone's life and are told from the perspective of another writer. **Autobiographies and memoirs** tell the story of the author's life and reflect the writer's thoughts and feelings about events. **Letters** are written forms of communication from one person to another. A letter might share information, thoughts, or feelings.	**Journals and diaries** are records of daily events and the writer's thoughts and feelings about them. **Essays and articles** are brief written works about a specific topic. Their purpose might be to explain, persuade, or inform. **Informational texts** are the written documents we come across in everyday life. Examples include textbooks, applications, instructions, and articles.

Nonfiction shares some elements with fiction, but it also has special features that set it apart from fiction.

Fiction
- Tells about made-up people and events and can retell historical events through an imagined perspective.
- Told from the **point of view** of a fictional character, an all-knowing narrator, or a limited narrator.

Both
- Have a **setting**, a time and place.
- Convey a **mood**, or overall feeling.
- Feature the writer's unique **style**, a characteristic way of using language and expressing ideas.

Nonfiction
- Deals exclusively with real people, events, or ideas. Nothing is made up or invented.
- Almost always told from the **point of view** of the writer, who is a real person.

Strategies for Reading Fiction and Nonfiction Use this strategy as you read fiction and nonfiction.

Visualize Picture the characters, setting, or other elements of the text in your mind. Allowing yourself to "see" what you are reading will help you to understand it better.

Introduction to Fiction and Nonfiction

1-2 Reading Skills
Making Predictions

In learning new reading skills, you will use special academic vocabulary. Knowing the right words will help you demonstrate your understanding.

Academic Vocabulary

Word	Meaning	Example Sentence
anticipate *v.* Related words: anticipating, anticipation	to look forward to, expect	I *anticipate* that Tommy will join the team.
modify *v.* Related words: modified, modifying	to change	Because of these new details, I have to *modify* my original prediction.
verify *v.* Related words: verified, verifying	to confirm	I had to bring my license to *verify* my identity.

Making predictions helps you make connections between events and actions. When you predict, you **anticipate** future events and possible outcomes.

How to Make Predictions

▶ **Preview** the selection by looking at graphic representations and text structures such as the title, chapter titles, captions, photos, organization, and headings to anticipate what the selection will be about.

▶ **Formulate** a prediction by using what you know about the topic of the selection, related personal life experiences, and knowledge of other similar selections.

▶ **Verify** your predictions as you read, and **modify** them when necessary.

Previewing a Text

Directions Preview the excerpt from a social studies textbook below and observe how a student completed the chart after previewing text features. Then, make a prediction based on the previewed information.

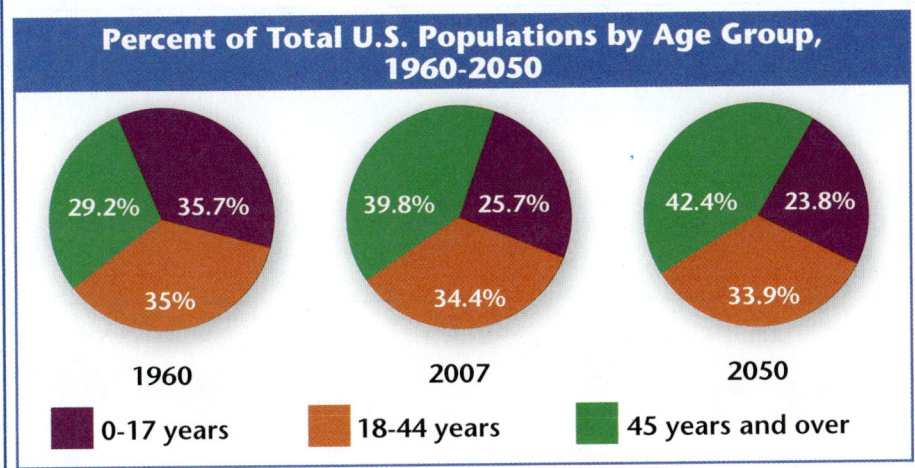

A Changing Society

The face of aging in the United States is changing, according to a new U.S. Census Bureau report. Higher levels of education, which are linked to better health, higher income, more wealth and a higher standard of living continue to increase among people 65 and older. Today's older Americans are living longer and more active lives. Future generations of the elderly will further challenge our understanding of what "being old" means.

Throughout this book, you will see student models, like the one below, that show you what applying a skill looks like.

Student Model

Text Feature to Preview	Tell(s) Me
Title	Society is changing
Images	Chart shows elderly population is growing

My Prediction: _____

_____

Making Predictions

Directions Now that you have learned how to make predictions, try it for yourself with the selection on the next page. Preview the selection and then make predictions in the chart below. If you have background knowledge related to the topic, use it to help you.

Text Feature to Preview	Tell(s) Me
Title	
Captions	
Images	

My Predictions:

Prediction 1

_____
_____

Prediction 2

_____
_____

Lesson 1-2

Preview the various text features, such as the title, introduction, and conclusion. Then, read this magazine article. *Guiding Question:* **What is the most important truth in this article that you would share with someone?**

Always to Remember:
The Vision of Maya Ying Lin

by Brent Ashabranner

In the 1960s and 1970s, the United States was involved in a war in Vietnam. Because many people opposed the war, Vietnam veterans were not honored as veterans of other wars had been. Jan Scruggs, a Vietnam veteran, thought that the 58,000 U.S. servicemen and women killed or reported missing in Vietnam should be honored with a memorial. With the help of lawyers Robert Doubek and John Wheeler, Scruggs worked to gain support for his idea.

The memorial had been authorized by Congress "in honor and recognition of the men and women of the Armed Forces of the United States who served in the Vietnam War." The law, however, said not a word about what the memorial should be or what it should look like. That was left up to the Vietnam Veterans Memorial Fund, but the law did state that the memorial design and plans would have to be approved by the Secretary of the Interior, the Commission of Fine Arts, and the National Capital Planning Commission.

What would the memorial be? What should it look like? Who would design it? Scruggs, Doubek, and Wheeler didn't know, but they were determined that the memorial should help bring closer together a nation still bitterly divided by the Vietnam War. It couldn't be something like the Marine Corps Memorial showing American troops planting a flag on enemy soil at Iwo Jima. It couldn't be a giant dove with an olive branch of peace in its beak. It had to soothe passions, not stir them up. But there was one thing Jan Scruggs insisted on: The memorial, whatever it turned out to be,

Making Predictions 11

would have to show the name of every man and woman killed or missing in the war.

The answer, they decided, was to hold a national design competition open to all Americans. The winning design would receive a prize of $20,000, but the real prize would be the winner's knowledge that the memorial would become a part of American history on the Mall in Washington, D.C. Although fundraising was only well started at this point, the choosing of a memorial design could not be delayed if the memorial was to be built by Veterans Day, 1982. H. Ross Perot contributed the $160,000 necessary to hold the competition, and a panel of distinguished architects, landscape architects, sculptors, and design specialists was chosen to decide the winner.

Announcement of the competition in October, 1980, brought an astonishing response. The Vietnam Veterans Memorial Fund received over five thousand inquiries. They came from every state in the nation and from every field of design; as expected, architects and sculptors were particularly interested.

Everyone who inquired received a booklet explaining the criteria. Among the most important: The memorial could not make a political statement about the war; it must contain the names of all persons killed or missing in action in the war; it must be in harmony with its location on the Mall.

A total of 2,573 individuals and teams registered for the competition. They were sent photographs of the memorial site, maps of the area around the site and of the entire Mall, and other technical design information. The competitors had three months to prepare their designs, which had to be received by March 31, 1981.

Of the 2,573 registrants, 1,421 submitted designs, a record number for such a design competition. When the designs were spread out for jury selection, they filled a large airplane hangar. The jury's task was to select the design which, in their judgment, was the best in meeting these criteria:

- a design that honored the memory of those Americans who served and died in the Vietnam War.
- a design of high artistic merit.
- a design which would be harmonious with its site, including visual harmony with the Lincoln Memorial and the Washington Monument.
- a design that could take its place in the "historic continuity" of America's national art.
- a design that would be buildable, durable, and not too hard to maintain.

The designs were displayed without any indication of the designer's name so that they could be judged anonymously, on their design merits alone. The jury spent one week reviewing all the designs in the airplane hangar. On May 1 it made its report to the Vietnam Veterans Memorial Fund; the experts declared Entry Number 1,026 the winner. The report called it "the finest and most appropriate" of all submitted and said it was "superbly harmonious" with the site on the

◀ The Vietnam Veterans Memorial

Mall. Remarking upon the "simple and forthright" materials needed to build the winning entry, the report concludes:

> This memorial, with its wall of names, becomes a place of quiet reflection, and a tribute to those who served their nation in difficult times. All who come here can find it a place of healing. This will be a quiet memorial, one that achieves an excellent relationship with both the Lincoln Memorial and Washington Monument, and relates the visitor to them. It is uniquely horizontal, entering the earth rather than piercing the sky.
>
> This is very much a memorial of our own times, one that could not have been achieved in another time and place. The designer has created an eloquent place where the simple meeting of earth, sky and remembered names contain messages for all who will know this place.

The eight jurors signed their names to the report, a unanimous decision. When the name of the winner was revealed, the art and architecture worlds were stunned. It was not the name of a nationally famous architect or sculptor, as most people had been sure it would be. The creator of Entry Number 1,026 was a twenty-one-year-old student at Yale University. Her name—unknown as yet in any field of art or architecture—was Maya Ying Lin.

How could this be? How could an undergraduate student win one of the most important design competitions ever held? How could she beat out some of the top names in American art and architecture? Who was Maya Ying Lin?

The answer to that question provided some of the other answers, at least in part. Maya Lin, reporters soon discovered, was a Chinese-American girl who had been born and raised in the small midwestern city of Athens, Ohio. Her father, Henry Huan Lin, was a ceramicist of considerable reputation and dean of fine arts at Ohio University in Athens. Her mother, Julia C. Lin, was a poet and professor of Oriental and English literature. Maya Lin's parents were born to culturally prominent families in China. When the Communists came to power in China in the 1940's, Henry and Julia Lin left the country and in time made their way to the United States. Maya Lin grew up in an environment of art and literature. She was interested in sculpture and made both small and large sculptural figures, one cast in bronze. She learned silversmithing and made jewelry. She was surrounded by books and read a great deal, especially fantasies such as *The Hobbit* and *Lord of the Rings*.[1]

But she also found time to work at McDonald's. "It was about the only way to make money in the summer," she said.

---

[1] *The Hobbit* and *Lord of the Rings* novels by the English author and scholar, J.R.R. Tolkien (1892–1973), chronicling the struggle between various good and evil kingdoms for possession of a magical ring that can shift the balance of power in the world.

Jan C. Scruggs, President of the Vietnam Veterans Memorial Fund, and Project Director Bob Doubek, display the final design for the memorial with Maya Ying Lin.

A co-valedictorian at high school graduation, Maya Lin went to Yale without a clear notion of what she wanted to study and eventually decided to major in Yale's undergraduate program in architecture. During her junior year she studied in Europe and found herself increasingly interested in cemetery architecture. "In Europe there's very little space, so graveyards are used as parks," she said. "Cemeteries are cities of the dead in European countries, but they are also living gardens."

In France, Maya Lin was deeply moved by the war memorial to those who died in the Somme[2] offensive in 1916 during World War I. The great arch by architect Sir Edwin Lutyens is considered one of the world's most outstanding war memorials.

Back at Yale for her senior year, Maya Lin enrolled in Professor Andrus Burr's course in funerary (burial) architecture. The Vietnam Veterans Memorial competition had recently been announced, and although the memorial would be a cenotaph—a monument in honor of persons buried someplace else—Professor Burr thought that having his students prepare a design of the memorial would be a worthwhile course assignment.

Surely, no classroom exercise ever had such spectacular results.

After receiving the assignment, Maya Lin and two of her classmates decided to make the day's journey from New Haven, Connecticut, to Washington to look at the site where the memorial would be built. On the day of their visit, Maya Lin remembers, Constitution Gardens was awash with a late November sun; the park was full of light, alive with joggers and people walking beside the lake.

"It was while I was at the site that I designed it," Maya Lin said later in an interview about the memorial with *Washington Post* writer Phil McCombs. "I just sort of visualized it. It just popped into my head. Some people were playing Frisbee. It was a beautiful park. I didn't want to destroy a living park. You use the landscape. You don't fight with it. You absorb the landscape.... When I looked at the site I just knew I wanted something horizontal that took you in, that made you feel safe within the park, yet at the same time reminding you of the dead. So I just imagined opening up the earth...."

When Maya Lin returned to Yale, she made a clay model of the vision that had come to her in Constitution Gardens. She showed it to Professor Burr; he liked her conception and encouraged her to enter the memorial competition. She put her design on paper, a task that took six weeks, and mailed it to Washington barely in time to meet the March 31 deadline.

A month and a day later, Maya Lin was attending class. Her roommate slipped into the classroom and handed her a note. Washington was calling and would call back in fifteen minutes. Maya Lin hurried to her room. The call came. She had won the memorial competition.

---

[2] **Somme offensive . . . World War I** a costly and largely unsuccessful Allied offensive that sustained roughly 615,000 casualties among British and French troops.

Thinking About the Selection

Always to Remember: The Vision of Maya Ying Lin

1 **Verify** Look at your predictions. Were you right? Identify the details that supported or contradicted your predictions.

_____
_____
_____

2 **Connect** Before reading this selection, did you have prior knowledge about the Vietnam War Memorial? How did this knowledge, or lack thereof, affect your predictions?

_____
_____
_____

3 **Predict** Based on Maya Ying Lin's accomplishments, what do you predict will happen to her next? What might she do?

_____
_____
_____

4 **Evaluate** What was the author's purpose in writing this article? How well did the author fulfill this purpose?

_____
_____
_____

5 **Conclude** Why is reading informational materials important? What can you gain from reading articles such as this one?

_____
_____
_____

Write Answer the following question on a separate piece of paper.

 6 **Assess** What is the most important truth in this article that you would share with someone?

Making Predictions 15

1-3 Vocabulary Building Strategies
Prefixes and Suffixes

Everyone has had the experience of encountering an unfamiliar word. When you get "stumped," try analyzing the parts of the word—prefixes, roots, and suffixes—to find clues to its meaning.

Prefix	Root	Suffix
A prefix is one or more syllables placed before the root to change its meaning.	A root is the basic meaning of a word.	A suffix is added to the end of a root to change its meaning or part of speech.

Common Prefixes		
pre-	before, in advance	predict: to tell in advance
re-	back, again	renew: make new again
ex-	from, out	extract: take out
in-	in, into	indent: bite into
inter-	between	international: between nations
mis-	wrong	misunderstand: understand incorrectly

Common Suffixes		
-yze	The suffixes -yze and -ize change words to verbs.	When you make an analysis, you *analyze* something.
-ize		When you make your decision final, you *finalize* it.
-tion	The suffixes -tion and –sion change verbs to nouns.	When you educate people, they receive an *education*.
-sion		When you persuade someone, you use *persuasion*.

Directions Figure out the meaning of each word below. Identify the prefix or suffix, then write your guess on the first line. Check your answers by looking up each word in either a bound or online dictionary, and write the definition on the second line.

1 misinterpret
My guess: _____

Dictionary meaning: _____

2 inflame
My guess: _____

Dictionary meaning: _____

3 location
My guess: _____

Dictionary meaning: _____

What to Do When You Encounter Unknown Words

Don't be held prisoner by words whose meaning you don't know. Remember that you have many tools, or strategies, to help you.

▶ Skip it! The word's meaning may be explained later.

Still struggling with the word? Try one of these steps.

▶ Use what you know about letters, sounds, and phonics to sound the word out to see if it is a word you know.

▶ Read the paragraph the word appears in aloud. See if you can use cueing systems, like context clues, to help you decode the word's meaning.

▶ Think about what you are reading. How might this word connect to the topic?

▶ Use the sentence structure to decide what part of speech the word may be.

▶ Associate the parts of the word (prefixes, root words, suffixes) with words you know.

Is not knowing the word's meaning preventing you from understanding the main idea of the reading?

▶ Look it up! Use a dictionary, thesaurus, glossary, or online resource to help you identify the word's meaning and pronunciation.

You may wish to keep a list of new words you have learned and identify connections among them (such as synonyms, antonyms, or words used to describe the same concept).

Ready? Start Reading Your Anchor Book It's time to get started. As you learn from this work text, your teacher will also give you reading assignments from your Anchor Book.

1-4 Writing About Your Anchor Book
Keeping a Reader's Journal

Introduction Throughout the year, you will keep a Reader's Journal for your Anchor Book. Your Reader's Journal will be a resource for you to help prepare you for discussions, assessments, and projects. You will use your journal for various purposes, such as the following.

- Answering questions in this book about your Anchor Book
- Writing notes recording ideas, thoughts, and questions about your Anchor Book
- Recording and analyzing important quotations from your Anchor Book

How to Set Up Your Reader's Journal

Whether you write your responses on a computer or in a notebook, be sure to set up your responses as demonstrated in the student model. If you are keeping your Reader's Journal in a notebook, write neatly in legible print or cursive.

As you read your Anchor Book, monitor your understanding of the book by writing down informal responses in your Reader's Journal. You can use these notes, questions, and ideas as the basis for discussions of your Anchor Book.

Student Model

Julio Melino   February 12

The Devil's Arithmetic by Jane Yolen
Confused about: Why does Fayge let herself get shot? How would the story be different if Rivka and Wolfe weren't related to Hannah?

Seems important: The image of a door—Chaya/Hannah chooses to enter the crematorium and that door brings her to her grandparents' home. The fact that the whole story happens on Passover

Tips for Writing Strong Responses

- Include specific details and quotations from your Anchor Book.
- Make connections among events, characters, and ideas in your Anchor Book to your own experience; to other books you have read; and to events, people, and ideas in the real world.

Julio Melino   February 15

Question: Why do authors of fiction sometimes use historical events as part of their fictional plots?

Answer: I think that authors of fiction use historical events to teach people about history in a way that is different from your typical history book. In *The Devil's Arithmetic,* Hannah gets a history book's version of the events from her grandparents. When she is transported back in time and taken to a concentration camp, the Holocaust becomes something she experiences first-hand. This book is a different way of learning about history because we learn it from a regular kid's perspective.

Directions Score the response and explain your scores in the "Comment" column.

RUBRIC FOR READER'S JOURNAL RESPONSES

Your response…	1 (Can Do Much Better) 2 (Okay) 3 (Nice Work) 4 (Excellent Job)	Comments
shows proof of deep thinking about what you are reading		
shows evidence that you are applying what you have learned about analyzing literature		
is long enough to explain your ideas fully		

while reading your anchor book

1-5 Analyzing an Informational Text

Reading a Diagram

There are many types of informational texts. Magazine articles, maps, schedules, newspaper articles, recipes, how-to manuals, and legal documents are just a few. Diagrams are an important part of many kinds of informational texts.

Examine how the diagram explains two versions of the greenhouse effect. Then, answer the questions that follow.

THE GREENHOUSE EFFECT:
Differences Between Natural and Amplified Warming

The Greenhouse Effect
The natural warming process by which gases in the Earth's atmosphere trap this energy is called the "greenhouse effect." Sunlight enters a greenhouse and is absorbed. The interior of the greenhouse radiates back energy in the form of infrared radiation, or heat. Much of the heat is trapped and held inside the greenhouse, warming it.

Most of the heat on the Earth comes from the Sun.

Amplified Greenhouse Effect
Many scientists hypothesize that human activities that add greenhouse gases to the atmosphere may increase the greenhouse effect and result in global warming, a gradual increase in the temperature of the Earth's atmosphere.

The Greenhouse Effect
1. Sunlight carries energy into the Earth's atmosphere.
2. The Earth's warmed surface emits infrared radiation.
3. This energy warms the lower atmosphere and is absorbed by greenhouse gases.
4. Some energy is released back toward the Earth's surface.
5. Some energy is released back into space.

Amplified Greenhouse Effect
1. Sunlight carries energy into the Earth's atmosphere.
2. The Earth's warmed surface emits infrared radiation.
3. This energy warms the lower atmosphere and is absorbed by greenhouse gases. Greater amounts of greenhouse gases mean that more heat is trapped in the atmosphere and radiated back toward the Earth's surface.

> A **diagram** is a graphic design that explains the relationships between parts of a whole.

> A **legend** is an important feature in informational texts. A legend is an explanatory list of the symbols on a map or chart.

while reading your anchor book

20 Lesson 1-5

1. **Examine** Analyzing a diagram involves reading in a different way. Instead of reading left to right, you read according to the path that the writer created. Do you have to start at one point for this diagram to make sense or can you start in different places? Explain.

2. **Identify** According to data included in the diagram, what happens when sunlight hits the Earth's surface and how does this affect the atmosphere?

3. **Compare** How does the author use the diagram to show the difference between natural and amplified warming?

4. **Infer** Think about what it means when a scientist hypothesizes. Why is the amplified greenhouse effect a hypothesis to explain global warming?

5. **Predict** Based on the information you learned in the diagram, what would cause a *decrease* in amplified warming?

6. **Evaluate** How does this diagram help you understand the greenhouse effect better than a text without a graphic would?

7. **Create** Complete the following task on a separate sheet of paper. Using a combination of words and pictures, create a diagram to explain the process of making a peanut butter and jelly sandwich.

Reading a Diagram

1-6 Literary Analysis
Narrative Texts

A narrative is a story. Every narrative shares the elements of character, conflict, plot, and setting. **Fiction** tells an imaginary narrative. A **nonfiction narrative** tells a story about real characters and events. In this type of narrative, the author must remain true to the facts.

Directions Think of an event in your life that introduced a problem or obstacle. Use that event to fill in the graphic organizer of narrative elements below.

Narrative Element	Question	Details of the Story
Character(s)	Who was involved?	
Conflict	What was the problem, challenge, or obstacle?	
Plot	What happened?	
Setting	Where and when did the event happen?	

You have just demonstrated how important details from your life can be given a narrative structure.

You have learned how to mark the text in order to make predictions. Now let's practice general guidelines for marking a text when you read.

Marking the Text

As you read, your eyes can quickly pass over a page without thinking too much about what you have just read. Marking the text helps slow you down so that you can identify the information you need and think more deeply about what it means. When you mark the text, you read first and then "talk back" to the text by deciding after each paragraph or section what is important enough to mark.

Guidelines for Marking the Text

In this book, you are going to read a variety of texts and learn how to mark the text for different purposes. You can mark any kind of text according to the following guidelines.

▶ **Use the margin to record your thoughts.**

- If a detail you read seems important, jot down notes to explain why you think it is important.

- Write down connections between what you are reading and what you have discussed in class, read about in other books, experienced yourself, or heard about happening in the world.

▶ **Ask yourself questions as you read.** To help train yourself to do this, try writing questions in the margin or in your Reader's Journal. These questions can serve as reminders of areas of confusion or disagreement with the author, as well as topics for discussion.

▶ **Draw a box around unfamiliar words.** See if you can get the meaning from context clues. If not, use a dictionary to find the meaning. Write the meaning in the margin.

▶ **Develop your own "code."** There is no need to write full sentences. Here are some symbol codes you can use.

✓	I knew that.
?	What does this mean? I am confused.
★	This seems important.
✗	I disagree.

Directions Read the passage and student model of marking the text. Then, answer the question that follows.

Student Model: Marking the Text

```
The Pledge of Allegiance

I pledge allegiance to the Flag           Flag = nation
of the United States of America,

and to the Republic for which it stands,
one Nation, under God, [indivisible,] ★   indivisible = cannot be
with liberty and justice for all.         broken
```

How does the student's marking of the text help you think about the text more deeply?

while reading your anchor book

Narrative Texts **23**

Directions Now read the following memoir, or nonfiction narrative. As you read, mark the text according to the guidelines.

from "Water Man Comics" by Dav Pilkey

I first started drawing the Water Man Comics in 1977, when I was eleven years old. My parents actually encouraged me to make these comics. They weren't too fond of my Captain Underpants and Diaper Man comics, and were trying to persuade me to make comics that were a little less "potty oriented."

So I began in November of 1977, and over the next few months compiled twenty issues of my Water Man Epic Saga. These comics featured not only Water Man and his crime-fighting pals Molecule Man and Mr. Shape-O, but also a cast of famous bad guys, including King Kong, the Invisible Man, and Jaws 2.

I started each comic by grabbing a big stack of paper. My dad always brought home paper from work for me to draw on (you might see the Republic Steel logo bleeding through some of the pages). I went through the paper as fast as my dad could bring it home.

I made my comics up as I went along. I started with the title, then made up the stories as I drew the pictures (much the same way I do today). Sometimes it worked out great … other times it didn't. For example, in the comic "We Must Destroy Water Man," there's only one bad guy. Who's the we? I didn't know then, and I don't know now. Often these comics contain misspelled words, and sometimes you can tell where my pen started running out of ink as the pages piled up. But that didn't stop me. I was on a roll.

While none of these comics are masterpieces, they always remind me of the homemade comics that children now send me every day. They have the same spirit. There's something about the work of a kid who is being creative on his or her own time. Nobody forces a kid to make a comic book. Kids just do it sometimes. And there is always something wonderful about that kind of spontaneous creativity. It's magic!

I'm really grateful that my parents encouraged me to make these comics, and even more grateful that they refused to let me bring them to school. I begged and pleaded, but they always said no. All of my other comics (including the ones I made in junior and high school) have disappeared. Some were torn up by angry teachers, others were borrowed by friends who never returned them, and some just got lost. But because my parents had forbidden me to take these comics to school, I still have every single one of them. They're the only childhood comics I have left. Don't you hate it when your parents are right?

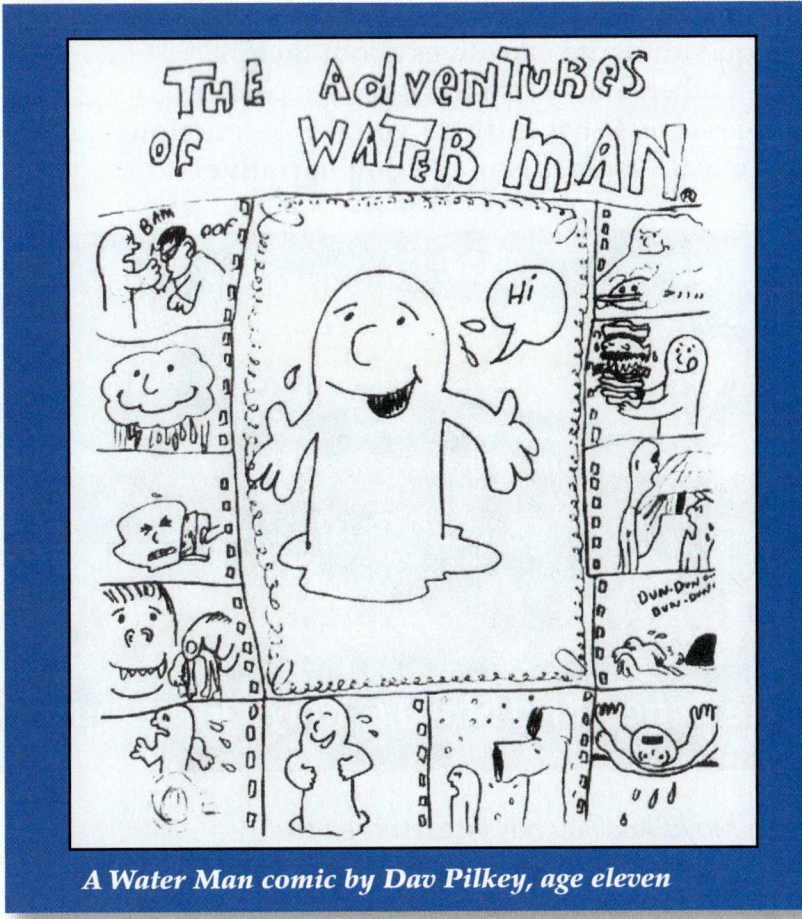

A Water Man comic by Dav Pilkey, age eleven

1 **Identify** What elements of narrative are in this memoir?

_____
_____

2 **Explain** Describe the plot. How do the characters and conflict influence the plot?

_____
_____
_____
_____
_____

3 **Respond** Pilkey is grateful to his parents for influencing his comics. How would you feel toward your parents if you were in a similar situation? Would you consider them meddlesome, intrusive, or concerned?

_____
_____
_____

while reading your anchor book

Narrative Texts 25

People frequently write narratives about their lives so that others may learn from their experience.
Guiding Question: What truth do you think Angelou wants us to learn from this nonfiction narrative?

Occupation: Conductorette

from *I Know Why the Caged Bird Sings* by Maya Angelou

Background The young Maya Angelou has just returned to San Francisco after an adventure-filled trip. Things are changing at home, she discovers, and her brother moves out soon after her return. Restless and discontented, Angelou ponders her next step.

Vocabulary Builder

Before you read, you will discuss the following words. In the Vocabulary Builder box in the margin, use a vocabulary building strategy to make the words your own.

self-sufficiency   dingy   supercilious

As you read, draw a box around unfamiliar words you could add to your vocabulary. Use context clues to unlock their meaning.

Marking the Text

Narrative Texts

As you read, analyze the text for elements of narrative nonfiction. Underline words and phrases that help you understand a nonfiction narrative. Write any questions you have in the margins.

I had it. The answer came to me with the suddenness of a collision. I would go to work. Mother wouldn't be difficult to convince; after all, in school I was a year ahead of my grade and Mother was a firm believer in **self-sufficiency.** In fact, she'd be pleased to think that I had that much gumption, that much of her in my character. (She liked to speak of herself as the original "do-it-yourself girl.")

Vocabulary Builder

self-sufficiency
(self sə fish' ən sē) *n.*

Meaning

Once I had settled on getting a job, all that remained was to decide which kind of job I was most fitted for. My intellectual pride had kept me from selecting typing, shorthand or filing as subjects in school, so office work was ruled out. War plants and shipyards demanded birth certificates, and mine would reveal me to be fifteen, and ineligible for work. So the well-paying defense jobs were also out. Women had replaced men on the streetcars as conductors and motormen, and the thought of sailing up and down the hills of San Francisco in a dark-blue uniform, with a money changer at my belt, caught my fancy.

Mother was as easy as I had anticipated. The world was moving so fast, so much money was being made, so many people were dying in Guam, and Germany,[1] that hordes of strangers became good friends overnight. Life was cheap and death entirely free. How could she have the time to think about my academic career?

To her question of what I planned to do, I replied that I would get a job on the streetcars. She rejected the proposal with: "They don't accept colored people on the streetcars."

I would like to claim an immediate fury which was followed by the noble determination to break the restricting tradition. But the truth is, my first reaction was one of disappointment. I'd pictured myself, dressed in a neat blue serge suit, my money changer swinging jauntily at my waist, and a cheery smile for the passengers which would make their own work day brighter.

From disappointment, I gradually ascended the emotional ladder to haughty indignation, and finally to that sad state

---

[1] **Guam** (gwäm) **and Germany** were places where World War II (1939–1945) was fought. Guam is an island in the Pacific Ocean.

Marking the Text

◀ **Good to Know!**
During World War II, women often worked in factories making equipment for the war. As a result of this social change, many women became more assertive in the workplace.

of stubbornness where the mind is locked like the jaws of an enraged bulldog.

I would go to work on the streetcars and wear a blue serge suit. Mother gave me her support with one of her usual terse asides, "That's what you want to do? Then nothing beats a trial but a failure. Give it everything you've got. I've told you many times, 'Can't Do is like Don't Care.' Neither of them have a home."

Translated, that meant there was nothing a person can't do, and there should be nothing a human being didn't care about. It was the most positive encouragement I could have hoped for.

In the offices of the Market Street Railway Company, the receptionist seemed as surprised to see me there as I was surprised to find the interior **dingy** and the décor drab. Somehow I had expected waxed surfaces and carpeted floors. If I had met no resistance, I might have decided against working for such a poor-mouth-looking concern. As it was, I explained that I had come to see about a job. She asked, was I sent by an agency, and when I replied that I was not, she told me they were only accepting applicants from agencies.

The classified pages of the morning papers had listed advertisements for motorettes and conductorettes and I reminded her of that. She gave me a face full of astonishment that my suspicious nature would not accept.

"I am applying for the job listed in this morning's *Chronicle* and I'd like to be presented to your personnel manager." While I spoke in **supercilious** accents, and looked at the room as if I had an oil well in my own backyard, my armpits were being pricked by millions of hot pointed needles. She saw her escape and dived into it.

"He's out. He's out for the day. You might call tomorrow and if he's in, I'm sure you can see him." Then she swiveled her chair around on its rusty screws and with that I was supposed to be dismissed.

"May I ask his name?"

She half turned, acting surprised to find me still there.

"His name? Whose name?"

"Your personnel manager."

We were firmly joined in the hypocrisy to play out the scene.

"The personnel manager? Oh, he's Mr. Cooper, but I'm not sure you'll find him here tomorrow. He's …Oh, but you can try."

"Thank you."

"You're welcome."

And I was out of the musty room and into the even mustier lobby. In the street I saw the receptionist and myself going faithfully through paces that were stale with familiarity, although I had never encountered that kind of situation before and, probably, neither had she. We were like actors who, knowing the

Vocabulary Builder

dingy
(din′ jē) *adj.*

Meaning

supercilious
(soo′ pər sil′ē əs) *adj.*

Meaning

play by heart, were still able to cry afresh over the old tragedies and laugh spontaneously at the comic situations.

The miserable little encounter had nothing to do with me, the me of me, any more than it had to do with that silly clerk. The incident was a recurring dream concocted years before by stupid whites and it eternally came back to haunt us all. The secretary and I were like Hamlet and Laertes[2] in the final scene, where, because of harm done by one ancestor to another, we were bound to duel to the death. Also, because the play must end somewhere.

I went further than forgiving the clerk, I accepted her as a fellow victim of the same puppeteer.

On the streetcar, I put my fare into the box and the conductorette looked at me with the usual hard eyes of white contempt. "Move into the car, please move on in the car." She patted her money changer.

Her Southern nasal accent sliced my meditation and I looked deep into my thoughts. All lies, all comfortable lies. The receptionist was not innocent and neither was I. The whole charade we had played out in that crummy waiting room had directly to do with me, Black, and her, White.

I wouldn't move into the streetcar but stood on the ledge over the conductor, glaring. My mind shouted so energetically that the announcement made my veins stand out, and my mouth tighten into a prune.

I WOULD HAVE THE JOB. I WOULD BE A CONDUCTORETTE AND SLING A FULL MONEY CHANGER FROM MY BELT. I WOULD.

---

[2] **Hamlet and Laertes** characters in William Shakespeare's tragedy *Hamlet* who duel at the end of the play.

▼ **Critical Viewing**
The photograph shows a streetcar in the 1940s, when racial segregation was accepted by many. Do you think the job might have been difficult for Angelou? Why or why not?

Literature in Context
San Francisco and the Gold Rushes

Link to Social Studies

When she looks at the buildings of San Francisco, Angelou thinks of names associated with the gold rushes of the 1800s:

- **Forty-Niners** the prospectors who poured into the San Francisco area in the California Gold Rush of 1849. They transformed San Francisco from a small town of 800 to a rough-and-tumble city of 25,000.

- **Robert Service** poet who portrayed the miners of the Yukon gold rush of the 1890s

- **John Augustus Sutter** owner of the sawmill where gold was first discovered in California

- **Jack London** writer who recreated his experiences in the Yukon Gold rush in stories and the novel *Call of the Wild* (1903)

The next three weeks were a honeycomb[3] of determination with apertures for the days to go in and out. The Negro organizations to whom I appealed for support bounced me back and forth like a shuttlecock on a badminton court. Why did I insist on that particular job? Openings were going begging that paid nearly twice the money. The minor officials with whom I was able to win an audience thought me mad. Possibly I was.

Downtown San Francisco became alien and cold, and the streets I had loved in a personal familiarity were unknown lanes that twisted with malicious intent. Old buildings, whose gray rococo façades[4] housed my memories of Forty-Niners, and Diamond Lil, Robert Service, Sutter and Jack London, were then imposing structures viciously joined to keep me out. My trips to the streetcar office were of the frequency of a person on salary. The struggle expanded. I was no longer in conflict only with the Market Street Railway but with the marble lobby of the building, which housed its offices, and elevators and their operators.

During this period of strain Mother and I began our first steps on the long path toward mutual adult admiration. She never asked for reports and I didn't offer any details. But every morning she made breakfast, gave me carfare and lunch money, as if I were going to work. She comprehended the perversity of life, that in the struggle lies the joy. That I was no glory seeker was obvious to her, and that I had to exhaust every possibility before giving in was also clear.

On my way out of the house one morning she said, "Life is going to give you just what you put in it. Put your whole heart in everything you do and pray, then you can wait."

---

[3] **honeycomb** (hun' ē kōm) wax structure, filled with holes, that bees build to store honey.

[4] **rococo façades** (rə kō' kō fə säds') elaborately designed front sides of buildings.

Marking the Text

Good to Know!
Footnotes are a common text feature. They provide information that helps your understanding of the text without distracting you from the body of the text.

while reading your anchor book

Another time she reminded me that "God helps those who help themselves." She had a store of aphorisms which she dished out as the occasion demanded. Strangely, as bored as I was with clichés, her inflection gave them something new, and set me thinking for a little while at least. Later, when asked how I got my job, I was never able to say exactly. I only knew that one day, which was tiresomely like all the others before it, I sat in the Railway office, ostensibly waiting to be interviewed. The receptionist called me to her desk and shuffled a bundle of papers to me. They were job application forms. She said they had to be filled in triplicate. I had little time to wonder if I had won or not, for the standard questions reminded me of the necessity for dexterous lying. How old was I? List my previous jobs, starting from the last held and go backward to the first. How much money did I earn, and why did I leave the position? Give two references (not relatives).

Sitting at a side table my mind and I wove a cat's ladder of near truths and total lies. I kept my face blank (an old art) and wrote quickly the fable of Marguerite Johnson, aged nineteen, former companion and driver for Mrs. Annie Henderson (a White lady) in Stamps, Arkansas.

I was given blood tests, aptitude tests, physical coordination tests, and Rorschachs,[5] then on a blissful day I was hired as the first Negro on the San Francisco streetcars.

Mother gave me the money to have my blue serge suit tailored, and I learned to fill out work cards, operate the money changer and punch transfers. The time crowded together and at an End of Days

Marking the Text

---

[5] **Rorschachs** (rôr′ shäks′) The Rorschach test is a method of analyzing an individual's personality using abstract images.

I was swinging on the back of the rackety trolley, smiling sweetly and persuading my charges to "step forward in the car, please."

For one whole semester the streetcars and I shimmied up and scooted down the sheer hills of San Francisco. I lost some of my need for the Black ghetto's shielding-sponge quality, as I clanged and cleared my way down Market Street, with its honky-tonk homes for homeless sailors, at the quiet retreat of Golden Gate Park and along closed undwelled-in-looking dwellings of the Sunset District.

My work shifts were split so haphazardly that it was easy to believe that my superiors had chosen them maliciously. Upon mentioning my suspicions to Mother, she said, "Don't worry about it. You ask for what you want, and you pay for what you get. And I'm going to show you that it ain't no trouble when you pack double."

She stayed awake to drive me out to the car barn at four thirty in the mornings, or to pick me up when I was relieved just before dawn. Her awareness of life's perils convinced her that while I would be safe on the public conveyances, she "wasn't about to trust a taxi driver with her baby."

When the spring classes began, I resumed my commitment for formal education. I was so much wiser and older, so much more independent, with a bank account and clothes that I had bought for myself, that I was sure that I had learned and earned the magic formula which would make me a part of the gay life my contemporaries led.

Vocabulary Builder

After you read, review the words you decided to add to your vocabulary. Write the meaning of words you have learned in context. Look up the other words in a dictionary, glossary, thesaurus, or electronic resource.

Maya Angelou (b. 1928)

Maya Angelou was born in St. Louis, Missouri. She is best known as the author of *I Know Why the Caged Bird Sings*. Angelou has had many accomplishments in her work as a writer, dancer, teacher, and actress. She was nominated for an Emmy for her role in the television miniseries *Roots*. She was nominated for a National Book Award and a Pulitzer Prize, and won Grammy Awards for spoken word poetry. She is an inspiration and a symbol of pride for women, especially African American women.

Thinking About the Selection

Occupation: Conductorette

1 **Recall** What is the conflict in this story? Describe it.

2 **Analyze** How does the historical setting affect Maya Angelou's experience in getting a job? Explain.

3 **Analyze** How did this life experience affect Maya Angelou's life and shape her perspective of the world around her? Use evidence from the story to prove your point.

4 **Speculate** What was the author's purpose for writing this story? Why did she choose to write it in the form of a nonfiction narrative?

Write Answer the following questions in your Reader's Journal.

5 **Interpret** What truth do you think Angelou wants us to learn from this nonfiction narrative? If Angelou had used a different literary genre—such as fiction—to express the theme of this text, would the text have been as powerful? Explain why or why not.

6 **Analyze** Describe one of the narrative elements in your Anchor Book. Explain the importance of that element to the book.

1-7 Literary Analysis
Conflict

Conflict is a problem that a character must overcome. It is the most important literary element of fiction and narrative non-fiction. If there is no conflict, there is no story.

Literary Terms

- **Conflict** is a struggle between opposing forces.
- An **external conflict** occurs when a character struggles against some outside force, such as another character, nature, or society.
- An **internal conflict** occurs within the mind of a character who struggles with opposing feelings, beliefs, needs, or choices.

Directions Read the following examples of external and internal conflicts. Then, write an example of each type of conflict.

EXTERNAL CONFLICT Character Versus Character

In this type of conflict, the main character struggles against another character.
Example Maria wants her mother to give her more independence.

---

1 Give an example of a conflict a character might have with another character.

EXTERNAL CONFLICT Character Versus the World

In this type of conflict, a character struggles against some aspect of nature or society.
Example Susan B. Anthony fought the U.S. government for women's rights.

---

2 Give an example of a conflict a character might have with society.

INTERNAL CONFLICT Character Versus Self

In this type of conflict, a character struggles to make a decision, or overcome a feeling.
Example Ethan wants to be in the school play, but he is too shy.

---

3 Give an example of a conflict a character might experience within his or her own mind.

Directions Read the following passage. Underline details that reveal the conflict, and then answer the questions that follow.

from *"Tears of Autumn"* by Yoshiko Uchida

Hana Omiya stood at the railing of the small ship that shuddered toward America in a turbulent November sea. She shivered as she pulled the folds of her silk kimono close to her chest and tightened the wool shawl about her shoulders.

She was thin and small, her dark eyes shadowed in her pale face, her black hair piled high in a pompadour that seemed too heavy for so slight a woman. She clung to the moist rail and breathed the damp salt air deep into her lungs. Her body seemed laden and lifeless, as though it were simply the vehicle transporting her soul to a strange new life, and she longed with childlike intensity to be home again in Oka Village.

She longed to see the bright persimmon dotting the barren trees beside the thatched roofs, to see the fields of golden rice stretching to the mountains where only last fall she had gathered plump white mushrooms, and to see once more the maple trees lacing their flaming colors through the green pine. If only she could see a familiar face, eat a meal without retching, walk on solid ground, and stretch out at night on a tatami mat instead of in a hard narrow bunk. She thought now of seeking the warm shelter of her bunk but could not bear to face the relentless smell of fish that penetrated the lower decks.

Why did I ever leave Japan? she wondered bitterly. Why did I ever listen to my uncle? And yet she knew it was she herself who had begun the chain of events that placed her on this heaving ship. It was she who had first planted in her uncle's mind the thought that she would make a good wife for Taro Takeda, the lonely man who had gone to America to make his fortune in Oakland, California.

4 **Analyze** What is the conflict? How does Hana Omiya's situation create this conflict? Explain.

_____
_____
_____
_____
_____

Understanding Plot

You have learned that without a conflict, there is no story. **Plot** is the sequence of events that shows how the conflict in a narrative develops and is finally resolved.

Literary Terms

Plot describes both events in the story and phases of the story (beginning, middle, and end). The plot in most stories follows a pattern that has five parts.

- The **exposition** is the beginning of the story. It introduces the characters, the setting, and the basic situation.

- The **rising action** introduces the central conflict. During the rising action, the conflict builds in intensity.

- The **climax** is the point in the plot when the conflict reaches its greatest intensity. This is also called a turning point.

- The **falling action** consists of everything that happens after the climax, as the conflict starts to wind down and move toward a resolution.

- The **resolution** resolves the conflict and ties up all the plot's loose ends.

Because most of you are familiar with the fairy tale "Snow White and the Seven Dwarfs," it is a good story to analyze in a plot diagram.

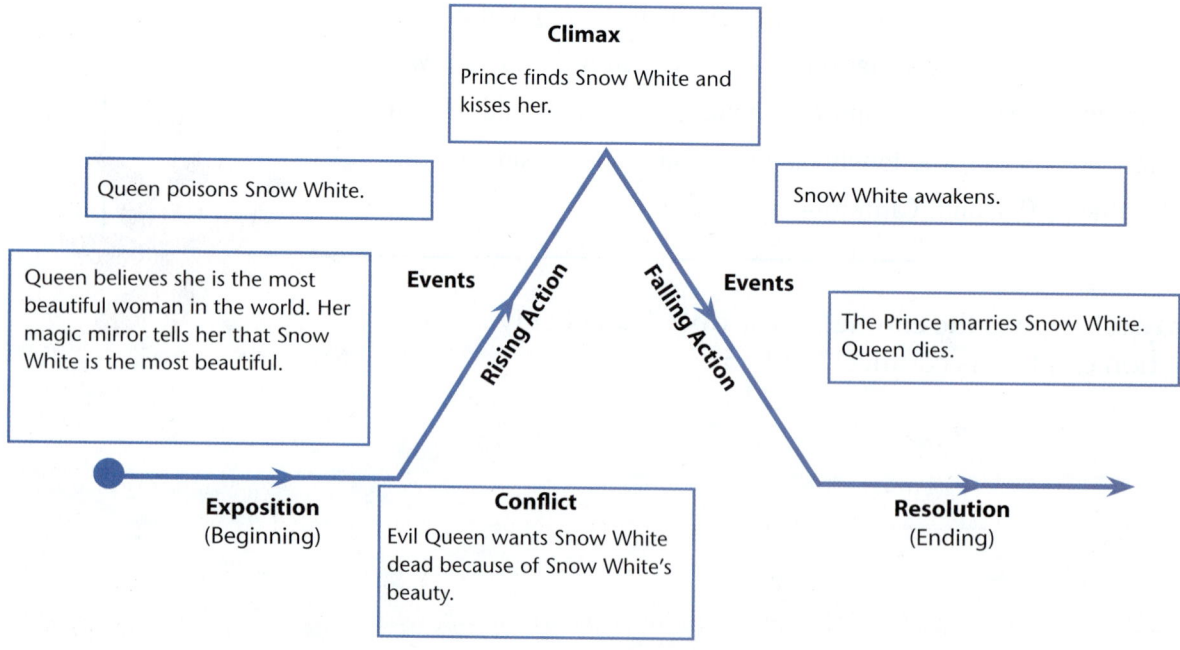

while reading your anchor book

Lesson 1-7

Marking the Text for Plot

Now see if you can identify the elements of plot in this selection.

▶ As you read, underline the most important events.

▶ After you read, identify each element of plot in the margin.

Note that neither rising action nor falling action is one specific event. They describe how the plot moves toward the climax (rising action) and toward the resolution (falling action).

The Attic by Alvin Schwartz

A man named Rupert lived with his dog in a house deep in the woods. Rupert was a hunter and a trapper. The dog was a big German shepherd named Sam. Rupert had raised Sam from a pup.

Almost every morning Rupert went hunting, and Sam stayed behind and guarded the house. One morning, as Rupert was checking his traps, he got the feeling that something was wrong at home.

He hurried back as fast as he could, but when he got there he found that Sam was missing. He searched the house and the woods nearby, but Sam was nowhere to be seen. He called and he called, but the dog did not answer. For days Rupert looked for Sam, but he could find no trace of him.

Finally he gave up and went back to his work. But one morning he heard something moving in the attic. He picked up a baseball bat. Then he thought, "I'd better be quiet about this."

So he took off his boots. And in his bare feet he began to climb the attic stairs. He slowly took one step—then another—then another, until at last he reached the attic door.

He stood outside listening, but he didn't hear a thing. Then he opened the door, and—

"AAAAAAAAAAH!"

(At this point, the storyteller stops, as if he has finished. Then usually somebody will ask,

"Why did Rupert scream?"

The storyteller replies, "You'd scream too if you stepped on a nail in your bare feet.")

Analyze What is the conflict in this passage? How do you know?

_____

_____

Now, read the following short story and focus on plot.
Guiding Question: Does the resolution seem true to life? Why or why not?

Amigo Brothers
by Piri Thomas

Background The annual Golden Gloves tournament is probably the most famous amateur boxing event in the United States. Local and regional elimination bouts lead to final championship matches. Notice that the title of the story is a mixture of Spanish and English: *amigo* is Spanish for "friend." (For English translations of other Spanish words in the story, see "Literature in Context.")

Vocabulary Builder

Before you read, you will discuss the following words. In the Vocabulary Builder box in the margin, use a vocabulary building strategy to make the words your own.

pensively   dispelled   feinted   savagery

As you read, draw a box around unfamiliar words you could add to your vocabulary. Use context clues to unlock their meaning.

Marking the Text

Conflict and Plot

As you read, underline important details that establish and develop the conflict. In the margin, write notes that identify the events that form the five main parts of the plot.

Antonio Cruz and Felix Vargas were both seventeen years old. They were so together in friendship that they felt themselves to be brothers. They had known each other since childhood, growing up on the lower east side of Manhattan in the same tenement building on Fifth Street between Avenue A and Avenue B.

Antonio was fair, lean, and lanky, while Felix was dark, short, and husky. Antonio's hair was always falling over his eyes, while Felix wore his black hair in a natural Afro style.

Each youngster had a dream of someday becoming lightweight champion of the world. Every chance they had the boys worked out, sometimes at the Boys Club on 10th Street and Avenue A and sometimes at the pro's gym on 14th Street. Early morning sunrises would find them running along the East River Drive, wrapped in sweat shirts, short towels around their necks, and handkerchiefs Apache style around their foreheads.

While some youngsters were into street negatives, Antonio and Felix slept, ate, rapped, and dreamt positive. Between them, they had a collection of *Fight* magazines second to none, plus a scrapbook filled with torn tickets to every boxing match they had ever attended, and some clippings of their own. If asked a question about any given fighter, they would immediately zip out from their memory banks divisions, weights, records of fights, knock-outs, technical knock-outs, and draws or losses.

Each had fought many bouts representing their community and had won two gold-plated medals plus a silver and bronze medallion. The difference was in their style. Antonio's lean form and long reach made him the better boxer, while Felix's short and muscular frame made him the better slugger. Whenever they had met in the ring for sparring sessions, it had always been hot and heavy.

Now, after a series of elimination bouts, they had been informed that they were to meet each other in the division finals that were scheduled for the seventh of August, two weeks away—the winner to represent the Boys Club in the Golden Gloves Championship Tournament.

The two boys continued to run together along the East River Drive. But even when joking with each other, they both sensed a wall rising between them.

One morning, less than a week before their bout, they met as usual for their daily work-out. They fooled around with a few jabs at the air, slapped skin, and then took off, running lightly along the dirty East River's edge.

Antonio glanced at Felix who kept his eyes purposely straight ahead, pausing from time to time to do some fancy leg work while throwing one-twos followed by upper cuts to an imaginary jaw. Antonio then beat the air with a barrage of body blows and short devastating lefts with an overhand jaw-breaking right. After a mile or so, Felix puffed and said, "Let's stop a while, bro. I think we both got something to say to each other." Antonio nodded. It was not natural to be acting as though nothing unusual was happening when two ace-boon buddies were going to be blasting each other within a few short days.

They rested their elbows on the railing separating them from the river. Antonio wiped his face with his short towel. The sunrise was now creating day.

Felix leaned heavily on the river's railing and stared across to the shores of Brooklyn. Finally, he broke the silence.

"Man, I don't know how to come out with it."

Antonio helped. "It's about our fight, right?"

"Yeah, right." Felix's eyes squinted at the rising orange sun.

"I've been thinking about it too, *panín*. In fact, since we found out it was going to be me and you, I've been awake at night, pulling punches on you, trying not to hurt you."

"Same here. It ain't natural not to think about the fight. I mean, we both are *cheverote* fighters and we both want to win. But only one of us can win. There ain't no draws in the eliminations."

Felix tapped Antonio gently on the shoulder. "I don't mean to sound like I'm bragging, bro. But I wanna win, fair and square."

Antonio nodded quietly. "Yeah. We both know that in the ring the better man wins. Friend or no friend, brother or no . . ."

Felix finished it for him. "Brother. Tony, let's promise something right here. Okay?"

"If it's fair, *hermano*, I'm for it." Antonio admired the courage of a tugboat pulling a barge five times its welterweight size.

"It's fair, Tony. When we get into the ring, it's gotta be like we never met. We gotta be like two heavy strangers that want the same thing and only one can have it. You understand, don'tcha?"

"*Sí*, I know." Tony smiled. "No pulling punches. We go all the way."

"Yeah, that's right. Listen, Tony. Don't you think it's a good idea if we don't see each other until the day of the fight? I'm going to stay with my Aunt Lucy in the Bronx. I can use Gleason's Gym for working out. My manager says he got some sparring partners with more or less your style."

Tony scratched his nose **pensively**. "Yeah, it would be better for our heads." He held out his hand, palm upward. "Deal?"

Marking the Text

Vocabulary Builder

pensively
(pen′ siv lē) *adv.*

Meaning

Literature in Context
Spanish Words

Throughout the story, the author uses Spanish words to reflect the flavor of life for the two Puerto Rican main characters:

- **amigo** (ə mē′ gō) *adj.* friend (usually a noun but used here as an adjective).
- **panín** (pä nēn′) *n.* pal.
- **cheverote** (che bā rō′tā) the greatest.
- **hermano** (er mä′ nō) *n.* brother.
- **suavecito** (swä ve sē′ tō) take it easy
- **sabe** (sä bā) *v.* understand. (Used here as part of a question.)
- **salsa** (säl′ sä) *n.* Latin American music.
- **Señores y Señoras** (se nyō′ res ē se nyō′ räs) Gentlemen and Ladies.
- **mucho corazón** (moō′ chō kô rä sôn′) much courage.

"Deal." Felix lightly slapped open skin.

"Ready for some more running?" Tony asked lamely.

"Naw, bro. Let's cut it here. You go on. I kinda like to get things together in my head."

"You ain't worried, are you?" Tony asked.

"No way, man." Felix laughed out loud. "I got too much smarts for that. I just think it's cooler if we split right here. After the fight, we can get it together again like nothing ever happened."

The amigo brothers were not ashamed to hug each other tightly.

"Guess you're right. Watch yourself, Felix. I hear there's some pretty heavy dudes up in the Bronx. *Suavecito*, okay?"

"Okay. You watch yourself too, *sabe*?"

Tony jogged away. Felix watched his friend disappear from view, throwing rights and lefts. Both fighters had a lot of psyching up to do before the big fight.

The days in training passed much too slowly. Although they kept out of each other's way, they were aware of each other's progress via the ghetto grapevine.

The evening before the big fight, Tony made his way to the roof of his tenement. In the quiet early dark, he peered over the ledge. Six stories below the lights of the city blinked and the sounds of cars mingled with the curses and the laughter of children in the street. He tried not to think of Felix, feeling he had succeeded in psyching his mind. But only in the ring would he really know. To spare Felix hurt, he would have to knock him out, early and quick.

Up in the South Bronx, Felix decided to take in a movie in an effort to keep Antonio's face away from his fists. The flick was *The Champion* with Kirk Douglas, the third time Felix was seeing it.

The champion was getting hit hard. He was saved only by the sound of the bell.

Felix became the champ and Tony the challenger.

The movie audience was going out of its head. The challenger, confident that he had the championship in the bag, threw a left. The champ countered with a dynamite right.

Felix's right arm felt the shock. Antonio's face, superimposed on the screen, was hit by the awesome blow. Felix saw himself in the ring, blasting Antonio against the ropes. The champ had to be forcibly restrained. The challenger was allowed to crumble slowly to the canvas.

When Felix finally left the theatre, he had figured out how to psyche himself for tomorrow's fight. It was Felix the Champion vs. Antonio the Challenger.

He walked up some dark streets, deserted except for small pockets of wary-looking kids wearing gang colors. Despite the fact that he was Puerto Rican like them, they eyed him as a stranger to their turf. Felix did a fast shuffle, bobbing and weaving, while letting loose a torrent of blows that would demolish whatever got in its way. It seemed to impress the brothers, who went about their own business.

Finding no takers, Felix decided to split to his aunt's. Walking the streets had not relaxed him, neither had the fight flick. All it had done was to stir him up. He let himself quietly into his Aunt Lucy's apartment and went straight to bed, falling into a fitful sleep with sounds of the gong for Round One.

Antonio was passing some heavy time on his rooftop. How would the fight tomorrow affect his relationship with Felix? After all, fighting was like any other profession. Friendship had nothing to do with it. A gnawing doubt crept in. He cut negative thinking real quick by doing some speedy fancy dance steps, bobbing and weaving like mercury.[1] The night air was blurred with perpetual motions of left hooks and right crosses. Felix, his amigo brother, was not going to be Felix at all in the ring. Just an opponent with another face. Antonio went to sleep, hearing the opening bell for the first round. Like his friend in the South Bronx, he prayed for victory, via a quick clean knock-out in the first round.

Large posters plastered all over the walls of local shops announced the fight between Antonio Cruz and Felix Vargas as the main bout.

The fight had created great interest in the neighborhood. Antonio and Felix were well liked and respected. Each had his own loyal following. Antonio's fans counted on his boxing skills. On the other side, Felix's admirers trusted in his dynamite-packed fists.

Felix had returned to his apartment early in the morning of August 7th and stayed there, hoping to avoid seeing Antonio. He

---

[1] **mercury** (mər′ kyə rē) *n.* element also known as quicksilver because it moves so quickly and fluidly.

turned the radio on to salsa music sounds and then tried to read while waiting for word from his manager.

The fight was scheduled to take place in Tompkins Square Park. It had been decided that the gymnasium of the Boys Club was not large enough to hold all the people who were sure to attend. In Tompkins Square Park, everyone who wanted could view the fight, whether from ringside or window fire escapes or tenement rooftops.

The morning of the fight Tompkins Square was a beehive of activity with numerous workers setting up the ring, the seats, and the guest speakers' stand. The scheduled bouts began shortly after noon and the park had begun filling up even earlier.

The local junior high school across from Tompkins Square Park served as the dressing room for all the fighters. Each was given a separate classroom with desk tops, covered with mats, serving as resting tables. Antonio thought he caught a glimpse of Felix waving to him from a room at the far end of the corridor. He waved back just in case it had been him.

The fighters changed from their street clothes into fighting gear. Antonio wore white trunks, black socks, and black shoes. Felix wore sky blue trunks, red socks, and white boxing shoes. Each had dressing gowns to match their fighting trunks with their names neatly stitched on the back.

Marking the Text

The loudspeakers blared into the open windows of the school. There were speeches by dignitaries, community leaders, and great boxers of yesteryear. Some were well prepared, some improvised on the spot. They all carried the same message of great pleasure and honor at being part of such a historic event. This great day was in the tradition of champions emerging from the streets of the lower east side.

Interwoven with the speeches were the sounds of the other boxing events. After the sixth bout, Felix was much relieved when his trainer Charlie said, "Time change. Quick knock-out. This is it. We're on."

Waiting time was over. Felix was escorted from the classroom by a dozen fans in white T-shirts with the word FELIX across their fronts.

Antonio was escorted down a different stairwell and guided through a roped-off path.

As the two climbed into the ring, the crowd exploded with a roar. Antonio and Felix both bowed gracefully and then raised their arms in acknowledgment.

Antonio tried to be cool, but even as the roar was in its first birth, he turned slowly to meet Felix's eyes looking directly into his. Felix nodded his head and Antonio responded. And both as one, just as quickly, turned away to face his own corner.

Bong—bong—bong. The roar turned to stillness.

"Ladies and Gentlemen. *Señores y Señoras*."

The announcer spoke slowly, pleased at his bilingual efforts.

"Now the moment we have all been waiting for—the main event between two fine young Puerto Rican fighters, products of our lower east side. In this corner, weighing 134 pounds, Felix Vargas. And in this corner, weighing 133 pounds, Antonio Cruz. The winner will represent the Boys Club in the tournament of champions, the Golden Gloves. There will be no draw. May the best man win."

The cheering of the crowd shook the window panes of the old buildings surrounding Tompkins Square Park. At the center of the ring, the referee was giving instructions to the youngsters.

"Keep your punches up. No low blows. No punching on the back of the head. Keep your heads up. Understand. Let's have a clean fight. Now shake hands and come out fighting."

Both youngsters touched gloves and nodded. They turned and danced quickly to their corners. Their head towels and dressing gowns were lifted neatly from their shoulders by their trainers' nimble fingers. Antonio crossed himself. Felix did the same.

BONG! BONG! ROUND ONE. Felix and Antonio turned and faced each other squarely in a fighting pose. Felix wasted no time. He came in fast, head low, half hunched toward his right shoulder, and lashed out with a straight left. He missed a right cross as Antonio slipped the punch and countered with one-two-three lefts that snapped Felix's head back, sending a mild shock coursing through him. If Felix had any small doubt about their friendship affecting their fight, it was being neatly **dispelled**.

Antonio danced, a joy to behold. His left hand was like a piston pumping jabs one right after another with seeming ease. Felix bobbed and weaved and never stopped boring in. He knew that at long range he was at a disadvantage. Antonio had too much reach on him. Only by coming in close could Felix hope to achieve the dreamed-of knock-out.

Antonio knew the dynamite that was stored in his amigo brother's fist. He ducked a short right and missed a left hook. Felix trapped him against the ropes just long enough to pour some punishing rights and lefts to Antonio's hard midsection. Antonio slipped away from Felix, crashing two lefts to his head, which set Felix's right ear to ringing.

Bong! Both *amigos* froze a punch well on its way, sending up a roar of approval for good sportsmanship.

Felix walked briskly back to his corner. His right ear had not stopped ringing. Antonio gracefully danced his way toward his stool, none the worse except for glowing glove burns, showing angry red against the whiteness of his midribs.

"Watch that right, Tony." His trainer talked into his ear. "Remember Felix always goes to the body. He'll want you to drop your hands for his overhand left or right. Got it?"

Antonio nodded, spraying water out between his teeth. He felt better as his sore midsection was being firmly rubbed.

Felix's corner was also busy.

Vocabulary Builder

dispelled
(di speld´) *v.*

Meaning

Conflict and Plot   45

"You gotta get in there, fella." Felix's trainer poured water over his curly Afro locks. "Get in there or he's gonna chop you up from way back."

Bong! Bong! Round two. Felix was off his stool and rushed Antonio like a bull, sending a hard right to his head. Beads of water exploded from Antonio's long hair.

Antonio, hurt, sent back a blurring barrage of lefts and rights that only meant pain to Felix, who returned with a short left to the head followed by a looping right to the body. Antonio countered with his own flurry, forcing Felix to give ground. But not for long.

Felix bobbed and weaved, bobbed and weaved, occasionally punching his two gloves together.

Antonio waited for the rush that was sure to come. Felix closed in and **feinted** with his left shoulder and threw his right instead. Lights suddenly exploded inside Felix's head as Antonio slipped the blow and hit him with a pistonlike left catching him flush on the point of his chin.

Bedlam[2] broke loose as Felix's legs momentarily buckled. He fought off a series of rights and lefts and came back with a strong right that taught Antonio respect.

Antonio danced in carefully. He knew Felix had the habit of playing possum when hurt, to sucker an opponent within reach of the powerful bombs he carried in each fist.

---

[2] **Bedlam** (bed ləm) *n.* condition of noise and confusion; chaos.

Marking the Text

Vocabulary Builder

feinted
(fānt´ əd) *v.*

Meaning

◀ **Critical Viewing**
How does this image convey the emotion of the story?

A right to the head slowed Antonio's pretty dancing. He answered with his own left at Felix's right eye that began puffing up within three seconds.

Antonio, a bit too eager, moved in too close and Felix had him entangled into a rip-roaring, punching toe-to-toe slugfest that brought the whole Tompkins Square Park screaming to its feet.

Rights to the body. Lefts to the head. Neither fighter was giving an inch. Suddenly a short right caught Antonio squarely on the chin. His long legs turned to jelly and his arms flailed out desperately. Felix, grunting like a bull, threw wild punches from every direction. Antonio, groggy, bobbed and weaved, evading most of the blows. Suddenly his head cleared. His left flashed out hard and straight catching Felix on the bridge of his nose.

Felix lashed back with a haymaker,[3] right off the ghetto streets. At the same instant, his eye caught another left hook from Antonio. Felix swung out trying to clear the pain. Only the frenzied screaming of those along ringside let him know that he had dropped Antonio. Fighting off the growing haze, Antonio struggled to his feet, got up, ducked, and threw a smashing right that dropped Felix flat on his back.

Felix got up as fast as he could in his own corner, groggy but still game. He didn't even hear the count. In a fog, he heard the roaring of the crowd, who seemed to have gone insane. His head cleared to hear the bell sound at the end of the round. He was very glad. His trainer sat him down on the stool.

In his corner, Antonio was doing what all fighters do when they are hurt. They sit and smile at everyone.

The referee signaled the ring doctor to check the fighters out. He did so and then gave his okay. The cold water sponges brought clarity to both amigo brothers. They were rubbed until their circulation ran free.

Bong! Round three—the final round. Up to now it had been tic-tac-toe, pretty much even. But everyone knew there could be no draw and this round would decide the winner.

This time, to Felix's surprise, it was Antonio who came out fast, charging across the ring. Felix braced himself but couldn't ward off the barrage of punches. Antonio drove Felix hard against the ropes.

The crowd ate it up. Thus far the two had fought with *mucho corazón*. Felix tapped his gloves and commenced his attack anew. Antonio, throwing boxer's caution to the winds, jumped in to meet him.

Both pounded away. Neither gave an inch and neither fell to the canvas. Felix's left eye was tightly closed. Claret red blood poured from Antonio's nose. They fought toe-to-toe.

---

[3] **haymaker** *n.* punch thrown with full force.

Marking the Text

while reading your anchor book

Conflict and Plot

The sounds of their blows were loud in contrast to the silence of a crowd gone completely mute. The referee was stunned by their **savagery**.

Bong! Bong! Bong! The bell sounded over and over again. Felix and Antonio were past hearing. Their blows continued to pound on each other like hailstones.

Finally the referee and the two trainers pried Felix and Antonio apart. Cold water was poured over them to bring them back to their senses.

They looked around and then rushed toward each other. A cry of alarm surged through Tompkins Square Park. Was this a fight to the death instead of a boxing match?

The fear soon gave way to wave upon wave of cheering as the two amigos embraced.

No matter what the decision, they knew they would always be champions to each other.

BONG! BONG! BONG! "Ladies and Gentlemen. *Señores* and *Señoras*. The winner and representative to the Golden Gloves Tournament of Champions is . . ."

The announcer turned to point to the winner and found himself alone. Arm in arm the champions had already left the ring.

Marking the Text

Vocabulary Builder

After you read, review the words you decided to add to your vocabulary. Write the meaning of words you have learned in context. Look up the other words in a dictionary, glossary, thesaurus, or electronic resource.

Vocabulary Builder

savagery
(sav´ ij rē) *n.*

Meaning

Piri Thomas (1928-2011)

Growing up in New York City's Spanish Harlem, the son of Puerto Rican and Cuban parents, Piri Thomas faced many challenges, including racism, poverty, and gangs. However, Thomas vowed that he would rise above the violence of street life, using his passion: reading.

Thomas also hoped to reach at-risk youth through his autobiography, *Down These Mean Streets.* This best-selling book not only captivated audiences nationwide but also introduced the Spanish term *el barrio,* "the neighborhood," to non-Spanish-speaking readers. "Amigo Brothers" comes from his collection *Stories From El Barrio.*

Thinking About the Selection

Amigo Brothers

1 **Compare and Contrast** What kind of conflicts do the characters face in "Operation: Conductorette" and "Amigo Brothers"? How are they similar? How are they different?

_____
_____
_____

2 **Describe** What is the conflict in the story? How is it resolved?

_____
_____
_____

3 **Analyze** How do Antonio and Felix's actions determine the outcome?

_____
_____

4 **Compare and Contrast** How are Antonio and Felix similar to each other? How are they different from the other kids in the neighborhood?

_____
_____

5 **Interpret** Compare how Antonio and Felix behave the night before the fight. How does the author use the structure of the story to show how they are alike or different?

_____
_____
_____

Write Answer the following questions in your Reader's Journal.

6 **Evaluate** Does the resolution seem true to life? Explain why.

7 **Write and Discuss** The conflicts in your Anchor Book are the causes for the actions of your characters. Identify a conflict in your Anchor Book and list at least two realistic solutions. Which solution would be the best for all characters? What would happen in the book if this solution was the actual outcome? Discuss your answer with your Literature Circle.

Conflict and Plot

1-8 Language Coach
Grammar and Spelling

The Writing Rules

In this book, you will learn how to improve your writing by practicing specific skills. Before you begin, there are some general rules you should always follow.

Directions The following sentences are intended to teach you some writing rules. However, each sentence breaks the writing rule that it explains. Rewrite each sentence so that it correctly represents the rule.

1 It is wrong to ever split an infinitive.

2 Just between you and I, case is important.

3 Parenthetical remarks (however relevant) are (usually) unnecessary.

4 Hyphens should be used to join compound adjectives before a noun, like hard working student.

5 Don't use no double negatives.

6 Eliminate commas, that are, not, necessary.

7 Use the apostrophe in it's proper place and omit it when its not needed.

8 Proofread carefully to see if you any words out.

9 Except the fact that you should check for commonly confused words.

Common and Proper Nouns

A **common noun** names any one of a group of people, places, things, or ideas. Common nouns are capitalized only when they begin a sentence. A **proper noun** names a specific person, place, thing, or idea. Proper nouns are always capitalized.

Common Nouns	Proper Nouns
athlete	Jackie Robinson
class	English Literature
book	*The Color Purple*
city	Tallahassee

Directions Underline each common noun once and each proper noun twice.

Example My <u>brother</u> <u>Brad</u> and I went to <u>Florida</u> to watch the <u>Dolphins</u> play in an important <u>game</u> against an undefeated <u>team</u>.

1. Ernest Hemingway was born in Oak Park, which is in Illinois.

2. During World War I, Hemingway was a volunteer for the Red Cross in Italy.

3. For six weeks, he drove an ambulance and worked at a canteen.

4. This important writer won a Pulitzer Prize in 1953.

An **appositive** is a noun or pronoun placed after another noun or pronoun to identify, rename, or explain it.

Example The naturalist <u>John James Audubon</u> identified several eagles.

An **appositive phrase** is a noun with modifiers.

Example Willa Cather, <u>an American novelist</u>, wrote *My Antonia*.

Directions Underline the appositive or appositive phrase and draw an arrow from it to the noun it renames

5. The bull of the American buffalo, Bison bison, may weigh more than 2,000 pounds.

6. The American buffalo, an enduring symbol of power and strength, is rich in Western imagery.

Author's Craft

There are four basic sentence types in English: declarative, interrogative, imperative, and exclamatory. **Declarative** is a statement or observation (I love sunflowers.). **Interrogative** is a question (Do you love sunflowers?). **Imperative** is a command or request (Please buy me some sunflowers.). **Exclamations** contain strong emotions or opinions (What lovely sunflowers!). Look back at "Occupation: Conductorette" on page 26. Find an example of each basic sentence type and identify the nouns in each sentence.

Language Coach continued

Concrete, Abstract, and Possessive Nouns

Nouns are words that name people, places, things, or ideas.
Concrete nouns name people, places, or things that can be perceived by the five senses (sight, hearing, taste, touch, smell). **Abstract nouns** name ideas, beliefs, qualities, or concepts—things that cannot be perceived by the senses.

Concrete Nouns: bicycle, house, sun, Kenneth, teacher

Abstract Nouns: freedom, confidence, joy, wealth, beauty

Possessive nouns are used to show ownership or belonging. To form the possessive of most singular nouns, add an apostrophe and an s. To form the possessive of a plural noun that ends in s, add an apostrophe. For plural nouns that do not end in s, form the possessive by adding an apostrophe and an s.

Singular Possessive Nouns	
uncle–**uncle's**	James–**James's**
parrot–**parrot's**	story–**story's**

Plural Possessive Nouns	
teenagers–**teenagers'**	the Gomezes–**the Gomezes'**
people–**people's**	countries–**countries'**

Directions Identify each noun as either concrete or abstract.

1. loyalty _____
2. Pacific Ocean _____
3. whale _____
4. generosity _____
5. basket _____

Directions Replace the underlined noun with its possessive form.

6. <u>Marks</u> favorite playwright is Neil Simon. _____
7. The <u>snowflakes</u> pattern is unique. _____

Author's Craft

Possessive nouns are one example of when to use an apostrophe. Look back at page 39 of "Amigo Brothers" for examples. With a partner, create a chart that shows when to use an apostrophe and how to use one.

Spelling Plural Nouns

A **plural noun** refers to more than one person, place, thing, or idea. The plural of most nouns is formed by adding -s or -es. Some nouns, however, form their plurals in different ways. Study the rules and examples below to learn how to form plurals.

Rule	Examples
For nouns that end in -s, -x, -ch, or -sh, add -es.	tax—taxes; dish—dishes; match—matches; pass—passes
For nouns that end in a consonant plus y, change the y to an i and add -es.	county—counties; berry—berries
For some nouns that end in -f or -fe, use -ves. (Some just add -s. Consult a dictionary.)	wolf—wolves; loaf—loaves; chief—chiefs; gulf—gulfs
Some nouns change their spelling to form the plural.	mouse—mice; child—children; foot—feet

Directions Proofread the following two informational passages. Underline and correct each misspelled plural noun.

Careers: Becoming a Professional Chef

You can train to become a professional chef by going to cooking school. After taking many courses, you will have learned skills such as how to make a variety of dishs and how to use sharp knifes carefully. You will also learn about the varietys of food there are: did you know there are nine kinds of berries?

Change How You See the World

Painting is one of those hobbys that can change how you see the world. When you paint an apple, you use the knowledge you already have about what apples look like. You also stop and look at a specific apple more closely so that you are certain not to leave out any important details. This act of looking makes you more aware of visual details.

Ready to start? You will need to buy paint, brushs, and a surface on which to paint. Maybe one day your paintings will be shown in gallerys all over the world!

1-9 Writer's Workshop
Description: Descriptive Essay

Many nonfiction writers enjoy describing the people who have influenced them. In this workshop, you will write a descriptive essay and reflect on a person who has had an important influence on your life.

Your description should feature the following elements.

- Your main impression of the person, supported by concrete examples and personal anecdotes
- Sensory details about appearance, behavior, and speech
- Your thoughts about how this person has influenced your life
- Error-free writing, including correct use of possessive nouns

Purpose To describe a person who has had an important influence on your life

Audience You, your teacher, and your classmates

Read through the rubric at the end of the lesson to preview the criteria for your descriptive essay. You may wish to add your own criteria, such as an aspect of descriptive writing you wish to focus on.

Prewriting—Plan It Out

Consider keeping a writer's notebook to record your ideas for writing. To choose the topic of your essay, follow these steps.

Choose the person you want to describe. Make a chart with four columns labeled *Family, Friends, Teachers,* and *Coaches*. In each column, list people who have influenced you in some important way. Review your list and select a person to describe.

Choose your focus. Identify what aspects of the person will be your focus. For example, if you choose to write about your older brother, your topic could focus on the various things he has taught you.

Gather details. In a character web like the one shown below, jot down specific details from observation or memory about the person. Also note examples of traits and actions that show why he or she is important to you. Review your web to decide what main impression you will convey in your writing.

54 Lesson 1-9

Drafting—Get It on Paper

Using your character web as an outline, write your first draft. The following steps will make your essay more creative and enjoyable.

Shape your writing. Your essay should keep readers' interest, focus on a main impression, and build up to your strongest point. Use the graphic organizer below to sequence your examples and details in *order of importance* from most important to least important.

Most Important ↓ Least Important

Examples and Details for Your Descriptive Essay

Provide elaboration. Focus on providing vivid details such as descriptions of or comparisons to your subject's movements, gestures, and expressions. Strengthen your descriptions by using figurative language such as similes and metaphors.

A **simile** compares one thing to another using the words *like* or *as*.	A **metaphor** compares two unlike things by setting them up as equals. It describes one object as if it were another.
Example My mother is like a drill sergeant, barking orders and running the house efficiently amid the chaos.	**Example** Carrie is my rock, always supportive, keeping me strong.
My simile:	**My metaphor:**

You may wish to add descriptive emphasis to your writing by also including an oxymoron. An **oxymoron** is a figure of speech that contains two contradictory terms, such as "act naturally."

Description: Descriptive Essay

Writer's Workshop continued

Directions Read this student descriptive essay as a model for your own.

Student Model: Writing

Brittany Barker, Somerset, Kentucky

Ding Bat

Amy has impacted my life since the day I was born. We are very close, and she is my favorite aunt. I resemble her in many ways. We both have caramel brown hair, sparkling brown eyes and cheerful smiles. My aunt is funny and sometimes seems less intelligent than she actually is. Once she made chocolate cupcakes for a party and for some unknown reason she bent over to sniff them while they were still hot. The steam from the cupcakes scorched her nose. (I guess the chocolate was too much for her to bear.) This incident, along with others, earned her the affectionate nickname of Ding Bat.

That's one reason I like her, though, because she is just like me—smart, yet very "ditzy." Amy influenced my own personality because I spent so much time with her when I was young. I loved having her as a babysitter because she would let me do anything, as long as it was safe. One time she taught me how to make paper snowflakes. I wasn't experienced with scissors and made several feeble attempts to cut on the gray lines she had traced onto the white paper. I got so involved that I snipped my index finger with the scissors. Tears began to dribble down my face and mix with the blood already on the paper. Amy carefully wrapped a bandage around my finger and helped me clean up the mess on the table. After we scrubbed the table, she told me a joke to make me laugh.

Amy is so easygoing and happy. She is also sincere and willing to forgive. Once, I accidentally broke a small bunny figurine of hers by knocking it off the table. It broke into a million tiny, brown pieces on her floor. She walked into the room and asked, "What happened here?" I tried to reply, but I choked up and tears came to my eyes. She wrapped her arms around me and said consolingly, "It's okay. Everyone has accidents."

In the introduction, the writer conveys her main impression of her aunt through sensory details.

This anecdote and the last sentence support the writer's impression of her aunt as funny and compassionate.

The writer illustrates part of Amy's personality through quotations, which support her impression.

Lesson 1-9

Revising—Make It Better

Mark words that are vague or dull and replace them with specific, vivid language using a dictionary, thesaurus, or electronic resource. Ask a teacher to review your draft. Paraphrase suggestions for revision to make sure you understand them.

Peer Review With a partner, discuss how your revisions enrich the meaning of your essay.

Editing—Be Your Own Language Coach

Review your descriptive essay for errors in grammar, spelling, and usage. Use resources such as a dictionary, thesaurus, computer spell checker, grammar handbook, or an online tool.

Publishing—Share It!

Make a photo scrapbook. Select a group of photos of you and your subject and organize them in a small photo album. On each page of the album, include a paragraph from your description.

Reflecting on Your Writing

Maintain a portfolio of your writing. Set writing goals and evaluate how well you meet them. Keep a list of writing ideas and explore topics that interest you, such as possible career choices.

Rubric for Self-Assessment Assess your essay. For each question, circle a rating.

CRITERIA	RATING SCALE
	NOT VERY VERY
IDEAS Is your paper clear and focused with rich details?	1 2 3 4 5
ORGANIZATION How logical and consistent is your organization?	1 2 3 4 5
VOICE Is your writing lively and engaging?	1 2 3 4 5
WORD CHOICE Are your words specific and powerful?	1 2 3 4 5
SENTENCE FLUENCY Does your writing consist of well-built sentences and a varied sentence structure?	1 2 3 4 5
CONVENTIONS How correct is your grammar?	1 2 3 4 5
ADD YOUR OWN CRITERIA	1 2 3 4 5

Description: Descriptive Essay

1-10 Discussing Your Anchor Book
Literature Circles

Introduction A Literature Circle is a small group of students who meet to discuss their personal reactions and connections to a book in a free-flowing, spontaneous conversation.

PART 1: Open Discussion

You have started reading your Anchor Book, had some class lessons about it, and made some entries in your Reader's Journal. Draw on these experiences to have a discussion about your book and to help inform your writing about it. Include everyone and ask follow-up questions to better understand others' ideas and opinions. Before you begin, read the discussion guidelines on the next page.

You may wish to start with some questions like these.

- What is your personal response or "gut reaction" to the book so far?
- What is your favorite part of the book so far, and why?
- What is your first impression of some key characters? Whom do you like, not like, feel suspicious of, etc?

PART 2: Discuss—Plot and Predictions

Now that your Literature Circle has shared some responses to your Anchor Book, try to dig deeper into the book using these prompts.

Plot Discuss the plot of your Anchor Book. How are the characters responding to the conflict? Do their reactions make sense to you? Why or why not? How do you think you would respond in a similar situation?

Make Predictions Predict future events in your Anchor Book, using details from the book to support your predictions. Based on what you have already read in your Anchor Book, what do you predict will happen next to the main character? What do you predict the ending of the book will be?

while reading your anchor book

58 Lesson 1-10

DISCUSSION GUIDELINES

1 LISTEN

To open up the widest possible range of ideas, a discussion needs each member's active involvement. Sit face-to-face, take turns, share "airtime," and listen actively.

2 BUILD

Think of ways to build on each other's comments. You could make a connection to the Big Question or give examples that support what a Literature Circle member said.

Sentence Starters for Building Discussion

To build off another Literature Circle member's comments

When Meena pointed out that … I thought about…

To show polite disagreement

I see your point, but I was looking at it in a different way…

3 QUESTION

Asking follow-up questions is a good way to have a member clarify unknown vocabulary or expand upon ideas.

Sentence Starters for Asking Questions

To ask for more information or an explanation of an idea
- Could you give me an example of what you mean?
- Can you say more about . . .?

REFER Before and during your meeting, use what you have written in your Reader's Journal to remind you of good topics for conversation. If the discussion lags, look through your Reader's Journal to find a new topic, a question, or a passage that can restart the discussion.

How did your discussion go? Summarize or paraphrase your first Literature Circle discussion in your Reader's Journal. Identify the best questions and ideas shared in the discussion.

Then, evaluate your discussion.

1 What characterizes a good discussion?

_____
_____

2 What did you and your Literature Circle members do to foster a good discussion?

_____
_____

3 What could you do to make your next Literature Circle discussion better?

Literature Circles 59

Monitoring Your Progress
Standardized Test Practice

Reading Skills: Making Predictions

Directions Read the following passage. Then, answer the questions.

> It was a beautiful day. Latisha put on her helmet, hopped on her bike, and headed to a desert bike path near her house. She was pedaling merrily along when suddenly she heard a loud, hissing sound. "Oh, no," she thought, "not a snake!" She pedaled faster but noticed that her bike was bouncing badly. When she looked back, she saw that her rear tire was flat.

1 What prior knowledge could someone use to predict that the tire was going flat?

A. Latisha hopped on her bike.
B. There was a hissing sound.
C. Latisha is in the desert.
D. She was pedaling fast.

2 Which kind of information might lead you to change a prediction about the snake?

F. Latisha was bouncing badly on the path.
G. She was pedaling merrily.
H. There was a loud hissing sound.
J. The hissing could be from the flat tire, not a snake.

3 Which prediction is most likely correct, based on details in the passage?

A. Something is wrong with the bicycle.
B. There is definitely a snake on the path.
C. Latisha will be stranded on the path for days.
D. Latisha might get hurt trying to pedal the bike home.

4 Which of the following events is most likely to happen next?

F. A snake will bite Latisha.
G. Latisha will walk her bike back home.
H. It will begin to rain.
J. Latisha will eat lunch.

Literary Analysis: Elements of Fiction and Nonfiction

Read the following passage. Then answer the questions.

> The Trojan War had ended, and Odysseus, a clever leader of the Greeks, set sail with his men toward home. Blown off course, they arrived at the island of the Cyclopses, the one-eyed giants. There, Odysseus and his men found a well-stocked cave. Before they could leave, a Cyclops arrived and trapped them inside. To Odysseus's horror, the Cyclops picked up two men, crushing them to death, and ate them.
>
> Odysseus knew he had to think of a way to escape before he, too, became the Cyclops's meal. The next day, while the Cyclops was tending his flock, Odysseus found a piece of wood and sharpened it into a spear. That night, Odysseus offered wine to the Cyclops, who drank greedily. Soon, the giant was asleep. With the spear in hand, Odysseus and his men lunged toward the Cyclops, piercing his one eye. The blinded Cyclops roared in pain. The next morning, Odysseus and his men escaped.

5 When does Odysseus realize he has to act in order to save himself?

  A. when Odysseus arrives at the island
  B. when the Cyclops eats two men
  C. when the Cyclops roars in pain
  D. when the Cyclops drinks the wine

6 What is the main type of **conflict**?

  F. character versus self
  G. character versus nature
  H. character versus society
  J. character versus character

7 What is part of the exposition of this story?

  A. The Trojan War had ended.
  B. The Cyclops comes to the cave.
  C. The Cyclops picks up two men.
  D. The Cyclops sees the men in the cave.

8 What is the **resolution** of this story?

  F. The Cyclops is blinded.
  G. Odysseus and his men find the cave.
  H. Odysseus and his men escape.
  J. The Trojan War has just ended.

Timed Writing: Explanation

A *stereotype* is a perception of an entire group, based on a single shared characteristic. Use some examples from literature and life to explain why stereotyping can be damaging. **(20 minutes)**

1-11 Reading Skills
Author's Purpose

In learning new reading skills, you will use special academic vocabulary. Knowing the right words will help you to demonstrate your understanding.

Academic Vocabulary

Word	Meaning	Example Sentence
convince v. Related words: convinced, convincing	to cause someone to agree	Lawyers *convince* the jury by providing relevant facts.
establish v. Related words: established, establishing	to create or prove	The players must *establish* the rules of the games before they begin.
achieve v. Related word: achiever	to carry out successfully	To *achieve* success you must be patient and persistent.

The **author's purpose** is the author's reason for writing. The most common purposes are *to inform, to entertain, to persuade*, and *to reflect*. The chart below lists some of the tools authors use to communicate their purpose in expository texts and literature. For example, in the novel *Animal Farm*, George Orwell used the theme of the danger of the few having power over the many to persuade his readers of the misuse of political power in a dictatorship.

Expository Texts	facts/details technical language sentence structure	figurative language word choice imagery
Literature	characters setting theme	imagery word choice genre

while reading your anchor book

Lesson 1-11

Directions Read the following e-mail. Underline clues in the text that tell you what the author's purpose is. Note whether the purpose is to inform, entertain, persuade, or reflect. Then answer the questions.

Link to Real Life

Cezar's b'day

Sasha,

All set for Cezar's b'day party tonight

Cake = great (IMHO)[1]

Decorations = took me four hours, but also great

BTW[2] Still need help so feel free to come early

Directions: Route 134 West to Exit 4A

Take right off exit

Take third left onto Evergreen Street

Take first right onto Prospect Place

We're #401A in the brick building on the left

CUL8R[3] ;) Aamir

---

1. IMHO – In my humble opinion
2. BTW – By the way
3. CUL8R – See you later

---

1 Identify What is the author's purpose for writing this e-mail?

2 Establish What is the relationship between the author and Sasha? What details tell you this?

3 Evaluate An e-mail is an informal way of communicating. What aspects of the e-mail identify it as informal? Which aspects are culture-specific?

Author's Purpose

The purpose of a memo is for formal communication in business. *Guiding Question:* **Does the author of this memo express a truth that one cannot argue against?**

Background The following memo was written by an employee of a business. Read this memo closely to determine the author's purpose.

Link to Real Life

MEMO
March 23

To: Todd Barker, Director of Facilities Management
From: Maria Furtado, Human Resources

RE: Changing from polyfoam products to paper in the company cafeteria

---

I am an employee of this company in the human resources department. I am writing with regard to the polyfoam that is currently being used as trays, bowls, and plates in the cafeteria. I suggest that we switch from polyfoam to paper.

By switching from polyfoam to paper we would be helping the environment, thereby eliminating unnecessary litter in our waste disposal site. Paper is recyclable; polyfoam is not. Also, paper products are less expensive than polyfoam, thereby saving the company a lot of money.

Please consider my proposal for switching from polyfoam products to paper products in the company cafeteria. I can be reached at extension 2431.

Thank you very much.

Thinking About the Selection
Memo

1 **Identify** The author's purpose is different from the message, or theme. What is the author's purpose for writing this memo? What is the message?

2 **Evaluate** Did Maria do an effective job of achieving her purpose? If so, explain. If not, what could she have done differently?

3 **Identify** What text features are part of a memo?

4 **Interpret** Rewrite the memo in the format of an e-mail, making sure to convey a friendly tone. Remember to include a greeting and closing.

Write Answer the following questions in your Reader's Journal.

5 **Analyze** Does the author of this memo express a truth that one cannot argue against? Explain two different ways of responding to this memo.

6 **Apply** With a partner, write a memo from the perspective of a character in your Anchor Book to a character with whom he or she is in conflict.

Ready for a Free-Choice Book? Your teacher may ask you if you would like to choose another book to read on your own. Select a book that fits your interest and that you'll enjoy. As you read, think about how your new book compares with your Anchor Book.

1-12 Literary Analysis
Setting and Mood

The **setting** of a narrative is where and when its action takes place. Setting is a key literary element because it affects the entire work. Imagine if *Romeo and Juliet* took place in Los Angeles in 2026. It would be a completely different play!

Literary Terms

- The **setting** of a literary work is the time and place of the action. The setting can also serve a more important function. For example, if a character is struggling against a force of nature, the setting is the source of the story's conflict.

- **Mood** is the overall feeling that a literary work conveys to the reader. Details of setting help establish the mood. A story set in an old, decaying castle on a dark, stormy night might convey a gloomy, frightening mood.

Directions Read the following passage. Underline details of setting that help convey the mood. Then, answer the questions that follow.

> ### from The Land I Lost *by Huynh Quang Nhuong*
>
> I was born on the central highlands of Vietnam in a small hamlet on a riverbank that had a deep jungle on one side and a chain of high mountains on the other. Across the river, rice fields stretched to the slopes of another chain of mountains.
>
> There were fifty houses in our hamlet, scattered along the river or propped against the mountainsides. The houses were made of bamboo and covered with coconut leaves, and each was surrounded by a deep trench to protect it from wild animals or thieves. The only way to enter a house was to walk across a "monkey bridge"—a single bamboo stick that spanned the trench. At night we pulled the bridges into our houses and were safe.
>
> There were no shops or marketplaces in our hamlet. If we needed supplies—medicine, cloth, soaps, or candles—we had to cross over the mountains and travel to a town nearby. We used the river mainly for traveling to distant hamlets, but it also provided us with plenty of fish.

1. **Describe** Look back at the details you underlined. Briefly describe the setting of the passage.

   _____
   _____

2. **Analyze** Describe the overall mood of the passage. Which details of setting are most important in conveying this mood?

   _____
   _____

3. **Analyze** What does the setting tell you about when and where the action in the passage takes place? Use details to support your answer.

   _____
   _____

4. **Apply** Imagine a setting that makes you feel a certain way. How would this place look, smell, and sound? What different tastes and textures might someone experience in this setting? Use the chart to list these sensory details.

Sight	
Sound	
Smell	
Taste	
Touch	

5. **Describe** On a separate sheet of paper, use the images from your chart to write a brief description of the setting you have imagined. Revise your description to make the setting and mood more vivid by substituting specific nouns and verbs.

In the following story, descriptive words help you understand the setting and mood. *Guiding Question:* What does this story express that is true for everyone?

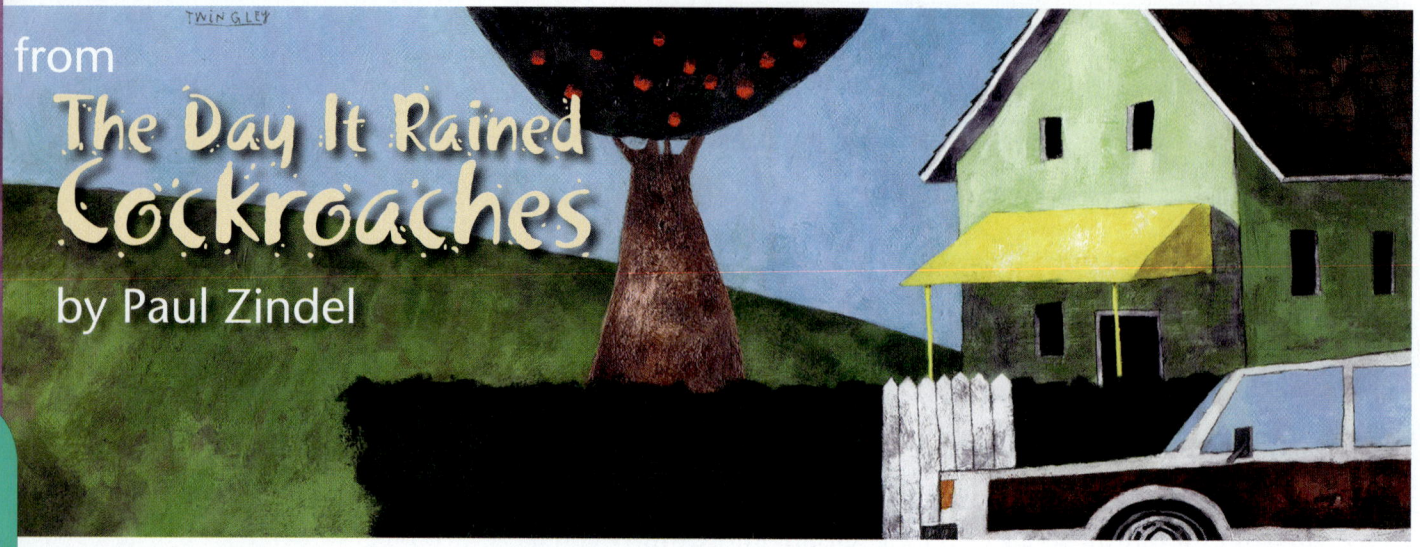

from
The Day It Rained Cockroaches
by Paul Zindel

Background *Paul Zindel was born in New York City, but he moved to many different places during his childhood.* The Day It Rained Cockroaches *tells of an event that left a lasting impression on him during one of these moves.*

Vocabulary Builder

Before you read, you will discuss the following words. In the Vocabulary Builder box in the margin, use a vocabulary building strategy to make the words your own.

kerchiefs   aghast   emblazoned

As you read, draw a box around unfamiliar words you could add to your vocabulary. Use context clues to unlock their meaning.

Marking the Text

Setting and Mood

As you read, underline key words and phrases that describe the setting and mood. In the margin, make notes about how the author is trying to help you visualize the place and feeling of the events that take place.

Vocabulary Builder

kerchiefs
(kʉr´chifs) *n.*

Meaning

About anything else you'd ever want to know about my preteen existence you can see in the photos in this book. However, I don't think life really started for me until I became a teenager and my mother moved us to Travis, on Staten Island.

When we first drove into the town, I noticed a lot of plain wood houses, a Catholic church, a war memorial, three saloons with men sitting outside on chairs, seventeen women wearing **kerchiefs** on their heads, a one-engine firehouse, a big redbrick school, a candy store, and a butcher shop with about 300 sausages hanging in the window. Betty shot me a private look,

68 Lesson 1-12

signaling she was **aghast**. Travis was mainly a Polish town, and was so special-looking that, years later, it was picked as a location for filming the movie *Splendor in the Grass*, which starred Natalie Wood (before she drowned), and Warren Beatty (before he dated Madonna). Travis was selected because they needed a town that looked like it was Kansas in 1920, which it still looks like.

The address of our new home was 123 Glen Street. We stopped in front, and for a few moments the house looked normal: brown shingles, pea-soup-green-painted sides, a tiny yellow porch, untrimmed hedges, and a rickety wood gate and fence. Across the street to the left was a slope with worn gravestones all over it. The best-preserved ones were at the top, peeking out of patches of poison oak.

The backyard of our house was an airport. I mean, the house had two acres of land of its own, but beyond the rear fence was a huge field consisting of a single dirt runway, lots of old propeller-driven Piper Cub-type planes, and a cluster of rusted hangars. This was the most underprivileged airport I'd ever seen, bordered on its west side by the Arthur Kill channel and on its south side by a Con Edison electric power plant with big black mountains of coal. The only great sight was a huge apple tree on the far left corner of our property. Its trunk was at least three feet wide. It had strong, thick branches rich with new, flapping leaves. It reached upward like a giant's hand grabbing for the sky.

"Isn't everything beautiful?" Mother beamed.

"Yes, Mom," I said.

Betty gave me a pinch for lying.

"I'll plant my own rose garden," Mother went on, fumbling for the key. "Lilies, tulips, violets!"

Mom opened the front door and we went inside. We were so excited, we ran through the echoing empty rooms, pulling up old, soiled shades to let the sunlight crash in. We ran upstairs and downstairs, all over the place like wild ponies. The only unpleasant thing, from my point of view, was that we weren't the only ones running around. There were a lot of cockroaches scurrying from our invading footfalls and the shafts of light.

"Yes, the house has a few roaches," Mother confessed. "We'll get rid of them in no time!"

"How?" Betty asked raising an eyebrow.

"I bought eight Gulf Insect Bombs!"

"Where are they?" I asked.

Mother dashed out to the car and came back with one of the suitcases. From it she spilled the bombs, which looked like big silver hand grenades.

"We just put one in each room and turn them on!" Mother explained.

Vocabulary Builder

aghast
(ə gast´) *adj.*

Meaning

She took one of the bombs, set it in the middle of the upstairs kitchen, and turned on its nozzle. A cloud of gas began to stream from it, and we hurried into the other rooms to set off the other bombs.

"There!" Mother said. "Now we have to get out!"

"Get out?" I coughed.

"Yes. We must let the poison fill the house for four hours before we can come back in! Lucky for us there's a Lassie double feature playing at the Ritz!"

Marking the Text

◀ **Critical Viewing**
Does this picture capture the mood of the story? Why or why not?

▼ **Good to Know!**
Cockroaches can survive on very little food. They will eat the glue from the back of postage stamps when little else is available.

We hadn't been in the house ten minutes before we were driving off again!

I suppose you might as well know now that my mother really loved Lassie movies. The only thing she enjoyed more were movies in which romantic couples got killed at the end by tidal waves, volcanos, or other natural disasters. Anyway, I was glad we were gassing the roaches, because they are the one insect I despise. Tarantulas I like. Scorpions I can live with. But ever since I was three years old and my mother took me to a World's Fair, I have had nightmares about cockroaches. Most people remember an exciting water ride this fair had called the Shoot-the-Chutes, but **emblazoned** on my brain is the display the fair featured of giant, live African cockroaches, which look like American cockroaches except they're six inches long, have furry legs, and can pinch flesh. In my nightmares about them, I'm usually lying on a bed in a dark room and I notice a bevy[1] of giant cockroaches heading for me. I try to run away but find out that someone has secretly tied me down on the bed, and the African roaches start crawling up the sides of the sheets. They walk all over my body, and then they head for my face. When they start trying to drink from my mouth is when I wake up screaming.

So after the movie I was actually looking forward to going back to the house and seeing all the dead cockroaches.

"Wasn't Lassie wonderful?" Mother sighed as she drove us back to Travis. "The way that brave dog was able to crawl hundreds of miles home after being kidnapped and beaten by Nazi Secret Service Police!"

"Yes, Mom," I agreed, although I was truthfully tired of seeing a dog movie star keep pulling the same set of tear-jerking stunts in each of its movies.

"Maybe we'll get a dog just like Lassie one day," Mother sighed.

When we got back to the house this time, we didn't run into it. We walked inside very slowly, sniffing for the deadly gas. I didn't care about the gas so much as I wanted to see a lot of roach corpses all over the place so I'd be able to sleep in peace.

But there were none.

"Where are all the dead cockroaches?" I asked.

We crept slowly upstairs to see if the bodies might be there. I knew the kitchen had the most roaches, but when we went in, I didn't see a single one, living or dead. The lone empty Gulf Insect Bomb sat spent in the middle of the floor. My sister picked up the bomb and started reading the directions. One thing my mother never did was follow directions. As Betty was reading, I noticed a closed closet door and reached out to turn its knob.

---

[1] **bevy** (bev´ē) a large number.

Vocabulary Builder

emblazoned
(em blā´zənd) v.

Meaning

Setting and Mood

"It says here we should've opened all the closet doors before setting off the bombs, so roaches can't hide." Betty moaned, her clue to me that Mom had messed up again.

I had already started to open the door. My mind knew what was going to happen, but it was too late to tell my hand to stop pulling on the door. It sprang open, and suddenly 5,000 very angry, living cockroaches rained down on me from the ceiling of the closet.

"Eeehhhhhh!" I screamed, leaping around the room, bathed in bugs, slapping at the roaches crawling all over me and down my neck! "Eeehhhhh! Eeehh! Ehhh! Ehh!"

"Don't worry. I'll get more bombs," Mother said comfortingly as she grabbed an old dishrag to knock the fluttering roaches off my back. Betty calmly reached out her foot to crunch as many as dared run by her.

Vocabulary Builder

After you read, review the words you decided to add to your vocabulary. Write the meaning of words you have learned in context. Look up the other words in a dictionary, glossary, thesaurus, or electronic resource.

Paul Zindel (1936–2003)

Although Paul Zindel studied chemistry at a college on Staten Island, the borough where he grew up, Zindel had been writing since he was a young boy. Because he, his mother, and his sister moved around so much, Zindel had a lot to write about. "By the time I was ten," Zindel wrote, "I had gone nowhere, but had seen the world."

Zindel used many of his unusual real-life experiences as a basis for his plays and young adult novels. He wrote his first play in high school, which earned him a literary award. During the ten years he spent teaching high school chemistry and physics, Zindel wrote the Pulitzer-Prize winning play *The Effect of Gamma Rays on Man-in-the-Moon Marigolds*. The play was performed on Broadway, winning an Obie Award in 1970 for Best American Play. In addition to writing plays, Paul Zindel wrote many novels for teenagers, including *The Pigman, Confessions of a Teenage Baboon,* and *The Undertaker's Gone Bananas*.

Thinking About the Selection

The Day It Rained Cockroaches

1 **Analyze** What mood does the story convey? How do the characters and the setting help to create the mood?

_____
_____
_____
_____

2 **Interpret** How do the narrator's sister and mother respond to the narrator's fear of cockroaches? What do their responses reveal about their attitude toward the narrator?

_____
_____
_____
_____

3 **Respond** At what point in the story did you know something was going to go wrong with the insect bombs? Explain your response.

_____
_____
_____

4 **Determine** What is the author's purpose for writing this story?

_____
_____
_____
_____

Write Answer the following questions in your Reader's Journal.

5 **Evaluate** What does this story express that is true for everyone?

6 **Analyze** How is the setting important in your Anchor Book? Compare the importance of this setting to one in your own life.

Setting and Mood 73

1-13 Comparing Literary Works
Theme

What does it all mean? All the elements of a piece of literature work together to help communicate the theme.

Literary Term

The **theme** of a literary work is different from the topic. A topic is the focus, while a theme is its unifying idea. The message can be a lesson about life or an observation about people. Often a work's theme is implied—not stated directly in the text—so you will need to think deeply about your reading to identify the theme.

Read the fable below to see how a student marked the text to identify theme.

Student Model: Marking the Text

> ### The Ant and the Dove by Leo Tolstoy
>
> An Ant went to the bank of a river to quench its thirst, and being carried away by the rush of the stream, was on the point of drowning. <u>A Dove sitting on a tree overhanging the water plucked a leaf and let it fall into the stream close to her. The Ant climbed onto it and floated safely into the bank.</u> — **Dove saves Ant's life.** Shortly afterward <u>a birdcatcher came and stood underneath the tree, and laid his lime-twigs for the Dove,</u> — **Dove will be trapped.** which sat in the branches. <u>The Ant, perceiving his design, stung him in the foot. In pain the birdcatcher threw down the twigs, and the noise made the Dove take wing.</u> — **Ant saves Dove's life.**
>
> **The Ant risked its life to save the Dove. The Dove saved the Ant's life first. Theme: One good turn deserves another.**

Here are some common themes in literature.

- ▶ A person grows with each challenge he or she overcomes.
- ▶ Enjoy life now, because life is short.
- ▶ Without courage, one might fail when life becomes difficult.
- ▶ Jealousy can cause a person to do things he or she may regret.

while reading your anchor book

Read the excerpt from *The Grass Harp* to compare its theme to the next selection, from *Child of the Owl*. *Guiding Question:* **What details make these fictional stories seem true?**

from The Grass Harp
by Truman Capote

Background *This excerpt takes place in the 1930s. The main character, Collin, had become an orphan and is now living with two quirky old ladies with whom he forms an unbreakable bond.*

Vocabulary Builder

Before you read, you will discuss the following words. In the Vocabulary Builder box in the margin, use a vocabulary building strategy to make the words your own.

    tantalizing   **kindled**   **preserves**

As you read, draw a box around unfamiliar words you could add to your vocabulary. Use context clues to unlock their meaning.

Marking the Text

Theme

As you read, *underline details that will help you to determine the theme. Write the theme at the end.*

    It was enough for Catherine that Dolly understood her: they were always together and everything they had to say they said to each other: bending my ear to an attic beam I could hear the **tantalizing** tremor of their voices flowing like sapsyrup through the old wood.
    To reach the attic, you climbed a ladder in the linen closet, the ceiling of which was a trapdoor. One day, as I started up, I saw that the trapdoor was swung open and, listening, heard above me an idle sweet humming, like

Vocabulary Builder

tantalizing
(tan´ tə līz´ iŋ) *adj.*

Meaning

Theme   **75**

pretty sounds small girls make when playing alone. I would have turned back, but the humming stopped, and a voice said: "Catherine?"

"Collin," I answered, showing myself.

The snowflake of Dolly's face held its shape; for once she did not dissolve. "This is where you come—we wondered," she said, her voice frail and crinkling as tissue paper. She had the eyes of a gifted person, **kindled,** transparent eyes, luminously green as mint jelly: gazing at me through the attic twilight they admitted, timidly, that I meant her no harm. "You play games up here—in the attic? I told Verena you would be lonesome." Stooping, she rooted around in the depths of a barrel. "Here now," she said, "you can help me by looking in that other barrel. I'm hunting for a coral castle; and sack of pearl pebbles, all colors. I think Catherine will like that, a bowl of goldfish, don't you? For her birthday. We used to have a bowl of tropical fish—devils, they were: ate each other up. But I remember when we bought them; we went all the way to Brewton, sixty miles. I never went sixty miles before, and I don't know that I ever will again. Ah see, here it is, the castle." Soon afterwards I found the pebbles; they were like kernels of corn or candy, and: "Have a piece of candy," I said, offering the sack. "Oh thank you," she said, "I love a piece of candy, even when it tastes like a pebble."

We were friends, Dolly and Catherine and me. I was eleven, then I was sixteen. Though no honors came my way, those were the lovely years.

I never brought anyone home with me, and I never wanted to. Once I took a girl to a picture show, and on the way home she asked couldn't she come in for a drink of water. If I'd thought she was really thirsty I would've said all right; but I knew she was faking just so she could see inside the house the way people were always wanting to, and so I told her she better wait until she got home. She said: "All the world knows Dolly Talbo's gone, and you're gone too." I liked that girl well enough, but I gave her a shove anyway, and she said her brother would fix my wagon, which he did: right here at the corner of my mouth. I've still got a scar where he hit me with a soda bottle.

I know: Dolly, they said, was Verena's cross, and said, too, that more went on in the house on Talbo Lane than a body cared to think about. Maybe so. But those were the lovely years.

On winter afternoons, as soon as I came in from school Catherine hustled open a jar of **preserves**, while Dolly put a foot-high pot of coffee on the stove and pushed a pan of biscuits into the oven; and the oven, opening, would let out a hot vanilla fragrance, for Dolly, who lived off of sweet foods, was always baking a pound cake, raisin bread, some kind of cookie or fudge:

Vocabulary Builder

kindled
(kin´ dəld) *adj.*

Meaning

preserves
(prē zurvs´) *n.*

Meaning

never would touch a vegetable, and the only meat she liked was the chicken brain, a pea-sized thing gone before you tasted it. What with a woodstove and an open fireplace, the kitchen was as warm as a cow's tongue. The nearest winter came was to frost the windows with its zero blue breath. If some wizard would like to give me a present, let him give me a bottle filled with the voices of that kitchen, the ha ha ha and fire whispering, a bottle brimming with its buttery sugary bakery smells–though Catherine smelled like a sow in the spring.

Vocabulary Builder

After you read, review the words you decided to add to your vocabulary. Write the meaning of words you have learned in context. Look up the other words in a dictionary, glossary, thesaurus, or electronic resource.

◀ **Critical Viewing**
The collage on the left is an artist's interpretation of the story. What details from the text support the artist's choices?

Now that you've read an excerpt from *The Grass Harp*, read this excerpt from *Child of the Owl* and compare the central message, or theme, in both readings.

FROM **CHILD** of the **OWL**
by Laurence Yep

Background In the following story, a twelve-year-old Asian-American girl is forced to live with her grandmother in San Francisco after her father, Barney, ends up in the hospital. The girl quickly learns that San Francisco is a place very different from her home, and finds herself feeling like a stranger in a strange land.

Vocabulary Builder

Before you read, you will discuss the following words. In the Vocabulary Builder box in the margin, use a vocabulary building strategy to make the words your own.

    momentary   swanky   truce

As you read, draw a box around unfamiliar words you could add to your vocabulary. Use context clues to unlock their meaning.

Marking the Text

Theme

As you read, underline details that will help you to determine the theme. Write the theme at the end.

It was like we'd gone through an invisible wall into another world. There was a different kind of air here, lighter and brighter. I mean, on the north side there were a series of small broken down stores; on the west, the mansions and hotels of Nob Hill; and on the other two sides were the tall skyscrapers where insurance men or lawyers spent the day. And they were pushing all the sunshine and all the buildings of Chinatown together like someone had taken several square miles of buildings and squeezed it until people and homes were compressed into a tiny little half of a square mile. I didn't know what to make of the buildings either. They were mostly three- or four-story stone buildings but some had fancy

78 Lesson 1-13

balconies, and others had decorations on them like curved tile roofs—one building had bright yellow balconies decorated with shiny, glazed purple dolphins—and there was a jumble of neon signs, dark now in the daytime, jammed all together. Most of the buildings, though, had some color to them—bright reds and rich golds with some green thrown in.

But it was the people there that got me. I don't think I'd ever seen so many Chinese in my life before this. Some were a rich, dark tan while others were as pale as Caucasians[1]. Some were short with round faces and wide, full-lipped mouths and noses squashed flat, and others were tall with thin faces and high cheekbones that made their eyes look like the slits in a mask. Some were dressed in regular American style while others wore padded silk jackets. All of them crowding into one tiny little patch of San Francisco.

Funny, but I felt embarrassed. Up until then I had never thought about skin colors because in the different places where Barney and I had lived, there were just poor people in all different colors. But now all of a sudden I saw all these funny brown people running around, a lot of them gabbling away at one another. I started to roll up the car window to try to shut out the sound and I noticed that my hand on the window handle was colored a honey kind of tan like some of the people outside. I took my hand off the handle and stared at it.

"What's the matter now?" Phil asked. We'd gotten caught in a **momentary** traffic snarl. I turned to see that Phil's face was brown as my hand. Phil adjusted his tie uneasily and growled, "What're you looking at?"

I looked ahead, keeping my eyes on the glove compartment. Barney and me had never talked much about stuff like this. I knew more about race horses than I knew about myself—I mean myself as a Chinese. I looked at my hands again, thinking they couldn't be my hands, and then I closed my eyes and felt their outline, noticing

Vocabulary Builder

momentary
(mō′mən ter′ē) *adj.*

Meaning

the tiny fold of flesh at the corners. Maybe it was because I thought of myself as an American and all Americans were supposed to be white like on TV or in books or in movies, but now I felt like some mad scientist had switched bodies on me like in all those monster movies, so that I had woken up in the wrong one.

Suddenly I felt like I was lost. Like I was going on this trip to this place I had always heard about and I was on the only road to that place but the signs kept telling me I was going to some other place. When I looked in the glove compartment to check my maps, I found I'd brought the wrong set of maps. And the road was too narrow to turn around in and there was too much traffic anyway so I just had to keep on going . . . and getting more and more lost. It gave me the creeps so I kept real quiet.

Phil headed up Sacramento Street—a steep, slanting street that just zoomed on and on up to the top of Nob Hill, where the rich people lived and where they had the **swanky** hotels. Phil turned suddenly into a little dead-end alley wide enough for only one car. On one side was a one-story Chinese school of brick so old or so dirty that the bricks were practically a purple color. On the other side as we drove by was a small parking lot with only six spaces for cars. Phil stopped the car in the middle of the alley and I could see the rest of it was filled with apartment houses. Somewhere someone had a window open and the radio was blaring out "I Want to Hold Your Hand" by that new group, the Beatles. I couldn't find the place where it was coming from but I did see someone's diapers and shirts hung in the windows and on the fire escape of one apartment.

"Why do they hang their laundry in the windows?" I asked Phil.

"That's what people from Hong Kong use for curtains," Phil grumbled.

The sidewalk in front of Paw-Paw's house was cracked like someone had taken a sledgehammer to it, and there were iron grates over the lower windows. The steps up to the doorway were old, worn concrete painted red. To the left were the mailboxes, which had Chinese words for the names or had no labels at all. To the right were the doorbells to all the nine apartments. Phil picked out the last and rang. He jabbed his thumb down rhythmically. Three short. Three long. Three short.

"Why are you doing that?" I asked.

"Signaling your Paw-Paw," he grumbled. "She never answers just one buzz like any normal person, or even just three bursts. It's got to be nine buzzes in that way or she doesn't open the door. She says her friends know what she means."

So did I. It was Morse code for SOS. The buzzer on the door sounded like an angry bee. Phil the Pill opened the door, putting his back against it and fighting against the heavy spring that tried to swing it shut. "Go on. Up three flights. Number nine."

Vocabulary Builder

swanky
(swaŋ' kē) *adj.*

Meaning

I walked into an old, dim hallway and climbed up the wooden steps. As I turned an angle on the stairs, I saw light burning fierce and bright from a window. When I came to it, I looked out at the roof of the Chinese school next door. Someone had thrown some old 45's and a pair of sneakers down there. If I were some kind of kid that felt sorry for herself, I would almost have said that was the way I felt: like some piece of old, ugly junk that was being kicked around on the discard pile while Barney was getting better.

I didn't stay by the window long, though, because Phil was coming up the stairs and I didn't want to act like his kids' stories about Paw-Paw had scared me. Anybody could be better than Phil the Pill and his family ... I hoped. I stopped by the number-nine room, afraid to knock. It could not be the right place because I could hear "I Want to Hold Your Hand" coming through the doorway. I scratched my head and checked the numbers on the other doors on the landing. Phil the Pill was still a flight down, huffing and puffing up the steps with my duffel bag—it wasn't that heavy; Phil was just that much out of shape. "Go on. Go on. Knock, you little idiot," he called up the stairwell.

I shrugged. It wasn't any of my business. I knocked at the door. I heard about six bolts and locks being turned. Finally the door swung open and I saw a tiny, pleasant, round-faced woman smiling at me. Her cheeks were a bright red. Her gray hair was all curly and frizzy around her head and a pair of rimless, thick eyeglasses perched on her nose. She was round and plump, wearing a sweater even on a hot day like this, a pair of cotton black slacks, and a pair of open-heeled, flat slippers.

"Paw-Paw?" I asked.

"Hello. Hello." She opened up her arms and gave me a big hug, almost crushing me. It was funny, but even though it was like I said—Barney and me never went in much for that sentimental stuff like hugging and kissing—I suddenly found myself holding on to her. Underneath all

Marking the Text

Critical Viewing ▶
Why does the sound of music make the narrator think she is at the wrong door?

while reading your anchor book

the soft layers of clothing I could feel how hard and tough she was. She patted me on the back three times and then left me for a moment to turn down her radio. It really was her old, white, beat-up radio playing rock music.

"Hey, how about a hand?" Phil puffed as he finally got to the landing.

Paw-Paw shuffled out to the landing in her slippered feet and made shooing motions. "You can go home now. We can do all right by ourselves."

Phil heaved his shoulders up and down in a great sigh and set the bag down. "Now, Momma—"

"Go on home." she said firmly. "We need time by ourselves."

I saw that Phil must have had some fine speech all prepared, probably warning Paw-Paw about me and warning me about ingratitude. He was not about to give up such an opportunity to make a speech.

"Now. Momma—"

"Go on. You're still not too old for a swat across the backside."

Phil ran his hand back and forth along the railing. "Really, Momma. You oughtn't—"

"Go on," Paw-Paw raised her hand.

Phil gulped. The thought of having a former district president of the lawyers spanked by his own mother must have been too much for him. He turned around and started down the steps. He still had to get in the last word though. "You mind your Paw-Paw, young lady. You hear me?" he shouted over his shoulder.

I waited till I heard the door slam. "Do you know what those buzzes stand for?"

"Do you?" Her eyes crinkled up.

"It stands for SOS. But where did you learn it?"

"When I worked for the American lady, her boy had a toy . . . what do you call it?" She made a tapping motion with her finger.

"Telegraph?"

"Yes. It's a good joke on such a learned man, no?" Her round red face split into a wide grin and then she began to giggle and when she put her hand over her mouth, the giggle turned into a laugh.

I don't think that I had laughed in all that time since Barney's accident a month ago. It was like all the laughter I hadn't been able to use came bubbling up out of some hidden well—burst out of the locks and just came up. Both of us found ourselves slumping on the landing, leaning our heads against the banister, and laughing.

Finally Paw-Paw tilted up her glasses and wiped her eyes. "Philip always did have too much dignity for one person. Ah." She leaned back against the railing on the landing before the stairwell, twisting her head to look at me. "You'll go far." she nodded. "Yes, you will. Your eyebrows are beautifully curved like silkworms. That means you'll be clever. And your ears are small and close to your head and shaped a certain way. That means you're adventurous and win much honor."

"Really?"

She nodded solemnly. "Didn't you know? The face is the map of the soul." Then she leaned forward and raised her glasses and pointed to the corners of her eyes where there were two small hollows, just shadows, really. "You see those marks under my eyes?"

"Yes." I added after a moment, "Paw-Paw."

"Those marks, they mean I have a temper."

"Oh." I wondered what was to happen next.

She set her glasses back on her nose. "But I will make a deal with you. I can keep my temper under control if you can do the same with your love of adventure and intelligence. You see, people, including me, don't always understand a love of adventure and intelligence. Sometimes we mistake them for troublemaking."

"I'll try." I grinned.

I went and got my bag then and brought it inside Paw-Paw's place and looked around, trying to figure out where I'd put it. Her place wasn't more than ten by fifteen feet and it was crowded with her stuff. Her bed was pushed lengthwise against the wall next to the doorway leading out to the landing. To the right of the door was another doorway, leading to the small little cubicle of a kitchen, and next to that door was her bureau. The wall opposite the bed had her one window leading out to the fire escape and giving a view of the alley, which was so narrow that it looked like we could have shaken hands with the people in the apartment house across from us. Beneath the window was a stack of newspapers for wrapping up the garbage. Next to the window was a table with a bright red-and-orange-flower tablecloth. Paw-Paw pulled aside her chair and her three-legged stool and told me to put my bag under the table. A metal cabinet and stacks of boxes covered the rest of the wall and the next one had hooks from which coats and other stuff in plastic bags hung.

In the right corner of the old bureau were some statues and an old teacup with some dirt in it and a half-burnt incense stick stuck into it. The rest of the top, though, was covered with old photos in little cardboard covers. They filled the bureau top and the mirror too, being stuck into corners of the mirror or actually taped onto the surface.

Next to the photos were the statues. One was about eight inches high in white porcelain of a pretty lady holding a flower and with the most patient, peaceful expression on her face. To her left was a statue of a man with a giant-sized, bald head. And then there were eight little statues, each only about two inches high. "Who are they?" I asked.

"Statues of some holy people," Paw-Paw said reluctantly.

There was something familiar about the last statue on Paw-Paw's bureau. It was of a fat, balding god with large ears, who had little children crawling over his lap and climbing up his shoulders. "Hey," I said. "Is that the happy god?"

Paw-Paw looked puzzled. "He's not the god of happiness."

"But they call him the happy god. See?" I pulled Barney's little plastic charm out of my pocket and pointed to the letters on the back.

Paw-Paw didn't even try to read the lettering. Maybe Barney had already shown it to her long ago. "He's not the god of happiness. He just looks happy. He's the Buddha—the Buddha who will come in the future. He's smiling because everyone will be saved by that time and he can take a vacation. The children are holy people who become like children again."

"What about the others, Paw-Paw?"

"I don't have the words to explain," Paw-Paw said curtly, like the whole thing was embarrassing her.

I sat down by the table on the stool, which was painted white with red flowers. "Sure you do. I think your English is better than mine."

"You don't want to know any of that stuff." With her index finger Paw-Paw rubbed hard against some spot on the tablecloth. "That stuff's only for old people. If I tell you any more, you'll laugh at it like all other young people do." There was bitter hurt and anger in her voice.

I should have left her alone, I guess; but we had been getting close to one another and suddenly I'd found this door between us—a door that wouldn't open. I wasn't so much curious now as I was desperate: I didn't want Paw-Paw shutting me out like that. "I won't laugh, Paw-Paw. Honest."

"That stuff's only for old people who are too stupid to learn American ways," she insisted stubbornly.

"Well, maybe I'm stupid too."

"No." Paw-Paw pressed her lips together tightly; and I saw that no matter how much I pestered her, I wasn't going to get her to tell me any more about the statues on her bureau. We'd been getting along so great before that I was sorry I'd ever started asking questions.

We both sat, each in our own thoughts, until almost apologetically Paw-Paw picked up a deck of cards from the table. "Do you play cards?"

"Some," I said. "Draw poker. Five-card stud. Things like that."

Paw-Paw shuffled the cards expertly. "Poker is for old men who like to sit and think too much. Now I know a game that's for the young and quick."

"What's that?"

"Slapjack." She explained that each of us took half of a deck and stacked it in front without looking at it. Then we would take turns taking the top card off and putting it down in the middle. Whenever a jack appeared, the first one to put her hand over the pile of cards

▲ **Good to Know!**
Buddhism was founded in the fifth century B.C.E. by Siddartha Gautama, who became known as the Buddha.

Marking the Text

got it. She then mixed the new cards with all the cards she still had in front of her. The first one to get all the cards won the game. It would sound like the advantage was with the person who was putting out the card at that time, but she was supposed to turn up the card away from her so she couldn't see it before the other player.

Paw-Paw had played a lot of card games, since she lived by herself, so she seemed to know when the jacks were going to come up. For a while all you could hear was the *slap-slap-slap*ping of cards and sometimes our hands smacking one another trying to get the pile. And sometimes I'd have more cards and sometimes Paw-Paw would. Eventually, though, she beat me. She shuffled the deck again. "You're a pretty good player," she grudged.

"Not as good as you, though."

Paw-Paw shuffled the cards, tapping them against the table so the cards in the pack were all even. "We used to play all the time. Your mother, Phil, everyone. We'd hold big contests and make plenty of noise. Only when Phil got older, he only wanted to play the games fancy Americans played like—what's that word for a road that goes over water?"

"A bridge? Phil wanted to play bridge."

"Yes." Paw-Paw put the deck on the table. I wandered over to the bed.

The radio was in a little cabinet built into the headboard of the bed. I lay down on the bed and looked at the radio dial. "Do you like rock music, Paw-Paw?"

"It's fun to listen to," Paw-Paw said, "and besides, *Chinese Hour* is on that station every night."

"*Chinese Hour*?"

"An hour of news and songs all in Chinese." Paw-Paw slipped the cards back carefully into their box. "They used to have some better shows on that station like mystery shows."

"I bet I could find some." I started to reach for the dial.

"Don't lose that station." Paw-Paw seemed afraid suddenly.

"Don't worry, Paw-Paw. I'll be able to get your station back for you." It was playing "Monster Mash" right then. I twisted the dial to the right and the voices and snatches of song slid past and then I turned the dial back to her station, where "Monster Mash" was still playing. "See?"

"As long as you could get it back," Paw-Paw said reluctantly.

I fiddled with the dial some more until I got hold of *Gunsmoke*. It'd gone off the air three years ago but some station was playing reruns. Paw-Paw liked that, especially the deep voice of the marshal. It was good to sit there in the darkening little room, listening to Marshal Dillon inside your head and picturing him as big and tall and striding down the dusty streets of Dodge City. And I got us some other programs too, shows that Paw-Paw had never been able to listen to before.

◀ Good to Know!
Physicists were developing innovative ideas for radio technology as early as the 1860s. It was not until the 1920s that commercial radio appeared.

Marking the Text

Don't get the idea that Paw-Paw was stupid. She just didn't understand American machines that well. She lived with them in a kind of **truce** where she never asked much of them if they wouldn't ask much of her.

"It's getting near eight," Paw-Paw said anxiously. It was only when I got the station back for her that she began to relax. "I was always so worried that I would not be able to get back the station, I never tried to listen to others. Look what I missed."

"But you have me now, Paw-Paw," I said.

"Yes," Paw-Paw smiled briefly, straightening in her chair. "I guess I do."

Vocabulary Builder

After you read, review the words you decided to add to your vocabulary. Write the meaning of words you have learned in context. Look up the other words in a dictionary, glossary, thesaurus, or electronic resource.

Vocabulary Builder

truce
(tro͞os) *n.*

Meaning

while reading your anchor book

86 Lesson 1-13

Thinking About the Selection
from The Grass Harp and from Child of the Owl

1. **Analyze** How are Paw-Paw's cultural and religious beliefs different from the narrator's? How does this difference affect their ability to communicate?

2. **Compare** *The Grass Harp* and *Child of the Owl* have similar themes, yet the ways in which their themes are revealed differ in each selection. What is the theme of these selections? What details from each selection are used to express the same theme?

3. **Analyze** The same themes that appear across literary texts are universal themes. Characters in these texts often share similarities. What issues, experiences, and emotions do the characters of both excerpts share?

4. **Evaluate** The *Child of the Owl* excerpt uses more contemporary language than the excerpt from *The Grass Harp*. Identify and explain an example from each that shows this difference in style.

Write Answer the following questions in your Reader's Journal.

5. **Evaluate** Is your Anchor Book genre fiction or nonfiction?

6. **Interpret** What is the theme of your Anchor Book, and how is it communicated through the genre? Support your response with details from the text.

1-14 Language Coach
Grammar and Spelling

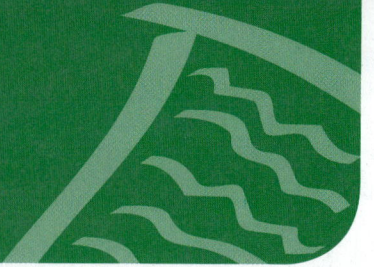

Personal Pronouns

A **personal pronoun** is used in place of a noun in a sentence. Personal pronouns change their form, or **case**, depending on how they function in a sentence.

Nominative Case Pronouns	I, you, he, she, it, we, they
Objective Case Pronouns	me, you, him, her, it, us, them
Possessive Case Pronouns	my, mine, your, yours, his, her, hers, its, our, ours, their, theirs

Case	When to Use	Examples
Nominative	the pronoun is the subject of a verb	<u>They</u> make memory chips for computers.
Objective	the pronoun is used as a direct or indirect object	Keith took the computer apart and studied <u>it</u>.
Possessive	to show ownership	Jasmine enjoys playing with <u>her</u> computer.

Avoid errors in pronoun case. If a pronoun is near the beginning of a sentence, it should probably be in the subjective case. If a pronoun is near the end of the sentence, it is most likely an example of the objective case.

Directions Proofread the following passage. Underline and correct the errors in pronoun case.

> Me and her went to the movies. I forgot me wallet, but she lent I some money. She gave the ticket to I. I will probably pay she back tomorrow. The movie was great, but the previews of upcoming movies were better. I can't wait to see them.

Author's Craft

See who can find the most personal pronouns in the excerpt from *The Day It Rained Cockroaches*. Label the pronouns as *nominative*, *objective*, or *possessive*.

Reflexive Pronouns

A **reflexive pronoun** reflects the action of the verb back to the subject. A reflexive pronoun always ends with *–self* or *-selves*.

Most domestic *cats* will groom *themselves*.

The reflexive pronoun *themselves* reflects the action of the verb *groom* back to the subject *cats*.

A reflexive pronoun always refers back to another word in the sentence (its **antecedent**). The reflexive pronoun should agree in number with the antecedent.

Mindy prides *herself* on being a good skater.

Mindy is the antecedent.

***Karen* and *I* found two seats and made *ourselves* comfortable.**

The antecedent of *ourselves* is the compound subject *Karen and I*.

Do not use a reflexive pronoun to take the place of a noun or pronoun.

INCORRECT	Dan, Lily, or myself will run the video camera.
CORRECT	Dan, Lily, or I will run the video camera.

Directions Underline the reflexive pronoun in each sentence. Then, circle the antecedent.

1. Viewers of television owe it to themselves to choose shows wisely.

2. Usually a producer of a TV show will not willingly censor himself.

3. My sisters and I make ourselves viewing schedules.

4. Because the TV does not turn itself off, we limit our viewing to one hour per night.

5. You can make yourself smarter by choosing interesting, informative shows to watch.

Author's Craft

Rewrite two sentences from the selection "The Day It Rained Cockroaches" on page 68 so that they contain reflexive pronoun errors. Then trade your sentences with a partner and correct your partner's sentences.

Language Coach continued

Pronoun Agreement

A **pronoun** usually stands for a noun or pronoun, which is called the **antecedent**. Pronouns should agree with their antecedents in person, gender, and number. **Person** tells whether the pronoun refers to the one speaking (first person), the one spoken to (second person), or the one spoken about (third person).

Number tells whether a pronoun is singular or plural.

    I would like to write **my** report on penguins.

    Penguins walk with a waddle because **they** have short legs and tall bodies.

Sometimes the antecedent of a pronoun is an indefinite pronoun.

Singular Indefinite Pronouns Example **One** of the penguins was feeding **its** baby.	anybody, anyone, anything, each, either everybody, everyone, everything, neither nobody, no one, nothing, one, somebody someone, something
Plural Indefinite Pronouns Example **Many** of the penguins were on **their** stomachs on the ice.	both, few, many

Certain indefinite pronouns can be plural or singular. Use the verb to identify whether the antecedent is plural or singular.

Plural *or* Singular Indefinite Pronouns Singular Example **Some** of the **money** <u>remains</u> unclaimed. Plural Example **Some** of the **children** <u>hide</u> from the babysitter.	all, any, most some, none, more

Directions Rewrite each sentence, correcting any errors in pronoun-antecedent agreement. If a sentence is correct as written, write *Correct*.

1. Each of the men took their uniform to the dry cleaners.

   _____

2. The maple and the oak lost its leaves in autumn.

   _____

3. Several of the homes had their roofs torn off during the storm.

   _____

Lesson 1-14

Spelling Tricky or Difficult Words

Sometimes, when saying a word, people make the mistake of adding or subtracting syllables. If this mistake leads them to mispronounce the word, they are likely to misspell the word as well.

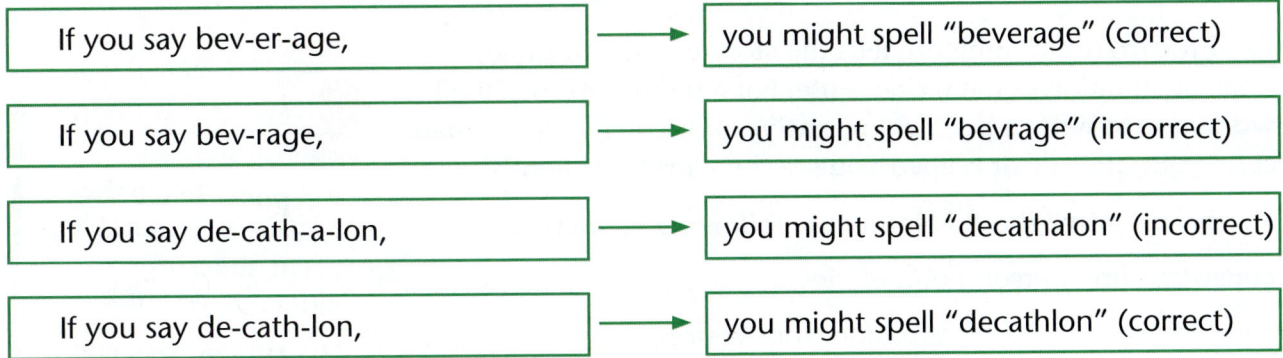

The best solution to this problem is to look in a dictionary. Check how to pronounce the word, as well as how to spell it. For practice in recognizing correct spelling, read through your Anchor Book. Say aloud tricky or difficult words to match their pronunciations to their spelling.

Directions Circle the letter of the sentence in which the underlined word is spelled correctly.

1.
   A. In the winter, everyone enjoys a hot <u>bevrage</u>.
   B. When I had the flu, the doctor told me to take <u>asprin</u>.
   C. Most soda pop is <u>basically</u> sugar water.
   D. Carla is a superb all-around <u>athalete</u>.

2.
   F. It can be dangerous to drive in <u>wintery</u> conditions.
   G. We <u>finely</u> finished painting the bedroom.
   H. Some nutritionists say that small amounts of <u>choclate</u> are good for you.
   J. My sister is a talented amateur <u>gardener</u>.

3.
   A. My dad and I have <u>basickly</u> different tastes in music.
   B. When we discuss this topic, the <u>atmossfhere</u> can grow pretty intense.
   C. My dad says that after listening to hours of my CDs, he has a headache and needs an <u>aspirin</u>.
   D. I tell him that I feel the same way after listening to his <u>opra</u> CDs.

1-15 Writer's Workshop
Narration: Personal Narrative

A **personal narrative,** or memoir, tells the story of a memorable event, time, or situation in the writer's life. Follow the steps outlined in this workshop to write a personal narrative about an event that had an effect on your attitude or helped you see the world differently.

Your personal narrative should feature the following elements.

- A consistent first-person point of view
- A clear incident, event, or situation from your life
- Relevant background information
- A central conflict, problem, or shift in perspective
- Vivid feelings you have about the experience
- Dialogue that helps reveal your and others' personalities
- Error-free writing, including correct use of pronouns

Purpose To tell the story of a memorable event, time, or situation in your life

Audience You, your teacher, and your classmates

Prewriting—Plan It Out

To choose a good topic to narrate, use any of the following strategies.

Free write. List ideas about special times in your life. Focus on getting ideas down — do not worry about grammar and punctuation. Instead, let one idea lead to another and jot down details to help you remember each specific time. Review your list and choose a topic.

Make a chart. In a chart like the one at right, list words and phrases that apply to each heading. You may use some of these words and phrases when you write.

People: Me, Matt, Pat
Time: 5 p.m.
Place: baseball field
Events: We played the Bulldogs, Pat got hurt, Matt had to take over.
Feelings: Nervous, excited

Refining Your Topic

Knowing why you want to tell your story and why it might interest your audience can help you decide what to write.

- If your purpose is to entertain your audience, focus on the funny, exciting, or moving parts of your story.
- If your purpose is also to share a lesson you learned, focus on details that illustrate the message. Be prepared to explain what you learned from your experience.

Lesson 1-15

Drafting—Get It on Paper

Before writing your draft, look over some of the techniques the authors in this unit and in your Anchor Book have used.

Shape your writing. Make sure you address the important elements in your narrative. Complete the graphic organizer below.

Narrative Elements	Your Narrative
Setting	
Conflict	
Climax	
Resolution	

Student Model: Shape Your Writing

> I remember the day my dad placed a glove in one of my hands and a bat in the other and told me the combination was an eight-letter word called baseball. Ever since then, most of my memories have been related to the sport. When I was eleven, I played in a game I'll remember forever.

The student starts his draft by introducing the situation and hinting at the conflict.

Provide elaboration. Describe the event, setting, situations, and people using rich details to create a vivid picture of the experience.

Dull:	Matt caught the ball and threw it to first base.
Vivid:	Matt made an awkward catch, then an even more clumsy lob toward first.
Create a vivid detail for your narrative:	

Describe your feelings. Tell your readers how you felt by using a consistent first-person point of view. As you draft, omit any information that is not appropriate or relevant to your topic.

Narration: Personal Narrative

Writer's Workshop continued

Directions Read the student model of a personal narrative below. Pay attention to specific details, the conflict, and dialogue.

Chris Kleinhen, Palos Verdes, CA

Baseball, a Sport I Love

I remember the day my dad placed a glove in one of my hands and a bat in the other and told me the combination was an eight-letter word called baseball. ==Ever since then, most of my memories have been related to the sport. When I was eleven, I played in a game I'll remember forever.==

We were facing the West Torrance Bull Dogs. We had a great team that year. Our pitcher, Frank (The Smasher) was tough to hit. The nicknames of other players—"Hot Glove," "Fireball," and "Maguire Jr."—were earned with outstanding play during the season. We had a team of stars. The only one who had not earned a "star" nickname was Matt.

==Nine starters took the field at five o'clock in the afternoon. The small crowd of parents and friends made enough noise for a major-league game.== For most of the game, the two teams were evenly matched. ==Then, in the last inning, Pat "The Runstopper" at third base was injured as one of the Bull Dogs accidentally rammed his ankle while sliding into third base. We had two choices: forfeit the game or play Matt.==

"You can do it, Matt!" the coach said as he sent Matt out to take Pat's place on third base.

"All right, Matt!" we encouraged from our places in the field as he trotted out nervously. The score was tied with two outs. Unfortunately, the next ball took a sharp bounce toward third–and toward Matt. Matt ran forward and made an awkward catch, followed by an even more awkward lob toward first. Amazingly it made it there in time!...

As we jogged back in, the players called out, ==ial"Way to go, Matt!"==

"You came through in the clutch!"

That's when I realized the truth of something the coach is always telling us. ==When you play as a team, everyone is a star.==

- The author uses a consistent first-person point of view, referring to himself with the first-person pronouns, *I*, *my*, and *me*.

- The author begins with a clear sequence of events from his life by identifying when the action begins.

- Precise details about the noise help bring the scene to life.

- The injury increases the suspense in the conflict between the two teams.

- Dialogue shows the peoples' feelings about the situation.

- Here, the author reveals how his personal experience has helped him look at his favorite sport in a new way.

Revising—Make It Better

Check that you have elaborated on your ideas with sufficient supporting details. Check for sentence variety. Look over your paragraphs to see the patterns of sentences you have used. When writing in the first person, you may find that many of the sentences begin with *I*. Use the rubric below to help you revise your narrative, and consider reviewing your essay with a classmate or your teacher.

Editing—Be Your Own Language Coach

Before you hand in your final draft, review it for grammatical errors. Pay special attention to proper spelling of plural nouns, along with pronoun agreement.

Publishing—Share It!

A work is published for a specific audience. Share your essay with friends or family, perhaps by creating a booklet or publishing it online.

Keep a log of your writing weaknesses and strengths and your goals to improve as a writer. Work on developing your personal voice.

Reflecting on Your Writing

Rubric for Self-Assessment Assess your essay. For each question, circle a rating.

CRITERIA	RATING SCALE
	NOT VERY · · · · · VERY
IDEAS Is your paper filled with rich details?	1 2 3 4 5
ORGANIZATION How consistent is your organization?	1 2 3 4 5
VOICE Does your writing draw the reader in?	1 2 3 4 5
WORD CHOICE Do your words convey a message?	1 2 3 4 5
SENTENCE FLUENCY Does your writing have an easy flow and rhythm with well-built, varied sentences?	1 2 3 4 5
CONVENTIONS How correct is your grammar, especially pronoun agreement?	1 2 3 4 5

1-16 Connecting to Your Anchor Book
Anchor Book Projects

Now that you have finished reading your Anchor Book, it is time to get creative! Complete one of the following projects.

A. What a Character!

Who we are affects the decisions we make. The decisions a character makes affect the outcome of a story. This project lets you change the outcome of your Anchor Book by changing the personality of a character.

1. Choose a character from your Anchor Book whose actions and decisions had an important impact on what happened.

2. List your character's personality traits. You can write a paragraph, make a list, or use another method to identify the character's traits.

3. Write a paragraph about how your character contributed to important events in the story. How would the story change if your character was different?

Your character rewrite should include the following elements.

- A description for your character using at least five new personality traits
- An explanation of how the changes in your character's personality would affect the outcome of main events in the story

B. Who Needs A Vacation?

In this project, you will create a travel brochure that identifies and advertises important locations in your Anchor Book.

1. List the important locations in your Anchor Book. Then, create a map of these places. If this is an actual place, provide an actual map. Next to each location, write a brief explanation of why the location is important to the book.

2. Choose two locations that are important to the plot. Write cardinal and ordinal directions from one location to another. Include landmarks in your directions.

Your travel brochure should include the following elements.

- A map of the book's most important settings, including a legend to explain the symbols on the map.
- An explanation of why these settings are important to the book
- A set of directions between two locations

Building Moments In Time

Imagine that you are a historian interested in the sequence of events that occurred in your Anchor Book. Here's your task.

1. Create a visual representation of the events of your Anchor Book. You might choose to build a timeline, or a collage.
2. Use both images and words in your visual representation to show the passage of time from the book's beginning to the end.
3. Write at least three paragraphs discussing the most important events in your Anchor Book. Explain why they were important.

Your completed project should include these elements.
- A visual representation of events
- Both images and words in the visual representation
- Three paragraphs discussing important events in your Anchor Book

Free-Choice Book Reflection

You have completed your free-choice book. Before you take your test, read the following instructions to write a brief reflection on your book.

My free-choice book is _____.

The author is _____.

1 Would you recommend this book to a friend? Yes ____ No ____

Briefly explain why. _____

_____

Write and Discuss Answer the following question in your Reader's Journal. Then, discuss your answer with a partner or your Literature Circle.

 2 **Compare and Contrast** *Is truth the same for everyone?* Compare and contrast how your Anchor Book, free-choice book, and your background knowledge from other subjects help you answer this question. Use specific details from both to support your ideas. To extend, consider how this question might be answered by a historian, a scientist, or a journalist.

Connecting to Your Anchor Book

Unit Review
Standardized Test Practice

Reading Skills: Making Predictions

Answer the questions below to check your understanding of this unit's skills. Read this selection. Then, answer the questions that follow.

> Milo is a little white mutt weighing only five pounds. He lives in Hawaii and he loves to surf. It all began accidentally when Milo fell off a fishing boat and went splashing into the sea. He paddled until a chunk of driftwood floated past. He climbed onto it, panting. He stood on it as it drifted closer to shore, where surfers were waiting for the waves to come in. Milo's driftwood caught a wave!

1 Which of the following is the BEST support for a **prediction**?

- A. Milo fell off a fishing boat.
- B. Milo caught a wave.
- C. Milo loves to surf.
- D. Milo was panting.

2 Which is most likely to happen next?

- F. Milo will wait for rescue.
- G. Milo will ride the wave.
- H. Milo will fall off the driftwood.
- J. Milo will catch a fish.

Reading Skills: Author's Purpose

Read this selection. Then, answer the questions that follow.

> Wherever and whenever you ride your bicycle, you should wear a helmet. You may not know it, but statistics show that a bike rider can expect to crash at least once for every 4,500 miles of riding. Every year, more than 600 people die in bicycle crashes, mostly from head injuries. Your bicycle helmet can protect you. Don't go biking without it!

3 You can predict that the **author's purpose** is

- A. to inform you of bicycle statistics.
- B. to entertain you with interesting information.
- C. to show that too many people ride bikes.
- D. to persuade you to wear a helmet.

4 To achieve his purpose, the author cites

- F. other experts' opinions.
- G. statistics about bicycle crashes.
- H. statistics about bicycle ownership.
- J. the opinions of bicyclists.

Literary Analysis: Elements of Fiction and Nonfiction

Choose the best answer for the following questions.

5 What is a **narrative**?
- A. a true account of a person's life
- B. the telling of a story
- C. a persuasive argument
- D. the author's purpose

6 When does the **plot** of a story reach its highest point?
- F. rising action
- G. falling action
- H. climax
- J. resolution

Read this selection and answer the questions that follow.

> A water nymph named Clytie was in love with the god of the sun, Apollo, but Apollo had no interest in Clytie. Clytie was so sad that she sat all day with her hair falling to the ground. She would not eat or drink, and lost interest in everything else. Each day she did nothing but watch the sun rise and set, rise and set. Finally, her legs rooted in the ground and her face became a flower. Now known as the sunflower, Clytie still turns her face to the sun.

7 Why did Clytie turn her face to the sun all day?
- A. She was lonely and it made her feel better.
- B. She loved Apollo, who was the god of the sun.
- C. She thought that it would make her beautiful.
- D. She knew Apollo loved flowers that turned to the sun.

8 What is the **resolution** in this story?
- F. She turned into the moon.
- G. Her hair fell to the ground.
- H. She turned into a sunflower.
- J. Apollo married her.

9 What is the **conflict** of the story?
- A. Clytie loves someone who doesn't love her back.
- B. Clytie becomes a sunflower.
- C. Clytie wants to live on land.
- D. There is too much sun and not enough rain.

10 What is the **theme** of the story?
- F. War is a terrible thing.
- G. You can let love control you.
- H. Friendship can help you in life.
- J. All flowers were once people.

11 Discuss in one paragraph how the **theme** of the passage you just read applies to your life or the world around you.

_____
_____
_____
_____

Read this selection and answer the questions that follow.

> Jamal sat waiting for the ski lift to take him up the slope. It was early yet, and the slopes had just opened. The snow was a perfect fluffy whiteness that lay undisturbed and peaceful. It is a brand new day, Jamal thought, looking out over the fresh snow. He took a deep breath and felt the crisp morning air fill his lungs. He felt better already, and he had not even gotten off the lift.

12 How does the story's **setting** seem to affect Jamal?

A. It makes him feel proud.
B. It seems to concern him.
C. It seems to inspire him.
D. It makes him feel lonely.

13 What can we **infer** from Jamal's thoughts?

F. He loves to ski.
G. Today will be a good day.
H. Jamal is a bad skier.
J. He will fall once off the lift.

Language Skills: Spelling

Choose the correct spelling for the following words.

14 occassion

A. ocassion
B. occasion
C. ocashun
D. occasiun

15 paralel

F. parrallel
G. parillel
H. parallel
J. parullel

Language Skills: Vocabulary

Choose the best meaning of the underlined word.

16 You can preview the movie by going to the website.

A. cancel the movie
B. view in advance
C. tell friends about the movie
D. pay for the movie.

17 I need to revise my paper.

F. to look over
G. to study carefully
H. to make improvements
J. to understand

18 It is time to finalize the paperwork.

A. begin
B. correct
C. throw away
D. complete

19 Timmy used persuasion to win the argument.

F. the act of convincing
G. the act of comedy
H. the act of crying
J. the act of yelling

Language Skills: Grammar

Choose the best answer.

20 Identify the **proper noun(s)** in the following sentence.

Jenna had spaghetti for lunch on Friday.

A. spaghetti
B. spaghetti and lunch
C. Jenna
D. Jenna and Friday

21 Identify the **common noun(s)** in the following sentence.

Frank went to a museum and saw paintings in Paris.

F. museum
G. Frank and Paris
H. museum and paintings
J. Paris

22 Choose the correct **personal pronoun** to complete the following sentence.

_____ names are Sara and Erin.

A. Their
B. I
C. Them
D. Yours

23 Identify the **reflexive pronoun** in the following sentence.

We thought we could solve it ourselves.

F. we
G. solve
H. it
J. ourselves

Unit Review 101

Can all *conflicts* be resolved?

Unit 2 Genre focus:
The Novel

Your Anchor Book
There are many good books that would work well to support both the Big Question and the genre focus of this unit. In this unit you will read one of these books as your Anchor Book. Your teacher will introduce the book you will be reading.

Free-Choice Reading
Later in this unit you will be given the opportunity to choose another book to read. This is called your free-choice book.

Thinking About What You Already Know

When you are reading a novel and think to yourself, "I know exactly what that feels like," you know that you are hooked. We read novels because we connect to the personalities and experiences of the characters, and get to experience someone else's life and different points of view.

Partner Activity

When you read a novel, you combine the details the author provides with your own knowledge of people and the way they behave. Read the narrative below and pay attention to details in the text that provide information about the narrator and what sort of person he is. Consider the following questions.

- Do you like this character? How would you describe him?
- Does he remind you of anyone you know or other characters in books you have read?
- Do you relate to this character? Explain why or why not.

from "The Scarlet Ibis" by James Hurst

When Doodle was five years old, I was embarrassed at having a brother of that age who couldn't walk, so I set out to teach him. We were down in Old Woman Swamp and it was spring and the sick-sweet smell of bay flowers hung everywhere like a mournful song. "I'm going to teach you to walk, Doodle," I said.

He was sitting comfortably on the soft grass, leaning back against the pine. "Why?" he asked.

I hadn't expected such an answer. "So I won't have to haul you around all the time."

"I can't walk, Brother," he said.

"Who says so?" I demanded.

"Mama, the doctor—everybody."

"Oh, you can walk," I said, and I took him by the arms and stood him up. He collapsed onto the grass like a half-empty flour sack. It was as if he had no bones in his little legs.

"Don't hurt me, Brother," he warned.

continued from "The Scarlet Ibis"

"Shut up. I'm not going to hurt you. I'm going to teach you to walk." I heaved him up again, and again he collapsed.

This time he did not lift his face up out of the rubber grass. "I just can't do it. Let's make honeysuckle wreaths."

"Oh yes you can, Doodle," I said. "All you got to do is try. Now come on," and I hauled him up once more.

It seemed so hopeless from the beginning that it's a miracle I didn't give up. But all of us must have something or someone to be proud of, and Doodle had become mine. I did not know then that pride is a wonderful, terrible thing, a seed that bears two vines, life and death. Every day that summer we went to the pine beside the stream of Old Woman Swamp, and I put him on his feet at least a hundred times each afternoon. Occasionally I too became discouraged because it didn't seem as if he was trying, and I would say, "Doodle, don't you want to learn to walk?"

He'd nod his head, and I'd say, "Well if you don't keep trying, you'll never learn." Then I'd paint for him a picture of us as old men, white-haired, him with a long white beard and me still pulling him around in the go-cart. This never failed to make him try again.

Finally, one day, after many weeks of practicing, he stood alone for a few seconds. When he fell, I grabbed him in my arms and hugged him, our laughter pealing through the swamp like a ringing bell. Now we knew it could be done.

Compare your conclusions with a partner. Then, answer the following question.

Use your imagination: If the narrator had a different personality, how might the excerpt have turned out differently? Why do you think so?

_____

_____

_____

Authors create characters to act out the comedy and drama of human nature. As you learn about the novel, think about the characters and imagine how you, or people you know, might behave when faced with situations presented in the selections in this unit.

Thinking About What You Already Know

2-1 Understanding the Big Question
Can all conflicts be resolved?

The resolution of a conflict can be affected by who is involved. Sometimes conflicts occur as a result of people seeing things differently. Someone who has a negative point of view will probably resolve a conflict differently than someone who has a positive point of view. One effective way to resolve a conflict is to consider the conflict from other points of view.

Your teacher will assign your group a conflict from the choices below. Put a check ✓ next to your group's assignment.

- ☐ A teenager wants to become a professional musician, but her parents think she needs to choose a more practical profession.

- ☐ A town needs a youth center but does not have the money to build one.

- ☐ A sports team has been losing every game, and no one knows how to reverse the losing streak.

- ☐ A teenager has just moved to a new city and is too shy to make new friends.

- ☐ Two best friends each want to be the captain of the basketball team. Both are qualified, but the competition is threatening their friendship.

- ☐ A student feels that her teacher is treating her unfairly. The student raises her hand but is not called upon and feels she is being graded too harshly.

Directions The chart on the next page lists five points of view and an example for each. Discuss your conflict with your group. Then, complete the chart by giving an example of each point of view for your group's conflict.

106 Lesson 2-1

FIVE POINTS OF VIEW

Point of View	Your Group's Conflict
Pessimistic Sees the negative side of a situation **Example** The cafeteria offering healthy food will not change teenagers' eating habits.	
Optimistic Sees what could work in a situation **Example** By offering teenagers healthy alternatives, the cafeteria will change their eating habits.	
Sensitive Focuses on emotional reactions **Example** Not offering junk food in the cafeteria is unfair because people want to choose their own food.	
Logical Focuses purely on facts and logic **Example** Eating junk food is unhealthy so a school cafeteria should not serve it to teenagers.	
Innovative Suggests new, creative approaches **Example** Create posters with nutritional value of different foods with the logo, "You make the choice."	

As you read your anchor book and the related readings, think about the kinds of conflicts characters face and how they are resolved. At the center of every theme in literature is the issue of conflict: good versus evil, growing up, seeking redemption.

Understanding the Big Question **107**

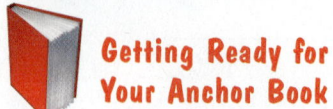

Getting Ready for Your Anchor Book

You will start reading your Anchor Book soon. The next few pages in this book give you some background information plus a reading skill.

Introduction to the Novel

A novel is a full-length work of fiction (a hundred pages or more). It is usually divided into chapters and includes some of the following literary elements and techniques.

- A **flashback** is an interruption of the chronological order of a narrative to show an event that happened at an earlier time.

- **Foreshadowing** is the use of clues to suggest events that will occur later.

- **Plot** is the sequence of events in a narrative. **Subplots** are smaller stories that add complexity to the main plot.

- A **character** is an individual who takes part in the action of a narrative. Most characters are people, but some are animals or other nonhuman beings that have human traits.

  - **Major characters** are the most important characters in a narrative.
    Minor characters are less important and are not the focus of attention.

  - The **protagonist** is the main character in a narrative. The **antagonist** is a character or a force that is in conflict with the protagonist.

  - A **round character** is a fully developed character with many personality traits. A **flat character** has only one or two personality traits.

- **Characterization** is the way or ways in which a writer reveals a character's personality.

  - With **direct characterization,** the writer makes direct statements that tell you what a character is like.

  - With **indirect characterization,** the writer hints at what a character is like through a variety of methods, such as showing the character's actions and revealing his or her thoughts.

- **Point of view** is the perspective from which a literary work is told.
  - With the **first-person point of view,** the narrator is a character who is part of the action and presents only his or her own perspective.
  - With the **third-person point of view,** the narrator is someone outside the action.
- **Irony** is a contrast between appearance and reality, between expectation and outcome, or between meaning and intention.

The Novel and the Short Story

A novel is not simply an overgrown short story. The following chart shows some of the key differences between these two genres of fiction.

Short Story	Novel
usually focuses on a protagonist and a few other characters	▶ usually presents several major characters ▶ may develop minor characters
usually tells about one important event or episode in a character's life	usually takes place over a longer period of time and weaves together many incidents and subplots
focuses on the protagonist's conflict and how it is resolved	focuses on the protagonist's conflict but usually includes several related conflicts
plot builds to a climax—a moment of decision or insight that often reveals the story's theme	▶ builds to a climax but is usually more complicated in structure ▶ presents one or more themes ▶ may use subplots to present a theme from different angles

The word *novel* comes from the French word for "new." The novel became firmly established as a literary genre, or form, in eighteenth-century England. Reading a novel became a social event, and people read novels to one another for entertainment. Although this type of entertainment may seem strange to you, think of how you and your friends may find today's forms of storytelling, such as blogs and graphic novels, just as exciting.

2-2 Reading Skills
Making Inferences

In learning new reading skills, you will use special academic vocabulary. Knowing the right words will help you demonstrate your understanding.

Academic Vocabulary

Word	Meaning	Example Sentence
infer v. *Related word:* inference	to draw conclusions based on facts	From the way the character speaks, you can *infer* that she is angry.
indicate v. *Related words:* indication, indicative	to show; to hint at	The author used a mountain to *indicate* the character's isolation.
deduce v. *Related word:* deduction	to use reasoning to figure something out	The footprints helped me *deduce* which way the animal went.

An **inference** is an educated guess or logical assumption based on available – though sometimes incomplete – information. Making inferences helps you understand information or ideas that are not stated directly. You must often "read between the lines" and look beyond what the words say to what they imply. Making inferences can also help you to determine the main idea.

Clues in the Text + **Your Background Knowledge** → **Leads to** → **Inference**

Clues in the Text (It Says . . .)	Your Background Knowledge (You Know . . .)	Inference (And So . . .)
A woman is smiling while she is reading a letter.	People smile when they are happy.	Information in the letter is making her happy.

Directions Read the poem on the next page. Notice the details a student underlined and the inferences she wrote based on those details. Then, complete the graphic organizer to help you make an inference about the last detail she underlined.

Lesson 2-2

Grandma Ling
by Amy Ling

If you dig that hole deep enough
you'll reach China, they used to tell me,
a child in a backyard in Pennsylvania.
Not strong enough to dig that hole,
5 I waited twenty years,
Then sailed back, half way around the world.

In Taiwan I first met Grandma.
Before she came to view, I heard
10 her slippered feet softly measure
the tatami[1] floor with even step;
the aqua paper-covered door slid open
and there I faced
my five foot height, sturdy legs and feet,
15 square forehead, high cheeks, and wide-set eyes;
my image stood before me,
acted on by fifty years.

She smiled, stretched her arms
to take to heart the eldest daughter
20 of her youngest son a quarter century away.
She spoke a tongue I knew no word of,
and I was sad I could not understand,
but I could hug her.

It wasn't until the speaker was a young adult that she visited China.

The speaker sees that her grandmother looks like her, but fifty years older.

[1] **tatami** (tä-tä-mē) *adj.* woven of straw matting

Clues in the Text (It Says . . .)	Your Background Knowledge (You Know . . .)	Inference (And So . . .)
"She spoke a tongue I knew no word of, and I was sad I could not understand, but I could hug her."		

Making Inferences

THE BIG Q

Use the text features to make inferences in the following article.
Guiding Question: How does the author use text features such as the title, headings, and captions to communicate conflict?

Link to Science

Animals AMONG US

In recent years, many wild animals that were once endangered have become more common. The number of deer, falcons, foxes, coyotes, and other species are steadily increasing. These animals are now a common sight in suburbs, and even in cities.

Falcons swoop down from New York City skyscrapers. Red foxes dig dens under porches in Washington, D.C. Black bears wander onto golf courses. Canada geese take over New Jersey soccer fields. All over the country, wild animals are moving from the countryside into the cities and towns. Why is this happening? Let's look at some of the reasons.

Urban Falcons

Peregrine falcons are the fastest birds in the world. They can travel the length of a football field in a single second. Normally these birds live in rugged mountain areas. Why, then, are peregrine falcons nesting in skyscrapers? At least 16 breeding pairs and their chicks were living in New York City in 2007.

In some ways, the city buildings are an ideal habitat for peregrine falcons. Skyscrapers offer the birds a high perch for hunting. There is also a steady supply of animals to hunt including city birds such as sparrows, starlings, and pigeons. The city also allows peregrine falcons to escape their own predators. In the wild, raccoons and owls feed on falcon eggs and chicks. The increase in urban falcons has another cause, too. Nearly 40 years ago the birds were in danger of dying out. That is because too many farmers were using a chemical called DDT, which killed insects and kept falcon eggs from hatching.

To protect the falcons, the U.S. government banned DDT. Scientists also began raising peregrine falcons in captivity. When the scientists released these birds, many settled in and around cities.

The Foxes Go to Town

Foxes are wily. These clever creatures can usually avoid people. In addition, foxes hunt mainly at night. As a result, no one has ever been able to count how many foxes there are in U.S. cities. We do know that people are seeing foxes more often, however. Golfers in Minneapolis, Minnesota, recently watched some fox cubs dash onto the green and steal a golf ball. Officials in Toronto, Canada, say that the city is home to at least 40 fox dens.

Why would foxes forsake the open meadows? Why would they abandon their homes in the country and move to the crowded city? One reason is that there are not as many open meadows as there used to be.

The last 50 years have been a time of suburban expansion. This growth has cut into the foxes' natural habitat. Many foxes have been forced to find new homes.

Moving to the city was a practical move for some foxes. Foxes are territorial animals. Each fox marks its own area and fights off other foxes. Because most city neighborhoods have not been claimed by foxes yet, it is easy for foxes to find "open territory" there.

Cities make a good habitat for foxes. Empty city lots are full of moles and mice, a fox's favorite foods. Hunting and trapping are not allowed in cities, so these foxes are safe from human predators.

In the city, foxes are good citizens. They go about their business silently, usually unseen. Weighing only about 12 pounds, foxes do not attack cats or dogs. They run away from young children. Foxes don't scavenge for garbage, either, unlike raccoons or dogs. Instead of searching for a free meal, they hunt, getting rid of pests such as mice and rats.

The Bear Raiders

The voters in Cross City, Michigan, got a big surprise one recent Election Day. A 400-pound black bear kept them from leaving the building where they were voting. That same fall, more than a dozen bears entered Colorado homes. Most of the bears headed straight for the kitchen.

In autumn, bears prepare to sleep away the winter. To survive the coming winter, they eat voraciously. They hungrily gobble up wild fruits and nuts. If the summer has been very dry, there may not be enough fruits and nuts for them all.

When bears cannot find enough food in the forest, they turn to dumpsters, landfills, garbage

> **FYI**
> *The city holds some dangers for peregrine falcons.*
> - *electric wires*
> - *moving vehicles*

cans, and bird feeders in cities and suburbs. As a result, people often see bears in the autumn.

Bear attacks on humans are very rare, but these powerful animals can be dangerous. To protect city residents, wildlife managers trap bears and release them into the wild. They may also try to scare the bears away by shooting them with stinging rubber bullets. However, some bears still return to the city, hoping to find an easy meal.

The Geese Mess

In the 1800s, many people hunted Canada geese for their meat. By 1900, these geese were very rare. Then in the 1960s, scientists found a group of Canada geese in Minnesota. The excited scientists took pairs of the birds to many different areas around the country, hoping the geese would start new flocks. The Canada geese loved their new homes. They were protected from hunters, and they had plenty of grass to eat. People also fed them bread. In fact, there was so much food that the geese no longer needed to migrate in winter. Because the geese had plenty of food and no predators, their numbers increased.

The goose population on golf courses, playgrounds, and parks began to skyrocket. Geese live for 20 years or more. A pair of geese can produce 100 new birds in just five years. At certain times of the year, more than 500 geese might gather in one place. Goose droppings can make

> **FYI**
> Bears adapt to city life by sleeping during the day and foraging through dumpsters at night.

parks unsafe. They pollute ponds and drinking water, and cleaning up the mess is expensive. To limit the number of geese, some cities and parks now use herding dogs to keep the geese from nesting. Officials also discourage the feeding of geese. Even so, the solution to the goose problem has not been found.

Problems and Solutions

As the human population increases, people will have more run-ins with wild animals. Some encounters are more frightening than others. For example, coyote attacks on humans and pets are very rare. However, coyotes have been rapidly extending their range. They have spread from the central United States to all of the lower 48 states, Alaska, and Canada. As a result, coyote attacks on pets and young children are increasing.

In the West, people have begun building houses in remote areas where mountain lions live. People are beginning to spot the big cats in and around parks and other public places. Attacks by mountain lions are very rare. Still, getting too close to these powerful creatures could be deadly.

Can people live in peace with wildlife? Most wildlife experts urge us to try. Some towns are setting aside special paths and areas for wild animals. Others use fences and chemical sprays to keep wildlife away. Experts urge people to enjoy wild animals only from a distance. Approaching or feeding them can be dangerous or can cause wild animals to become pests. Experts say that it is always better to keep the "wild" in wildlife.

Thinking About the Selection
Animals Among Us

1 **Explain** Reread the concluding sentence. Why does the author say that we should "keep the 'wild' in wildlife"?

_____

_____

2 **Infer** What effect might an increase in the falcon population have on a city's pigeon population? Look back at the text. Put an asterisk (*) by the details that help support your answer. Complete the graphic organizer below.

Clues in the Text (It Says…)	Your Background Knowledge (You Know…)	Inference (And So…)

3 **Support** What are some solutions that animals have found to the problem of being in the "wrong" place? Cite specific details from the selection to support your answer.

_____

_____

4 **Evaluate** Based on the information provided in the reading, is the inference that there should be no wild animals in the city valid or invalid? Explain why.

_____

_____

_____

Write Answer the following question in your Reader's Journal.

5 **Analyze** How does the author use text features such as the title, headings, and captions to communicate the conflict?

Making Inferences 115

2-3 Vocabulary Building Strategies
Word Origins

A **root** is the most important piece of a word because it contains the word's basic meaning. The **origin** of a word is the word's history.

This chart shows some English words whose roots have origins from the Latin and Greek languages. The root of the word is underlined. Read the related words in the chart aloud to practice pronunciation and to help you learn to recognize these root words in new words.

Origin	Meaning	Related Words
differe (Latin)	"to carry apart"	difference: "unlikeness" differentiate: "to separate, set apart"
specere (Latin)	"to see"	perspective: "view" spectator: "observer"
similis (Latin)	"same"	similar: "alike" assimilate: "to absorb"
videre (Latin)	"to see"	evident: "easy to see" evidence: "proof"
tekhne (Greek)	"art, skill, craft"	technician: "someone who has practical knowledge of a mechanical or scientific subject" technique: "a method of accomplishing a desired aim"
tele (Greek)	"far, far off"	television: "an electronic system of transmitting moving images and sound through space" telescope: "an optical instrument for viewing distant objects"
logos (Greek)	"reason"; "word"	logical: "reasonable" monologue: "words spoken by one person"

Spelling Tip Knowing word roots not only helps you increase your vocabulary but also helps you check your spelling. Notice that the word root is spelled the same way in different words.

Directions Identify the word that completes each sentence.

1 Two things that are alike share many _____.

   A. differences   B. similarities   C. monologues

2 I can _____ between the twin sisters because Liz has a scar and Laura doesn't.

   A. speculate   B. indicate   C. differentiate

3 Which _____ of the story did you enjoy more, its suspense or its humor?

   A. aspect   B. similar   C. prologue

4 Scientists look for _____ to prove their findings.

   A. perspectives   B. evidence   C. spectators

5 Jose learned his brother's _____ of shooting a perfect basket from across the court.

   A. television   B. technique   C. evidence

6 Scientists can observe weather phenomena on other planets by high-powered _____.

   A. indications   B. spectators   C. telescopes

7 Snow was a _____ expectation given the time of the year.

   A. respective   B. video   C. logical

Vocabulary Inventor

William Shakespeare invented many words when he wrote his plays. Many of them worked so well that now they are in the dictionary. Simple words like "hurry" and "disgraceful" came from Shakespeare. Look back at the chart. How many words can you create? Complete the first item and choose two more word roots from the chart to complete the activity. Your new words must include the word root. The meaning of your word must reflect the root's meaning.

Your Word   **Meaning**

Word Roots and Origins

Ready? Start Reading Your Anchor Book It's time to get started. As you learn from this work text, your teacher will also give you reading assignments from your anchor book.

2-4 Writing About Your Anchor Book
Reader's Journal

Using Self-Stick Notes Marking the text is a great way to keep track of your ideas and important details. However, you cannot always write directly on the pages.

How to Use Self-Stick Notes Supporting your Reader's Journal responses with important details from the text is an essential skill. You can use self-stick notes to track details and plan your writing as you read your anchor book.

- **As you read,** track your ideas and important details (such as plot development and character clues) by placing self-stick notes next to the passages where the details were found. On each self-stick note, explain what the details tell you about your anchor book.

- **After you read,** review your self-stick notes for details to use in your Reader's Journal response. You can use self-stick notes for other tasks that require supporting your ideas with details from the text.

In the passage that follows, the student wrote the word *character* to indicate the type of detail referred to on her self-stick note. Then she drew an image that she associated with the character and wrote a brief note to explain the passage's importance.

Student Model: Marking the Text

from Bad Boy: A Memoir by Walter Dean Myers

Being good in class was not easy for me. I had a need to fill up all the spaces in my life, with activity, with talking, sometimes with purely imagined scenarios that would dance through my mind, occupying me while some other student was at the blackboard. I did want to get good marks in school, but they were never of major importance to me, except in the sense of "winning" the best grade in a subject. My filling up the spaces, however, kept me in trouble.

118 Lesson 2-4

1. **Justify** What details in the passage support the student's statement on her self-stick note?

_____
_____
_____

Directions Read this passage and add details to the self-stick note. Then answer the questions.

> ### from *The Giver* by Lois Lowry
>
> It was almost December, and Jonas was beginning to be frightened. No. Wrong word, Jonas thought. Frightened meant that deep, sickening feeling of something terrible about to happen. Frightened was the way he had felt a year ago when an unidentified aircraft had overflown the community twice. He had seen it both times. Squinting toward the sky, he had seen the sleek jet, almost a blur at its high speed, go past, and a second later heard the blast of sound that followed.

Character

2. **Justify** What details in the passage did you use to help you fill in the self-stick note?

_____
_____
_____

3. **Analyze** Why might using self-stick notes to track important details help you analyze your anchor book more deeply?

_____
_____
_____

4. **Analyze** What do you think is the author's purpose in this passage? How does the author set a mood that accomplishes this? Support your answer with an example from the passage.

_____
_____
_____

while reading your anchor book

Reader's Journal 119

2-5 Literary Analysis
Flashback

Have you ever watched a character in a movie say, "I remember…" and then the story jumps to a scene from the character's past? That is a flashback.

Literary Terms

Flashback is an interruption of the **chronological order**, or time order, of a story to show an event that happened earlier.

Directions Read the following passage. Underline the details that indicate that this experience is a flashback. In the margin, explain what the narrator's flashback tells you about how his relationship with Mitchell Thomas has changed.

from the novel The Land *by Mildred D. Taylor*

I loved my daddy. I loved my brothers too. But in the end it was Mitchell Thomas and I who were most like brothers, with a bond that couldn't be broken. The two of us came into Mississippi together by way of East Texas, and that was when we were still boys, long after we had come to our understanding of each other. Seeing that we were a long way from our Georgia home and both of us being strangers here in Mississippi, the two of us depended on each other and became as family.

But it wasn't always that way.

In the beginning the two of us didn't get along at all. Fact to business, there was a time it seemed like to me Mitchell Thomas lived just to taunt me. There were other boys too who picked on me, but Mitchell was the worst. I recall one time in particular when I was about nine or so and I was reading beside a creek on my daddy's land, and Mitchell came up from behind me and just whopped me on the head. For no reason. Just whopped me on the head! Course I jumped up mad. "What ya do that for?" I cried.

"Felt like it," he said. That's all; he felt like it. "Ya wanna do somethin' bout it?" But I said nothing. Sure, I wanted to do something about it, all right, but I was no fool.

while reading your anchor book

Foreshadowing

Think about a scary or suspenseful movie that you have seen. How do you know something is about to happen? A man is walking alone down a dark road. He looks around nervously. Then, the background music changes. The tempo of the music quickens. The pitch gets higher. These are details that hint at, or **foreshadow,** something that is to come.

Writers often use the same technique to give clues about what is to happen later. This technique is called **foreshadowing.**

Literary Terms

Foreshadowing is the use of clues to suggest events that have yet to occur. Foreshadowing can also help to create suspense.

Directions Create your own clues to foreshadow one of the endings below.

1 Choose an ending. Circle your choice.

　　A. A bully changes his ways.　　B. Someone falls in love.

　　C. Two friends drift apart.　　D. An "underdog" team wins the game.

2 See how the examples in the following chart foreshadow a story ending in a shipwreck. Write clues for your ending. Each clue should foreshadow the same ending.

FORESHADOWING CLUES		
Detail	Shipwreck Example	My Example
Setting	At sea that night, the dense fog made it impossible to see.	
Dialogue	"The sea certainly is rough tonight," the captain said.	
Action	Below deck, with no one watching, the engine quietly began to break down.	
Comment by Narrator	The crew slept soundly, dreaming of returning home. They did not realize what problem lay ahead.	

while reading your anchor book

Directions Read the following passage. Underline the details that the author uses to foreshadow events to come. Then answer the questions.

from "The Birds"
by Daphne du Maurier

The sky was hard and leaden, and the brown hills that had gleamed in the sun the day before looked dark and bare. The east wind, like a razor, stripped the trees, and the leaves, crackling and dry, shivered and scattered with the wind's blast. Nat stubbed the earth with his boot. He had never known a change so swift and sudden. Black winter had descended in a single night.

The children were awake now. Jill was chattering upstairs and young Johnny crying once again. Nat heard his wife's voice, soothing, comforting. Presently he came down. He had breakfast ready for them, and the routine of the day began.

"Did you drive away the birds?" asked Jill, restored to calm because of the kitchen fire, because of day, because of breakfast.

"Yes, they've all gone now," said Nat. "It was the east wind brought them in. They were frightened and lost; they wanted shelter."

"They tried to peck us," said Jill. "They went to Johnny's eyes."

"Fright made them do that," said Nat. "They didn't know where they were in the dark bedroom."

"I hope they won't come again," said Jill. "Perhaps if we put bread for them outside the window they will eat that and fly away."

3 Analyze What kind of detail does the author use to foreshadow (setting, dialogue, action, comments made by narrator)?

4 Predict What prediction can you make based on the foreshadowing?

In this story, flashback and foreshadowing are tools to serve the author's purpose. *Guiding Question:* **How are flashback and foreshadowing used to communicate the conflict?**

The Scarlet Ibis
by James Hurst

Background James Hurst grew up along the coast of North Carolina, a place of quiet landscapes and violent storms. His story of the relationship between two brothers uses the beauty of the setting to communicate the emotional life of its characters.

Vocabulary Builder

Before you read, you will discuss the following words. In the Vocabulary Builder box in the margin, use a vocabulary building strategy to make the words your own.

**billowed   careen   sullenly   imminent
infallibility   precariously**

As you read, draw a box around unfamiliar words you could add to your vocabulary. Use context clues to unlock their meaning.

Marking the Text

Flashback and Foreshadowing

As you read, underline details that indicate flashback and foreshadowing. Write notes in the margin explaining how these techniques help to develop the characters and the conflict.

It was in the clove[1] of seasons, summer was dead but autumn had not yet been born, that the ibis lit in the bleeding tree. The flower garden was stained with rotting brown magnolia petals, and ironweeds grew rank amid the purple phlox. The five o'clocks by the chimney still marked time, but the oriole nest in the elm was untenanted and rocked back and forth like an empty cradle. The last graveyard flowers were blooming, and

---

[1] **clove** (klōv) *n.* dividing point

Flashback and Foreshadowing

Good to Know!
This photograph of two young boys was taken by Lewis Wickes Hines, a sociologist who lived at the time of this story's setting. His pictures of children at work helped change the labor laws in the United States.

their smell drifted across the cotton field and through every room of our house, speaking softly the names of our dead.

It's strange that all this is still so clear to me, now that the summer has long since fled and time has had its way. A grindstone stands where the bleeding tree stood, just outside the kitchen door, and now if an oriole sings in the elm, its song seems to die up in the leaves, a silvery dust. The flower garden is prim, the house a gleaming white, and the pale fence across the yard stands straight and spruce. But sometimes (like right now), as I sit in the cool, green-draped parlor, the grindstone begins to turn, and time with all its changes is ground away – and I remember Doodle.

Doodle was just about the craziest brother a boy ever had. Of course, he wasn't a crazy crazy like old Miss Leedie, who was in love with President Wilson and wrote him a letter every day, but was nice crazy, like someone you meet in your dreams. He was born when I was six and was, from the outset, a disappointment. He seemed all head, with a tiny body which was red and shriveled like an old man's. Everybody thought he was going to die – everybody except Aunt Nicey, who had delivered him. She said he would live because he was born in a caul[2] and cauls were made from Jesus' nightgown. Daddy had Mr. Heath, the carpenter, build a little mahogany coffin for him. But he didn't die, and when he was three months old Mama and Daddy decided they might as well name him. They named him William Armstrong, which was like tying a big tail on a small kite. Such a name sounds good only on a tombstone.

I thought myself pretty smart at many things, like holding my breath, running, jumping, or climbing the vines in Old Woman

---
[2] **caul** (kôl) *n.* membrane enclosing a baby at birth.

Swamp, and I wanted more than anything else someone to race to Horsehead Landing, someone to box with, and someone to perch with in the top fork of the great pine behind the barn, where across the fields and swamps you could see the sea. I wanted a brother. But Mama, crying, told me that even if William Armstrong lived, he would never do these things with me. He might not, she sobbed, even be "all there." He might, as long as he lived, lie on the rubber sheet in the center of the bed in the front bedroom where the white marquisette curtains **billowed** out in the afternoon sea breeze, rustling like palmetto fronds.[3]

It was bad enough having an invalid brother, but having one who possibly was not all there was unbearable, so I began to make plans to kill him by smothering him with a pillow. However, one afternoon as I watched him, my head poked between the iron posts of the foot of the bed, he looked straight at me and grinned. I skipped through the rooms, down the echoing halls, shouting, "Mama, he smiled. He's all there! He's all there!" and he was.

When he was two, if you laid him on his stomach, he began to try to move himself, straining terribly. The doctor said that with his weak heart this strain would probably kill him, but it didn't. Trembling, he'd push himself up, turning first red, then a soft purple, and finally collapse back onto the bed like an old worn-out doll. I can still see Mama watching him, her hand pressed tight across her mouth, her eyes wide and unblinking. But he learned to crawl (it was his third winter), and we brought him out of the front bedroom, putting him on the rug before the fireplace. For the first time he became one of us.

As long as he lay all the time in bed, we called him William Armstrong, even though it was formal and sounded as if we were referring to one of our ancestors, but with his creeping around on the deerskin rug and beginning to talk, something had to be done about his name. It was I who renamed him. When he crawled, he crawled backwards, as if he were in reverse and couldn't change gears. If you called him, he'd turn around as if he were going in the other direction, then he'd back right up to you to be picked up. Crawling backward made him look like a doodlebug so I began to call him Doodle, and in time even Mama and Daddy thought it was a better name than William Armstrong. Only Aunt Nicey disagreed. She said caul babies should be treated with special respect since they might turn out to be saints. Renaming my brother was perhaps the kindest thing I ever did for him, because nobody expects much from someone called Doodle.

Although Doodle learned to crawl, he showed no signs of walking, but he wasn't idle. He talked so much that we all quit

---

[3] **palmetto fronds** (pal me tō fränds) *n.* palm leaves.

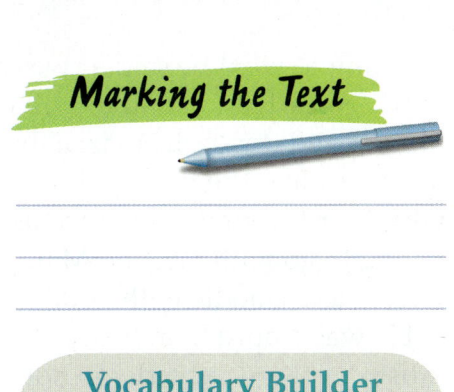

Marking the Text

Vocabulary Builder

billowed
(bi′lōd) *v.*

Meaning

while reading your anchor book

Flashback and Foreshadowing

listening to what he said. It was about this time that Daddy built him a go-cart, and I had to pull him around. At first I just paraded him up and down the piazza, but then he started crying to be taken out into the yard and it ended up by my having to lug him wherever I went. If I so much as picked up my cap, he'd start crying to go with me, and Mama would call from wherever she was, "Take Doodle with you."

He was a burden in many ways. The doctor had said that he mustn't get too excited, too hot, too cold, or too tired and that he must always be treated gently. A long list of don'ts went with him, all of which I ignored once we got out of the house. To discourage his coming with me, I'd run with him across the ends of the cotton rows and **careen** him around corners on two wheels. Sometimes I accidentally turned him over, but he never told Mama. His skin was very sensitive, and he had to wear a big straw hat whenever he went out. When the going got rough and he had to cling to the sides of the go-cart, the hat slipped all the way down over his ears. He was a sight. Finally, I could see I was licked. Doodle was my brother, and he was going to cling to me forever, no matter what I did, so I dragged him across the burning cotton field to share with him the only beauty I knew, Old Woman Swamp. I pulled the go-cart through the saw-tooth fern, down into the green dimness where the palmetto fronds whispered by the stream. I lifted him out and set him down in the soft rubber grass beside a tall pine. His eyes were round with wonder as he gazed about him, and his little hands began to stroke the rubber grass. Then he began to cry.

"For heaven's sake, what's the matter?" I asked, annoyed.

"It's so pretty," he said. "So pretty, pretty, pretty."

After that day Doodle and I often went down into Old Woman Swamp. I would gather wildflowers, wild violets, honeysuckle, yellow jasmine, snakeflowers, and water lilies, and with wire grass we'd weave them into necklaces and crowns. We'd bedeck ourselves with our handiwork and loll about thus beautified, beyond the touch of the everyday world. Then when the slanted rays of the sun burned orange in the tops of the pines, we'd drop our jewels into the stream and watch them float away toward the sea.

There is within me (and with sadness I have watched it in others) a knot of cruelty borne by the stream of love, much as our blood sometimes bears the seed of our destruction, and at times I was mean to Doodle. One day I took him up to the barn loft and showed him his casket, telling him how we all had believed he would die. It was covered with a film of Paris green[4] sprinkled to kill the rats, and screech owls had built a nest inside it.

---

[4] **Paris green** poisonous green powder used chiefly as an insecticide.

Marking the Text

Vocabulary Builder

careen
(kə rēn´) v.

Meaning

Doodle studied the mahogany box for a long time, then said, "It's not mine."

"It is," I said. "And before I'll help you down from the loft, you're going to have to touch it."

"I won't touch it," he said **sullenly**.

"Then I'll leave you here by yourself," I threatened, and made as if I were going down.

Doodle was frightened of being left. "Don't go leave me, Brother," he cried, and he leaned toward the coffin. His hand, trembling, reached out, and when he touched the casket he screamed. A screech owl flapped out of the box into our faces, scaring us and covering us with Paris green. Doodle was paralyzed, so I put him on my shoulder and carried him down the ladder, and even when we were outside in the bright sunshine, he clung to me, crying, "Don't leave me. Don't leave me."

When Doodle was five years old, I was embarrassed at having a brother of that age who couldn't walk, so I set out to teach him. We were down in Old Woman Swamp and it was spring and the sick-sweet smell of bay flowers hung everywhere like a mournful song. "I'm going to teach you to walk, Doodle," I said.

He was sitting comfortably on the soft grass, leaning back against the pine. "Why?" he asked.

I hadn't expected such an answer. "So I won't have to haul you around all the time."

"I can't walk, Brother," he said.

"Who says so?" I demanded.

"Mama, the doctor – everybody."

"Oh, you can walk," I said, and I took him by the arms and stood him up. He collapsed onto the grass like a half-empty flour sack. It was as if he had no bones in his little legs.

"Don't hurt me, Brother," he warned.

"Shut up. I'm not going to hurt you. I'm going to teach you to walk." I heaved him up again, and again he collapsed.

This time he did not lift his face up out of the rubber grass. "I just can't do it. Let's make honeysuckle wreaths."

"Oh yes you can, Doodle," I said. "All you got to do is try. Now come on," and I hauled him up once more.

It seemed so hopeless from the beginning that it's a miracle I didn't give up. But all of us must have something or someone to be proud of, and Doodle had become mine. I did not know then that pride is a wonderful, terrible thing, a seed that bears two vines, life and death. Every day that summer we went to the pine beside the stream of Old Woman Swamp, and I put him on his feet at least a hundred times each afternoon. Occasionally I too became discouraged because it didn't seem as if he was trying, and I would say, "Doodle, don't you want to learn to walk?"

Vocabulary Builder

sullenly
(sə´ lən lē) *adv.*

Meaning

Flashback and Foreshadowing   127

He'd nod his head, and I'd say, "Well, if you don't keep trying, you'll never learn." Then I'd paint for him a picture of us as old men, white-haired, him with a long white beard and me still pulling him around in the go-cart. This never failed to make him try again.

Finally one day, after many weeks of practicing, he stood alone for a few seconds. When he fell, I grabbed him in my arms and hugged him, our laughter pealing through the swamp like a ringing bell. Now we knew it could be done. Hope no longer hid in the dark palmetto thicket but perched like a cardinal in the lacy toothbrush tree, brilliantly visible. "Yes, yes," I cried, and he cried it too, and the grass beneath us was soft and the smell of the swamp was sweet.

With success so **imminent**, we decided not to tell anyone until he could actually walk. Each day, barring rain, we sneaked into Old Woman Swamp, and by cotton-picking time Doodle was ready to show what he could do. He still wasn't able to walk far, but we could wait no longer. Keeping a nice secret is very hard to do, like holding your breath. We chose to reveal all on October eighth, Doodle's sixth birthday, and for weeks ahead we mooned

Marking the Text

Vocabulary Builder

imminent
(i´ mə nənt) *adj.*

Meaning

◀ **Good to Know!**
North Carolina features many swamps, including the Great Dismal Swamp, one of the largest protected swamp wildernesses in the eastern United States.

around the house, promising everybody a most spectacular surprise. Aunt Nicey said that, after so much talk, if we produced anything less tremendous than the Resurrection,[5] she was going to be disappointed.

At breakfast on our chosen day, when Mama, Daddy, and Aunt Nicey were in the dining room, I brought Doodle to the door in the go-cart just as usual and had them turn their backs, making them cross their hearts and hope to die if they peeked. I helped Doodle up, and when he was standing alone I let them look. There wasn't a sound as Doodle walked slowly across the room and sat down at his place at the table. Then Mama began to cry and ran over to him, hugging him and kissing him. Daddy hugged him too, so I went to Aunt Nicey, who was thanks praying in the doorway, and began to waltz her around. We danced together quite well until she came down on my big toe with her brogans, hurting me so badly I thought I was crippled for life.

Doodle told them it was I who had taught him to walk, so everyone wanted to hug me, and I began to cry.

"What are you crying for?" asked Daddy, but I couldn't answer. They did not know that I did it for myself; that pride, whose slave I was, spoke to me louder than all their voices, and that Doodle walked only because I was ashamed of having a crippled brother.

Within a few months Doodle had learned to walk well and his go-cart was put up in the barn loft (it's still there) beside his little mahogany coffin. Now, when we roamed off together, resting often, we never turned back until our destination had been reached, and to help pass the time, we took up lying. From the beginning Doodle was a terrible liar, and he got me in the habit. Had anyone stopped to listen to us, we would have been sent off to Dix Hill.

My lies were scary, involved, and usually pointless, but Doodle's were twice as crazy. People in his stories all had wings and flew wherever they wanted to go. His favorite lie was about a boy named Peter who had a pet peacock with a ten-foot tail. Peter wore a golden robe that glittered so brightly that when he walked through the sunflowers they turned away from the sun to face him. When Peter was ready to go to sleep, the peacock spread his magnificent tail, enfolding the boy gently like a closing go-to-sleep flower, burying him in the gloriously iridescent, rustling vortex.[6] Yes, I must admit it. Doodle could beat me lying.

Doodle and I spent lots of time thinking about our future. We decided that when we were grown we'd live in Old Woman Swamp and pick dog-tongue for a living. Beside the stream, he

Marking the Text

---

[5] **the Resurrection** when Jesus Christ rose from the dead after his death and burial.

[6] **vortex** (vôr´ teks) *n.* rushing whirl, drawing in all that surrounds it.

Flashback and Foreshadowing

planned, we'd build us a house of whispering leaves and the swamp birds would be our chickens. All day long (when we weren't gathering dog-tongue) we'd swing through the cypresses on the rope vines, and if it rained we'd huddle beneath an umbrella tree and play stickfrog. Mama and Daddy could come and live with us if they wanted to. He even came up with the idea that he could marry Mama and I could marry Daddy. Of course, I was old enough to know this wouldn't work out, but the picture he painted was so beautiful and serene that all I could do was whisper yes, yes.

Once I had succeeded in teaching Doodle to walk, I began to believe in my own **infallibility** and I prepared a terrific development program for him, unknown to Mama and Daddy, of course. I would teach him to run, to swim, to climb trees, and to fight. He, too, now believed in my infallibility, so we set the deadline for these accomplishments less than a year away, when, it had been decided, Doodle could start to school.

That winter we didn't make much progress, for I was in school and Doodle suffered from one bad cold after another. But when spring came, rich and warm, we raised our sights again. Success lay at the end of summer like a pot of gold, and our campaign got off to a good start. On hot days, Doodle and I went down to Horsehead Landing, and I gave him swimming lessons or showed him how to row a boat. Sometimes we descended into the cool greenness of Old Woman Swamp and climbed the rope vines or boxed scientifically beneath the pine where he had learned to walk. Promise hung about us like leaves, and wherever we looked, ferns unfurled and birds broke into song.

That summer, the summer of 1918, was blighted. In May and June there was no rain and the crops withered, curled up, then died under the thirsty sun. One morning in July a hurricane came out of the east, tipping over the oaks in the yard and splitting the limbs of the elm trees. That afternoon it roared back out of the west, blew the fallen oaks around, snapping their roots and tearing them out of the earth like a hawk at the entrails of a chicken. Cotton bolls were wrenched from the stalks and lay like green walnuts in the valleys between the rows, while the cornfield leaned over uniformly so that the tassels touched the ground. Doodle and I followed Daddy out into the cotton field, where he stood, shoulders sagging, surveying the ruin. When his chin sank down onto his chest, we were frightened, and Doodle slipped his hand into mine. Suddenly Daddy straightened his shoulders, raised a giant knuckly fist, and with a voice that seemed to rumble out of the earth itself began cursing heaven, hell, the weather, and the Republican Party. Doodle and I, prodding each other and giggling, went back to the house, knowing that everything would be all right.

Marking the Text

Vocabulary Builder

infallibility
(in fa lə biˊ lə tē) *n.*

Meaning

Good to Know!
A single cotton plant may grow up to 100 bolls.

Literature in Context
World War I

This story is set during World War I (1914–1918). By the end of the war, more than 9 million soldiers had been killed. About 13 million civilians, or non-soldiers had also died. The horrors of this war left people with the hope that this had been "the war to end all wars." Much of the literature and art in Europe and America during this time describe this experience through the theme of a loss of innocence.

Link to Social Studies

And during that summer, strange names were heard through the house: Château-Thierry, Amiens, Soissons, and in her blessing at the supper table, Mama once said, "And bless the Pearsons, whose boy Joe was lost at Belleau Wood."[7]

So we came to that clove of seasons. School was only a few weeks away, and Doodle was far behind schedule. He could barely clear the ground when climbing up the rope vines, and his swimming was certainly not passable. We decided to double our efforts, to make that last drive and reach our pot of gold. I made him swim until he turned blue and row until he couldn't lift an oar. Wherever we went, I purposely walked fast, and although he kept up, his face turned red and his eyes became glazed. Once, he could go no further, so he collapsed on the ground and began to cry.

"Aw, come on, Doodle," I urged. "You can do it. Do you want to be different from everybody else when you start school?"

"Does it make any difference?"

"It certainly does," I said. "Now, come on," and I helped him up.

As we slipped through the dog days, Doodle began to look feverish, and Mama felt his forehead, asking him if he felt ill. At night he didn't sleep well, and sometimes he had nightmares, crying out until I touched him and said, "Wake up, Doodle. Wake up."

It was Saturday noon, just a few days before school was to start. I should have already admitted defeat, but my pride wouldn't let me. The excitement of our program had now been gone for weeks, but still we kept on with a tired doggedness. It was too late to turn back, for we had both wandered too far into a net of expectations and had left no crumbs behind.

Daddy, Mama, Doodle, and I were seated at the dining-room table having lunch. It was a hot day, with all the windows and doors open in case a breeze should come. In the kitchen Aunt

---

[7] **Château-Thierry, Amiens, Soissons, . . . Belleau Wood** places in France where battles were fought during World War I.

while reading your anchor book

Flashback and Foreshadowing

Nicey was humming softly. After a long silence, Daddy spoke. "It's so calm, I wouldn't be surprised if we had a storm this afternoon."

"I haven't heard a rain frog," said Mama, who believed in signs, as she served the bread around the table.

"I did," declared Doodle. "Down in the swamp."

"He didn't," I said contrarily.

"You did, eh?" said Daddy, ignoring my denial.

"I certainly did," Doodle reiterated, scowling at me over the top of his iced-tea glass, and we were quiet again.

Suddenly, from out in the yard, came a strange croaking noise. Doodle stopped eating, with a piece of bread poised ready for his mouth, his eyes popped round like two blue buttons. "What's that?" he whispered.

I jumped up, knocking over my chair, and had reached the door when Mama called, "Pick up the chair, sit down again, and say excuse me."

By the time I had done this, Doodle had excused himself and had slipped out into the yard. He was looking up into the bleeding tree. "It's a great big red bird!" he called.

The bird croaked loudly again, and Mama and Daddy came out into the yard. We shaded our eyes with our hands against the hazy glare of the sun and peered up through the still leaves. On the topmost branch a bird the size of a chicken, with scarlet feathers and long legs, was perched precariously. Its wing hung down loosely, and as we watched, a feather dropped away and floated slowly down through the green leaves.

"It's not even frightened of us," Mama said.

"It looks tired," Daddy added. "Or maybe sick."

Doodle's hands were clasped at his throat, and I had never seen him stand still so long. "What is it?" he asked.

Daddy shook his head. "I don't know, maybe it's—"

At that moment the bird began to flutter, but the wings were uncoordinated, and amid much flapping and a spray of flying feathers, it tumbled down, bumping through the limbs of the bleeding tree and landing at our feet with a thud. Its long, graceful neck jerked twice into an S, then straightened out, and the bird was still. A white veil came over the eyes, and the long white beak unhinged. Its legs were crossed and its clawlike feet were delicately curved at rest. Even death did not mar its grace, for it lay on the earth like a broken vase of red flowers, and we stood around it, awed by its exotic beauty.

"It's dead," Mama said.

"What is it?" Doodle repeated.

"Go bring me the bird book," said Daddy.

I ran into the house and brought back the bird book. As we watched, Daddy thumbed through its pages. "It's a scarlet ibis,"

Vocabulary Builder

precariously
(pri ker´ ē əs lē) *adv.*

Meaning

he said, pointing to a picture. "It lives in the tropics—South America to Florida. A storm must have brought it here."

Sadly, we all looked back at the bird. A scarlet ibis! How many miles it had traveled to die like this, in our yard, beneath the bleeding tree.

"Let's finish lunch," Mama said, nudging us back toward the dining room.

"I'm not hungry," said Doodle, and he knelt down beside the ibis.

"We've got peach cobbler for dessert," Mama tempted from the doorway.

Doodle remained kneeling. "I'm going to bury him."

"Don't you dare touch him," Mama warned. "There's no telling what disease he might have had."

"All right," said Doodle. "I won't."

Daddy, Mama, and I went back to the dining-room table, but we watched Doodle through the open door. He took out a piece of string from his pocket and, without touching the ibis, looped one end around its neck. Slowly, while singing softly "Shall We Gather at the River," he carried the bird around to the front yard and dug a hole in the flower garden, next to the petunia bed. Now we were watching him through the front window, but he didn't know it. His awkwardness at digging the hole with a shovel whose handle was twice as long as he was made us laugh, and we covered our mouths with our hands so he wouldn't hear.

When Doodle came into the dining room, he found us seriously eating our cobbler. He was pale and lingered just inside the screen door. "Did you get the scarlet ibis buried?" asked Daddy.

Doodle didn't speak but nodded his head.

"Go wash your hands, and then you can have some peach cobbler," said Mama.

"I'm not hungry," he said.

"Dead birds is bad luck," said Aunt Nicey, poking her head from the kitchen door. "Specially red dead birds!"

As soon as I had finished eating, Doodle and I hurried off to Horsehead Landing. Time was short, and Doodle still had a long way to go if he was going to keep up with the other boys when he started school. The sun, gilded with the yellow cast of autumn, still burned fiercely, but the dark green woods through which we passed were shady and cool.

When we reached the landing, Doodle said he was too tired to swim, so we got into a skiff and floated down the creek with the tide. Far off in the marsh a rail was scolding, and over on the beach locusts were singing in the myrtle trees. Doodle did not speak and kept his head turned away, letting one hand trail limply in the water.

After we had drifted a long way, I put the oars in place and made Doodle row back against the tide. Black clouds began to gather in the southwest, and he kept watching them, trying to pull the oars a little faster. When we reached Horsehead Landing, lightning was playing across half the sky and thunder roared out, hiding even the sound of the sea. The sun disappeared and darkness descended, almost like night. Flocks of marsh crows flew by, heading inland to their roosting trees, and two egrets, squawking, arose from the oyster-rock shallows and careened away.

Doodle was both tired and frightened, and when he stepped from the skiff he collapsed onto the mud, sending an armada of fiddler crabs rustling off into the marsh grass. I helped him up, and as he wiped the mud off his trousers, he smiled at me ashamedly. He had failed and we both knew it, so we started back home, racing the storm. We never spoke (What are the words that can solder cracked pride?), but I knew he was watching me, watching for a sign of mercy. The lightning was near now, and from fear he walked so close behind me he kept stepping on my heels. The faster I walked, the faster he walked, so I began to run. The rain was coming, roaring through the pines, and then, like a bursting Roman candle, a gum tree ahead of us was shattered by a bolt of lightning. When the deafening peal of thunder had died, and in the moment before the rain arrived, I heard Doodle, who had fallen behind, cry out, "Brother, Brother, don't leave me! Don't leave me!"

Marking the Text

Marking the Text

The knowledge that Doodle's and my plans had come to naught was bitter, and that streak of cruelty within me awakened. I ran as fast as I could, leaving him far behind with a wall of rain dividing us. The drops stung my face like nettles, and the wind flared the wet glistening leaves of the bordering trees. Soon I could hear his voice no more.

I hadn't run too far before I became tired, and the flood of childish spite evanesced[8] as well. I stopped and waited for Doodle. The sound of rain was everywhere, but the wind had died and it fell straight down in parallel paths like ropes hanging from the sky. As I waited, I peered through the downpour, but no one came. Finally I went back and found him huddled beneath a red nightshade bush beside the road. He was sitting on the ground, his face buried in his arms, which were resting on his drawn-up knees. "Let's go, Doodle," I said.

He didn't answer, so I placed my hand on his forehead and lifted his head. Limply, he fell backward onto the earth. He had been bleeding from the mouth, and his neck and the front of his shirt were stained a brilliant red.

"Doodle! Doodle!" I cried, shaking him, but there was no answer but the ropy rain. He lay very awkwardly, with his head thrown far back, making his vermilion neck appear unusually long and slim. His little legs, bent sharply at the knees, had never before seemed so fragile, so thin.

I began to weep, and the tear-blurred vision in red before me looked very familiar. "Doodle!" I screamed above the pounding storm and threw my body to the earth above his. For a long, long time, it seemed forever, I lay there crying, sheltering my fallen scarlet ibis from the heresy[9] of the rain.

---

[8] **evanesced** (e və nest´) *v.* dissipated gradually

[9] **heresy** (her´ə sē) *n.* idea opposed to the beliefs of a religion or philosophy.

Vocabulary Builder

After you read, *review the words you decided to add to your vocabulary. Write the meaning of words you have learned in context. Look up the other words in a dictionary, glossary, thesaurus, or electronic resource.*

Flashback and Foreshadowing

Thinking About the Selection
The Scarlet Ibis

1 **Respond** Do you blame the narrator for Doodle's death? Explain.

2 **Recall** Why does the narrator cry when everyone congratulates him for teaching Doodle to walk? Incorporate a quotation from the story in your answer.

3 **Analyze** An **allusion** is a reference to a well-known person, event, place, literary work, or work of art. How might the allusion to the Resurrection on page 129 represent something happening within the story?

4 **Compare and Contrast** How is Doodle's reaction to the death of the ibis different from the way the rest of the family reacts? What motivates Doodle to react in this way?

5 **Analyze** Look back at the foreshadowing clues you marked in the text. Write the details and what they foreshadow in the graphic organizer below.

Details From the Story	What the Details Foreshadow

6 **Analyze** A dynamic character is one who learns something important that changes him or her by the end of the story. Is the narrator a dynamic character? If so, how did he change and what did he learn? Support your answer with evidence from the story.

_____

_____

Write Answer the following questions in your Reader's Journal.

7 **Evaluate** How are flashback and foreshadowing used to communicate the conflict?

8 **Interpret** Describe an example of flashback or foreshadowing in your Anchor Book. Explain how the example adds to your understanding of the novel's central conflict.

Flashback and Foreshadowing **137**

2-6 Language Coach
Grammar and Spelling

Action and Linking Verbs

An **action verb** indicates an action. The action may be visible (*run, write, return, practice, give*) or mental (*think, like, dream, believe*). A **linking verb** connects the subject with a word that describes it or identifies the subject. Common linking verbs include *seem, appear, feel, sound, taste, smell, look,* and forms of *be* (*am, is, are, was, were, have been*). Depending on how they are used, some verbs may be action or linking.

Action Verbs	Linking Verbs
He <u>acted</u> mean.	I <u>was</u> mean to Doodle. (*mean* describes *I*)
The sun <u>hurts</u> his skin.	His skin <u>is</u> very sensitive. (*sensitive* describes *skin*)

Directions Underline the verb in each sentence. Then, write *A* if it is an action verb or *L* if it is a linking verb.

1. Our neighbor remained a close friend for years. _____
2. Your perfume smells too strong today. _____
3. Grandmother tasted our fresh bread. _____
4. This red sweater is the one I made. _____
5. My grandmother is my favorite relative. _____

Directions Each sentence contains a linking verb. Underline the subject with one line and the verb with two lines. Circle the word that either describes or identifies the subject.

Example <u>Doodle</u> <u><u>was</u></u> (paralyzed).

6. Her rug is too small for her room.
7. Television is an important tool of education.
8. Dana may be the most likely choice for the office.
9. The girls were hoarse from cheering.

Author's Craft

"Show, don't tell" describes how a good writer uses action and dialogue to show who his or her characters are. Sometimes too many linking verbs indicate that the writer is telling you too much ("She was tired"). Look back at the excerpt from the novel *The Land* on page 120. Identify the places where the author uses action verbs to show information about the narrator and Mitchell.

Principal Parts of Regular Verbs

Every verb has four principal parts that are used to form tenses, which show action occurring at different times. These principal parts are the *present (basic form)*, the *present participle*, the *past*, and the *past participle*. A regular verb forms its past and past participle by adding -ed or -d to the basic form. Sometimes you will have to double a final consonant, add a -d if the verb ends in e, or change y to i before adding -ed or -ing.

Principal Part	Description	Examples
Present	Basic form	She *tries* hard.
Present Participle	Add – ing. Use after *is* or *are*.	She *is trying* hard.
Past	Add –ed or –d.	She *tried* hard.
Past Participle	Add –ed or –d. Use after *has, have, had*.	She *has tried* hard.

Directions Underline the verb or verb phrase in each sentence. Then, identify the principal part used to form the verb.

Example The scarlet ibis <u>lives</u> in the tropics. _____**present**_____

1. Barbara filled the fish tank with fresh water. _____
2. The president is holding a press conference tomorrow. _____
3. My brother is enrolling in college in the fall. _____
4. Have the judges announced the winner? _____
5. The sweater always shrinks in the wash. _____

Directions Cross out the incorrect principal part of the verb in the sentence. In the space provided, write the correct principal part of the verb to complete the sentence.

6. Doodle and I are cry together in the rain. _____
7. Kevin has live in Kentucky all his life. _____
8. I still exercising every day. _____
9. We have agree to meet at 7 P.M. _____
10. Before he spoke, the entertainer smile at the audience. _____

Regular Verbs

Language Coach continued

Irregular Verbs

Irregular verbs are verbs whose past and past participle forms do not follow a predictable pattern. For regular verbs, the past tense is formed by adding *–ed* or *-d*, as in *follow, followed*. Irregular verbs are not formed according to this rule.

Present Tense: School begins at 8:00.
Past Tense: School began at 8:00.
Past Participle: School has begun at 8:00 for years.

SOME IRREGULAR VERBS			
Present	**Present Participle**	**Past**	**Past Participle**
bring	(is) bringing	brought	(have) brought
rise	(is) rising	rose	(have) risen
go	(is) going	went	(have) gone
choose	(is) choosing	chose	(have) chosen
do	(is) doing	did	(have) done
see	(is) seeing	saw	(have) seen

Directions Underline the correct form of the verb.

1. Doodle had (chose, chosen) to bury the bird.

2. You mean I (did, done) the wrong page of math homework?

3. Now I wish that I had (went, gone) with you.

Directions Circle the incorrect form of the verb. Revise each sentence, using the correct form of the verb.

4. I had grow to love my brother Tyrell.

_____

5. I had swore never to get rid of it.

_____

6. The seat belt buzzer has rang its last warning.

_____

Lesson 2-6

Subject/Verb Agreement

A **simple sentence** is a single independent clause, which means that it contains at least one subject and verb. In grammar, the number of a word can be either *singular* (indicating *one*) or plural (indicating *more than one*). See the diagram below of a simple sentence. More sentence diagrams are available online.

To check that your sentences are correct, make sure that the verb agrees with the subject in number.

Example 1 <u>Doodle and I</u> (is, <u>are</u>) walking to Old Woman Swamp.

Plural Subject   **Plural Verb**

Example 2 <u>The scarlet ibis</u> (<u>sits</u>, sit) in the tree.

Singular Subject   **Singular Verb**

Directions Underline the subject. Write an "S" above it if the subject is singular and a "P" if the subject is plural. Circle the correct singular or plural form of the verb in parentheses.

Example Mama and Daddy (believes, (believe)) in Doodle. [P]

1. Two dogs and a cat (lives, live) in that house.

2. They (is, are) always playing together.

3. Both Megan and Moneshia (has, have) agreed to help.

4. Enriquez (has, have) entered a contest.

Directions Rewrite the sentences. Correct the agreement mistakes.

Example We enjoys making honeysuckle wreaths.
   We enjoy making honeysuckle wreaths.

5. The cities closes the beaches in September.

6. My brother and sister has been very cooperative lately.

7. A box of cookies are in the cupboard.

Author's Craft

Look back at the excerpts from *Bad Boy: A Memoir* and *The Giver* on pages 118 and 119. Rewrite one passage with errors in subject-verb agreement. Then, trade your passage with a partner and correct each other's errors.

2-7 Writer's Workshop
Narration: Short Story

A short story can entertain readers, taking them to new places or showing them unfamiliar sides of life. By following the steps outlined in this workshop, you can write your own short story. You will write a realistic story with believable characters who face a conflict.

Your short story should include the following elements.

- One or more characters, developed throughout the story
- A clear setting, a time and place in which the action occurs
- A conflict, or problem, faced by a main character
- A suspenseful plot that leads to a climax and a resolution
- A theme—an idea about life or human nature
- Precise language, including dialogue, vivid verbs, and descriptive adjectives

Purpose To tell a story about a character who faces a conflict.

Audience You, your teacher, and your classmates

Prewriting—Plan It Out

To imagine the people and action of your story, use these strategies.

Begin with a main character. Get to know the character by drawing a picture, listing details about the character's goals and personality traits, or asking questions such as "How do you spend your time?"

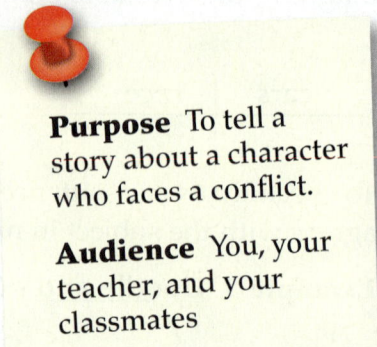

Picture the scene. Imagine your character in a particular time and place. Use action and sensory details, including vivid verbs and descriptive adjectives, to help readers experience the setting, plot, and characters. Complete a five senses chart.

SIGHT	SOUND	SMELL	TOUCH	TASTE
Open windows Curtains blowing	Music Laughter	Neighbor's barbecue	Cool breeze from window	Sweet apple Lemonade

Determine point of view. A narrator's presentation of information influences how a story is told and received and how characters are developed. Decide who you want your narrator to be.

First-person narrator: I felt a surge of energy as I launched the ball.

Third-person narrator: They held their breath as Pam shot the ball.

Lesson 2-7

Identify a conflict. Ask yourself questions about the characters that help you identify the conflict.

What does he or she want?	
What problem prevents this?	

Drafting—Get It on Paper

Build to a climax. In the exposition, give your readers background information. Include foreshadowing and flashbacks to build and develop the story. Develop an engaging plot, building suspense until you reach the climax. End with a resolution that gives a sense of closure to the story. Use this Plot diagram to help you. If you prefer, use a story map to sketch out the key plot events in your narrative.

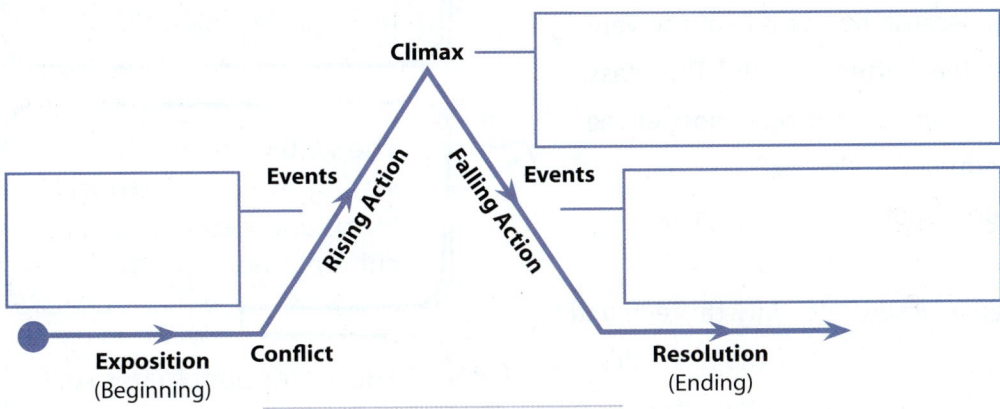

Use dialogue. Dialogue moves the action forward, and develops the characters. An interjection like "Hey!" makes it more realistic.

Create a mood and tone. Use imagery and figurative language to communicate mood and tone.

Revising—Make It Better

Add detail. Help your readers imagine characters and settings.

- Review your draft, highlighting situations and events to which a character would have a strong reaction.
- Use characterization to develop major and minor characters. Ask yourself: What words, facial expressions, thoughts, or actions reflect this reaction? Jot down your answers to these questions.
- Influence your audience's reactions by describing your characters with strong details. Use setting details to create a mood.

Peer Review Ask for a partner's response to your story. Revise to achieve the reaction you intended. Discuss usage and mechanics issues and explain the choices you made, such as using sentence fragments to achieve realistic dialogue.

Writer's Workshop continued

Directions Read this student short story as a model for your own.

Student Model: Writing

Michael Casey, Tiverton, Rhode Island

Sailing to Freedom

The hot sun was beating down on Anuk as he finished the final words on the tomb in which the Pharaoh would be buried two days later. As he looked back to examine his work, his mind began to wander. Anuk thought about his situation. The only reason he was standing there, half-heartedly working, was because he was one of the very few teenagers accepted into the "Gifted Society." This class of servants who were smarter and stronger than most of the others were permitted to perform the "better" jobs and were honored with the closest burial spot next to the Pharaoh inside the pyramid.

"Great," thought Anuk sarcastically, "I'm only thirteen and I'm already being sent to my death." Most of the Pharaoh's servants would jump at the chance to go into the afterlife with their king. But Anuk was no ordinary boy. There was something inside him that made him want to live – a drive that all the servants in Egypt didn't have... Anuk wanted and needed to escape, and no matter how hard the challenges, he was going to accomplish this.

Talla was hoeing in his fields again. He hated hoeing because it made huge calluses and blisters on his hands. Talla was almost finished with the first row when he saw a boy his age, dressed in fine clothes, walking toward him.

As the boy walked closer he said, "You boy! Listen. I have a proposal for you. I'd like to offer you a large payment if you will help me sail to Lower Egypt."

Talla could clearly see the boy now. It was Anuk, the son of the royal scribe.

"Aren't you supposed to be buried with the Pharaoh in his tomb – " He was cut short by the hand of Anuk.

> First, the writer introduces and develops the main character, Anuk, in this third-person narrative.

> The writer conveys the setting by using historical terms and describing cultural traditions.

> The writer punctuates split dialogue correctly and uses it to show the character's personality.

> Conflict and theme are introduced early.

> This dialogue reveals differences between the two boys. It also moves the plot forward.

Lesson 2-7

Editing—Be Your Own Language Coach

Review your story for errors. Revise your sentences, paying attention to subject/verb agreement. Check that the verb tenses and point of view between paragraphs, passages, and ideas are consistent. Also check for correct spelling. Use a dictionary or thesaurus if necessary.

Publishing—Share It!

When you publish a work, you produce it for a specific audience. Consider the following idea to share your writing.

Tell your story aloud. Focus on the most important events in your story and show how they affected the plot and characters. Include dialogue, descriptions, and actions. Use various facial expressions, hand gestures, and tones of voice to help tell your story.

Reflecting on Your Writing

Write a letter. Write a letter to your teacher reflecting on your writing by answering the following questions. What new insights did you gain about writing a short story? What do you do well? What do you need to work on? Set a goal you can meet in your next workshop.

Rubric for Self-Assessment Assess your short story. For each question, circle a rating.

CRITERIA	RATING SCALE
IDEAS How compelling are your plot, characters, setting, and theme?	NOT VERY VERY 1 2 3 4 5
ORGANIZATION How clearly is your story organized, especially by developing conflict and building to a climax?	1 2 3 4 5
VOICE How well do you set a tone and tell the story in an engaging way?	1 2 3 4 5
WORD CHOICE Did you use precise language, including vivid verbs and descriptive adjectives?	1 2 3 4 5
SENTENCE FLUENCY How varied is your sentence structure?	1 2 3 4 5
CONVENTIONS How correct is your grammar, especially your use of verb tenses and subject/verb agreement?	1 2 3 4 5

2-8 Discussing Your Anchor Book
Literature Circles

Subplots In this Literature Circle, your group members will start with an open discussion and then you will explore the role of subplots in your Anchor Book.

Part 1: Open Discussion

Divide into your Literature Circles. Use your memory as well as your notes, ideas, and questions from your Reader's Journal to start talking about your Anchor Book. Refer to or read aloud passages from your Anchor Book to support your conclusions.

If you need some ideas to start your conversation, form a question or statement using at least one word from each row below.

A	conflict	change	theme	setting	mood
B	wealth	gender	religion	disability	race

Example: How is the main character's disability important to the theme of the book?

Part 2: Discuss—Subplots

Now that you have discussed your Anchor Book, you are going to explore the topics of plot and subplot.

Plot is the sequence of main events in a literary work. It is structured around characters involved in a conflict.

Subplots are smaller stories contained in a literary work. They either add interest to or provide relief from the main plot. They also enrich the main plot by adding complexity to the story.

Imagine a story about a boy who has just enrolled in a new middle school and is having a hard time making friends. This is the plot. Then, imagine that his older sister attends the same school and is very popular. This is a subplot.

1 **Discuss** Identify three subplots and explain what they add to the plot.

Subplots	What They Add to the Plot

2 **Analyze** Choose one subplot. Consider what it adds to the plot. What is the author's purpose in using this subplot to contribute to the overall meaning of the work?

_____

_____

3 **Synthesize** Identify details and characters in your Anchor Book that could be made into interesting stories of their own.

Details and Characters from Your Anchor Book	Possible Plots

Your Literature Circle may choose to extend this activity by creating a videotaped dramatization of one of these subplots.

Literature Circles 147

Monitoring Your Progress
Standardized Test Practice

Reading Skills: Making Inferences

Directions Read the following passage. Then answer the questions.

> Marlena wheeled her cart down the aisle and paused in front of a bin of oranges. She filled a plastic bag without counting to see that she had enough for each member of her family. Her mind was elsewhere—on the science test her teacher had announced a few hours before. Marlena always got high grades in school, but she still worried about tests. She was worrying now as she went into the cereal aisle and absently dropped a package of Sugar Os cereal into her cart even though no one in her family ate cereal with sugar. As she approached the checkout area, Marlena hoped the lines were not too long because she wanted to get home and study before supper.

1 What inference can you make about Marlena's location?

   A. She is in a supermarket.
   B. She is in a drug store.
   C. She is in a department store.
   D. She is on her way to school.

2 Which detail helps you infer that the events take place on a weekday?

   F. "as she approached the checkout"
   G. "wheeled her cart down the aisle"
   H. "her teacher had announced a few hours before"
   J. "get home and study before supper"

3 From the details in the passage, what inference can you make about the character of Marlena?

   A. She is smart but lazy.
   B. She is foolish and impulsive.
   C. She is selfish and unkind.
   D. She is studious but absent-minded.

4 Which detail helps you infer what type of student Marlena is?

   F. "absently dropped a package of Sugar Os cereal into her cart"
   G. "she went into the cereal aisle"
   H. "always got high grades"
   J. "She was worrying now"

5 What do the details about Marlena's purchases suggest about her family?

   A. They eat healthy food.
   B. They eat a lot of red meat.
   C. They don't like oranges.
   D. They pay little attention to costs.

6 From the details in the passage, what inference can you make about the time of day the events take place?

   F. It is early morning.
   G. It is late afternoon.
   H. It is noontime.
   J. It is midnight.

Literary Analysis: Elements of the Novel

Read the following passage. Then answer the questions.

> ### From the novel Tuck Everlasting
> ### by Natalie Babbitt
>
> The sky was a ragged blaze of red and pink and orange, and its double trembled on the surface of the pond like color spilled from a paintbox. The sun was dropping fast now, a soft red sliding egg yolk, and already to the east there was a darkening to purple. Winnie, newly brave with her thoughts of being rescued, climbed into the rowboat. The hard heels of her buttoned boots made a hollow banging sound against its wet boards, loud in the warm and breathless quiet. Across the pond, a bullfrog spoke a deep note of warning.

7 Which phrase from the passage indicates foreshadowing?

  A. "newly brave"

  B. "climbed into the rowboat"

  C. "Across the pond"

  D. "a deep note of warning"

8 What is a flashback?

  F. the sequence of events in a story

  G. an interruption in a story that shows what happened earlier

  H. an unexpected outcome in a story that is often humorous

  J. a word or phrase that hints at what will happen later in a story

9 What prediction can you make based on the foreshadowing in the passage?

  A. Winnie will find danger.

  B. Winnie will sleep in the boat.

  C. Winnie will find a bullfrog.

  D. Winnie will be rescued soon.

10 Why might a writer use a flashback?

  F. to help the reader picture the events in the story

  G. to provide background for the character's motives

  H. to give a vivid description of the setting

  J. to confuse the reader

Timed Writing: Response to Literature

Directions Identify and analyze how the historical period in which a specific story or novel is set influences how the characters behave. Use details and information from the text to support your answer.
(20 minutes)

2-9 Reading Skills
Compare and Contrast

In learning new reading skills, you will use special academic vocabulary. Knowing the right words will help you demonstrate your understanding.

Academic Vocabulary

Word	Meaning	Example Sentence
examine *v.* *Related words:* exam, examination	to study carefully	If you carefully *examine* the man's actions, you can understand his motivations.
differentiate *v.* *Related words:* different, differentiation	to show how things are not alike	Bob and Tim's unequal heights can help you *differentiate* between them.
signify *v.* *Related word:* significance	to have a meaning or represent	A red traffic light *signifies* "stop your car."

When you **compare,** you show how things are similar. When you **contrast,** you show how things are different. Comparing and contrasting will help you clarify the relationships among people, places, and things that you read about.

Directions You are going to read a consumer report that compares and contrasts two kinds of televisions. Review these questions. After reading the report, return to this page and answer the questions.

1. **Assess** Why does the author organize the report in this way? Does it help you understand similarities and differences between the two television sets? Explain.

   _____
   _____

2. **Respond** Which television would you choose, based on the report?

   _____
   _____

while reading your anchor book

Weighing Your Options: Plasma or LCD TV?

Link to Real Life

When it comes to flat panel high-definition televisions, the choice between Plasma or LCD is a matter of personal taste. A comparison chart of two of the best televisions on the market will help you make the right choice for your needs.

HiDef Plasma TV

42-inch Widescreen

Resolution: 1366 x 768 Pixels

$$ expensive

Modex Flat Panel LCD

42-inch Widescreen

Resolution: 1366 x 768 Pixels

$$$ more expensive

Strengths

- Flat screen
- Produces a bright image with the best color accuracy of any television
- The highest quality image available from any viewing angle
- Bright, lively image

Drawbacks

- Images that stay on screen for a long time can leave traces on the screen. If you watch programs where the same images stay on screen, such as a news channel with a news ticker, this may not be the TV for you.
- If you like watching old black–and–white movies, this is not the TV for you. Plasma televisions have difficulty reproducing pure black.

Strengths

- Flat screen
- Bright picture that can be viewed in very bright conditions
- The most energy efficient television on the market
- Warmer, deeper image

Drawbacks

- A "screen-door effect" can occasionally happen (where an image looks as if it is being viewed through a screen door).
- Outlines of moving people or objects can appear jagged or blocky due to image delays.

Compare and Contrast

THE BIG Q

In the following article, the author uses two methods of organization: chronological and compare-contrast.
Guiding Question: **How do the two forms of organization work together to help you understand the conflict these storms create?**

Extreme Weather
Hurricanes and Tornadoes

Link to Science

Hurricanes and tornadoes are both destructive storms, but they are different in many ways. The following earth science article helps explain the differences between the two kinds of severe weather.

Imagine having your dinner interrupted by a deadly guest—a tornado. That's what happened to Carson and his family as they enjoyed a simple dinner of pancakes in their Kansas home. The sky out one window turned a dark gray, warning sirens blared, and the electricity went out. Carson, his mother, and his four sisters fled to the basement and listened as the storm grew louder and louder, like a train rumbling toward them. Then it was silent.

When they went upstairs, they saw that their neighborhood in Hesston, Kansas, had changed forever. The family's roof had fallen in. Other houses had been blown away. One car had been picked up and blown into a tree. Miraculously, nobody died in the storm, but it left a scar on the town that would linger for years.

Like tornadoes, hurricanes also send people running to basements and shelters for cover. After Hurricane Andrew hit Florida, many people returned to the surface to find that their homes had been flattened. Victims of Hurricane Katrina were forced to flee their homes when ocean water flooded their neighborhoods. The hurricanes devastated communities, killed many people, and left others homeless.

Hurricanes and tornadoes can both have a severe impact on a community, but they are vastly different. Learning about the nature of these powerful storms can help us better understand how to prepare for them.

BACKGROUND IMAGE: September 2003: The eye of Hurricane Isabel, as seen from the International Space Station (ISS).

HURRICANES

A hurricane is a storm that forms over oceans in the tropics. It begins with a low-pressure area that creates winds that grow increasingly violent. These winds move at high speeds in a circle around the low-pressure center, which is called "the eye" of the storm. Hurricane winds can move at 74 to more than 155 miles (199 to more than 250 kilometers) per hour, although most hurricanes are at the low end of the range. In the Northern Hemisphere, the winds circle in a counterclockwise direction. In the Southern Hemisphere, they blow clockwise.

Inside the eye of the storm, the winds are still, but the sea is turbulent. The eye can cover 20 miles (32 kilometers), while the entire hurricane is often 300 miles (483 kilometers) in diameter. From the edge of the eye outward, heavy rains pour down and gale winds whip up the sea. Huge waves billow up. The winds also push water violently ahead, creating a storm tide along the shore. If a high tide meets the storm tide, the rapid rush of water can cause devastation on shore. The violent winds and heavy rains of the hurricane follow the storm tide with more destruction of lives and property. Then as the hurricane moves across the land, its winds begin to slow down. The storm subsides into heavy rainfall, and the destruction ceases.

TORNADOES

A tornado is also a violent wind storm, but it is much more concentrated in its damage. Most tornadoes are less than 300 yards (275 meters) across. However, the winds can reach speeds of 300 or more miles (483 kilometers) per hour. In the Northern Hemisphere, the wind moves around the center of the storm in a counterclockwise direction. In the Southern Hemisphere, the winds move clockwise. Tornadoes occur most often on land, but they can also form at sea. Those tornadoes are known as "waterspouts." Although tornadoes form all over the world, they are most common in the Midwest and West, particularly in Kansas, Iowa, Texas, and Oklahoma.

A tornado often forms on a hot, moist, spring afternoon. A cloud becomes heavy and dark and begins to whirl and twist. Rain, hail, and lightning follow. A narrow column of whirling air that resembles a funnel reaches down from the cloud and touches the ground. On contact, great destruction occurs. Trees and buildings are blown down. People, animals, and objects fly through the air. Sometimes buildings explode because of the severe drop in air pressure. However, this violent destruction only lasts a very short time. The tornado only causes destruction when it touches the ground, and this contact is brief. Unlike hurricanes, which can cover 300 miles (483 kilometers), tornadoes normally cover less than 16 miles (26 kilometers) before they are spent.

SURVIVING EXTREME WEATHER

Carson and his family were able to survive their ordeal with a tornado because the sirens warned them that a storm was on its way. The family also knew that the safest place to go during a tornado was the basement, where they would be protected from the dangers of the violent winds. These two factors—technology and education—are the best protection against extreme weather.

While tornado sirens might only give a few minutes' notice, satellites can help us predict where a hurricane will strike days in advance. Armed with advance warning, people in a storm's path can get out of the way before disaster strikes, either by rushing to a basement or, in the case of a hurricane, leaving town for a few days. This is good news, because while extreme weather might be fascinating to read about or watch on TV, the last thing you want to do is get caught in its path.

September 2005: Hurricane Katrina aftermath.

Stormchasers save lives by following and studying the path of severe storms. The information they collect helps meteorologists to predict the paths of storms.

Thinking About the Selection

Extreme Weather: Hurricanes and Tornadoes

1 **Compare and Contrast** Complete the Venn diagram with sentences from the selection that tell how hurricanes and tornadoes are alike and how they are different.

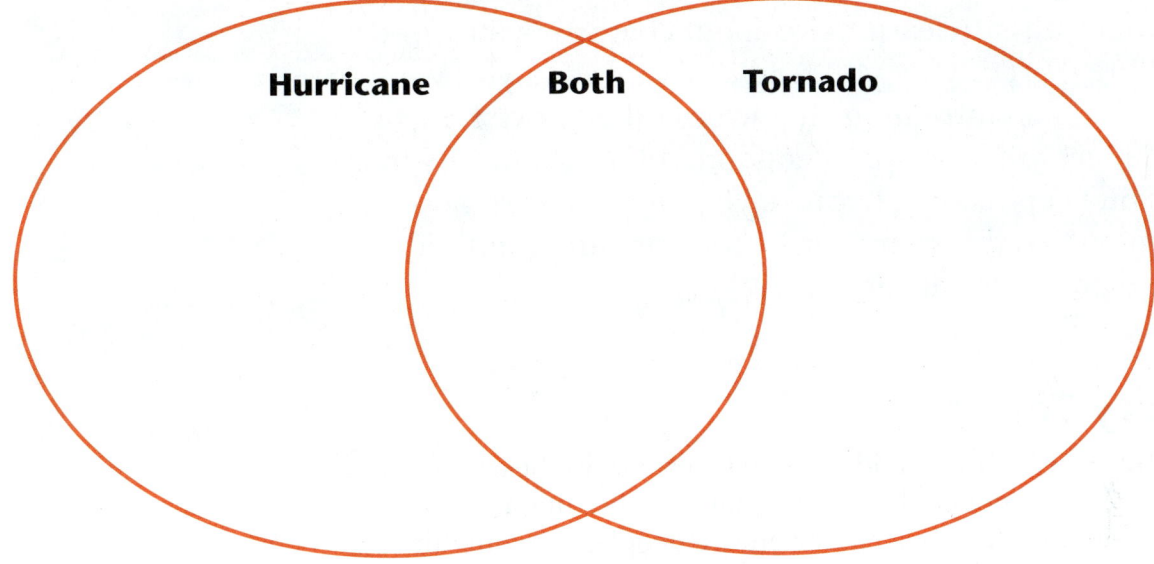

2 **Analyze** What text features does the author use to show that he is comparing and contrasting hurricanes?

_____

_____

Write Answer the following questions in your Reader's Journal.

3 **Interpret** To what extent do the two forms of organization (chronological and compare-contrast) help clarify the main idea and help you understand the conflict these storms create?

4 **Compare and Contrast** Choose two characters from your Anchor Book. Compare and contrast the personalities of the two characters. How do they both serve the author's purpose in the novel?

Ready for a Free-Choice Book? Your teacher may ask you if you would like to choose another book to read on your own. Select a book that fits your interest and that you'll enjoy. As you read, think about how your new book compares with your Anchor Book.

Compare and Contrast **155**

2-10 Literary Analysis
Character

"What a character!" We use this expression to describe people whose personality and behavior intrigue us. Writers know that readers want to learn more about characters they find compelling. Part of why you read a novel is that you want to find out what an intriguing character will do next: how he or she will react to events, problems, and other characters in the novel. You keep reading because you want to learn how things will turn out for this character—this captivating individual you have grown to care about.

Literary Terms

- A **character** is an individual who takes part in the action of a narrative (a novel, short story, play, or other literary work that tells a story). Most characters are people, but sometimes a character is an animal or other nonhuman being (such as a robot or an alien) that has human traits.

- **Major characters** are the most important characters in a narrative. **Minor characters** are characters that enrich a narrative and take part in the action but are not the focus of attention.

- The **protagonist** is the main character in a narrative—the character you care the most about and whose conflict is central to the plot. The **antagonist** is a character or a force that is in conflict with the protagonist.

- A **dynamic character** is one who changes over the course of a narrative. A dynamic character develops and learns something as a result of what happens. A **static character** is one who does not change over the course of a narrative. Minor characters are usually static characters.

- A **round character** is a complex, fully developed character with many aspects to his or her personality, both strengths and weaknesses. A **flat character** is a one-dimensional character who has only one or two personality traits. Minor characters are often flat characters.

Directions Read the following passage. Identify the protagonist, and underline details that provide information about this character. Then, answer the questions that follow.

from Raymond's Run
by Toni Cade Bambara

I don't have much work to do around the house like some girls. My mother does that. And I don't have to earn my pocket money by hustling; George runs errands for the big boys and sells Christmas cards. And anything else that's got to get done, my father does. All I have to do in life is mind my brother Raymond, which is enough. Sometimes I slip and say my little brother Raymond. But as any fool can see he's much bigger and he's older too. But a lot of people call him my little brother cause he needs looking after cause he's not quite right. And a lot of smart mouths got lots to say about that too, especially when George was minding him. But now, if anybody has anything to say to Raymond, anything to say about his big head, they have to come by me. And I don't play the dozens[1] or believe in standing around with somebody in my face doing a lot of talking. I much rather just knock you down and take my chances even if I am a little girl with skinny arms and a squeaky voice, which is how I got the name Squeaky. And if things get too rough, I run. And as anybody can tell you, I'm the fastest thing on two feet.

[1] the **dozens** game in which the players insult one another; the first to show anger loses.

1. **Analyze** Summarize what we learn about the protagonist and the conflict she is facing.

2. **Infer** Will she become a dynamic character—one who is likely to undergo a change during the course of the story? Explain why or why not.

Character 157

Characterization

Writers reveal what their characters are like in many ways. If a writer simply tells the reader that a character is funny, the reader will probably be bored. Instead, the writer must show that the character is funny. In a novel, the writer uses characterization not only to show what a character is like but also to show how he or she changes.

© Scott McCloud

Literary Terms

- **Character traits** are the qualities, attitudes, and values that a character possesses, such as dependability, intelligence, stubbornness, or selfishness.

- **Characterization** is the way or ways in which a writer reveals a character's traits.

- With **direct characterization,** the writer comes right out and tells you what a character is like, making direct statements about his or her character traits.

▶ With **indirect characterization**, the writer hints at what a character is like by showing the character's actions, presenting the character's words and thoughts, describing the character's appearance, and revealing character traits in other ways.

Directions Read the following selection. Underline details that reveal Jim's mother's character traits, either directly or indirectly. Then, answer the questions that follow.

from the novel *Jim the Boy*
by Tony Earley

Jim's mother opened the stove door with a dishrag. Mama was tall and pale and handsome; her neck was long and white. Although she was not yet thirty years old, she wore a long, black skirt that had belonged to her mother. The skirt did not make her seem older, but rather made the people in the room around her feel odd, as if they had wandered into an old photograph, and did not know how to behave. On the days mama wore her mother's long clothes, Jim didn't let the screen door slam.

"There he is," Mama said. "The birthday boy."

Jim's heart rose up briefly, like a scrap of paper on a breath of wind, and then quickly settled back to the ground. His love for his mother was tethered by a sympathy Jim felt knotted in the dark of his stomach. The death of Jim's father had broken something inside her that had not healed. She pulled the heaviness that had once been grief behind her like a plow. The uncles, the women of the church, the people of the town, had long since given up on trying to talk her into leaving the plow where it lay. Instead they grew used to stepping over, or walking inside, the deep furrows she left in her wake. Jim knew only that his mother was sad, and that he figured somehow in her sadness. When she leaned over to kiss him, the lilaced smell of her cheek was as sweet and sad at once as the smell of freshly turned earth in the churchyard.

while reading your anchor book

1 Identify What do you learn about Jim's mother through direct characterization?

_____
_____

2 Classify What do you learn about Jim's mother through indirect characterization? Use the following chart to classify the details the writer provides.

Method of Indirect Characterization	Details
Actions	
Words and Thoughts	
Appearance and Clothing	
Effect on Other Characters	

3 Analyze Use these details to write a sentence analyzing the character of Jim's mother.

_____
_____
_____

4 Compare Compare how the author presents characters in your Anchor Book with how Tony Earley describes his characters on the previous page.

_____
_____
_____

In the following short story, the author focuses on helping you understand how important the character Hamadi is to Susan, the protagonist.
Guiding Question: **How does Hamadi help Susan through a conflict?**

HAMADI
by Naomi Shihab Nye

Background *This story focuses on Susan, a teenage girl, and Saleh Hamadi, a Palestinian refugee. Before 1948, the region that is now Israel was known as Palestine. When ethnic fighting broke out in the late 1940s, many Palestinians fled the violence and settled in other nations. Older members of these refugee communities, like Hamadi, kept alive the traditions of the homeland they left behind.*

Vocabulary Builder

Before you read, *you will discuss the following words. In the Vocabulary Builder box in the margin, use a vocabulary building strategy to make the words your own.*

distinctions   refugees   melancholy

As you read, *draw a box around unfamiliar words you could add to your vocabulary. Use context clues to unlock their meaning.*

Marking the Text

Character and Characterization

As you read, underline details that reveal what Susan and Hamadi are like. In the margin, explain what the author is trying to reveal about these characters through these details.

Susan didn't really feel interested in Saleh Hamadi until she was a freshman in high school carrying a thousand questions around. Why this way? Why not another way? Who said so and why can't I say something else? Those brittle women at school in the counselor's office treated the world as if it were a yardstick and they had tight hold of both ends.

Character and Characterization   **161**

Sometimes Susan felt polite with them, sorting attendance cards during her free period, listening to them gab about fingernail polish and television. And other times she felt she could run out of the building yelling. That's when she daydreamed about Saleh Hamadi, who had nothing to do with any of it. Maybe she thought of him as escape, the way she used to think about the Sphinx at Giza[1] when she was younger. She would picture the golden Sphinx sitting quietly in the desert with sand blowing around its face, never changing its expression. She would think of its wry, slightly crooked mouth and how her grandmother looked a little like that as she waited for her bread to bake in the old village north of Jerusalem. Susan's family had lived in Jerusalem for three years before she was ten and drove out to see her grandmother every weekend. They would find her patting fresh dough between her hands, or pressing cakes of dough onto the black rocks in the taboon, the rounded old oven outdoors. Sometimes she moved her lips as she worked. Was she praying? Singing a secret song? Susan had never seen her grandmother rushing.

Now that she was fourteen, she took long walks in America with her father down by the drainage ditch at the end of their street. Pecan trees shaded the path. She tried to get him to tell stories about his childhood in Palestine. She didn't want him to forget anything. She helped her American mother complete tedious kitchen tasks without complaining—rolling grape leaves around their lemony rice stuffing, scrubbing carrots for the roaring juicer. Some evenings when the soft Texas twilight pulled them all outside, she thought of her far-away grandmother and said, "Let's go see Saleh Hamadi. Wouldn't he like some of that cheese pie Mom made?" And they would wrap a slice of pie and drive downtown. Somehow he felt like a good substitute for a grandmother, even though he was a man.

Usually Hamadi was wearing a white shirt, shiny black tie, and a jacket that reminded Susan of the earth's surface just above the treeline on a mountain—thin, somehow purified. He would raise his hands high before giving advice.

"It is good to drink a tall glass of water every morning upon arising!" If anyone doubted this, he would shake his head. "Oh Susan, Susan, Susan," he would say.

He did not like to sit down, but he wanted everyone else to sit down. He made Susan sit on the wobbly chair beside the desk and he made her father or mother sit in the saggy center of the bed. He told them people should eat six small meals a day.

They visited him on the sixth floor of the Traveler's Hotel, where he had lived so long nobody could remember him ever

---

[1] **Sphinx** (sfinks) **at Giza** huge statue with the head of a man and the body of a lion.

Literature in Context
Guided by Gibran

Kahlil Gibran's most famous work, *The Prophet,* has appealed to millions of readers looking for meaning and dignity in ordinary life. It was first published in 1923 in English and has been translated into at least twenty languages.

Born in Bsharri, Lebanon, in 1883, Gibran eventually settled in New York City, where he began to publish his short stories and exhibit his paintings. The novelist, poet, philosopher, essayist, and artist died in 1931 at the age of forty-eight and was buried in his hometown. Gibran once summarized *The Prophet* this way: "You are far greater than you know, and all is well."

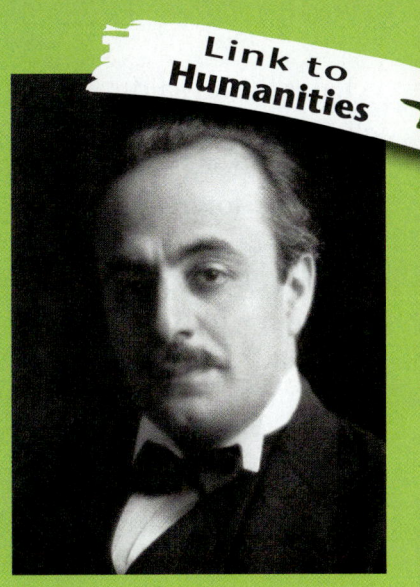

Link to Humanities

traveling. Susan's father used to remind him of the apartments available over the Victory Cleaners, next to the park with the fizzy pink fountain, but Hamadi would shake his head, pinching kisses at his spartan room. "A white handkerchief spread across a tabletop, my two extra shoes lined by the wall, this spells 'home' to me, this says 'mi casa.' What more do I need?"

Hamadi liked to use Spanish words. They made him feel expansive, worldly. He'd learned them when he worked at the fruits and vegetables warehouse on Zarzamora Street, marking off crates of apples and avocados on a long white pad. Occasionally he would speak Arabic, his own first language, with Susan's father and uncles, but he said it made him feel too sad, as if his mother might step into the room at any minute, her arms laden with fresh mint leaves. He had come to the United States on a boat when he was eighteen years old and he had never been married. "I married books," he said. "I married the wide horizon."

"What is he to us?" Susan used to ask her father. "He's not a relative, right? How did we meet him to begin with?"

Susan's father couldn't remember. "I think we just drifted together. Maybe we met at your uncle Hani's house. Maybe that old Maronite priest who used to cry after every service introduced us. The priest once shared an apartment with Kahlil Gibran[2] in New York—so he said. And Saleh always says he stayed with Gibran when he first got off the boat. I'll bet that popular guy Gibran has had a lot of roommates he doesn't even know about."

Susan said, "Dad, he's dead."

"I know, I know," her father said.

---

[2] **Kahil Gibran,** (kəlēl jə brän), Lebanese writer and artist who lived from 1883 to 1931; his most famous book is *The Prophet* (see Literature in Context).

Later Susan said, "Mr. Hamadi, did you really meet Kahlil Gibran? He's one of my favorite writers." Hamadi walked slowly to the window of his room and stared out. There wasn't much to look at down on the street—a bedraggled³ flower shop, a boarded-up tavern with a hand-lettered sign tacked to the front, GONE TO FIND JESUS. Susan's father said the owners had really gone to Alabama.

Hamadi spoke patiently. "Yes, I met brother Gibran. And I meet him in my heart every day. When I was a young man—shocked by all the visions of the new world—the tall buildings—the wild traffic—the young people without shame—the proud mailboxes in their blue uniforms—I met him. And he has stayed with me every day of my life."

"But did you really meet him, like in person, or just in a book?"

He turned dramatically. "Make no such **distinctions,** my friend. Or your life will be a pod with only dried-up beans inside. Believe anything can happen."

Susan's father looked irritated, but Susan smiled. "I do," she said. "I believe that. I want fat beans. If I imagine something, it's true, too. Just a different kind of true."

Susan's father was twiddling with the knobs on the old-fashioned sink. "Don't they even give you hot water here? You don't mean to tell me you've been living without hot water?"

On Hamadi's rickety desk lay a row of different "Love" stamps issued by the post office.

---

³ **bedraggled** (bi dra′ gəld) *adj.*, limp and dirty as if dragged through the mud.

Vocabulary Builder

distinctions
(di stingk′shəns) *n.*

Meaning

▼ **Critical Viewing**
How does the collage below help communicate who Hamadi is?

"You must write a lot of letters," Susan said.

"No, no, I'm just focusing on that word," Hamadi said. "I particularly like the globe in the shape of a heart," he added.

"Why don't you take a trip back to his village in Lebanon?" Susan's father asked. "Maybe you still have relatives living there."

Hamadi looked pained. "'Remembrance is a form of meeting,' my brother Gibran says, and I do believe I meet with my cousins every day."

"But aren't you curious? You've been gone so long! Wouldn't you like to find out what has happened to everybody and everything you knew as a boy?" Susan's father traveled back to Jerusalem once every year to see his family.

"I would not. In fact, I already know. It is there and it is not there. Would you like to share an orange with me?"

His long fingers, tenderly peeling. Once when Susan was younger, he'd given her a lavish ribbon off a holiday fruit basket and expected her to wear it on her head. In the car, Susan's father said, "Riddles. He talks in riddles. I don't know why I have patience with him." Susan stared at the people talking and laughing in the next car. She did not even exist in their world.

Susan carried *The Prophet* around on top of her English textbook and her Texas history. She and her friend Tracy read it out loud to one another at lunch. Tracy was a junior—they'd met at the literary magazine meeting where Susan, the only freshman on the staff, got assigned to do proofreading. They never ate in the cafeteria; they sat outside at picnic tables with sack lunches, whole wheat crackers and fresh peaches. Both of them had given up meat.

Marking the Text

while reading your anchor book

Character and Characterization 165

Tracy's eyes looked steamy. "You know that place where Gibran says, 'Hate is a dead thing. Who of you would be a tomb?'"

Susan nodded. Tracy continued. "Well, I hate someone. I'm trying not to, but I can't help it. I hate Debbie for liking Eddie and it's driving me nuts."

"Why shouldn't Debbie like Eddie?" Susan said. "You do."

Tracy put her head down on her arms. A gang of cheerleaders walked by giggling. One of them flicked her finger in greeting.

"In fact, we all like Eddie," Susan said. "Remember, here in this book—wait and I'll find it—where Gibran says that loving teaches us the secrets of our hearts and that's the way we connect to all of Life's heart? You're not talking about liking or loving, you're talking about owning."

Tracy looked glum. "Sometimes you remind me of a minister."

Susan said, "Well, just talk to me someday when I'm depressed."

Susan didn't want a boyfriend. Everyone who had boyfriends or girlfriends all seemed to have troubles. Susan told people she had a boyfriend far away, on a farm in Missouri, but the truth was, boys still seemed like cousins to her. Or brothers. Or even girls.

A squirrel sat in the crook of a tree, eyeing their sandwiches. When the end-of-lunch bell blared, Susan and Tracy jumped—it always seemed too soon. Squirrels were lucky; they didn't have to go to school.

Susan's father said her idea was ridiculous: to invite Saleh Hamadi to go Christmas caroling with the English Club. "His English is archaic⁴, for one thing, and he won't know any of the songs."

"How could you live in America for years and not know 'Joy to the World' or 'Away in a Manger'?"

"Listen, I grew up right down the road from 'Oh Little Town of Bethlehem' and I still don't know a single verse."

"I want him. We need him. It's boring being with the same bunch of people all the time."

So they called Saleh and he said he would come—"thrilled" was the word he used. He wanted to ride the bus to their house, he didn't want anyone to pick him up. Her father muttered, "He'll probably forget to get off." Saleh thought "caroling" meant they were going out with a woman named Carol. He said, "Holiday spirit—I was just reading about it in the newspaper."

Susan said, "Dress warm."

Saleh replied, "Friend, my heart is warmed simply to hear your voice."

All that evening Susan felt light and bouncy. She decorated the coffee can they would use to collect donations to be sent to the children's hospital in Bethlehem. She had started doing this last

---

⁴ **archaic**, (är kā ik) *adj.*, old-fashioned; out-of-date.

year in middle school, when a singing group collected $100 and the hospital responded on exotic onion-skin stationery that they were "eternally grateful."

Her father shook his head. "You get something into your mind and it really takes over," he said. "Why do you like Hamadi so much all of a sudden? You could show half as much interest in your own uncles."

Susan laughed. Her uncles were dull. Her uncles shopped at the mall and watched TV. "Anyone who watches TV more than twelve minutes a week is uninteresting," she said.

Her father lifted an eyebrow.

"He's my surrogate grandmother," she said. "He says interesting things. He makes me think. Remember when I was little and he called me The Thinker? We have a connection." She added, "Listen, do you want to go too? It is not a big deal. And Mom has a great voice, why don't you both come?"

A minute later her mother was digging in the closet for neck scarves, and her father was digging in the drawer for flashlight batteries.

Saleh Hamadi arrived precisely on time, with flushed red cheeks and a sack of dates stuffed in his pocket. "We may need sustenance on our journey." Susan thought the older people seemed quite giddy as they drove down to the high school to meet the rest of the carolers. Strands of winking lights wrapped around their neighbors' drainpipes and trees. A giant Santa tipped his hat on Dr. Garcia's roof.

Her friends stood gathered in front of the school. Some were smoothing out song sheets that had been crammed in a drawer or cabinet for a whole year. Susan thought holidays were strange; they came, and you were supposed to feel ready for them. What if you could make up your own holidays as you went along? She had read about a woman who used to have parties to celebrate the arrival of fresh asparagus in the local market. Susan's friends might make holidays called Eddie Looked at Me Today and Smiled.

Two people were alleluia-ing in harmony. Saleh Hamadi went around the group formally introducing himself to each person and shaking hands. A few people laughed behind their hands when his back was turned. He had stepped out of a painting, or a newscast, with his outdated long overcoat, his clunky old men's shoes and elegant manners.

Susan spoke more loudly than usual. "I'm honored to introduce you to one of my best friends, Mr. Hamadi."

"Good evening to you," he pronounced musically, bowing a bit from the waist.

What could you say back but "Good evening, sir." His old-fashioned manners were contagious.

Character and Characterization

They sang at three houses which never opened their doors. They sang "We Wish You a Merry Christmas" each time they moved on. Lisa had a fine, clear soprano. Tracy could find the alto harmony to any line. Cameron and Elliot had more enthusiasm than accuracy. Lily, Rita, and Jeannette laughed every time they said a wrong word and fumbled to find their places again. Susan loved to see how her mother knew every word of every verse without looking at the paper, and her father kept his hands in his pockets and seemed more interested in examining people's mailboxes or yard displays than in trying to sing. And Saleh Hamadi—what language was he singing in? He didn't even seem to be pronouncing words, but humming deeply from his throat. Was he saying, "Om?" Speaking Arabic? Once he caught her looking and whispered, "That was an Aramaic word that just drifted into my mouth—the true language of the Bible, you know, the language Jesus Christ himself spoke."

By the fourth block their voices felt tuned up and friendly people came outside to listen. Trays of cookies were passed around and dollar bills stuffed into the little can. Thank you, thank you. Out of the dark from down the block, Susan noticed Eddie sprinting toward them with his coat flapping, unbuttoned. She shot a glance at Tracy, who pretended not to notice. "Hey, guys!" shouted Eddie. "The first time in my life I'm late and everyone else is on time! You could at least have left a note about which way you were going." Someone slapped him on the back.

Saleh Hamadi, whom he had never seen before, was the only one who managed a reply. "Welcome, welcome to our cheery group!"

Eddie looked mystified. "Who is this guy?"

Susan whispered, "My friend."

Eddie approached Tracy, who read her song sheet intently just then, and stuck his face over her shoulder to whisper, "Hi." Tracy stared straight ahead into the air and whispered "Hi" vaguely, glumly. Susan shook her head. Couldn't Tracy act more cheerful at least? They were walking again. They passed a string of blinking reindeer and a wooden snowman holding a painted candle. Ridiculous!

Eddie fell into step beside Tracy, murmuring so Susan couldn't hear him anymore. Saleh Hamadi was flinging his arms up high as he strode. Was he power walking? Did he even know what power walking was? Between houses, Susan's mother hummed obscure songs people never remembered: "What Child Is This?" and "The Friendly Beasts."

Lisa moved over to Eddie's other side. "I'm so excited about you and Debbie!" she said loudly. "Why didn't she come tonight?"

Eddie said, "She has a sore throat."

Tracy shrank up inside her coat.

Lisa chattered on. "James said we should make our reservations now for dinner at the Tower after the Sweetheart Dance, can you believe it? In December, making a reservation for February? But otherwise it might get booked up!"

Saleh Hamadi tuned into this conversation with interest; the Tower was downtown, in his neighborhood. He said, "This sounds like significant preliminary planning! Maybe you can be an international advisor someday." Susan's mother bellowed, "Joy to the World!" and voices followed her, stretching for notes. Susan's father was gazing off into the sky. Maybe he thought about all the **refugees** in camps in Palestine far from doorbells and shutters. Maybe he thought about the horizon beyond Jerusalem when he was a boy, how it seemed to be inviting him, "Come over, come over." Well, he'd come all the way to the other side of the world, and now he was doomed to live in two places at once. To Susan, immigrants seemed bigger than other people, and always slightly **melancholy.** They also seemed doubly interesting. Maybe someday Susan would meet one her own age.

Two thin streams of tears rolled down Tracy's face. Eddie had drifted to the other side of the group and was clowning with Cameron, doing a tap dance shuffle. "While fields and floods, rocks hills and plains, repeat the sounding joy, repeat the sounding joy . . ." Susan and Saleh Hamadi noticed her. Hamadi peered into Tracy's face, inquiring, "Why? Is it pain? Is it gratitude? We are such mysterious creatures, human beings!"

refugees
(re´ fyū jēz) *n.*

Meaning

melancholy
(me´ lən kä lē) *adj.*

Meaning

Tracy turned to him, pressing her face against the old wool of his coat, and wailed. The song ended. All eyes on Tracy, and this tall, courteous stranger who would never in a thousand years have felt comfortable stroking her hair. But he let her stand there, crying as Susan stepped up to stand firmly on the other side of Tracy, putting her arms around her friend. Hamadi said something Susan would remember years later, whenever she was sad herself, even after college, a creaky anthem sneaking back into her ear, "We go on. On and on. We don't stop where it hurts. We turn a corner. It is the reason why we are living. To turn a corner. Come, let's move."

Above them, in the heavens, stars lived out their lonely lives. People whispered, "What happened? What's wrong?" Half of them were already walking down the street.

Vocabulary Builder

After you read, review the words you decided to add to your vocabulary. Write the meaning of words you have learned in context. Look up the other words in a dictionary, glossary, thesaurus, or electronic resource.

Naomi Shihab Nye (b. 1952)

An award-winning poet and fiction writer, Naomi Shihab Nye is concerned with "paying attention to the world." Perhaps the richness of her multicultural heritage and her time spent living in the Middle East inspired her. The daughter of a Palestinian father and an American mother, Nye grew up in St. Louis, Missouri, but she and her family lived in Jerusalem and Ramallah, Jordan, when she was in high school. Nye's most recent poetry collections include *You and Yours* (2005) and *19 Variations of Gazelle: Poems of the Middle East* (2002). Nye is also the author of the young adult novels *Going Going* (2005) and *Habibi* (1997). She currently lives in San Antonio, Texas, the setting of "Hamadi."

Thinking About the Selection
Hamadi

1. **Speculate** Is Tracy a major or minor character? What was the author's purpose for including her in the story? Explain.

2. **Analyze** Describe Susan's connection to Hamadi. Why do you think they get along well?

3. **Interpret** Explain how the following quotation reflects the story's theme. Use specific details from the story in your response. "We go on. On and on. We don't stop where it hurts. We turn a corner. It is the reason why we are living. To turn a corner. Come, let's move."

4. **Analyze** Look back at the character details you underlined in the story and your notes in the margin. Which method of characterization—direct or indirect—does the author use most often to reveal what Susan and Hamadi are like? Are these characters round or flat? Dynamic or static? Support your character analysis with evidence from the story.

Write Answer the following questions in your Reader's Journal.

5. **Interpret** How does Hamadi help Susan through a conflict?

6. **Adapt** The short story "Hamadi" clearly communicates Hamadi's importance to Susan. If you were going to rewrite your anchor book as a short story, which aspect of the novel would you focus on as you adapted it to a shorter, more focused form? Describe and explain your choice.

Character and Characterization

2-11 Literary Analysis
Point of View

Imagine a situation in which a runner in a relay race drops the baton and costs her team a victory. How would the runner's account of the event differ from that of a sportswriter?

Runner's Account	Sportswriter's Account
Oh no! I can't believe I dropped the baton. I've got no other choice than to go back and get it. We'll lose the race now and it's my fault.	As Chiara sprinted to what looked like an easy win, she stumbled and dropped the baton. The other team's runner raced ahead of her to victory.

Literary Terms

Point of view is the perspective from which a literary work is told.

- In a narrative told from the **first-person point of view**, the narrator is a character who is part of the action and uses the pronouns *I*, *me*, and *my*. With a first-person point of view, the reader sees, hears, and understands only what this character sees, hears, and understands—and only what this character chooses to reveal. The runner's account above is an example of the first-person point of view.

- In a narrative told from the **third-person point of view**, the narrator is someone outside the action who uses the character names and the pronouns *he*, *she*, *they*, *them*, and *their*. There are two types of third-person points of view.

    - With the **omniscient third-person point of view**, the narrator is an all-knowing observer who can describe everything that happens and can reveal every character's thoughts and feelings.

    - With the **limited third-person point of view**, the narrator views the world through a single character's eyes and reveals only what that character is experiencing. The sportswriter's account above is an example of limited third-person point of view.

Directions Read the following passage. Underline details that identify the point of view. Then answer the questions.

from *"Beauty Lessons"*
by Judith Ortiz Cofer

Paco is watching me again, I can feel it. I'm taking my math book out of my locker while everyone else stampedes down the hall, but I just know that he's somewhere in the crowd, staring a hole right through me. It's just that I haven't caught him doing it yet. Paco is shy and the best student in Mrs. Laguna's algebra class, the one class we have together, but this year he's trying to be tough instead of smart. It's only because he's getting a lot of pressure from the other boys, Luis Cintrón and them, to join their "social club," as they call their gang at school. If I was good-looking and popular, I'd be getting offers to hang out with them too.

1 **Identify** What point of view is used in this passage? What words does the author use to help you understand the narrator's point of view?

2 **Analyze** How does the point of view affect your understanding of and reaction to the passage?

3 **Apply** Rewrite this passage, using the omniscient third-person point of view.

Point of View 173

Irony

What do you think the writer is saying in this sentence?

"Don't be nervous—it's only the most important test of your life!"

The writer seems to be saying that the test is not a cause for worry, but the sentence actually conveys the opposite message. The writer is being ironic, creating a deliberate contrast between what these words seem to mean and what they really do mean.

Literary Terms

Irony is a contrast or contradiction between appearance and reality, between expectation and outcome, or between meaning and intention. There are three types of irony.

Type of Irony	Definition	Example
Verbal Irony	A writer, speaker, or character says something that is the opposite of what that person really means.	A mother looks into her daughter's messy room and says, "Great job cleaning up your room!"
Situational Irony	Something happens that contradicts what the reader, the audience, or a character expects to happen.	In the state championship, the worst player on the baseball team ends up hitting the game-winning home run.
Dramatic Irony	The reader or audience knows or understands something that a character does not.	A character in a play disguises himself, but the audience realizes that the other characters recognize him.

Directions Complete the following chart with your own example of each type of irony.

Type of Irony	Example
Verbal Irony	
Situational Irony	
Dramatic Irony	

Directions Read the cartoon, and then answer the questions that follow.

1 **Identify** What type or types of irony is the cartoon showing?

_____

2 **Analyze** Explain why this cartoon is ironic.

_____
_____
_____
_____

3 **Identify** What type of irony is each of the following an example of?

The Titanic, a massive ship hailed by the media as "unsinkable" before its fateful voyage, was too large and too slow to avoid the iceberg that caused the ship to sink.	A contestant auditioning for a singing competition sings so badly, yet so memorably, that he becomes popular, appearing on cable music channels and producing his own album.
Type of irony: _____	Type of irony: _____

Irony **175**

THE BIG Q

In the following story, the author uses the first-person point of view to place you inside the main character's head.
Guiding Question: **How does the character's point of view affect your understanding of the conflict?**

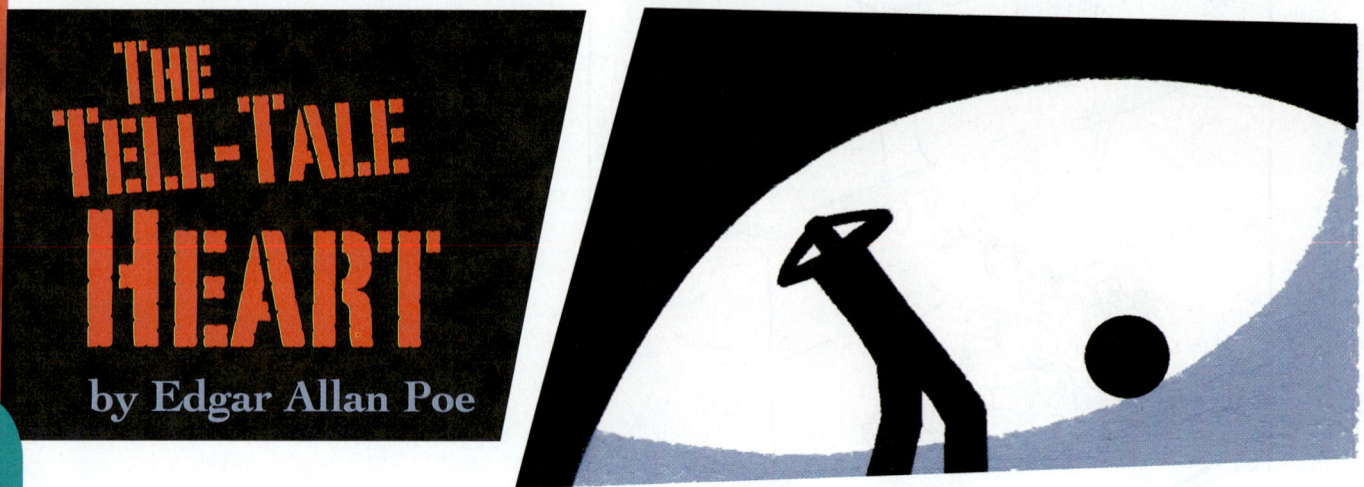

The Tell-Tale Heart
by Edgar Allan Poe

Background *Edgar Allan Poe led a short and troubled life and died in poverty. Yet his terrifying tales that keep readers wide awake at night have made him a literary star long after his death.*

Vocabulary Builder

Before you read, you will discuss the following words. In the Vocabulary Builder box in the margin, use a vocabulary building strategy to make the words your own.

acute   distinctness   ceased   derision

As you read, draw a box around unfamiliar words you could add to your vocabulary. Use context clues to unlock their meaning.

Marking the Text

Point of View and Irony

As you read, underline details suggesting that the narrator's point of view might not be accurate or trustworthy. Also underline details that strike you as ironic. Take notes in the margins about what you marked.

Vocabulary Builder

acute
(ə kyüt´) *adj.*

Meaning

TRUE!—nervous—very, very dreadfully nervous I had been, and am; but why *will* you say that I am mad? The disease had sharpened my senses—not destroyed—not dulled them. Above all was the sense of hearing **acute**. I heard all things in the heaven and in the earth. I heard many things in hell. How, then, am I mad? Hearken![1] and observe how healthily—how calmly I can tell you the whole story.

It is impossible to say how first the idea entered my brain; but, once conceived, it haunted me day and night. Object[2] there was none. Passion there was none. I loved the old man. He had never wronged me. He had never given me insult. For his gold I had

---

[1] **Hearken!** (här´ kən) *v.* Listen!

[2] **Object** (äb´ jekt) *n.* purpose; objective.

176 Lesson 2-11

while reading your anchor book

no desire. I think it was his eye!—yes, it was this! He had the eye of a vulture—a pale blue eye, with a film over it. Whenever it fell upon me, my blood ran cold; and so, by degrees—very gradually—I made up my mind to take the life of the old man, and thus rid myself of the eye forever.

Now this is the point. You fancy me mad. Madmen know nothing. But you should have seen *me.* You should have seen how wisely I proceeded—with what caution—with what foresight—with what dissimulation[3] I went to work! I was never kinder to the old man than during the whole week before I killed him. And every night, about midnight, I turned the latch of his door and opened it—oh so gently! And then, when I had made an opening sufficient for my head, I first put in a dark lantern, all closed, closed, so that no light shone out, and then I thrust in my head. Oh, you would have laughed to see how cunningly I thrust it in! I moved it slowly—very, very slowly, so that I might not disturb the old man's sleep. It took me an hour to place my whole head within the opening so far that I could see the old man as he lay upon his bed. Ha!—would a madman have been so wise as this? And then, when my head was well in the room, I undid the lantern cautiously—oh, so cautiously (for the hinges creaked)—I undid it just so much that a single thin ray fell upon the vulture eye. And this I did for seven long nights—every night just at midnight—but I found the eye always closed; and so it was impossible to do the work; for it was not the old man who vexed[4] me, but his Evil Eye. And every morning, when the day broke, I went boldly into his chamber, and spoke courageously to him, calling him by name in a hearty tone, and inquiring how he had passed the night. So you see he would have been a very profound old man, indeed, to suspect that every night, just at twelve, I looked in upon him while he slept.

Upon the eighth night I was more than usually cautious in opening the door. A watch's minute-hand moves more quickly than did mine. Never, before that night, had I *felt* the extent of my own powers—of my sagacity.[5] I could scarcely contain my feelings of triumph. To think that there I was, opening the door, little by little, and the old man not even to dream of my secret deeds or thoughts. I fairly chuckled at the idea. And perhaps the old man heard me; for he moved in the bed suddenly, as if startled. Now you may think that I drew back—but no. His room was as black as pitch with the thick darkness, (for the shutters were close fastened, through fear of robbers,) and so I knew that

---

[3] **dissimulation** (di sim yə lā′ shən) *n.* concealing or disguising of one's true feelings or intentions.

[4] **vexed** (vekst) *v.* annoyed.

[5] **sagacity** (sə ga′ sə tē) *n.* wisdom and sound judgment.

Point of View and Irony

he could not see the opening of the door, and I kept on pushing it steadily, steadily.

I had got my head in, and was about to open the lantern, when my thumb slipped upon the tin fastening, and the old man sprang up in the bed, crying out—"Who's there?"

I kept quite still and said nothing. For another hour I did not move a muscle, and in the meantime I did not hear the old man lie down. He was still sitting up in the bed, listening;—just as I have done, night after night, hearkening to the death-watches[6] in the wall.

Presently I heard a slight groan, and I knew that it was the groan of mortal terror. It was not a groan of pain, or of grief—oh, no!—it was the low, stifled sound that arises from the bottom of the soul when overcharged with *awe*. I knew the sound well.

---

[6] **death-watches** *n.* wood-boring beetles whose heads make a tapping sound; they are superstitiously regarded as an omen of death.

Many a night, just at midnight, when all the world slept, it has welled up from my own bosom, deepening, with its dreadful echo, the terrors that distracted me. I say I knew it well. I knew what the old man felt, and pitied him, although I chuckled at heart. I knew that he had been lying awake ever since the first slight noise, when he had turned in the bed. His fears had been, ever since, growing upon him. He had been trying to fancy them causeless, but could not. He had been saying to himself—"It is nothing but the wind in the chimney—it is only a mouse crossing the floor," or "it is merely a cricket which has made a single chirp." Yes, he had been trying to comfort himself with these suppositions; but he had found all in vain. *All in vain:* because death, in approaching the old man, had stalked with his black shadow before him, and the shadow had now readied and enveloped the victim. And it was the mournful influence of the unperceived shadow that caused him to feel—although he neither saw nor heard me—to *feel* the presence of my head within the room.

When I had waited a long time, very patiently, without hearing the old man lie down, I resolved to open a little—very, very little crevice in the lantern. So I opened it—you cannot imagine how stealthily, stealthily—until, at length, a single dim ray, like the thread of the spider, shot from out the crevice and fell full upon the vulture eye.

It was open—wide, wide open—and I grew furious as I gazed upon it. I saw it with perfect **distinctness**—all a dull blue, with a hideous veil over it that chilled the very marrow in my bones; but I could see nothing else of the old man's face or person; for I had directed the ray, as if by instinct, precisely upon the damned spot.

And now—have I not told you that what you mistake for madness is but over acuteness of the senses?—now, I say, there came to my ears a *low, dull, quick sound – much such a sound as a watch makes when enveloped in cotton.* I knew *that* sound well, too. It was the beating of the old man's heart. It increased my fury, as the beating of a drum stimulates the soldier into courage.

But even yet I refrained and kept still. I scarcely breathed. I held the lantern motionless. I tried how steadily I could maintain the ray upon the eye. Meantime the hellish tattoo of the heart increased. It grew quicker, and louder and louder every instant. The old man's terror *must* have been extreme! It grew louder, I say, louder every moment:—do you mark me well? I have told you that I am nervous:—so I am. And now, at the dead hour of the night, and amid the dreadful silence of that old house, so strange a noise as this excited me to uncontrollable wrath. Yet, for some minutes longer, I refrained and kept still. But the beating grew louder, *louder*! I thought the heart must burst! And now a new anxiety seized me—the sound would be heard by a neighbor! The old man's hour had come! With a loud yell, I threw

Vocabulary Builder

distinctness
(di stingkt´nes) *n.*

Meaning

open the lantern and leaped into the room. He shrieked once—once only. In an instant I dragged him to the floor, and pulled the heavy bed over him. I then sat upon the bed and smiled gaily, to find the deed so far done. But, for many minutes, the heart beat on, with a muffled sound. This, however, did not vex me; it would not be heard through the walls. At length it **ceased.** The old man was dead. I removed the bed and examined the corpse. Yes, he was stone, stone dead. I placed my hand upon the heart and held it there many minutes. There was no pulsation. The old man was stone dead. His eye would trouble *me* no more.

If, still, you think me mad, you will think so no longer when I describe the wise precautions I took for the concealment of the body. The night waned, and I worked hastily, but in silence. First of all I dismembered the corpse. I cut off the head and the arms and the legs. I then took up three planks from the flooring of the chamber, and deposited all between the scantlings.[7] I then replaced the boards so cleverly, so cunningly, that no human eye—not even *his*—could have detected anything wrong. There was nothing to wash out—no stain of any kind—no blood-spot whatever. I had been too wary for that. A tub had caught all—ha! ha!

When I had made an end of these labors, it was four o' clock—still dark as midnight. As the bell sounded the hour, there came a knocking at the street door. I went down to open it with a light heart—for what had I *now* to fear? There entered three men, who introduced themselves, with perfect suavity, as officers of the police. A shriek had been heard by a neighbor during the night; suspicion of foul play had been aroused; information had been lodged at the police-office, and they (the officers) had been deputed[8] to search the premises.

I smiled,—for *what* had I to fear? I bade the gentlemen welcome. The shriek, I said, was my own in a dream. The old man, I mentioned, was absent in the country. I took my visitors all over the house. I bade them search—search *well*. I led them, at length, to *his* chamber. I showed them his treasures, secure, undisturbed. In the enthusiasm of my confidence, I brought chairs into the room, and desired them *here* to rest from their fatigues; while I myself, in the wild audacity of my perfect triumph, placed my own seat upon the very spot beneath which reposed the corpse of the victim.

The officers were satisfied. My *manner* had convinced them. I was singularly at ease. They sat, and, while I answered cheerily, they chatted of familiar things. But, ere long, I felt myself getting pale and wished them gone. My head ached, and I fancied

Vocabulary Builder

ceased
(sēst) *v.*

Meaning

---

[7] **scantlings** (skant' liŋs) *n.* small beams or timbers.
[8] **deputed** (dep yoot'ed) *v.* appointed.

▼ **Critical Viewing**
What do these illustrations convey about the narrator's point of view?

a ringing in my ears: but still they sat and still chatted. The ringing became more distinct: I talked more freely, to get rid of the feeling; but it continued and gained definitiveness—until, at length, I found that the noise was *not* within my ears.

No doubt I now grew very pale;—but I talked more fluently, and with a heightened voice. Yet the sound increased—and what could I do? It was a *low, dull, quick sound—much such a sound as a watch makes when enveloped in cotton.* I gasped for breath – and yet the officers heard it not. I talked more quickly—and yet the officers heard it not. I talked more quickly—more vehemently;—but the noise steadily increased. I arose, and argued about trifles, in a high key and with violent gesticulations[9];—but the noise steadily increased. Why *would* they not be gone? I paced the floor to and fro, with heavy strides, as if excited to fury by the observations of the men;—but the noise steadily increased. Oh God! What *could* I do? I foamed—I raved—I swore! I swung the chair upon which I had sat, and grated it upon the boards;—but the noise arose over all, and continually increased. It grew

---

[9] **gesticulations** (je sti kyə lā′ shənz) *n.* energetic hand or arm movements.

louder—louder—*louder!* And still men chatted pleasantly, and smiled. Was it possible they heard not? Almighty God!—no, no! They heard!—they suspected!—they *knew!*—they were making a mockery of my horror!—this I thought, and this I think. But anything better than this agony! Anything was more tolerable than this **derision**! I could bear those hypocritical smiles no longer! I felt that I must scream or die!—and now—again! hark! louder! louder! louder! *louder!*—

"Villains!" I shrieked, "dissemble[10] no more! I admit the deed!—tear up the planks!—here, here!—it is the beating of his hideous heart!

---

[10] **dissemble** (di sem′ bəl) *v.* conceal one's true feelings or intentions.

Vocabulary Builder

After you read, *review* the words you decided to add to your vocabulary. Write the meaning of words you have learned in context. Look up the other words in a dictionary, glossary, thesaurus, or electronic resource.

Vocabulary Builder

derision
(di ri′ zhən) *n.*

Meaning

Edgar Allan Poe (1809–1849)

Edgar Allan Poe is considered the inventor of both the horror story and the detective story. His dark exploration of our deepest fears have inspired contemporary writers like Stephen King, and his ideas about the short story have influenced generations of literary critics.

Born in Boston, Poe was the son of professional traveling actors. His father deserted the family when Poe was a baby, and his mother died before he turned three. Young Edgar was then taken in by a wealthy couple. Poe grew into a romantic, irresponsible young man who dreamed of writing poetry and who constantly quarreled with his foster father over money. Forced to withdraw from the University of Virginia during his first year, after his foster father refused to pay his gambling debts, Poe moved to Boston. Soon he published his first book of poetry. Poe went on to achieve some success as a writer, but he was never able to escape from poverty.

Thinking About the Selection
The Tell-Tale Heart

1 **Analyze** What was the author's purpose for writing this story? What is one characteristic of short stories the author used to accomplish his purpose?

2 **Recall** According to the narrator, why does he kill the old man? What argument does he use to try to persuade the reader that he is sane?

3 **Evaluate** Does the point of view of the story make the plot more believable?

4 **Analyze** The story is written from the first-person point of view, revealing only the narrator's thoughts. How would the meaning of the story be different if it revealed the police officers' point of view?

5 **Interpret** Why is the ending of the story ironic? How does the author's use of irony impact the reader's reaction?

Write Answer the following questions in your Reader's Journal.

6 **Explain** Is the main character credible? How does the main character's point of view affect your understanding of the conflict?

7 **Evaluate** Identify the point of view in your anchor book. Is there more than one? Explain how the point of view is important to the novel. Why does the author use this point of view?

Point of View and Irony 183

2-12 Listening and Speaking Workshop
Oral Interpretation of Literature

In this activity, you and your group members will deliver a formal presentation about a term you have learned. Your presentation will include literary terms and formal language that fit your audience and purpose.

Your Task

- Choose a literary term that is represented in your anchor book.
- Analyze your book, considering the author's purpose for using this literary element.
- Review the term for your classmates in an oral presentation.
- Present an oral interpretation of how that term is represented in your book.

Organize Your Presentation

1 **Choose your literary term.** Define the term carefully—your group is responsible for your classmates' understanding. Make sure that your definition is correct and clear.

LITERARY TERM	DEFINITION

2 **Identify a story that will effectively demonstrate your literary term.** All stories demonstrate multiple literary terms. Focus only on the parts of the story that will help you teach your literary term. Support your interpretation with examples and evidence from the text.

3 **Create a visual.** Display your term, its definition, the title, and key words you want your audience to remember. Use visuals to support your instruction. For example, if your term is "characterization," you might use a graphic organizer to explain the different ways an author can create a character.

while reading your anchor book

Rehearse your presentation. As you practice, think about the way you want to express your personal style. Use a clear, consistent voice and tone for your presentation, but adjust your volume, phrasing, enunciation, tone, and inflection to stress important ideas and impact audience response.

 Check for understanding. After your presentation, ask questions to test your audience's understanding of your term. Encourage your listeners to respond by paraphrasing, elaborating, or connecting ideas beyond the scope of your presentation. Have your listeners identify missing, conflicting, or unclear information during your presentation.

Directions Assess your performance. For each question, circle a rating.

SPEAK: Rubric for Oral Interpretation

CRITERIA	RATING SCALE
	NOT VERY VERY
CONTENT How well did the group match the message and vocabulary to the audience and purpose?	1 2 3 4 5
ORGANIZATION How well did the group present clear ideas and logical organization?	1 2 3 4 5
DELIVERY How well did the group demonstrate appropriate eye contact, pacing, and tone?	1 2 3 4 5
DELIVERY How well did the group demonstrate effective use of voice modulation, expression, and correct use of grammar?	1 2 3 4 5
COOPERATION How well did the group work together?	1 2 3 4 5

LISTEN: Rubric for Audience Self-Assessment

CRITERIA	RATING SCALE
	NOT VERY VERY
ACTIVE LISTENING How well did you focus your attention on the speakers? Did you ask questions at the end?	1 2 3 4 5
ACTIVE LISTENING How well did you demonstrate active listening with appropriate silence, responses, and body language?	1 2 3 4 5

2-13 Language Coach
Grammar and Spelling

Verbs—Simple Tenses

The tense of a verb shows the time of an action or a condition. The three simple tenses are *present, past,* and *future*. A regular verb forms its past tense by adding *-ed* or *-d* to the base form. Sometimes you will have to double a final consonant, add a *–d* if the verb ends in *e*, or change *y* to *i* before adding *-ed*.

Present Tense	Past Tense	Future Tense
Base Form	Add *–d* or *–ed* to base form.	Use *will* before the base form.
I play you play he, she, it plays	I played you played he, she, it played	I will play you will play he, she, it will play

Directions Underline each verb, and tell what tense it is.

1. In 1969, American astronauts landed on the moon. _____

2. The idea of space travel started long ago. _____

3. Maybe we will travel to the moon again. _____

4. In 1957, the Soviet Union launched *Sputnik* I into orbit. _____

5. The shuttle crews continue the launching of satellites today. _____

Directions Fill in the blanks with the verb form called for in parentheses.

Example We _____ a train on our vacation. (*use*, past)
We <u>used</u> a train on our vacation.

6. The band _____ their rehearsal. (*stop*, past)

7. By next week, the workers _____ the job. (*finish*, future)

8. Only one train _____ at this station. (*stop*, present)

9. The audience _____ closely to the speaker. (*listen*, past)

Author's Craft

In fiction, writers frequently move between the past and the present. Scan the short story "Hamadi" on page 161 for Hamadi's description of his past. How is this description of the past important to the present moment of the story?

Verbs—Perfect Tenses

The perfect tense describes an action that was or will be completed at a certain time. In perfect tenses, the helping verb changes tense. The perfect tenses are made by adding the appropriate form of *have* to the past participle of the verb. The chart lists the perfect tenses.

Verb Tense	Example: invite (invited)
Present Perfect: action begun in the past that continues up to the present **have + past participle**	I *have invited* my friends to the party.
Past Perfect: action begun in the past that ended **had + past participle**	I *had invited* my friends to the party, but some couldn't make it.
Future Perfect: action begun in the past or present, completed in the future **will have + past participle**	By tonight, I *will have invited* everyone.

Directions Underline the perfect tense verbs in the sentences. Write what tense forms they are.

Example I <u>have enjoyed</u> all kinds of sports. _present perfect_

1. I have taken swimming lessons since October. _____
2. By June 20, I will have attended thirty lessons. _____
3. My teacher has complimented me on my backstroke. _____
4. I have practiced even more lately. _____
5. By the end of August, I will have raced in several events. _____
6. Neither of them had swum before. _____

Directions Rewrite the sentences, adding the indicated form of the verb.

7. By tomorrow, I _____ a great experiment. (*complete*, future perfect)

   _____

8. I _____ about life on Mars. (*wonder*, present perfect)

   _____

Author's Craft

Look back at the short story "The Tell-Tale Heart" on page 176. Identify three examples of the present perfect and past perfect tenses. Rewrite a section of the story using only present tense. How is it different?

Perfect Tenses

Language Coach continued

Vowel Sounds in Unstressed Syllables

In many words, the vowel sounds in one or more syllables are not clear. Because these unclear vowel sounds occur in syllables that are not stressed or accented, they can lead to spelling mistakes.

Example   The *i* in *episode*, for example, sounds the same as the *e* in *competent*.

ep-*i*-sode   com-p*e*-tent

This "uh" sound may be spelled by any vowel, and it may occur in more than one syllable, as in *a*ccomp*a*ny.

Directions Study the word list, and note the spelling of sounds in unstressed syllables. Rewrite the word, breaking it into syllables. Underline the unstressed syllable or syllables that represent the "uh" sound.

1 bargain _____

2 hesitate _____

3 anonymous _____

4 benefit _____

5 epilogue _____

Directions Underline the six misspelled words in the following paragraph. Give the correct spelling for each on the lines below.

> The jurors were desparate to get to the end of the trial. They hoped the judge would edjourn the trial so they could leave. Nevertheless, they did their duty by listening to every syllible of the presentation. They even hoped the defense lawyer would try to plea bargaon to cut the trial short. It was a pleasunt surprise when the prosecuter finally ended his remarks.

_____

_____

Lesson 2-13

Choosing the Right Word

Words are the tools of authors. A good author makes careful **word choices** to build vivid description and action. Using specific words and appropriate details will make your writing clearer and more interesting.

Read the following sentence. *A big dog went by.* Can you create a picture in your mind of what this looks like? You probably find yourself asking questions such as, "What kind of dog?" The words are not specific enough to communicate effectively. The right words should create an image in your mind.

Now read this sentence. *An enormous dog with curly black hair trotted down the gravel driveway.* Which words give you a more specific image?

Directions Read the following sentences. Review the verbs and adjectives. Make at least two changes to each of the following sentences to make them more specific and vivid.

1. The nice trip to the beach made me happy. _____

2. Jim was eating a sandwich. _____

3. The car looks old. _____

4. Angela went home in the rain. _____

5. The police officer was going fast. _____

6. Rusty is a good dog. _____

7. My dinner was not good. _____

8. The boy carried a backpack. _____

2-14 Writer's Workshop
Exposition: Compare-and-Contrast Essay

A **compare-and-contrast essay** examines the similarities and differences between two or more related subjects. A good compare-and-contrast essay can even change your perspective—as when a reviewer compares the latest hit song with an old album.

Your essay should include the following elements.

- A topic involving two or more subjects that share similarities, but are also different in some ways
- An introduction that presents the main point of the essay
- Paragraphs describing both similarities and differences
- An organization that highlights the points of comparison

Purpose To write an essay that communicates the similarities and differences between two or more related subjects.

Audience Your teacher and your classmates

Prewriting—Plan It Out
Choosing Your Topic

To choose a topic for your essay and to evaluate your information, use these graphic organizers.

Quicklist Fold a sheet of paper in thirds. In the first column, list recent choices you have made—for instance, products you have bought or activities you have completed. In the second column, next to each choice, write a descriptive phrase. In the third column, give an alternative to your choice.

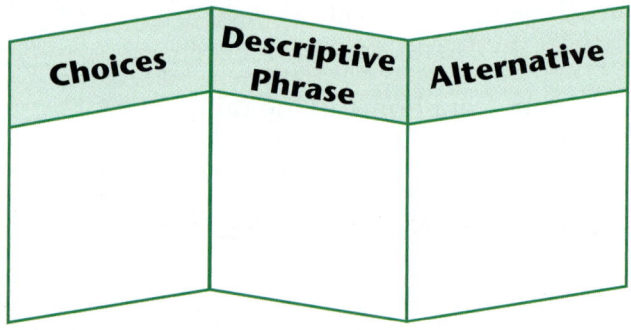

Review your list. Choose a topic that is not too narrow or too broad in order to make sure you are able to support your topic with enough details.

BUT Chart Write the word BUT in the center of a sheet of paper. On the left, list items or ideas with something in common. List differences among them on the right. Choose your topic from this list.

Things That Are Similar		Differences Between Them
My bike and Kara's bike: blue frame and two wheels	B U T	Kara's has thick, heavy tread tires. My bike has thin, smooth tires.

190 Lesson 2-14

Develop Your Ideas

Follow these steps to develop and organize your ideas.

1 For each of the two subjects you chose to compare and contrast, use one of these strategies to help you flesh out your ideas.

Describe it to someone who is not familiar with it.

Explain what you can do with it, on it, or to it.

Analyze it by breaking it into parts.

Argue for or against it, explaining good and bad points.

2 A graphic organizer can enhance your comprehension of main ideas and supporting details. Use the Venn diagram below to gather details that show similarities and differences between your subjects. Write ideas that are true of the first subject on the left. Write ideas that are true about the second subject on the right. Write ideas that are true of both subjects in the overlap area.

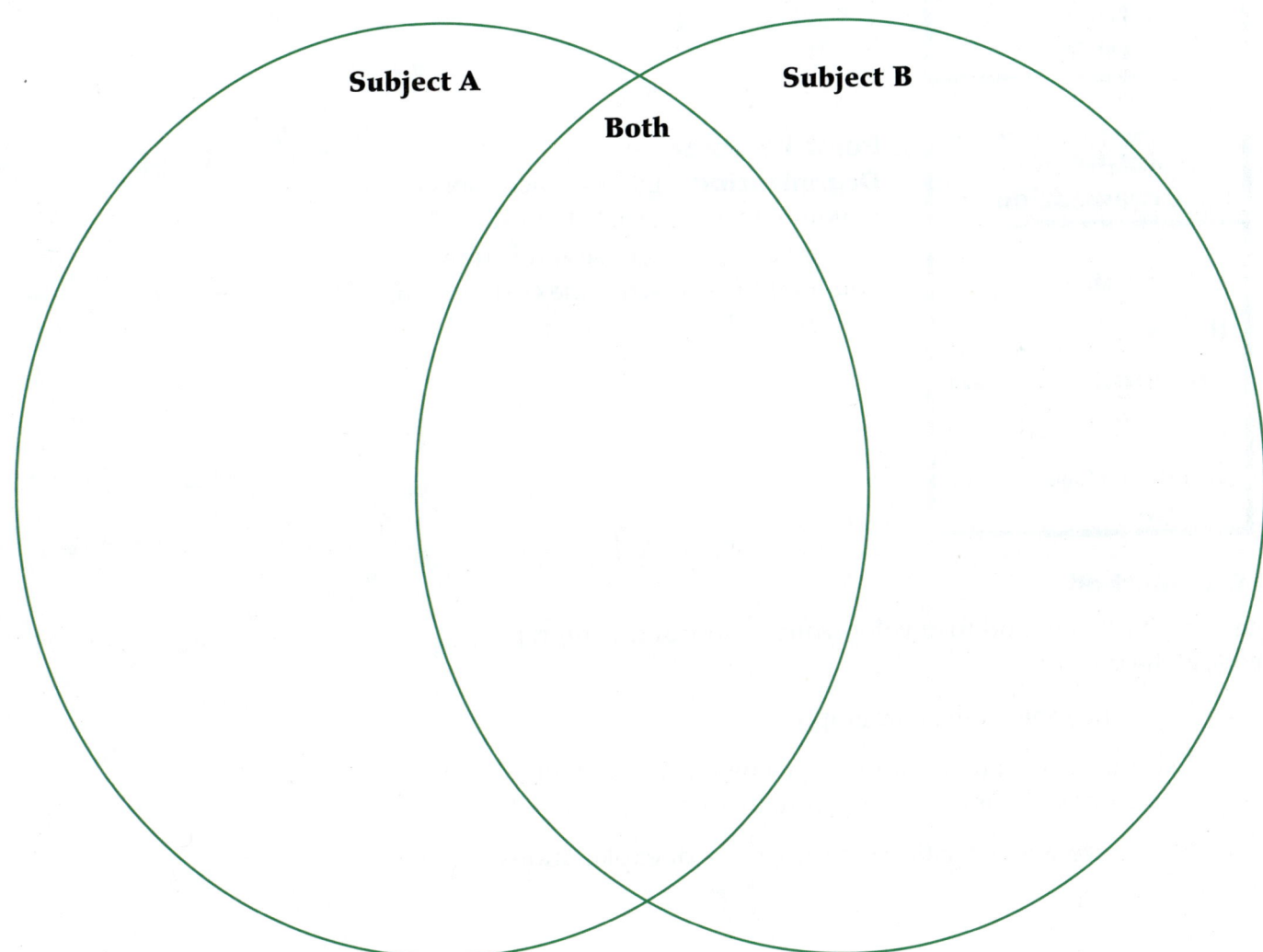

Exposition: Compare-and-Contrast Essay 191

Writer's Workshop continued

Drafting—Get It on Paper
Organize Your Essay

There are two common ways to organize a compare-and-contrast essay. Choose a structure that seems the best way to make your points.

Block Method

I. Buses
   a. cheaper
   b. more routes
   c. better views

II. Trains
   a. better seats
   b. faster
   c. quieter

Block Method Present all the details about one subject first, then present all the details about the next subject. The block method works well if your topic is complicated.

Point-by-point Organization

I. Introduction
II. Costs of each
III. Accessibility of each
IV. View from each
V. Disadvantages of each

Point-by-point Organization Discuss each aspect of your subjects in turn. For example, if you are comparing buses and subways, you might first discuss the cost of each, then accessibility, and so on.

"SEE" Method

Use the "SEE" method to develop your supporting paragraphs. Follow these steps.

▶ **State** the topic of the paragraph.

▶ **Extend** the idea by restating it in a new way, applying it to a particular case, or contrasting it with another point.

▶ **Elaborate** with specific examples, facts, or explanations.

Student Model: "SEE" Method

Statement: Two civil rights movements protested in nonviolent ways.

Extension: They held marches, boycotts, and demonstrations.

Elaboration: In 1917, Alice Paul and other women picketed at the White House. In 1963, more than 200,000 Americans marched on Washington, D.C.

> In the first sentence, the student states a main idea. The SEE Method allows her to provide details to support the main idea.

Directions Read this student essay as a model for your own.

Student Model: Writing

Carolyn Sienko, Williamstown, MI

The civil rights movement of the 1950s and 1960s had a lot in common with the women's suffrage movement that began with the Seneca Falls Convention in 1848. Both movements involved a group of people who were denied rights and who fought to obtain those rights.

Although in most ways the two struggles were similar, the specific rights each group fought for were different. Women wanted the right to vote in elections, the right to own property in their own names, and the right to keep their own wages. African Americans fought for the end to segregation. Like the women, they wanted to be treated with equal rights. However, the civil rights movement was about fairness in schools, jobs, and public places like buses and restaurants.

Both movements protested in nonviolent ways. They held marches, boycotts, and demonstrations to raise the public's consciousness and get the laws changed. In 1917, Alice Paul and other women picketed at the White House. In 1963, more than 200,000 Americans, led by Dr. Martin Luther King, Jr., marched on Washington, D.C. They wanted Congress to pass laws to end discrimination.

> The writer begins her essay with a statement that introduces the subjects of her comparison. She indicates that she will focus more on similarities.

> The writer focuses first on the differences in the specific rights being sought.

Writer's Workshop continued

Both movements were about equality. The Declaration of Independence, an important document in the struggle for equality, states: "We hold these truths to be self-evident, that all men are created equal; that they are endowed by their Creator with certain unalienable rights; that among these are life, liberty, and the pursuit of happiness."

Protesters in both the civil rights movement and the women's suffrage movement felt that they were being denied rights that were given to them by this statement from the Declaration of Independence.

Both groups were able to change the laws so that they could have their rights. Women were given the right to vote in 1920 by Amendment 19 to the Constitution. Similarly, the Civil Rights Act of 1964 outlawed discrimination in hiring and ended segregation in public places.

In conclusion, the civil rights movement of the 1950s and 1960s and the women's suffrage movement were both about equality under the law. They are both good examples of how much work and determination it takes to change the laws. It is good to know, however, that the laws can be changed.

> The writer uses point-by-point organization to compare the movements.

> The writer provides a quotation to elaborate on an idea.

Revising—Make It Better

Reread your draft. A well-organized essay conveys ideas and information effectively while reflecting the writer's voice or personality. Color-code to check organization and balance. Use different colors to highlight supporting details about each of your subjects. If your draft has more of one color, add or subtract details to represent both positions well. If your highlights do not show a consistent organization, such as the block method or the point-by-point method, consider revising for balance. Then, make certain you have developed reader's interest by creating an effective voice.

Peer Review Have a classmate read your draft to evaluate the organization, balance, and voice. Ask your reader whether your essay presents enough information about each subject, or to suggest points that need more detail. Ask whether your voice comes through. Add details based on this feedback.

Editing—Be Your Own Language Coach

Check your writing to correct errors in spelling, grammar, and punctuation. Use a grammar or spell checker to help. Review your work to delete redundant and irrelevant words, as well as ideas that do not add value or meaning.

Publishing—Share It!

When you publish a work, you produce it for a specific audience. Consider one of these ways to share your writing.

Publish a newsletter. For example, if you have compared and contrasted two restaurants or several stores, publish it as a newsletter and distribute it in your community.

Be a consumer watchdog. If your essay tells about a product that students can buy, form a Consumer Information Panel with classmates. Present your essays as a series of consumer reports, using any of these visual aids to enhance your presentation: photos, charts, diagrams, and cartoons.

Reflecting on Your Writing

Rubric for Self-Assessment Assess your essay's strengths and weaknesses using the criteria. For each question, circle a rating.

CRITERIA	RATING SCALE
	NOT VERY VERY
IDEAS How well did you maintain the central idea of your essay?	1 2 3 4 5
ORGANIZATION How effectively are points of comparison and contrast organized?	1 2 3 4 5
VOICE How well do you set a tone for your essay?	1 2 3 4 5
WORD CHOICE How appropriate is the language for your audience?	1 2 3 4 5
SENTENCE FLUENCY How varied is your sentence structure? Are your sentence beginnings purposeful? Do they show connections between ideas?	1 2 3 4 5
CONVENTIONS How correct is your grammar, especially your use of simple and perfect tenses?	1 2 3 4 5

2-15 Discussing Your Anchor Book
Literature Circles

Power and Conflict In this Literature Circle, you and your group members will start with an open discussion, and then you will consider the topic of power and conflict.

Part 1: Open Discussion

Meet with your Literature Circle. Discuss your Anchor Book using your Reader's Journal as a reference for specific notes, ideas, questions, and passages. Remember to follow the guidelines from Unit 1 for a successful discussion.

Part 2: Discuss—Power and Conflict

Now that you have completed your student-led discussion, consider the topic of power and conflict. Look at the following types of power in human relationships and the examples of each. Then, with your group, discuss the questions that follow.

A person who has power over another person

- A superhero has physical strength that allows him or her to defeat a villain.
- A comedian has the ability to make you laugh.
- Your parent or guardian has the authority to tell you how to behave.

A person who has power over a group

- A general has the authority to command soldiers.
- A musician has the ability to make an audience feel the power of a song.
- In some cultures, the oldest person in the family has the authority to make decisions for the rest of the family.

A group that has power over an individual or another group

- Peer pressure is the power a social group (such as a clique) uses to make an individual or another group feel the need to behave in the same way the social group behaves.
- In WWII, the Nazis used their military strength to force individuals and groups to enter concentration camps.
- Today, the American Civil Liberties Union (ACLU) uses the law and court system to make individuals and groups who violate the rights of others responsible for their actions.

▲ **Good to Know!**
Bono, the lead singer of the band U2, is known for inspiring thousands of people through his socially-conscious lyrics and humanitarian efforts.

1 Identify Which characters in your Anchor Book have power and how do they use it? Which characters do not have power and how does that lack of power affect them?

Has Power	Does Not Have Power
Character	Character
How Character Uses His/Her Power	How Lack of Power Affects Him/Her

2 Analyze What kinds of power does each character have? How does each character use or misuse his or her power?

Characters	Kinds of Power	How Are They Using or Misusing Power?

3 Propose How could characters who do not have power gain it? What types of power would they gain? Also, are there characters who do not realize they have power? What kind of power do they have? What might help them realize they have power?

4 Extend Characters who misuse their power are sometimes called **villains,** while characters who use their power to help others are often called **heroes.** Find an event from a magazine or newspaper about an ordinary person who has done something heroic. Discuss it with your group. How is being a hero related to realizing that you can use your power to solve a conflict?

Literature Circles

2-16 Connecting to Your Anchor Book
Anchor Book Projects

Now that you have finished reading your Anchor Book, it is time to get creative! Complete one of the following projects.

A. Body Biography

A "body biography" communicates all the important information about who a character is. By using images, words, and symbols, you can create a clearer picture of a character's appearance, personality, situation, and goals.

1. Choose a character from your Anchor Book who is integral to the novel. Think about how that character reflects the author's purpose. Sketch a large figure (one that fills a sheet of poster board) to represent that character. Draw the character's physical features and clothing.

2. Use words, phrases, and sentences from the text to convey information about the character's traits. Include reasons why you chose to use these words and symbols to describe the character.

Your body biography should include the following.

- A drawing that shows your character's physical features
- Words and symbols that convey unique and clear character traits
- Evidence and reasons that support your choices

B. Create the Soundtrack

In a film, each song chosen in a soundtrack serves an important purpose. A soundtrack helps tell a story through the medium of music. Retell your novel by creating a soundtrack. Each song must communicate important information such as one character's point of view, the mood of the story, an important change in plot, or the theme.

1. Choose ten songs that would work in a soundtrack of your novel. Analyze each song to make certain it communicates ideas from the book. Include at least one song that relates to the message, or theme, of the book, and one song that reflects the author's purpose.

2. Make a list of the ten songs. For each song, include its title, the part of the novel it supports, and the reasons why you chose it.

Your soundtrack should include the following.

- A retelling of your book's story through music
- Songs that relate to specific events and aspects of the story, including the theme

Be the Bad Guy

In every novel, there is a character who makes life more difficult for other characters. Frequently, the character you would least like to meet in real life is the most fun to read about. In *Wicked*, Gregory Maguire has fun rewriting *The Wizard of Oz* from the Wicked Witch's point of view.

1. Write a first-person narrative in which the villain, or antagonist, from your Anchor Book explains why he or she is not "bad," just misunderstood.

2. Make sure that the antagonist talks from his or her point of view using details and events from the story. Be sure to describe the antagonist's background.

3. Reveal the antagonist's character through his or her words, thoughts, and actions, and how he or she compares or contrasts with the other characters.

Your narrative should include the following.

- A story that is told from the first-person point of view of the antagonist
- Important story events that are retold from another perspective
- Information that reveals how the antagonist views himself or herself
- Dialogue and information that reveals traits of the antagonist

Free-Choice Book Reflection

You have completed your free-choice book. Before you take your test, read the following instructions to write a brief reflection on your book.

My free-choice book is _____.

The author is _____.

1 Would you recommend this book to a friend? Yes _____ No _____

Briefly explain why. _____

_____

Write and Discuss Answer the following question in your Reader's Journal. Then, discuss your answer with a partner or your literature circle.

 2 **Compare and Contrast** *Can all conflicts be resolved?* Compare and contrast how your Anchor Book, your free-choice book, and your knowledge from other subjects help you answer this question. Use specific details from both books to support your ideas.

Connecting to Your Anchor Book

Unit Review
Standardized Test Practice

Reading Skills: Making Inferences

Answer the questions below to check your understanding of this unit's skills.
Read this selection. Then answer the questions that follow.

> Above all, Tomaso loved writing his own music. He could hear the rhythms of new songs in his head, and someday he would record them. He hummed as he walked from class to class. He jotted down lyrics as he thought of them, sometimes in the middle of chemistry class or Spanish.
>
> "What's this, Mr. Efraimov?" asked Ms. Tern, his chemistry teacher. "Are you writing a formula? Or just fooling with your music lyrics?"

1 What does Tomaso want to do?
  A. become an actor
  B. get an "A" in chemistry
  C. go to a concert
  D. write and record his own music

2 What details in the paragraph support your answer?
  F. "He jotted down lyrics as he thought of them"
  G. "Are you writing a formula?"
  H. "in the middle of chemistry class"
  J. "he walked from class to class"

Reading Skills: Compare and Contrast

Read this selection. Then answer the questions that follow.

> Jake called up his friend, Sharona, who had moved to New York City. She described how much she loved taking walks in the city so that she could look at all the huge buildings and different kinds of people. He laughed and said it sounded great—but he was going to stay right where he was, in Kansas. He liked the broad flat land, with its glowing wheat fields. He felt as though he could see for miles and miles.

3 What or who is being compared or contrasted?
  A. New York City and Kansas
  B. people from New York City and people from Kansas
  C. Sharona and Jake
  D. teenagers in the United States

4 What clue helps you identify the differences in this passage?
  F. The word *but* shows a difference of opinion.
  G. Jake and Sharona are friends.
  H. Jake laughs.
  J. Three sentences begin with pronouns.

Literary Analysis: Elements of the Novel

Choose the best answer for the following questions.

5 When a story is told from the **limited third-person point of view,** what do the readers know?

A. only what one character experiences

B. what most characters experience

C. what all characters experience

D. only what one character does

6 What is the term for the part of a story that interrupts the chronological order to tell what happened earlier?

F. exposition

G. flashback

H. falling action

J. resolution

Read this selection and answer the questions that follow.

> Luiz and Harry were always playing elaborate practical jokes. If people got upset, the boys laughed and told them to get a sense of humor. Simone lived in the same neighborhood as Luiz and Harry. Like them, she enjoyed a good joke, but she didn't like to upset people. She thought the friends' jokes sometimes went too far. She decided it was time they learned a lesson. A few nights before Halloween, Simone went from door to door, telling her neighbors about her plan to beat the friends at their own game. Most of the neighbors were happy to play along. The only holdout was Mr. Carrini. He was a grumpy man who never said hello to anyone and always kept his lights off on Halloween. He didn't even answer the door when Simone knocked, although she knew he was home.

7 Which **character trait** does Harry show in this selection?

A. thoughtfulness

B. cruelty

C. unfriendliness

D. insensitivity

8 Which character trait does Mr. Carrini show in this selection?

F. boredom

G. playfulness

H. grouchiness

J. carelessness

9 In one paragraph, explain which character(s) from the passage you would describe as **flat** and which character(s) you would describe as **round.**

Unit Review 201

10 Which of these is an example of situational irony?

   A. A little brother, who is always a brat, brightens the day for some nursing-home residents.

   B. A lazy and friendly cat turns out to be a very good pet.

   C. Grandparents get together with their grandchildren and enjoy an outing.

   D. A gymnast trains so hard for a meet that he wins a medal.

11 How might an author use irony in a short story?

   F. He or she might use lots of dialogue so that the action moves quickly.

   G. He or she might include lots of description so that readers can get a good sense of the story's setting.

   H. He or she might lead readers to expect a certain outcome and then make the plot shift in an unexpected way.

   J. He or she might choose a serious theme to make the story believable.

Language Skills: Vocabulary

Choose the best answer.

12 The view from the top of the mountain is _____.

   A. similar
   B. different
   C. spectacular
   D. simulated

13 What is the origin of the word *indicate*?

   F. It comes from a Latin word meaning "follow."
   G. It comes from a Latin word meaning "show."
   H. It comes from a Greek word meaning "believe."
   J. It comes from a Greek word meaning "prove."

14 There was significant _____ for the jury's decision.

   A. logical
   B. reasonable
   C. conclusion
   D. evidence

15 What is the origin of the word *logical*?

   F. It comes from a Latin word meaning "proof."
   G. It comes from a Latin word meaning "sign."
   H. It comes from a Greek word meaning "reason."
   J. It comes from a Latin word meaning "decision."

Language Skills: Spelling

Circle the letter of the word that completes each sentence correctly.

16 I was _____ to know the answer.
- A. desprete
- B. desperate
- C. desperet
- D. desperete

17 Winning the prize was a great _____.
- F. benafit
- G. benfit
- H. benufit
- J. benefit

Language Skills: Grammar

Choose the best answer.

18 Identify the **principal part** used to form the verb.

We are planning a trip to San Francisco next summer.
- A. Present Participle
- B. Present
- C. Past
- D. Past Participle

19 Identify the correct form of the **irregular verb**.

The referee had _____ the whistle.
- F. blew
- G. blown
- H. blowing
- J. blew out

20 Identify the **simple tense** used to form the verb.

I will play in next week's basketball tournament.
- A. Present Tense
- B. Past Tense
- C. Future Tense

21 Identify the **perfect tense** used to form the verb.

I have enjoyed all kinds of sports.
- F. Present Perfect Tense
- G. Past Perfect Tense
- H. Future Perfect Tense

22 Identify the **perfect tense** used to form the verb.

I had invited Sandra to the movies, but she couldn't make it.
- A. Present Perfect Tense
- B. Past Perfect Tense
- C. Future Perfect Tense

23 Choose the correct **singular** or **plural form** of the verb to complete the sentence.

At sunrise, the ships _____ from the harbor.
- F. is sailing
- G. sails
- H. sail
- J. was sailing

Unit Review 203

How much *information* is enough?

Unit 3 Genre focus:
Types of Nonfiction

Your Anchor Book
There are many good books that would work well to support both the Big Question and the genre focus of this unit. In this unit you will read one of these books as your Anchor Book. Your teacher will introduce the book you will be reading.

Free-Choice Reading
Later in this unit you will be given the opportunity to choose another book to read. This is called your free-choice book.

Thinking About What You Already Know

Whether you are reading, listening to someone speak, or watching TV, it can be tricky to separate out the facts from the opinions. Nonfiction writers—the people behind advertisements, political speeches, news programs, and newspapers, for instance—tend to use a mix of facts and their own opinions to influence what readers or viewers think.

Partner Activity

With a partner, read the following four excerpts. Discuss which parts you think are fact, and which parts you think are opinion. Once you have reached a decision together, mark the statements with "O" for "opinion" and "F" for "fact." Then, take turns reading each passage aloud as if you were the author. Discuss and answer the questions.

A group of local teens showed their town pride Tuesday by cleaning up an area park. The students, from Hoover High School, cleaned up Memorial Park as part of Earth Day.

The students picked up garbage, raked leaves, and planted a variety of flowers along the entrance.

Students said they wanted to give back to the community, but also to improve a park they enjoy.

"We play baseball here in the summer and soccer in the fall," said 14-year-old Mark Johnson. "That's much easier to do when there aren't leaves and trash everywhere."

Cars are everywhere. We have 130 million cars on the U.S. roads right now, and add 15 million more each year. But there is another transportation option, bicycles, and it seems that most motorists are unaware of them. People should realize that bicycles are often a better way of getting around than cars.

from "The Trouble With Television" by Robert MacNeil

It is difficult to escape the influence of television. If you fit the statistical averages, by the age of 20 you will have been exposed to at least 20,000 hours of television. You can add 10,000 hours for each decade you have lived after the age of 20. The only things Americans do more than watch television are work and sleep.

Calculate for a moment what could be done with even a part of those hours. Five thousand hours, I am told, are what a typical undergraduate spends working on a bachelor's degree. In 10,000 hours you could have learned enough to become an astronomer or engineer. You could have learned several languages fluently. If it appealed to you, you could be reading Homer[1] in the original Greek or Dostoevski[2] in Russian. If it didn't, you could have walked around the world and written a book about it.

[1] **Homer** *n.* Greek epic poet of the 8th century B.C.
[2] **Dostoevski** (dôs tô yef′ skē) *n.* (1821–1881) Russian novelist.

from "America the Not-So-Beautiful"
by Andrew A. Rooney

Ten years ago most people thought nothing of dumping an old bottle of weed or insect killer in a pile of dirt in the backyard or down the drain in the street, just to get rid of it. The big companies in America had the same feeling, on a bigger scale. For years, the chemical companies dumped their poisonous wastes in the rivers behind the mills or they put it in fifty-gallon drums in the vacant lots, with all the old, rusting machinery in it, up behind the plants. The drums rusted out in ten years and dumped their poison into the ground. It rained, the poison seeped into the underground streams and poisoned everything for miles around. Some of the manufacturers who did this weren't even evil. They were dumb and irresponsible. Others were evil because they knew how dangerous it was but didn't want to spend the money to do it right.

Class Discussion

As a class, discuss what methods you used to tell the difference between fact and opinion in the selections. What do your conclusions indicate about how you should read nonfiction texts?

3-1 Understanding the Big Question
How much information is enough?

Every day we receive information from television, the Internet, newspapers, the radio, and books about the world we live in. How do we decide when we have enough information? Part of deciding how much information is enough is identifying what information is useful and what is not.

The answer to the question "How much information is enough?" depends upon what you already know and for what purpose you need the information.

Advertisements present themselves as sources of information that will help you decide what to buy. With a partner, look at the advertisement below and analyze the information given to you about Crunchie's peanut butter.

THE BEST PEANUT BUTTER IN THE WORLD

Are you ready for your life to change? If so, try **Crunchie's Peanut Butter**. One bite and you are guaranteed to become the person you always wanted to be. Do what all your friends and neighbors are doing! Buy **Crunchie's**. Be careful of imitators: other peanut butter brands claim to be as good as **Crunchie's**, but they don't include all-natural ingredients like **Crunchie's** does.

1 What information from the newspaper ad is not useful? Why is that information included?

2 What additional information from the newspaper ad would be useful in deciding whether or not to buy Crunchie's Peanut Butter?

3 Do you have enough information to decide whether you want to buy Crunchie's Peanut Butter? Explain why or why not.

_____
_____

The word "media" describes all the forms of communication that provide the public with information, including news, entertainment, and advertising.

On your own, consider the ways that you use the media in a week.

Complete the chart below.

▶ First, identify what you use the information source for. Is it to be entertained and/or to learn more about something? It is possible to use an information source for multiple purposes. You could watch television to learn more, and to be entertained, when you watch a nature program.

▶ Then, record the average amount of time you spend gathering information from each of the sources below.

Information Source	Purpose	Amount of Time Per Day
Television		
Radio		
Print Media (books, newspapers, magazines)		
Internet		

4 Now, discuss your chart with your classmates. What did you learn about how you and your peers use information sources?

_____
_____

When you receive information, you should first evaluate the quality of the information and then decide what you will do with it. As you read your Anchor Book and the related readings, think about how you can benefit from the information and ideas they share.

Understanding the Big Question **209**

Getting Ready for Your Anchor Book

You will start reading your Anchor Book soon. The next few pages in this book give you some background information plus a reading skill.

Types of Nonfiction

Nonfiction writing, such as essays and articles, discusses real people, events, places, and ideas. You can learn about others' lives, find information, explore new ideas, or weigh arguments on issues.

Elements of Nonfiction

There are four kinds of nonfiction writing you will read about in this unit.

Type of Nonfiction	Definition	Example
Reflective	Addresses an experience and includes the writer's insights about the event's importance	Letter
		Memoir or journal
Persuasive	Tries to convince the reader to adopt a particular point of view or take a particular course of action	Editorial
		Sales brochure
Narrative	Tells the story of real-life experiences	Biography
		Autobiography
Expository	Presents facts and ideas, or explains a process	Media account
		Essay or article
		How-to writing

Purposes of Nonfiction

Nonfiction is written with at least one, and often more than one, specific purpose in mind. Look for language that teaches, persuades, or amuses to determine why the work was written. Here are some common purposes of nonfiction and examples from this unit.

You Will Read		
To inform	➤	from *Narrative of the Life of Frederick Douglass* by Frederick Douglass
To persuade	➤	"America the Not-So-Beautiful" by Andy Rooney
To entertain	➤	"Interview" by Sara Henderson Hay
To reflect	➤	"Volar: To Fly" by Judith Ortiz Cofer

Organization Methods for Nonfiction

Nonfiction can be organized in one or more of the following ways.

- **Chronological organization** presents details in time order.
- **Compare-and-contrast organization** shows the ways in which two or more subjects are similar and different.
- **Cause-and-effect organization** shows the relationship among events.
- **Problem-and-solution organization** identifies a problem and then proposes a solution

The Author

You can identify the author's style and perspective in nonfiction by paying attention to the two following literary elements.

- **Tone** is the writer's attitude about the audience and subject.
- **Voice** is the writer's distinctive way of "speaking" based on word choice, sentence structure, and tone.

The Information Age

Today, many people rely on the Internet as their source for nonfiction information.

1 What examples of nonfiction can you think of that are specific to the Internet? List them below.

2 Compare your ideas with your classmates'. What types of nonfiction did you identify? Did you identify any new types?

Introduction to Nonfiction

3-2 Reading Skills
Identifying Main Idea and Supporting Details

In learning new reading skills, you will use special academic vocabulary. Knowing the right words will help you demonstrate your understanding.

Academic Vocabulary

Word	Meaning	Example Sentence
suggest v. Related words: suggesting, suggested	to mention as something to think over	Jeff *suggested* that he and Anna should leave Carlos's house because it was getting late.
imply v. Related words: implied, implying	to mean or suggest without specifically saying	She *implied* by her remark that she was joking.
support v. Related words: supporting, supported	to take the side of, uphold or help; to help prove	Everything I've read *supports* the idea that he is innocent.

The main idea is the major topic of what you read or write. Writers usually convey their main ideas in an introduction. The main idea is **supported** by related details in the paragraphs that follow. The writer may then restate the main idea in the final paragraph. Many informational texts follow this structural pattern.

Sometimes the main idea is stated, usually in a topic sentence at the beginning of the paragraph or the concluding sentence. Even if it is not stated, there is still a main idea. You just have to read carefully for what the details **suggest** or **imply** the main idea is. When you do this, you are making inferences to determine the main idea.

How to Identify the Main Idea and Supporting Details

1. What is this selection about? In the margin, identify the topic.

2. What is the author trying to tell me about the topic? In the margin, identify the main idea.

3. What information does the author use to support or prove the main idea? Underline supporting ideas.

Directions Practice these steps on the selection below.

IN THE NEWS   07

Local Kids Clean Up Playground

A group of local teens showed their town pride Tuesday by cleaning up an area park. The students, from Hoover High School, cleaned up Memorial Park as part of Earth Day.

The students picked up garbage, raked leaves, and planted a variety of flowers along the entrance.

Students said they wanted to give back to the community, but also to improve a park that they enjoy.

"We play baseball here in the summer and soccer in the fall," said 14-year-old Mark Johnson. "That's much easier to do when there aren't leaves and trash everywhere."

The flowers were donated by Carol's Nursery. Owner Carol Haim said she was proud to pitch in to make her community look a little nicer.

"It just gives me a good feeling to see the park looking so nice," Haim said.

Hoover High Students planted flowers for Earth Day.

1. **Locate** What is this article's topic sentence?

2. **Evaluate** Which supporting details are most important to the main idea?

3. **Analyze** How do the headline and photograph in this news article help you understand the main idea?

Identifying Main Idea and Supporting Details **213**

Think about how the author organizes the main idea and supporting details in this article. *Guiding Question:* Does this article provide you with enough information to repair a car? What is the author's purpose?

What Makes a Car Run?

The automobile has come a long way from the time when people stood in awe as they watched Henry Ford turn a crank to start his Model-T.

The heart of the automobile is the engine. In the 1870s, Karl Benz, Gottlieb Daimler, and Wilhelm Maybach developed the gasoline engine that is similar to the one used today. The gas engine became successful very quickly. Blacksmith shops that made horseshoes soon changed into service stations and garages. The gasoline engine has become more complicated over the years, but the idea is still the same. In short, the engine mixes gasoline and air and then burns the mixture at a high temperature. Although it sounds simple, the engine is a piece of machinery whose inner workings are complex and fascinating.

How the Gasoline Engine Works

All the parts of a car engine work together. An important part of the engine is a hollow metal tube called a cylinder. Tightly fitted inside the cylinder is a solid piece of steel called a piston. It is here, in the cylinder, that air and gasoline mix and that the mixture burns. The air and gasoline mixture burns so fast and at such a high temperature that it produces hot gases. When the air and gasoline mixture burns, the cylinder is tightly closed. The gases are under great pressure. This rapid burning makes an explosion. The spark that causes the explosion is made by a spark plug. An automobile engine gets its power from hundreds of small but powerful explosions. The earliest gasoline engines had only one cylinder. Today's gasoline engines have four, six, or eight cylinders.

How the Cylinders Work

Look at the diagrams in Figure 1. Each diagram shows one of the four steps that occur in a cylinder. Each step is called a stroke. **Step 1** is the intake stroke. In this step, the piston moves down. At the same time, the air and gasoline mixture moves into the cylinder. **Step 2** is the compression stroke. In this step, the piston moves upward. This motion compresses, or squeezes, the air and gasoline into a smaller space. **Step 3** is the power stroke. In this step, the spark plug makes a spark. The spark explodes the air and gasoline mixture. The pressure of the explosion then forces the piston down. **Step 4** is the exhaust stroke. In this step, the gases produced by the explosion are forced out of the cylinder.

FIGURE 1. These diagrams show the four strokes in the operation of a cylinder.

How the Power Is Sent to the Wheels

The up-and-down motion of the pistons produces power. However, to move a car forward, the up-and-down motion has to be changed to a turning or spinning motion. Piston rods connect the pistons to the backbone of the engine, the crankshaft (KRANK shaft). As the pistons move up and down, they move the piston rods. The piston rods then turn the crankshaft. The crankshaft changes the up-and-down motion to a spinning motion. As the crankshaft turns, it spins the flywheel. In most cars, the spinning power is carried to the rear wheels that move the car. Look at Figure 2.

▼ **FIGURE 2.** The diagram shows how the pistons turn the crankshaft and the crankshaft turns the flywheel, which produces power that is carried to the wheels.

How the Engine Is Cooled

When the air and gasoline mixture burns in the cylinders, the temperature can reach 4,500 degrees Fahrenheit (2,481 degrees Celsius). This much heat can melt iron and speed up rusting. That is why a gasoline engine needs a cooling system. The cooling system removes heat from the metal parts. Water stored in the radiator (RAY dee ayt r) does the job. A pump moves the water through the engine and cools the cylinders. In doing this, the water also gets very hot. It has to be cooled. This is the job of the fan. Look at Figure 3. In very cold weather, antifreeze is added to the water. The antifreeze helps keep the water from freezing.

Although the gasoline engine began as a basic piece of machinery, its process has become more complex over the years. The steps have become more elaborate, but the basis for how this marvelous invention works remains the same.

Partner Activity

With a partner use the features in this informational text to create your own informational text. Choose instructions for assembling an object, for a procedure, or for an experiment. Include diagrams, captions, and headings.

▲ **FIGURE 3.** The engine is cooled by water. The water is cooled by air that is blown by the fan.

Thinking About the Selection
What Makes a Car Run?

1 **Explain** How do the headings and illustrations in this article impact the meaning of the text?

_____
_____

2 **Apply** Each paragraph of an essay has one main point that supports the main idea. The paragraph then has details that support the point. Identify a supporting detail for each main point. Complete the graphic organizer below.

Main Point	Supporting Detail
How a Gasoline Engine Works	
How the Cylinders Work	
How Power Is Sent to the Wheels	
How the Engine Is Cooled	

3 **Evaluate** How well do the details support the main idea? Are any details included that do not support a main idea? What type of information do these details represent, and what is the purpose of including these details?

_____
_____
_____

4 **Evaluate** Does the article provide you with enough information to repair a car? What is the author's purpose?

_____
_____

5 **Connect** How useful is this article to its readers? How can you apply the information in this article for personal use?

_____

Write Answer the following question in your Reader's Journal.

6 **Summarize** Now that you have read this article, explain in your own words how a car runs.

Identifying Main Idea and Supporting Details **217**

3-3 Vocabulary Building Strategies
Synonyms and Antonyms

When you encounter a new word, you can identify synonyms and antonyms to help you learn the word and make it your own.

Synonyms are words that have nearly the same meaning. Some synonyms are interchangeable, which means that you can use either synonym in the same sentence without changing the meaning.

Example I practiced a new song for the concert.
I rehearsed a new song for the concert.

Directions Write the two words that are synonyms in the sentence.

1 I tried to focus on my homework, but I just couldn't concentrate. _____

Antonyms are words that are opposite in meaning. You can often use the prefixes *un-* or *in-* to form an antonym. In the example below, the word is underlined and its antonym is underlined twice.

Example The facts in this newspaper article are accurate, but one TV station reported inaccurate details about the same story.

Directions Write a definition of the underlined antonym.

2 *Biased* means "unfair", so unbiased means _____.

Directions Turn to Lesson 3-5. Preview the reading *The Trouble With Television* for a word whose meaning you do not yet know. Complete the graphic organizer for this word.

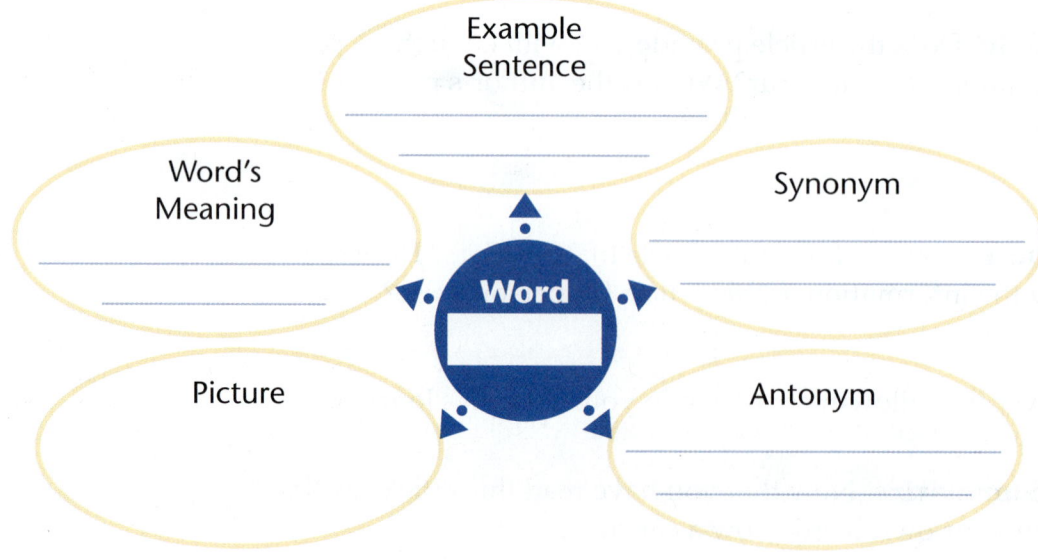

before reading your anchor book

218 Lesson 3-3

Using a Thesaurus

A thesaurus is a book of synonyms, or words that have similar meanings. Use a thesaurus to increase your vocabulary or to find alternative words to express your meaning.

- ▶ Do not choose a word just because it sounds interesting or smart. Choose the word that expresses exactly the meaning you intend.

- ▶ When choosing a word, note both its denotative and connotative meanings. A word's **denotation** is its literal meaning. A word's **connotation** is the emotional association that it calls to mind. The connotation may not reflect your intentions even if the denotation does so.

- ▶ To avoid errors, look up an unfamiliar word in a dictionary to check its precise meaning and to make sure you are using it properly.

Here is an example from a thesaurus.

> **book** *noun*
> A printed and bound work: tome, volume. *See* WORDS.
> **book** *verb* 1. To register in or as if in a book: catalog, enroll, inscribe, list, set down, write down. *See* REMEMBER. 2. To cause to be set aside, as for one's use, in advance: bespeak, engage, reserve. *See* GET.

If a word can be used as different parts of speech, as *book* can, the thesaurus entry provides synonyms for the word as each part of speech. A thesaurus entry gives specific synonyms for each connotation, or emotional association, of the word.

Look up the word *deception* in a thesaurus. Then, answer the questions.

3 What are three synonyms for this word?

_____

4 How do the connotations of the synonyms differ?

_____

Some words, called **homonyms**, have several meanings depending upon how they are used in a sentence. For example, the word "bat" could be a flying mammal or a wooden tool used to hit a ball. It could also be a verb that describes the act of hitting a ball.

Synonyms and Antonyms

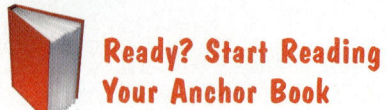

Ready? Start Reading Your Anchor Book — It's time to get started. As you learn from this work text, your teacher will also give you reading assignments from your Anchor Book.

3-4 Literary Analysis
Expository Writing

One type of nonfiction, or factual writing, is expository writing. Expository writing explains or gives information about a topic. It focuses on facts about the topic, not on opinions.

Literary Terms

Expository writing is factual writing that explains or informs. Four methods of organizing or arranging the information in expository writing are shown below. You may think of others.

- Information may be organized to show a **cause-and-effect** relationship among events.
- **Chronological** organization is the arrangement of events in the order they happen.
- **Compare-and-contrast** organization shows how two or more subjects are similar and different.
- In the **problem-and-solution** method, a problem is identified and a solution is given.

Understanding the methods of organization can help you predict what the text will be about and the author's purpose for writing it.

Organization Method	Example
Cause–and–effect	an article about how the sun can be harmful to your skin if you don't use sunscreen
Chronological	a manual that tells you how to put a desk together
Compare–and–contrast	an essay about the similarities and differences between city life and country life
Problem–and–solution	an article about global warming and what we can do to help slow it down

Lesson 3-4

Authors frequently use a combination of organization methods. Pay attention to how the shift in organization reflects a change in the author's purpose. To help you identify the method of organization, look for clue words and phrases.

Cause–and–effect	look for	*because, why, therefore, so, then, since, as a result*
Chronological	look for	*first, then, since, next, once, before, after, later, afterward, when, finally, eventually*
Compare–and–contrast	look for	(compare) *like, same, similarly, both* (contrast) *different, however, unlike, instead, but*
Problem–and–solution	look for	*if/then, therefore, the problem is, the question is*

Directions Read the following passage. Then, answer the questions.

People pluck eyebrows, apply makeup to them, and pierce them. They also use their eyebrows to communicate. You know the code—two raised eyebrows indicate amazement or questioning, a single raised brow expresses skepticism, scrunched eyebrows indicate deep thought, and pinched eyebrows communicate anger. In some periods of history, it was fashionable to shave eyebrows. Take a close look at Leonardo da Vinci's famous painting of the Mona Lisa.

What is the real reason for eyebrows? Most scientists believe the primary purpose is to keep moisture out of the eyes. The arched shape of our eyebrows and the direction of the hair growth help to divert rain and sweat to the sides of the face. In addition, our brows catch snow, dust, and other small debris. This may have given early humans a slight edge in the fight for survival. Someone looking for shelter or trying to outrun a predator would have had a distinct advantage if salty, irritating sweat were diverted from the eyes. Today, humans don't depend on eyebrows for survival, but our brows still perform the useful function of helping to keep our vision clear.

1 **Analyze** Reread the passage for the author's craft. Underline all clue words and phrases. In the margin, identify what methods of organization are used.

2 **Apply** Think of an emotion such as excitement, sadness, or anger and then use your eyebrows to reflect it. Have a partner guess what emotion you are expressing.

Expository Writing

As you read this article, self-monitor for comprehension. Read difficult sections aloud. Look at how an author uses some methods of organization. *Guiding Question:* Does this article provide enough information to choose forensic science as a career?

Link to Science

The World of the Forensic Scientist

Background With interest in forensic science increasing, more and more people are pursuing a career in the field. This article is a mere glimpse into the intricate details involved in forensic science.

Vocabulary Builder

Before you read, you will discuss the following words. In the Vocabulary Builder box in the margin, use a vocabulary building strategy to make the words your own.

> database   genetic   cells

As you read, draw a box around unfamiliar words you could add to your vocabulary. Use context clues to unlock their meaning.

Marking the Text

Expository Writing

As you read, underline important details about a forensic scientist's job. In the margin, identify the method used to organize those details (cause and effect, chronological, compare and contrast, problem and solution).

Books and movies glamorize it, and television shows make those who figure it out into intelligent heroes of skill and extensive knowledge. What is it? Forensic science!

Forensic science is the term applied to the scientific techniques used to solve crimes and find criminals. Identifying fingerprints and analyzing chemical compounds on objects found at a crime scene are some of the tasks set before the forensic scientist.

When It Begins

It all begins when a crime has been committed. It might be any crime, from burglary or counterfeiting to kidnapping or murder. No matter how careful a criminal may be, he or she usually leaves behind evidence, or something that can provide information about the crime. It is up to the investigators on the scene—the crime scene investigators—to find that evidence. The investigators then determine how the evidence is linked to the crime and how that links a suspect to the crime. The evidence is taken to a lab and analyzed, and the crime scene investigators put their forensic science knowledge to work.

Fingerprints

One kind of evidence is a fingerprint. On the pads of everyone's fingers are patterns of raised skin, or ridges. It is these ridges that create fingerprints. Because no two sets of fingerprints are alike, fingerprints can be used as a means of identification.

Scientists have been able to divide fingerprints into different pattern groups. Figure 1 shows the types of fingerprints common to most people. However, even though fingerprint types might be the same, the actual layout of ridges on the fingers is different for each and every person.

Figure 1.

Fingerprints are not always visible to the naked eye. For this reason, crime scene investigators dust a crime scene with fingerprint powder, which sticks to the fingerprints and reveals them. Tape is then pressed to the fingerprints and gently lifted, enabling the crime scene team to take the fingerprints back to the lab for further examination.

Once at the lab, the fingerprints are scanned into a computer. The fingerprints of other suspects and criminals are also stored in a massive computer **database**. Investigators run a computer program that can access the database and look for a fingerprint match. The fingerprints found at a crime scene are placed alongside fingerprints stored in the computer database. When enough matches exist, there is a positive identification of the suspect.

Vocabulary Builder

database
(dā′ tə bās) *n.*

Meaning

while reading your anchor book

▲ The image above is an artist's rendition of DNA.

DNA Evidence

If a criminal wears gloves, he or she will not leave fingerprints behind. The criminal may, however, leave evidence in the form of DNA. DNA is the abbreviation for deoxyribonucleic acid, a molecule found in the body of every human being. Everybody has DNA, and everybody's DNA is unique. The DNA holds the **genetic** makeup of a person. Every cell in a person's body except red blood cells has the same DNA.

The body of every human being is made up of **cells**. A person's blood, sweat, skin, muscles, saliva, and hair all have cells. The cell membrane is the outer wall, which holds the cell together. The cytoplasm is like a thick liquid in which other cell components are found. The middle of the cell is the nucleus, and it is here that DNA molecules are found.

DNA is responsible for a person's genes and physical makeup. A strand of DNA does not look like a cell; rather, it looks like a ladder that has been twisted. Each side of the "ladder," shown in the illustration above, is part of a chain, bound together by chemical compounds called nucleotides. The DNA structure is also called a double helix.

Marking the Text

Vocabulary Builder

genetic
(jə net´ ik) *adj.*

Meaning

cells
(sels) *n.*

Meaning

224 Lesson 3-4

Scientists believe that it would be nearly impossible for two people to share the same identical DNA structure, except for identical twins. Since each person's DNA is different, any type of body cell left behind can lead scientists to a suspect. A strand of hair or a drop of sweat is all that the forensic scientist needs in order to figure out the DNA.

Analyzing DNA is done through a process called DNA fingerprinting. DNA is removed from a body sample—such as hair or sweat—with chemicals. Then the DNA is cut and analyzed with radioactive probes and x-rays. Finally the DNA is presented in a series of patterned bands. Because the bands could have 10 billion possible patterns, scientists believe that each person's pattern of bands is unique. They believe that it is highly unlikely that any two people would have the same DNA pattern. Therefore DNA fingerprinting, or analyzing DNA from body cells found at a crime scene, has become part of a forensic scientist's job.

Other Kinds of Evidence

Other parts of the body can also be used for identifying a suspect or even a victim. Tooth marks can be matched to dental records. Faces can be reconstructed from skulls. In the future, scientists believe that the iris, the colored part of the eye, will be used for identification, as well. Like fingerprints, no two people have the same irises.

Forensic scientists also examine other items at a crime scene. A plaster cast can be made of tracks left by shoes or tires to find a match. Clothing fibers can be analyzed through magnification under a microscope and matched with clothing worn by a suspect or a victim.

Foreign substances such as food stains, dirt, or paint found on clothing can also be chemically analyzed. For example, dirt or paint on a suspect's clothing can be isolated, and then its chemical compound can be identified. The chemical compound of dirt or paint found at a crime scene is run through the same tests. If the chemical compounds prove to be the same, the forensic scientist has linked the suspect to the crime scene through the matching dirt or paint samples.

Weapon and Bullet Evidence

During many crimes, a tool or weapon has been used. These tools often leave behind impressions or toolmarks. Forensic scientists investigate these toolmarks as well. If a door has been indented by being knocked open by a heavy force, the scientists might experiment with different objects to discover which one makes an indentation exactly like the one that was left in the door. If telephone wires or cables have been cut, the forensic scientist will experiment with different cutting tools to see which makes cuts in exactly the same way.

Ballistics, the study of bullets, is a well-known tool used by forensic scientists. When a gun is fired, a bullet travels down the barrel of the gun and outward. As the bullet moves, it scrapes along the barrel's insides. This scraping forms lines on the bullet. These lines, or markings, identify the gun from which the bullet was fired. Crime scene investigators run a bullet that is found at a crime scene through a microscope to magnify these markings. Once they believe they have found the gun, they fire a bullet from it, usually into a big tub of water to lessen the impact. Then, under a microscope, they examine the bullet they fired and compare its markings with those on the bullet they found at the crime scene. If the bullets have the same identifying markings, the gun they have found is the gun that was used for the crime.

Forensic science has helped crime scene investigators solve more and more crimes that were once considered unsolvable. Sometimes a crime scene contains so little evidence that even modern forensics cannot help, but these cases are few. Forensic scientists continue their pursuit of those hard-to-find clues that enable them to solve seemingly unsolvable crimes, and to demonstrate that those who break the law will eventually be caught.

Thinking About the Selection
The World of the Forensic Scientist

1 **Evaluate** What kind of organization did the author use for this article? Why do you think the author chose to use this method of organization? How does it impact the meaning of the text? Use details to support your answer.

_____
_____
_____

2 **Describe** What is the author's point of view toward forensic science? Is it favorable or unfavorable, and how does it determine the type of information the author used in the article?

_____
_____
_____
_____

3 **Compare and Contrast** Compare the organization of this selection to that of "What Makes a Car Run?" How are they similar? How are they different?

_____
_____
_____

4 **Explain** How did the diagrams help you understand the text?

_____
_____

Write Answer the following questions in your Reader's Journal.

5 **Evaluate** Does this article provide enough information to choose forensic science as a career? Explain why or why not.

6 **Explain** Is your Anchor Book an example of expository writing? How can you tell?

Expository Writing 227

3-5 Literary Analysis
Persuasive Writing

The world is noisy with people trying to persuade others of their opinions. Learning how to persuade, and how to recognize when others are trying to persuade you, are both valuable skills.

Literary Terms

- A writer uses **persuasion** to convince the reader to take action.
- The writer's **position** is his or her opinion or point of view about the topic. Persuasive writing attempts to make the reader agree with this position.

Depending on the context or situation, a person may use different methods to convince his or her audience of a position. Look at the chart for methods used when speaking or writing persuasively.

How to Persuade	
Persuasive words such as *should*, *must*, and *ought* are often used to cause listeners or readers to change their minds. "We must come together as a community to solve the issue of pollution."	**Facts** can provide a strong base for persuading an audience. "Seat belts save an estimated 9,500 lives in America each year."
A person can communicate **opinions** to try to persuade an audience to agree. "As soon as you open the first page, you will find this book as entertaining as I did."	**Ethical appeals** are based on the audience's perception of the person. If the speaker is seen as ethical, the audience is more likely to be convinced. "This is the right thing to do."
Rhetorical questions (questions with obvious answers) make readers more likely to agree with a person's position. "Do you want to live in a better world? Together, we can make a difference."	**Emotional appeals** can aid in changing people's minds about particular subjects. "The children you help will be so grateful if you give to this worthy cause."
Repetition of words and phrases can emphasize a point a person is trying to make. "We won last year; we won the year before that. This year, we will win again."	

Directions Read the following selection. Underline persuasive words the writer uses to convince readers. In the margin, identify the author's position.

Dear Editor:

Cars are everywhere. We have 130 million cars on U.S. roads right now, and add 15 million more each year. But there is another transportation option, bicycles, and it seems that most motorists are unaware of them. People should realize that bicycles are often a better way of getting around than cars.

There are benefits to traveling by bicycle. Bicycles are powered by muscle, not non-renewable fossil fuels. When you ride a bike, you are burning calories.

The problem is that cars and bicycles cannot always share the same space. Roads can be a dangerous place for bicyclists. Many serious injuries result from bicycle-car collisions. I am not suggesting that automobiles be banned from roads, but I feel that people on bicycles will feel safer when there is coordination between automobile and bicycle traffic. Shouldn't everyone be allowed to feel safe on the road?

— A Concerned Citizen

---

1 **Interpret** Which persuasive techniques does the author use? How effective are these techniques?

_____
_____
_____

2 **Evaluate** Are the author's opinions well-supported and clear? Does the author use examples, details, or reasons to support his or her opinions? How does the author develop his or her argument?

_____
_____
_____
_____

3 **Assess** Does this letter fairly represent the bike/car debate? Does it include an opposing point of view?

_____
_____

Persuasive Writing

Propaganda

What do all advertisements have in common? They are propaganda that use words and images to convince you to make decisions without thinking deeply. **Propaganda** is a form of persuasion that can be used for good and bad purposes.

Literary Terms

The following are some propaganda techniques.

- The **bandwagon technique** tries to convince you that since everyone else is doing it (or buying it), you should, too.

- **Glittering generalities** are statements that sound positive but have no real meaning. Words such as *freedom*, *good*, and *evil* are ambiguous, but because they have a strong emotional meaning, or connotation, for people, they are effective.

- **Card stacking** seeks to manipulate audience perception of an issue by emphasizing one side and de-emphasizing another.

- **Testimonials** are quotations, stories, or personal experiences of individuals used to make a product or idea sound worthwhile.

- **Celebrity endorsements** are testimonials by famous people. Similarly, an **appeal to authority** cites an expert as a persuasive tool.

▼ Positive use of propaganda

Directions Look at this World War II poster. Then answer the questions.

1 **Interpret** What is the poster's message?

_____
_____
_____

2 **Analyze** Which propaganda techniques does this poster use to communicate its message? Is it effective? Explain why.

_____
_____
_____

Understanding Tone

When you think about tone, perhaps you think of someone's tone of voice. Works of literature have their own tones, as well. For example, a work's tone can be joyful or angry, informal or formal. An author carefully chooses words to convey a certain tone.

Literary Terms

- The **tone** of a literary work is the writer's attitude toward his or her audience and subject. Elements such as word choice, figurative language, sentence structure, line length, punctuation, rhythm, rhyme, and repetition are some of the details the writer chooses to include to communicate tone.

Example	Tone
Watching television can be a wonderful way to learn about the world!	excited
One might wish to consider alternatives to television viewing.	formal
Don't waste your time sitting in front of a television.	critical

- **Diction** is the author's word choice. The words the author chooses can conjure up specific feelings for a reader, helping to set a tone. Diction might be formal and eloquent or plain and simple. For example, the diction of the sentence "I didn't know what hit me" sets a different tone than the sentence "I found myself caught quite off guard." Authors frequently use variation in word choice for emphasis.

- The **denotation** of a word is its literal dictionary meaning. The **connotation** of a word is the positive or negative feelings associated with that word. Choosing words with a specific connotation can help set a tone.

Word	Denotation	Connotation
stubborn	unwilling to change	negative
strong-willed	unwilling to change	positive
slender	thin	positive
skinny	thin	negative

Understanding Tone

Directions Read the poem below. Circle word choices (diction) that reveal the speaker's tone. For example, is it objective, personal or impersonal, enthusiastic, humorous, or disapproving? Describe the speaker's tone in the margin.

Interview
by Sara Henderson Hay

Yes, this is where she lived before she won
The title Miss Glass Slipper of the Year,
And went to the ball and married the king's son.
You're from the local press, and want to hear
About her early life? Young man, sit down.
These are my *own* two daughters; you'll not find
Nicer, more biddable girls in all the town,
And lucky, I tell them, not to be the kind
That Cinderella was, spreading those lies,
Telling those shameless tales about the way
We treated her. Oh, nobody denies
That she was pretty, if you like those curls.
But looks aren't everything, I always say.
Be sweet and natural, I tell my girls,
And Mr. Right will come along, someday.

1. **Describe** How would you describe the overall tone of the poem? How does the tone connect to the main idea?

2. **Interpret** Does the phrase "spreading those lies" carry a positive or negative connotation? How does the phrase contribute to the tone of the poem?

3. **Listen and Speak** Read the poem aloud to a partner in a way that communicates the speaker's tone.

THE BIG Q: A writer chooses which details to include, and which to exclude, in order to persuade his or her readers.
Guiding Question: **Does the author provide you with enough information to convince you of his opinion?**

The Trouble with Television

by Robert MacNeil

Background Many people participate in debates about whether television plays a positive or negative role in today's society. Robert MacNeil is a novelist, playwright, and was the co-host of PBS' *MacNeil-Lehrer NewsHour* for twenty years.

Vocabulary Builder

Before you read, you will discuss the following words. In the Vocabulary Builder box in the margin, use a vocabulary building strategy to make the words your own.

diverts   usurps   august   pervading

As you read, draw a box around unfamiliar words you could add to your vocabulary. Use context clues to unlock their meaning.

Marking the Text

Persuasive Writing and Tone

As you read, underline the key points the author makes to persuade his readers. In the margin, identify the author's tone as he makes his points, as conveyed through word choice, figurative language, sentence structure, line length, punctuation, rhythm, rhyme, and repetition.

It is difficult to escape the influence of television. If you fit the statistical averages, by the age of 20 you will have been exposed to at least 20,000 hours of television. You can add 10,000 hours for each decade you have lived after the age of 20. The only things Americans do more than watch television are work and sleep.

Persuasive Writing, Propaganda, and Tone **233**

Calculate for a moment what could be done with even a part of those hours. Five thousand hours, I am told, are what a typical college undergraduate spends working on a bachelor's degree. In 10,000 hours you could have learned enough to become an astronomer or engineer. You could have learned several languages fluently. If it appealed to you, you could be reading Homer[1] in the original Greek or Dostoevski[2] in Russian. If it didn't, you could have walked around the world and written a book about it.

The trouble with television is that it discourages concentration. Almost anything interesting and rewarding in life requires some constructive, consistently applied effort. The dullest, the least gifted of us can achieve things that seem miraculous to those who never concentrate on anything. But television encourages us to apply no effort. It sells us instant gratification. It **diverts** us only to divert, to make the time pass without pain.

Television's variety becomes a narcotic,[3] not a stimulus.[4] Its serial, kaleidoscopic[5] exposures force us to follow its lead. The viewer is on a perpetual guided tour: thirty minutes at the museum, thirty at the cathedral, then back on the bus to the next attraction—except on television, typically, the spans allotted are on the order of minutes or seconds, and the chosen delights are more often car crashes and people killing one another. In short, a lot of television **usurps** one of the most precious of all human gifts, the ability to focus your attention yourself, rather than just passively surrender it.

---

[1] **Homer** *n.* Greek epic poet of the 8th century B.C.

[2] **Dostoevski** (dôs tô yef´ skē) *n.* (1821–1881) Russian novelist.

[3] **narcotic** *n.* something that soothes or dulls the senses.

[4] **stimulus** (stim´yə ləs) *n.* something that rouses to action.

[5] **kaleidoscopic** (kə lī də skäp´ik) *adj.* constantly changing.

Marking the Text

Vocabulary Builder

diverts
(di vurts´) *v.*

Meaning

usurps
(yōō surps´) *v.*

Meaning

Capturing your attention—and holding it—is the prime motive of most television programming and enhances its role as a profitable advertising vehicle. Programmers live in constant fear of losing anyone's attention—anyone's. The surest way to avoid doing so is to keep everything brief, not to strain the attention of anyone but instead to provide constant stimulation through variety, novelty, action and movement. Quite simply, television operates on the appeal to the short attention span.

It is simply the easiest way out. But it has come to be regarded as a given, as inherent[6] in the medium itself: as an imperative, as though General Sarnoff, or one of the other **august** pioneers of video, had bequeathed to us tablets of stone commanding that nothing in television shall ever require more than a few moments' concentration.

In its place that is fine. Who can quarrel with a medium that so brilliantly packages escapist entertainment as a mass-marketing tool? But I see its values now **pervading** this nation and its life. It has become fashionable to think that, like fast food, fast ideas are the way to get to a fast-moving, impatient public.

In the case of news, this practice, in my view, results in inefficient communication. I question how much of television's nightly news effort is really absorbable and understandable. Much of it is what has been aptly described as "machine gunning with scraps." I think its technique fights coherence[7]. I think it tends to make things ultimately boring and dismissable (unless they are accompanied by horrifying pictures) because almost anything is boring and dismissable if you know almost nothing about it.

I believe that TV's appeal to the short attention span is not only inefficient communication but decivilizing as well. Consider

Marking the Text

Vocabulary Builder

august
(ô gust´) *adj.*

Meaning

pervading
(pər vād´ iŋ) *v.*

Meaning

---

[6] **inherent (in hir´ ənt)** *adj.* natural.
[7] **coherence (kō hir´ əns)** *n.* the quality of being connected in an intelligible way.

Persuasive Writing, Propaganda, and Tone

the casual assumptions that television tends to cultivate: that complexity must be avoided, that visual stimulation is a substitute for thought, that verbal precision is an anachronism[8]. It may be old-fashioned, but I was taught that thought is words, arranged in grammatically precise ways.

There is a crisis of literacy in this country. One study estimates that some 30 million adult Americans are "functionally illiterate" and cannot read or write well enough to answer a want ad or understand the instructions on a medicine bottle.

Literacy may not be an inalienable human right, but it is one that the highly literate Founding Fathers might not have found unreasonable or even unattainable. We are not only not attaining it as a nation, statistically speaking, but we are falling further and further short of attaining it. And, while I would not be so simplistic as to suggest that television is the cause, I believe it contributes and is an influence.

Everything about this nation—the structure of the society, its forms of family organization, its economy, its place in the world—has become more complex, not less. Yet its dominating communications instrument, its principal form of national linkage, is one that sells neat resolutions to human problems that usually have no neat resolutions. It is all symbolized in my mind by the hugely successful art form that television has made central to the culture, the thirty-second commercial: the tiny drama of the earnest housewife who finds happiness in choosing the right toothpaste.

When before in human history has so much humanity collectively surrendered so much of its leisure to one toy, one mass diversion? When before has virtually an entire nation surrendered itself wholesale to a medium for selling? Some years ago Yale University law professor Charles L. Black, Jr. wrote: ". . . forced feeding on trivial fare is not itself a trivial matter." I think this society is being force fed with trivial fare, and I fear that the effects on our habits of mind, our language, our tolerance for effort, and our appetite for complexity are only dimly perceived. If I am wrong, we will have done no harm to look at the issue skeptically and critically, to consider how we should be resisting it. I hope you will join with me in doing so.

---

[8] **anachronism** (ənak´rə niz´əm) *n.* anything that seems to be out of its proper place in history.

Vocabulary Builder

After you read, review the words you decided to add to your vocabulary. Write the meaning of words you have learned in context. Look up the other words in a dictionary, glossary, thesaurus, or electronic resource.

Marking the Text

▼ **Critical Viewing**
What does this image communicate about the effects of television?

Thinking About the Selection
The Trouble with Television

1 **Make a Judgment** What are the author's beliefs about television? Judging from the author's arguments and other evidence from the text, do you think he is biased? Explain.

2 **Speculate** In the first paragraph what does the author assume about his readers?

3 **Interpret** Identify three places where MacNeil repeats that television appeals to the short attention span. Why does he repeat this idea and use variation to build his argument?

4 **Analyze** Read the last paragraph of the essay aloud. How would you describe the tone? Identify and analyze details that support your response.

5 **Identify** One method of persuasion is analogy. An analogy is the comparison between two things that are otherwise dissimilar ("a *strand of DNA* is like a *ladder* that has been twisted"). Identify and explain one analogy in this essay.

Write Answer the following questions in your Reader's Journal.

 6 **Evaluate** Does the author provide you with enough information to convince you of his opinion? Explain why or why not.

 7 **Evaluate** What is the author of your Anchor Book trying to persuade you to believe? Do you agree? Explain.

Persuasive Writing, Propaganda, and Tone

3-6 Listening and Speaking Workshop
Delivering a Persuasive Speech

Have you ever had a disagreement? Using the right tools can help you persuade others of your opinion.

Your Task

- Select a topic for your speech.
- Determine key points and gather information to support them.
- Rehearse and present your persuasive speech.

Prepare Your Presentation

1 CHOOSE YOUR TOPIC
- Consider your audience.
- Choose a position, or thesis, you can support with reasoning.

2 GATHER INFORMATION
- Research your topic and consider whether the opinions you read are valid. Revise your position if necessary.
- Identify facts, quotations, ideas, and personal experiences that will strengthen your position and add interest.
- Include details, reasons, arguments, and analogies in support of your ideas that will convince your audience and answer their concerns. Use wording that has the denotations and connotations you intend. Incorporate persuasive techniques, such as hyperbole and understatement, and use jargon appropriate to your topic.

3 CREATE AN EXCITING VISUAL
- Use a picture, illustration, or chart to make your point.

4 SHAPE YOUR PRESENTATION
- Write each idea and visual on a separate index card and rearrange to find the best order for your presentation. Then, create a script from your notes.

5 PRACTICE YOUR PRESENTATION
- Present in front of friends, relatives, or your teacher. Have them use the script as a reference point. Practice changing your delivery to suit each audience.

- Use their responses and feedback to assess your performance. Respond to their concerns orally, paraphrasing the suggestions or directions, and give counterarguments. Then, modify the speech's organization and reword unclear sentences.

- Speak slowly, clearly, and loudly enough to be easily understood. Use a tone of voice and precise, active language that fits your topic and audience. Try to entertain your audience with your unique voice and style.

- Speak in a steady rhythm, making eye contact and using posture to emphasize your message.

Directions For each assessment question, circle a rating.

SPEAK: Rubric for Oral Interpretation

CRITERIA	RATING SCALE NOT VERY VERY
TOPIC Was your topic interesting and your viewpoint clear?	1 2 3 4 5
LANGUAGE How well did you demonstrate persuasive techniques?	1 2 3 4 5
ORGANIZATION How persuasive were your facts, quotes, anecdotes, and other forms of information?	1 2 3 4 5
DELIVERY How well did you make eye contact, and control pacing, posture, pronunciation, tone, and volume?	1 2 3 4 5

LISTEN: Rubric for Audience Self-Assessment

CRITERIA	RATING SCALE NOT VERY VERY
ACTIVE LISTENING How well did you pay attention and understand the message of each speaker?	1 2 3 4 5
ACTIVE LISTENING Did you ask relevant questions about the speech? Were the speaker's opinions persuasive?	1 2 3 4 5

Explain Was your opinion of a subject changed or reinforced by a particular speech you heard? Explain why or why not.

while reading your anchor book

Delivering a Persuasive Speech

3-7 Language Coach
Grammar and Spelling

Adjectives, Articles, and Adverbs

An **adjective** is a word that describes a noun or pronoun. A **proper adjective** is an adjective that is capitalized because it is derived from a proper noun. An adjective adds detail to a noun by answering one of these questions.

What kind?	Which one?	How many?	How much?	Whose?
The black cat jumped out of the way.	The Siamese cat ran under the sofa.	There were seven cats in my closet.	I watched a tiny kitten eat an entire can of tuna	My cat is the grey one.

Three common adjectives, *a, an,* and *the,* are called **articles**. These three articles answer the question *Which one?*

An **adverb** modifies a verb, an adjective, or another adverb. Adverbs often end in the suffix *–ly* and answer one of these questions.

When?	Where?	In What Manner?	To What Extent?
Yesterday I decided on a special project.	Many students live close to the school.	A firefighter ran swiftly past her.	The Perfect Storm is an extremely exciting story.

Directions Create a list of adjectives to describe the two nouns below.

1. car _____
2. wolf _____

Directions Create an example of each use of adverb shown in the chart below.

Adverb use	Example	Your Sentence
Opener	*Frantically*, Alejandro searched for his keys.	
Interrupter	Moneshia, *meanwhile*, was running late.	
Closer	Jerome waited *patiently*.	

Comparative and Superlative Forms

When using adjectives and adverbs to compare items, use the comparative and superlative forms. Use the **comparative form** to compare two items. Use the **superlative form** to compare three or more items.

Comparative: One road is narrower than the other.
Superlative: This road is the narrowest of these three roads.

- Form these degrees by adding *-er* or *-est* to most one- or two-syllable words.
- Use *more* and *most* (and *less* and *least*) with most adverbs ending in *-ly* and with modifiers of three or more syllables.
- Irregular adjectives and adverbs have unpredictable patterns that must be memorized.

Positive	Comparative	Superlative
happy	happier	happiest
interesting	more interesting	most interesting
bad, badly	worse	worst
good, well	better	best
many, much	more	most
far (distance)	farther	farthest
far (extent)	further	furthest

Author's Craft

Look back at the selection "The Trouble With Television" on page 233. When writers try to persuade you of their opinion they frequently use superlative adjectives. Find three superlative adjectives in the selection and analyze how they are being used.

Directions Fill in each blank with the correct form of the modifier in parentheses.

Example This is the (good) story I have ever written. ____best____

1. I feel (bad) today than I did yesterday. _____
2. Of all my friends, Joseph lives the (far) from school. _____
3. Air travel is (safe) than travel by car. _____
4. This is the (good) news I've heard all day. _____
5. John is the (old) of their four nephews. _____
6. It is (sunny) this week than it was last week. _____

Language Coach continued

Modifiers

Adjectives and adverbs are modifiers. A **modifier** is a word, phrase, or clause that changes a noun, verb, or entire sentence by adding information. Good writers use modifiers for effective description and dramatic effect. Look back at the chart on page 240 to see how a modifier can go in different places in a sentence.

It is easy to make mistakes with modifiers, however. Modifiers need to be near the idea (noun) they are meant to describe or modify. There are two kinds of mistakes people make when they use modifiers incorrectly.

A **misplaced modifier** is too far from the noun it describes.

1 They bought a puppy for my sister *they call Fido.*

What does the writer think the sentence says, and what does it really say?

_____

A **dangling modifier** often has no subject to modify and the doer of the phrase is not stated. The subject is unclear, and its meaning is often humorous.

2 *Having finished her homework,* the TV was turned on.

What does the writer think the sentence says, and what does it really say?

_____
_____

3 Choose one of these sentences and rewrite it to correct the modifier.

_____
_____

Directions Experiment with modifiers. Create a sentence using a series of modifiers.

Example Marika sighed, *head in her hands, exhausted and exasperated, waiting for Tomas.*

_____
_____
_____

> **Author's Craft**
> Look back at the selection "The World of the Forensic Scientist" on page 222. Find two sentences containing modifiers. Rewrite each sentence so that the modifier's position is different (opener, interrupter, closer). Which placement is most effective?

Lesson 3-7

Prepositions and Prepositional Phrases

A **preposition** relates the noun or pronoun following it to another word in the sentence.

The categorized list below will help you identify some common prepositions and their functions.

Location			Time	Other Relationships
above	between	out	after	about
across	beyond	outside	as	despite
against	by	over	before	except for
along	down	past	during	like
among	from	through	since	of
around	in, inside	to	until	per
at	into	toward		than
behind	near	under, underneath		with
below	off	up		without
beside	on	within		

The group of words beginning with a preposition and ending with a noun or pronoun is called a **prepositional phrase**. In the example sentence below, the preposition is circled and the prepositional phrase is underlined.

Example We were sitting (on) the front porch.

Directions Circle each preposition and underline each prepositional phrase in these sentences.

1. The actress with red hair held a book in her hand.

2. She stood in the very center of the huge stage.

3. She was auditioning for the director and for the producer.

4. The stage manager sat inside the wings to the right.

5. Behind him stood various members of the cast.

Directions Prepositional phrases are great for helping to build specific, descriptive details in your writing. Write a description of an imagined setting using as many prepositional phrases as possible.

_____
_____
_____

Author's Craft

Look back at the selection "Interview" on page 232. Identify three prepositional phrases. Why are they important to the meaning of the sentences in which they appear?

Language Coach

3-8 Writer's Workshop
Exposition: Cause-and-Effect Essay

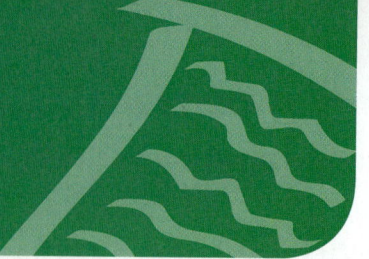

Whether the subject is historical trends or weather patterns, cause-and-effect reasoning explains why things happen. A **cause-and-effect** essay examines the relationship between or among two or more events, explaining how one causes another. In this workshop, you will write your own cause-and-effect essay about an issue that interests you.

To be effective, your essay should include the following elements.

- a clear and consistent organization
- an explanation of how one or more events or situations resulted in another event or situation
- a thorough presentation of facts, statistics, and other details that support the explanation presented

Purpose To write a cause-and-effect essay about an issue that interests you

Audience You, your teacher, and your classmates

Prewriting—Plan It Out

Use the following to select the topic of your essay.

Choose your topic. With a partner, brainstorm topics that interest you from your everyday life. Review your answers and choose the topic that you find most interesting.

Narrow your focus. Make sure your topic is narrow enough to cover in depth. Jot down subtopics of your main topic.

Gather details. Do some research. Gather facts, examples, and details through research, observation, and memory that you need to thoroughly illustrate cause-and-effect relationships. Use a K-W-L chart to plan and guide your research, and consider incorporating relevant questions from the middle column into your essay.

Topic
NASA Technology

Satellites

Benefits

Improved weather forecasts

Student Model: Using a K-W-L Chart

K-W-L Chart		
What I Know	What I Want to Know	What I Learned
Sleep is important for good health. People do not get enough sleep.	What are the effects of not getting enough sleep? Is there a solution?	Lack of sleep can harm the body. Sleeping well benefits the body.

244 Lesson 3-8

Drafting—Get It on Paper

Using your K-W-L chart as an outline, write your draft. The following steps will help make your essay engaging and organized.

Shape your writing. Review your research and list the main causes and effects. Identify which description below best fits your topic. Use the chart on the right to organize the cause(s) and effect(s) in one paragraph.

Cause(s)	Effect(s)

- **Many Causes/Single Effect** If your topic has several causes of a single effect, develop a paragraph to discuss each cause.

- **Single Cause/Many Effects** For one cause with several effects, devote a paragraph to discuss each one.

- **Chain of causes and effects** If you are presenting a chain of causes and effects, present them in chronological order with transitions to show the connections.

Provide elaboration. Add details to elaborate on the connection you are showing.

> **Weak connection** *The stores were crowded the weekend before the holiday.*
>
> **Cause-and-effect connection** *With reduced prices and the pressure of last-minute shopping, the stores were crowded before the holiday.*

Write a conclusion. Conclude with a detailed summary of your essay.

Revising—Make It Better

Using the following strategies, revise your draft to make it more precise.

Student Model: Revising to Define Key Terms

> Sleep deprivation occurs when someone receives fewer hours of sleep than his or her body needs. Many different things can cause sleep deprivation. **A few of them are drinking caffeine, living in a noisy sleep environment, and working long hours.**

This information will help a reader who is unfamiliar with the term sleep deprivation.

The writer helped clarify the definition by giving an example.

Add or delete details to better elaborate on the stated central idea.

Peer Review Read your essay aloud to a partner. Identify at least three goals for the revision of your essay.

Exposition: Cause-and-Effect Essay

Writer's Workshop continued

Directions Read this student essay as a model for your own.

Student Model: Writing

Sleep, It's Healthy
Max Norowzi, Raleigh, NC

Since the beginning of time, sleep has been an important factor in maintaining good health. While people sleep, they refuel their bodies and minds to help them through the next day. Many people do not get the proper amount of sleep, however, and this has a negative effect on their health.

During the day our bodies and minds consume a great deal of energy. Sleep recharges our bodies and minds, giving our bodies and minds a chance to recover the energy that we have lost. We wake up feeling refreshed because, while we sleep, our brains do not need to focus and our muscles can relax.

Sleep deprivation occurs when someone receives fewer hours of sleep than his or her body needs. Many different things can cause sleep deprivation. A few of the main causes are drinking caffeine, living in a noisy environment, and working long hours. The effect on a person who does not get enough sleep can be devastating.

Some effects of sleep deprivation are stress, anxiety, inability to concentrate, and loss of coping skills. Another effect is weight gain, which is very unhealthy for most people. Mood shifts, including depression, increased irritability, and loss of a sense of humor all result from not getting enough sleep.

I have observed some of these sleep deprivation effects in people I know. My friend Tim had to stay up late several nights in a row to finish a term paper on time. Here is how Tim describes how the loss of sleep affected him: "The first thing I noticed was that I couldn't concentrate in class. My attention would wander and I couldn't understand ideas that would ordinarily be very easy for me to grasp. My body was achy, my head was cloudy, and I was snapping at everyone..."

In conclusion, adequate sleep promotes good health and helps us feel better about ourselves. Sleep deprivation can seriously harm our minds and bodies. To counter these harmful effects, the answer is to simply get more sleep. Sleeping well can guarantee us better health and a better life.

The writer clearly outlines the cause-and-effect relationship he will address.

This paragraph identifies the causes of sleep deprivation.

To support his explanation, the writer offers detailed descriptions of sleep deprivation's effects.

The writer concludes his essay effectively by summarizing the health benefits of sleep.

Editing—Be Your Own Language Coach

Before you hand in your essay, review it for language convention errors, using a language or style handbook. Pay special attention to your use of prepositional phrases.

Publishing—Share It!

When you publish a work, you produce it for a specific audience. Consider one of the following ideas to share your writing.

- ▶ **Present a public service announcement.** Create a video or audio recording of your essay to raise awareness of your topic or to inspire people to get involved.

- ▶ **Publish a feature article.** Submit your essay to your local or school newspaper.

Reflecting on Your Writing

1. Respond to the following questions on the back of your final draft. What new insights did you gain about the form of the cause-and-effect essay by writing one? What do you do well? What do you need to work on? Set a goal you can meet in your next workshop.

2. **Rubric for Self-Assessment** Assess your essay. For each question, circle a rating.

CRITERIA	RATING SCALE
	NOT VERY — VERY
IDEAS Does your paper include clear causes and effects?	1 2 3 4 5
ORGANIZATION How well do you employ a clear and logical organization?	1 2 3 4 5
VOICE Is your writing lively and engaging, drawing the reader in?	1 2 3 4 5
WORD CHOICE How appropriate is the language for your audience?	1 2 3 4 5
SENTENCE FLUENCY How varied is your sentence structure?	1 2 3 4 5
CONVENTIONS How correct is your grammar, especially your use of prepositions?	1 2 3 4 5

Exposition: Cause-and-Effect Essay

3-9 Discussing Your Anchor Book
Literature Circles

Cause and effect In this Literature Circle, you and your group members will start with an open discussion, and then you will analyze cause-and-effect relationships in your Anchor Book.

Part 1: Open Discussion

In this part of your Literature Circle, it is up to you and your group members to decide which events, ideas, passages, and/or characters from your Anchor Book you wish to discuss. For discussion ideas, check Reader's Journal notes you have made or questions, ideas, and observations you wrote on self-stick notes in your Anchor Book.

Part 2: Discuss—Cause and Effect

Now, consider how cause-and-effect relationships are important to your Anchor Book. Cause and effect is the relationship between an event and its result or results. As we grow up, we learn that our actions have consequences, or effects. We also learn that we can cause certain things to happen based on how we behave.

Although cause-and-effect relationships explain the connection between events, they do not always follow a simple pattern of a single cause producing a single effect. Sometimes, a single cause produces multiple effects. Alternatively, multiple causes can produce a single effect as shown in the model below.

What happened first?	**Cause**	You drop a large rock through the bottom of the boat in which you are sitting.
And then what happens?	**Effect**	There is a large hole in your boat.
And then what happens?	**Effect**	Water begins to fill up your boat.
And then what happens?	**Effect**	Your boat starts to sink.
And then what happens?	**Effect**	You are all wet.

With your group, discuss important cause-and-effect relationships in your Anchor Book using the guidelines that follow.

What role do these cause-and-effect relationships play in your Anchor Book? How might the chain of cause and effect change if a character behaved differently or if an event happened in a different way? Speculate on how two events in your Anchor Book might have gone differently. Record your group members' ideas in the chart below.

If this cause were different in this way,	then the effect(s) would be different in this way.

How can you make discussions better? Brainstorm thoughtful questions and supportive behavior that made your discussion interesting and entertaining (while remaining on topic). Then discuss what else you could have asked or done to make the discussion better. Remember these points for your next Literature Circle!

Thoughtful Questions
We asked:
We could ask:

Supportive Behavior
We said or did:
We could say or do:

while reading your anchor book

Monitoring Your Progress
Standardized Test Practice

Reading Skills: Identifying Main Ideas and Supporting Details

Read the passage. Then, answer the questions.

> About 20,000 years ago, Earth was experiencing a big chill, or what is commonly called the "Ice Age," in which glacial ice covered most of North America, northern Europe and Russia, and Siberia. Because so much water was locked in these glaciers, sea level was lowered by as much as 300 feet. Therefore, land that had been submerged during warmer periods was now exposed and dry.
>
> One exposed strip of land became the gateway for the first inhabitants to the Americas. Referred to as "Beringia" by anthropologists, this strip was about 1,000 miles wide, connecting Siberia to Alaska where the Bering Strait now exists. If early humans were standing on the Siberian side of Beringia, however, they would not have been able to see across to the land that lay beyond—the unknown continent of North America. Though they were not aware of exactly where they were headed some 11,000 years ago, and despite the ice and the cold in the stark landscape, early humans traveled into new territory, making history along the way.

1 What is the **main idea** of the passage?

   A. Beringia was a land bridge connecting Siberia to Alaska.
   B. As recently as 20,000 years ago, Earth experienced the Ice Age.
   C. Water taken up by glaciers lowered sea level.
   D. Earth's cold climate exposed a stretch of land that allowed early humans to cross into North America.

2 What is an important **detail** supporting the main idea in the first paragraph?

   F. Earth rotated away from the sun.
   G. Beringia was about 11,000 miles wide.
   H. The decrease in sea level caused some land to be exposed.
   J. Earth's cold period is also known as the "Stone Age."

3 What is one possible title of this passage?

   A. "The 11,000-Mile Strip"
   B. "A Stark Landscape"
   C. "Early Human Beings"
   D. "From Siberia to Alaska"

4 Based on the details in the second paragraph, what can be inferred about early human beings?

   F. Early human beings existed about 11,000 years ago.
   G. Early human beings had occupied lands in, east of, and west of Siberia.
   H. Early human beings knew that there was a whole continent beyond Beringia.
   J. Early human beings were not able to survive in to the cold.

Literary Analysis: Elements of Nonfiction

Read the following passage. Then, answer the questions.

> Do you own an MP3 player? If you answered *Yes,* you may be at risk for hearing loss. Currently, more than 28 million Americans have experienced some hearing loss, according to the National Institute on Deafness. "Everything is louder—phones ring louder, movies are louder . . . And rock & roll is a big part of it," says Marshall Chasin, director of auditory research at the Musicians' Clinic of Canada.
>
> Digital-music players, such as the popular iPod, pose a new threat to our hearing. Studies show that continued listening, even at moderate volume, can be harmful. Brian Fligor, audiologist at Boston Children's Hospital, warns that in-the-ear headphones—the MP3 player ear buds, for example—are capable of producing high sound levels because they are closer to the eardrum. In fact, portable music players comparable to the MP3 player can go as high as 130 decibels, or as loud as a jackhammer. Fligor has determined that individuals can safely listen to a portable music player with in-the-ear headphones around 30 minutes a day. If you can't limit your music play, Fligor suggests, then buy better headphones that mute external noise to allow you to lower the volume. But Marshall Chasin offers just this: give your ears a break.

5 What kind of writing is this passage an example of?

A. expository writing

B. humorous writing

C. persuasive writing

D. cause-and-effect writing

6 Which word best describes the **tone** of this passage?

F. cautionary

G. sarcastic

H. humorous

J. light-hearted

7 The **diction** used in the last sentence of the passage can be best described by which words?

A. eloquent and poetic

B. simple but effective

C. abstract and hard to understand

D. formal and academic

8 What is the primary message the author is conveying in this passage?

_____
_____
_____

Timed Writing: Exposition

Directions Persuasive writing is often used to question the values of a society. Think of a piece of persuasive writing you have read and explain what the author questions about society. **(20 minutes)**

3-10 Reading Skills
Differentiating Between Fact and Opinion

In learning new reading skills, you will use special academic vocabulary. Knowing the right words will help you demonstrate your understanding.

Academic Vocabulary

Word	Meaning	Example Sentence
cite v. Related word: cited, citing	to refer to or quote by way of example	I *cited* three articles to back up my information on renewable energy.
justify v. Related words: justified, justifiable	to prove or show to be just, right, or reasonable	His anger was *justified* considering what had happened.
bias n., v. Related words: biasing, biased	a personal and sometimes unreasoned judgment	I may be *biased*, but my mom is the best cook in the world.

A **fact** is something that actually happened or that can be **justified,** or proved. To determine if something is a fact, you can do some research. You can check encyclopedias, almanacs, or reliable Web sites to **cite** as sources.

An **opinion** is a person's **bias**, or judgment or belief about something or someone. An opinion cannot be proved. To determine if something is an opinion, look for statements that suggest judgments that cannot be proved, such as *In my opinion, I believe,* and *I think*. Specific words that reveal a writer's feelings, such as *best* or *worst*, often indicate an opinion.

Fact The movie was two hours long.

Opinion That was the best movie ever!

Direction Read the following passage. Then, underline the statements that are facts, and circle words that signal opinion. Then, answer the questions.

"Women's Suffrage"

The Founding Fathers believed in a government that would promote the welfare of its people. Curiously, though, they let the states decide who had a say in running that government. Over the years, laws that kept people from voting were endured by the poor, Catholics, non-Christians, Indians, African Americans, and women.

Wyoming allowed women to vote while it was still a territory. Other territories and states let women vote in local elections. Finally, one by one, states started to let women take part in elections. Women even began to hold elected office. Still, it was not until 1920 that they could vote everywhere in the United States.

It took many years and various changes in our laws to give all adult citizens the right to vote. We should all have a downright feeling of pride that we can vote. That right gives us the ability to direct the course of our own lives and that of our country's history.

1 **Infer** Not all states granted women the right to vote at the same time. Which fact in the above text is this statement based on?

_____
_____

2 **Analyze** "Over the years, laws that kept people from voting were endured by the poor, Catholics, non-Christians, Indians, African Americans, and women." How could you prove this statement?

_____
_____

3 **Analyze** In which part of the passage do the facts appear? The opinions? Why would the author structure the passage's information this way?

_____
_____

Differentiating Between Fact and Opinion

THE BIG ? Strong opinions can lead you to view facts differently.
Guiding Question: **Does the author provide enough factual information, or is the essay mostly opinion?**

AMERICA the Not-So- BEAUTIFUL

The amount of garbage the United States population produces has quickly surpassed the amount of space where it can be disposed of. In the following article, one man discusses the consequences of trash disposal.

by Andrew A. Rooney

Next to saving stuff I don't need, the thing I like to do best is throw it away. My idea of a good time is to load up the back of the car with junk on a Saturday morning and take it to the dump. There's something satisfying about discarding almost anything. Throwing things out is the American way. We don't know how to fix anything and anyone who does know how is too busy to come so we throw it away and buy a new one. Our economy depends on us doing that. The trouble with throwing things away is, there is no "away" left.

Sometime around the year 500 B.C., the Greeks in Athens passed a law prohibiting people from throwing their garbage in the street. This Greek law was the first recognition by civilized people that throwing things away was a problem. Now, as the population explodes and people take up more room on earth, there's less room for everything else. The more civilized a country is, the worse the trash problem is. Poor countries don't have the same problem because they don't have much to discard. Prosperity in the United States is based on using things up as fast as we can, throwing away what's left and buying new ones. We've been doing that for so many years that 1) we've run out of places to throw things because houses have been built where the dump was, and 2) some of the things we're throwing away are poisoning the earth and will eventually poison all of us and all living things.

Ten years ago most people thought nothing of dumping an old bottle of weed or insect killer in a pile of dirt in the backyard or down the drain in the street, just to get rid of it. The big companies in America had the same feeling, on a bigger scale. For years the chemical companies dumped their poisonous wastes in the rivers behind the mills or they put it in fifty-gallon drums in the vacant lots, with all the old, rusting machinery in it, up behind the plants. The drums rusted out in ten years and dumped their poison into the ground. It rained, the poisons seeped into the underground streams and poisoned everything for miles around. Some of the manufacturers who did this weren't even evil. They were dumb and irresponsible. Others were evil because they knew how dangerous it was but didn't want to spend the money to do it right.

The problem is staggering. I often think of it when I go in a hardware store or a Sears Roebuck and see shelves full of poison. You know that, one way or another, it's all going to end up in our rivers and lakes.

I have two pint bottles of insecticide with 5 percent DDT in them in my own garage that I don't know what to do with. I bought them years ago when I didn't realize how bad they were. Now, I'm stuck with them.

The people of the City of New York throw away nine times their weight in garbage and junk every year. Assuming other cities come close to that, how

The people of the City of New York throw away nine times their weight in garbage every year.

255

Of all household waste, 30 percent of the weight and 50 percent of the volume is the packaging that stuff comes in. Not only that, but Americans spend more for the packaging of food than all our farmers together make in income growing it. That's some statistic.

Trash collectors are a lot more independent than they used to be because we've got more trash than they've got places to put it. They have their own schedules and their own holidays. Some cities try to get in good with their trash collectors or garbagemen by calling them "sanitation engineers." Anything just so long as they pick it up and take it away. We often call the dump "the landfill" now, too. I never understood why land has to be filled, but that's what it's called. If you're a little valley just outside town, you have to be careful or first thing you know you'll be getting "filled." If five billion people had been living on earth for the past thousand years as they have been in the past year, the planet would be nothing but one giant landfill and we'd have turned America the beautiful into one huge landfill. The best solution may be for all of us to pack up, board a spaceship and move out. If Mars is habitable, everyone on Earth can abandon this planet we've trashed, move to Mars and start trashing that. It'll buy us some time.

Of all household waste, 30 percent of the weight and 50 percent of the volume is the packaging that stuff comes in.

Thinking About the Selection
America the Not-So-Beautiful

1 **Evaluate** What facts did you learn about trash that you did not already know?

2 **Identify** Look back at how you marked your text. Find three examples of author bias. Write them below.

3 **Compare** How does Rooney's tone in "America the Not-So-Beautiful" compare to MacNeil's tone in "The Trouble with Television"? Use details from both selections to support your response.

Write Answer the following questions in your Reader's Journal.

4 **Evaluate** Does the author provide enough factual information, or is this essay mostly opinion? Use details from the selection to support your answer.

5 **Support** Write three facts about a character from your Anchor Book. Then, write three statements that illustrate your opinion about that character. Use details from the text to support your facts and opinion.

Ready for a Free-Choice Book? Your teacher may ask you if you would like to choose another book to read on your own. Select a book that fits your interest and that you'll enjoy. As you read, think about how your new book compares with your Anchor Book.

Differentiating Between Fact and Opinion

3-11 Literary Analysis
Biography and Autobiography

Biographies and autobiographies are life stories. They may tell the account of a person's whole life, or only a part of it. Most biographies are written about people who are famous, but they may also tell the story of an "ordinary" person.

Literary Terms

- A **biography** is a story of one person's life written by another person. It is told from a third-person point of view.

- An **autobiography** is a writer's account of his or her own life. It is told from a first-person point of view.

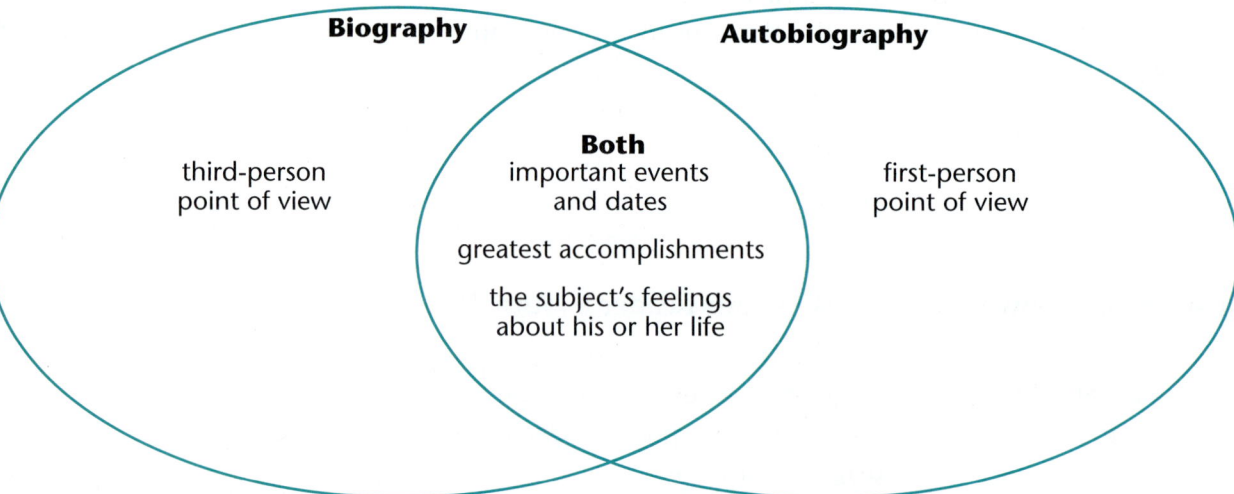

Biography: third-person point of view

Both: important events and dates; greatest accomplishments; the subject's feelings about his or her life

Autobiography: first-person point of view

Directions Read the following passage. As you read, underline the most important events in Harriet Beecher Stowe's life. For example, where was she born? What were the most important things that happened to her? What was the most interesting thing she did?

Link to Social Studies

Harriet Beecher Stowe

Harriet Beecher Stowe was a writer in a time when few women were publishing their writing. Today she is best known as the writer of *Uncle Tom's Cabin,* a novel about enslaved African Americans. It sold over 10,000 copies in the first week and convinced many people that slavery was wrong.

In 1832, when Stowe was in her early twenties, her family moved from Connecticut to Cincinnati, Ohio, a northern state that didn't allow slavery. It was directly across the Ohio River from Kentucky, a southern state that did allow slavery.

One day, Stowe heard the story of a young woman who had run across the frozen river from Kentucky to Cincinnati, clutching a baby in her arms. This later became one of the most famous scenes in *Uncle Tom's Cabin*. In the scene, the desperate Eliza runs across a frozen river with her son in her arms to prevent him from being sold and taken away from her.

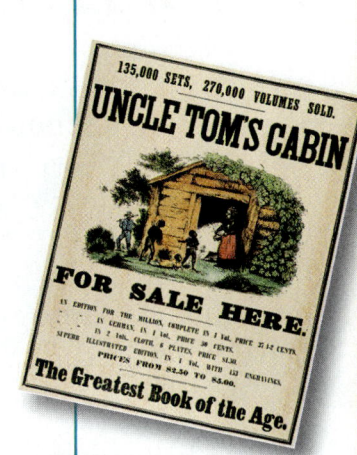

When you read a biography or autobiography, it can help to use a graphic organizer to keep track of important events in the person's life.

Directions Complete the biography graphic organizer with important events in Harriet Beecher Stowe's life. Answer the questions that follow.

Biography Graphic Organizer
Person: Harriet Beecher Stowe
Important event: Stowe's family moves from Connecticut to Cincinnati, Ohio.
Important event:
Important event:

1. **Apply** How do you know this is a biography?

   _____

   _____

2. **Analyze** Select an event you listed in the graphic organizer and explain why it was important.

   _____

   _____

3. **Infer** What can you infer about why Harriet Beecher Stowe wrote *Uncle Tom's Cabin*? Explain your reasoning.

   _____

   _____

Biography and Autobiography

Author's Perspective

Experiences shape who we are. Our age, gender, social position, and surroundings are just a few things that affect how we perceive the world around us.

In autobiographies, the authors' perspectives and attitudes are reflected through their own life stories. Readers are able to see the world directly through the authors' eyes.

You can better understand an **author's perspective** by learning about when and how he or she lived. When reading an autobiography, keep an eye out for details that tell you about the following things.

Directions As you read the following selection, complete this graphic organizer with words and phrases the author used that help clue you in to aspects of his or her life.

- Time period—When did the author live?
- Social position—What role did the author have in society?
- Surroundings—Where did the author live?
- Attitude—How did the author feel?
- Age—How old was the author?

Lesson 3-11

Now that you have learned about autobiography, read about an event that was of great importance in the author's life—learning to read and write. *Guiding Question:* **Does the author provide you with enough information to understand why this event was important to him?**

Narrative of THE LIFE of FREDERICK DOUGLASS
by Frederick Douglass

Background *Frederick Douglass was an enslaved African American who was born on a plantation in Maryland. When he was about eight years old, he was sent to live with a family in Baltimore.*

Vocabulary Builder

Before you read, *you will discuss the following words. In the Vocabulary Builder box in the margin, use a vocabulary building strategy to make the words your own.*

depravity   pious   prudence

As you read, *draw a box around unfamiliar words you could add to your vocabulary. Use context clues to unlock their meaning.*

Marking the Text

Autobiography and Author's Perspective

As you read, *underline important events and details that identify the author's perspective. In the margin, explain why you chose these events.*

I lived in Master Hugh's family about seven years. During this time, I succeeded in learning to read and write. In accomplishing this, I was compelled to resort to various stratagems. I had no regular teacher. My mistress, who had kindly commenced to instruct me, had, in compliance with the advice and direction of her husband, not only ceased to instruct, but had set her face against my being instructed by any one else. It is due, however, to my mistress to say of her, that she did not adopt this course of treatment immediately. She at first lacked the **depravity** indispensable to shutting me up in mental darkness. It was at least necessary for her to have some training in the exercise of irresponsible power, to make her equal to the task of treating me as though I were a brute.

Vocabulary Builder

depravity
(dē prav´ ə tē) *n.*

Meaning

Biography, Autobiography, and Author's Perspective **261**

My mistress was, as I have said, a kind and tender-hearted woman; and in the simplicity of her soul she commenced, when I first went to live with her, to treat me as she supposed one human being ought to treat another. In entering upon the duties of a slaveholder, she did not seem to perceive that I sustained to her the relation of a mere chattel,[1] and that for her to treat me as a human being was not only wrong, but dangerously so. Slavery proved as injurious to her as it did to me. When I went there, she was a **pious,** warm, and tender-hearted woman. There

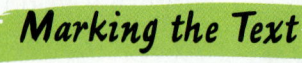

---

[1] **chattel** (chat´ əl) *n.* personal property

1. Frederick Douglass was brought to Wye House plantation. It was under the ownership of the sixth Edward Lloyd, who in the 1850s was the largest land proprietor in Talbot County and the largest slaveholder in Maryland.

2. Frederick Douglass's original copy of the Columbian Orator, which he obtained while learning to read.

3. Letter dated August 8, 1863, from George L. Stearns of Philadelphia authorizing Frederick Douglass to go to Washington, D.C., as his agent for the recruiting service for the United States Colored Volunteers.

4. A recruitment poster soliciting black soldiers to fight for the Union army in the Civil War, with signatures including that of Frederick Douglass, 1860s.

5. Frederick Douglass at his desk in Haiti.

6. This letter informed Douglass of his appointment as Minister of Counsel General to Haiti. Enclosed with the letter was a bond for $5,000 and two oath-of-office forms.

Literature in Context
The Abolitionists

Link to Social Studies

The abolitionists' goal was to abolish, or end, the enslavement of Africans and their descendants in Europe and North and South America. After Frederick Douglass escaped from slavery, he became one of the leading speakers for the abolitionist movement. The debate over slave ownership became so bitter that it was one of the major causes for the Civil War that was fought in the United States (1861–1865).

Johnson, William H. (1901-1970) © Copyright
Three Great Abolitionists:
A. Lincoln, F. Douglass, J. Brown. Ca. 1945.

was no sorrow or suffering for which she had not a tear. She had bread for the hungry, clothes for the naked, and comfort for every mourner that came within her reach. Slavery soon proved its ability to divest her of these heavenly qualities. Under its influence, the tender heart became stone, and the lamblike disposition gave way to one of tiger-like fierceness. The first step in her downward course was in her ceasing to instruct me. She now commenced to practice her husband's precepts. She finally became even more violent in her opposition than her husband himself. She was not satisfied with simply doing as well as he had commanded; she seemed anxious to do better. Nothing seemed to make her more angry than to see me with a newspaper. She seemed to think that here lay the danger. I have had her rush at me with a face made all up of fury, and snatch from me a newspaper, in a manner that fully revealed her apprehension. She was an apt woman; and a little experience soon demonstrated, to her satisfaction, that education and slavery were incompatible with each other.

From this time I was most narrowly watched. If I was in a separate room any considerable length of time, I was sure to be suspected of having a book, and was at once called to give an account of myself. All this, however, was too late. The first step had been taken. Mistress, in teaching me the alphabet, had given me the *inch*, and no precaution could prevent me from taking the *ell*.[2]

The plan which I adopted, and the one by which I was most successful, was that of making friends of all the little white boys whom I met in the street. As many of these as I could, I converted into teachers. With their kindly aid, obtained at different times and in different places, I finally succeeded in learning to read. When I was sent on errands, I always took my book with me,

Vocabulary Builder

pious
(pī´ əs) *adj.*

Meaning

Marking the Text

while reading your anchor book

---
[2] ***ell*** (el) *n.* a measure equal to 45 inches

Biography, Autobiography, and Author's Perspective   **263** and by doing one part of my errand quickly, I found time to get a lesson before my return. I used also to carry bread with me, enough of which was always in the house, and to which I was always welcome; for I was much better off in this regard than many of the poor white children in our neighborhood. This bread I used to bestow upon the hungry little urchins, who, in return, would give me that more valuable bread of knowledge. I am strongly tempted to give the names of two or three of those little boys, as a testimonial of the gratitude and affection I bear them; but **prudence** forbids; not that it would injure me, but it might embarrass them; for it is almost an unpardonable offence to teach slaves to read in this Christian country. It is enough to say of the dear little fellows, that they lived on Philpot Street, very near Durgin and Bailey's ship-yard. I used to talk this matter of slavery over with them. I would sometimes say to them, I wished I could be as free as they would be when they got to be men. "You will be free as soon as you are twenty-one, *but I am a slave for life!* Have not I as good a right to be free as you have?" These words used to trouble them; they would express for me the liveliest sympathy, and console me with the hope that something would occur by which I might be free.

Marking the Text

Vocabulary Builder

prudence
(prōō´ dəns) *n.*

Meaning

Vocabulary Builder

After you read, review the words you decided to add to your vocabulary. Write the meaning of words you have learned in context. Look up the other words in a dictionary, glossary, thesaurus, or electronic resource.

while reading your anchor book

Frederick Douglass

Frederick Douglass was born into slavery in 1818. After escaping from a cruel master at age 20, Douglass settled in Massachusetts, where he worked hard to continue the education he had begun as a young boy. Soon he was speaking in front of abolitionists, telling his life story in eloquent and popular speeches.
Douglass advised President Lincoln during the Civil War, and recruited African Americans for the Union Army. After the war, he continued to fight for the rights of African Americans as well as women. He spent much of his long life writing and traveling the world on speaking tours.

Thinking About the Selection
Narrative of the Life of Frederick Douglass

1 **Deduce** Which words or phrases helped you understand the social position Frederick Douglass held? How did his position affect his perspective?

_____
_____

2 **Analyze** What was Frederick Douglass's attitude? How do you know? Use details from the text to support your answer.

_____
_____
_____

3 **Analyze** Why is Douglass's autobiography an especially valuable source for people such as historians who are interested in slavery in America? What role does this knowledge play in today's world?

_____
_____
_____

4 **Compare and Contrast** Compare Frederick Douglass's struggle for equality with women's struggle for suffrage. How are they the same? How are they different? What effect did these struggles have on today's society?

_____
_____

Write Answer the following questions in your Reader's Journal.

5 **Analyze** Does the author provide enough information for you to understand why this event was important to him? Explain your response with details from the selection.

6 **Evaluate** Use the chart on page 260 to help you identify the perspective of the author of your Anchor Book.

3-12 Comparing Literary Works
Author's Style

When you write an e-mail to a friend, what kind of words, sentences, and tone do you use? What if you were writing a letter to apply for a job? How would the writing differ from an e-mail to a friend? Just as each of these letters would have its own style, each author has his or her own distinctive style.

An author's style may be playful or serious, informal or formal, poetic or informative, sympathetic or critical. The style of a piece of writing should fit its purpose. For example, a personal essay might use vivid, informal language, whereas a letter to an editor might use formal, persuasive language.

Literary Terms

An **author's style** is shaped by many elements including word choice, tone, length of sentences, author's purpose, figurative language, and changes in the English language over time. The way the author uses these elements also impacts the meaning of the text. When you look for an author's style in text, ask yourself the following questions.

Diction	What vocabulary does the author use? How appropriate are the word choices? How vivid is the language? Does the author use formal or informal language?
Tone	What is the author's attitude toward his or her subject?
Sentence length	Does the writer use short or long sentences? Does the writer vary the sentence length?
Author's purpose	How does the author's style fit his or her message or purpose?
Figurative language	Does the author use hyperbole, personification, simile and/or metaphor to communicate his or her ideas?

266 Lesson 3-12

Directions Read each of the following paragraphs, paying close attention to the author's style. Then answer the questions.

Personal Essay: A Beach Diary

My sister and I have spent the morning lazing on a beautiful beach in Bermuda. Now, as we prepare to leave, the ocean shimmers under the noon sun, the waves lap against the shell-pink sand. As we pack up our beach gear and leave, other beachgoers take our place, armed with sunglasses, lotion, and ice-cold drinks. Like imitation sandpipers, we pick our way through umbrellas and beach chairs to make our way back to Ocean Avenue. As we walk down the street, we turn to each other and say at the same time, "I wish I could live here!"

Travel Advertisement: Come to Bermuda!

You will find much to enjoy on the beautiful island of Bermuda. Our beaches are world-famous for their pink sands, contrasting with the turquoise ocean waters. When you want a break from the sun, try exploring an offshore reef or shopping for souvenirs. At night, you can eat at a gourmet restaurant or dance to a local band. We promise that it will be a trip to remember!

1 Compare and Contrast How are the two descriptions of Bermuda alike? How are they different?

2 Analyze How would you describe the style of each paragraph? What words and phrases contribute to their styles?

3 Evaluate Is the style of each paragraph appropriate to the author's purpose in each case? Explain.

Author's Style

Now that you've read an excerpt from *Narrative of the Life of Frederick Douglass,* read "Volar: To Fly" to compare the authors' styles.
Guiding Question: **How does an author's style contribute to the information that is delivered through his or her writing?**

Volar: To Fly

by Judith Ortiz Cofer

Background Born in Puerto Rico, Judith Ortiz Cofer moved to the United States with her family as a child. Her writing often explores the Puerto Rican experience in America, as in this excerpt from her book, *The Latin Deli.*

Vocabulary Builder

Before you read, you will discuss the following words. In the Vocabulary Builder box in the margin, use a vocabulary building strategy to make the words your own.

recurring   obsession

As you read, draw a box around unfamiliar words you could add to your vocabulary. Use context clues to unlock their meaning.

Marking the Text

Author's Style

As you read, underline examples of diction, tone, and figurative language, such as hyperbole, simile, and metaphor, that show the author's style. In the margin, write notes about her style. Is her writing formal or informal? Light or serious?

Vocabulary Builder

recurring
(rē kʉr´ iŋ) *adj.*

Meaning

At twelve I was an avid consumer of comic books—*Supergirl* being my favorite. I spent my allowance of a quarter a day on two twelve-cent comic books or a double issue for twenty-five. I had a stack of *Legion of Super Heroes* and *Supergirl* comic books in my bedroom closet that was as tall as I. I had a **recurring** dream in those days: that I had long blond hair and could fly. In my dream I climbed the stairs to the top of our apartment building as myself, but as I went up each flight, changes would be taking place. Step by step I would fill out: my legs would grow long, my arms harden into steel, and my hair would magically go straight and turn a golden color. . . . Once on the roof, my parents safely asleep in their beds, I would get on tip-toe, arms outstretched in the position for flight and jump out my fifty-story-high window

268 Lesson 3-12

▸ **Critical Viewing**
How does the style of this image communicate the mood and tone of the selection?

into the black lake of the sky. From up there, over the rooftops, I could see everything, even beyond the few blocks of our barrio[1]; with my X-ray vision I could look inside the homes of people who interested me. Once I saw our landlord, whom I knew my parents feared, sitting in a treasure-room dressed in an ermine coat and a large gold crown. He sat on the floor counting his dollar bills. I played a trick on him. Going up to his building's chimney, I blew a little puff of my super-breath into his fireplace, scattering his stacks of money so that he had to start counting all over again. I could more or less program my Supergirl dreams in those days by focusing on the object of my current **obsession**. This way I "saw" into the private lives of my neighbors, my teachers, and in the last days of my childish fantasy and the beginning of adolescence, into the secret room of the boys I liked. In the mornings I'd wake up in my tiny bedroom with the incongruous—at least in our tiny

Vocabulary Builder

obsession
(əb seˊ shən) n.

Meaning

[1] **barrio** (bäˊ rē ō) n. a mostly Spanish-speaking community or neighborhood

Author's Style

apartment—white "princess" furniture my mother had chosen for me, and find myself back in my body: my tight curls still clinging to my head, skinny arms and legs. . . .

In the kitchen my mother and father would be talking softly over a café con leche.[2] She would come "wake me" exactly forty-five minutes after they had gotten up. It was their time together at the beginning of each day and even at an early age I could feel their disappointment if I interrupted them by getting up too early. So I would stay in my bed recalling my dreams of flight, perhaps planning my next flight. In the kitchen they would be discussing events in the barrio. Actually, he would be carrying that part of the conversation; when it was her turn to speak she would, more often than not, try shifting the topic toward her desire to see her *familia* on the Island: *How about a vacation in Puerto Rico together this year, Querido? We could rent a car, go to the beach. We could . . .* And he would answer patiently, gently, *Mi amor, do you know how much it would cost for all of us to fly there? It is not possible for me to take the time off . . . Mi vida, please understand. . . .* And I knew that soon she would rise from the table. Not abruptly. She would . . . look out the kitchen window. The view was of a dismal alley that was littered with refuse thrown from windows. The space was too narrow for anyone larger than a skinny child to enter safely, so it was never cleaned. My mother would check the time on the clock over her sink, the one with a prayer for patience and grace written in Spanish. A birthday gift. She would see that it was time to wake me. She'd sigh deeply and say the same thing the view from her kitchen window always inspired her to say: *Ay, si yo pudiera volar.*[3]

---

[2] **café con leche** (kä fā′ kän lā′ chā) *n.* a strong, black coffee mixed with hot milk

[3] Oh, if only I could fly.

✦ JUDITH ORTIZ COFER (b. 1952) ✦

Judith Ortiz Cofer was born in Puerto Rico. Before Ortiz Cofer was five years old, she and her parents moved to the United States, settling in New Jersey. Ortiz Cofer and her mother returned to Puerto Rico on many occasions to visit their family when her father was overseas on naval missions.

While in Puerto Rico, Ortiz Cofer spent extended periods of time with her grandmother. She was so influential in Ortiz Cofer's life that a powerful grandmother character appears in many of her narratives. Her writing also features strong-willed Puerto Rican women and young characters who are torn between their Puerto Rican culture and American culture.

Thinking About the Selections

Volar: To Fly *and* Narrative of the Life of Frederick Douglass

1 **Compare and Contrast** Complete this chart to compare and contrast the authors' styles in the two selections.

Author's Style	Volar: To Fly	Narrative of the Life of Frederick Douglass
Diction	Vivid, poetic language; appropriate word choices	Formal, straightforward language; appropriate word choices
Tone		
Length of sentences		
Figurative language		

2 **Evaluate** Is the author's style appropriate? How does the style reflect changes in the English language? Explain.

_____

_____

3 **Compare and Contrast** What is the theme of each selection? How are they alike? How are they different?

_____

_____

4 **Analyze** "In *Volar: To Fly*," how does the author shift from the dream to the present? Explain.

_____

Write Answer the following questions in your Reader's Journal.

5 **Analyze** How does an author's style contribute to the information that is delivered through his or her writing?

6 **Interpret** Describe an example of figurative language in your Anchor Book. Explain how the example adds to your understanding of the author's style.

Author's Style 271

3-13 Language Coach
Grammar and Spelling

Combining Sentences With Conjunctions

Conjunctions connect words or groups of words. They can be used to create a compound or complex sentence. There are two categories of conjunctions that serve different functions.

Coordinating conjunctions join words of the same kind and equal rank, such as two nouns or two verbs. When they join two independent clauses, these conjunctions make a compound sentence.

Example: Jerry enjoys playing tennis. Tommy enjoys playing tennis.
Compound Sentence: Jerry and Tommy enjoy playing tennis.

Example: Crocodiles look slow. They can move swiftly.
Compound Sentence: Crocodiles look slow, but they can move swiftly.

Subordinating conjunctions create complex sentences by connecting two complete ideas and showing that one is dependent on the other.

Example: Carol had searched for several days. She found the perfect gift.
With Subordinating Conjunction After Carol had searched for several days, she found the perfect gift.

Author's Craft
Look back at the selection "Volar: To Fly" on page 268. Identify two sentences that use conjunctions to combine two independent clauses. How would the selection read differently if each sentence was broken into two sentences?

Common Conjunctions	
Coordinating	and, but, for, nor, or, so, yet
Subordinating	after, although, as, because, before, if, since, unless, until, when, while, whenever

Directions Combine the pair of sentences, using the coordinating or subordinating conjunction in parentheses.

1. We were late for school. We missed the bus. (because)

2. We stood by the Washington Monument. We felt very small. (when)

3. My schedule varies. I try to exercise every day. (although)

272 Lesson 3-13

Spelling Homophones

Homophones are words that sound alike but have different meanings and spellings. The words *cite, sight,* and *site* are homophones. You might have used the wrong word but spelled it correctly.

Notice the different ways the words are used in the chart below.

Homophone	Part of Speech	Meaning	Example
cite	verb	"to quote"	What sources did he cite in his report?
sight	noun	"the act of seeing"	The sight of the shark's teeth made me shiver.
site	noun	"place"	The site of the new library is on Main Street.

Directions Underline the correct homophone in each sentence.

1. It was so dark that (knight/night) that I could hardly see a thing.

2. The dove is a symbol of (peace/piece).

3. I used my birthday money to (by/buy) a new shirt.

4. The umpires could not agree on whether the ball was (fair/fare) or not.

5. Her (presents/presence) in the room was intimidating.

Directions Proofread the paragraph below. Underline the six misspelled words, and then write the correct spellings on the lines below.

I was hoping to get a new surf bored for my birthday. But my parents thought that would be a waist of money. Instead, they through out the idea of a chess set with hand-carved game pieces. The thought of sitting indoors playing chess put me in such a fowl mood. My father asked me to give chess just one our of my time. Surprisingly, I loved it! I gladly decided to except their offer.

6. _____   7. _____   8. _____
9. _____   10. _____ 11. _____

3-14 Writer's Workshop
Persuasion: Persuasive Essay

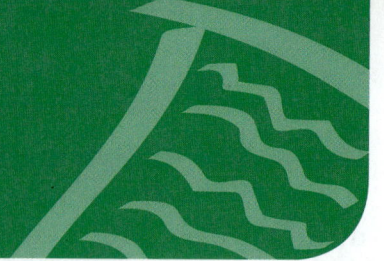

When you use words to change people's thinking or influence their actions, you are using persuasion. A **persuasive essay** is written in first or third—person and states and defends an opinion on a current issue. Some forms of this type of writing are political speeches, editorials, and reviews. In MacNeil's essay, he talks about the negative impact of television. Using the steps outlined in this workshop, take a positive or negative position on the impact of non-print media, such as talk radio or the Internet, on modern society.

Purpose To take a position on the impact of non-print media on modern society

Audience You, your teacher, and your classmates

To be effective, your editorial should include the following elements.

▶ a clear statement of your position supported by strong evidence

▶ a clear organization that builds toward your position and develops into a clear and informed conclusion

▶ a response to possible opposing arguments

▶ persuasive techniques that convey a powerful message

▶ error-free writing, including correct use of conjunctions

Prewriting—Plan It Out

You will do your best job writing if you choose a problem that concerns you. Follow these steps to plan your essay.

▶ **Choose your topic.** Create a list of problems that need solving and choose the issue that concerns you most. You can also conduct a media review and note topics that spark your interest in a chart like the one shown here.

Newspapers	Television News
overweight teens a national epidemic (National Gazette)	health care costs continue to rise (The Nightly News)
town needs new recycling plan (My Town Newspaper)	residents protest building of stadium (Local Channel News)

▶ **Narrow your topic.** Ask the "reporter's questions"—*Who? What? Where? When? Why?* and *How?* Circle the most interesting issues your answers raise in order to choose a narrowed topic.

▶ **Gather details.** Compile evidence such as statistics, expert opinions, facts, analogies, anecdotes, and personal observations to help explain and support your thesis and ideas. You may also find it helpful to conduct an interview or a survey and to create a graph that shows the results. Be sure to differentiate between facts and opinion as you compile your evidence. You might reference sources such as consumer, workplace, and public documents.

Who?
What?
When?
Where?
Why?
How?

274 Lesson 3-14

Drafting—Get It on Paper

The following steps will help make your essay focused and effective.

Shape your writing. Establish a logical organization with supporting details that are substantial, specific, and relevant. Being able to anticipate and answer readers' questions will make your essay well-rounded and show an understanding of your audience. Meet opposing ideas with counterarguments of your own.

Provide elaboration. Make your editorial as convincing as possible. Use a variety of persuasive techniques.

- **Logical Arguments** Present accurate evidence to earn your readers' trust by using sincere language. Develop a persona that your readers will find engaging and trustworthy by posing and answering your own questions.

- **Emotional Appeals** Spark an emotion in your readers such as pride, surprise, anger, or fear.

- **Charged Words, Expressions** Use words that pack entire arguments into a few syllables and provide powerful imagery.

- **Repetition and Parallelism** Use sentences that begin with identical forms to emphasize ideas.

Student Model: Using Persuasive Techniques

> My old grandfather says, "A problem always has a solution if you want to find it." Well, we need to find that solution!

The writer makes an emotional appeal to readers' feelings of respect for their elders.

Revising—Make It Better

Revise for clarity. In an effective persuasive essay, a few strong arguments are usually enough to make the case. Exclude any arguments that seem irrelevant or repetitive.

Revise for coherence. Ideas and paragraphs should connect logically. Rearrange words, sentences, and paragraphs to clarify meaning and/or use transitions. Two ways to add a word, phrase, or sentence that links the paragraphs together are repeating a key word or phrase and using a transitional word or phrase.

Revise for point of view and voice. Make certain you have expressed your point of view clearly. Vary your word choice and sentence structure to sustain the interest of your readers, to emphasize important ideas, and to let your own personality come through.

Peer Review. Read your essay aloud to a partner or group. Discuss your essay and revise based on the feedback you receive.

Writer's Workshop continued

Directions Read this student persuasive essay as a model for your own.

Student Model: Writing

Jordanna Oliveira, Newark, NJ

Editorial: Save The Brazilian Voice

Our Ironbound neighborhood of Newark is like a little Brazil. A lot of us who live here came from Brazil, and most of us read *The Brazilian Voice* every week. Now, however, this paper is going to close because there isn't enough money to keep publishing it. My old grandfather says, "A problem always has a solution if you want to find it." We need to find a solution to the problem of losing this neighborhood newspaper. It is my belief that *The Brazilian Voice* should not stop publishing. The people need it.

There are a lot of reasons why the people need *The Brazilian Voice*. For one thing, as all the readers know, it is an important source of information. It contains news about things happening in New Jersey and the rest of the country, and also about things happening in Brazil. The articles in Portuguese are important for people who don't know English very well. By reading *The Brazilian Voice*, they learn about the security of the city and about projects that the city is planning. Furthermore, the paper contains ads for people who are looking for jobs and all the announcements for special events like new restaurants opening, festivals, shows, sales, and activities for older people and young people. It lists all programs for the weekends and holidays. It is the heartbeat of a city that pulses with life and energy.

Some people might think that if we have a Brazilian television channel in New Jersey, we don't need the newspaper. However, the Brazilian channel only shows news from Brazil. *The Brazilian Voice* gives the news about our community that affects our lives every day. The people in the Ironbound depend on this paper . . .

> The writer presents the problem and clearly states her position.

> The writer supports her position with a series of reasons.

> The writer anticipates and addresses a potential argument against her position.

There are 45,000 people in the Ironbound. According to a poll by the paper, over half of them read *The Brazilian Voice* every week. If 20,000 people would pay 50 cents for the paper, that would be an extra $10,000. This money would mean that the citizens of the neighborhood could keep their paper.

In summation, I want to repeat that it is really important to have *The Brazilian Voice* in the Ironbound, and 50 cents isn't too much to pay for something that important.

> Statistics provide solid support for logical arguments.

> The writer has used evidence to build up to her conclusion.

Editing—Be Your Own Language Coach

Review your essay for errors using a language or style handbook. Pay special attention to your use of conjunctions.

Publishing—Share It!

Consider one of these ideas to share your writing.

- **Start a public forum.** Send out invitations to your community announcing a public debate. Then, share your persuasive essay with an audience of adults and peers and invite discussion.

- **Submit your persuasive essay.** Send your persuasive essay to your local or school newspaper to appear as an editorial or letter to the editor.

Rubric for Self-Assessment Assess your essay. For each question, circle a rating.

CRITERIA	RATING SCALE
	NOT VERY　　　　　VERY
IDEAS Does your essay include strong arguments and evidence that supports them?	1　2　3　4　5
ORGANIZATION How well do you employ a clear and logical organization?	1　2　3　4　5
VOICE Is your writing lively and engaging?	1　2　3　4　5
WORD CHOICE How well do you use persuasive techniques, including charged words?	1　2　3　4　5
SENTENCE FLUENCY How varied are your sentences?	1　2　3　4　5
CONVENTIONS How correct is your grammar, especially your use of conjunctions?	1　2　3　4　5

3-15 Connecting to Your Anchor Book
Anchor Book Projects

Now that you have finished reading your Anchor Book, it is time to get creative! Complete one of the following projects.

A — Create an Ad Campaign

An advertising campaign is designed to persuade people to change a habit, try a new product, or look at an issue in a different way.

1. Choose an issue that you have read about in your Anchor Book.
2. Think about how you could convince people to feel a certain way about the issue.
3. Use the persuasive techniques you have already learned in this unit. Incorporate **symbols** that convey a positive connotation and **irony** to humorously dismiss the other point of view.
4. Decide how your advertisement will be presented visually.

Your ad campaign should include the following elements.
- An engaging visual image that captures your stand on the issue
- A written message that informs and persuades readers

B — Write a Letter to the Editor

When people write letters to the editor of their local newspaper, they express their opinions or judgments about an issue. People write these letters to share information, expose an issue, or change a reader's stance on an issue.

1. Choose an issue from your Anchor Book. Decide your purpose for writing.
2. Research your topic. Use the library, Internet, or other resources, such as public and workplace documents and non-print media, to gather accurate information.
3. Write a rough draft. Provide factual information, including statistics, definitions, and personal knowledge. When appropriate, summarize or paraphrase the opinions and statements of opponents of your issue. If your letter includes unfamiliar terms, provide definitions to support your ideas.
4. Write a final draft to share with classmates. Ask them if they find it convincing, and why.

Your letter to the editor should include the following elements.
- Accurate and factual information
- Clearly stated and well-supported opinions

after reading your anchor book

Conduct an Interview

People who have significant accomplishments are often interviewed so that others can learn about their experiences. Interviewers prepare by reading about their subjects and writing up a list of questions before conducting their interviews.

1. Choose someone you have read about in your Anchor Book. Learn more about that person by researching on the Internet or at the library.
2. Write up a list of ten questions to ask your interviewee.
3. Based on what you know about your interviewee and his or her work, answer your questions based on how you would imagine your interviewee would respond.

Your interview should include the following elements.
- Ten well-thought-out and relevant questions that are organized in a logical manner
- Ten answers that reflect the interviewee's experiences and achievements

Free-Choice Book Reflection

You have completed your free-choice book. Before you take your test, read the following instructions to write a brief reflection on your book.

My free-choice book is _____.

The author is _____.

1 Would you recommend this book to a friend? Yes _____ No _____

Why or why not? _____

Write and Discuss Answer the following question in your Reader's Journal. Then, discuss your answer with a partner or your Literature Circle.

 2 **Compare and Contrast** *How much information is enough?* Compare and contrast how your Anchor Book and free-choice book provide information about a nonfiction topic. Use specific details from both books to support your ideas. Then, to extend the discussion, consider how information drives decisions in other subject areas, such as social studies, math, current events, or science.

Connecting to Your Anchor Book **279**

Unit Review
Standardized Test Practice

Answer the questions below to check your understanding of this unit's skills.

Reading Skills: Identifying Main Ideas and Supporting Details

Read this selection. Then answer the questions that follow.

> When sailors long ago glimpsed a smooth body, round head, and fluked tail parting the surface of the sea, they believed they had just sighted a mermaid. Biologists now know that what these sailors had seen was no mermaid: it was the dugong, a sea mammal related to the manatee. The dugong is bulky, its skin thick and tough, and it has two front flippers that are used for steering and a fluked tail for propulsion. It can grow as long as 11 ft and weigh up to 800 lbs—as much as a cow. Indeed, dugongs are also called "sea cows" because they graze on beds of sea grass.

1 What is the **main idea** of the selection?
  A. Dugongs are known as "sea cows."
  B. Dugongs have been mistaken for mermaids.
  C. The dugong is a sea mammal that resembles other creatures.
  D. The dugong has a smooth body, round head, and fluked tail.

2 Which of the following is a **supporting detail** of the main idea?
  F. Sailors discovered that the dugong was actually a mermaid.
  G. The dugong has several names.
  H. The dugong uses its nose for steering.
  J. The dugong is related to another large sea mammal.

Reading Skills: Differentiating Between Fact and Opinion

Read this selection. Then answer the questions that follow.

> Singing is a lot like sports. It takes physical stamina to produce a good sound. Like swimming or tennis, singing takes coordination, practice and exercise. In fact, singing is probably harder than most sports.
>
> A tennis player coordinates her muscles when she serves a ball. When a performer sings she coordinates muscles in the diaphragm, the voice box, and the throat.
>
> When you saw a singer perform, you probably were not aware of how much effort it took. The goal is to make singing look effortless. Now you know that it's not!

3 The following sentence can be supported by which **fact**?

"Singing is a lot like sports."

A. Both singing and sports require coordination.

B. I'll bet you didn't realize how much work went into music making.

C. The best singers do not let the audience realize how much effort it requires.

D. The goal is to make singing look and sound effortless.

4 Which statement is an **opinion**?

F. "Singing takes coordination, practice, and exercise."

G. "A tennis player coordinates her muscles when she serves a ball."

H. "In fact, singing is probably harder than most sports."

J. "A tennis player coordinates her muscles."

Literary Analysis: Elements of Nonfiction

Choose the best answer for the following questions.

5 Which choice defines the **tone** of a literary work?

A. the writer's attitude toward the reader or subject

B. a character's feelings

C. the mood or atmosphere

D. the writer's style

6 What is the term for the choice of words a writer makes?

F. style

G. connotation

H. diction

J. denotation

Read this selection and answer the questions that follow.

> Honey shouldn't be just food for the bees—with all its amazing properties, it should be a household and nutritional staple in our lives. This golden treat was prized by the ancient Greeks, who recognized honey's remarkable healing properties. Indeed, when diluted honey is applied to a moist wound, it produces hydrogen peroxide, a known antibacterial agent. In addition, the sweet sticky stuff helps the body on the inside. Researchers have found that honey provides a heaping dose of antioxidants, substances that protect the body's cells from harmful chemicals called free radicals. Of course, honey is also superb as a sugar alternative, perfect in teas, desserts, and other dishes.

Unit Review 281

7 This selection is an example of which kind of writing?

A. expository writing
B. autobiographical writing
C. humorous writing
D. persuasive writing

8 Based on the information in the selection, what is the author's opinion about honey?

F. Honey should be an important part of our lives.
G. Honey is a magical substance.
H. Honey helps to heal wounds.
J. Honey benefits the body in several ways.

9 In one paragraph, describe the author's **tone** from the selection.

_____
_____
_____

10 What type of organization is used when the relationship between events and their results is described?

A. cause—and—effect
B. main idea—and—fact
C. problem—and—solution
D. compare—and—contrast

11 Which statement carries a negative **connotation**?

F. Eliza thought he was a lying snake for accusing her of another's crime.
G. The electrician snaked the wire through the wall.
H. When my brother was young, he wanted to be a snake so he could slither around.
J. Some snakes are so poisonous that the venom in one bite is enough to kill several people.

Language Skills: Vocabulary

Choose the best answer.

12 Since the author only hinted at a deeper meaning, the novel's message remained _____.

A. hopeless   B. stated
C. strange   D. implied

13 What is a synonym of *rehearse*?

F. practice   G. quit
H. perform   J. applaud

14 Although there was not enough proof to publish her work, the scientist's discoveries were _____ for further research.

  A. unimportant   B. adequate
  C. not necessary D. criticized

15 What is an antonym of <u>believable</u>?

  F. convincing   G. honest
  H. incredible   J. weak

Language Skills: Spelling

Circle the letter of the word that completes each sentence correctly.

16 The construction _____ is located near Central Park.

  A. cite   B. site   C. sight

17 The pitcher _____ three strikes in a row.

  F. thru   G. through   H. threw

Language Skills: Grammar

Choose the best answer.

18 Identify the sentence containing a **superlative adjective** and an **adverb.**

  A. My parents gladly donated money to the best charity.
  B. Franklin hoped he would play well during the baseball game.
  C. My friend said the movie was the worst she had seen in over a year.
  D. The librarian quietly led us to the poetry section.

19 Identify the **preposition** in the following sentence.

  We should order the appetizers before our main course.

  F. order
  G. should
  H. main
  J. before

20 Identify the **article** in the following sentence.

  Without water, the dog remained thirsty.

  A without
  B. thirsty
  C. the
  D. remained

21 Which of the following sentences contains a **coordinating conjunction** and an **adverb**?

  F. You can eat slowly or get indigestion.
  G. The opera singer raised his hands and took a graceful bow.
  H. Should you ask for extra credit if you are doing well in class?
  J. Our school recycles glass, plastic, and paper.

What is the secret to *reaching someone* with words?

Unit 4 Genre focus:
Prose and Poetry

Your Anchor Book
There are many good books that would work well to support both the Big Question and the genre focus of this unit. In this unit you will read one of these books as your Anchor Book. Your teacher will introduce the book you will be reading.

Free-Choice Reading
Later in this unit you will be given the opportunity to choose another book to read. This is called your free-choice book.

Thinking About What You Already Know

It is often assumed that poetry has to be "formal" and "serious." Anyone who has ever gone to a poetry slam or spoken word performance, however, knows that this is not true. The great thing about poetry is that it can be one of the most creative, playful, and fun ways to put words on a page.

Partner Activity

The trick to understanding poetry is seeing that the ideas being expressed are not any more complicated than those in prose. With a partner, read the following poem.

Poetry

Fences by Pat Mora

Mouths full of laughter,
The *turistas*[1] come to the tall hotel
with suitcases full of dollars.

Every morning my brother makes
the cool beach sand new for them.
With a wooden board he smooths
away all footprints.

I peek through the cactus fence
and watch the women rub oil
sweeter than honey into their arms and legs
while their children jump waves
or sip drinks from long straws,
coconut white, mango yellow.

Once my little sister
ran barefoot across the hot sand
for a taste.

My mother roared like the ocean,
"No. No. It's their beach.
It's their beach."

[1] **turistas** (tōō rēs′ täz) *n.* Spanish word meaning *tourists*.

Now, in your own words, write a paragraph with a sentence for each stanza that explains the meaning of the poem.

_____
_____
_____
_____
_____
_____
_____

Class Discussion

Have a class discussion about the experience of putting the poem into your own words. Consider the following questions as you discuss.

- ▶ Did putting the poem into your own words help you to understand the poem better? Why or why not?
- ▶ What do you think the poem is about?

Jot down some notes about the discussion in the space provided.

_____
_____
_____
_____
_____
_____
_____

4-1 Understanding the Big Question
What is the secret to reaching someone with words?

Have you ever heard the expression, "It's not what you said, but how you said it"? The content of what you communicate is affected by how you say it — the form you express it in.

For the first part of this activity, you and your classmates will work in small groups. One member of the group will be a note-taker. Another member will be an actor, or model. This classmate will be the key to the development of your understanding of one another's inclusive methods of communication.

With your group, brainstorm a number of emotions. Write them in the following chart. Then think of ways to express these emotions when talking to another person or group of people. Be as specific as possible in your descriptions.

Emotions	Actions
Example: surprise	sudden gasp; eyes wide open; hand over mouth; head pushed back

Once you have completed your chart, you're ready for the next step. Your group's model will act out the actions your group has listed for each emotion. Challenge your classmates to identify the emotions being expressed.

Keep in Mind

Your classmates' ability to identify these emotions will depend on your group's ability to communicate your material.

After the class has completed the exercise, answer the following questions.

1 Which were the most popular emotions chosen by the class? Why do you think that these were so common?

_____

2 Was it easier for your group to describe a particular emotion on the chart, or was it easier to direct your model/actor in front of the class? How was the form of communication important?

_____
_____
_____
_____

3 Why do you think you were successful or unsuccessful in portraying the emotions you chose?

_____
_____
_____
_____

Further Exploration

On a separate sheet of paper, write a half-page reflection on how important the descriptions were in portraying emotions. Did the model stick closely to the descriptions? Would you go back and re-work your written descriptions? What changes would you make? Be prepared to discuss your thoughts with the class.

As you read your Anchor Book, pay attention to the emotions that you think your author is trying to convey and the form the author uses to communicate them. Pay attention to how simple things, like word choice and punctuation, can change the meaning.

Understanding the Big Question 289

Getting Ready for Your Anchor Book — You will start reading your Anchor Book soon. The next few pages in this book give you some background information plus a reading skill.

Introduction to Prose and Poetry

Prose and poetry are two major genres of literature. **Prose** occurs in two forms: fiction and nonfiction. **Poetry** describes the use of extremely concise, musical, and emotionally charged language. There are few absolutes in poetry. Perhaps the only rule is that with poetry every word counts.

When you read, you will find that some techniques you associate with poetry also appear in prose. All good writers use some of the following techniques.

- **Sensory language** is writing or speech that appeals to one or more of the five senses—sight, sound, smell, taste, and touch.

- **Figurative language** is imaginative and not meant to be taken literally. Types of figurative language include personification, which gives human qualities to nonhuman things; simile, which compares two unlike things using *like* or *as*; and metaphor, which describes one thing as if it were something else.

- **Sound devices** add a musical quality to written language. Here are some examples.

Type of Sound Device	Definition
Repetition	the repeated use of a sound, word, or phrase
Alliteration	the repetition of consonant sounds at the beginnings of words, as in *feathered friend*
Rhyme	the repetition of sounds at the ends of words
Rhythm	the pattern of beats, or stresses, in spoken or written language

Prose and Poetry: Different but Alike

Read the prose sentence. Then read the lines from Langston Hughes' poem "Dreams."

Prose   Hold fast to dreams, for if dreams die, life is a broken-winged bird that cannot fly.

Poetry   Hold fast to dreams
For if dreams die
Life is a broken-winged bird
That cannot fly.

In prose, sentences are used to express complete thoughts. In poetry, the equivalent is a **line**. Although poetry may use punctuation, the poet wants his or her audience to experience a poem line by line. These lines combine together to create the full effect of the poem.

Found Poem Exercise

Found poetry describes poetry that is made out of prose. It is the literary equivalent of a collage.

1 Find a prose passage from fifty to one hundred words long. Choose a passage that contains descriptive language and a strong emotional tone. Copy it onto a piece of paper or into a word processing document.

2 Choose the most powerful words and phrases from the prose text and arrange them in lines in a way that communicates the message and connotations of the original prose text.

3 Read your found poem aloud to see if your word choices and arrangement effectively communicate your message. Change as needed.

Strategies for Reading Prose and Poetry   As you read both poetry and prose, self-monitor and self-correct using the following strategies.

Reread the Text   If you feel lost while reading, go back to where you felt you understood the text. Then, slowly reread the material that follows that section.

Read Aloud   Read difficult sections aloud to help you monitor your comprehension.

Check Your Understanding   Check your understanding by asking yourself questions about the text, marking the text, summarizing, paraphrasing, or using graphic organizers.

Introduction to Prose and Poetry

4-2 Reading Skills
Paraphrasing

In learning new reading skills, you will use special academic vocabulary. Knowing the right words will help you demonstrate your understanding.

Academic Vocabulary

Word	Meaning	Example Sentence
convey v. Related word: conveyed	to make known; express	Please *convey* my concerns to your principal.
emphasize v. Related words: emphasizing, emphasis	to give special attention; stress	The coach *emphasized* that good sportsmanship was just as important as winning.
adapt v. Related words: adapted, adapting, adaptable	to change so as to make fit or usable; to change oneself to fit new conditions	The transfer student *adapted* easily to her new classes.

When you **paraphrase,** you restate a text in your own words. Before you paraphrase a line or a passage, reread to clarify the writer's meaning. First, identify the most basic information. Then put that information into your own words.

Paraphrasing helps you **convey** your own interpretation of important information to others. It is also a good way to check your own understanding of the text. Paraphrasing can help to **emphasize** what information is important. Paraphrasing also allows you to avoid plagiarism, or using someone else's words as your own.

How to Paraphrase

When attempting to communicate a concept to your audience, you should refrain from making your message obscure and vague.

- **Restate details more simply.** Communication needs to be clear to reach your audience.
- **Use synonyms for the writer's words.** Choose synonyms for difficult words to help your audience understand your ideas.
- **Look up unfamiliar words.** Replace unusual words and sentence structures with language that is more like everyday speech.

Directions Sometimes prose contains poetic language. Read the following passage. Then answer the questions.

> ### From *Rumblefish* by S.E. Hinton
>
> "Rusty-James," Steve said. I didn't look up. He sounded like he felt sorry for me and I didn't want to see him feeling sorry for me, because if I did I would hit him, no matter what.
>
> "I've tried to help you," he said. "But I've got to think about myself some."
>
> I wondered what he was talking about.
>
> "You're just like a ball in a pinball machine. Getting slammed back and forth; and you never think about anything, about where you're going or how you're going to get there...."
>
> I didn't understand what he was talking about.... I did think about where I was going. I wanted to be like the Motorcycle Boy. I wanted to be tough like him, stay calm and laughing when things got dangerous. I wanted to be the toughest street-fighter and most respected hood on our side of the river. I had tried everything.... Even though nothing had worked so far, that didn't mean nothing ever would.

1 **Restate** Paraphrase what the character Steve says to Rusty-James.

2 **Listen and Speak** Choose a powerful passage from your Anchor Book. Paraphrase this passage with your partner. Discuss how paraphrasing powerful writing makes you more aware of the choices the author made.

Now that you've learned to paraphrase, read the following article. *Guiding Question:* How can writers and other artists use synesthesia to communicate their ideas?

For Some, Pain Is Orange

By Susan Hornick

People with synesthesia experience "extra" sensations. The letter *T* may be navy blue; a sound can taste like pickles. The occurrence of synesthesia is rare and occurs differently in every person who experiences it, so people who are born with this condition are often misunderstood.

When New York artist Carol Steen was seven and learning to read, she exclaimed to a classmate as they walked home from school, "Isn't *A* the prettiest pink you've ever seen?" Her little chum responded with a withering look. "You're weird," she said.

Shabana Tajwar was a bit older when she discovered that her world was more colorful than most. In 1991, as a twenty-year-old intern, she and a group of friends were trying to remember someone's name over lunch. "I knew the name was green. It started with *F* and *F* is green," says Tajwar, now an environmental engineer. "But when I mentioned that, everyone said, 'What are you talking about?'" She shrugs. "I was sort of in shock. I didn't know everyone didn't see things the same way."

While most of us experience the world through orderly, segregated senses, for some people two or more sensations are commingled. For Steen and Tajwar, hearing a name or seeing a letter or word in black and white causes an involuntary sensation of color. To Tajwar the letter *T* is always navy blue. "I don't see the actual letter as colored," she says. "I see the color flash, sort of in my mind's eye." Steen not only delights in pink *A*'s and gold *Y*s, she experiences colored taste as well. "I see the most brilliant blue after I eat a salty pretzel," she says.

Others with synesthesia—from the Greek *syn*, meaning together, and *aisthesis*, perception—may feel or taste sounds, or hear or taste shapes. The chords of a strumming guitar may be a soft brushing sensation at the back of an ankle, a musical note may taste like pickles, a trumpet may sound "pointed," the taste of chicken may feel "round." A teenager once confessed that her boyfriend's kiss made her see "orange-sherbet foam."

Even more baffling to outsiders: while synesthetes' perceptions are consistent over time, they are not shared. Letters, for instance, don't evoke the same color for everyone. Steen jokes that her good friend and fellow synesthete Patricia Duffy is "great" but misguided. "She thinks L is pale yellow, not black with blue highlights," says Steen with a grin, as she pours a mug full of coffee in her downtown New York loft. Separately, over lunch in a sunny bistro, Duffy, a language instructor at the United Nations, confides, "Some of Carol's colors are so wrong!"

Even relatives who have synesthesia—it seems to run in families—see things differently. The Russian novelist Vladimir Nabokov tells in his memoirs about playing with a set of wooden blocks when he was seven years old. He complained to his mother that the letters on the blocks weren't the right colors. She was sympathetic. She, too, objected to the shades—though she also disagreed with some of her son's color choices. According to one study, only one letter elicits consensus among a majority of synesthetes; apparently some 56 percent see O as a shade of white. For Nabokov, it radiated the hue of an "ivory-backed hand-mirror."

People with synesthesia have described their unusual perceptions to intrigued but baffled researchers for more than two hundred years. At times they were viewed as mentally defective, at other times idealized as artistically gifted. Often, they weren't believed at all. Only in the past decade or so, using controlled studies, in-depth interviews and computer-aided visual tests, have scientists begun to identify and catalog the staggering variety of these automatically induced sensations.

"We've gone to great lengths to identify the range of forms," says Peter Grossenbacher, a cognitive neuroscientist and one of the foremost U.S. researchers on synesthesia. "We understand it's a real experience. But we don't know yet how it comes to pass."

Already, scientists have discovered that synesthetes frequently have more than one form of the trait. Carol Steen's tall-windowed loft—part living space, part art studio—is jammed with her synesthesia-inspired paintings and sculptural models. Pulling letters painted on business-card-size pieces of paper off a shelf, she struggles to make clear the unique sensations that color her life and work. "It's like viewing the world in multimedia," she says. "I want to show other people what I'm seeing."

What Steen is seeing is not only color triggered by certain sounds, smells and flavors; when listening to music, she also sees shapes, which are reflected in her sculpture.

Steen also feels pain in color. When on vacation in British Columbia two years ago, she jumped down from a rock and tore a ligament. "All I saw was orange," she says. "It was like wearing orange sunglasses." In her paintings she depicts similar color sensations that she experiences during acupuncture. One abstract oil shows a green slash arcing through a field of red; in another a tiny red triangle drifts off into the distance on a sea of bright blue.

Researcher Peter Grossenbacher and a small cadre of scientists in this country, the United Kingdom, Canada, Germany, and elsewhere are currently doing research with volunteers to try to figure out why Steen sees orange when the rest of us just ache. So far, they agree that

▸ **Critical Viewing** How does this painting describe the experience of someone wih synesthesia?

synesthesia is more common in women than in men and is an international phenomenon. Grossenbacher primarily employs sophisticated screening and interviewing methods. Others, bolstered by dramatic advances in imaging techniques, are observing the neural activity of synesthetes and measuring the unique ways their brains respond to stimuli. In the process, they are shedding light on how we all perceive the world around us.

"It's the only way I know of perceiving," Steen points out. "If someone said they were going to take it away, it would be like saying they were going to cut off my leg." Although Steen delights in exploring her sensations, others remain ambivalent. When she was twenty and eating dinner with her family, Steen mentioned that the number five was yellow. "No," her father said. "It's yellow ocher."

Thinking About the Selection
For Some, Pain Is Orange

1 **Convey** How does each subject experience letters, numbers, or feelings? Paraphrase their experiences in the chart.

Subject	Experiences
Carol Steen	
Vladimir Nabokov	
Shabana Tajwar	

2 **Restate** Look back at the first page of the reading. Paraphrase what synesthesia is.

_____
_____

3 **Emphasize** When you paraphrase, you identify the main idea of the text. How does knowing the main idea help you to understand the text better?

_____
_____

4 **Analyze** How can writers and other artists use synesthesia to communicate their ideas?

_____

Write Answer the following question in your Reader's Journal.

 5 **Apply** Describe a place in your Anchor Book using your senses of sight, hearing, and taste. For example, instead of saying something tasted fresh, you could say it tasted green. Translate your descriptive details from one sense into another.

Paraphrasing 297

4-3 Vocabulary Building Strategies
Word Origins and Roots

You have learned a variety of strategies to help you unlock the meaning of words you do not know. In this lesson, you will learn more word origins and roots.

Let's practice unlocking the meaning of unknown words by identifying the word root and associating it with words you know. The word root is underlined in the English word.

Latin Origin	Meaning	English Words
reflectere	"to bend back"	reflector: "something that reflects"
recipere	"to get; to receive"	receive: "to take; to get"
gratus	"pleasing"	congratulate: "to express one's pleasure in another's success"
adaptare	"to fit; to adjust"	adaptable: "able to adjust"

Directions Read the passage below. Then, identify the word root for each of the words underlined and explain the word's meaning.

I put on the sweater I had just bought. I looked at my reflection in the mirror. Perhaps buying a sweater with a giant mouse on it wasn't the best idea after all. Luckily, I still had the receipt. I went back to the store and was gratified that the salespeople had no problem in giving me my money back. I really need to rethink what I buy. I need to adapt to changes in style.

reflection
_____

receipt
_____

gratified
_____

adapt
_____

Directions Now build your vocabulary by making three new words your own. Circle the word root in each word. Then, complete the boxes for each word.

Word Origins and Roots

Ready? Start Reading Your Anchor Book It's time to get started. As you learn from this work text, your teacher will also give you reading assignments from your Anchor Book.

4-4 Literary Analysis
Imagery

When you see a picture of a fresh, hot pizza, does it make you hungry? You can probably recall the way a pizza smells and tastes just by seeing a photograph of one. That's because the picture was created to appeal to your senses. Writers do the same thing by painting pictures with words that trigger a reaction in your senses, whether through memory or imagination.

Literary Terms

- Writers use **imagery**—word pictures or descriptions of sights, sounds, tastes, smells, and textures—to appeal to your five senses. This is also known as **sensory language.**

- A writer's **diction,** also referred to as **word choice,** is an important part of creating effective imagery. The words writers choose must paint the pictures they want you to see.

- Readers can **visualize,** or picture images in their minds, to better understand imagery.

Authors use words that describe the five senses to make vivid images.

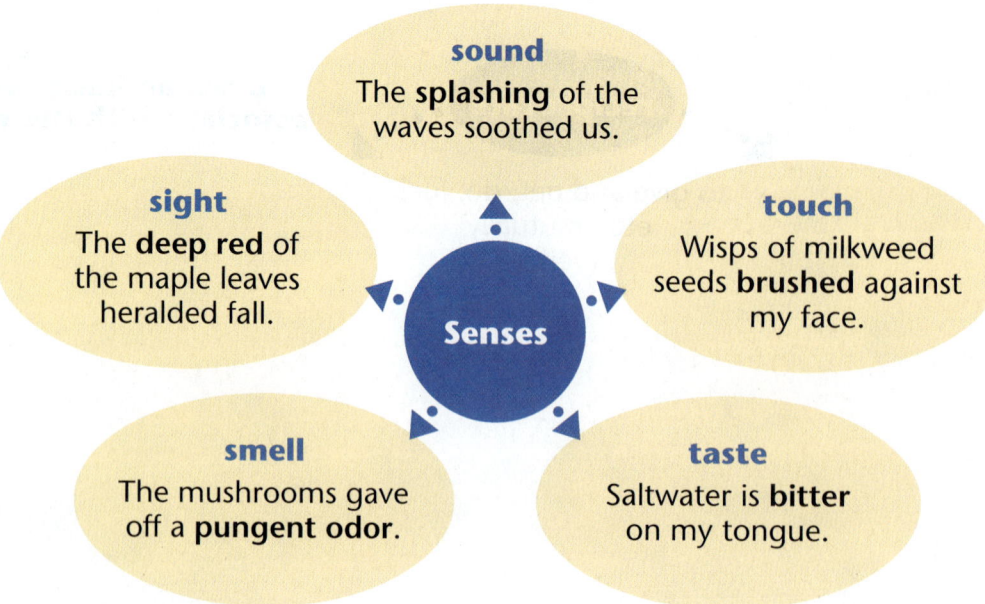

sound — The **splashing** of the waves soothed us.
sight — The **deep red** of the maple leaves heralded fall.
touch — Wisps of milkweed seeds **brushed** against my face.
smell — The mushrooms gave off a **pungent odor.**
taste — Saltwater is **bitter** on my tongue.

Directions Read the following selection. Underline words and phrases that use strong imagery. On the right, write whether each example of imagery relates to sight, sound, touch, smell, or taste.

At First, It Is True, I Thought There Were Only Peaches & Wild Grapes by Alice Walker

To my delight
I have found myself
Born
Into a garden
5 Of many fruits.

At first, it is true,
I thought
There were only
Peaches & wild grapes.
10 That watermelon
Lush, refreshing
Completed my range.

But now, Child,
I can tell you
15 There is such
A creature
As the wavy green
Cherimoya
The black loudsmelling
20 & delicious
Durian
The fleshy orange mango
And the spiky, whitehearted
Soursop.

25 In my garden
Imagine!
At first I thought
I could live
On blue plums
30 That fresh yellow pears
Might become
My sole delight.

I was naïve, Child.

Infinite is
35 The garden
Of many fruits.
Tasting them
I myself
Spread out
40 To cover
The earth.

Savoring each &
Every
One—date, fig, persimmon,
45 passion fruit—
I am everywhere
At home.

1 Assess How does visualizing the imagery the author uses affect your comprehension of the poem? Explain.

_____

_____

2 Connect Remember synesthesia, from the article "For Some, Pain Is Orange"? Poets frequently use synesthesia as a kind of imagery. For example, consider the word "loudsmelling." The word "loud," an adjective that describes sound, is used to describe smell. Create an example of synesthetic imagery.

_____

_____

In the following poems, the authors use vivid imagery to appeal to the reader's senses.
Guiding Question: How does the imagery help communicate the author's purpose?

Alabanza: In Praise of Local 100
by Martín Espada

Vocabulary Builder

Before you read, you will discuss the following words. In the Vocabulary Builder box in the margin, use a vocabulary building strategy to make the words your own.

diminutive   plagued

As you read, draw a box around unfamiliar words you could add to your vocabulary. Use context clues to unlock their meaning.

Marking the Text

Imagery

As you read, circle places where Espada uses imagery. In the margin, explain how that imagery helps communicate the author's purpose.

For the 43 members of Hotel Employees and Restaurant Employees Local 100, working at the Windows on the World restaurant, who lost their lives in the attack on the World Trade Center.

Alabanza[1]. Praise the cook with the shaven head
and a tattoo on his shoulder that said *Oye*,
a blue-eyed Puerto Rican with people from Fajardo,
the harbor of pirates centuries ago.
Praise the lighthouse in Fajardo, candle
glimmering white to worship the dark saint of the sea.
Alabanza. Praise the cook's yellow Pirates cap

---
[1] **Alabanza** (äl ə ban´ za) *n.* Spanish for "praise"

worn in the name of Roberto Clemente², his plane
that flamed into the ocean loaded with cans for Nicaragua,
for all the mouths chewing the ashes of earthquakes.
Alabanza. Praise the kitchen radio, dial clicked
even before the dial on the oven, so that music and Spanish
rose before bread. Praise the bread. *Alabanza.*
Praise Manhattan from a hundred and seven flights up,
like Atlantis³ glimpsed through the windows of
an ancient aquarium.
Praise the great windows where immigrants from the kitchen
could squint and almost see their world, hear the chant of nations:
*Ecuador, México, Republica Dominicana,
Haiti, Yemen, Ghana, Bangladesh.*
Alabanza. Praise the kitchen in the morning,
where the gas burned blue on every stove
and exhaust fans fired their **diminutive** propellers,
hands cracked eggs with quick thumbs
or sliced open cartons to build an altar of cans.
Alabanza. Praise the busboy's music, the chime-chime
of his dishes and silverware in the tub.
Alabanza. Praise the dish-dog, the dishwasher
who worked that morning because another dishwasher
could not stop coughing, or because he needed overtime
to pile the sacks of rice and beans for a family
floating away on some Caribbean island **plagued** by frogs.
Alabanza. Praise the waitress who heard the radio in the kitchen
and sang to herself about a man gone. *Alabanza.*

---

² **Roberto Clemente** a Puerto Rican-born Major League baseball player.

³ **Atlantis** (at lan´tis) *n.* A legendary island in the Atlantic Ocean said to have sunk beneath the sea during an earthquake.

Marking the Text

Vocabulary Builder

diminutive
(də min´ yoo tiv) *adj.*

Meaning

plagued
(plāgd) *adj.*

**Meaning*

◀ **Critical Viewing**
Discuss how this photo adds to your understanding of the poem. How does the photo contribute to the poem's mood?

Imagery

After the thunder wilder than thunder,
after the booming ice storm of glass from the great windows,
after the radio stopped singing like a tree full of terrified frogs,
after night burst the dam of day and flooded the kitchen,
for a time the stoves glowed in darkness like the lighthouse in Fajardo,
like a cook's soul. Soul I say, even if the dead cannot tell us
about the bristles of God's beard because God has no face,
soul I say, to name the smoke-beings flung in constellations
across the night sky of this city and cities to come.
Alabanza I say, even if God has no face.

Alabanza. When the war began, from Manhattan to Kabul
two constellations of smoke rose and drifted to each other,
mingling in icy air, and one said with an Afghan tongue:
Teach me to dance. We have no music here.
And the other said with a Spanish tongue:
I will teach you. Music is all we have.

Vocabulary Builder

After you read, review the words you decided to add to your vocabulary. Write the meaning of words you have learned in context. Look up the other words in a dictionary, glossary, thesaurus, or electronic resource.

Literature in Context
Out of Tragedy: Art and Community

National tragedies leave no one untouched: Family and friends mourn the passing of loved ones; sympathy and compassion for the terrible loss crosses ocean and land. It would seem, then, that the country, if not the world, is united in its suffering. Following the terrorist attacks on Sept. 11, 2001, the first memorials appeared on New York fences and telephone poles. Photographs of ones lost were memorialized with flowers and candles. Here people came together to honor those who had died. Art can express what words cannot, and it can bring people together. In memory of those who died in the attack on the World Trade Center, a memorial on the scale of the original towers was designed. The memorial, called Reflecting Absence, is a landscaped public plaza with two large one-acre gaps where the Twin Towers once stood. Around the edges of these gaps, water cascades into the voids to make two reflecting pools. Memorials of those who have died serve two purposes: they not only memorialize the dead but also create community.

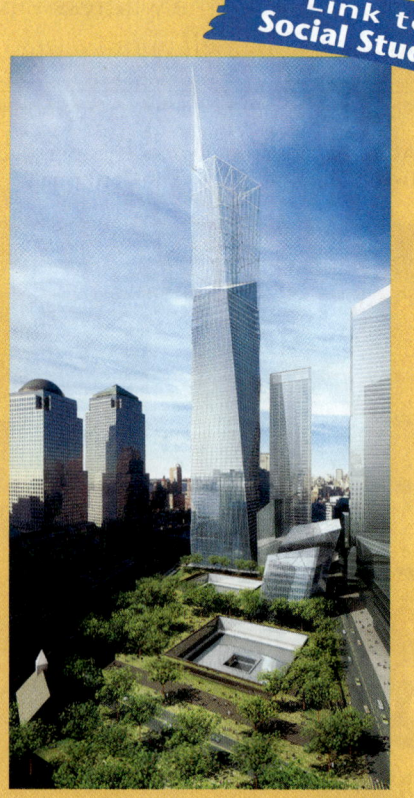

Thinking About the Selection
Alabanza: In Praise of Local 100

1 **Respond** Use your notes from the poem to fill in the chart with sensory language. Which sense does Espada appeal to the most?

Sight	Sound	Smell	Taste	Touch

2 **Explain** How does visualizing the sensory language enhance your response to the poem?

_____
_____

3 **Analyze** How does Espada's diction, as well as significant phrases and words, contribute to the meaning of "Alabanza" as a poem about immigrants who died in the attack on the World Trade Center?

_____
_____

4 **Analyze** How does the use of descriptive language contribute to the poem's mood and meaning?

_____
_____

5 **Compare and Contrast** Compare this poem to "The Vision of Maya Ying Lin." How are they similar? How do they differ?

_____
_____
_____

Directions Answer the following questions in your Reader's Journal.

6 **Explain** How does the tool of imagery help communicate the author's purpose?

7 **Evaluate** Find a passage in your Anchor Book with effective imagery. Copy it into your Reader's Journal. What important information does the imagery communicate about characters, mood, and/or theme?

4-5 Literary Analysis
Symbolism

When you see a heart, you might think of love. When you see a four-leaf clover, you might be reminded of luck. A heart and a four-leaf clover can be thought of as symbols. A symbol is a person, place, or thing that represents something beyond its literal meaning.

Familiar Symbols	Meaning
the color red	anger, passion, love
dove	peace
Liberty Bell	freedom
shackles or chains	slavery, oppression
thunderstorm	dark times ahead

Symbolism, or the use of symbols, plays an important role in poetry and prose. It can highlight certain elements the author wishes to emphasize and also add levels of meaning.

Some symbols are universal. We recognize them right away in different kinds of writing. For example, light has often symbolized life and goodness. In contrast, darkness has represented death and evil.

Other literary symbols take on meaning as we read. At the beginning of a story, a small room is just a small room. By the end, it might suggest a horrible prison. A mirror might start out as a harmless household item, but it might take on the meaning of deception in a story. Alternatively, the mirror might come to represent truth in a story.

Directions What do fire and ice represent to you? Write down some words that come to mind. Then read the poem and answer the questions that follow.

fire _____

ice _____

> ### Fire and Ice *by Robert Frost*
> Some say the world will end in fire,
> Some say in ice.
> From what I've tasted of desire
> I hold with those who favor fire.
> 5 But if it had to perish twice,
> I think I know enough of hate
> To say that for destruction ice
> Is also great
> And would suffice.

1 **Interpret** Complete the chart below.

- In the first column, identify which emotions the speaker in "Fire and Ice" associates with fire and ice.
- In the second column, explain why fire and ice are fitting symbols for these emotions.
- In the third column, explain how the poem's message applies to you.

What Is the Emotion?	Why Does It Work?	What Does It Mean?

2 **Synthesize** Good literature doesn't tell us what to think. Instead, it asks us to think about how we would answer certain big questions about life. What is the poem asking us to think about?

_____

_____

Symbolism 307

In the following selections, the authors use symbolism.
Guiding Question: **Do the authors' choices of symbols matter? Could a different symbol have communicated the same message?**

Kim
by Paul Fleischman

Background *Paul Fleischman grew up in a house with a printing press, a grand piano, a shortwave radio, and his father—children's author Sid Fleischman. This selection is taken from a series of short vignettes about a vacant lot that was converted into a community garden. Living in a rundown section of Cleveland, Ohio, the characters are changed by the simple act of growing vegetables or flowers.*

Vocabulary Builder

Before you read, you will discuss the following words. In the Vocabulary Builder box in the margin, use a vocabulary building strategy to make the words your own.

teetered   scouted   diverged

As you read, draw a box around unfamiliar words you could add to your vocabulary. Use context clues to unlock their meaning.

Marking the Text

Symbolism

As you read, underline important details. In the margin, explain why these details are important. Identify the main symbol of the story when you discover it.

I stood before our family altar. It was dawn. No one else in the apartment was awake. I stared at my father's photograph—his thin face stern, lips latched tight, his eyes peering permanently to the right. I was nine years old and still hoped that perhaps his eyes might move. Might notice me.

The candles and the incense sticks, lit the day before to mark his death anniversary, had burned out. The rice and meat offered him were gone. After the evening feast, past midnight, I'd been wakened by my mother's crying. My oldest sister had joined in. My own tears had then come as well, but for a different reason.

308 Lesson 4-5

I turned from the altar, tiptoed to the kitchen, and quietly drew a spoon from a drawer. I filled my lunch thermos with water and reached into our jar of dried lima beans. Then I walked outside to the street.

The sidewalk was completely empty. It was Sunday, early in April. An icy wind **teetered** trash cans and turned my cheeks to marble. In Vietnam we had no weather like that. Here in Cleveland people call it spring. I walked half a block, then crossed the street and reached the vacant lot.

I stood tall and **scouted**. No one was sleeping on the old couch in the middle. I'd never entered the lot before, or wanted to. I did so now, picking my way between tires and trash bags. I nearly stepped on two rats gnawing and froze. Then I told myself that I must show my bravery. I continued farther and chose a spot far from the sidewalk and hidden from view by a rusty refrigerator. I had to keep my project safe.

I took out my spoon and began to dig. The snow had melted, but the ground was hard. After much work, I finished one hole, then a second, then a third. I thought about how my mother and sisters remembered my father, how they knew his face from every angle and held in their fingers the feel of his hands. I had no such memories. I'd been born eight months after he'd died. Worse, he had no memories of me. When his spirit hovered over our altar, did it even know who I was?

I dug six holes. All his life in Vietnam my father had been a farmer. Here our apartment house had no yard. But in that vacant lot he would see me. He would watch my beans break ground and spread, and would notice with pleasure their pods growing plump. He would see my patience and my hard work. I would show him that I could raise plants, as he had. I would show him that I was his daughter.

My class had sprouted lima beans in paper cups the year before. I now placed a bean in each of the holes. I covered them up, pressing the soil down firmly with my fingertips. I opened my thermos and watered them all. And I vowed to myself that those beans would thrive.

Marking the Text

Vocabulary Builder

teetered
(tēt´ərd) v.

Meaning

scouted
(skou´ ted) v.

Meaning

The Road Not Taken
BY ROBERT FROST

Background This poem takes place in the fall woods where a traveler is walking. Frost spent most of his life in New England, the setting for much of his poetry. He struggled there for many years as a farmer and teacher before his poetry gained acceptance. Today, he is recognized as one of America's greatest poets whose simple language holds profound truths.

Two roads **diverged** in a yellow wood,
And sorry I could not travel both
And be one traveler, long I stood
And looked down one as far as I could
5 To where it bent in the undergrowth;

Then took the other, as just as fair,
And having perhaps the better claim,
Because it was grassy and wanted wear;
Though as for that, the passing there
10 Had worn them really about the same,

And both that morning equally lay
In leaves no step had trodden black.
Oh, I kept the first for another day!
Yet knowing how way leads on to way,
15 I doubted if I should ever come back.

I shall be telling this with a sigh
Somewhere ages and ages hence:
Two roads diverged in a wood, and I—
I took the one less traveled by,
20 And that has made all the difference.

Marking the Text

Symbolism

As you read, circle the main symbol in the poem and underline words that help explain it. In the margin, suggest meanings of this symbol.

Vocabulary Builder

diverged
(dī vʉrjd´) v.

Meaning

Vocabulary Builder

After you read, review the words you decided to add to your vocabulary. Write the meaning of words you have learned in context. Look up the other words in a dictionary, glossary, thesaurus, or electronic resource.

310 Lesson 4-5

Thinking About the Selection
Kim *and* The Road Not Taken

1 **Deduce** In "The Road Not Taken," how does the traveler feel about his decision? Are the traveler's feelings clear from the poem, or ambiguous? Explain.

_____
_____
_____

2 **Interpret** Explain how "The Road Not Taken" is symbolic of choices we make in life.

_____
_____
_____

3 **Analyze** How does the setting contribute to the meaning of "The Road Not Taken"?

_____
_____
_____

4 **Interpret** What emotions does the speaker reveal in the fourth stanza? Why does the speaker feel this way? Explain.

_____
_____
_____

5 **Analyze** Identify a symbol in "Kim." Explain its significance to the story.

_____
_____
_____

Write Answer the following questions in your Reader's Journal.

6 **Analyze** Do the authors' choices of symbols matter? Could a different symbol have communicated the same message?

7 **Interpret** Identify a symbol in your Anchor Book and explain what the symbol means. Support your explanation with details from the book, placing the symbol in the context of the story.

4-6 Comparing Literary Works
Figurative Language

Have you ever described someone as an "angel"? You probably did not mean that this person has wings and a halo. Instead, you were trying to emphasize his or her virtues, such as kindness. You were using figurative language to make a point.

Literary Terms

▶ **Figurative language** is language that is used imaginatively rather than literally. Writers use figurative language to make interesting connections and express their thoughts or emotions more vividly.

▶ Figurative language includes one or more **figures of speech.** A figure of speech is an expression or even just a word that is not meant to be understood literally.

Figure of Speech	Meaning	Example
simile	uses *like* or *as* to compare two different ideas or things	The sea sparkled like a diamond.
metaphor	compares two different ideas or things without using *like* or *as*	My friend Joe is a walking encyclopedia.
personification	language in which a nonhuman subject is given human traits	The tree reached its arms to the sky.
hyperbole	exaggeration of speech for emphasis or effect	I'm so hungry, I could eat a horse.
analogy	comparison that is used to increase understanding	an ant colony is like an underground city

The example in the chart is a **direct metaphor.** There are two other types of metaphor—extended metaphor and implied metaphor.

▶ In an **extended metaphor,** several connected comparisons are made. For example, a poem about a conversation could contain details that compared it to a game of catch.

▶ In an **implied metaphor,** the comparison is not stated directly. For example, "The supervisor barked orders." It is implied that the supervisor is like an aggressive dog.

Directions Read the following poem. Notice how the student marked the text to identify figures of speech. Then, answer the questions.

Ode to Enchanted Light
by Pablo Neruda

Under the trees light	
has dropped from the <u>top of the sky</u>,	implied metaphor
<u>light</u>	
<u>like a green</u>	simile
5 <u>lattice work of branches</u>,	
shining	
on every leaf,	
<u>drifting down like clean</u>	simile
<u>white sand.</u>	
10 A cicada sends	
its <u>sawing song</u>	implied metaphor
high into the <u>empty air.</u>	implied metaphor
The <u>world is</u>	direct metaphor
<u>a glass</u> overflowing	
15 with water.	

1   **Analyze** Identify an example of analogy in the poem. How does this type of figurative language contribute to the poem's meaning?

2   **Interpret** Reread the second stanza of the poem and determine which two items are compared in the metaphor. What is the metaphor's literal meaning?

3   **Analyze** Describe the mood of the poem. How does figurative language help to create the poem's mood?

4   **Apply** The above poem is an ode, which is a meditative reflection on a theme. On a separate piece of paper, write an ode to a person, place, or thing you admire. Use at least two literary devices in your ode.

The following poems include similes, metaphors, and personification. **Guiding question:** Why is figurative language an effective way of communicating the way in which we respond to the world?

Vocabulary Builder

Before you read, you will discuss the following words. In the Vocabulary Builder box in the margin, use a vocabulary building strategy to make the words your own.

abash   barren   quake

As you read, draw a box around unfamiliar words you could add to your vocabulary. Use context clues to unlock their meaning.

Marking the Text

Figurative Language

As you read, underline examples of figures of speech. In the margin, name the type of figurative language, tell what two items are being compared, and explain for what purpose the author is making the comparison.

"Hope" is the thing with feathers
by Emily Dickinson

"Hope" is the thing with feathers—
That perches in the soul—
And sings the tune without the words—
And never stops—at all—

5   And sweetest—in the Gale—is heard—
And sore[1] must be the storm—
That could **abash** the little Bird
That kept so many warm—

I've heard it in the chillest land—
10 And on the strangest Sea—
Yet, never, in Extremity,
It asked a crumb—of Me.

Vocabulary Builder

abash
(ə bash´) v.

Meaning

---

[1] **sore** (sôr) *adj.* full of distress or sorrow.

Dreams
by Langston Hughes

Hold fast to dreams
For if dreams die
Life is a broken-winged bird
That cannot fly.

5 Hold fast to dreams
For when dreams go
Life is a **barren** field
Frozen with snow.

Vocabulary Builder

barren
(bar´ ən) *adj.*

Meaning

Critical Viewing ▶
Explain how this illustration could be used to describe the message of both poems.

Figurative Language

The City Is So Big
by Richard Garcia

The city is so big
Its bridges **quake** with fear
I know, I have seen at night

The lights sliding from house to house
5   And trains pass with windows shining
Like a smile full of teeth

I have seen machines eating houses
And stairways walk all by themselves
And elevator doors opening and closing
10 And people disappear.

Marking the Text

Vocabulary Builder

quake
(kwāk) *v.*
Meaning

Vocabulary Builder

After you read, review the words you decided to add to your vocabulary. Write the meaning of words you have learned in context. Look up the other words in a dictionary, glossary, thesaurus, or electronic resource.

Thinking About the Selection
"Hope" is the thing with feathers, Dreams, *and* The City Is So Big

1 **Describe** Explain how personification is used in "The City Is So Big." What items are personified, and how?

_____
_____
_____

2 **Analyze** In Emily Dickinson's poem, hope is metaphorically compared to a bird. Explain how the metaphor "extends" throughout the poem and what it communicates about the poem's message.

_____
_____
_____

3 **Connect** What symbol appears in both Dickinson's poem and Hughes's poem? How does the historical context of each poem affect the way the symbol is portrayed?

_____
_____
_____

4 **Deduce** Why do you think Hughes used metaphors instead of literal statements to describe life without dreams? Use details from the poem to support your explanation.

_____
_____
_____

Write Answer the following questions in your Reader's Journal.

5 **Analyze** Identify a simile in your Anchor Book. What is its function? Explain its literal meaning, and discuss why figurative language is an effective way of communicating the way in which we respond to the world.

6 **Evaluate** Identify a passage from your Anchor Book that uses analogy. Explain the literal meaning of the analogy. Then, explain its figurative meaning. How does this analogy contribute to the tone of the passage?

Figurative Language **317**

4-7 Language Coach
Grammar and Spelling

Active and Passive Voice

A verb is in the **active voice** when its subject performs the action.

Active Voice   Tina hits two home runs.
　　　　　　　　The subject is *Tina*. Tina performs the action of hitting.

A verb is in the **passive voice** when the action is done to the subject. Passive voice uses a form of *be* plus the past participle.

Passive Voice   Two home runs are hit by Tina.
　　　　　　　　　The subject is *home runs*. The action of hitting is done to the home runs.

Using active voice will make your writing sound stronger and more direct. However, passive voice is appropriate upon occasion. The passive voice is correctly used when the writer wants to emphasize the receiver of the action and/or de-emphasize the performer, as in the famous example "Mistakes were made."

Effective Use of Passive Voice   An umpire was injured in an unfortunate collision.
　　　　　　　　　　　　　　　　Umpire, the receiver of the action, is emphasized.

The announcer's booth was vandalized in the middle of the night. The writer does not know who did the vandalizing.

Directions Why is active voice usually the better choice? Read the following passage to find out. Circle all examples of passive voice and passive construction.

> The river was crossed by Panos. Rocks were banged by his feet. Beneath the water slipped Panos. His head was rushed over by water. A branch from a low-hanging tree was grabbed by Panos. He pulled himself onto the riverbank and collapsed in exhaustion.

Now rewrite the passage in active voice. Add details such as adverbs to emphasize the action of the passage.

_____
_____
_____
_____

Author's Craft

On page 308, the selection "Kim" uses first-person narration and active voice. Reread the selection. Why is active voice the most effective choice for first-person narration?

Spelling Words With Suffixes

Sometimes you have to change the spelling of the base word when adding a suffix.

Base Word + Suffix	Rule	Correct Spelling
collapse + -ible = ?	**If** the suffix begins with a vowel, **then** drop the final *e*.	collapsible
hazy + -ness = ? hurry + -ed = ? hurry + -ing = ?	**If** the base word ends with a consonant followed by *y*, **then** change the *y* to *i* except when the suffix begins with *i*.	haziness hurried hurrying
knit + -ing = ?	**If** the suffix begins with a vowel and the base word has one syllable, **then** double the final consonant of the base word.	knitting
occur + -ence = ?	**If** the suffix begins with a vowel and the base word ends in a single vowel followed by a single consonant and the accent falls on the last syllable, **then** double the final consonant of the base word.	occurrence

Apply Create words using suffixes. In the examples below, add the base word to its suffix, spell the new word, and use it in a sentence.

1 response + ible _____

2 dizzy + ness _____

3 edit + ing _____

4 recur + ence _____

Spelling Words With Suffixes

4-8 Writer's Workshop
Response to Literature: Critical Review

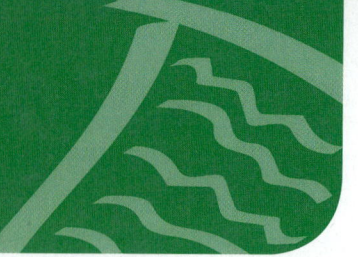

If you are uncertain whether you would like the latest blockbuster movie or would enjoy reading a recent bestseller, you might turn to a **critical review** for information and the reviewer's opinion. This form of writing may also be used to write assessments, newspaper reviews, and book reviews. Follow the steps outlined here to write your own critical review of two or more works of literature that are similar in theme or topic.

To be effective, your critical review should include the following elements.

- A discussion of two works by two different authors
- A coherent thesis statement, or main idea
- An opinion on the value of each work
- Examples from both texts and authors to support ideas and make connections
- Ideas and arguments that demonstrate independent thinking
- A clear and well-supported conclusion
- Error-free writing with appropriate use of active voice

Purpose To write a critical review of two or more works of literature that are similar in theme or topic

Audience You, your teacher, and your classmates

Prewriting—Plan It Out

Use the following steps to select the topic and gather information for your critical review.

Choose your topic and gather details. Browse this textbook, your own bookshelf, the library, or a bookstore. Look for works that have enough similarities to be addressed in a single essay. Then, choose at least two works to compare. On a separate sheet of paper, take notes in a comparison chart like the one shown below.

Author	Theme	Characters	Your Evaluation

Drafting—Get It on Paper

Using your comparison chart as an outline, write your draft. The following steps will help.

Shape your writing. Use block organization to arrange the structure of your critical review.

> **Introduction** Identify both the works and the idea that fits both works of literature. State your reaction to both works.
>
> ▼
>
> **Body** Develop your ideas about each work.
> Work 1
>
> ▼
>
> **Body** Develop your ideas about each work.
> Work 2
>
> ▼
>
> **Conclusion** Evaluate each work, noting similarities or differences, and explain why these ideas are important.

I. Stories about the consequences of greed
   A. "The Giving Tree"
   B. "Story of King Midas"
II. Details that show greed
   A. "The Giving Tree"
     1. Takes things from tree
     2. Uses for his own needs
   B. "King Midas"
     1. Gift of a golden touch
     2. Isolates himself
III. Conclusion
   A. Messages about greed
     1. Loss and heartbreak
     2. Moral responsibilities

Provide elaboration. Support your opinion with specific examples in each text that will strengthen your position and develop readers' interest. Follow the outline as shown here.

Revising—Plan It Out

Now that you have a draft, you can revise your critical review to make it more precise. Revise using the following steps.

Add modifiers. Use precise words to convey praise or criticism. Review your draft, bracketing any modifiers you have used. If you have chosen vague or overused words, replace them with words that more accurately capture your response. Consider these suggestions.

   High Praise: brilliant, hilarious, entertaining
   Mild Praise: accurate, intelligent, sad
   Mild Disapproval: confusing, dull, predictable
   Strong Disapproval: biased, pointless, misguided

Peer Review Ask for a partner's response to your critical review. Revise to achieve the reaction you had intended.

Directions Read the following student critical review as a model.

Response to Literature: Critical Review

Writer's Workshop continued

Student Model: Writing

Joyce McShane, Clackamas, OR

A lot of stories are written to teach lessons to readers. Sometimes stories can have different plots, settings, and characters but still have the same message.

Although *The Giving Tree*, by Shel Silverstein, and the story of King Midas are different in many ways, they both share an important theme. Both stories are about the unhappy consequences of greed.

The Giving Tree is the story of a boy who keeps taking pieces of a tree to try to make himself happy. In the beginning of the story, there is an apple tree who loves a little boy. Every day he comes to play with her leaves, climb her trunk, and eat her apples. However, as the boy grows older, other things become more important. From then on, all he wants to do is take things from the tree and use them for his own needs. In the end, when the boy comes back for the last time, he is an old man and the tree has nothing left to give him. Instead of taking something from her, all he does is sit on the tree's stump.

The story of King Midas is also a story about greed. King Midas spares the life of a satyr who is caught sleeping in his royal rose bed, a crime punishable by death. Because King Midas decides to spare the satyr's life, he is granted one wish. Being a greedy man, he immediately wishes for the gift of a golden touch. One day, his beloved daughter comes running up to him and gives him a hug. She is instantly turned to gold and King Midas is heartbroken.

Both of these stories show men who ask for more than they should have... Given another chance, neither character would probably act the same way. However, neither the boy nor King Midas can change the consequences of their actions.

Both stories show why people should not be greedy. There are some people who could greatly benefit from reading these stories and some whose unselfish attitudes would be reinforced. The tales of King Midas and of *The Giving Tree* are important and everyone should read them and learn from them.

> In her second paragraph, the writer introduces both works and their common theme.

> The writer summarizes both works, offers details from the text, and explains how each one connects to the theme of greed.

> In her conclusion, the writer offers an opinion on the value of each work that reflects independent thought.

Editing—Be Your Own Language Coach

Before you hand in your critical review, review it for language convention errors. Pay special attention to your use of active and passive voice.

Publishing—Share It!

When you publish a work, you produce it for a specific audience. Consider one of the following ideas to share your writing with classmates or a larger audience.

Present a book talk. Use your critical review as the basis for an informal oral presentation.

Publish a "Teens Review" column. Contact a local newspaper and arrange for your work to be part of a series of critical reviews by young people. Make sure your writing is legible and follows the correct format for publication.

Reflecting On Your Writing

Rubric for Self-Assessment Assess your essay. For each question, circle a rating.

CRITERIA	RATING SCALE
IDEAS Is your paper clear and focused with rich details?	NOT VERY — VERY 1 2 3 4 5
ORGANIZATION How well do you employ a clear and logical organization?	1 2 3 4 5
VOICE Is your writing lively and engaging, drawing the reader in?	1 2 3 4 5
WORD CHOICE How appropriate is the language for your audience?	1 2 3 4 5
SENTENCE FLUENCY How varied is your sentence structure?	1 2 3 4 5
CONVENTIONS How correct is your grammar, especially your use of active and passive voice?	1 2 3 4 5

4-9 Discussing Your Anchor Book
Literature Circles

Cultural Context In this Literature Circle, you and your group members will start with an open discussion and then you will analyze the cultural context of your Anchor Book.

Earlier in the unit, you read the poems listed below. The authors of these poems wrote about things that were familiar to them personally, so each poem reflects the author's background and culture.

Part 1: Open Discussion

As you participate in this open discussion with your Literature Circle, remember to incorporate all the aspects of effective discussion you have been practicing. Encourage your group members to support their ideas with specific details from your Anchor Book and, if the conversation lags, look in your Reader's Journal for ideas to spark discussion.

Part 2: Discuss—Cultural Context

The **cultural context** of a literary work is the social and historical environment in which the characters live. Literary works set in similar cultural contexts often share common themes and values.

Use the biographical and cultural information on the right to identify the author of each poem.

"Dreams"

1. Author ____

"The City Is So Big"

2. Author ____

"'Hope' is the thing with feathers—"

3. Author ____

Author A
- Born in 1941
- Lives in San Francisco
- First-generation American with parents from Mexico and Puerto Rico

Author B
- Lived 1830–1886
- Educated in classical literature from an early age
- Sensitive, insightful
- Innovative style

Author C
- Lived 1902–1967
- African American
- Promoted equality and justice
- Encouraged pride among blacks

Now think about the cultural context of your Anchor Book. Discuss the clues in your Anchor Book that help you identify the cultural context. Complete the chart below to explain the cultural context.

Anchor Book Cultural Context	
▸ When written ▸ Place ▸ Time Period ▸ Traditions and Values ▸ Impact of Cultural Issues on Storyline ▸ Author Background	

How would your Anchor Book be different if the cultural context changed? For example, if it was set in a different time period, in the city instead of the country, etc. With your group, discuss how a different cultural context would affect the book's plot and characters and record your answers below.

Change	Impact

A book is always a product of its time, but there are also aspects of great books that make them timeless. What makes your Anchor Book timeless? Discuss how literary elements used in your Anchor Book, such as characterization, theme, plot, and imagery reflect universal human experience, and then list them below.

_____
_____
_____
_____

while reading your anchor book

Literature Circles 325

Monitoring Your Progress
Standardized Test Practice

Reading Skill: Paraphrasing

Read the passage. Then answer the questions.

> Spider-Man has a great weapon, but it's not X-ray vision or super strength. It's simpler than that: spider silk. Indeed, spider silk is several times stronger than steel of the same thickness. Perhaps Spider-Man could give Superman, the "Man of Steel", a run for his money!
>
> Spider silk starts off as liquid protein in the spider's body, and somehow this liquid becomes the sticky solid fibers we see in spider webs. A spider produces this liquid substance inside special silk glands in its abdomen. Then the spider forces the liquid through spinnerets, where it instantly solidifies.
>
> With its strength and varying elasticity, spider silk could be used to make a variety of products: paper, material for aircrafts, artificial ligaments and tendons, textiles, ropes, body armor, and more. First, however, scientists need to figure out how to reproduce spider silk. Where's Spider-Man when you need him?

1 Which is the definition of the term *paraphrase*?

   A. to state in your own words
   B. to state an opinion
   C. to analyze a problem
   D. to solve a problem

2 Which statement best paraphrases the first paragraph?

   F. Spider-Man would win in a fight with Superman.
   G. Spider silk is stronger than steel.
   H. Spider silk is so strong even super heroes use it.
   J. Spider silk is a great weapon.

3 Which statement best paraphrases the second paragraph?

   A. Spider silk somehow forms from a liquid to a solid.
   B. Scientists do not know exactly how spiders spin silk.
   C. Two organs, the silk glands and the spinnerets, produce the silk.
   D. Spider webs are made of solid fibers.

4 Which statement best paraphrases the entire passage?

   F. Scientists do not yet know all of spider silk's properties.
   G. Spider silk is so strong it has been the weapon of super heroes.
   H. Spider silk comes from spiders.
   J. Spider silk is an amazingly strong natural substance that could improve the way we live.

Literary Analysis: Prose and Poetry

Read the following passage. Then answer the questions.

> The spring snow fell thick and wet, sticking like balls of lint to the evergreen's clothes: muted green needles pointing downward, sideways, and up. The evergreen was prepared. It always had on a winter coat.
>
> The sugar maple, however, shuddered its annoyance at the storm's unexpected visit. Its bare boughs rattled in the wind, desperately trying to shake off the clingy flakes. The sugar maple, nearly in a tantrum, flung its arms wildly, hoping to prove to the storm that spring was here: one had only to look at the sugar maple's opening buds to see that winter's time had come and gone.
>
> A half-buried stream gurgled its amusement from below. It was neither prepared nor unfit for this sudden blizzard. It simply carried itself through the forest, taking with it chunks of melting ice around turns and curves, carving into the forest floor a superhighway that would later transport the fallen fiery leaves of the sugar maple. But those leaves would be dead leaves. The stream didn't want to tell the sugar maple the inevitable truth: its time would come and go, too, just like the snow. But the maple needed to figure that out on its own.

5 "A half-buried stream gurgled its amusement from below" is an example of which type of **figurative language**?

A. imagery
B. metaphor
C. personification
D. symbolism

6 Which best explains the **symbolism** in this passage?

F. The maple tree symbolizes spring.
G. The stream symbolizes wisdom and experience.
H. The evergreen symbolizes a winter coat.
J. Winter symbolizes death.

Timed Writing: Interpretation of Literature

Directions Think about books and stories you have read. Identify an important symbol in a book or story you have read and explain its significance. Use specific details from the book or story to support your answer. **(20 minutes)**

4-10 Reading Skills
Using Context to Determine Meaning

In learning new reading skills, you will use special academic vocabulary. Knowing the right words will help you demonstrate your understanding.

Academic Vocabulary

Word	Meaning	Example Sentence
confirm v. Related words: confirming, confirmation	to prove to be true; to verify	After I ordered the game, I received an e-mail *confirming* my purchase.
clarify v. Related words: clarifying, clarified	to make or become easier to understand	Thank you for taking the time to *clarify* those confusing directions for me.
restate v. Related words: restated, restatement	to state again, especially in a new way	Our teacher asked us to *restate* the poem in our own words as part of the assignment.

A word's **context** is made up of the other words or phrases that surround it. The following types of clues can help you **confirm** the meanings of unfamiliar words, multiple-meaning words, and **idioms**, expressions with overall meanings different from the literal meanings of their words.

Context Clue	Definition	Example
Synonym	a word that means the same as the unfamiliar word or idiom	Jed has always found unsolved mysteries *fascinating*, so it's no surprise that he thought the documentary was *intriguing*.
Antonym	a word that means the opposite of the unfamiliar word or idiom	Unlike pygmy chimpanzees, which are known for their *peace-loving* nature, their relatives, the chimpanzees, are *bellicose*.
Explanation	words that give information about the unfamiliar word or idiom	My brother is a *stick-in-the-mud*! As a result, we never have that much fun together.

while reading your anchor book

Directions The following passage contains words or phrases that might be unfamiliar to you. Read the passage, looking for context clues that can help you **clarify** the meaning of the unfamiliar word. Then, answer the questions that follow.

Short-Sided Soccer

Because of my diminutive size, opposing soccer players always tease me. They call me "shorty" at almost every game. It doesn't matter that I'm the best player on the soccer team; the teasing is nonstop. Their incessant teasing bothers me so much that I've decided to give them a dose of their own medicine. Won't they be surprised when my teammates and I carry signs that say, "Shorty will be your demise! Shorty will be your defeat!"

Link to Real Life

1. **Apply** What does the word *diminutive* mean? What context clue points to its meaning?

2. **Evaluate** What type of context clue for *incessant* is the word *nonstop*?

3. **Interpret** Based on the passage's context, what does the idiom "give them a dose of their own medicine" mean? Use a dictionary to check your response, and correct as necessary.

4. **Evaluate** How does the idiom make this passage seem more realistic? How did you know not to take the words in the idiom literally?

Using Context to Determine Meaning

THE BIG Q Use context clues to help you learn new words in this article. *Guiding Question:* How does the form of rap help communicate its message?

Rap music, as we know it today, began in the 1970s. However, its roots go back 250 years in African American culture. In this article, the author tells about the popularity of rap music and how listeners interpret its styles.

The RHYTHMS of RAP

BY KATHIANN M. KOWALSKI

Rap is about society; some songs get notoriety. But do your feet tap when you hear rap?

Lots of rap tracks make you move along with them. Rap is about words, but rhythm makes them more powerful.

"Rhythm is the feeling of movement in time," explains Miami University (OH) music professor Chris Tanner. "Rhythm is the term we use in music for dividing time. Music can't exist without rhythm." In other words, one sound with no break is just noise. Play a sequence of notes for a certain time each, and you get music.

As music moves forward in time, your brain notes the duration of individual sounds and groups them together into bunches that let you perceive rhythm in the music. It could be the hammering lyrics of a rap artist. Or, it could be the beginning of Beethoven's Fifth Symphony: "Bum, bum, bum, bummm. Bum, bum, bum, bummm."

SAYING THEIR SONGS

Rap as a popular music style started in the late 1970s. But, notes music professor Adam Krims at the University of Alberta, "In some form or another, this kind of music has been around for about 250 years. It continues very old practices of rhyming and rhythm among African Americans."

Rap's style of rhythmic delivery sets it apart from talking or other styles of declamatory (words recited with music) delivery. "In rap, you're not just talking," notes Krims, "you're really foregrounding [bringing up front] the rhythmic aspects of what you're doing."

It's somewhat like the difference between reading a textbook and reading Dr. Seuss's *Green Eggs and Ham* aloud. However, stresses Krims, "Rap actually takes a lot of practice to do even slightly well." Effective rhythmic phrasing really draws listeners into the lyrics of an MC ("MC" is the same as "emcee" and stands for "master of ceremonies"—a name rap artists commonly use).

Often an MC works with words' natural emphasis. Other times, the artist may deform words. "You purposely deliver them in a way that's a little perverse," explains Krims. So instead of "California," an MC might say "Californ-eye-ay."

IN THE BACKGROUND

Sampling serves up yet more rhythms in rap. "Sampling is taking a little bit of music from another source," says Krims. Sampling may be the artist's own composition. It may be a segment from another popular song or even a classical piece.

The musician then makes a "loop" of the segment, which means that it's played over and over. Sampling adds background melody and harmony. Each bit of sampling also adds its own rhythms to a rap song.

THE BEAT GOES ON

Underlying rap and almost all music is its pulse, or beat. "There are all kinds of rhythms going on in a Sousa march, but what do people march to?" says Tanner. It's not the rhythmic phrasing of the melody. Instead, he says, "They move their feet to the underlying pulse of the music."

Rap and other popular music forms often spell out the beat explicitly with drums. "Any

◀ Artist: Paul Berry, Commissioned graffiti on wall, St. Peters, Sydney, Australia
▼ Disc jockey at a turntable

Using Context to Determine Meaning 331

popular music that we're used to usually has that characteristic," notes Tanner. "That's why it's fun to dance to. In fact, popular music is often designed for movement."

"Meter is simply organizing pulses into a regular cyclical pattern," adds Tanner. Instead of an endless series of beats, the musician may play cycles of "ONE, two, Three, four." This meter, known as "common time," stresses the first beat most. The third beat gets slight emphasis, too. Meter sets up a hierarchy, which the listener's brain can then remember and anticipate. That makes it possible for you to tap your foot or clap in time with the music.

Tempo is how fast a piece of music delivers its meter. Too slow, and a rap song sounds like a *dirge*, or funeral song. Too fast, and the brain can't perceive individual sounds. The music becomes one big blur. Choose a tempo that's just quick enough, and listeners want to move with the music. Speed it up slightly or slow it down in places, and listeners respond to the music's different moods.

WHAT MAKES IT COOL?

Hearing rhythm patterns in a song, listeners form expectations of what comes next. If music doesn't give enough for listeners to form those expectations, it sounds chaotic and grating. If music gets too predictable, however, it becomes boring.

Sophisticated rap music provides an innovative mix that satisfies and sometimes surprises listeners' expectations. With lyrics, an MC might stop in the middle of a line or give some offbeat accents. Sampling or the drum track may stress different notes than those that would usually be emphasized in the meter—a technique called *syncopation*.

Revel in the rhythms of your favorite music. Innovative rhythms not only move music forward in time, but they also make rap—and many other types of music—cool.

▼ Artist: Paul Berry, Museum of Contemporary Art Detroit, Commissioned Graffiti art.

Thinking About the Selection
The Rhythms of Rap

1 Recall How does the author confirm the meaning of the word *declamatory*?

_____

_____

2 Analyze What context clue(s) helped you clarify the meaning of the word *syncopation*?

_____

_____

3 Apply The following chart shows some words from the article with which you may be unfamiliar. Read aloud the section of text that the word appears in to help understand its context. Identify types of context clues to help you determine the meaning of each word. Then, complete the chart to show how each word can be restated.

Unfamiliar Word	Type of Context Clue	Restated Meaning
tempo	explanation—"how fast a piece of music delivers its meter"	how fast or slow
innovative		
foregrounding		

Write Answer the following questions in your Reader's Journal.

4 Interpret How does the form of rap help communicate its message?

5 Identify Find three words in your Anchor Book that are new to you. Determine the meaning of the words by using context clues and restate them in your own words. What kind of context clues are used?

Ready for a Free-Choice Book? Your teacher may ask you if you would like to choose another book to read on your own. Select a book that fits your interest and that you'll enjoy. As you read, think about how your new book compares with your Anchor Book.

Using Context to Determine Meaning

4-11 Literary Analysis
Sound Devices

Many readers are afraid of poetry because they think it's too hard to understand. But poetry is all around you—in the rhythm of a train passing, the sound of your friends' laughter, a written word or phrase that reflects your feelings perfectly. Poetry has many layers: one of them is sound. Poets use the sound of a poem to create a mood.

Literary Terms

Poetry often includes **sound devices** that make the poem pleasing to the ear. Here are a few kinds of sound devices.

- A **rhyme** is a repeated sound at the ends of words. **Rhyme scheme** is the pattern of rhymes in a poem. Lines that rhyme get the same letter. For example, a poem's rhyme scheme can be *abab*. A group of lines in a poem is called a **stanza**, which can contain patterns of meter and rhyme.

- **End rhyme** is the repeated sound at the ends of lines. **Internal rhyme** is the repeated sound within a line.

- Poets may use repetition—words, phrases, sounds, or sentences used more than once—to emphasize an idea.

Alliteration	Consonance	Assonance
the repetition of consonant sounds at the beginning of words	the repetition of consonant sounds at the end of words	the repetition of vowel sounds in words
The big ball bounded by.	The brush swished as we pushed past.	I see the sheen of the deep green sea.

- **Onomatopoeia** is the use of words that imitate sounds. In the chart below, notice that the meaning of the word describes the sound.

Words That Imitate	Meaning
crash	a collision
boom	a loud noise
bang	a slamming noise
swish	the sound of a tail wagging; the sound of windshield wipers

Another kind of literary device, a **pun**, is a phrase that plays with sound and meaning. A pun treats words that sound the same as if they mean the same thing. Puns frequently appear in bad jokes (such as "Q: What instrument do fish like to play? A: A *bass* guitar").

Directions Read the following poem and circle those words that are unfamiliar to you. With a classmate, say each circled word aloud and try to imitate the sound or action you think the author is describing. Then, answer the questions that follow.

Onomatopoeia by Eve Merriam

The rusty spigot

sputters,

utters

a splutter,

5   spatters a smattering of drops,

gashes wider;

slash,

splatters,

scatters,

10   spurts,

finally stops sputtering

and plash!

gushes rushes splashes

clear water dashes.

1 **Identify** Locate two examples of internal rhyme. What effect do they have on the poem?

_____
_____
_____
_____

2 **Analyze** What image does each sound device bring to mind?

_____
_____
_____
_____

Sound Devices   335

Rhythm and Meter

Think you don't have rhythm? You do. **Rhythm** is the rise and fall in intensity of sounds. Have you ever recognized that a friend was approaching simply by the sound of his or her footsteps? Rhythm is all around us. Poets make us more aware of these rhythms by using **meter**, the rhythmical pattern in a line of poetry.

Rhythm is a sound device. One way to understand and appreciate the rhythms in poetry is to read it aloud. Some poems follow very specific rhythmic patterns, whereas prose and free verse use the natural rhythms of everyday speech.

Literary Terms

In literature, **rhythm** describes the pattern of beats in language. Prose and free verse use the natural rhythms of everyday speech, but some poems have a very specific pattern, or **meter.**

- Let's start with your heartbeat. You hear two sounds or beats: da DUM. This is one of the most basic forms of poetic meter: an **iamb**. The first sound is softer and is an unstressed syllable (da). The second sound is stronger and is a stressed syllable (DUM). Say the words "upon" and "arise" aloud. These are iambs.

- To identify the meter of a poem, you determine the number of stressed and unstressed syllables in each line. You can do this by **scanning**, marking the poetry to show its meter. Strong stresses are marked with a slanted line (') called an **accent**. Unstressed syllables are marked with a horseshoe symbol (˘).

- Weak and strong stresses are divided by vertical lines (|). The group of weak and strong stresses between the lines is called a **foot**. A line of poetry is measured by how many feet it has.

- **Iambic pentameter** is the most common type of meter. It is a line of iambs with five feet: da DUM da DUM da DUM da DUM da DUM.

Nearly all of Shakespeare's plays and poetry are written in iambic pentameter, as in this line from *Romeo and Juliet*:

˘	´	˘	´	˘	´	˘	´	˘	´
But,	soft!	what	light	through	yon	der	win	dow	breaks?

Directions Read this poem. Circle examples of repetition used as a poetic device. Scan the first and last lines of the poem. Use a dictionary to help you identify the syllables. With a partner, read the poem aloud, emphasizing the use of repetition and meter.

I Hear America Singing
by Walt Whitman

I hear America singing, the varied carols I hear,
Those of mechanics, each one singing his as it should be blithe and strong,
The carpenter singing his as he measures his plank or beam,
The mason singing his as he makes ready for work, or leaves off work,
5 The boatman singing what belongs to him in his boat, the deckhand singing on the steamboat deck,
The shoemaker singing as he sits on his bench, the hatter singing as he stands,
The wood-cutter's song, the ploughboy's on his way in the morning, or at the noon intermission or at sundown,
The delicious singing of the mother, or of the young wife at work, or of the girl sewing or washing,
Each singing what belongs to her, and to none else,
The day what belongs to the day—at night the party of young fellows, robust, friendly,
10 Singing with open mouths their strong melodious songs.

1 Examine How is the word "singing" used as poetic device in the poem?

_____

_____

2 Analyze How do the first and last lines help frame the poem?

_____

_____

_____

Read the following selections aloud. Listen for how sound devices make an impact on the audience.
Guiding Question: How do the tools of sound devices help communicate the author's purpose?

The Gettysburg Address
BY ABRAHAM LINCOLN

Background This speech by President Lincoln was presented on Nov. 19, 1863, at the ceremony dedicating the battlefield of Gettysburg as a cemetery for soldiers who fell in the Civil War. During a perilous time of national crisis, Lincoln's words were an attempt to provide comfort to the soldiers who had survived the battle.

Vocabulary Builder

Before you read, you will discuss the following words. In the Vocabulary Builder box in the margin, use a vocabulary building strategy to make the words your own.

consecrate   hallow

As you read, draw a box around unfamiliar words you could add to your vocabulary. Use context clues to unlock their meaning.

Marking the Text

Sound Devices

As you read, circle places where sound devices are used. In the margin, note the kinds of sound devices you find and explain how they help communicate the author's message.

Fourscore[1] and seven years ago our fathers brought forth on this continent a new nation, conceived in liberty, and dedicated to the proposition that all men are created equal.

Now we are engaged in a great civil war, testing whether that nation, or any nation so conceived and so dedicated, can long endure. We are met on a great battlefield of that war. We have come to dedicate a portion of that field as a final resting place for those who here gave their lives that that nation might live. It is altogether fitting and proper that we should do this. But, in

---

[1] **Fourscore** (for′ skor′) *adj.* eighty

Literature in Context
The Battle of Gettysburg

The result of an accidental clash between the 75,000 soldiers in the Army of Northern Virginia and 80,000-plus soldiers in the Union Army of the Potomac, the Battle of Gettysburg raged for three days between July 1 and 3, 1863. The battle helped turn the tide for the Union Army, but at a great cost. There were over 51,000 casualties; more men fought and more men died here than in any other battle before or since on North American soil. Lincoln was to say later, in his speech, that his words would be long forgotten before the deeds of the men who lost their lives in battle.

Link to Social Studies

a larger sense, we cannot dedicate, we cannot **consecrate**, we cannot **hallow,** this ground. The brave men, living and dead, who struggled here have consecrated it, far above our poor power to add or detract. The world will little note, nor long remember, what we say here, but it can never forget what they did here. It is for us the living, rather, to be dedicated here to the unfinished work which they who fought here have thus far so nobly advanced. It is rather for us to be here dedicated to the great task remaining before us—that from these honored dead we take increased devotion to that cause for which they gave the last full measure of devotion—that we here highly resolve that these dead shall not have died in vain—that this nation, under God, shall have a new birth of freedom and that government of the people, by the people, for the people, shall not perish from the earth.

Marking the Text

Vocabulary Builder

consecrate
(kän´ si krāt) v.

Meaning

hallow
(hal´ ō) v.

Meaning

while reading your anchor book

Vocabulary Builder

Before you read, you will discuss the following words. In the Vocabulary Builder box in the margin, use a vocabulary building strategy to make the words your own.

      insignia   **labyrinth**   **lyric**

As you read, draw a box around unfamiliar words you could add to your vocabulary. Use context clues to unlock their meaning.

Marking the Text

Sound Devices

As you read, circle places where sound devices are used. In the margin, note the kinds of sound devices you find and explain how they help communicate the author's message.

    Fast breaks. Lay ups. With Mercury's
    Insignia on our sneakers,
    We outmaneuvered the footwork
    Of bad angels. Nothing but a hot
5 Swish of strings like silk
    Ten feet out. In the roundhouse
    Labyrinth our bodies
    Created, we could almost
    Last forever, poised in midair
10 Like storybook sea monsters.
    A high note hung there
    A long second. Off
    The rim. We'd corkscrew
    Up & dunk balls that exploded
15 The skullcap of hope & good
    Intention. Bug-eyed, lanky,
    All hands & feet . . . sprung rhythm.

Vocabulary Builder

insignia
(in sig´ nē ə) *n.*

Meaning

labyrinth
(lab´ ə rinth) *n.*

Meaning

Marking the Text

We were metaphysical[1] when girls
Cheered on the sidelines.
20 Tangled up in a falling,
Muscles were a bright motor
Double-flashing to the metal hoop
Nailed to our oak.
When Sonny Boy's mama died
25 He played nonstop all day, so hard
Our backboard splintered.
Glistening with sweat, we jibed[2]
& rolled the ball off our
Fingertips. Trouble
30 Was there slapping a blackjack
Against an open palm.
Dribble, drive to the inside, feint,
& glide like a sparrow hawk.
Lay ups. Fast breaks.
35 We had moves we didn't know
We had. Our bodies spun
On swivels of bone & faith,
Through a **lyric** slipknot
Of joy, & we knew we were
40 Beautiful & dangerous.

---

[1] **metaphysical** (met´ ə fiz´ i kəl) *adj.* without bodily form.

[2] **jibed** (jībd) *v.* worked together; *also*, teased.

Vocabulary Builder

lyric
(lir´ ik) *adj.*

Meaning

YUSEF KOMUNYAKAA (b. 1947)

Yusef Komunyakaa was raised in Bogalusa, Louisiana. To escape the lack of opportunities there, he joined the United States Army during the Vietnam War. His writing ability led him to positions as a combat journalist and managing editor of an army newspaper. For his service reporting news amid the dangers of the battlefield, he was awarded the Bronze Star Medal.

After the military, he attended college in California. Later, Komunyakaa was a professor at various universities. During this time, he published more than eight books of poetry, including *Neon Vernacular*, which earned him the Pulitzer Prize.

Besides his 1994 Pulitzer Prize, Komunyakaa has been awarded the William Faulkner Prize, the Thomas Forcade Award, and the Hanes Poetry Prize, as well as fellowships from the Fine Arts Work Center in Provincetown, the Louisiana Arts Council, and the National Endowment for the Arts. Additionally, he was presented with the Robert Creeley Poetry Award on March 28, 2007.

The Eagle
by Alfred, Lord Tennyson

He clasps the crag[1] with crooked hands;
Close to the sun in lonely lands,
Ring'd with the azure[2] world, he stands.

The wrinkled sea beneath him crawls;
He watches from his mountain walls,
And like a thunderbolt he falls.

---

[1] **crag** (krag) *n.* steep, rugged rock that juts out from a rock mass.
[2] **azure** (azh' ə r) *adj.* blue.

Vocabulary Builder

After you read, review the words you decided to add to your vocabulary. Write the meaning of words you have learned in context. Look up the other words in a dictionary, glossary, thesaurus, or electronic resource.

Literature in Context
History of Literature

Alfred Tennyson (1809-1892) is one of the most famous poets in English literature. As a young man, Tennyson met Arthur Henry Hallam, who became his closest friend and encouraged Tennyson to publish his poems. When Hallam died suddenly in 1833, Tennyson was devastated but his grief inspired one of his greatest works, *In Memoriam, A.H.H.* Tennyson remains a major figure in the history of literature because of the musical quality of his language and his ability to communicate the melancholy that we all feel at times.

Thinking About the Selections

The Gettysburg Address; Slam, Dunk, & Hook; and The Eagle

1 **Evaluate** What impact does repetition have on "The Gettysburg Address"? Would the speech have the same impact if it was not based on a real event? Explain.

2 **Distinguish** Does the rhythm in "The Gettysburg Address" differ from the rhythm found in a poem? Why or why not?

3 **Analyze** In "Slam, Dunk, & Hook," what sound devices does the author use, and why?

4 **Interpret** The tone of "The Eagle" is formal. How does this tone give meaning to the subject of the poem, the eagle?

5 **Identify** What sound devices are used to help create an image of the eagle? How do they help set the tone?

6 **Contrast** How are the rhythm, meter, and rhyme/rhyme scheme of "Slam, Dunk, & Hook" different from those of "The Eagle"? How do these elements contribute to the poems' mood/meaning?

Write Answer the following questions in your Reader's Journal.

 7 **Evaluate** How do the tools of sound devices help communicate the author's purpose?

 8 **Analyze** Identify a passage from your Anchor Book that uses sound devices. Explain how the sound devices contribute to the description.

Sound Devices 343

4-12 Listening and Speaking Workshop
Reading Poetry Aloud

In this activity, you and your group members will read a poem aloud. Your goal will be to deliver the poem in a clear and effective way that communicates the poem's meaning to your listeners.

Your Task

- Work with your group to select a poem of between six and eight stanzas that represents a diverse perspective.
- Analyze the poem together and identify elements such as alliteration, assonance, and consonance that contribute to the poem's meaning.
- Read the poem to the class and provide a brief explanation of its meaning. Be prepared to answer clarifying questions.

Organize and Practice Your Presentation

1 Choose a poem. Work with your group to select a poem from this unit. Your teacher may provide other poems from which to choose.

2 Read and discuss the poem. Read the poem to yourself. Think of how your poem represents diverse cultures, ethnicities, and time periods. How is race, gender, disability, religion, or age portrayed? Discuss with your group how these different perspectives give meaning to your poem. Then, identify elements of poetry, such as mood and tone, and how they are conveyed—for example, through word choice, figurative language, sentence structure, line length, punctuation, rhythm, rhyme, and repetition. Think about how these elements add to the poem's meaning. Decide on an interpretation of the poem.

3 Create a visual. Display the terms and provide examples from your poem. Use visuals to support your instruction. For example, if one term is "symbolism," you might use a graphic organizer to identify the symbol, explain what it means, and explain how it contributes to the meaning of the poem.

4 Plan your delivery. Your voices and actions help convey and express the poem's content, mood, and meaning. Consider

while reading your anchor book

adjusting your pitch, volume, pacing, and tone to emphasize the poem's meaning. Ask yourself these questions as you prepare.

- ▶ Which words will you emphasize? Why?
- ▶ What gestures will you use?
- ▶ Which parts will be read by individuals?

Experiment with different ideas. Remember that all group members should read at least one line. Be prepared to answer questions about the poem's language and its meaning.

5 **Rehearse your presentation.** Speak clearly. Rehearse until all members are able to read their parts as planned. Review the rubric below to make sure you are meeting all criteria.

Directions Assess your performance. For each question, circle a rating.

SPEAK: Rubric for Oral Interpretation

CRITERIA	RATING SCALE
CONTENT How well did the group convey the poem's meaning through its analysis of different perspectives, such as culture, ethnicity, time period, race, gender, disability, or religion?	NOT VERY VERY 1 2 3 4 5
CONTENT How well did the group convey the poem's meaning through its explanation of the poetic elements used?	1 2 3 4 5
ORGANIZATION Did group members seem to know when and how to read their lines?	1 2 3 4 5
DELIVERY How well did the group use voice modulation and expression to convey the poem's meaning?	1 2 3 4 5
COOPERATION How well did the group work together?	1 2 3 4 5

LISTEN: Rubric for Audience Self-Assessment

CRITERIA	RATING SCALE
ACTIVE LISTENING How well did you demonstrate active listening with appropriate silence, responses, and body language?	NOT VERY VERY 1 2 3 4 5

Be prepared to ask questions to clarify each group's interpretation.

Reading Poetry Aloud

4-13 Literary Analysis
Forms of Poetry

Is the form of communication important? Poems come in all shapes and sizes. In poetry, the form is connected to the poet's purpose. Poets use different forms to talk about different subjects.

Literary Terms

There are three main types of poetry.

Narrative poetry tells a story and has a plot, characters, and a setting. An *epic* is a long narrative poem about the adventures of gods or heroes. A *ballad* is a songlike narrative that has short stanzas and a refrain.	**Dramatic poetry** tells a story using a character's own thoughts or spoken statements.	**Lyric poems** express the feelings of a single speaker. Lyrics are the most common type of poem. An example of a lyric poem is an elegy, a poem of mourning.

Poetic forms are defined by the way lines are organized using devices such as stanzas, rhythm, and rhyme.

- **Free verse** has neither a set pattern of rhythm nor rhyme.
- **Concrete poems** look like their subject. A poem about the ocean, for example, might take the shape of a wave.
- A **sonnet** is a fourteen-line lyric poem with formal patterns of rhyme, rhythm, and line structure that traditionally follows a problem/resolution pattern, where a proposition or question is posed and then, at the end of the poem, gets resolved or answered.

Directions With a partner, discuss connotations of the word "night." Then, read the sonnet aloud. Scan the poem and identify the rhyme pattern.

Acquainted With the Night by Robert Frost

I have been one acquainted with the night,
I have walked out in rain – and back in rain.
I have outwalked the furthest city light.

I have looked down the saddest city lane.
5 I have passed by the watchman on his beat
And dropped my eyes, unwilling to explain.

I have stood still and stopped the sound of feet
When far away an interrupted cry
Came over houses from another street,

10 But not to call me back or say good-bye;
And further still at an unearthly height,
One luminary clock against the sky

Proclaimed the time was neither wrong nor right
I have been one acquainted with the night.

Draw a picture to describe the poem in the space below.

Directions A **haiku** is a form of Japanese verse that often captures a perfect moment in nature. A haiku contains only three unrhymed lines of five, seven, and five syllables. Read the poems. Then, write a haiku of your own on a separate sheet of paper.

Temple bells die out.
The fragrant blossoms remain.
A perfect evening!
—Bashõ

Dragonfly catcher,
How far have you gone today
In your wandering?
—Chiyojo

Forms of Poetry 347

Speaker

When you read or listen to a poem, do you get the sense that there is a specific voice speaking the words? Don't assume that this is the poet's voice. Like the narrator in a story or novel, the speaker in a poem is a kind of character who may be nothing at all like the person who wrote the poem. This speaker may not even be human!

Literary Terms

The **speaker** is the imaginary voice that is speaking in a poem. You know what a narrator is. The speaker is like the narrator of a poem. A narrator always tells a story, but a speaker may only express thoughts or feelings.

Whenever you read a poem, ask yourself these questions to help you locate important information about the speaker.

> **Questions About the Speaker**
> 1. Who is the speaker (man, woman, child, animal, plant, object)?
> 2. How does he, she, or it seem to be feeling?
> 3. What subject is the speaker talking about?
> 4. What is the speaker's tone? Does it change?
> 5. Examine the poem's diction. How do the speaker's words convey the tone?
> 6. Is the speaker doing anything? If so, what?

The answers to all these questions help you **infer the speaker's attitude,** determining the speaker's views of ideas and events.

Directions Recall Walt Whitman's poem "I Hear America Singing" from page 337. Look at the first stanza below to see how a student underlined details from the poem to infer the speaker's attitude.

> ### I Hear America Singing
> #### by Walt Whitman
> I hear America singing, the varied carols I hear,
>
> Those of mechanics—each one singing his as it should be blithe and strong,

Directions The following dramatic poem is a direct response to Walt Whitman's poem "I Hear America Singing" (page 337). As you read, answer the questions about the speaker from the previous page in the margin. Circle diction that communicate the speaker's tone.

I, Too by Langston Hughes

I, too, sing America.

I am the darker brother.
They send me to eat in the kitchen
When company comes,
5 But I laugh,
And eat well,
And grow strong.

Tomorrow,
I'll be at the table
10 When company comes.
Nobody'll dare
Say to me,
"Eat in the kitchen,"
Then.

15 Besides,
They'll see how beautiful I am
And be ashamed—

I, too, am America.

1 Interpret What is the poem's historical setting, and how is it relevant to the speaker's tone? Explain what the speaker means by the lines "Nobody'll dare say to me 'Eat in the kitchen.'"

_____
_____
_____

2 Apply On a separate sheet of paper, write a dramatic poem whose speaker addresses a problem in society. Make careful diction choices to express your speaker's attitude.

The following poems are written in very different forms.
Guiding Question: How does the style and structure of each poem affect how its message is communicated?

Vocabulary Builder

Before you read, you will discuss the following words. In the Vocabulary Builder box in the margin, use a vocabulary building strategy to make the words your own.

brazen   wretched

As you read, draw a box around unfamiliar words you could add to your vocabulary. Use context clues to unlock their meaning.

Fences
by Pat Mora

Marking the Text

Forms of Poetry and Speaker

As you read, underline words that help you understand the speaker and the speaker's attitudes. In the margin, write what you learn about the speaker.

Mouths full of laughter,
the *turistas*[1] come to the tall hotel
with suitcases full of dollars.

Every morning my brother makes
5 the cool beach sand new for them.
With a wooden board he smooths
away all footprints.

I peek through the cactus fence
and watch the women rub oil
10 sweeter than honey into their arms and legs
while their children jump waves
or sip drinks from long straws,
coconut white, mango yellow.

Once my little sister
15 ran barefoot across the hot sand
for a taste.

My mother roared like the ocean,
"No. No. It's their beach.
It's their beach."

---

[1] **turistas** (too rēs′ täz) *n.* Spanish word meaning *tourists*

Lesson 4-13

THE NEW COLOSSUS
by Emma Lazarus

Not like the **brazen** giant of Greek fame,
With conquering limbs astride from land to land;
Here at our sea-washed, sunset gates shall stand
A mighty woman with a torch, whose flame
Is the imprisoned lightning, and her name
Mother of Exiles.[1] From her beacon-hand
Glows world-wide welcome; her mild
    eyes command
The air-bridged harbor that twin
    cities frame.
"Keep, ancient lands, your storied
    pomp!"[2] cries she
With silent lips. "Give me your tired,
    your poor,
Your huddled masses yearning to
    breathe free,
The **wretched** refuse of your teeming
    shore.
Send these, the homeless, tempest-tossed
    to me,
I lift my lamp beside the golden door!"

Vocabulary Builder

brazen
(brā′ zən) *adj.*

Meaning

wretched
(rech′ id) *adj.*

Meaning

[1.] **Exiles** (ek′sils) people who are forced out of their country or home
[2.] **pomp** (pämp) show of magnificence

Forms of Poetry and Speaker 351

Forsythia
by Mary Ellen Solt

Vocabulary Builder

After you read, review the words you decided to add to your vocabulary. Write the meaning of words you have learned in context. Look up the other words in a dictionary, glossary, thesaurus, or electronic resource.

Thinking About the Selection
Fences, The New Colossus, and Forsythia

1 **Apply** Which form and/or type of poetry is each poem an example of? Explain.

2 **Infer** Which lines in "The New Colossus" tell you what the poem is about? Paraphrase the lines, using a sentence structure that is more like everyday speech. Now read your lines aloud using the rhythm, meter, and flow of everyday speech.

3 **Compare and Contrast** The poems "I, Too" and "The New Colossus" have different cultural contexts. How does the speaker of each poem communicate a different perspective on America?

4 **Interpret** Find an example of figurative language in "Fences." What does the phrase mean and how does it help set the poem's tone?

5 **Analyze** How does the graphic element in "Forsythia" contribute to the meaning/mood of the poem?

Write Answer the following questions in your Reader's Journal.

6 **Analyze** How does the style of each poem affect how its message is communicated?

7 **Interpret** Describe the speaker in your Anchor Book. Use the questions about the speaker as a guide.

while reading your anchor book

Forms of Poetry and Speaker 353

4-14 Language Coach
Grammar and Spelling

Sentence Structure

The four basic sentence structures are simple, compound, complex, and compound-complex. Sentence diagrams and exercises are online.

You have learned what a simple sentence is, now let's focus on the other three.

A **compound sentence** consists of two or more independent clauses usually joined by a comma and a conjunction.

Independent clause + **, conjunction** + **independent clause**

Example Nicole likes popular music, **but** I prefer jazz.

1 Create an example of a compound sentence on the line below.

A **complex sentence** consists of one independent clause and one or more subordinate clauses (also known as modifiers, or describers).

Independent clause + **subordinate clause**

Example Mom and Dad will take us to a movie **when we finish our homework.**

2 Create an example of a complex sentence on the lines below.

Author's Craft

Look back at "The Gettysburg Address" beginning on page 338. Find an example of each of the following sentence structures: simple, compound, and complex.

A **compound-complex sentence** consists of two or more independent clauses and one or more subordinate clauses. As the name indicates, a compound-complex sentence contains the elements both of a compound sentence and a complex sentence.

Example Tools and weapons **that date back to before 500 B.C.** show great skill**, and** they serve as evidence that their makers were very talented.

3 Create an example of a compound-complex sentence on the lines below.

354 Lesson 4-14

Revising to Vary Sentence Patterns

When you review your writing, you might notice that many of your sentences begin with nouns. This construction is probably the subject followed by the verb. To avoid this dull subject-verb pattern, try varying your sentence beginnings. For example, you can start your sentence with an adjective, an adverb, or a prepositional phrase.

DULL: Sam walked to the stage to accept his award.

Try beginning with	Examples
an adjective or adjective phrase	Thrilled by the applause, Sam walked to the stage to accept his award.
an adverb or adverb phrase	Finally winning after years of only being nominated, Sam walked to the stage to accept his award.
a prepositional phrase	After a long pause, Sam walked to the stage to accept his award.

Directions Revise each sentence according to the directions in parentheses.

1. The park was crowded on that early Saturday morning.
   (Move the prepositional phrase to the beginning.)

2. Sara approached the soccer field.
   (Add an adjective at the beginning.)

3. She asked the coach to let her try out for the team.
   (Add an adverb at the beginning.)

4. She emptied her gym bag's contents onto the grass.
   (Add a prepositional phrase at the beginning.)

5. Sara retied the laces on her running shoes, and then she continued the race. (Add an adverb to the beginning.)

Vary Sentence Patterns

4-15 Writer's Workshop
Exposition: Writing for Assessment

When you **write for assessment,** you usually have to respond to a writing prompt and prepare an answer in a limited time. This form of writing may be used in end-of-course exams and standardized tests. Following the steps outlined, practice writing for assessment. You will write an essay about a technique that an author uses in writing.

Purpose To identify elements of an author's technique

Audience You, your teacher, and your classmates

To be effective, your writing for assessment should include the following elements.

- A response that addresses all parts of a writing prompt
- A main idea supported by evidence
- A clear and logical organization
- Error-free writing with appropriate use of active and passive voice

Prewriting—Plan It Out

You should spend about one quarter of your time prewriting. To choose your topic, use the following strategies.

Consider the prompt. When you write for assessment, study the instructions to determine what you need to write. The chart identifies key words that show the type of information the response requires. If given a choice of topics, choose the one you know best or have studied the most.

Prompt Think of a book you have read. Identify one technique the author uses to develop the story, such as foreshadowing, flashback, point of view, or characterization. Discuss how this technique contributes to your understanding of the story.

Words	Essay Objectives
Analyze	Examine how elements contribute to the whole
Compare/Contrast	Stress how subjects are alike/different
Define	Give examples to explain meaning
Discuss	Support generalizations with facts and examples

Gather details. Use an **idea web** to jot down ideas to use in your draft. Do not worry about punctuation and spelling while you are compiling your ideas.

Lesson 4-15

Drafting—Get It on Paper

Using your idea web as an outline, write out your assessment. You should spend about half your time drafting. The following steps will help you make your assessment focused and logical.

Shape your writing. Use an organization that supports your goals.

- **Order of Importance** For persuasion, or to stress key points, organize your ideas from most important to least important.

- **Chronological Order** For a summary, an explanation, or a narrative, organize details in the order in which they happen.

Provide elaboration. For each idea, include a variety of supporting details from the text, such as facts, names, explanations, and examples.

Student Model: Supporting Ideas with Details

> **Prompt** How does the point of view used in *Flowers for Algernon* affect your understanding of the characters?
>
> **Idea** The first-person point of view helps the reader see how Charlie changes.
>
> **Detail** The reader can follow how much he changes by watching his writing improve.
>
> **Detail** His writing also reflects his ability to think more deeply and clearly about things.

The writer's notes help her quickly gather evidence for her essay.

Revising—Make It Better

Now that you have a draft, you can revise your assessment to make it clearer and more precise. You should spend about one quarter of your time revising and editing. Revise using these steps.

Check your structure. Review your introduction and conclusion. Ask yourself these questions.

- Does my introduction clearly reflect the instructions?
- Does it clearly state what I will cover in the rest of the essay?
- Do the ideas in my introduction and conclusion match?

Identify vague words. Replace vague words with more specific ones.

Vague	**Specific**
He had *good* ideas.	He had *innovative* ideas.

Peer Review: Ask for a partner's response to your writing for assessment. Revise to achieve the reaction you had intended.

Exposition: Writing for Assessment

Writer's Workshop continued

Directions Read this student writing for assessment as a model for your own.

Writing Prompt How does the point of view used in *Flowers for Algernon* affect your understanding of the characters?

Isabel Garcia, Miami, FL
Point of View in Flowers for Algernon

In *Flowers for Algernon,* the point of view of the narrator is very important. The story is told in the first person by Charlie, who is keeping a diary as the story takes place. This allows you to see things as he sees them, and also to understand how his mind changes during the story.

At the beginning of the story, Charlie is not very smart, and he sees things in a very simple way. We can tell how much trouble he has writing from the way he spells words and uses punctuation. He gets happy when he gets something right, such as when he tells the doctor that he sees an inkblot. He also talks about how badly he wants to become smart, which helps the reader understand his motivations.

As the story goes on, Charlie's writings get better and better. He also starts to have more complicated ideas and to think more clearly. Seeing things from his point of view helps you follow his progress as his treatments start to work. However, the reader also sees that being smart isn't always great, because he realizes ways people took advantage of him in the past.

By telling the story from a first-person point of view, the author leaves some things out. The reader can't tell how other people perceive Charlie at first. We also don't know anything that Charlie doesn't know, so it is not clear at first exactly what type of experiment is being tried on Charlie.

In the introduction, the writer introduces the main ideas that she will write about in her essay.

The writer uses specific examples to show how the point of view affects the beginning of the story.

Here, the writer uses chronological order as she discusses different parts of the story.

Editing—Be Your Own Language Coach

Before you hand in your writing for assessment, review it for language convention errors. Pay special attention to proper placement of modifiers and the variety of your sentence patterns. When editing a sentence for variety, maintain parallel structure. For example, if surrounding sentences are in the active voice don't switch to the passive voice (and vice versa).

Publishing—Share It!

When you publish a work, you produce it for a specific audience. Consider one of the following ideas to share your writing.

Discuss with a group. Compare your test responses to those of others by using your essays as the springboard for a class discussion.

Create a review folder. Set aside a folder for old tests, and place a copy of your writing assessment in it. When you study for future tests, use your essays to remind you of the effective writing strategies you used.

Reflecting On Your Writing

1 What did you learn through practicing writing for assessment?

2 **Rubric for Self-Assessment** Assess your essay. For each question, circle a rating.

CRITERIA	RATING SCALE
IDEAS Is your paper clear and focused with details that support the main idea?	NOT VERY VERY 1 2 3 4 5
ORGANIZATION How well do you employ a clear and logical organization?	1 2 3 4 5
VOICE Is your writing lively and engaging, drawing the reader in?	1 2 3 4 5
WORD CHOICE How appropriate is the language for your audience?	1 2 3 4 5
SENTENCE FLUENCY How varied is your sentence structure?	1 2 3 4 5
CONVENTIONS How correct is your grammar?	1 2 3 4 5

Exposition: Writing for Assessment

4-16 Connecting to Your Anchor Book
Anchor Book Projects

Now that you have finished reading your Anchor Book, it is time to get creative! Complete one of the following projects.

It's a Trial — A

In almost every book, the major character comes into conflict with another character. Usually the conflict gets resolved, but you may not agree with the outcome. Holding a mock trial gives you a chance to have your own say. With other students reading the same Anchor Book, choose one of the characters in a conflict to put on trial.

1. Review the conflict and combine your notes on the event and the characters involved in the conflict.
2. Research the components of a trial and choose what role each of you will play. There will be the defendant and the plaintiff, two attorneys, witnesses for each side, a bailiff, and a judge.
3. Prepare loose scripts for the opening statements, interrogation and cross-examinations of witnesses, and closing arguments.
4. Stage your trial in front of the class, who will play the jurors.

Your mock trial should include the following elements.
- An outline combining the notes of all your teammates
- A summary of your team's research on the components of a trial
- Scripts for the performers

Create a Visual Poem — B

If a poem uses powerful and vivid imagery, you might be able to "see" the poem in your head. What if you were to put those images on paper or record them on a video? What would the poem look like? By using a poem's imagery you can retell a poem using only images.

1. Choose a poem or poetic passage from your Anchor Book. Underline any strong imagery or figurative language, such as symbols, similes, metaphors, and personification.
2. Decide how you want to represent these elements. Draw, paint, photograph, or use photos from the Internet to create your images.
3. On several sheets of paper or on a poster board, display your images in such a way that they retell the poem. Include the title of the poem. If you record the images on a video, play the video for the class.

Your visual poem should include the following elements.
- Clear and identifiable images that are related to the imagery and figurative language in your poem
- A logical order of images that matches the poem
- The title of the poem

Create a Poetry Anthology

An anthology is a collection of literary texts. Use details from your Anchor Book to write five poems for a class anthology. Choose from these forms: epic poem, elegy, ballad, haiku, concrete poem, dramatic poem, found poem, sonnet, and ode.

1. Think of specific images, feelings, ideas, or events from your Anchor Book. Which interest you the most? Can you extend or elaborate on any of these elements to make thoughtful, organized, and creative poems? List your ideas for topics of your poems.

2. Read examples of poetic forms, which you can find in this unit or in a poetry anthology from your local library. Analyze language technique of published poets, such as the way these writers use rhythm and varied sentence structure. You might apply these techniques in your own writing. Take notes on the relationship between the *purposes* and the *characteristics* of the forms. For example, the purpose of an elegy is to mourn someone or something, therefore, characteristics of an elegy might include somber tone, solemn mood, and simile. Think about how each form influences the poem's meaning, purpose, and emotional effect on the audience.

3. Write your poems using evocative language and any of these sound devices: rhythm, meter, rhyme, repetition, alliteration, and assonance.

Your poems should include the following elements.
- Appropriate titles, poetic language, and sound devices
- Extension or elaboration of ideas, events, or other elements from your Anchor Book
- Clearly defined organization and structure

Free-Choice Book Reflection

My free-choice book is _____.

The author is _____.

1 Would you recommend this book to a friend? Yes ____ No ____

Briefly explain why. _____

Write and Discuss Answer the following question in your Reader's Journal. Then, discuss your answer with a partner or your Literature Circle.

 2 **Compare and Contrast** *What is the secret to reaching someone with words?* Select a passage from your Anchor Book and one from your free-choice book that communicate a similar idea. Explain how each author's style affects what is communicated. To extend the discussion, consider how a journalist, a scientist, or an artist might answer the question.

Connecting to Your Anchor Books

Unit Review
Standardized Test Practice

Answer the questions below to check your understanding of this unit's skills.

Reading Skills: Paraphrasing

Read this selection. Then, answer the questions that follow.

> Dr. Martin Luther King, Jr. brought about many important changes in American life. His words and deeds have served as a model for creating change without violence or foul actions. At age thirty-five, King became the youngest person to receive the Nobel Peace Prize. By this time, he had helped many African Americans begin to feel the triumph of gaining equal rights.

1 Which statement best **paraphrases** the last two sentences?

A. King won a prize for being young.
B. King's actions gained him notoriety.
C. King helped many people.
D. King won an award for his pursuit of equality.

2 Which statement best **paraphrases** the selection?

F. America did not change because of King.
G. King acted through nonviolence.
H. King worked peacefully.
J. King spent his life promoting equality for African Americans.

Reading Skills: Using Context to Determine Meaning

Read this selection. Then, answer the questions that follow.

> Soon I saw lines of cars parked by the sand, all with signs that said, "Santoro Family Reunion." Even the vehicles seemed to have a familial likeness—there were several that looked the same as ours, as if they were relatives. We parked and jumped out of the car to join the party. Aromas of grilling meats and vegetables filled my nose, and those delicious smells made me hungry right away. I was given a T-shirt with the family name on it, and before I knew it, I was in the middle of a game of beach volleyball.

3 What is the meaning of *familial*?

A. closely acquainted

B. very pleasing or satisfying

C. of, relating to, or suggestive of a family

D. partly or totally unlike in nature

4 What is the meaning of *aroma*?

F. the state of having different forms

G. an offensive smell

H. a portion

J. an agreeable odor

Literary Analysis: Elements of Poetry and Prose

Read this poem and answer the questions that follow.

> From **Worth While** by Ella Wheeler Wilcox
>
> It is easy enough to be pleasant
>   When life flows by like a song,
> But the man worth while is the one who will smile
>   When everything goes dead wrong.
> For the test of the heart is trouble,
>   And it always comes with the years,
> And the smile that is worth the praises of earth
>   Is the smile that shines through tears.

5 Which of the following is used in the second line?

A. free verse

B. metaphor

C. personification

D. simile

6 What is the **rhyme scheme** of this poem?

F. ABAB

G. ABCB

H. AABB

J. ABCD

Choose the best answer for the following questions.

7 What is the definition of **meter**?

A. the repetition of sounds at the ends of words

B. the use of words that imitate sounds

C. the arrangement and number of stressed and unstressed syllables in a poem

D. the repetition of consonant sounds at the beginnings of words

8 A three-line poem with five syllables in the first and third lines and seven syllables in the second line is known as a _____.

F. haiku

G. ballad

H. limerick

J. narrative

9 Which of the following sentences is an example of **personification**?

A. Carlos is as tall as an elm tree.

B. Her anger was a raging fire.

C. He whooshed down the hill on his new snowboard.

D. The wind whispered in Jackie's ear as it blew by.

10 *The plates clattered and clanged* is an example of _____.

F. onomatopoeia and simile

G. onomatopoeia and alliteration

H. alliteration and metaphor

J. personification and assonance

Language Skills: Vocabulary

Choose the best answer.

11 Which of these words contains a **suffix**?

A. happy

B. glorious

C. many

D. mentor

12 What does the **origin** of *congratulate* mean?

F. "to bend back"

G. "pleasing"

H. "to fit"

J. "water"

13 What is the meaning of the **root** *recipere* in *receive*?

A. "to recite"

B. "to give"

C. "to go"

D. "to get"

14 What is the most likely meaning of *receiver* in the following sentence?

Because of the quarterback's tremendous throw, the wide **receiver** scored a touchdown.

F. "one who runs the ball"

G. "one who throws the ball"

H. "one who catches the ball"

J. "one who kicks the ball"

Language Skills: Spelling

Circle the letter that contains the correctly spelled word to complete the sentence.

15 Twirling around in a circle can cause _____.

A. dizzieness

B. dissiness

C. dizziness

D. dizzyness

16 She was a _____ person.

F. likable

G. likeable

H. likible

J. likeabel

17 Any lawyer can tell you that stealing is _____.

A. illegal
B. ilegal
C. illeagle
D. illigal

18 The _____ was an obscure one.

F. reverence
G. referrence
H. referee
J. reference

Language Skills: Grammar

Choose the best answer.

19 Identify the sentence written in the **passive voice**.

A. She smiled every time I walked by.
B. They lived in a small but affluent town.
C. The question was asked by the senator.
D. People love to shop on sunny days.

20 When is it appropriate to use the **passive voice**?

F. to make a strong statement
G. when the subject is unclear
H. to add vivid description
J. to improve communication

21 What type of sentence is the following?
My friend Tom picked me up.

A. simple sentence
B. complex sentence
C. compound sentence
D. compound-complex sentence

22 Which is a **compound sentence**?

F. The walk to the end of the mall was exhausting.
G. "What were you thinking?" he exclaimed.
H. A talented speaker, the announcer answered the question.
J. I like rap music, but my dad listens to rock.

23 A **complex sentence** contains

A. two independent clauses
B. a conjunction
C. an independent clause and at least one subordinate clause
D. a participial phrase

24 Which of these sentences has been revised with a **prepositional phrase**?

F. Cautiously, he opened the window.
G. Before evening fell, he opened the window.
H. He opened the window.
J. Hoping to let in some air, he opened the window.

Is it our *differences* or our *similarities* that matter most?

Unit 5 Genre focus:
Drama

Your Anchor Book
There are many good books that would work well to support both the Big Question and the genre focus of this unit. In this unit you will read one of these books as your Anchor Book. Your teacher will introduce the book you will be reading.

Free-Choice Reading
Later in this unit you will be given the opportunity to choose another book to read. This is called your free-choice book.

Thinking About What You Already Know

Have you ever watched a movie and found yourself sitting on the edge of your seat wondering what will happen next? What you are feeling is suspense, a key element of drama.

Edgar Allan Poe is famous for making hearts beat faster with his stories of suspense. You are about to read an excerpt from a Poe story. The excerpt has been divided in half, and each half stops at a suspenseful moment. Read the excerpt and answer the questions.

from "The Tell-Tale Heart" by Edgar Allan Poe

Upon the eighth night I was more than usually cautious in opening the door. A watch's minute-hand moves more quickly than did mine. Never, before that night, had I *felt* the extent of my own powers—of my sagacity.[1] I could scarcely contain my feelings of triumph. To think that there I was, opening the door, little by little, and the old man not even to dream of my secret deeds or thoughts. I fairly chuckled at the idea. And perhaps the old man heard me; for he moved in the bed suddenly, as if startled. Now you may think that I drew back—but no. His room was as black as pitch with the thick darkness, (for the shutters were close fastened, through fear of robbers,) and so I knew that he could not see the opening of the door, and I kept on pushing it steadily, steadily.

[1] **sagacity** (sə gaʹ sə tē) *n.* wisdom and sound judgment

How has the author made you curious about what happens next?

continued from "The Tell-Tale Heart"

I had got my head in, and was about to open the lantern, when my thumb slipped upon the tin fastening, and the old man sprang up in the bed, crying out—"Who's there?"

I kept quite still and said nothing. For another hour I did not move a muscle, and in the meantime I did not hear the old man lie down. He was still sitting up in the bed, listening;—just as I have done, night after night, hearkening to the death-watches[2] in the wall.

[2] **death-watches** *n.* wood-boring beetles whose heads make a tapping sound; they are superstitiously regarded as an omen of death.

How has the author made you curious about what happens next?

_____
_____
_____
_____
_____
_____
_____
_____
_____

Now that you have thought about how this author made his story suspenseful, consider how other authors create suspense as you read the selections in this unit.

5-1 Understanding the Big Question

Is it our differences or our similarities that matter most?

Our differences as people can be a cause for both celebration and frustration. Sometimes you may feel like another person is too different for you to relate to him or her. What do you find yourself doing next?

In this activity, you will think about how you can be unique and still find something in common with different people.

First, let's think about who you are. In the left column of the chart, list six of your personality traits. In the right column, explain how you demonstrate each personality trait. For example, if your trait is being outgoing, you might show it by talking to who ever seems shy in a group.

My Personality Trait	How I Show It

Now, let's think about how you can be different and still find something to connect to in others. Talk with your group members. Identify which group members share personality traits.

Each circle in the graphic organizer on the next page represents a group member. Write your names in the center of the circles. Complete the ring of circles so that each overlapping area identifies a trait you share with the adjacent group member. Put the traits that are unique to you in the center of your circle.

before reading your anchor book

Our Group: *Unique but Not Completely Different*

before reading your anchor book

Apply Many themes in literature stem from the conflict caused by differences between characters. These differences can be based on culture, experience, gender, and class. As you read your Anchor Book and the related readings, think about how differences cause conflict between characters. Are there important similarities that the characters cannot see?

Understanding the Big Question

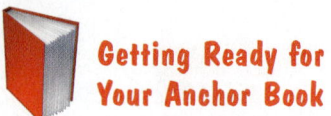

Getting Ready for Your Anchor Book

You will start reading your Anchor Book soon. The next few pages in this book give you some background information plus a reading skill.

Introduction to Drama

Before there were radios, movie theaters, televisions, DVDs, and computers, people watched drama for entertainment—and to learn more about the world.

Drama Tells a Story

Drama is one of many forms of storytelling. Unlike a novel or a short story, however, a play tells a story using only dialogue and action. There are some elements that are specific to drama.

Literary Terms

- A **drama** is a story written to be performed by actors. A drama is also known as a **play,** and the author is known as a playwright.

- A play is usually divided into large units called **acts.** Acts are often divided into smaller units called **scenes.**

- The story of a play is told through **dialogue,** the words the characters speak to one another. A **dramatic speech,** such as a monologue or soliloquy, is a long speech.

- **Stage directions** guide the performance of a play. These directions give background, indicate character movement, and tell about the sets, costumes, lighting, and sound effects.

- The director and production designers use the stage directions for the **staging** of the play. Staging includes all the elements that bring a drama to life, such as sets, costumes and props. **Sets** are the scenery, backdrops, and furnishings that create the setting of the action. **Props** are objects that are used onstage.

- Some plays are not performed live on a stage. A **radio play** is written for radio, and a **teleplay** is written for television. A **screenplay** is the script for a movie. A **dramatization** is a play that has been adapted from another source, such as a novel.

▲ Edward Scissorhands is the hero of a drama. Based on this picture, think of some of the positives and negatives of his predicament. Create a story based on either the positives or the negatives.

Drama shares the following elements with fiction and other forms of storytelling.

- The **plot** of a drama focuses on characters in **conflict.**

- The playwright must create characters whose actions are believable. **Character motivation** is the reason or reasons behind a character's behavior. Once we understand a character's motivation, we start to care about what happens to that character.

- The plot of a play creates **suspense,** the growing uncertainty we feel about what will happen. The **climax** is the point at which the suspense reaches its greatest intensity. The **resolution** occurs when the conflict is resolved. Every play should generate suspense about the outcome of the story.

Comedy and Tragedy

Plays are often divided into two broad categories based on the nature of this outcome. Comedy and tragedy are frequently just different ways of looking at the same problem.

- A **comedy** is a play that has a happy ending. Comedies often show ordinary characters in conflict with society. Although comedies are usually written to entertain, they can also point out human weaknesses or the faults of society.

- A **tragedy** is a play that ends with the downfall or death of the main character. In modern tragedies, the main character is usually an ordinary person. However, in ancient Greek and Shakespearean tragedies, the main character is always a person of great significance, such as a king or a hero.

Many plays contain elements of both comedy and tragedy. The best way to tell if a play is a comedy or a tragedy is to think about how it ends. If a play ends happily, it's a comedy. If it ends unhappily, it's a tragedy.

Directions In the following chart, identify some stories you have read or movies you have seen that are comedies and some that are tragedies.

Comedy	Tragedy

Introduction to Drama 373

5-2 Reading Skills
Cause and Effect

In learning new reading skills, you will use special academic vocabulary. Knowing the right words will help you demonstrate your understanding.

Academic Vocabulary

Word	Meaning	Example Sentence
perceive v. Related word: perception	to understand; to become aware of	The information you have affects how you *perceive* reality.
impact v. Related word: impacted	to have an effect on	The lack of available food will negatively *impact* the polar bear population.
influence v. Related word: influenced	to affect something	The politician hopes his advertisement will *influence* citizens to vote for him.

A **cause** is an event or situation that produces a result. An **effect** is the result that is produced. Identifying cause and effect helps you **perceive** the relationships among situations or events.

▶ **Look for a cause-and-effect relationship.** Pick one event or condition as a starting point. As you read, ask yourself, "Why did this happen?" or "How did this happen?" Examine how earlier events or conditions may have **influenced** the outcome.

▶ **Look for clue words.** Look for clue words, or transitional words, that signal causes and effects. Words such as *because, due to,* and *for this reason* signal a cause. Words such as *as a result, consequently, so,* and *therefore* can signal the effect.

Cause-and-effect relationships can sometimes form a chain. Effects can **impact** and become causes for further effects, and so on.

Cause	Effect/Cause	Effect/Cause	Effect/Cause	Effect
You wake up late on Monday morning.	You miss the school bus.	You are late to school.	You miss a quiz in first-period class.	You need to stay after school to take the quiz.

before reading your anchor book

Directions Read the following selection. As you read, follow the steps to identify cause and effect. Mark the text for clue words and phrases that signal causes and effects. Then identify two cause-and-effect relationships in the graphic organizer below.

Link to Science

Moving Plates of Rock

The uniqueness of New Zealand and Australia is the result of forces beneath Earth's surface. According to the theory of plate tectonics, the outer "skin," or crust of Earth, is broken into huge, moving slabs of rock called tectonic plates. These plates move independently, which sometimes causes them to collide and slide against one another. Australia, New Zealand, and the Pacific islands are all part of the Indo-Australian plate. Once, it was part of a landmass that included Africa. Then, several hundred million years ago, the Indo-Australian plate broke away. Consequently, at a rate of an inch or two each year, it moved northeast toward Asia.

As the plates moved, Australia and the Pacific islands moved farther from Africa. Over the centuries, small changes have occurred naturally in the animals and plants of Australia and the islands. For instance, many birds have lost the ability to fly, even though they still have small wings. Because Australia and the islands are so isolated, these animals have not spread to other regions.

Cause	→	Effect

Cause	→	Effect

before reading your anchor book

Cause and Effect 375

Now that you have learned about the reading skill of cause and effect, read the following article.

Guiding Question: **What can the Tuskegee Airmen teach us about dealing with unfair perceptions of differences?**

The Red Tail Angels

On July 2, 1943, German fighter planes surrounded 16 American bombers. The bombers had just attacked the enemy over Italy. Now the Americans were returning to their base in North Africa. Would they make it?

The swift German fighters closed in on the American bombers. Before the Germans could fire, however, the American fighter planes dived down on them. The lead German plane exploded in a ball of flames. The other German fighters were under attack, too. The crews of the American bombers sighed in relief. The Tuskegee Airmen, America's first African American combat pilots, saved the lives of the American bombers.

Left: Congressional Medal of Honor, U.S. Military Award
Below: Tuskegee Airmen in Italy, ca. 1944

Before the Tuskegee Airmen

Today there are many African American combat pilots. Before the Tuskegee Airmen, however, no African Americans had ever flown in combat. As in many areas of American life, African Americans had limited opportunities in the armed services.

Racial segregation was the official policy of the United States military. In a racially segregated society, people of different races are kept separate in their daily life and work.

In the navy, for example, African Americans could work only at kitchen jobs. The army accepted black and white volunteers, but soldiers of different races fought in separate units. The coast guard and marines, however, did not accept any African Americans in 1941.

As early as 1939, African American leaders asked President Franklin D. Roosevelt to desegregate the army. They wanted black soldiers to fight in the same units as white soldiers. Most white army leaders, however, were against such a plan. These officers tended to believe stereotypes about the races. The most general stereotype they believed was that all blacks were inferior in some way to white people. The white military leaders also thought that black and white soldiers would not get along in combat.

A Breakthrough at Tuskegee

As the war effort heated up, the demand for pilots grew. Some African Americans already knew how to fly. Others were ready and able to learn. They wanted to serve their country as pilots, but their country would not let them.

Black leaders pressured lawmakers to let African Americans fly. One African American pilot sued the government for the right to fly. In July of 1941, a breakthrough came. The army announced that it would open its first pilot-training school for blacks. During World War II, the Air Force was part of the Army.

The school would be at Tuskegee Institute in Tuskegee, Alabama. Tuskegee is a well-known college founded by Booker T. Washington. Since 1881, African Americans had studied science and technology there. Now the school would also train pilots.

Hundreds of African American men applied to enter the first flight-training classes. Many had college degrees from top universities. Their test scores on a qualifying test were so high that white officers suspected them of cheating. Forced to take a second test, they scored just as high.

Getting Into the Fight

In 1942, the first class of Tuskegee Airmen got their wings. More trainees were arriving at the Alabama airfield every month. They were all eager to defend their country.

The army, however, would not send the Tuskegee Airmen into combat. White military officials were prejudiced against the Tuskegee pilots. They had a low opinion of the pilots just because of their race. They also questioned their flying ability. Frustrated, the Tuskegee airmen felt like second-class citizens.

Things began to change when First Lady Eleanor Roosevelt, the wife of President Franklin D. Roosevelt, visited Tuskegee. She took a test flight with one of the Tuskegee Airmen. The visit created good publicity for the airmen. Newspapers and magazines took photos and wrote about the flight. People wanted to know where and when the pilots would be fighting. Early in 1943, the Tuskegee Airmen became the 99th Squadron. A typical squadron in the air force was a group of eight or more airplanes that flew and fought together. The all-black unit was under the leadership of Lieutenant Colonel Benjamin O. Davis, Jr. Davis would later become the first African American major general.

Lieutenant Colonel Benjamin O. Davis, Jr., was only the fourth African American to graduate from West Point.

Fighting in Tunisia

In 1943, the 99th Squadron was posted to Tunisia in North Africa. The 99th Squadron was finally an official member of the Allies, which was the group of countries, including the United States, fighting together in World War II. The Allies were fighting against the Germans and Italians in North Africa.

The Tuskegee Airmen's orders were to stop the enemy from delivering supplies to its troops. Part of their task was to bomb enemy trucks, tanks, and railroads and blow up bridges and fuel supplies.

It was a very dangerous assignment. The airmen had to fly deep into enemy territory to reach their targets. They also had to fly low, only a few hundred feet above the ground. That was the only way to hit small targets. Deadly enemy guns pounded away at them constantly.

The 99th Squadron did an amazing job. They blew up hundreds of supply trains and trucks. Without supplies, the enemy could not fight. Unfortunately the Tuskegee Airmen got little praise at first. There was still much bigotry, or narrow-mindedness, that they had to overcome.

We think of the Tuskegee Airmen as only pilots. For every pilot, however, there were Airmen soldiers supporting him on the ground. Some were airplane mechanics. Others maintained airfields. There were office workers, doctors, and cooks. Because the squadron was segregated, all of these support people were African Americans, too.

Tuskegee Airmen waving on gangway, 1945. The squadron was the first all African American combat unit activated as part of the 15th Air Force in Italy.

A New Assignment in Europe

Late in 1943, the Tuskegee Airmen were transferred to Italy. There the 99th Squadron joined the 332nd Squadron. This larger, all-black unit was given an important new assignment.

The United States was bombing enemy targets in Europe. Bombers, however, were large and slow airplanes. They could not maneuver easily. They flew out to their targets, dropped their bombs, and flew home. Along the way, they became easy targets for enemy fighter planes.

The job of the Tuskegee Airmen was to escort, or to follow along and protect, the bombers. When German fighter planes attacked, the 332nd Squadron had to fight them off. It was another challenging assignment. The Tuskegee Airmen would be going up against Germany's best pilots.

To identify themselves, the pilots of the 332nd Squadron painted the tails of their planes bright red. They called themselves "The Red Tail Angels." When an enemy pilot saw the red tails, he knew the message was "Try to get us!" When an American bomber pilot saw a red tail, however, he knew he would be protected.

The air fighting over Europe was fierce. In just ten months, pilots of the 332nd Squadron shot 136 enemy planes out of the air. Altogether the 332nd squadron flew 1,578 missions. They won 150 Distinguished Flying Crosses and 744 air medals. They received more medals than any other pilots in the war.

The Tuskegee Airmen had an impressive record. In all, they escorted thousands of bombers during the war. Yet few of those bombers were ever shot down.

The news of the Red Tails' skill got around. Their bravery became well known. When white bomber pilots flew a mission, they asked for the Tuskegee Airmen to protect them.

Top: African American cadets receive a salute
Right: Tuskegee Airmen Poster, 1943

A Job Well Done

By the end of the war, the Tuskegee Airmen had nothing left to prove. They had shot down hundreds of airplanes and destroyed more on the ground. They had sunk 40 enemy boats. They even sank a German destroyer, using just a machine gun. They were as good as any other pilots the military had ever seen.

Like all pilots in World War II, the Tuskegee Airmen had a high casualty rate. Many were killed or wounded in battle. Some 992 men had graduated from pilot training at Tuskegee. Of them, 150 lost their lives in combat or on training flights. Another 32 were shot down and held as prisoners of war.

The brave accomplishments of the Tuskegee Airmen helped President Truman make a decision. In 1948, Truman ordered the military to integrate black soldiers and white soldiers in the same units. Segregation would no longer be allowed. African Americans would finally get equal treatment in the armed services. In the end, this could be the greatest achievement of the Tuskegee Airmen.

Thinking About the Selection
The Red Tail Angels

1 **Analyze** Use causes and effects from the article to complete the graphic organizer.

Causes	Effects
	There were no African American fighter pilots before 1941.
	The American public learned about the Tuskegee Airmen and wanted them to join the fighting.
Bombers were big and slow and they could not maneuver easily.	
President Truman was very impressed by the Tuskegee Airmen.	

2 **Analyze** Consider the article's organization. How did the organization help you know where you could find why there were no African American fighter pilots before 1941? How does the organization serve the author's purpose of telling the story of the Tuskegee Airmen?

_____
_____
_____

3 **Compare** What does this selection have in common with *Operation: Conductorette*? Why is it important to know the time period in which these stories are set?

_____
_____
_____

Write Answer the following question in your Reader's Journal.

4 **Reflect** What can the Tuskegee Airmen teach us about dealing with unfair perceptions of differences?

Cause and Effect **381**

5-3 Vocabulary Building Strategies
Using a Dictionary

Although you shouldn't stop reading every time you encounter an unfamiliar word, sometimes it is a good idea to interrupt yourself and look up a confusing word in a dictionary.

You can find the following information in a print dictionary or online.

- the definitions of words
- pronunciation
- the part of speech of a word
- the word's etymology, or its origin

Here is an entry from a dictionary. Notice what it tells about the word.

> **anthology** (an THAL ə jē) ***n.***, *pl.* **–gies** [Gr. *anthologia*, a garland, collection of short poems < *anthologos*, gathering flowers <*anthos*, flower + *legein*, to gather] a collection of poems, stories, songs, excerpts, etc., chosen by the compiler

Etymology explains how words change, how they are borrowed from other languages, and how new words are invented. The symbol < means "comes from" or "is derived from."

1 Identify What is the word "anthology" derived from?

_____

_____

2 Interpret Why might the word for a collection of literature have originated from the word for a garland of flowers?

_____

_____

3 Locate You can find pieces of words in the etymology, too. One of the most important parts of a word is its root, the basic meaning of a word. Find the root of "anthology." What is the root's definition?

_____

_____

Idiomatic Expressions Dictionaries also provide information about idiomatic expressions. An idiomatic expression is a phrase that means something different from the combined meanings of its individual words. For example, "lay eyes on" is an idiomatic expression meaning "to see."

Directions Look up the word *gauntlet* in a dictionary.

1 What idiomatic expressions are associated with it?

_____

Analogies A dictionary definition is just one way of understanding a word's meaning. Understanding the relationship between two words leads to a higher level of comprehension. This is called **analogy**.

In an analogy, two things are compared because they have something in common. Sometimes these two things share a similarity; sometimes they are opposites. An example of analogy is *cinnamon* is to *spice* as *almond* is to *nut*. Here, the two things share a similarity, as both items belong to a larger group (cinnamon is a spice, and an almond is a nut). Now you have not only a definition of both words but also a higher level of understanding, as you have placed the words in a context.

Directions Complete each analogy by writing the best word in the blank. You may use a dictionary to look up unfamiliar words.

2 *Glass* is to *breakable* as *velvet* is to _____.
  soft   fabric   dress   shiny

3 *Bow* is to *arrow* as *pen* is to _____.
  ink   pencil   paper   write

4 *Car* is to *driver* as *stove* is to _____.
  food   chef   oven   cooking

5 *Pleased* is to *overjoyed* as *sad* is to _____.
  happy   angry   emotional   miserable

6 *Three* is to *six* as *four* is to _____.
  two   twelve   eight   double

7 *Cat* is to *cats* as *dog* is to _____.
  animals   dogs   pets   mammals

Good to Know! ▶
There are many types of dictionaries, such as this one for language learners.

before reading your anchor book

383

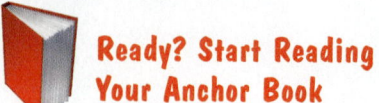

Ready? Start Reading Your Anchor Book It's time to get started. As you learn from this work text, your teacher will also give you reading assignments from your Anchor Book.

5-4 Literary Analysis
Dialogue and Stage Directions

Drama is a unique kind of storytelling because a play is written to be performed by actors in front of an audience. All the writing in a play is either dialogue or stage directions.

Literary Terms

- **Dialogue** is the words that characters speak. Dialogue reveals what characters are like and advances the plot.

- **Dialect** is the form of language spoken by people in a particular region or group. Dialects differ in pronunciation, grammar, and word choice.

- **Stage directions** tell where and when a scene takes place and how the characters move and speak. They also describe the sets, costumes, lighting, and sound effects. Sometimes they even explain what a character is feeling.

Directions Read the following selection, underlining dialogue and stage directions that reveal important information. Then, answer the questions.

from *Let Me Hear You Whisper* by Paul Zindel

Setting: *The action takes place in the hallway, laboratory and specimen room of a biology experimentation association located in Manhattan near the Hudson River.*

Time: *The action begins with the night shift on a Monday and ends the following Friday.*

Act I, Scene 1
(DR. CROCUS *and* MR. FRIDGE *are leaving the laboratory where they have completed their latest experimental tinkering with a dolphin, and they head down a corridor to the elevator. The elevator opens and* MISS MORAY *emerges with* HELEN.)

MISS MORAY. Dr. Crocus. Mr. Fridge. I'm so glad we've run into you. I want you to meet Helen.

HELEN. Hello.

(DR. CROCUS *and* MR. FRIDGE *nod and get on elevator.*)

MISS MORAY. Helen is the newest member of our Custodial Engineering Team.

(MISS MORAY *and* HELEN *start down the hall.*)

MISS MORAY. Dr. Crocus is the guiding heart here at the American Biological Association Development for the Advancement of Brain Analysis. For short, we call it "Abadaba."

HELEN. I guess you have to.

(They stop at a metal locker at the end of the hall.)

MISS MORAY. This will be your locker and your key. Your equipment is in this closet.

HELEN. I have to bring in my own hangers, I suppose.

MISS MORAY. Didn't you find Personnel pleasant?

HELEN. They asked a lot of crazy questions.

MISS MORAY. Oh, I'm sorry. (*pause*) For instance.

HELEN. They wanted to know what went on in my head when I'm watching television in my living room and the audience laughs. They asked me if I ever thought the audience was laughing at me.

MISS MORAY. (*laughing*) My, oh, my! (*pause*) What did you tell them?

HELEN. I don't have a TV.

---

1 Classify What different types of information do the stage directions provide? How did you find this information?

2 Infer What details from the dialogue suggest that Helen is not going to get along with the people at her new job?

3 Apply Writers often listen to the dialogue they hear every day and use it in their stories and plays. On a separate sheet of paper, jot down interesting lines of dialogue you hear. Think of ways you could use these words in your own writing.

Dialogue and Stage Directions

Character Motivation

"Why did she do that?" "What could he have been thinking?" There are times when someone's behavior makes us wonder what motivated the person to act that way. Characters in literature can make us wonder exactly the same thing.

Literary Terms

- **Character motivation** is the reason or reasons for a character's actions. One of the ways a writer creates believable characters is by making us understand all the different factors that motivate their behavior. A character's motivation may be external, internal, or both.

  - External motivation comes from external situations like poverty or danger. Example: *Dale looked for a new place to live after a fire destroyed his apartment building.*

  - Internal motivation comes from internal emotions like loneliness or jealousy. Example: *Clara insulted Alex because she couldn't stand the fact that he had won the speech competition.*

Often, a character's motivation is a combination of internal and external causes, such as fear in response to danger. Sometimes a character's motivation is directly stated, but usually the reader or audience must piece together clues.

Directions Read the passage and underline details that explain Eliza's motivation for visiting Professor Higgins. Then, answer the questions.

---

from *Pygmalion* by George Bernard Shaw

Background *A poor girl, Eliza Doolittle, arrives at the home of a famous professor of phonetics, Henry Higgins. The previous night he had boasted to Colonel Pickering that he could pass this girl off as a duchess by teaching her to speak proper English.*

THE FLOWER GIRL. Oh, we are proud! He aint above giving lessons, not him: I heard him say so. Well, I aint come here to ask for any compliment; and if my money's not good enough I can go elsewhere.

HIGGINS. Good enough for what?

THE FLOWER GIRL. Good enough for yə-oo.[1] Now you know, dont you? I'm coming to have lessons, I am. And to pay for em tə-oo[2]: make no mistake.

HIGGINS. [*stupent*[3]] Well!!! [*Recovering his breath with a gasp*] What do you expect me to say to you?

THE FLOWER GIRL. Well, if you was a gentleman, you might ask me to sit down, I think. Dont I tell you I'm bringing you business?

HIGGINS. Pickering: shall we ask this baggage[4] to sit down, or shall we throw her out of the window?

THE FLOWER GIRL. [*running away in terror to the piano, where she turns at bay*] Ah-ah-oh-ow-ow-ow-oo! [*Wounded and whimpering*] I wont be called a baggage when Ive offered to pay like any lady.

Motionless, the two men stare at her from the other side of the room, amazed.

PICKERING. [*gently*] But what is it you want?

THE FLOWER GIRL. I want to be a lady in a flower shop stead of sellin at the corner of Tottenham Court Road. But they wont take me unless I can talk more genteel.[5] He said he could teach me. Well, here I am ready to pay him—not asking any favor—and he treats me zif[6] I was dirt.

---

[1] **yə-oo** her pronunciation of "you"
[2] **tə-oo** her pronunciation of "too"
[3] **stupent** *adj.* extremely surprised
[4] **baggage** *n.* shamelessly bold girl or woman
[5] **genteel** *adj.* refined
[6] **zif** her pronunciation of "as if"

---

1 Identify Why does Eliza Doolittle come to see Professor Higgins? In other words, what does she want from him?

2 Analyze What is Eliza's motivation for making this request? Is her motivation internal, external, or both? Explain.

3 Interpret Eliza uses specific dialect in her speech. How does this language impact the plot and characters? How does it affect her motivation?

Character Motivation

Now you will apply what you have learned about dialogue and character motivation to a story.

Guiding Question: How does Mrs. Jones show Roger to have different expectations of himself?

Thank You, M'am
by Langston Hughes

Background *The author Langston Hughes (1902–1967) was born in Joplin, Missouri. As a young man he held a variety of jobs, including teacher and ship steward. He drew on these experiences when he wrote of the generosity of ordinary people—like Mrs. Luella Bates Washington Jones—who help other people realize that they do have dignity.*

Vocabulary Builder

Before you read, you will discuss the following words. In the Vocabulary Builder box in the margin, use a vocabulary building strategy to make the words your own.

    frail   contact   presentable   barren

As you read, draw a box around unfamiliar words you could add to your vocabulary. Use context clues to unlock their meaning.

Marking the Text

Dialogue and Character Motivation

As you read, underline important dialogue and descriptions that show the characters' motivations. In the margin, explain what the dialogue reveals.

She was a large woman with a large purse that had everything in it but hammer and nails. It had a long strap, and she carried it slung across her shoulder. It was about eleven o'clock at night, and she was walking alone, when a boy ran up behind her and tried to snatch her purse. The strap broke with the single tug the boy gave it from behind. But the boy's weight and the weight

388 Lesson 5-4

of the purse combined caused him to lose his balance. Instead of taking off full blast as he had hoped, the boy fell on his back on the sidewalk, and his legs flew up. The large woman simply turned around and kicked him right square in his blue-jeaned sitter. Then she reached down, picked the boy up by his shirt front, and shook him until his teeth rattled.

After that the woman said, "Pick up my pocketbook, boy, and give it here." She still held him. But she bent down enough to permit him to stoop and pick up her purse. Then she said, "Now ain't you ashamed of yourself?"

Firmly gripped by his shirt front, the boy said, "Yes'm."

The woman said, "What did you want to do it for?"

The boy said, "I didn't aim to."

She said, "You a lie!"

By that time two or three people passed, stopped, turned to look, and some stood watching.

"If I turn you loose, will you run?" asked the woman.

"Yes'm," said the boy.

"Then I won't turn you loose," said the woman. She did not release him.

"I'm very sorry, lady, I'm sorry," whispered the boy.

"Um-hum! And your face is dirty. I got a great mind to wash your face for you. Ain't you got nobody home to tell you to wash your face?"

"No'm," said the boy.

"Then it will get washed this evening," said the large woman starting up the street, dragging the frightened boy behind her.

He looked as if he were fourteen or fifteen, **frail** and willow-wild,[1] in tennis shoes and blue jeans.

The woman said, "You ought to be my son. I would teach you right from wrong. Least I can do right now is to wash your face. Are you hungry?"

"No'm," said the being dragged boy. "I just want you to turn me loose."

"Was I bothering you when I turned that corner?" asked the woman.

"No'm."

"But you put yourself in **contact** with *me*," said the woman. "If you think that that contact is not going to last awhile, you got another thought coming. When I get through with you, sir, you are going to remember Mrs. Luella Bates Washington Jones."

Sweat popped out on the boy's face and he began to struggle.

Mrs. Jones stopped, jerked him around in front of her, put a half-nelson about his neck, and continued to drag him up the street. When she got to her door, she dragged the boy inside,

---

[1] **willow-wild** *adj.* slender and flexible, like a reed blowing in the wind

Vocabulary Builder

frail
(frāl) *adj.*

Meaning

contact
(kän' takt) *n.*

Meaning

down a hall, and into a large kitchenette-furnished[2] room at the rear of the house. She switched on the light and left the door open. The boy could hear other roomers laughing and talking in the large house. Some of their doors were open, too, so he knew he and the woman were not alone. The woman still had him by the neck in the middle of her room.

She said, "What is your name?"

"Roger," answered the boy.

"Then, Roger, you go to that sink and wash your face," said the woman, whereupon she turned him loose—at last. Roger looked at the door—looked at the woman—looked at the door—*and went to the sink.*

"Let the water run until it gets warm," she said. "Here's a clean towel."

"You gonna take me to jail?" asked the boy, bending over the sink.

"Not with that face, I would not take you nowhere," said the woman. "Here I am trying to get home to cook me a bite to eat and you snatch my pocketbook! Maybe, you ain't been to your supper either, late as it be. Have you?"

"There's nobody home at my house," said the boy.

"Then we'll eat," said the woman, "I believe you're hungry—or been hungry—to try to snatch my pocketbook."

"I wanted a pair of blue suede shoes," said the boy.

"Well, you didn't have to snatch *my* pocketbook to get some suede shoes," said Mrs. Luella Bates Washington Jones. "You could of asked me."

"M'am?"

The water dripping from his face, the boy looked at her. There was a long pause. A very long pause. After he had dried his face and not knowing what else to do dried it again, the boy turned around, wondering what next. The door was open. He could make a dash for it down the hall. He could run, run, run, run, *run!*

The woman was sitting on the day-bed. After a while she said, "I were young once and I wanted things I could not get."

There was another long pause. The boy's mouth opened. Then he frowned, but not knowing he frowned.

The woman said, "Um-hum! You thought I was going to say *but,* didn't you? You thought I was going to say, *but I didn't snatch people's pocketbooks.* Well, I wasn't going to say that." Pause. Silence. "I have done things, too, which I would not tell you, son—neither tell God, if he didn't already know. So you set down while I fix us something to eat. You might run that comb through your hair so you will look **presentable**."

---

[2] **kitchenette-furnished** *adj.* having a small, compact kitchen

Vocabulary Builder

presentable
(prē zent′ə bəl) *adj.*

Meaning

◀ Painting by William H. Johnson (1901–1970). *Woman in Calico*, 1944

◀ **Critical Viewing**
How would you describe the personality of the woman in this portrait? How is she like Mrs. Jones?

In another corner of the room behind a screen was a gas plate and an icebox. Mrs. Jones got up and went behind the screen. The woman did not watch the boy to see if he was going to run now, nor did she watch her purse which she left behind her on the day-bed. But the boy took care to sit on the far side of the room where he thought she could easily see him out of the corner of her eye, if she wanted to. He did not trust the woman *not* to trust him. And he did not want to be mistrusted now.

"Do you need somebody to go to the store," asked the boy, "maybe to get some milk or something?"

"Don't believe I do," said the woman, "unless you just want sweet milk yourself. I was going to make cocoa out of this canned milk I got here."

"That will be fine," said the boy.

She heated some lima beans and ham she had in the icebox, made the cocoa, and set the table. The woman did not ask the boy anything about where he lived, or his folks, or anything else that would embarrass him. Instead, as they ate, she told him about her

Marking the Text

Dialogue, Stage Directions, and Character Motivation

Literature in Context
The Harlem Renaissance

In the Harlem neighborhood of New York City in the 1920s, a talented group of African American artists took part in a cultural movement. It was called the Harlem Renaissance, which means "rebirth," because it gave birth to new ideas and artistic achievements. Langston Hughes was one of its most important writers and thinkers. Other important contributions were made by musicians Bessie Smith and Duke Ellington, artists James Van Der Dees and Aaron Douglas, and writers Zora Neale Hurston and Countee Cullen.

▲ The Sam Wooding Orchestra, c1925.

job in a hotel beauty-shop that stayed open late, what the work was like, and how all kinds of women came in and out, blondes, red-heads, and Spanish. Then she cut him a half of her ten-cent cake.

"Eat some more, son," she said.

When they were finished eating she got up and said, "Now, here, take this ten dollars and buy yourself some blue suede shoes. And next time, do not make the mistake of latching onto *my* pocketbook *nor nobody else's*—because shoes come by devilish like that will burn your feet. I got to get my rest now. But I wish you would behave yourself, son, from here on in."

She led him down the hall to the front door and opened it. "Good-night! Behave yourself, boy!" she said, looking out into the street.

The boy wanted to say something else other than "Thank you, m'am" to Mrs. Luella Bates Washington Jones, but he couldn't do so as he turned at the **barren** stoop and looked back at the large woman in the door. He barely managed to say "Thank you" before she shut the door. And he never saw her again.

Vocabulary Builder

After you read, review the words you decided to add to your vocabulary. Write the meaning of words you have learned in context. Look up the other words in a dictionary, glossary, thesaurus, or electronic resource.

Marking the Text

Vocabulary Builder

barren
(bar′ ən) *adj.*

Meaning

Thinking About the Selection
Thank You, M'am

1 **Recall** Why does Mrs. Jones take Roger home? Use dialogue from the story to support your answer.

2 **Infer** Why doesn't Roger run away when Mrs. Jones lets him go?

3 **Predict** Has Roger grown as a person? What effect might his experience with Mrs. Jones have on his future behavior?

4 **Create** Look back at how you marked the text. Use these details to create stage directions in the margins of the story to show what the characters are thinking and feeling.

5 **Connect** Compare a historical figure who has similar motivations to Mrs. Jones.

Write Answer the following questions in your Reader's Journal.

 6 **Analyze** How does Mrs. Jones show Roger to have different expectations of himself?

 7 **Interpret** Think of a character in your Anchor Book who, like Roger, wants something he or she cannot get. How are this character's motivations similar to and different from Roger's? How do the time period and the culture influence each character's motivations? Now, compare the character in your Anchor Book to someone in your life. How are the motivations of the Anchor Book character similar to and different from those of the person you know?

Dialogue, Stage Directions, and Character Motivation

5-5 Language Coach
Grammar and Spelling

Participles and Participial Phrases

A **participle** is a verb form that is used as an adjective. Participles commonly end in *-ing* (present participle) or *-ed* (past participle). Some past participles are formed in irregular ways (for example, *broken, shaken, known, born*).

Present Participle   **Laughing,** the girl chased the the dog outside

Past Participle   The parents, **worried,** stayed at the hospital.

Sometimes you can combine two related sentences by changing one sentence into a participial phrase and adding it to the other sentence. A **participial phrase** is a group of words (or phrase) that begins with a participle and forms a unit of meaning. A phrase does not contain its own subject and verb.

Original   The suspect was arrested by the local police.
                The suspect cooperated with the authorities.

Combined   **Arrested by the local police,** the suspect cooperated with the authorities.

Directions Underline the participle in each sentence, and circle the word or words it modifies. Then, write *PrP* if the participle is a present participle or *PaP* if it is a past participle.

1 Mosaic artists set small pieces of colored glass or stone into mortar. _____

2 William Blake was one of the leading engravers of the 1800s. _____

Directions Combine each pair of sentences by changing one into a participial phrase.

3 The ancient Romans believed in many gods and goddesses. The ancient Romans developed a mythology.

_____

_____

4 The god of war was known as Mars. He was important in their mythology.

_____

> **Author's Craft**
>
> Reread page 390 of the selection "Thank You, M'am." One of the paragraphs begins with a participial phrase. Discuss what the participial phrase adds to the paragraph.

Sentence Combining with Gerunds and Participles

A **gerund** is a verb form ending in *-ing* that is used as a noun.

> **Playing** chess is Inara's favorite pastime.

Sometimes you can combine two related sentences by using a gerund or a participle.

Original	Kade enjoys hiking. She also likes to jog.
Combined	Kade enjoys hiking and **jogging**. [gerund]
Original	The kitten rubbed against my arm. It purred softly.
Combined	**Purring** softly, the kitten rubbed against my arm. [participle]

Directions Combine each pair of sentences using either a gerund or a participle.

1 The butterfly can be a graceful swim stroke. It has to be performed correctly.

2 Isaiah enjoys learning new swim strokes. He also enjoys practicing them.

3 Baby Jeremiah rarely cries. This makes his parents very happy.

Directions Combine each pair of sentences using a participle. Circle the word your participle modifies.

4 "The Tortoise and the Hare" is a fable about a race. It is well known.

5 The hare becomes too sure of himself. He stops to take a nap.

Sentence Combining

5-6 Writer's Workshop
Exposition: Manual

A **manual** is a short, focused piece of expository writing that offers guidance or information on a particular topic. Manuals focus on how-to topics. The writer breaks the process down into steps and explains them in the order in which they should be done.

If you buy a new game, bake cookies, or design a Web page, you probably refer to the how-to instructions. You might look at the features of each and the way they present information to get ideas for your own manual.

Your manual should include these elements.

- A focused topic that can be fully explained in the manual
- An informed tone
- A list of logical steps explained in chronological order
- A list of materials needed
- Transitional words and phrases to make the order clear
- Optional illustrations that help clarify the directions
- Error-free writing, especially the correct use of participles

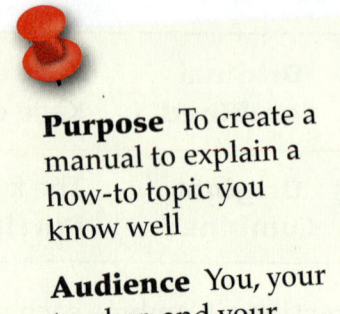

Purpose To create a manual to explain a how-to topic you know well

Audience You, your teacher, and your classmates

Prewriting—Plan It Out

To choose the focus of your manual, use the following strategies.

Choose your focus. Create a list of topic ideas. Use the list at right to help you think of ideas. Choose a topic from your list.

Topic Ideas
- sports
- activities
- things I can repair
- things I can cook
- crafts

Gather details. Complete the following spider web for your topic. Write your topic in the center and details in the ovals around it. Add more ovals as needed.

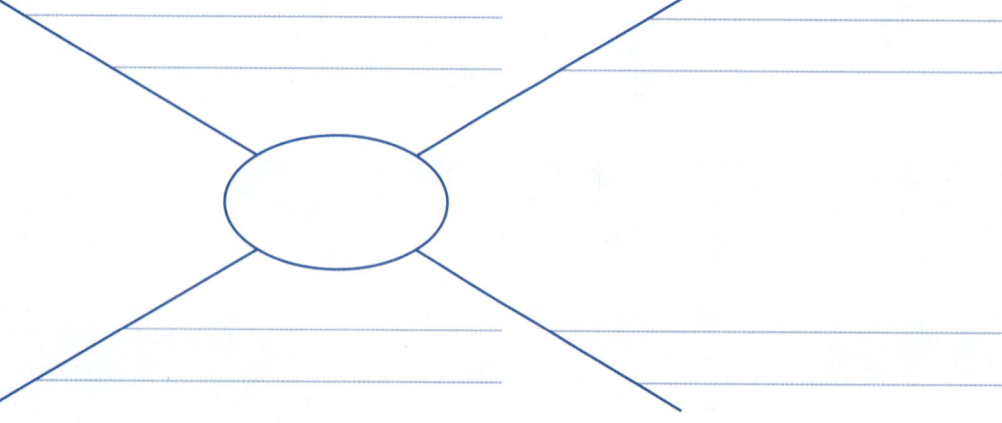

Lesson 5-6

Drafting—Get It on Paper

Using your spider web as an outline, write your first draft. The following steps will make your manual focused and clear.

Shape your writing. Create a chain-of-events organizer using sticky notes or note cards, so that you can arrange the steps in sequential order.

Provide elaboration. Make your instructions as complete as possible. Look for places to add details that show how much, how long, or how to complete a step. Circle any step that seems incomplete and then add the appropriate information. Add headings, bold face words, italicized words, or different fonts to emphasize your steps and to give your manual a technical format.

Revising—Make It Better

A great way to improve your essay is to insert transitions between paragraphs, passages, and ideas. Time words are words that show sequential order. They include words such as *first, later, next,* and *finally,* as well as phrases such as *in about an hour.*

Student Model: Inserting Transitions

> To begin,
> ^Use a volleyball that is heavier than normal. It will be harder at the beginning, but when you finally get your serve over it will be worth it.
>
> Next is the toss,
> ^The most important part of the serve ~~is the toss.~~

The writer added a few transitions to show time.

Use specific vocabulary. Include the names of specific objects. Replace general words with precise words that help clarify your instructions. Use a thesaurus to help you find the right words and add the words that fit best. Find two examples of general language from your draft and replace them with specific terms.

General	Specific
tools ⟶	spatula, whisk, eggbeater

Peer Review Have a group of people, such as classmates, adults, or community members, try to follow your how–to manual. Watch for any difficulties they have and revise your work if necessary.

Writer's Workshop continued

Directions Read this online how-to manual as a model for your own.

How to Spin a Pencil Around Your Thumb

Have you ever watched somebody in class or at the office skillfully twirl a pencil around his or her thumb and wondered how that person did it? Have you tried to do it on your own and found that it's not as easy as it looks? ==By following these steps and practicing—a lot—you can amaze curious onlookers with your brilliant pencil spinning, too!==

> The author focuses on how to spin a pencil.

Things You'll Need Pens or pencils. ==Unsharpened pencils are the best,== as they are long, moderately heavy, and perfectly balanced.

> The author identifies list of materials needed. Author explains best materials for the task.

Steps

1. ==First,== hold the pencil between your index, middle finger, and thumb. Your index and middle finger should be spaced about the width of your thumb apart (your thumb should be able to fit between your index and middle fingers). Your fingers should point upwards about 20-45 degrees. Your middle finger should be against the center of gravity of the pencil (towards the middle, slightly closer to the eraser).
2. ==Next,== fold your middle finger in (at the joint closest to your hand) and extend your index finger. Your middle finger should end up resting with the inside of its last joint on the thumb.
3. Catch the pencil after it wraps around your thumb and hits your middle finger, by moving your index finger back to its original position.
4. Practice this by holding the pencil in your non-dominant hand and guiding it around, so that you get a feel for how it should move. Also, the angle to hold your hand at varies from person to person. Experiment to find your preferred angle.

> Steps for spinning the pencil are presented in the order they should be done. Transitional words help make the order of steps clear.

Lesson 5-6

Editing—Be Your Own Language Coach

Review your draft for errors. Use patterns you have learned to check the spelling of difficult words. A grammar or spell checker can also help. Where you have added details to clarify and expand on your instructions, consider combining sentences using participial phrases.

Publishing—Share It!

When you publish a work, you produce it for a specific audience. Consider the following way to share your writing.

Publish your manual. Incorporate elements of spacing and design for graphics, such as tables, drawings, charts, and graphs, to enhance the appearance of your manual. Put it on display in your classroom or school library.

Give a demonstration. Demonstrate your topic by using props to show how to perform a process step by step.

Reflecting on Your Writing

Respond to the following questions on a separate piece of paper and hand it in with your final draft. What new insights did you gain about writing a manual? What did you do well? What do you need to work on?

Rubric for Self-Assessment Assess your manual. For each question, circle a rating.

CRITERIA	RATING SCALE
	NOT VERY VERY
IDEAS Is your manual focused? Does it include all the necessary instructions?	1 2 3 4 5
ORGANIZATION How logical and consistent is your organization?	1 2 3 4 5
VOICE Is your writing clear and engaging?	1 2 3 4 5
WORD CHOICE How appropriate is the language for your audience?	1 2 3 4 5
SENTENCE FLUENCY How varied is your sentence structure?	1 2 3 4 5
CONVENTIONS How correct is your grammar, especially your use of participial phrases?	1 2 3 4 5

Monitoring Your Progress
Standardized Test Practice

Reading Skills: Identifying Cause and Effect

Directions Read the passage. Then answer the questions.

> Few books have had as great an impact on American history as Harriet Beecher Stowe's *Uncle Tom's Cabin*. Published in 1852, the novel tells the story of a slave named Uncle Tom, who is cruelly treated by his overseer, Simon Legree. The book sold 300,000 copies in its first year, soon sold over 7 million copies worldwide, and was adapted into a play.
>
> Reactions to the book were dramatic. Northerners were horrified to read its descriptions of how slaves were mistreated, and the novel built support for the movement to abolish slavery. It intensified the conflict between the North and the South about slavery, which was one issue that led to the Civil War. It's been reported that when Abraham Lincoln met Stowe, he was only half joking when he said, "So you're the little lady who made this big war."

1 What does the passage focus on?
- A. several causes of the Civil War
- B. several effects of the Civil War
- C. the dramatic effects of one book
- D. the causes of Harriet Beecher Stowe's success

2 According to the passage, what was a result of the publication of *Uncle Tom's Cabin*?
- F. It intensified the conflict between North and South.
- G. It helped Stowe's political career.
- H. 7 million copies were distributed
- J. It caused the Civil War

3 What background information might help you link the causes and effects in the passage?
- A. President Abraham Lincoln and the Emancipation Proclamation
- B. the childhood of Harriet Beecher Stowe
- C. opposing views of Northerners and Southerners in the 1850s.
- D. what kinds of books Americans enjoyed in the 1850s

4 Which sentence in the passage prepares you to read about effects?
- F. sentence 2 of paragraph 1
- G. sentence 3 of paragraph 1
- H. sentence 1 of paragraph 2
- J. the quotation at the end

Literary Analysis: Elements of Drama

Read the following passage. Then, answer the questions.

> As she and Romero casually walked down the school steps, Ena prayed, almost begged her body not to shake out of her control like it had done too many times before. Not now, she silently told herself, with Romero here, right next to her. She didn't want him to witness the convulsions.
>
> "So," Romero asked, "what do you feel like doing?"
>
> Ena nearly said escape, but she knew Romero was genuinely interested in her. She had to tell him—but now?
>
> Ena looked at Romero, shrugged, then looked away.
>
> "Ena?" He asked. "Is something wrong?" He stopped walking.
>
> Ena glanced at the ground. "I," she said. "I didn't know if I should tell you…"
>
> "Ena?" Romero repeated, encouraging her to continue.
>
> Maybe she could tell him.
>
> "Romero," Ena began, "I have epilepsy." This was it, Ena thought. Romero would not want to be her friend because she was epileptic. Then he surprised her.
>
> "Please," Romero said, smiling. "I would like to know all about it."

5 Why doesn't Ena want Romero to witness her convulsions?

A. She is afraid he will make fun of her.
B. She is afraid she might injure him.
C. She is afraid he will not want to be friends with her.
D. She is afraid he will tell everyone else.

6 Which line of **dialogue** shows you that Romero is concerned for Ena?

F. "I would like to know all about it."
G. "I didn't know if I should tell you …"
H. "Is something wrong?"
J. "Ena?"

7 **Explain** in your own words what motivates Ena to tell Romero about her epilepsy.

_____
_____

Timed Writing: Response to Literature

Directions Think about a character from your Anchor Book. Think of an important action the character takes in the book. Then, write a paragraph explaining the character's motivation for taking this action. Tell whether this motivation was internal, external, or both.
(20 minutes)

5-7 Reading Skills
Drawing Conclusions

In learning new reading skills, you will use special academic vocabulary. Knowing the right words will help you demonstrate your understanding.

Academic Vocabulary

Word	Meaning	Example Sentence
assume v. Related word: assumption	to suppose to be a fact without proof	When we don't have all the information, we sometimes *assume* what the facts are.
evaluate v. Related word: evaluation	to judge; determine the worth or strength of something	*Evaluate* the evidence carefully before making a decision.
conclude v. Related word: conclusion	to decide by reasoning	What can you *conclude* from the details in the story?

Drawing conclusions means arriving at an overall judgment or idea by **evaluating** several details. A conclusion is often based on a series of inferences. By drawing conclusions, you recognize meanings that are not directly stated.

Asking the following questions can help you draw a conclusion.

- What details does the writer include and emphasize?
- How are the details related?
- What do all the details mean all together?

If you are reading a work of nonfiction, you might draw a conclusion about the **assumptions** the author is making or about information in the text. If you are reading a narrative or drama, you might draw a conclusion about a character's personality or about how the situation will turn out.

You can use a graphic organizer to record details and draw conclusions from them. Notice how details in the following passage help the reader to draw a conclusion.

> Dad looked out the window and smiled. I had never been so happy to see such a gray morning. The back steps were surrounded by small puddles, and the previously dusty field had turned a darker brown. Today everyone would be a bit lighter, not quite so afraid that this year's harvest would be another failure. For one day, at least, our prayers had been answered.

Detail	Detail	Detail
Puddles around steps, field darker brown	Dad smiled; everyone is a bit lighter	Not so afraid harvest would be a failure

CONCLUSION

I can conclude that it has rained for the first time in a long time, and people are happy because their fields need water.

Directions Read the following passage, and then answer the questions that follow.

KEVIN. What is that roaring sound? I've been hearing it ever since I got here.

LUIS. Roaring sound? [Listens] Oh, you mean that. That, farm boy, is the sound of the Pacific Ocean. And those crying sounds? Seagulls. And that blue thing over our heads? Out here we call it "sky."

KEVIN. Very funny, cousin. I never realized you live close to the ocean. You'll have to teach me how to surf, right away.

LUIS. Sure, Kev, but it's late. We've got all summer, after all. Let's take it easy today. I want to hear about your thousand-mile journey in a twelve-year-old car. What was your junior year like?

KEVIN. Can we at least wade in the surf while we talk?

while reading your anchor book

Drawing Conclusions 403

1. **Connect** Think about the details from the selection you just read. Consider how they are related. Write the details in the following graphic organizer and write a conclusion you could draw from the details.

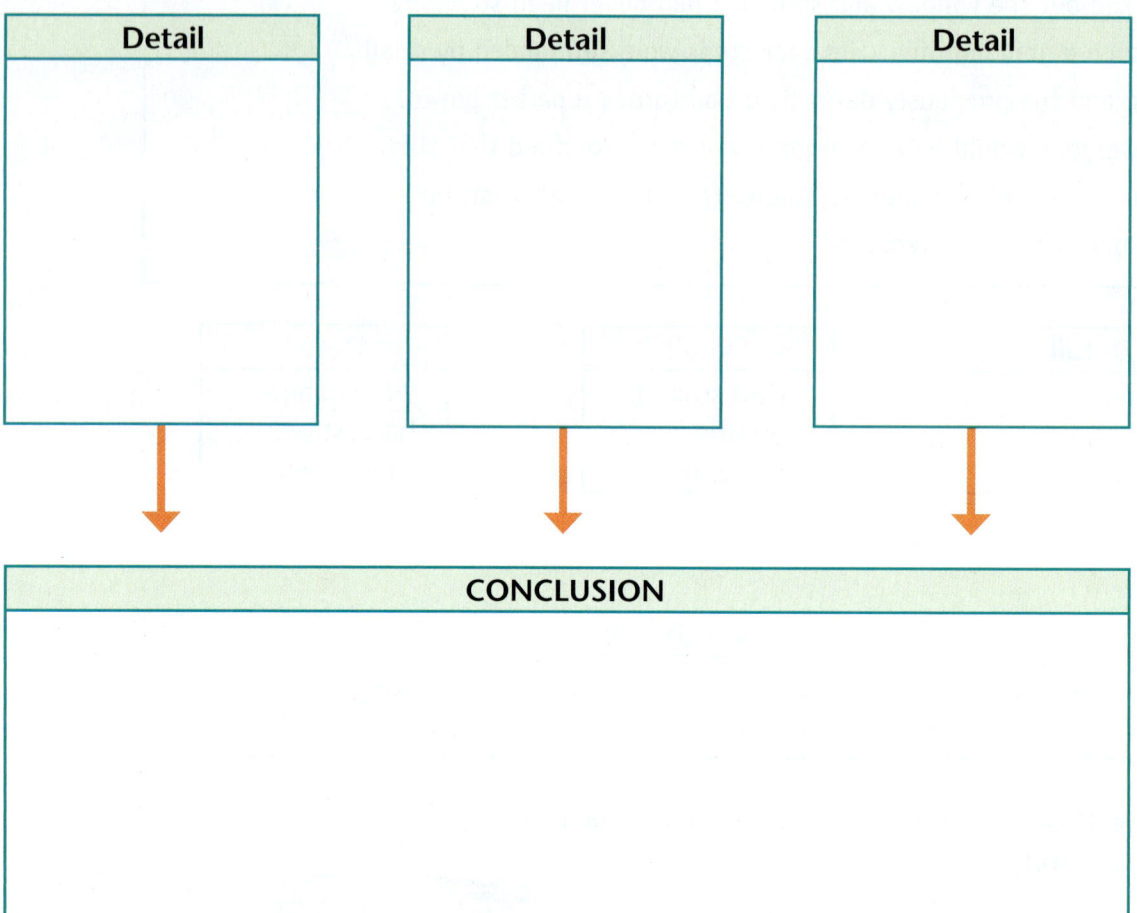

2. **Explain** How did the details you wrote lead you to the conclusion you drew?

_____
_____
_____

3. **Draw Conclusions** What conclusion can you draw about whether Kevin has visited Luis's house before? Explain.

_____
_____
_____

The way we perceive things can affect the conclusions we draw.
Guiding Question: How does the author show us that looking for the value in something different can help us learn about ourselves?

Golden Years

by Joel Achenbach

Link to Science

You've probably never pondered the aging process of the cockroach. You've never looked at a cockroach and thought: That one's a little long in the tooth.

Or: That one must be looking for the early bird special. No, you've thought: Where'd I put the Raid?

But a creature we find repulsive in ordinary life may help us solve some of the mysteries of human aging. Is getting old primarily a mechanical problem, a decrepitude in joints and muscles? Or is it a bigger problem located somewhere in our worn-out brains?

Roaches are good research subjects because they're big by insect standards, which makes it easy to study their relatively simple nervous systems. They don't require a lot of care either. You can chuck them in a plastic garbage bin, slather Vaseline around the rim to discourage escapes, toss them some dog food once in a while, and everyone's happy.

There are reasons roaches have been around for more than 300 million years. One is that they're fabulous at running away from danger. Although even the swiftest roaches only go three miles an hour, that's all the velocity they need to sprint to the nearest crack in the baseboard.

Cockroaches suffer from creaky joints too.

Christopher Comer, a neuroscientist at the University of Illinois at Chicago, studies roach escape behavior. "When you puff wind on a cockroach, it's off and running in 50 milliseconds," Comer says. "If you smack a roach's antenna abruptly, it can turn and run in 15 to 20 milliseconds. Quicker than the blink of

Drawing Conclusions 405

an eye." Compare that with a human, whose brain usually needs about 200 milliseconds (a fifth of a second) to respond to a stimulus.

But roaches, like all of us, get old. Angela Ridgel of Case Western Reserve University recently shot high-speed video images (125 frames per second) as roaches ran down a little hallway with a see-through floor. Ridgel discovered that about 60 weeks after its final molting, a roach starts to trip. The front legs literally snag on the middle legs. Old roaches also begin to slip while walking uphill.

Studies of escape behavior by Comer and Ridgel show another sign of roach senescence: When they get older, roaches react less reliably to being touched or hit by a puff of wind.

Sometimes they run; sometimes they just stand there.

In addition to aiding in the study of human aging, roach research can help the space program, Comer says. He points out that the roach escape mechanism has an admirable redundancy. The hairs on a roach's cerci, two rear appendages extending from the abdomen, are tied into one sensory system, but the antennae are tied into another. So the roach can operate with one system deactivated. In some experiments researchers remove the insect's head, and it still manages to get around.

"Suppose you wanted to build controlling circuitry for a rover on Mars," Comer says. "You might want to base the design on the kind of dual circuitry that insects use. With a simple nervous system roaches achieve rather sophisticated control."

And if the system breaks down, the engineers could blame it on a bug in the engine.

Bottom: Each wheel of this Mars rover has its own individual motor. The two front and two rear wheels also have individual steering motors (one each).

Far Right: Many senior athletes continue to exhibit high levels of mobility.

Thinking About the Selection
Golden Years

1 Recall What assumptions does the author make about his audience's perception of cockroaches? Support your answer with quotations from the article.

2 Define Review the words "senescence" and "appendages" from the last page of the article. What do you think these words mean? What context clues can help you guess their meaning?

3 Evaluate How well does the author structure and support his arguments? Cite specific examples of two conclusions the author makes and the support he provides for them.

Write Answer the following questions in your Reader's Journal.

4 Draw Conclusions How does the author show us that looking for the value in something different can help us learn about ourselves?

5 Apply How do differences cause conflict between the characters in your Anchor Book? Use details from the book to support your answer.

Ready for a Free-Choice Book? Your teacher may ask you if you would like to choose another book to read on your own. Select a book that fits your interest and that you'll enjoy. As you read, think about how your new book compares with your Anchor Book.

5-8 Literary Analysis
Suspense

Have you ever sat on the edge of your seat watching a play, or movie, wondering what would happen next? That nail-biting, edge-of-your-seat feeling is called suspense.

Literary Terms

- **Suspense** is the growing tension or uncertainty that the reader or audience feels about the outcome of events in a literary work. Writers use a variety of techniques to create suspense.

- **Foreshadowing** is the use of clues that hint at events that will occur later in the plot (see Unit 2). Foreshadowing helps create suspense by grabbing the reader's curiosity without actually giving the plot away.

- **Dramatic irony** is a contradiction between what a character believes is true and what the reader or audience knows is true. In a play, particularly a mystery or thriller, dramatic irony creates suspense by making the audience wonder whether a character will discover the truth before it is too late.

- The **climax** of a play or story is the moment when the suspense reaches its greatest intensity (see Unit 1). Suspense usually increases with the **rising action** of the plot, then winds down with the **falling action**. However, in some short plays and stories, the climax occurs at the very end.

Directions Read the passage, underlining details that create suspense. Then, answer the questions.

from *The Diary of Anne Frank*
by Frances Goodrich and Albert Hackett

Background *The Frank family and four other Jews are hiding from the Nazis during World War II. They are living in a secret annex in the attic of Mr. Frank's office building in Amsterdam, Holland. Mr. Kraler is an employee who protects the occupants of the secret annex. Margot is Anne's older sister.*

MR. KRALER. [*He rises*] If we could go downstairs . . . [MR. FRANK *starts ahead;* MR. KRALER *speaks to the others.*] Will you forgive us? I won't keep him but a minute. [*He starts to follow* MR. FRANK *down the steps.*]

MARGOT. [*With sudden foreboding*] What's happened? Something's happened! Hasn't it, Mr. Kraler?

[MR. KRALER *stops and comes back, trying to reassure* MARGOT *with a pretense of casualness.*]

MR. KRALER. No, really. I want your father's advice . . .

MARGOT. Something's gone wrong! I know it!

MR. FRANK. [*Coming back, to* MR. KRALER] If it's something that concerns us here, it's better that we all hear it.

MR. KRALER. [*Turning to him, quietly*] But . . . the children . . . ?

MR. FRANK. What they'd imagine would be worse than any reality.

[*As* MR. KRALER *speaks, they all listen with intense apprehension.* MRS. VAN DAAN *comes down the stairs and sits on the bottom step.*]

MR. KRALER. It's a man in the storeroom . . . I don't know whether or not you remember him . . . Carl, about fifty, heavy-set, nearsighted . . . He came with us just before you left.

MR. FRANK. He was from Utrecht?

MR. KRALER. That's the man. A couple of weeks ago, when I was in the storeroom, he closed the door and asked me . . . how's Mr. Frank? What do you hear from Mr. Frank? I told him I only knew that there was a rumor that you were in Switzerland. He said he'd heard that rumor too, but he thought I might know something more. I didn't pay any attention to it . . . but then a thing happened yesterday . . . He'd brought some invoices to the office for me to sign. As I was going through them, I looked up. He was standing staring at the bookcase . . . your bookcase. He said he thought he remembered a door there . . . Wasn't there a door there that used to go up to the loft? Then he told me he wanted more money. Twenty guilders more a week.

MRS. VAN DAAN. Blackmail!

1 **Analyze** How do the words and actions of the characters create suspense in the plot?

_____

_____

2 **Analyze** What dramatic irony is at work in this passage? How does it create suspense?

_____

_____

In this story, the author uses suspense to keep you wondering if the main character will survive. **Guiding Question:** How is Brian's struggle different from the experience of the average teenager? How is it the same?

FROM
Hatchet
BY GARY PAULSEN

Background The main character in the novel **Hatchet** is a thirteen-year-old boy named Brian Robeson. Traveling to visit his father, Brian is the only passenger in a single-engine plane that crashes in the Canadian wilderness, killing the pilot. In the following excerpt, Brian has found shelter in a cave and is struggling to light a fire.

Vocabulary Builder

Before you read, you will discuss the following words. In the Vocabulary Builder box in the margin, use a vocabulary building strategy to make the words your own.

tinder   exasperation   smoldered   gratified

As you read, draw a box around unfamiliar words you could add to your vocabulary. Use context clues to unlock their meaning.

Marking the Text

Suspense

As you read, underline details that build suspense in the story. In the margin, explain how the details you have marked create suspense.

His eyes opened and there was light in the cave, a gray dim light of morning. He wiped his mouth and tried to move his leg, which had stiffened like wood. There was thirst, and hunger, and he ate some raspberries from his jacket. They had spoiled a bit, seemed softer and mushier, but still had a rich sweetness. He crushed the berries against the roof of his mouth with his tongue and drank the sweet juice as it ran down his throat. A flash of metal caught his eye and he saw his hatchet in the sand where he had thrown it at the porcupine in the dark.

410 Lesson 5-8

He scootched up, wincing a bit when he bent his stiff leg, and crawled to where the hatchet lay. He picked it up and examined it and saw a chip in the top of the head.

The nick wasn't too large, but the hatchet was important to him, was his only tool, and he should not have thrown it. He should keep it in his hand, and make a tool of some kind to help push an animal away. Make a staff, he thought, or a lance, and save the hatchet. Something came then, a thought as he held the hatchet, something about the dream and his father and Terry, but he couldn't pin it down.

"Ahhh . . ." He scrambled out and stood in the morning sun and stretched his back muscles and his sore leg. The hatchet was still in his hand, and as he stretched and raised it over his head it caught the first rays of the morning sun. The first faint light hit the silver of the hatchet and it flashed a brilliant gold in the light. Like fire. That is it, he thought. What they were trying to tell me.

Fire. The hatchet was the key to it all. When he threw the hatchet at the porcupine in the cave and missed and hit the stone wall it showered sparks, a golden shower of sparks in the dark, as golden with fire as the sun was now.

The hatchet was the answer . . . Somehow he could get fire from the hatchet. The sparks would make fire.

Brian went back into the shelter and studied the wall. It was some form of chalky granite, or a sandstone, but imbedded in it were large pieces of a darker stone, a harder and darker stone. It only took him a moment to find where the hatchet had struck. The steel had nicked into the edge of one of the darker stone pieces. Brian turned the head backward so he would strike with the flat rear of the hatchet and hit the black rock gently. Too gently, and nothing happened. He struck harder, a glancing blow, and two or three weak sparks skipped off the rock and died immediately.

He swung harder, held the hatchet so it would hit a longer, sliding blow, and the black rock exploded in fire. Sparks flew so heavily that several of them skittered and jumped on the sand beneath the rock and he smiled and struck again and again.

There could be fire here, he thought. I will have a fire here, he thought, and struck again—I will have fire from the hatchet.

Brian found it was a long way from sparks to fire.

Clearly there had to be something for the sparks to ignite, some kind of **tinder** or kindling—but what? He brought some dried grass in, tapped sparks into it, and watched them die. He tried small twigs, breaking them into little pieces, but that was worse than the grass. Then he tried a combination of the two, grass and twigs.

Nothing. He had no trouble getting sparks, but the tiny bits of hot stone or metal—he couldn't tell which they were—just sputtered and died.

He settled back on his haunches in **exasperation**, looking at the pitiful clump of grass and twigs.

He needed something finer, something soft and fine and fluffy to catch the bits of fire.

Shredded paper would be nice, but he had no paper.

"So close," he said aloud, "so close . . . "

He put the hatchet back in his belt and went out of the shelter, limping on his sore leg. There had to be something, had to be. Man had made fire. There had been fire for thousands, millions of years. There had to be a way. He dug in his pockets and found the twenty-dollar bill in his wallet. Paper. Worthless paper out here. But if he could get a fire going . . .

He ripped the twenty into tiny pieces, made a pile of pieces, and hit sparks into them. Nothing happened. They just wouldn't take the sparks. But there had to be a way—some way to do it.

Not twenty feet to his right, leaning out over the water were birches and he stood looking at them for a full half-minute before they registered on his mind. They were a beautiful white with bark like clean, slightly speckled paper.

Paper.

He moved to the trees. Where the bark was peeling from the trunks it lifted in tiny tendrils, almost fluffs. Brian plucked some of them loose, rolled them in his fingers. They seemed flammable, dry and nearly powdery. He pulled and twisted bits off the trees, packing them in one hand while he picked them with the other, picking and gathering until he had a wad close to the size of a baseball.

Then he went back into the shelter and arranged the ball of birchbark peelings at the base of the black rock. As an afterthought he threw in the remains of the twenty-dollar bill. He struck and a stream of sparks fell into the bark and quickly died. But this time one spark fell on one small hair of dry bark—almost a thread of bark—and seemed to glow a bit brighter before it died.

The material had to be finer. There had to be a soft and incredibly fine nest for the sparks.

Vocabulary Builder

tinder
(tin' dər) *n.*

Meaning

exasperation
(eg zas pər ā' shən) *n.*

Meaning

Marking the Text

I must make a home for the sparks, he thought. A perfect home or they won't stay, they won't make fire.

He started ripping the bark, using his fingernails at first, and when that didn't work he used the sharp edge of the hatchet, cutting the bark in thin slivers, hairs so fine they were almost not there. It was painstaking work, slow work, and he stayed with it for over two hours. Twice he stopped for a handful of berries and once to go to the lake for a drink. Then back to work, the sun on his back, until at last he had a ball of fluff as big as a grapefruit—dry birchbark fluff.

He positioned his spark nest—as he thought of it—at the base of the rock, used his thumb to make a small depression in the middle, and slammed the back of the hatchet down across the black rock. A cloud of sparks rained down, most of them missing the nest, but some, perhaps thirty or so, hit in the depression and of those six or seven found fuel and grew, **smoldered** and caused the bark to take on the red glow.

Then they went out.

Close—he was close. He repositioned the nest, made a new and smaller dent with his thumb, and struck again.

More sparks, a slight glow, then nothing.

It's me, he thought. I'm doing something wrong. I do not know this—a cave dweller would have had a fire by now, a Cro-Magnon man would have a fire by now—but I don't know this. I don't know how to make a fire.

Maybe not enough sparks. He settled the nest in place once more and hit the rock with a series of blows, as fast as he could. The sparks poured like a golden waterfall. At first they seemed to take; there were several, many sparks that found life and took briefly, but they all died.

Starved.

He leaned back. They are like me. They are starving. It wasn't quantity, there were plenty of sparks, but they needed more.

I would kill, he thought suddenly, for a book of matches. Just one book. Just one match. I would kill.

What makes fire? He thought back to school. To all those science classes. Had he ever learned what made a fire? Did a teacher ever stand up there and say, "This is what makes a fire . . ."

He shook his head, tried to focus his thoughts. What did it take? You have to have fuel, he thought—and he had that. The bark was fuel. Oxygen—there had to be air.

He needed to add air. He had to fan on it, blow on it.

He made the nest ready again, held the hatchet backward, tensed, and struck four quick blows. Sparks came down and he leaned forward as fast as he could and blew.

Too hard. There was a bright, almost intense glow, then it was gone. He had blown it out.

Vocabulary Builder

smoldered
(smōl' dərd) v.

Meaning

Another set of strikes, more sparks. He leaned and blew, but gently this time, holding back and aiming the stream of air from his mouth to hit the brightest spot. Five or six sparks had fallen in a tight mass of bark hair and Brian centered his efforts there.

The sparks grew with his gentle breath. The red glow moved from the sparks themselves into the bark, moved and grew and became worms, glowing red worms that crawled up the bark hairs and caught other threads of bark and grew until there was a pocket of red as big as a quarter, a glowing red coal of heat.

And when he ran out of breath and paused to inhale, the red ball suddenly burst into flame.

"Fire!" He yelled. "I've got fire! I've got it, I've got it, I've got it . . ."

But the flames were thick and oily and burning fast, consuming the ball of bark as fast as if it were gasoline. He had to feed the flames, keep them going. Working as fast as he could, he carefully placed the dried grass and wood pieces he had tried at first on top of the bark and was **gratified** to see them take. But they would go fast. He needed more, and more. He could not let the flames go out.

He ran from the shelter to the pines and started breaking off the low, dead small limbs. These he threw in the shelter, went back for more, threw those in, and squatted to break and feed the hungry flames. When the small wood was going well he went out and found larger wood and did not relax until that was going. Then he leaned back against the wood brace of his door opening and smiled.

I have a friend, he thought—I have a friend now. A hungry friend, but a good one. I have a friend named fire.

Marking the Text

Vocabulary Builder

gratified
(grat' i fīed) v.

Meaning

Vocabulary Builder

After you read, review the words you decided to add to your vocabulary. Write the meaning of words you have learned in context. Look up the other words in a dictionary, glossary, thesaurus, or electronic resource.

414 Lesson 5-8

Thinking About the Selection
Hatchet

1. **Interpret** What is Brian's attitude toward his surroundings and the events that led him there?

2. **Identify** Briefly describe the exposition, rising action, and the climax of the story. What role do the exposition and rising action have in advancing the plot to its climax?

3. **Analyze** How does the author use details about the setting and tone to contribute to the sense of suspense? Cite specific examples.

4. **Infer** At the end of the selection, Brian states, "I have a friend now…a friend named fire." Why would Brian call fire his "friend"? What does this statement reveal about his character?

5. **Connect** What is the theme of this selection? How is it universal? Support your answer with details from the text and from your own experience.

Write Answer the following questions in your Reader's Journal.

6. **Respond** How is Brian's struggle different from the experience of the average teenager? How is it the same?

7. **Evaluate** Find a suspenseful event in your Anchor Book. Is the author successful in creating suspense? Use details from the text to support your answer.

5-9 Literary Analysis
Staging

Because plays are written to be performed in front of an audience, the playwright, director, set designer, and other members of the production staff must plan how the text will come to life onstage.

Literary Terms

- **Staging** is the act of putting on a play. It includes elements such as sets, costumes, props and lighting. The director and the production designers use the stage directions to help them stage a play, but often add their own ideas.
- **Sets** are the scenery, backdrops, and furnishings that create the setting for a scene or the whole play. Some plays feature realistic sets. Others are performed on a bare stage.
- **Props** are movable objects like books and lamps that are used onstage during the performance.

Directions The following passage is the opening of a one-act play. *Downstage* and *upstage* refer to the parts of the stage that are closest to and farthest from the audience. Read the passage, underlining details that help you visualize the staging. Then do the activity that follows.

from *The Dancers* by Horton Foote

[Scene: The stage is divided into four acting areas: downstage left is the living room of INEZ and HERMAN STANLEY. Downstage right is part of a small-town drugstore. Upstage right is the living room of ELIZABETH CREWS. Upstage left, the yard and living room of MARY CATHERINE DAVIS. Since the action should flow continuously, only the barest amount of furnishings should be used to suggest what each area represents. The lights are brought up on the drugstore, downstage right. WAITRESS is there. INEZ STANLEY comes into the drugstore. She stands for a moment thinking. The WAITRESS goes over to her.]

Create Imagine that you are a set designer. On a separate sheet of paper, sketch the layout of the stage as described in these stage directions. Include as many details as possible.

Dramatization

Have you ever read a novel, a short story, or even a newspaper article that you thought would make a great play or movie? Many playwrights have created their plays by dramatizing some other form of writing.

Literary Terms

- A **dramatization** is a play that has been adapted from another source. For example, Frances Goodrich and Albert Hackett adapted their play *The Diary of Anne Frank* from Anne Frank's actual diary, *The Diary of a Young Girl*.

- When you adapt another form of writing into a play, you need to think about how to present the same story using **dialogue** and **stage directions.** You also need to think about how **staging** will bring the dramatization to life for an audience.

Directions The following chart shows a letter and a dramatization based on the letter. Read both columns, and think about how the letter and dramatization are alike and different.

Letter	Dramatization
Dear Mom and Dad, My internship is going really well and I love D.C. You'll never believe what happened! Senator Ross sent me to the White House to pick up some documents. In the main hall, I saw Secretary of State Carson. You guys know how much I admire her, so I introduced myself and told her how I felt. She asked me if I worked in Washington, and I told her about my internship. Then, she asked me if I would meet her to talk about jobs in the State Department! I'll let you know how the meeting goes . . . Love, Carla	Scene 2. Main hall in the White House CARLA. [*shyly*] Secretary Carson! I so admire what you've accomplished at the State Department. SEC. CARSON. [*shakes her hand*] Why, thank you. Do you have a summer job here? CARLA. [*showing badge*] Yes, I'm working for Senator Ross on an environmental project, but I'd rather work in diplomacy or foreign service. SEC. CARSON. Well! [*looks at watch*] I'm on my way to a meeting, can you come to my office next Tuesday? Maybe I could suggest ways for you to work on that goal. CARLA. I am definitely available!

while reading your anchor book

1 **Analyze** How do stage directions help develop Carla's character in the dramatization? Explain.

_____
_____
_____

Directions The following chart lists some of the things you might need if you were dramatizing and staging the fairy tale "Rapunzel." Read the chart. Then, do the activity that follows.

Sets and Props	painted set showing tall castle or tower with one window high up, but no door or windows low to ground table, chair, jug of water, cup
Costumes	velvet or satin princess gown wig with long braid for Rapunzel's hair tunic, tights, and plumed hat for prince
Sound Effects	eerie, amplified voice of witch (she is never shown on stage) sound of sirens when witch arrives at castle or tower
Lighting	scary police searchlights when witch's voice is heard

2 **Apply** Write a one-act play on a separate piece of paper. Use the chart below to help you. Dramatize and stage a selection in this book or a chapter from an Anchor Book you have read for another unit.

Source	
Sets and Props	
Costumes	
Sound Effects	
Lighting	

Think about how you might stage a dramatization of this myth. *Guiding Question:* **How do the characters of Coyote and Eagle represent two different types of people?**

Coyote Steals the Sun and Moon

Zuñi Myth retold by Richard Erdoes and Alfonso Ortiz

Background The Zuñi belong to a group of Native American peoples known as the Pueblos. According to Zuñi beliefs, the Great Spirit and other sacred beings guided the people to their homelands, showed them how to plant corn, and taught them to live in peace with one another. Zuñi myths often involve the sun and the moon, as well as the mischievous character Coyote.

Vocabulary Builder

Before you read, you will discuss the following words. In the Vocabulary Builder box in the margin, use a vocabulary building strategy to make the words your own.

sacred   pestering   shriveled   pursuit

As you read, draw a box around unfamiliar words you could add to your vocabulary. Use context clues to unlock their meaning.

Marking the Text

Staging and Dramatization

As you read, underline details and events that seem essential to the story. In the margin, write notes about how you might dramatize and stage these elements of the story, and mark the text for scenes and acts, keeping in mind how their interrelationship advances the plot.

Coyote is a bad hunter who never kills anything. Once he watched Eagle hunting rabbits, catching one after another—more rabbits than he could eat. Coyote thought, "I'll team up with Eagle so I can have enough meat." Coyote is always up to something.

"Friend," Coyote said to Eagle, "we should hunt together. Two can catch more than one."

Staging and Dramatization   419

"Why not?" Eagle said, and so they began to hunt in partnership. Eagle caught many rabbits, but all Coyote caught was some little bugs.

At this time the world was still dark; the sun and moon had not yet been put in the sky. "Friend," Coyote said to Eagle, "no wonder I can't catch anything; I can't see. Do you know where we can get some light?"

"You're right, friend, there should be some light," Eagle said. "I think there's a little toward the west. Let's try and find it."

And so they went looking for the sun and moon. They came to a big river, which Eagle flew over. Coyote swam, and swallowed so much water that he almost drowned. He crawled out with his fur full of mud, and Eagle asked, "Why don't you fly like me?"

"You have wings; I just have hair," Coyote said. "I can't fly without feathers."

At last they came to a pueblo,[1] where the Kachinas[2] happened to be dancing. The people invited Eagle and Coyote to sit down and have something to eat while they watched the **sacred** dances. Seeing the power of the Kachinas, Eagle said, "I believe these are the people who have light."

Coyote, who had been looking all around, pointed out two boxes, one large and one small, that the people opened whenever they wanted light. To produce a lot of light, they opened the lid of the big box, which contained the sun. For less light they opened the small box, which held the moon.

Coyote nudged Eagle. "Friend, did you see that? They have all the light we need in the big box. Let's steal it."

"You always want to steal and rob. I say we should just borrow it."

"They won't lend it to us."

"You may be right," said Eagle. "Let's wait till they finish dancing and then steal it."

---

[1] **pueblo** (pweb' lō) *n.* Native American village in the southwestern United States.

[2] **Kachinas** (kə chē' nəz) *n.* spiritual counterparts of elements in the real world.

Good to Know! ▶ During annual ceremonies, dancers give religious figures made of cottonwood and cloth to children to help them learn about the different Kachinas.

Vocabulary Builder

sacred
(sā' krid) *adj.*

Meaning

while reading your anchor book

Lesson 5-9

After a while the Kachinas went home to sleep, and Eagle scooped up the large box and flew off. Coyote ran along trying to keep up, panting, his tongue hanging out. Soon he yelled up to Eagle, "Ho, friend, let me carry the box a little way."

"No, no," said Eagle, "you never do anything right."

He flew on, and Coyote ran after him. After a while Coyote shouted again: "Friend, you're my chief, and it's not right for you to carry the box; people will call me lazy. Let me have it."

"No, no, you always mess everything up." And Eagle flew on and Coyote ran along.

So it went for a stretch, and then Coyote started again. "Ho, friend, it isn't right for you to do this. What will people think of you and me?"

"I don't care what people think. I'm going to carry this box."

Again Eagle flew on and again Coyote ran after him. Finally Coyote begged for the fourth time: "Let me carry it. You're the chief, and I'm just Coyote. Let me carry it."

Eagle couldn't stand any more **pestering.** Also, Coyote had asked him four times, and if someone asks four times, you'd better give him what he wants. Eagle said, "Since you won't let up on me, go ahead and carry the box for a while. But promise not to open it."

"Oh, sure, oh yes, I promise." They went on as before, but now Coyote had the box. Soon Eagle was far ahead, and Coyote lagged behind a hill where Eagle couldn't see him. "I wonder what the light looks like, inside there," he said to himself. "Why shouldn't I take a peek? Probably there's something extra in the box, something good that Eagle wants to keep to himself."

And Coyote opened the lid. Now, not only was the sun inside, but the moon also. Eagle had put them both

Vocabulary Builder

pestering
(pes′ tər ing) *adj.*

Meaning

together, thinking that it would be easier to carry one box than two.

As soon as Coyote opened the lid, the moon escaped, flying high into the sky. At once all the plants **shriveled** up and turned brown. Just as quickly, all the leaves fell off the trees, and it was winter. Trying to catch the moon and put it back in the box, Coyote ran in **pursuit** as it skipped away from him. Meanwhile the sun flew out and rose into the sky. It drifted far away, and the peaches, squashes, and melons shriveled up with cold.

Eagle turned and flew back to see what had delayed Coyote. "You fool! Look what you've done!" he said. "You let the sun and moon escape, and now it's cold." Indeed, it began to snow, and Coyote shivered. "Now your teeth are chattering," Eagle said, "and it's your fault that cold has come into the world."

It's true. If it weren't for Coyote's curiosity and mischief making, we wouldn't have winter; we could enjoy summer all the time.

> **Vocabulary Builder**
>
> **shriveled**
> (shriv' əld) v.
> Meaning
>
> **pursuit**
> (pər so͞ot') n.
> Meaning

> **Vocabulary Builder**
>
> **After you read,** review the words you decided to add to your vocabulary. Write the meaning of words you have learned in context. Look up the other words in a dictionary, glossary, thesaurus, or electronic resource.

Literature in Context
Kachinas

The Kachina dancers mentioned in the story serve as links between the earthly world and the spirit world in the culture of the Zuñi and other Pueblo peoples, such as the Hopi. Every year, between late December and July, Pueblo men and women spend days apart in preparation for the ceremony. During the ceremony, dancers perform, wearing masks representing various supernatural beings, or Kachinas.

The dancers play a central role in Zuñi religion, where the blessings of the powerful spirits are sought every year for a good harvest and good fortune. Children are given miniature versions of the Kachinas made of wood and fabric, and special food is eaten. This old tradition is still observed by Pueblo peoples today.

Link to Humanities

Thinking About the Selection

Coyote Steals the Sun and Moon

1 **Interpret** What elements of nature does this myth explain? What lesson, or moral, regarding nature does the myth contain?

___

2 **Connect** What can you learn about Zuñi culture and beliefs from studying this myth?

___

3 **Interpret** Look back at the details and events you underlined and your notes in the margin. If you were dramatizing the myth, what staging ideas (sets and props, costumes and makeup, lighting and visual effects) could you add to your "scenes" to communicate important aspects of the original story?

___

while reading your anchor book

Write Answer the following questions in your Reader's Journal.

4 **Analyze** How do the characters of Coyote and Eagle represent two different types of people?

5 **Apply** Cast your Anchor Book. If you were going to stage a production of the play, who would play each role, and why? Support your answers with details from the text.

Staging and Dramatization 423

5-10 Comparing Literary Works
Dramatic Speeches

Sometimes a playwright interrupts the regular flow of conversation in a play to have a character deliver a dramatic speech. In a dramatic speech, a character might speak directly to another character, or the audience might get the feeling that it is overhearing a character's innermost secrets.

Literary Terms

- A **dramatic speech** is a speech or remark that a character makes during a play. There are three types of dramatic speech: a monologue, a soliloquy, and an aside.

- A **monologue** is a long speech by one character that is addressed to another character or characters. Sometimes a character addresses a monologue directly to the audience.

- A **soliloquy** is a long speech in which a character reveals private thoughts and feelings to the audience. This character is usually alone on stage, and the audience feels as if it is overhearing someone thinking out loud.

- An **aside** is a brief remark that a character directs privately to the audience or to another character. The other characters on stage do not hear this remark.

Directions The following passage is a monologue spoken by a girl who is struggling to fit into a new culture. Read the passage, and then answer the questions that follow.

from FOB by David Henry Hwang

GRACE. Yeah, it's tough trying to live in Chinatown. But it's tough trying to live in Torrance, too. It's true. I don't like being alone. You know, when Mom could finally bring me to the U.S., I was already ten. But I never studied my English very hard in Taiwan, so I got moved back to the second grade. There were a few Chinese girls in the fourth grade, but they were American-born, so they wouldn't even talk to me. They'd just stay with themselves and compare how much clothes they all had, and make fun of the way we all talked.

I figured I had a better chance of getting in with the white kids than with them, so in junior high I started bleaching my hair and hanging out at the beach—you know, Chinese hair looks pretty lousy when you bleach it. After a while, I knew what beach was gonna be good on any given day, and I could tell who was coming just by his van. But the American-born Chinese, it didn't matter to them. They just giggled and went to their own dances. Until my senior year in high school—that's how long it took me to get over this whole thing. One night I took Dad's car and drove on Hollywood Boulevard, all the way from downtown to Beverly Hills, then back on Sunset. I was looking and listening—all the time with the window down, just so I'd feel like I was part of the city. And that Friday, it was—I guess—I said, "I'm lonely. And I don't like it. I don't like being alone." And that was all. As soon as I said it, I felt all of the breeze—it was really cool on my face—and I heard all of the radio—and the music sounded really good, you know? So I drove home.

1 **Analyze** What emotions does the narrator reveal in this passage? Why does the narrator feel this way? Support your answer with evidence from the passage.

2 **Evaluate** How does the monologue form emphasize the narrator's feelings?

3 **Contrast** How is this character's experience specific to a time and place? How is it universal?

Dramatic Speeches 425

Compare the monologues in *The Piano Lesson* and *A Raisin in the Sun.* **Guiding Question:** How does each monologue help emphasize the speaker's differentness?

from

The PIANO LESSON

by August Wilson

Background Set in 1936, The Piano Lesson is part of August Wilson's cycle of ten plays exploring the African American experience in the twentieth century. In this excerpt, Boy Willie is arguing with his sister Berniece about an ornately carved family piano that he wants to sell. Boy Willie wants to use the money from the sale of the piano to buy the Mississippi land where his family once worked as slaves.

Vocabulary Builder

Before you read, you will discuss the following words. In the Vocabulary Builder box in the margin, use a vocabulary building strategy to make the words your own

    shrivel   sentimental

As you read, draw a box around unfamiliar words you could add to your vocabulary. Use context clues to unlock their meaning.

Marking the Text

Dramatic Speeches

As you read, underline details in the dialogue and monologue that reveal the conflict between Boy Willie and Berniece. In the margins, explain what these details mean.

BERNIECE. … Now set that piano back over there. I done told you a hundred times I ain't selling that piano.

BOY WILLIE. I'm trying to get me some land, woman. I need that piano to get me some money so I can buy Sutter's land.

426 Lesson 5-10

BERNIECE. Money can't buy what that piano cost. You can't sell your soul for money. It won't go with the buyer. It'll **shrivel** and shrink to know that you ain't taken on to it. But it won't go with the buyer.

BOY WILLIE. I ain't talking about all that, woman. I ain't talking about selling my soul. I'm talking about trading that piece of wood for some land. Get something under your feet. Land the only thing God ain't making no more of. You can always get you another piano. I'm talking about some land. What you get something out the ground from. That's what I'm talking about. You can't do nothing with that piano but sit up there and look at it.

BERNIECE. That's just what I'm gonna do. Whining Boy, you want me to fry you some pork chops?

BOY WILLIE. Now, I'm gonna tell you the way I see it. The only thing that make that piano worth something is them carvings Papa Willie Boy put on there. That's what make it worth something. That was my great-grandaddy. Papa Boy Charles

Vocabulary Builder

shrivel
(shriv' əl) *v.*

Meaning

brought that piano into the house. Now, I'm supposed to build on what they left me. You can't do nothing with that piano sitting up here in the house. That's just like if I let them watermelons sit out there and rot. I'd be a fool. Alright now, if you say to me, Boy Willie, I'm using that piano. I give out lessons on it and that help me make my rent or whatever. Then that be something else. I'd have to go on and say, well, Berniece using that piano. She building on it. Let her go on and use it. I got to find another way to get Sutter's land. But Doaker say you ain't touched that piano the whole time it's been up here. So why you wanna stand in my way? See, you just looking at the **sentimental** value. See, that's good. That's alright. I take my hat off whenever somebody say my daddy's name. But I ain't gonna be no fool about no sentimental value. You can sit up here and look at the piano for the next hundred years and it's just gonna be a piano. You can't make more than that. Now I want to get Sutter's land with that piano. I get Sutter's land and I can go down and cash in the crop and get my seed. As long as I got the land and the seed then I'm alright. I can always get me a little something else. Cause that land give back to you. I can make me another crop and cash that in. I still got the land and the seed. But that piano don't put out nothing else. You ain't got nothing working for you. Now, the kind of man my daddy was he would have understood that. I'm sorry you can't see it that way. But that's why I'm gonna take that piano out of here and sell it.

BERNIECE. You ain't taking that piano out of my house.

[She crosses to the piano.]

Look at this piano. Look at it. Mama Ola polished this piano with her tears for seventeen years. For seventeen years she rubbed on it till her hands bled. Then she rubbed the blood in…mixed it up with the rest of the blood on it. Every day that God breathed life into her body she rubbed and cleaned and polished and prayed over it. "Play something for me, Berniece. Play something for me, Berniece." Every day. "I cleaned it up for you, play something for me, Berniece." You always talking about your daddy but you ain't never stopped to look at what his foolishness cost your mama. . . .

Marking the Text

Vocabulary Builder

sentimental
(sen tə ment' 'l) *adj.*

Meaning

Vocabulary Builder

After you read, review the words you decided to add to your vocabulary. Write the meaning of words you have learned in context. Look up the other words in a dictionary, glossary, thesaurus, or electronic resource.

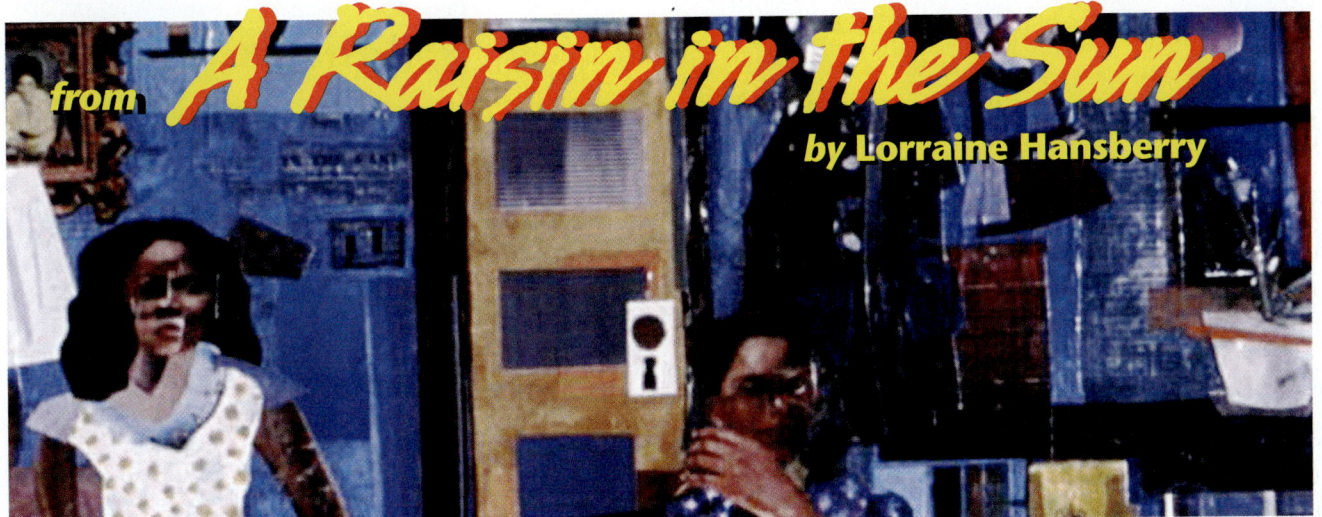

from A Raisin in the Sun
by Lorraine Hansberry

Background *A Raisin in the Sun chronicles the struggles and dreams of an African American family living in Chicago during the 1950s. In this excerpt, Walter, a man in his mid-thirties, has just learned that his mother is going to give him part of her insurance settlement money to start a business. Travis is Walter's son.*

Vocabulary Builder

Before you read, you will discuss the following words. In the Vocabulary Builder box in the margin, use a vocabulary building strategy to make the words your own.

    transaction   **hysterical**

As you read, draw a box around unfamiliar words you could add to your vocabulary. Use context clues to unlock their meaning.

Marking the Text

Dramatic Speeches

As you read, underline details in the dialogue and monologue that reveal Walter's character. In the margin, write notes about what Walter is trying to tell Travis and how he wants his son to perceive him.

TRAVIS. Well, good night, Daddy.

[*The father has come from behind the couch and leans over, embracing his son*]

WALTER. Son, I feel like talking to you tonight.

TRAVIS. About what?

WALTER. Oh, about a lot of things. About you and what kind of man you going to be when you grow up…. Son—son, what do you want to be when you grow up?

TRAVIS. A bus driver.

WALTER. [*Laughing a little*] A what? Man, that ain't nothing to want to be!

TRAVIS. Why not?

WALTER. 'Cause, man—it ain't big enough—you know what I mean.

TRAVIS. I don't know then. I can't make up my mind. Sometimes Mama asks me that too. And sometimes when I tell her I just want to be like you—she says she don't want me to be like that and sometimes she says she does….

WALTER. [*Gathering him up in his arms*] You know what, Travis? In seven years you going to be seventeen years old. And things is going to be very different with us in seven years, Travis…. One day when you are seventeen I'll come home—home from my office downtown somewhere—

TRAVIS. You don't work in no office, Daddy.

WALTER. No—but after tonight. After what your daddy gonna do tonight, there's going to be offices—a whole lot of offices….

TRAVIS. What you gonna do tonight, Daddy?

WALTER. You wouldn't understand yet, son, but your daddy's gonna make a **transaction** … a business transaction that's going to change our lives…. That's how come one day when you 'bout seventeen years old I'll come home and I'll be pretty tired, you know what I mean, after a day of conferences and secretaries getting things wrong the way they do…'cause an executive's life is hell, man—[*The more he talks the farther away he gets.*] And

Vocabulary Builder

transaction
(tran zak' shən) *n.*

Meaning

◀ **Critical Viewing**
How does this collage, by artist Chandra Dieppa Ortiz, match your vision of the characters?

I'll pull the car up on the driveway…just a plain black Chrysler, I think, with white walls—no—black tires. More elegant. Rich people don't have to be flashy…though I'll have to get something a little sportier for Ruth—maybe a Cadillac convertible to do her shopping in…. And I'll come up the steps to the house and the gardener will be clipping away at the hedges and he'll say, "Good evening, Mr. Younger." And I'll say, "Hello, Jefferson, how are you this evening?" And I'll go inside and Ruth will come downstairs and meet me at the door and we'll kiss each other and she'll take my arm and we'll go up to your room to see you sitting on the floor with the catalogues of all the great schools in America around you…. All the great schools in the world! And—and I'll say, all right son—it's your seventeenth birthday, what is it you've decided?… Just tell me where you want to go to school and you'll *go*. Just tell me, what it is you want to be—and you'll *be* it…. Whatever you want to be—Yessir! [*He holds his arms open for Travis*] You just name it, son… [*Travis leaps into them*] and I hand you the world!

[*Walter's voice has risen in pitch and* **hysterical** *promise and on the last line he lifts Travis high*]

Marking the Text

Vocabulary Builder

After you read, review the words you decided to add to your vocabulary. Write the meaning of words you have learned in context. Look up the other words in a dictionary, glossary, thesaurus, or electronic resource.

Vocabulary Builder

hysterical
(hi ster′ i kal) *adj.*

Meaning

Lorraine Hansberry
(1930-1965)

Lorraine Hansberry was born in Chicago, the youngest of four children in an activist family that fought to end segregation decades before the civil rights movement. Hansberry drew on her family's experience of desegregating a white neighborhood in her first play, *A Raisin in the Sun*.

When *A Raisin in the Sun* opened in 1959, it made theatrical history because it was the first play by an African American woman to be produced on Broadway. It also won the New York Drama Critic's Circle Award as Best Play of the Year, making Hansberry the youngest American and the first African American to earn this prestigious honor. Hansberry's early success as a playwright was cut tragically short when she died of cancer at the age of 34.

Dramatic Speeches

The following poem inspired the title of *A Raisin in the Sun*. Read the poem and identify its theme.

Theme _____

Harlem
by Langston Hughes

What happens to a dream deferred?
Does it dry up
like a raisin in the sun?
Or fester like a sore—
And then run?
Does it stink like rotten meat?
Or crust and sugar over—
like a syrupy sweet?

Maybe it just sags
like a heavy load.

Or does it explode?

Thinking About the Selections

from *The Piano Lesson*, from *A Raisin in the Sun*, and Harlem

1 **Analyze** In the excerpt from *A Raisin in the Sun*, why does Walter ask his son what he wants to be when he grows up? What is Walter's dream for his son?

2 **Interpret** In the excerpt from *The Piano Lesson*, explain the different attitudes that Willie Boy and Berniece have toward the piano. Why does Willie Boy dream of owning land? Why does Berniece believe that he doesn't understand the value of the piano?

3 **Compare and Contrast** Both Hansberry and Wilson use the form of the monologue to convey the intense feelings of their characters. Compare and contrast the way Walter in *A Raisin in the Sun* and Willie Boy in *The Piano Lesson* express their dreams in these excerpts. What similarities and differences do you see between their dreams?

4 **Connect** How does the dialogue of each play connect to the Langston Hughes poem "Harlem"?

Write Answer the following questions in your Reader's Journal.

5 **Evaluate** How does each monologue help emphasize the speaker's differentness?

6 **Synthesize** Identify a character in your Anchor Book who has something important to say, but is not being heard. Write a soliloquy for that character, and recite it to the class.

5-11 Listening and Speaking Workshop
Reading Drama Aloud

In this activity, you and your group members will prepare and present a scene from your Anchor Book. You will pay special attention to dialogue delivery, stage directions, and setting.

Your Tasks

- Work with your group to choose a scene from your Anchor Book to present to the class.
- Work with your group to prepare and rehearse the scene.
- Present your prepared scene to the class.

Organize and Present Your Scene

1. Choose a scene.

- Choose a scene from your Anchor Book that everyone in your group can participate in. Pick a scene that will be interesting for your audience to watch.
- Reread the scene and discuss how you might convey the meaning through gestures, visuals, and tone. Review sentence structure and punctuation to help understand unclear dialogue. Pay attention to how dialect, if used, reveals character.

2. Prepare the scene.

- Work with your group to assign a role to each member. All group members need to be speaking participants, so divide work accordingly.
- Imagine how your character feels so you can portray your character's emotions when performing.

3. Create a visual for your audience.

- Decide with your group what the set should look like.
- Use visuals to support your performance and props to make the setting more realistic.

4. Rehearse your presentation.

- Practice the scene together. Decide how you will deliver your lines and follow stage directions.

- Adjust your pitch, volume, pacing, and tone based on the characters and action. Use punctuation in the script to guide your expression. Remember that the way you present your scene will affect your audience's interpretation.

- Rehearse your lines until you can speak with ease and control. Monitor yourself as you read. If you lose your place or mispronounce a word, correct yourself and continue with your presentation.

Speak: Rubric for Oral Interpretation

Assess your performance. For each question, circle a rating.

CRITERIA	RATING SCALE
CONTENT How well did the group's presentation reflect the content of the scene?	NOT VERY VERY 1 2 3 4 5
ORGANIZATION How organized was the group when presenting their scene? For example, did the group members follow stage directions and know when it was their turn to speak?	1 2 3 4 5
DELIVERY How well did the group demonstrate eye contact, pitch, volume, pacing, and tone appropriate to the characters?	1 2 3 4 5
COOPERATION How well did the group work together?	1 2 3 4 5

Listen: Rubric for Audience Self-Assessment

Assess your role as an audience. For each question, circle a rating.

CRITERIA	RATING SCALE
ACTIVE LISTENING How well did you focus your attention on the performance and listen for the meaning of the scene?	NOT VERY VERY 1 2 3 4 5
ACTIVE LISTENING How well did you demonstrate active listening with appropriate silence, responses, and body language?	1 2 3 4 5

Interpret How did the performers' body language, expressions, and silences help you listen for unspoken meanings in the scene?

5-12 Language Coach
Grammar and Spelling

Independent and Subordinate Clauses

A **clause** is a group of words that has a subject and a verb. An **independent clause** expresses a complete thought and can stand by itself as a complete sentence. A **subordinate clause** cannot stand by itself as a sentence because it does not express a complete thought. Subordinate clauses begin with **subordinating conjunctions** such as *since, that, until, which, because, although, when, if, after,* and *before.*

In the following examples, the subjects are underlined once, and the verbs are underlined twice.

Independent Clause	the letters were old and dusty [complete thought] The letters were old and dusty. [stands alone as a sentence]
Subordinate Clauses	that Judy found in the attic [incomplete thought] if they had been written by her grandfather [incomplete thought] when he was courting her grandmother [incomplete thought]

Each of the following sentences has both an independent clause and a subordinate clause. The subordinate clauses are in bold.

> The letters **that Judy found in the attic** were old and dusty.
> She wondered **if they had been written by her grandfather.**
> **When he was courting her grandmother,** he had sent her some love letters.

Directions Underline each independent clause once and each subordinate clause twice.

1. Mammals that bear extremely underdeveloped offspring are called marsupials.

2. Kangaroos are in the macropodidae family, which also includes wallabies.

3. The Israel Museum, which is found in West Jerusalem, displays artifacts dating back to prehistoric man, and the museum has an online exhibit.

4. Because Israelites picked up many customs from the Egyptians, idols and extravagant jewelry are also on display; some of these artifacts date back to the time of Moses.

Author's Craft

Good writers use subordinate clauses to add description and avoid too many short choppy sentences. Scan page 421 of the selection "Coyote Steals the Sun and the Moon" for three subordinate clauses. Rewrite them as complete sentences. Does the passage work best with shorter sentences or sentences with subordinate clauses? Explain why.

Sentence Combining with Subordinate Clauses

Writing that has mostly short sentences sounds choppy and dull. You can combine short sentences into longer ones to make your writing smoother and more interesting.

First, make sure the two sentences are related. Then, rewrite the less important idea as a subordinate clause, and add it to the other sentence. Make sure the word you use to begin your subordinate clause shows the correct relationship between the two ideas.

Subordinate clauses can be divided into three types. A **noun clause** answers questions like *who(m)?* or *what?*. An **adjective clause** answers questions like *which (one)?*. An **adverb clause** answers questions like *when?*, *where?*, *why?*, *with what goal/result?*, and *under what conditions?*.

Original	Nathan finished his homework. Then, he took a bike ride.
Combined	**After Nathan finished his homework,** he took a bike ride. [The adverb clause shows a time relationship.]
Original	The bicycle is broken. Nathan has been riding it for years.
Combined	The bicycle **that Nathan has been riding for years** is broken. [The adjective clause tells which bicycle is broken.]

Directions Combine each pair of sentences by changing one sentence into a subordinate clause and adding it to the other. Use the subordinating conjunction in parentheses to begin your subordinate clause. Then, identify the type of clause: noun, adjective, or adverb.

Example: My family visited Philadelphia. It is a historic city. (which)
My family visited Philadelphia, <u>which is a historic city.</u>

1. William Penn was an English Quaker. Penn founded Philadelphia in 1682. (who)

2. Many of the early settlers were Quakers. The city became known as the Quaker City. (because)

3. It was located near trade routes. Philadelphia became an important shipping center. (since)

4. We toured Independence Hall. The U.S. Constitution was signed there. (where)

Sentence Combining 437

5-13 Writer's Workshop
Workplace Writing: Business Letter

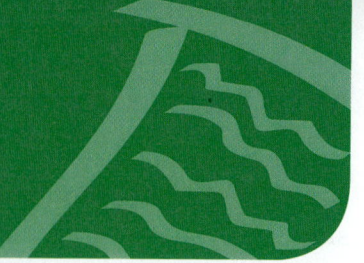

People read **workplace writing** because they want information that will help them take action, solve a problem, or make a decision. A business letter is one form of workplace writing.

A **business letter** is a document written for a formal purpose. There are many different types of business letters, including job application letters, letters of complaint, letters of recommendation, and requests for information. By following the steps outlined in this workshop, you can write your own letter.

Purpose To write a business letter to obtain a job

Audience A future potential employer, you, your teacher, and your classmates

Your letter should include the following elements.

- Correct business letter format
- A statement of purpose
- Content that is clear, concise, and focused
- Points supported by fact and details
- A voice and style appropriate to your audience and purpose
- Error-free grammar

Prewriting—Plan It Out

To choose the focus of your letter, use the following strategies.

Brainstorm for job options. Think of jobs for which you are qualified, such as newspaper delivery or babysitting. List each option and choose which job you find most desirable.

Possible Jobs	My Qualifications

Gather details. In the following chart, identify three qualities that make you a good candidate for the job. See the model to the right. List examples of accomplishments that demonstrate these qualities.

Qualities	Accomplishments
Dependable	Never missed a day of basketball practice
Honest	Found a wallet and turned it in to police
Punctual	Always on time for school

Lesson 5-13

Qualities	Accomplishments

Drafting—Get It on Paper

Write your draft in a direct, focused voice. In the first paragraph, state your purpose for writing. Next, include supporting information in the following paragraphs. To conclude, restate the purpose of your letter and tell what you will do to follow up.

Revising—Make It Better

A great way to make your letter successful is to stay focused on your purpose. Business letters should be brief and to the point. Review your letter for wordiness and unnecessary repetition. Cut and condense any passages that are too long.

Student Model: Revising for conciseness

> I have a passion for great music. ~~My mom gets upset because she says I listen to the radio too much. She thinks I should have quiet time without any distractions.~~ My love of music is not just restricted to listening to music for myself. Whenever I go to a party, I am the official DJ.

The writer cut words that were not directly connected to the purpose of the letter.

Use parallel structures. Use the same structures to show two related ideas, to juxtapose ideas for emphasis, or to present items in a series. For example, the last two sentences in the student model can be made parallel by writing, "My love of music is not restricted to listening for myself; as a DJ, my love of music extends to playing music for others."

Revise your word choice. Business writing should not include slang, rude comments, or details from your personal life. Use serious, polite language that communicates respect.

Unprofessional tone I think the job sounds totally cool.

Professional tone I look forward to speaking with you.

Writer's Workshop continued

Directions Read this student business letter as a model for your own.

Student Model: Writing

555 Any Street
Brooklyn, New York 11201
chantelle.baron@gmail.com
(555) 235-3517
November 12, 20XX

Ms. Susan Blackmore
Internship Coordinator
The Cloisters Summer Internship Program
Fort Tryon Park
New York, New York 10040

Dear Ms. Blackmore:

I am writing to apply for the Cloisters Summer Internship Program which I learned about from Carl Jimenez, a participant in the program last summer. I feel I am particularly suited for the internship because of my interest in art and experience working with children.

I first became interested in art as a child during school trips to the Metropolitan Museum of Art. Recent visits to the Met and other museums have deepened my appreciation for art as a vehicle for expressing important truths about life.

As my resume shows, for two summers I assisted an art teacher in Garden City, New York. I helped lead crafts programs for groups of children ages 6-10. I developed weekly projects, instructed the children on using materials, and coordinated craft birthday parties. Because of these experiences, I am confident that I will be able to work with students in the Cloisters Summer Art Program.

I am available by phone or in person for an interview. I look forward to discussing with you my strong interest in the Cloisters Summer Internship Program.

Sincerely,
Chantelle Baron
Chantelle Baron
Enclosures: resume

HEADING
The heading includes the writer's address, phone number, e-mail address, and the date.

INSIDE ADDRESS
The inside address includes the name and address of the recipient.

OPENING PARAGRAPH
The writer identifies the purpose for writing her letter.

BODY
In these two paragraphs, the writer explains what makes her qualified and interested in the job.

CONCLUSION
Purpose is restated and follow-up is proposed.

CLOSING
The closing begins with a capital letter and ends with a comma. The writer's name is typed below the closing. The writer adds a handwritten signature.

"Enclosures" indicates that her resume is included with the letter.

Lesson 5-13

Editing—Be Your Own Language Coach

Review your draft for grammatical errors. Check all names, events, dates, and addresses for accuracy. Make sure that you have followed the correct format for a business letter and used a variety of sentence structures to reinforce your ideas. Look for sentences to combine using subordinate clauses.

Publishing—Share It!

Read your letter to a partner. Ask your partner to imagine he or she is a business person and comment on your letter. If you would really like to apply for the job, include a resume and drop them in the mail!

Reflecting on Your Writing

Respond Answer the following questions on a separate piece of paper and hand it in with your final draft. What new insights did you gain about writing a business letter? What did you do well? What do you need to work on?

Rubric for Self-Assessment Assess your letter. For each question, circle a rating.

CRITERIA	RATING SCALE NOT VERY VERY
IDEAS Is your letter clear and focused?	1 2 3 4 5
ORGANIZATION How logical and consistent is your organization?	1 2 3 4 5
VOICE Is your writing lively and engaging, drawing the reader in?	1 2 3 4 5
WORD CHOICE How appropriate is the language for your audience?	1 2 3 4 5
SENTENCE FLUENCY How varied is your sentence structure?	1 2 3 4 5
CONVENTIONS How correct is your grammar, especially your use of subordinate clauses?	1 2 3 4 5

5-14 Discussing Your Anchor Book
Literature Circles

Asking Questions In this Literature Circle, you and your group members will start with an open discussion, and then you will practice asking questions.

Part 1: Open Discussion

Talk about your responses to your Anchor Book with your Literature Circle. If you need help, begin the discussion by having each group member share one good insight from his or her Reader's Journal.

Part 2: Discuss—Asking Questions

Effective reading and discussion involves asking questions. This helps you to clarify any confusion and to better engage with and interpret the text. With your group members, use the question stems provided below to create more than one question for each category.

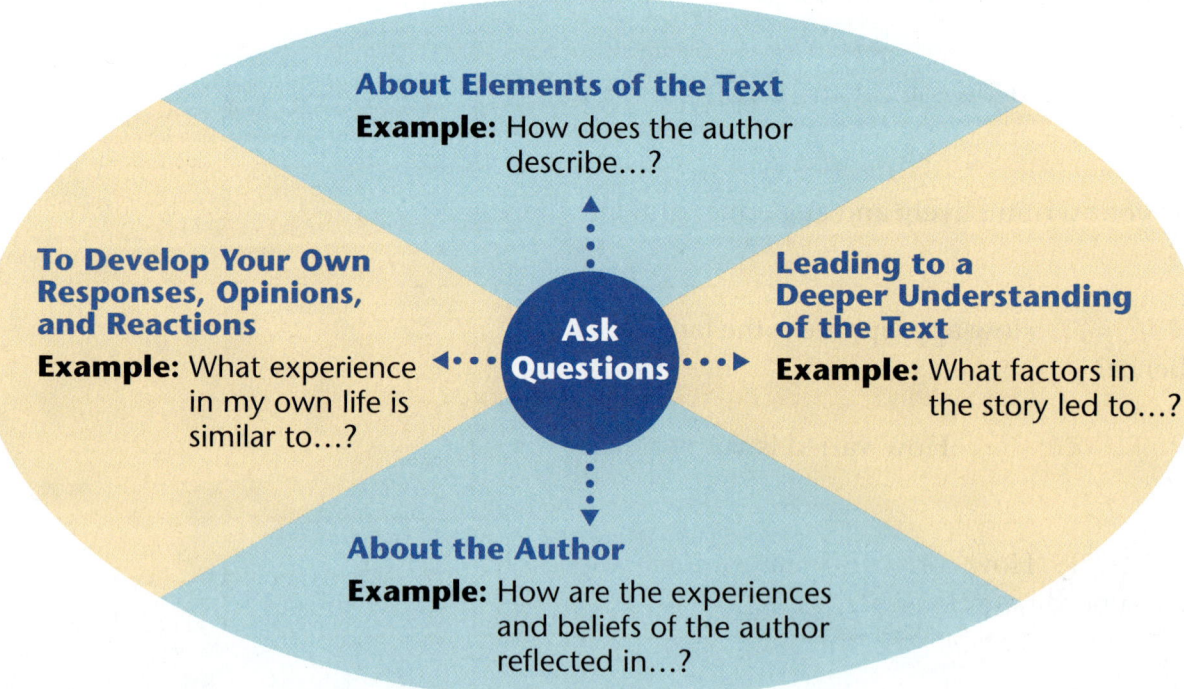

Remember that a good discussion involves not only asking questions but also asking follow-up questions after someone has answered the initial ones. These follow-up questions help clarify responses as well as probe more deeply for understanding.

Question: What experience in my own life is similar to Shayla's trouble with her brother?

Follow-up Question: How is Shayla's trouble with her brother important to the play?

With your Literature Circle, identify the best questions you created. Then, create a follow-up question for each initial question.

Best Questions	Follow-Up Questions

How did these questions help you probe deeper into the meaning of your Anchor Book?

_____
_____

1 Select the best questions from each member of your group. Write them on the following lines.

_____
_____

2 What makes these good questions?

_____

while reading your anchor book

443

5-15 Connecting to Your Anchor Book
Anchor Book Projects

Now that you have finished reading your Anchor Book, it is time to get creative! Complete one of the following projects.

Design a Set A

A set designer identifies physical elements of the play that are essential to the meaning of the story. He or she creates these elements in a way that helps the audience emotionally connect to the story.

1. As set designer, you will focus on the sets for the play. Write a description of how the set from your Anchor Book will change from scene to scene or act to act. Think about how plays or movies you have seen use sets to help visually enhance their meaning. You may also include drawings of your designs.

2. Write an explanation of why you would choose to design the set in this way. Support your choices with details from the play.

Your completed set design project should include the following elements.

- A written design that addresses essential details about the setting
- Design choices that explain important information about your play
- An explanation that supports your design choices with details from your play and tells how they reflect the author's purpose

Be a Critic B

A critic evaluates something, but a really good critic makes his or her evaluation as interesting (or more so) than the performance itself. A theater or film critic assesses how elements of narrative (setting, plot, theme, characterization) and staging work together to communicate a story to its audience.

1. Watch a media presentation—such as a film, video, television show, or theatrical production—of your Anchor Book.

2. Using critical reviews from the newspaper as your model, write your own review, explaining the media presentation's strengths and weaknesses, and why, or why not, audiences should see it.

Your review should feature the following elements.

- An explanation of your opinion supported by specific details from the media presentation
- Reference to elements of staging and narrative
- Lively and entertaining language

Create a Storyboard

A movie is a kind of drama that is filmed. A filmmaker can affect the audience's perception by controlling the camera shots. Filmmakers use storyboards to plan how they will film a scene. A storyboard resembles a cartoon strip, with each square representing a different camera shot.

1. Create a storyboard with at least fifteen squares to show one scene from your Anchor Book. You may draw or photograph the camera shots. Under each square, write a brief caption that uses dialogue or describes the action.

2. Write an explanation of why you chose to film the scene in this way. Refer to specific details from the play to support your choice.

Your completed storyboard project should feature these elements.

- Images that communicate important information about your play
- Captions that describe each image or show dialogue
- An explanation that supports your storyboard choices with details from your play

Free-Choice Book Reflection

You have completed your free-choice book. Before you take your test, read the following instructions to write a brief reflection on your book.

My free-choice book is _____.

The author is _____.

1 Would you recommend this book to a friend? Yes _____ No _____

Briefly explain why. _____

Write and Discuss Answer the following question in your Reader's Journal. Then, discuss your answer with your partner or your Literature Circle.

 2 **Compare and Contrast** *Is it our differences or our similarities that matter most?* Compare and contrast how differences cause conflict between the characters in your Anchor Book and in your free-choice book. Are there important similarities that the characters cannot see? Use specific details from both books to support your ideas. Then, to extend the discussion, consider the way differences create conflict or influence decisions in other subject areas, such as history or science.

Unit Review
Standardized Test Practice

Answer the questions below to check your understanding of this unit's skills.

Reading Skills: Identifying Cause and Effect

Read this selection. Then answer the questions that follow.

> The night of the big basketball game, Tim ate pizza for dinner and then rushed to catch the team bus. Traffic was backed up on the highway because of an accident, so the team arrived late, which meant they had very little practice time before the game. Nevertheless, they were ahead at halftime, thanks to Zach's hot shooting arm and Tim's five rebounds. However, Zach fouled out in the fourth quarter, so the rest of the team had to step up their defense and also pass the ball more to maintain their lead.

1 What causes the team to be ahead at halftime?

   A. Zach's shots

   B. Tim's rebounds

   C. both A and B

   D. neither A nor B

2 What is the relationship between Zach's fouling out and other events?

   F. It is a cause with one important effect.

   G. It is a cause with two important effects.

   H. It is an effect with one cause.

   J. It has no relationship to other events.

Reading Skills: Drawing Conclusions

Read this selection. Then answer the questions that follow.

> **TASHA.** [*pouting*] I'm not going! I hate dances!
>
> **LIZ.** [*sighing*] But it won't be any fun without you.
>
> **TASHA.** I'm not fun…[*hopefully*] Right?
>
> **LIZ.** You are fun when you stop thinking about yourself so much. [*in a coaxing voice*] Come on, there's going to be a really good DJ…[*grinning and handing* TASHA *a sweater*] You can wear this.
>
> **TASHA.** [*with a big smile*] Really? Oh, all right. You talked me into it…again. [*with enthusiasm*] Who else is going to be there?
>
> **LIZ.** Everybody! I knew you'd change your mind.

3 What can you conclude about Tasha from this passage?

A. She hates dances.

B. She dislikes Liz.

C. She depends on Liz for reassurance.

D. She has a lot of confidence.

4 Which is the most logical **conclusion** about this type of situation between Tasha and Liz?

F. It has never occurred before.

G. It will never occur again.

H. It has occurred only once before.

J. It occurs often.

Literary Analysis: Elements of Drama

Choose the best answer for the following questions.

5 Which of these best defines **mood** in a literary work?

A. the reader's opinion about the work

B. language that describes the physical sense

C. the overall feeling the work creates in the reader

D. the writer's purpose in writing

6 A **character's motivation** is best defined as

F. reasons for his or her actions

G. his or her way of speaking

H. his or her worldview

J. his or her internal conflicts

Read this selection. Then answer the questions that follow.

> **GRASSHOPPER.** [*knocking on Ant's door*] Mr. Ant! I'm freezing and starving to death out here in the cold, while you have a warm home and plenty to eat. Could you spare a grain of corn for me?
> **ANT.** I warned you about this, Mr. Grasshopper, but you wouldn't listen. All summer, you played and sang, while I was working hard, storing food for winter.
> **GRASSHOPPER.** Come on, Mr. Ant, have a heart. Take me in, and I'll sing and dance for you all winter. We'll have fun.
> **ANT.** I'm truly sorry, but I have no food to spare. If I share with you, I may not survive the winter myself. Goodbye! [*slams his door*]

7 Which of the following terms best describes the selection?

A. narration

B. nonfiction

C. dialogue

D. monologue

8 What does the selection reveal about the character of Grasshopper?

F. He is fun-loving and practical.

G. He is fun-loving but impractical.

H. He is kind and compassionate.

J. He is sneaky and dishonest.

9 What is a **dramatization**?

_____
_____
_____
_____

Language Skills: Vocabulary

Choose the best answer.

10 Where can you find the **origin** of the word *factor*?

   A. in a dictionary definition
   B. in a dictionary pronunciation
   C. in a dictionary etymology
   D. in a thesaurus

11 What is the **root** of the word *accept*?

   F. acc-
   G. -cept
   H. -cep-
   J. -ept

12 What is the meaning of the root *seq-* in *sequence*?

   A. to make
   B. to follow
   C. to join
   D. to appear

13 Which of these is true about a root word?

   F. It is always the beginning a word.
   G. It is the basic meaning of a word.
   H. It is the least important piece of a word.
   J. It is only used in certain words.

Language Skills : Spelling

Circle the letter that contains the correctly spelled word to complete the sentence.

14 Television shows are produced in _____.

   A. studioes
   B. studioze
   C. studioses
   D. studios

15 Cold sliced _____ are an excellent addition to salads.

   F. tomatose
   G. tomatoes
   H. tomatos
   J. tomatoze

16 The _____ were arrested by the police.

A. thiefs
B. thieves
C. theifes
D. thievze

17 She ate _____ with her dinner.

F. frys
G. fris
H. fryze
J. fries

Language Skills: Grammar

Choose the best answer.

18 Identify the **participial phrase** in the sentence.

The god of war, known as Mars, was important in their mythology.

A. "in their mythology"
B. "The god of war"
C. "known as Mars"
D. "was important"

19 Identify the **participle** in the sentence.

Exhausted, I fell asleep in a minute.

F. Exhausted
G. fell
H. asleep
J. minute

20 Which of the following is true for every **clause**?

A. It is a complete thought.
B. It contains a subject and a verb.
C. It contains a subordinating conjunction.
D. It is an incomplete thought.

21 Which of these contains both an **independent clause** and a **subordinate clause**?

F. The CDs that I ordered on the Internet were from a popular Web site.
G. Many people were walking on the sidewalk and it was a warm summer day.
H. After reading for hours, I strained my eyes.
J. Coiled under a rock was a large rattlesnake.

22 Which of the following is true of a **subordinate clause**?

A. It expresses a complete thought.
B. It is missing either a subject or a verb.
C. It cannot stand alone as a sentence.
D. It is found in every sentence.

23 Which of the following could be used to introduce a **subordinate clause**?

F. walking
G. although
H. and
J. however

Are yesterday's *heroes* and *events* important today?

Unit 6 Genre focus:
The Research Process

Your Anchor Book
There are many good books that would work well to support both the Big Question and the genre focus of this unit. In this unit you will read one of these books as your Anchor Book. Your teacher will introduce the book you will be reading.

Free-Choice Reading
Later in this unit you will be given the opportunity to choose another book to read. This is called your free-choice book.

Thinking About What You Already Know

How many times have you heard someone say, "It's a fact?" How do you know whether what they say is really true? When you come head to head with an unknown fact—whether it is in a book, a movie, or something said by a friend—dig into some research and see what you can uncover.

Partner Activity

With a partner, look at the "fact" below. Then, look at the sources found online using the keywords *teen* and *prefrontal cortex*. Determine which would be the best one to help you verify whether the statement is fact or not.

> Teens cannot always be blamed for impulsive behavior. There is a biological reason: the final part of the brain to develop fully in young people—the prefrontal cortex—is the part that is capable of deciding, *first* I'll do my homework and get ready for school, *then* I'll play a video game and IM my friends.

News Magazine

Timely Magazine

Why Do Teens Do What They Do?
By Julio Medina
July 15, 2008
Web edition

Where exactly does all that moodiness, attitude, and risk-taking behavior in teens come from? According to a study done by the University of Pittsburgh, there is a biological reason why teens and risky behavior go hand-in-hand. The study shows that when making decisions, teenagers use less of the prefrontal region of their brains—which governs planning, judgment, and goal-oriented functions—than do grownups, because it does not fully develop until adulthood. The amygdala region of the brain—which governs emotion and gut response—is the primary region that is activated, and it is activated far more than in adults. The question that parents of all teens ask across the globe—"Why didn't you stop and think?!"—finally has an answer: "I did, Mom/Dad, but my amygdala took over!"

Blog

This Is Your Brain on Puberty

Submitted by tbone on Wed, 09/27/2008 – 11:48 am.

They say now that you'd better keep a close watch on your kids during those tumultuous years of puberty. Ha! Newsflash: that's not news. Apparently, a teen's prefrontal cortex barely rates a blip on the screen when tested for activity during decision-making. Instead, the amygdala (wasn't that the Star Wars queen of the planet Naboo?), which governs the emotions and gut reaction, lights up like the Milky Way. Now, when your sixteen-year-old junior driving champion asks for the keys to the car, you can say, "Not on your amygdala!"

Online Science Newspaper for Teens

Scientific Teens Online

Teens: Get Your Bliss On!
By Alina Tan
June 30, 2004

New research suggests that there is a link between prefrontal cortex activity and happiness. According to a study by the University of Wisconsin, happiness isn't just a feeling—it's a physical state of the brain, and it can be induced by—guess what?—meditation. Scientists observed monks while they were meditating, and saw that their brains sparked with activity when they reached the trancelike stage in meditation described as a sensation of bliss. So next time you feel overloaded by stress, sit down, fold your legs in a pretzel, and say, "Om."

Which do you think is the best source to verify the fact? Explain.

_____
_____
_____
_____
_____
_____

Thinking About What You Already Know

6-1 Understanding the Big Question
Are yesterday's heroes and events important today?

If you were born in a different time would you still be you? There are some experiences that we all share as part of being human and some experiences that are dictated by the attitudes and beliefs of the culture and time in which we are born.

In this activity, you will compare your present to the past. How does the time in which we live control our life experience? Consider the following ideas about children in earlier times.

▶ In Europe in the Middle Ages, childhood lasted to about the age of seven. After that, children were expected to be active participants in the adult world.

▶ Until the twentieth century in the United States, if you were a child as young as five years old, it was considered legal for you to be working in a factory as many as 18 hours a day.

1 How is our understanding of childhood different today from what it was in the two examples described above?

_____
_____
_____

Work in Groups Now think about other aspects of life besides childhood. In your group, identify at least four examples for each of the two questions that follow.

What aspects of your own life are specific to the time and place in which you live?			

What aspects of your own life are universal (shared) to human experience?			

before reading your anchor book

2 Look back at the examples shared in your group of universal aspects of human life. How could yesterday's heroes and events help you understand your own life?

_____
_____
_____
_____

On Your Own Think about how the past has relevance to our lives today. Choose one of the following two questions to answer.

▶ What time in history would have been fun or interesting to live in?

▶ Who is a person from history who has traits you admire?

Complete this graphic organizer based on your choice.

_____ [Historical Person/Time]

I admire this person or find this event interesting because…

_____
_____
_____
_____
_____
_____
_____

In this unit you will learn about the research process. You may find that you want to explore the historical time or person you identified above in your research project.

 As you read your Anchor Book and related readings, think about how yesterday's heroes and events can help us better understand our own lives.

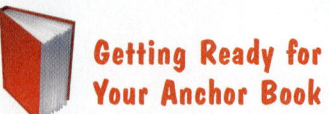

Getting Ready for Your Anchor Book

You will start reading your Anchor Book soon. The next few pages in this book give you some background information plus a reading skill.

Introduction to the Research Process

When you think of research, you might think of boring facts. Actually, research changes the way we live. It gives us new tools and improves our understanding of the world.

What Is Research?

Research describes a process of investigation. People investigate a topic to discover and understand facts, theories, and laws. When you research a subject, you gather information about it. Many people write a research paper about the information they learned.

Why Do We Do Research?

Good researchers don't just accept the way things are. They question the ways things are and think of ways to change them. Here are two examples.

- The inventor of the cell phone, Martin Cooper, wondered why people couldn't carry their phones with them anywhere. He researched this question and invented the cell phone in 1973.

- In the fourth century, the Greek philosopher Aristotle created a theory that forms of life could suddenly appear out of something not alive (spontaneous generation). He noticed that when a river flooded and created mud, large numbers of frogs appeared that weren't around when the mud wasn't there. He decided that mud must create frogs.

  It wasn't until 1668 that the Italian doctor Francisco Redi decided to do research to see if he could prove that Aristotle was wrong. He did.

Research also allows us to learn about historical people, places, and events. By doing research, we can move forward by understanding what came before us.

How Do I Begin My Research?

You will be writing a research report that will vary in length from about four to ten pages. Pick a topic that you find interesting and want to learn more about. The more appealing the topic is to you, the more enjoyable it will be to research and write about.

Your Research Process

Writing a research report requires many steps. The main ones are shown here. You will learn more about these steps in this unit in the lessons indicated. When you finish each step, fill in the chart, recording your completion date.

PREWRITING (Lesson 6–4)
Choose a topic. Narrow it if it is too general. Fill in the due date beforehand to keep track of your time.

Date due _____ **Date completed** _____

▼

RESEARCHING (Lessons 6–5 and 6–6)
Gather information and take notes about your topic.

Date due _____ **Date completed** _____

▼

DRAFTING (Lesson 6–11)
Formulate a thesis statement.   Write and organize your first draft.
Create an outline.   Cite your sources accurately.

Date due _____ **Date completed** _____

▼

REVISING (Lesson 6–12)
Rework your rough draft to improve it. Revise its content and structure to make your message clear and well supported. Eliminate irrelevant information.

Date due _____ **Date completed** _____

▼

PUBLISHING (Lesson 6–13)
Present the final draft of your research report.

Date due _____ **Date completed** _____

6-2 Reading Skills
Setting a Purpose for Reading

In learning new reading skills, you will use special academic vocabulary. Knowing the right words will help you demonstrate your understanding.

Academic Vocabulary

Word	Meaning	Example Sentence
critique v. Related words: critical, criticism	to review or discuss critically	The writer *critiqued* the film and was less than pleased.
skim v. Related words: skimmed, skimming	to read quickly to note only important information	She turned on her light and *skimmed* the last page of the novel.
revise v. Related word: revision	to change something based on new ideas	After hearing the responses of his classmates, José *revised* his essay.

People read for different purposes: to gain general knowledge about a topic, to find specific information, or to analyze an author's ideas.

The author's purpose and the reader's purpose can be the same. Stephen King writes horror stories to scare and entertain, and most people read his stories for that reason. However, if you were writing an essay on how he uses animal characters, then you might read through a Stephen King novel once for an understanding of the story and then **skim** for specific references to animal characters.

Make your reading more focused by setting a purpose, or goal.

How to Set a Purpose for Reading

Before You Read

- If the text is unfamiliar, preview the text to identify the topic. **Skim** for key words and scan the organization and features such as headings, photos, and diagrams, subheadings, charts, maps, illustrations, captions, and graphs. Look for font treatment, such as bold print, type set in color, and italics, which may be clues to meaning or structure.

- Once you have identified the topic of the text, determine what you already know about the topic, and what you want to know.

While You Read

▶ **Adjust** your reading rate to fit the type of text you are reading. Slow down when reading technical information or difficult text. You might read a magazine or a novel more quickly.

▶ **Revise** your ideas of what you would like to know. You can develop the questions you already have or ask new questions.

After You Read

Critique what you read to determine whether it met your expectations. Was your purpose for reading the selection fulfilled?

Directions Before you read the following instructions for an answering machine, preview to set a purpose for your reading.

Partner Activity
Find technical directions for a mechanical device, such as your cell phone or MP3 player. Paraphrase a difficult section of the directions so that it is easier for someone to follow.

1 **Identify** What is the purpose for reading this selection? Why is knowing how to follow written instructions important?

_____
_____
_____

2 **Explain** What text features helped you identify the purpose?

_____
_____

Instructions

Recording Your Announcement

Before using this answering system, you should record the announcement (up to one minute long) that callers will hear when the system answers a call. If you choose not to record an announcement, the system answers with a prerecorded announcement: "Hello. Please leave a message after the tone."

1. Press and hold [ANNC.]. The system beeps. Speak toward the microphone normally, from about nine inches away. While you are recording, the Message Window displays ---.

2. To stop recording, release [ANNC.]. The system automatically plays back your announcement.

To review your announcement, press and release [ANNC.].

Setting a Purpose for Reading

Directions Set a purpose for reading the following contract, an employment agreement, by choosing to be either the "Company" or the "Employee" (circle your choice). Think about the answer to the following question before you read. After you finish reading, answer the question.

> Locate a job application at a local store, or find one online. Identify three types of information you would need to include to complete the application.

3 **Summarize** What did you, as the Company Manager or the Employee, agree to do by signing this contract?

_____

_____

EMPLOYMENT AGREEMENT

between _Green Iguana Music Store_ (the "Company") and _Maria Fuentes_ (the "Employee").

1. The Company employs the Employee based on the following terms and conditions.

2. **Employment Start Date.** Under this agreement, the Employee will begin work on _April 21_.

3. **Compensation.** The Company shall pay Employee a wage of _$11.00_ per hour for the services of the Employee, payable at two-week intervals.

4. **Basis of employment.** Employee is hired _part-time_, to work no more than _15 hours_ per week.

5. **Position.** The Company hires the Employee in the capacity of _Sales Associate_. From time to time and within reason, Employee's duties may change at the Company's discretion.

6. **Dedication.** While working, Employee will focus on the business of the Company, and will not engage in any other activity, whether business or personal, unless Employee is on a break.

7. **Confidentiality.** Employee agrees not to reveal confidential company information to any person.

8. **Vacation.** The Employee is entitled to a yearly vacation of _2 days_ at _regular_ pay.

9. **Termination of Agreement.** With just cause, the Company may terminate this agreement at any time upon five days' written notice to the Employee. If the Company requests, the Employee may continue to perform his/her duties and will be paid his/her regular salary up to the date of termination.

10. **Changes to Agreement.** This instrument is the entire agreement of the Company and the Employee. It may be altered only by a written agreement signed by both the Company and the Employee.

Signed this _18th_ day of _April_.

Suzanne Conversano   _Maria Fuentes_
Company Manager   **Employee**

Directions Complete Part 1 of this graphic organizer to help you set a purpose before you read the next selection. While you read, return to Part 2 of the graphic organizer to adjust your purpose as necessary.

Now, set a purpose for reading this selection.
Guiding Question: **Why are heroic characters and the authors who created them important today?**

from The World Book Encyclopedia

Detective story is a work of fiction about a puzzling crime, a number of clues, and a detective who solves the mystery. In most detective stories, the crime is murder and the clues lead to or away from the solution.

The pattern of most detective stories is the same, whether the tale is a novel, a novelette, or a short story. The author presents the crime, the detective, and several clues and suspects. The detective follows the clues and may even discover additional crimes. The climax of the story comes when the detective reveals the criminal and tells how the mystery was solved.

Certain conventions have developed from the detective story pattern. The author is expected to "play fair" with the reader. That is, the reader should be given exactly the same information that the detective uses to find the criminal. Readers can treat the story as a battle of wits between themselves and the detective.

The detective in most of these stories is not a professional police officer but a private consultant. For example, G. K. Chesterton's Father Brown is a priest, Rex Stout's Nero Wolfe is a gourmet and intellectual, and S. S. Van Dine's Philo Vance is a sophisticated socialite. Fictional professional detectives include Wilkie Collins's Sgt. Cuff, John Creasey's Inspector Gideon (written under the name of J. J. Marric), and Georges Simenon's Inspector Maigret. Romance or financial gain may be a factor in a detective story, but the main theme is the mystery and its solution.

History of the detective story began with Edgar Allan Poe's "The Murders in the Rue Morgue" (1841). With this story and "The Mystery of Marie Rogêt" and "The Purloined Letter," Poe created the literary tradition of detective fiction. His detective was C. Auguste Dupin, a brilliant amateur who uses logic to solve mysteries.

Charles Dickens tried the new form in *Bleak House* (1852–1853) and in his unfinished novel, *The Mystery of Edwin Drood*. Wilkie Collins's *The Moonstone* (1868) was one of the most important early detective novels. Sherlock Holmes and his comrade, Dr. John Watson, appeared in 1887 in Sir Arthur Conan Doyle's *A Study in Scarlet*. Holmes is the most famous character in detective fiction—and perhaps in all fiction.

—David Geherin

Related articles in *World Book* include:
Collins, Wilkie
Doyle, Sir Arthur Conan
Holmes, Sherlock
Poe, Edgar Allan
Stout, Rex

Additional resources
Henderson, Lesley, ed. *Twentieth-Century Crime and Mystery Writers,* 3rd ed. St. James Pr., 1991.
Symons, Julian. *Bloody Murder: From the Detective Story to the Crime Novel.* 3rd ed. Mysterious Pr., 1992.

Thinking About the Selection
Detective Story

1 Explain How did your preview of the selection help you understand it?

_____
_____
_____

2 Reflect What might you do differently before you read next time?

_____
_____
_____

3 Review Why would an encyclopedia be a good place to begin the research process?

_____
_____
_____

4 Apply Name a topic that you would like to learn more about, then complete the chart below.

Topic		
What I Think I Know	What I Want to Know	Five Possible Sources

Write Answer the following question in your Reader's Journal.

5 Support Why are heroic characters and the authors who created them important today?

Setting a Purpose for Reading   463

6-3 Vocabulary Building Strategies
Words from Mythology and Borrowed Words

No spoken language exists in a vacuum. Language is influenced by the meeting of cultures, such as through immigration. Many English words originated in other cultures.

Day of the Week	Mythological Origin
Sunday	**Sun's Day**
Monday	**Moon's Day**
Tuesday	**Tiw's Day** Tiw, or Tyr, was an Anglo-Saxon (Scandinavian) god of war.
Wednesday	**Woden's Day** Woden was the most powerful Anglo-Saxon god.
Thursday	**Thor's Day** Thor was the Norse god of thunder.
Friday	**Frigga's Day** Frigga was the Norse goddess of marriage and hearth.
Saturday	**Saturn's Day** Saturn was the Roman god of time and the harvest.

Some adjectives that describe behavior come from mythical characters whose personalities reflect those behaviors.

English word	Meaning	Mythological Origin
mercurial (adj.)	having rapid, unpredictable moods	Mercury, swiftest of the Roman gods
jovial (adj.)	jolly; of good humor	Jove, king of the Roman gods and the god of light and sky
herculean (adj.)	of extraordinary power, intensity, or difficulty	Hercules, a Greek hero, who had to perform twelve seemingly impossible tasks to win his freedom

before reading your anchor book

Lesson 6-3

Directions Write the word originating from mythology that completes each sentence.

1. Demonstrating _____ strength, Rita lifted up the desk by herself.

2. First, he's happy, then one minute later he's sad. His moods are so _____.

3. I enjoy being around Carlos. He's always in a _____ mood.

Modern world languages are the source of some English words. Here are a few examples.

Borrowed Word	Meaning	Original Language
gumbo (n.)	okra, or a stew containing okra	Bantu (African)
kayak (n.)	canoe with a small opening	Inuit (Eskimo)
incognito (n., adv., or adj.)	with one's identity concealed	Italian
moccasin (n.)	heelless shoe of soft leather	Algonquian (Native American)
leprechaun (n.)	mischievous elf	Gaelic (Irish)
finale (n.)	last part of a dramatic presentation	Italian
gung-ho (adj.)	very enthusiastic	Chinese
yoga (n.)	a series of exercises to build strength and to help think clearly	Hindi

Directions Write the borrowed word that completes each sentence.

4. When I neared the end of my presentation, I shouted, "And now, the grand _____!"

5. I wasn't too excited about the field trip to the aquarium, but Rafael was _____.

6. When movie stars get tired of all the attention, they sometimes travel in disguise or _____.

7. Carl's uncle is a famous New Orleans chef and his recipe for _____ is incredible.

Directions Using the Internet or print resources, research the origins of the following topics: *kayak*, *moccasin*, *leprechaun*, and *yoga*. Find an early image of each from the culture it originated in. Compare that image to one found in contemporary American culture.

Words from Mythology and Borrowed Words

Ready? Start Reading Your Anchor Book It's time to get started. As you learn from this work text, your teacher will also give you reading assignments from your Anchor Book.

6-4 The Research Process
Choosing Your Topic

When choosing a topic for your research paper, think about what interests you most. Is it a person, a faraway place, a social or personal issue, or a historical event?

To find your topic, use the strategies below. These strategies can be helpful even if your teacher has asked you to research within a specific academic area, category, or general topic.

Strategy	How to Use It
Newswatch	Flip through recent magazines or newspapers for thought-provoking topics. Tune in to television and radio broadcasts, or flip to the history, science, and other educational channels. Add ideas to your list.
Net Browse	Many Internet sites cover a variety of topics. Log on and look over the topics to generate more thoughts. Add ideas to your list.
Self-Interview	Ask yourself questions to generate interesting subject ideas. What people or places fascinate you? What objects or events have a special meaning for you? Create a list of people, places, things, and events. Look over the topics and choose one that is particularly interesting or relevant to your life.
Brainstorm or Free-Write	Jot down research ideas as they come to mind. Make a list or use a sentence starter for free-writing, such as "I like learning about_____."

Apply On a separate sheet of paper, make a list of topics. Circle the five topics that are the most interesting or relevant to your life. From those, choose the one topic that you would most like to research.

Narrowing Your Topic

The scope of your topic should not be too broad. If your topic is too general, there will be too much information for you to cover. Doing a little research and asking good questions can help you refine your topic and make it more specific.

Conduct preliminary research. Before you settle on a topic, conduct a first round of research on the Internet or at the library. As you research, look for key words that relate to specific ideas about a topic. Use those key words as you conduct your research.

Type of Source	How It Helps
Search engine	Using search engines can help you narrow your topic. Using a search engine can give you results that are more specific than your original topic. If so, you may want to focus on that part of the topic.
Library index	An index provides the titles of books or magazines available and tells you where to find them in your school or public library. These lists can also help you figure out how to narrow a topic. A book or magazine title may suggest a more specialized topic of interest. Many library indexes are also online.
Research texts	Skimming the **tables of contents, glossaries,** and **indexes** of books and magazines on your topic. This can help you generate ideas and gain an understanding of key words related to your topic. You can also scan text features like headings and captions for your key words.

Ask open-ended questions. Ask yourself: What do I want to learn about this topic? Why am I interested in it? Aim for variety, keeping in mind the five *W*'s and *H*: *who, what, when, where, why,* and *how.* Use your questions to guide your research. As you gather information, modify your questions to reflect changes in your topic.

Research

Now, think about your own research paper.

Apply Write three questions that you would like to answer about the topic you chose.

_____

_____

_____

Directions The picture below shows the results of a student's preliminary Internet search on environmental conservation efforts led by teens. The student used the key words *teens* and *earth conservation* in a search engine. Study the results this search produced and then answer the questions.

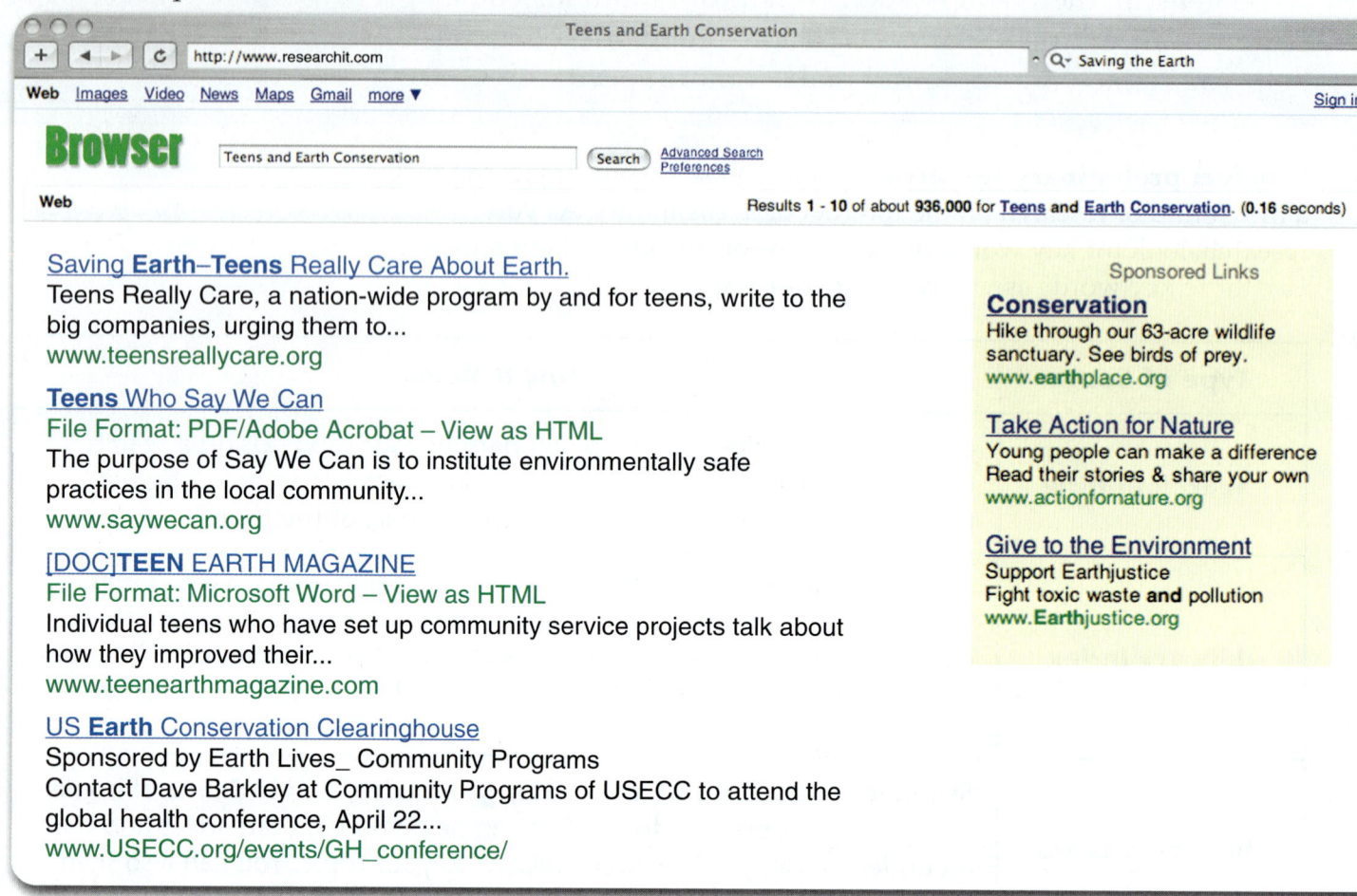

1. **Synthesize** Write two questions that the student might use to help narrow the focus of research.

_____
_____
_____

Research

Now, think about your own research paper.

2. **Apply** Create a list of key words that you could use to search for your topic on the Internet.

_____
_____
_____

468 Lesson 6-4

Directions This library index page shows the results of a student's preliminary research for a report about careers. The student used the key words *home businesses* in the electronic index. Study the results and then answer the questions.

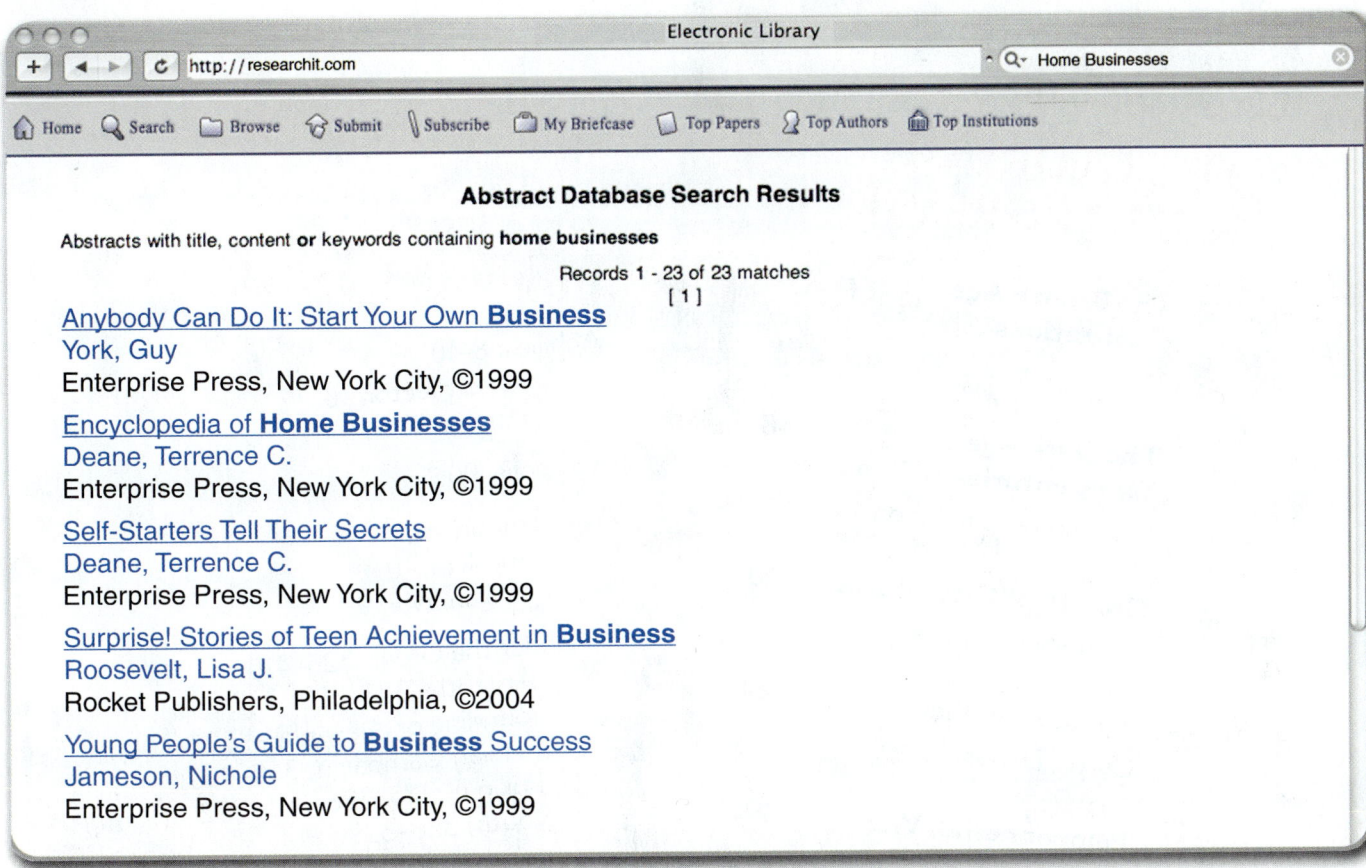

3. **Apply** Use the index above to identify two specific topic ideas with a narrower focus than the student's original idea of "home businesses."

_____
_____

Research

Now, think about your own research project.

4. **Apply** Find a book in the library on your topic. Use the index to identify more specific topic ideas for your project. List those specific topic ideas below. Circle the ones that are most interesting to you.

_____
_____
_____

Choosing and Narrowing Your Topic

Directions The sample table of contents and partial index pages come from a student's preliminary research on the topic "Ancient Greece." Study the materials and then answer the question.

6. **Research** What pages might you search to find information about wars with Persia?

_____

_____

7. **Speculate** A student researching the topic of "Ancient Greece" is interested in the lives of unusual people. How might she use this interest along with the table of contents and index above to help narrow her topic?

_____

_____

Thinking About the Research Process
Choosing and Narrowing Your Topic

1 **Organize** If you made a plan to use all three methods of preliminary research (search engine, library index, research texts), what order would you follow? Why?

_____
_____
_____
_____

2 **Analyze** Based on the table of contents and index, write two questions that the student might use to begin research on Alexander the Great.

_____
_____
_____
_____

Research

Now, think about your own research paper.

3 **Synthesize** Follow the steps outlined in this lesson to help you choose a topic to research. Identify your topic below.

_____
_____
_____

4 **Apply** Narrow your topic by conducting preliminary research and asking yourself questions. Write down two questions about your topic in the space below.

_____
_____
_____
_____
_____

6-5 The Research Process
Finding Reliable Sources

How do you learn about a scientific discovery, the latest news about your community, or a historical place you would like to visit? You probably gather information from many sources, such as the Internet, newspapers, encyclopedias, or your own observations. These sources, along with others, can also provide details, facts, and information for research papers.

Research Terms

To make sure that the sources you use for a research report are reliable, balanced, and accurate, follow these guidelines.

- Check copyright dates for **currency,** or how up-to-date your source is. This helps ensure that the information you gather from books and on Web sites is the most recent available.

- Review the author's background and credentials. An **unbiased source** is one written by an author with no special ties to the subject.

- Avoid personal and most ".com" Web sites. For **credible** and **valid** information, use the sites of educational institutions (.edu), reliable organizations (.org), and government agencies (.gov).

- Evaluate a source for its **relevancy** to your topic. Scan the introduction, topic sentences, and conclusion to look for information related to your topic. Look over footnotes and a source's bibliography or index to help you determine if it is relevant.

- Use multiple sources to **verify** information. If you find discrepancies between two sources, use a third to check the accuracy of your facts and details. Use information from additional sources to cross-check information from interviews or Internet sites.

1 **Draw Conclusions** What problems might occur if you are not careful about choosing your sources?

_____
_____
_____
_____

Directions Read the information in the following sources. Then answer the questions.

PETS IN AMERICA

There are now over 73.9 million dogs, 90.5 million cats, and 16.6 million birds owned as pets in America. This can only be seen as an indication that the pet overpopulation crisis is growing. Too many people take on pet ownership without understanding the responsibilities. This hurts both people and pets. Think carefully before adding to this problem by buying a pet you cannot properly care for!

http://www.petsinthestates.com

HOUSEHOLD PET OWNERSHIP IN THE UNITED STATES: 2007
[Based on a sample survey of 80,000 households in 2007]

TYPE OF PET	Dog	Cat	Bird
NUMBER OWNED (IN MILLIONS)	74.8	88.3	16
NUMBER OF HOUSEHOLDS OWNING PETS (IN MILLIONS)	44.8	38.4	6.4

Source: American Pet Products Manufacturers Association, *National Pet Owners Survey*, 2007.

2 **Evaluate** Which source do you think is more reliable? Explain.

3 **Analyze** What would be the advantages and disadvantages of using the table "Household Pet Ownership in the United States" as a source?

Finding Reliable Sources

Avoiding Plagiarism

When someone mentions the word *stealing* or *theft*, do you immediately think of money or items of value? You would not be alone if you do, but written ideas and words can also be stolen. When that happens, it is called **plagiarism.**

Presenting someone else's ideas, research, or opinions as your own, even if you have rephrased it in different words, is **plagiarism**, the equivalent of academic stealing, or fraud.

Careful note-taking and the use of direct quotations and paraphrasing with proper citations are all ways to avoid plagiarism.

Directions Read each paragraph. Underline sentences in the student's paragraph that are examples of plagiarism. Then, answer the question.

AUTHOR'S PARAGRAPH	STUDENT'S PARAGRAPH
Benjamin Franklin was born on January 17, 1706, in Boston, Massachusetts. He was one of 17 children. A prolific writer, he was primarily self-taught. His formal education consisted of a single year at a grammar school and one additional year with a private tutor. Schooling for young Ben Franklin was over by the time he turned 10. (*Encyclopædia Britannica* article 22465) By age 12, he was working as a printer's apprentice for one of his brothers. **Works cited** **Franklin, Benjamin.** *Encyclopædia Britannica.* 2007. *Encyclopædia Britannica Online.* 25 Apr. 2007. <http://www.britannica.com/eb/article-22465	Benjamin Franklin, born in Boston, Massachusetts, on January 17, 1706, had 16 siblings. Although he is known for his writing, he had little formal education. Schooling for young Ben Franklin was over by the time he turned 10. Two years later, one of his brothers apprenticed Ben in his printing shop.

4   Explain Why are your underlined sentences examples of plagiarism?

_____

_____

_____

5   Describe What should the student have done to avoid plagiarism?

_____

_____

while reading your anchor book

Lesson 6-5

Note-Taking

You should take notes throughout the process of gathering information. Always use the same procedure for note-taking, but use the method that works best for you.

Note-Taking Procedures

By following these procedures, you will give proper credit for information you use from any source.

NOTE-TAKING PROCEDURE	HOW TO DO IT
Create a source card	Create one for every source you use. Assign each card a number to help you keep track of your information.
Record the source	Record necessary information about the source. Include the page number(s) of where you found the information.
Record quotations	When copying words from a text, put them in quotes. Double-check the accuracy of any direct quote.
Paraphrase text	Restate the text in your own words to check your understanding.
Summarize information from a text	Write only the main points and most important details.
Use visual aids	Include visuals (charts, graphs, maps) as part of your note-taking.

Note-Taking Methods

► One way to take notes is to use a **note card.** Follow these steps.

- **Identify the source** by author or title at the top of each card. Include the source card number of the book or article.
- **Write the topic** that describes the card's contents at the top.
- **Write one main idea with supporting details** on each card.

> Wepman and Schlesinger (p. 4) (topic) Aristotle and Alexander
> Philip knew tutor couldn't prepare son for ruling. (347 B.C.)
> 1. Greek philosopher, in his early 40s, not yet famous
> 2. Prepared Alex to be a wise king (Plato's philosopher-king)
> 3. Alex returned to Pella to take over; Philip at war. (340 B.C.)

while reading your anchor book

- A second method of note-taking is to create an **idea map.** This is a diagram of the main idea and supporting details in a book or article. If a text organizes ideas by listing qualities of a topic, then an idea map is a good tool. Idea maps may be used in conjunction with any other note-taking method.

- The **Cornell method** is laid out in a special format on a piece of paper.
  - Divide the top 3/4 of the page into two columns. Label the right column Notes and the left column Prompts.
  - The bottom 1/4 of the page is for summarizing. Label it Summary.
  - In the right column take notes on one source. These notes may be fairly extensive. Remember to follow basic note-taking procedures.
  - Write questions and key words in the left column.
  - Write a one or two sentence summary of your notes at the bottom of the page.

Student Model: Cornell Method

Wepman, Dennis and Schlesinger (p. 4)	
Prompts	**Notes**
How did Aristotle affect Alex.? Iliad Philosopher king	1. Philip knew that Leonides could only prepare Alex for war; wanted somebody to prepare his mind, too. 2. Chose Greek philosopher, Aristotle, in his early 40s, not yet famous. 3. Huge influence: instilled love of Greek arts, science; especially Homer; slept with Iliad. 4. Wanted to be Plato's philosopher-king.
Summary	
Aristotle, who became Alexander's tutor, instilled in him a love of Greek art and science.	

As you read the following selection, take notes. Think, too, about the Big Question. *Guiding Question:* **How can remembering heroes and events affect the lives of people today?**

Flying to Fame

Amelia Earhart and Sally Ride were pioneers in the history of flight and for their gender. Amelia Earhart was the first woman to fly solo across the Atlantic. Sally Ride became the first American woman in space.

Amelia Earhart

Amelia Earhart was born on July 24, 1897, in Atchison, Kansas. While growing up, she liked to experiment with daring stunts. At the age of 19, Earhart discovered flying. She was working as a nurse's aide in a Canadian military hospital. One of her friends was a pilot in the Royal Flying Corps. She spent her free time watching him fly planes at a nearby airfield.

In 1921, Earhart began taking flying lessons. At this time, flying was still a risky new endeavor. It was a difficult task that required skill, courage, and the determination to keep trying to succeed. In her first two months of flying, she made two crash landings. Bravely, she continued flying. Six months later, she bought her own plane.

Earhart became the first woman to fly solo across the Atlantic. Her flight brought her international fame. It also inspired her to set one new record after another. In 1935, Earhart became the first person to fly nonstop alone from Honolulu, Hawaii, to the U.S. mainland. Later she became the first person to fly nonstop from Los Angeles to Mexico City and from Mexico City to Newark, New Jersey.

Earhart's greatest challenge came on June 1, 1937. She had decided to attempt another record-breaking flight. She was ready to make a 29,000-mile trip around the world. She asked Fred Noonan,

> Take notes on the first paragraph on a note card.

> On a separate sheet of paper, take notes on the rest of this section using the Cornell Method.

Good to Know! ▶
Amelia Earhart broke the women's altitude record by flying 14,000 feet in the air.

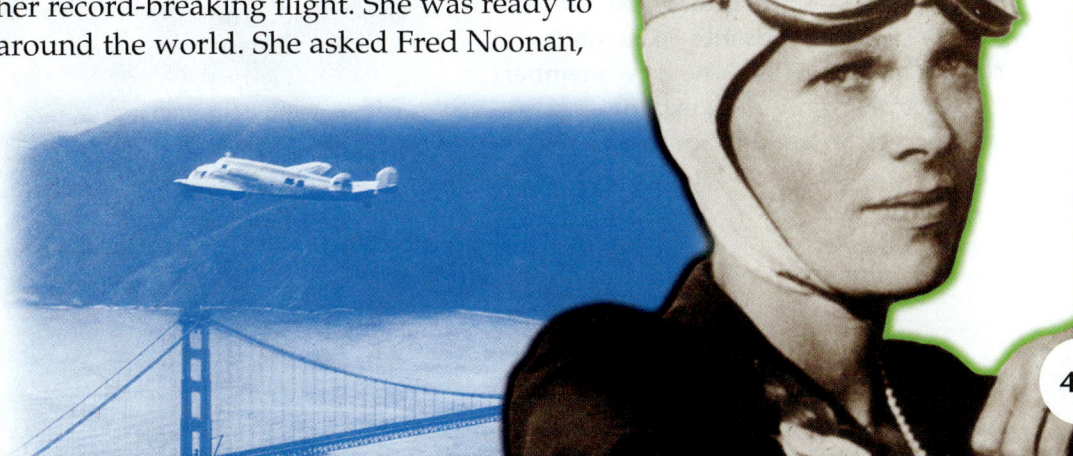

an experienced navigator, to fly with her. Taking off from Florida, they flew on to South America, across the Atlantic to Africa, and on to Asia. Finally they arrived on the island of New Guinea. From there, they faced the most dangerous part of their journey. They would have to fly 2,556 miles across the Pacific Ocean to reach Howland Island. On July 2, Earhart and Noonan took off across the Pacific. Somewhere between New Guinea and Howland Island, however, they disappeared and have never been found.

Sally Ride

As a young girl, Sally Ride enjoyed challenges. For example, she often competed successfully when playing sports with children in her neighborhood. Also, at the age of 12, Ride began to play tennis. She was soon winning tournaments and became a nationally ranked tennis player.

> On a separate sheet of paper, make an idea map of the information about Sally Ride.

In college, Ride studied hard, spending nine years earning degrees in English, science, and physics. "Then one day in 1977," Ride said, "I read an announcement in the paper that NASA (National Aeronautics and Space Administration) was accepting applications. And all of a sudden, I realized that I wanted to do it. There was no question in my mind." Ride wrote to NASA and expressed her interest in becoming an astronaut. She was admitted, along with five other women, into the first class to accept women.

In 1978, Ride joined NASA. After years of training, she was chosen to go up in the *Challenger* space shuttle. It was on this shuttle where Ride became the first American woman astronaut to reach outer space.

Amelia Earhart took off across the Pacific Ocean to achieve a dream. Sally Ride faced an even greater vastness as she blasted off into outer space. They both proved that women have the courage and determination to make history.

June 18, 1983—Cape Canaveral, Florida: ▶
Dr. Sally Ride heads into space on board shuttle mission STS-7. The crew members conduct pharmaceutical experiments and are the first to use a robot arm to release a satellite into space.

Sally Ride, ▶
the first American woman sent into space, totes her luggage following her arrival at the Kennedy Space Center.

Thinking About the Selection
Flying to Fame

1 **Compare and Contrast** Which method of note-taking did you find easiest to use? Which was the hardest? Explain your answer.

_____
_____
_____
_____

2 **Analyze** Which method helped you to understand the information best? Why do you think so?

_____
_____
_____
_____

3 **Compare** Which method do you think would be best for a short research paper? Which method do you think would be best for a long research paper? Why?

_____
_____
_____
_____

Research

Now, think about your own research paper.

4 **Apply** Find a primary and secondary source on your research topic. Cite the source and take notes according to the format that works best for you.

Write Answer the following questions in your Reader's Journal.

5 **Draw Conclusions** How can remembering heroes and events affect the lives of people today?

6 **Connect** Find out information about the author of your Anchor Book. Is your book a reliable source on its topic? Explain why or why not.

6-6 Comparing Source Texts
Primary and Secondary Sources

When conducting research before writing a paper, it's important to know what types of sources to use to gather information. Sources are divided into two main categories: primary sources and secondary sources.

▶ **Primary sources** are firsthand accounts of the experiences and observations of the writer or speaker. Writers frequently cite primary sources in their work to provide evidence or support for their arguments. Here are some examples of primary sources.

- interviews
- diaries and letters
- speeches
- autobiographies

▶ **Secondary sources** provide information that is not firsthand, but they bring together ideas from other sources about a subject. Often, they include quotations or paraphrases from primary sources or other secondary sources. Here are some examples of secondary sources.

- textbooks
- some nonfiction books
- encyclopedias
- newspaper articles

The following models show a primary source and a secondary source. As you read, notice how the secondary source uses quotations from the primary source as well as paraphrasing (the writer uses his or her own words).

PRIMARY SOURCE	SECONDARY SOURCE
Preamble to the Constitution of the United States We the People of the United States, in Order to form a more perfect Union, establish Justice, insure domestic Tranquility, provide for the common defence,[1] promote the general Welfare, and secure the Blessings of Liberty to ourselves and our Posterity,[2] do ordain and establish this Constitution for the United States of America.	The Preamble, which states the philosophical need for the creation of the Constitution, possesses language that is timeless yet not entirely clear. For instance, the phrases "insure domestic Tranquility" and "secure the Blessings of Liberty to ourselves and our Posterity" may lead U.S. citizens of different backgrounds to question what the words "tranquility" and "liberty" really mean.

[1] **defence**, also spelled as **defense** *n.* protection from harm.
[2] **Posterity** (päs ter′ ə tē) *n.* future generations; descendants.

while reading your anchor book

Read the following primary and secondary sources.
Guiding Question: How might Chief Joseph's words and actions be seen as heroic today?

A GREAT and HONORABLE Leader

Background *Chief Joseph was a courageous leader and military strategist who relied on diplomacy in his dealings with conflict. At age 30, he became leader of the Nez Percé people. The following article describes his experiences with the United States government.*

Vocabulary Builder

Before you read, you will discuss the following words. In the Vocabulary Builder box in the margin, use a vocabulary building strategy to make the words your own.

treaty   retreat   misrepresentations

As you read, draw a box around unfamiliar words you could add to your vocabulary. Use context clues to unlock their meaning.

Marking the Text

Primary and Secondary Sources

As you read, underline details in each selection that show what type of source this is. In the margins, identify the source as primary or secondary and explain your reasoning.

In 1863, the U.S. government demanded that the Nez Percé[1] give up about 6 million acres of land on their reservation. This was land the U.S. government had set aside for them earlier. The Nez Percé refused. Then a government agent bribed several chiefs, who sold the land and signed the **treaty.**

A Nez Percé leader called Old Joseph was angry about the land sale. Near his death, he warned his son Joseph against ever signing a treaty to sell their homeland. Upon his father's death,

Vocabulary Builder

treaty
(trēt′ ē) *n.*

Meaning

---

[1] **Nez Percé** (nā per sā′) a Native American people originally occupying the lands where Washington, Oregon, and Idaho now meet.

Joseph became the peace chief of his father's band. Chief Joseph held many councils, or meetings, with leaders from the U.S. government. In 1873, Joseph convinced the government that it did not buy the reservation lands legally. The government ordered the whites to move out of the territory. However, the government then changed its mind under pressure from Oregon settlers. Several Nez Percé men took revenge by killing four of the settlers. Knowing that U.S. troops would come after them, the bands began a remarkable **retreat.** To avoid death or capture, the Nez Percé outwitted one military force after another for four months, trying to reach safety in Canada.

The soldiers who fought Chief Joseph thought that he was a great and honorable man. The soldiers knew that the Nez Percé never killed without reason. Chief Joseph and his people fought only to defend themselves and their land.

The end finally came. After a five-day battle, Chief Joseph decided to surrender on October 5, 1877. He rode into the army camp alone and handed his rifle to the soldiers. He said:

> I am tired of fighting. . . . It is cold and we have no blankets. The little children are freezing to death. . . . Hear me, my chiefs, my heart is sick and sad. From where the sun now stands I will fight no more against the white man.

After Chief Joseph's surrender, the U.S. government ordered the Nez Percé onto a reservation in Kansas, then to a reservation in Oklahoma. Many of the Nez Percé died from diseases they caught while on these reservations.

Chief Joseph pleaded on behalf of his people to return to a reservation in the Northwest. In 1879, Chief Joseph traveled to Washington, D.C., to plead his case to President Rutherford B. Hayes. There, he delivered a speech that included the following words:

> If the white man wants to live in peace with the Indian, he can live in peace. There need be no trouble. Treat all men alike. Give them the same laws. Give them all an even chance to live and grow.

Vocabulary Builder

retreat
(ri trēt') *n.*

Meaning

from
A Visit to Washington, D.C., 1879

by Chief Joseph

Nez Percé infant wrapped in a papoose

At last I was granted permission to come to Washington and bring my friend Yellow Bull and our interpreter with me. I am glad I came. I have shaken hands with a good many friends, but there are some things I want to know which no one seems able to explain.... I have heard talk and talk, but nothing is done.

Good words do not last long unless they amount to something. Words do not pay for my dead people. They do not pay for my country, now overrun by white men. They do not protect my father's grave. They do not pay for my horses and cattle. Good words will not give me back my children. Good words will not make good the promise of your war chief, General Miles.... Good words will not give my people a home where they can live in peace and take care of themselves. I am tired of talk that comes to nothing. It makes my heart sick when I remember all the good words and all the broken promises. There has been too much talking by men who had no right to talk. Too many **misrepresentations** have been made; too many misunderstandings have come up between the white men about the Indians.

If the white man wants to live in peace with the Indian he can live in peace. There need be no trouble. Treat all men alike. Give them the same law. Give them all an even chance to live and grow. All men were made by the same Great Spirit Chief. They are all brothers. The earth is the mother of all people, and all people should have equal rights upon it. You might as well expect all rivers to run backward as that any man who was born a free man should be contented penned up and denied liberty to go where he pleases. If you tie a horse to a stake, do you expect he will grow fat? If you pen an Indian up on a small spot of earth, and compel him to stay there, he will not be contented, nor will he grow and prosper. I have asked some of the Great White Chiefs where they get their authority to say to the Indian that he shall stay in one place, while he sees white men going where they please. They cannot tell me.

Vocabulary Builder

misrepresentations
(mis rep rē zen tā′ shəns) *n.*

Meaning

Primary and Secondary Sources **483**

from The SURRENDER in the BEAR PAW MOUNTAINS

by Chief Joseph

Tell General Howard I know his heart. What he told me before, I have in my heart. I am tired of fighting. Our chiefs are killed; Looking Glass[1] is dead. Tu-hul-hil-sote[2] is dead. The old men are all dead. It is the young men who say yes or no. He who led on the young men is dead. It is cold and we have no blankets. The little children are freezing to death. My people, some of them, have run away to the hills and have no blankets, and no food; no one knows where they are—perhaps freezing to death. I want to have time to look for my children and see how many of them I can find. Maybe I shall find them among the dead. Hear me, my chiefs, my heart is sick and sad. From where the sun now stands I will fight no more against the white man.

---

[1] **Looking Glass** a Nez Percé warrior.
[2] **Tu-hul-hil-sote** a wise elder.

Vocabulary Builder

After you read, review the words you decided to add to your vocabulary. Write the meaning of words you have learned in context. Look up the other words in a dictionary, glossary, thesaurus, or electronic resource.

Thinking About the Selections

A Great and Honorable Leader *and* Speeches of Chief Joseph

1 **Distinguish** Why is *A Great and Honorable Leader* considered a secondary source rather than a primary source? Why are the speeches of Chief Joseph primary sources?

2 **Connect** In what type of book might you find the passage *A Great and Honorable Leader*? Support your statement with information from the passage.

3 **Evaluate** How does each reading deal with the topic differently in terms of treatment, scope, and organization?

Research

Now, think about your own research paper.

4 **Evaluate** Identify the sources you have gathered for your research project as primary or secondary. Find a primary source for your topic and explain what new perspective it offers.

Write Answer the following questions in your Reader's Journal.

5 **Explain** How might Chief Joseph's words and actions be seen as heroic today?

6 **Explain** Is your Anchor Book a primary or secondary source? Cite a passage from your book in your explanation.

6-7 Analyzing an Informational Text
Interview Transcript

An **interview** is a discussion between an interviewer and another person or group of people. Often the subject is someone of special interest. The interviewer asks questions or makes statements, and the subject responds. A coherent, well-formed interview uses this structure to reveal information about the subject.

Interviews may be recorded in a variety of ways, such as written notes, an audio recorder, or a video recorder. A written copy of an interview is called a **transcript**.

Directions Read the following transcript of an interview with acclaimed horror writer Stephen King. Note how the interview's structure reveals information about the subject. Then answer the questions that follow.

Stephen King: *His Books, His Life, His Wife*

LESLEY STAHL (CO-HOST): There's hardly anybody in America who hasn't read a Stephen King novel or seen a Stephen King movie. Let's face it, he's the world's best-selling novelist, the most successful horror writer in history. As we reported in February last year, even including entertainers, King is one of the highest paid in the country, earning more than $30 million in a single year. That's all because his mind works this way: A man screams . . .

STEPHEN KING (NOVELIST): . . . and this rat jumps into his mouth and gets halfway down his throat. And if you can imagine, OK, not just the taste of it and the rear legs sort of kicking in air, but the feel of the whiskers way back in your throat as it sort of gobbles away at your soft palate.

STAHL: You know what? I'm completely grossed out. You've accomplished . . .

KING: I'm sorry.

STAHL: No, you're not. That's what you wanted to do.

> The names of the co-host and novelist are called out in **bold capital letters.**

KING: No . . .

STAHL: Yes, this is . . .

> Ellipses (. . .) appear where dialogue is interrupted.

KING: . . . I'm not sorry.

STAHL: Have you ever gone to a psychiatrist?

> Text Structure The interviewer asks a question and the subject responds, revealing information.

KING: No, no. I've never gone to a psychiatrist, because I feel like what you do at a psychiatrist is you pay $75, $90 an hour to get rid of your fears, whereas if I write them down, people pay me. It's good.

(footage[1] of Stephen King thrillers; Stephen King working on a computer; Stephen King singing)

STAHL: (Voiceover[2]) Since 1974, people have paid good money for 32 novels, five collections of short stories, nine screenplays, and one non-fiction study of horror. Except for his birthday, the Fourth of July and Christmas, King writes at least four hours every day.

KING: The ideas come and they have to be let out. That's all. They just have to be let out.

(footage of King home)

> Parentheses contain directions for voiceovers and film footage.

STAHL: (Voiceover) All that stands between those ideas and the rest of the world are these wrought-iron gates. King can afford to live anywhere, but the hometown of horror is Bangor, Maine.

No, this is not happening. This is not happening.

KING: Bring me the ball.

(footage of King's Welsh Corgi[3])

---

[1] A collection of filmed images and sounds about a certain subject

[2] An offscreen voice that speaks about the subject a viewer sees

[3] **Welsh Corgi** (Welsh Kôr gē) *n.* squat, short-legged dog with a foxlike head and pointy ears

Critical Viewing ▶
What does Stephen King's house, shown here, tell you about him? Were you surprised or not?

while reading your anchor book

487

STAHL: (Voiceover) A vicious canine beast also lives here.

KING: Oops! He stole the ball!

(footage of Stephen King with Corgi; excerpt from *Cujo*)

STAHL: (Voiceover) In Stephen King's world, Welsh Corgis play basketball, and St. Bernards become demons, as in the movie *Cujo*. He wants to scare us. But what scares him?

KING: Everything that scares you, everything that scares anybody. That's part of the reason for my success.

STAHL: Well, for instance, is it true, or is this kind of part of your humor to tell us that you sleep with a night-light?

KING: So what if it is true? It's not hurting anybody. I tend to keep a night-light on, but, like anybody else—particularly if you're in a strange place—you don't want to stub your toe if you have to go to the bathroom in the night.

STAHL: It's not like anybody else. Trust me.

KING: No, no. It's like anybody else, or else I wouldn't be as successful as I am.

STAHL: Is his story that he sleeps with a night-light . . .

TABITHA KING (STEPHEN'S WIFE): Not true. Not true.

STAHL: Not true.

TABITHA KING: No.

(footage of Tabitha King)

STAHL: (Voiceover) Tabitha King is certain because she and her husband Stephen have been married for 26 years.

TABITHA KING: There's a lot of mythologizing.

STAHL: Yeah, but he . . . he created that.

TABITHA KING: And he encourages it. Yes, he does. He does. He encourages it.

KING: Tabby keeps the monsters away so . . . yeah, it's true. Over the years, you have kept a lot of monsters away.

▼ Tabitha King, writer and wife of Stephen King

Thinking About the Selection
Stephen King: His Books, His Life, His Wife

1 **Recall** According to the information presented in the interview, why are Stephen King's works so scary?

_____
_____
_____

2 **Evaluate** Why would Lesley Stahl have chosen to interview Stephen King? What value does this interview have?

_____
_____
_____
_____

3 **Infer** Why does the interview show footage of King playing with his real-life dog and an excerpt from the movie *Cujo*?

_____
_____
_____

4 **Evaluate** How does the structure of this interview help reveal information about the subject? Is the structure consistent?

_____
_____
_____

5 **Connect** Why is the structure of this interview like a play and not like a narrative?

_____
_____
_____

Write Answer the following questions in your Reader's Journal.

6 **Identify** If you could interview someone from your Anchor Book, who would it be, and why?

Interview Transcript **489**

6-8 Language Coach
Grammar and Spelling

Revising Run-on Sentences and Sentence Fragments

A **sentence fragment** does not express a complete thought. Although writers sometimes use them for effect, it is best to avoid them in formal writing. Either add the fragment to a nearby sentence or add words to make a complete thought.

Sentence Fragment	Revised Sentence
When I finished my homework. It was nine o'clock.	When I finished my homework, it was nine o'clock.

A **run-on sentence** has two or more complete sentences that are not properly joined or separated. Either separate the sentence into two sentences, or join them with a comma and a conjunction or with a semicolon.

Run-On Sentence	Revised Sentence
The pilot landed the plane in Chicago it was a bumpy flight.	**Separate sentences:** The pilot landed the plane in Chicago. It was a bumpy flight.
	Add a comma and a conjunction: The pilot landed the plane in Chicago, and it was a bumpy flight.
	Use a semicolon: The pilot landed the plane in Chicago; it was a bumpy flight.

Directions Revise the following fragments and run-on sentences.

1. Here is the package you ordered it was delivered this morning.

2. Since my last visit to Los Angeles.

3. Karen writes music she is a fine pianist.

Revising to Use Quotation Marks and Block Quotes

When you use quotations to support your points, you must set them off so the reader knows they are someone else's words. **Brief quotations** have five or fewer lines and are treated like the quotations in a story's dialogue. **Block quotations,** or quotations more than five lines long, should be indented. When you quote from another source, copy the words exactly as they appear in the work.

Example: Brief quotation

According to the story, the narrator's greatest interest is running because she says, "I'm serious about running, and I don't care who knows it."

Example: Block quotation

These lines of *Raymond's Run* by Toni Cade Bambara show what kind of person the character Squeaky is.

> And I don't play the dozens or believe in standing around with somebody in my face doing a lot of talking. I much rather just knock you down and take my chances even if I am a little girl with skinny arms and a squeaky voice. Which is how I got the name "Squeaky."

Clearly, Squeaky is a determined person with little fear.

Author's Craft

All writers aim to create something quotable, or memorable. Choose a memorable passage from something you have read in this book. Incorporate the quotation, using the proper format, into a paragraph that explains why the passage is memorable.

Directions Rewrite each sentence, adding any missing punctuation marks or capital letters.

Example: Melissa said there's my mom at the front door
Melissa said, "There's my mom at the front door."

1 My mother felt my forehead and said you get into bed this minute

2 I heard him ask can you tell me where a drinking fountain is

3 We won the championship the boys shouted

4 Let me see your license the police officer said

6-9 Writer's Workshop
Research: Interview Report

An **interview** is an information-gathering technique in which you ask someone questions and record his or her answers. In an interview report, a living person is your primary source. Follow the steps outlined in this workshop to write your own interview report.

Your interview report should include the following elements.

- a detailed background of your subject, to create context
- thought-provoking questions
- important points provided by the subject (person being interviewed)
- accurate recording of the subject's statements
- a clear organizational format
- error-free grammar

Purpose To write an interview report

Audience You, your teacher, and your classmates

Prewriting—Plan It Out

To choose a subject, use the following strategy.

Choose your subject. In this chart, list people that you want to interview. Think of someone whom you find interesting or who has knowledge of your research topic. Then, choose the most interesting person.

Interesting People	What Makes Them Interesting

Gather questions. Prepare a list of questions to ask your subject. Write each question on a separate note card. If it is difficult to speak with your interview subject directly, write him/her a friendly letter or email with your questions. Structure your questions in an order that allows the interview to move smoothly.

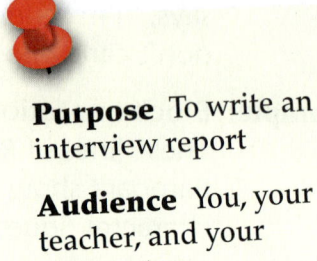

Conduct the interview. Be polite when interviewing your subject. Ask questions slowly and take notes on each note card. You may wish to use a recording device during the interview.

492 Lesson 6-9

Drafting—Get It on Paper

Using your note cards, write your draft. The following step will help make your report engaging and organized.

Shape your writing. Write an outline to structure your report. Start the report by giving background information about your subject. This will help to engage the reader. Order your questions based on their importance and how they fit together. For instance, if you interview a musician, you might arrange them by training, favorite artists, and inspiration.

To determine which information should be included, ask yourself these questions and write down your answer.

What part of the interview was the most insightful?	
Which questions received the best answers?	
Was anything surprising?	

> I. Introduction
> II. First question
>   A. Answer detail
>   B. Answer detail
> III. Second question
>   A. Answer detail
>   B. Answer detail

Revising—Make It Better

Now that you have a draft, revise your report to make it more precise. Review your draft to make sure that your subject's quotations are noted accurately. Consult your notes and make the appropriate changes. Then think of ways to use tables, charts, or graphs to enhance the appearance of your report.

Student Model: Revising for Accuracy

```
No, no. I've never gone to a psychiatrist because, I feel like
                                  ^pay $75, $90 an hour
what you do at a psychiatrist is to get rid of your fears.
                                ^whereas if I write
                                 them down, people
                                 pay me. It's good.
```

The writer's revision makes the quote accurate.

Peer Review Ask for a partner's response to your interview report. Your partner can look at the rubric at the end of this lesson to help formulate a response. Revise to achieve the reaction you had intended.

Research: Interview Report 493

Writer's Workshop continued

Directions Read this interview report as a model for your own.

Student Model: Writing

Michael Palermo, Haverhill, MA

A Sea Man on Land

In 1942, during World War II, there was a great need not only for soldiers but also engineers. Norman DeBrosky was a member of the Seabees. He developed skills as a carpenter. He served and worked alongside men fighting for a common goal, and he is my grandfather.

Why did you decide to join the Navy?
I felt a sense of duty: a sense of duty to my country and to myself, to my friends and family. The world was at war. There was a terrible power trying to change the world.

Why were you called "Seabees"?
Because we'd sting you if you got too close. Actually, it comes from Construction Battalion that was abbreviated "C.B." and later turned into "Seabee."

What did you do as a Seabee?
I built bases, roads, airstrips, hospitals, and storage facilities. Anything that needed to be constructed, we'd do it. When you're a Seabee, your motto is "Can Do!"

You say that with a lot of pride. What do you think being a Seabee taught you?
Being a Seabee taught me to work hard and measure everything twice. You couldn't afford to mess up. I was always good with math, but I never had the opportunity to put it to good use. Serving as a Seabee gave me that opportunity. I'm proud that I was able to be a part of something important.

Do you consider yourself a hero?
A hero? No. I helped heroes get to where they needed to be.

> In his opening paragraph, the writer introduces his subject in an interesting way.

> This quotation provides insight into the subject's personality.

> In his final question, the writer asks a thought-provoking question.

Lesson 6-9

Editing—Be Your Own Language Coach

Before you hand in your interview report, review it for language convention errors. Pay special attention to your use of quotations and be sure that you've structured your interview in a way that makes sense.

Publishing—Share It!

Consider one of the following ideas to share your writing.

Submit it. Offer your report to your local or school newspaper.

Share your report. Discuss your report with a group of classmates. Invite classmates to respond with their opinions.

Be courteous. Remember to send your interview subject a copy of your report and a thank-you note.

Reflecting on Your Writing

1 Respond to the following questions on the back of your final draft. What new insights did you gain about the form of the interview report by writing one? What do you do well? What do you need to work on? Set a goal you can meet in your next workshop.

2 **Rubric for Self-Assessment** Assess your essay. For each question, circle a rating.

CRITERIA	RATING SCALE
IDEAS Does your report give a clear understanding of your subject?	NOT VERY VERY 1 2 3 4 5
ORGANIZATION Is your report well organized?	1 2 3 4 5
VOICE How well do you set a tone for your essay?	1 2 3 4 5
WORD CHOICE How appropriate is the language for your audience?	1 2 3 4 5
SENTENCE FLUENCY How varied is your structure?	1 2 3 4 5
CONVENTIONS How correct is your grammar, especially your avoidance of run-ons and fragments?	1 2 3 4 5

Monitoring Your Progress
Standardized Test Practice

Reading Skill: Setting a Purpose for Reading

Read the passage. Then, answer the questions.

> We've all seen them in pictures: flat, coal-black, and about the size and shape of a small pizza. They are LPs: long-playing record albums, also known as "vinyl."
>
> CDs, or compact discs, are produced by converting sound to digital signals that are burned onto a disc with lasers. So, what goes into making, and listening to, an LP? First, an analog, or likeness, of the audio is transformed into jagged waves. These waves are stored in tiny channels called grooves on a disc's surface. Then, the sound is reproduced by a phonograph. This machine consists of the following parts:
> - A delicately balanced turntable
> - A finely-tuned motor that spins the disc at a precise, constant speed
> - A tone arm that holds a stylus, or needle, that rides along the grooves
>
> The waves in each groove cause the stylus to vibrate. The vibrations are then transformed into electric signals. The signals are converted back into sound using speakers.

1 Which best states what this passage is about?
- A. a delicately balanced turntable
- B. waves that cause the stylus to vibrate
- C. what goes into making, and listening to, an LP
- D. sound reproduced by a phonograph

2 Which of the following states a valid purpose for reading this passage?
- F. to find out how compact discs are made
- G. to learn about the science of LP recordings
- H. to get information for a paper on lasers
- J. to critique the author's presentation of opinions

3 Which term in the passage describes the process of copying sound for use on an LP?
- A. analog
- B. grooves
- C. phonograph
- D. stylus

4 Which question is not answered by information in the passage?
- F. How is sound stored on the surface of an LP?
- G. What are the parts of a phonograph?
- H. How do CDs reproduce sound so listeners can hear it?
- J. How does a stylus help reproduce sound on an LP?

The Research Process

Read the following selection. Then, answer the questions.

> No one knows exactly when the first library was founded. The earliest records were kept on clay tablets and scrolls of papyrus, a primitive form of paper. About 2,000 years ago, the rulers of ancient Egypt borrowed papyrus scrolls from distant lands and made copies of them. The establishment of the Alexandrian Library made Alexandria, Egypt, a great center of culture and learning. It contained more than 700,000 scrolls. Scholars came from far and wide to study them.
>
> The oldest library in the United States was started at Harvard University in 1638. A century later, Benjamin Franklin founded the first subscription library in the country. For a small fee, subscribers could borrow books in exchange for their solemn pledge to return the books to the library. The first tax-supported free libraries in the United States appeared in the early 1800s. Today, public libraries can be found in almost every community in the nation.

5 For what research project topic do you think this selection would be a good source?

  A. the history of papyrus
  B. the history of paper
  C. the history of libraries
  D. the history of Alexandria, Egypt

6 A student is researching the history of libraries. Which is a primary source the student could use?

  F. a book on the history of Harvard University
  G. a newspaper article about the discovery of the oldest scrolls ever found in Egypt
  H. a biography about Benjamin Franklin
  J. an interview with a librarian

7 Which of the following is the most appropriate method for taking notes about this selection?

  A. idea map
  B. Cornell method
  C. paraphrasing
  D. copying and pasting

8 To find reliable and accurate information about the history of libraries, a student could use _____.

  F. a library index
  G. Harvard University's Web site
  H. one source about clay tablets
  J. all of the above

Timed Writing: Interpretation

Directions What opinions do you have about your research topic so far? Support your opinion with specific details from your research.
(20 minutes)

Monitoring Your Progress 497

6-10 Reading Skills
Summarizing

In learning new reading skills, you will use special academic vocabulary. Knowing the right words will help you demonstrate your understanding.

Academic Vocabulary

Word	Meaning	Example Sentence
sequence *n.* Related words: sequencing, sequential	to follow one thing after another	I want to stick to the *sequence*, so I won't read any book in the series out of order.
pertinent *adj.* Related words: pertinence, pertain	related to the topic	After her presentation, the speaker answered *pertinent* questions from the audience.
determine *v.* Related words: determining, determined	to figure out	To *determine* the author's purpose, study the work's details.

A **summary** is a brief passage that restates the most important points in a piece of writing. Summarizing is a great tool to check and correct errors in comprehension. To summarize a selection, you need to do the following.

- ▶ **Determine** the main idea for each paragraph. Write it in the margin.
- ▶ Review each idea to determine the main idea of the passage.
- ▶ Identify the **sequence** in which events occur or information is listed.
- ▶ Select the **pertinent** information you need to write a strong summary.
- ▶ Write your summary in paragraph form, including the main idea and the sequence of pertinent details or events.

Directions Read the following excerpt from a Dynamo Bicycle Company warranty, then read the summary and answer the questions that follow.

while reading your anchor book

498 Lesson 6-10

DYNAMO BICYCLES

Limited Warranty

Time Period
Warranty coverage on all Dynamo bicycle frames is for the life of the bicycle while owned by the original purchaser. Coverage on bicycle components (excluding tires, tubes, and cables) is for two years. Warranty coverage on tires, tubes, and cables is not through Dynamo, and the purchaser is responsible for seeking coverage through the companies manufacturing these components.

This warranty does not cover the following:
- Normal wear and tear as a result of riding and/or transporting the bicycle.
- Damage or loss due to theft, accident, misuse, or failure to follow instructions in owner's manual.
- Damage or mechanical failure caused as a result of stunt riding, jumping, or racing.
- Damage caused by the modification of bicycle from its original form, such as the installation of non-factory components or power engines.

Labor Charges
The original purchaser shall pay all labor charges connected with the repair or replacement of parts under warranty. This warranty does not include shipping or other transportation costs to or from a Dynamo bicycle dealer, other business, or private residence.

Student Model

> ### Summary
> Dynamo bike frames and parts are covered under warranty for a certain amount of time. The warranty does not cover certain events, such as damage due to wear and tear, bike modification, and dangerous riding. The warranty does not cover loss due to theft. The warranty also states that the purchaser is responsible for labor and shipping charges.

1 **Compare** Does the summary accurately capture the main idea and important details of the warranty? Is there any information not included in the summary that could help clarify the main idea? Explain your answer.

_____
_____
_____

2 **Speculate** In what situations might it be better to provide a summary rather than giving all of the information? In what situations might it be better to provide all of the information rather than a summary?

_____
_____
_____

3 **Interpret** The warranty states which bicycle components are covered and for how long. If the frame cracks after one year of normal wear, what should the bicycle owner do?

_____
_____
_____

Research

Now, think about your own research paper.

4 On a separate piece of paper, summarize what you have learned about your topic in your research. What is the main idea you want to convey?

while reading your anchor book

In this article, the author summarizes historical events as part of his writing. *Guiding Question:* Why would Barbara Johns's actions from the past still be considered heroic today?

Link to Social Studies

Kids on the Bus
The Overlooked Role of Teenagers in the Civil-Rights Era
by Jeffrey Zaslow

You probably know that Martin Luther King, Jr., fought for racial equality, and that Rosa Parks set an example by refusing to give up her seat on a segregated bus. But have you heard of sixteen-year-old Barbara Johns?

▲ School bus transporting African American high school children to a run-down segregated school.

There's a true story we should tell our children about a bus, an African American citizen, and her yearning for equality in the segregated South of the 1950s.

No, Rosa Parks is not part of this story. This story is about Barbara Johns. In 1951, Barbara was a 16-year-old student at a segregated school in Farmville, Virginia. About 450 black students were crowded into a school built for 200. Overflow classes were held in leaky, tar-paper shacks and on

501

school buses, with kids shivering in the winter. Books and supplies were in tatters.

One day, Barbara missed the bus to school, and waited by the road, hoping someone would pick her up. A bus, filled with children heading to their far-superior school, passed by. After it drove off, Barbara bravely decided to organize a walkout of her entire student body. Her leadership would help change America.

Our children are taught about Rosa Parks's refusal to give up her seat on the bus in 1955. They know about the Rev. Martin Luther King Jr. and his "I Have a Dream" speech. But many don't realize that the early civil-rights movement was often led by unsung teens. Some academics and activists now argue that by not sharing this hidden history, parents and teachers are missing crucial opportunities to energize and inspire today's kids, especially African Americans.

"Rosa Parks, an older woman, is a wonderful symbol, but most black teenagers don't have a sense of the role played by the people of their own age," says Clayborne Carson, director of the Martin Luther King Jr. Research and Educational Institute at Stanford University. "When we speak about Rosa Parks, let's speak about these other people."

▼ **Students who took part in a strike against inadequate African American schools posing for a photo in Prince Edward County. Inset: Graduation photo of Barbara Johns.**

Thinking About the Selection

from Kids on the Bus: The Overlooked Role of Teenagers in the Civil-Rights Era

1 **Identify** In informational texts, authors frequently organize their ideas around key vocabulary. In this reading, words like *racial equality* and *segregated* are essential to the text's meaning. Use the chart below to identify and categorize the key words/phrases in order of importance. Then, identify any salient features of the key words, such as prefixes, suffixes, or roots, and give their definition. An example is shown.

Key Words	Important Word Parts
segregated school	Root, *segregare*, meaning *to set apart*

2 **Summarize** Write a summary of the passage you read.

_____
_____
_____
_____
_____

Write Answer the following questions in your Reader's Journal.

3 **Explain** Why would Barbara Johns's actions from the past still be considered heroic today?

4 **Apply** Choose one or two paragraphs from your Anchor Book and summarize the main idea and important details. How might this summary be helpful to you or to others?

Ready for a Free-Choice Book? Your teacher may ask you if you would like to choose another book to read on your own. Select a book that fits your interest and that you'll enjoy. As you read, think about how your new book compares with your Anchor Book.

Summarizing **503**

6-11 The Research Process
Drafting

You are ready to begin producing a draft. In it, you present your ideas at their earliest stages. Articulate your thoughts so that you can begin to shape your report.

Step 1: Identify Your Purpose and Perspective

▶ Your **main purpose** in writing a research report is to inform readers about your topic. However, you may also be trying to persuade readers to accept your perspective—your point of view. Depending on which perspective you take, you will need to focus on finding information to back up your point of view.

1 **Identify** Define your purpose and perspective for your paper.

_____
_____

▶ Could you tell a friend the main idea of your research report in a sentence or two? This brief summary, called a **thesis statement**, is one of the most important parts of your report. It should be clear and focused, and prove your perspective.

Too Broad   Alexander deserved the name "Great" due to a lifetime of achievement.

Too Narrow   Alexander's education in philosophy served him well, and he was known as the "Philosopher King."

Clear Focus   Out of this turmoil came a boy, Alexander III, a hero and perhaps the greatest military strategist in history.

▶ The background of your **audience** will determine what you write and how you present it. If your readers know little about your topic, you would need to provide simple explanations using everyday language. However, if your readers are experts in the field, you would want to provide complex definitions using specialized terminology.

2 **Synthesize** Write a thesis statement for your report. Ask a partner to review your statement. Revise it based on feedback.

_____
_____
_____

504 Lesson 6-11

Step 2: Organizing Your Ideas

Once you have written a strong thesis statement and gathered information to support it, you can begin to organize your report. Decide on a structure that is logical and easy to follow.

Begin by organizing your report into **main ideas.** Then find **details** that support each main idea—facts and examples that provide evidence or elaborate on your point. Cover each main idea and its **supporting details** in a paragraph or paragraph block—two or more paragraphs that develop the same main idea.

While all reports use main ideas and details, many use an additional organizational structure, or method of organizing information. Here are some examples.

- **Chronological order** presents events in the order in which they happened. This structure works well for topics about historical events or the lives of people. For example, a report on the life of Alexander the Great would probably be organized chronologically to relate the narrative of his life.

- **Compare-and-contrast** organization shows the ways in which two subjects are both alike and different. This structure suits topics that examine two or more people, places, things, or events. For example, compare-and-contrast would work well for a report about solar energy versus wind energy.

- **Cause-and-effect** organization explains how an event, an action, or a situation causes another event, action, or situation to occur. A report that uses this structure might analyze one or more causes and effects. For example, a cause-and-effect report might explain the multiple causes and effects of the Great Depression.

Evaluate Which type of organization do you think best suits your topic? Why?

_____
_____
_____
_____

Step 3: Creating an Outline

Once you have decided on the best organizational structure for your report, you can develop an outline. This outline will serve as your plan or map while you are writing your first draft. As you develop your outline, keep your thesis statement in mind. Every main idea, detail, fact, and example should support your thesis statement.

Graphic Organizer Method

Some writers move right into the outlining stage. Others begin with a looser writing plan, such as a main idea and supporting details in a graphic organizer. They then use this plan to create an outline.

Directions Complete the graphic organizer for your research report.

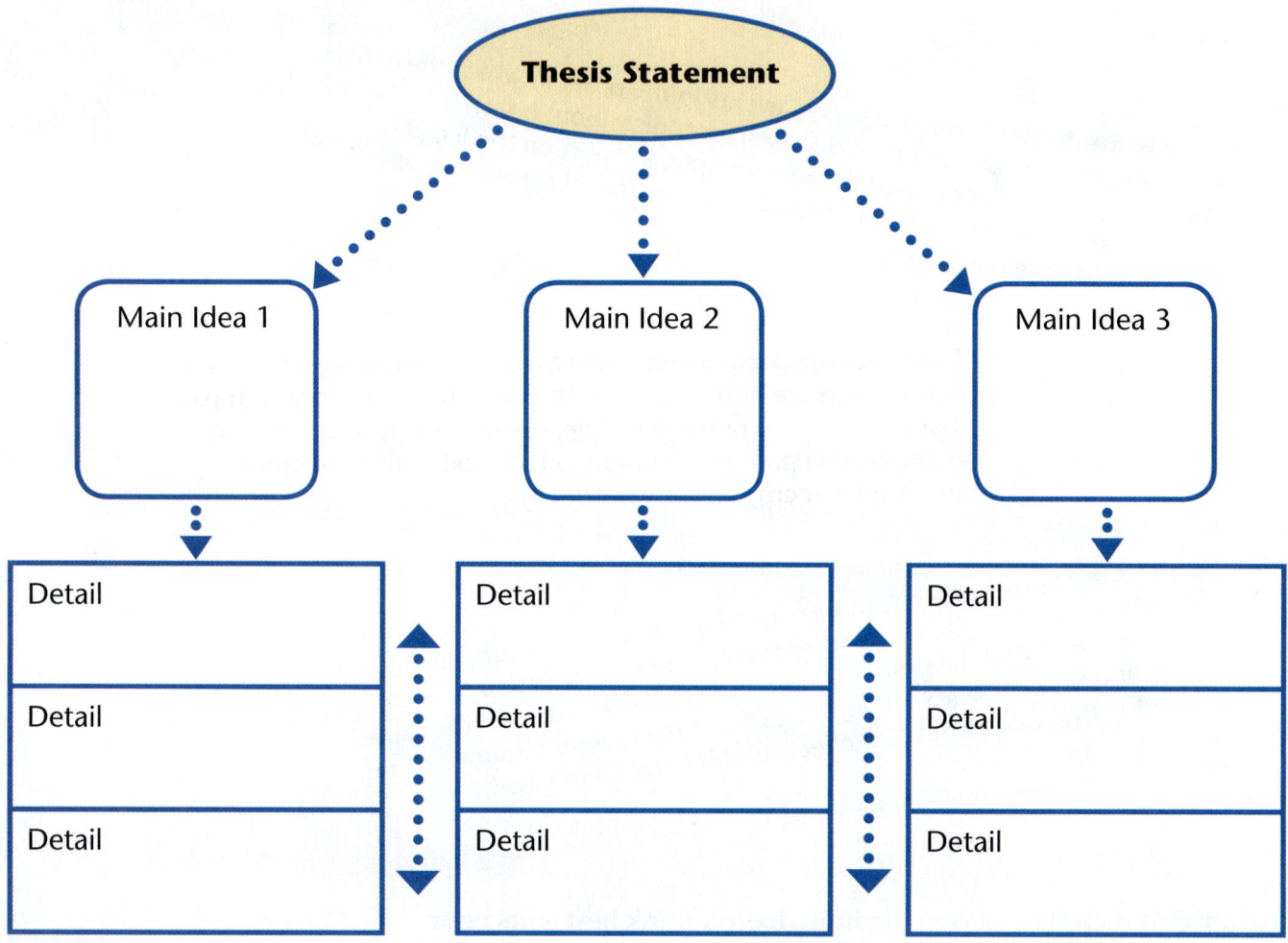

Depending on the type of organization you have chosen, you can use a different graphic organizer to plan your ideas. For example, if you are using chronological order, you can use a **sequence chain** to show the order of the events you are presenting. If you are using compare-and-contrast, you can use a **Venn diagram** or a **comparison chart** to list the similarities and differences you are analyzing. If you prefer, you can use technology by entering your data into a spreadsheet or by using an online mind-mapping program.

506 Lesson 6-11

Formal Outline Method

You can now use your graphic organizer to create an outline. Under each Roman numeral, present all the supporting details that back up your main idea. Use capital letters for the most important details and the numbers 1, 2, 3, and so on for minor details.

Directions Study the outline for the first part of a research report on Alexander the Great. Then answer the questions that follow.

> I. Introduction
> Thesis Statement: Alexander conquered most of the known world.
> II. Alexander's first 20 years
>   A. Parents: Philip II of Macedonia; Olympias, princess of Epirus
>   1. Close with mother; religious influence of mother
>   2. Military genius; bravery of father
>   B. Road to kingship
>   1. Philip's assassination—336 b.c.
>   2. Continuation of Philip's Persian campaign
> III. Alexander's campaign against Persia
>   A. Army of Alexander
>   1. 30,000 men
>   2. 5,000 Companions: cavalry
>   B. Army of Darius III
>   1. Persian cavalry
>   2. Greek mercenaries
>   C. Battle at the Hellesponte
>   1. Alexander's innovative strategy
>   2. Destruction of Persians

1 **Analyze** How does the writer's thesis statement determine the organizational structure of this outline? Explain your thinking.

2 **Synthesize** Look through your research notes. What main idea will you cover after your introduction? Why?

Step 4: Writing Your Rough Draft

It is time to start drafting your report. As you write, keep referring to both your outline and your research notes. Your outline is your plan, but your notes provide the details you need to turn that plan into an informative, well-documented research report.

> The following checklist will help you write your draft. Review your draft and put a ✔ next to each item that you have successfully completed.
>
> ❏ **Stick to your thesis.** In your introduction, present your thesis statement plus any background information that will provide context and catch readers' interest. In the body of the report, include only those details that are most relevant to your thesis. In your conclusion, restate your thesis and add a final comment.
>
> ❏ **Connect your ideas.** Think about how to connect, compare, and contrast your information. Use transitions to show the connections within and between paragraphs—signal words and phrases like *because, as a result, although, therefore,* and *however.*
>
> ❏ **Prepare to credit your sources.** Circle every idea and quotation that comes directly from a source. After each circled item, include the author's name and the source page number in parentheses, or, put a number in parentheses and create footnotes or endnotes.

Directions Read the excerpt from the first draft of a student report on Alexander the Great. Then, answer the questions that follow.

> (1) Alexander inherited his military genius and bravery from his father, who conquered all of the Greek city-states and then united them under his rule. (2) Because Philip felt that his son's education was important, he hired Aristotle, considered the wisest man in Greece, to tutor him. (3) Even as a child, Alexander had enough ambition for several men. (4) After Philip had conquered a city, Alexander made this comment: "My father will have everything, and I will have nothing left to conquer." (Wepman)

1 **Analyze** Refer to the outline on the previous page. Which sentence in the draft contains an irrelevant detail? Explain why.

2 **Evaluate** Where could the writer have used a transition to connect ideas more clearly? Explain your thinking.

Thinking About the Research Process
Drafting

1 **Explain** Is it a good idea to include statistics in a thesis statement? Why or why not?

_____
_____
_____
_____

2 **Apply** Which type of organization would you choose for a research report on the topic "Dogs Versus Cats as Pets"? Why?

_____
_____
_____
_____

Research

Now, think about your own research paper.

3 **Apply** Look through your research notes and find one main idea that you want to include in your report. On a separate sheet of paper, use a chart or web to plan what details you will use to support this main idea. Then, turn the information in the chart into a section of an outline in the space below.

_____
_____
_____
_____
_____

Write Answer the following question in your Reader's Journal.

4 **Evaluate** What is the thesis of your Anchor Book? Do you agree with it? Explain why or why not.

6-12 The Research Process
Revising Your Research Report

Every form of writing—a magazine article, a biography, a novel, or even a poem—was revised before it was published. Revising is a key step when you are writing a research report. It lets you improve the overall structure of your paper, clarify your ideas, and enliven your writing.

The following checklists will help you revise your draft. Put a check ✔ next to each item as you complete your revisions.

Create a Unified Structure

All the parts of your report should fit together into a unified whole.

- ❑ Compare the organization of your draft to that of your outline. What sequence works best?
- ❑ Move paragraphs and sentences around to communicate ideas effectively and to maintain a parallel structure.
- ❑ Does every paragraph develop your thesis statement? If not, cut the paragraph, or revise it to show the connection.

Create Well-structured Paragraphs

The sentences in a paragraph should work together to express the main idea.

- ❑ Identify the main idea of each paragraph. Include a topic sentence that states the main idea.
- ❑ Evaluate each paragraph. Do the sentences work together to express the main idea? Are the details stated in a logical order?
- ❑ Evaluate the connections between sentences. Add transitions within paragraphs where they can improve the connections between sentences.
- ❑ Look for paragraphs that are missing information. Also look for conflicting information: ideas and facts that contradict each other. Consider doing additional research to fill in the gap or resolve the contradiction.

while reading your anchor book

Create More Effective Sentences

Your sentences should flow smoothly and express your ideas using precise and vivid words.

> ❏ Evaluate your sentence structure. Consider restructuring sentences to create emphasis. Try combining short sentences to avoid a choppy rhythm and to show connections.
>
> ❏ Consider your word choice. Look for places where you can replace tired, overused words with precise action verbs and vivid nouns and adjectives. Also look for unnecessary words that you can cut.

Directions Read the following excerpt from a rough draft of a research report about Alexander the Great. Read the student's ideas for revision, and then answer the questions that follow.

Student Model: Revising

James Barraclough, Los Alamos, NM
Alexander the Great

Southeastern Europe and western Asia were continually plagued by wars and rebellions in the fourth century B.C. Out of all this strife rose a boy, Alexander III, a hero whose name would be remembered for thousands of years. Alexander was born in July 356 B.C. to King Philip II of Macedonia, and Olympias, daughter of the King of Epirus.

Alexander became King of Macedonia at the young age of twenty and commenced to conquer the Persian Empire and part of modern-day India using brilliant battle strategy and a quickness to act that kept his enemies guessing. He earned his reputation as "Alexander the Great" by carving an empire of approximately one million square miles out of a land filled with enemies who were often intent on overthrowing him. Throughout his life, Alexander was very close with his mother, Olympias. From his mother, he learned to pray and to deeply believe in the gods. However, Alexander inherited his military genius and bravery from his father. His father conquered all of the Greek city-states and then united them under his rule.

There is no thesis statement in the introduction.

Sentence doesn't fit. Move to the second paragraph, which tells about Alexander's childhood.

Choppy — need to combine these four sentences into two.

Even as a child, Alexander had enough ambition for several men, as shown by his comment after his father had conquered a city, "My father will have everything, and I will have nothing left to conquer."

After uniting Greece, King Philip began a campaign to conquer the Persian Empire, but his efforts were cut short when he was assassinated in 336 B.C. Alexander was only twenty years old, though he had been commanding troops with his father for four years. ==He quickly claimed the throne with the army's support.== Picking up where his father left off, Alexander III, King of Macedonia, began a campaign that would change the world.

> Confusing — something is missing here.

In the spring of 334 B.C., Alexander led a relatively small army of 30,000 infantry, comprised mostly of soldiers called hoplites, who carried 16-foot spears, and 5,000 cavalry, called the Companions, across the Hellespont, a narrow strait. There he met a force of Persian cavalry and Greek mercenaries, sent by Darius III, King of the Persian Empire, which was intended to throw back the invaders.

==The Macedonians cut them to shreds by employing Alexander's innovative military strategy.== After that battle, Alexander led his army down along the coast of Asia Minor, taking cities for Greece until he met Darius at Issus. There, Alexander's outnumbered soldiers again routed the Persians, but Darius escaped. As the ancient historian Arrian reports, Darius fled in such a panic, he abandoned his royal chariot. "He even left his bow in the chariot, and mounting a horse continued his flight."

> Needs transition to show its connection to the previous sentence.

==At the age of twenty-five, Alexander became ruler of the Persian Empire and the most powerful man in the world.==

Choosing not to pursue Darius further, Alexander continued along the eastern Mediterranean coast into Egypt, liberating the Egyptians from their hated Persian overlords. In exchange for their liberation, the Egyptians named Alexander pharaoh of Egypt. After his victory, he planned a city called Alexandria to be built on the Mediterranean Sea. As Alexander pressed back into Asia he conquered many cities, but again Darius confronted him—this time better prepared for the man who was such a grave threat to the Persian Empire. However, Alexander employed a cunning ruse to distract the Persians during the battle and crashed back to the middle, ==defeating== the unsuspecting Persians. When Darius fled, the empire was left to Alexander's control.

> Move this sentence to the end of the next paragraph to emphasize the consequence of the events the paragraph describes.

> Need a more vivid word to emphasize this crucial event.

while reading your anchor book

Lesson 6-12

Thinking About the Research Process
Revising

1 **Apply** In the second paragraph, how could the writer combine sentences so that the highlighted passage is not so choppy?

2 **Analyze** In the third paragraph, what cause-and-effect relationship does the writer need to explain so that the highlighted sentence is not so confusing?

3 **Apply** In the fourth paragraph, what transitional word or phrase could the writer add to clarify the connection between the highlighted sentence and the previous sentence? What kind of relationship does this transition establish?

4 **Synthesize** If you were peer-reviewing these paragraphs, what other revisions would you suggest? Revise one sentence or passage, and then explain what you are trying to accomplish with this change.

Research

Now, think about your own research paper.

5 **Revise** Review a partner's draft and on a separate sheet of paper, suggest some areas for revision. Share your revision suggestions with your partner and come up with a follow-up plan for further revision based on your partner's feedback.

Write Answer the following question in your Reader's Journal.

6 **Evaluate** Find an effective passage from your Anchor Book. Explain why it is effective, and identify what techniques the author uses.

6-13 The Research Process
Sources and Publishing

After the revising process, it is time to proofread your report from start to finish, including your list of sources. This step helps you figure out the smaller, but very important, changes that need to be made to ensure that the information contained in your report is accurate.

Cite Your Sources

Your sources are an important part of your report because they are where you gathered your information. You must give credit to your sources so that a reader can refer to them if he or she wants to.

If your report contains quotations, facts that are not commonly known, or ideas that are not your own, you need to cite the sources from which they came.

Locate an **internal citation** within your report. Put it at the end of the sentence to which it refers.

> According to Ovid, the Latin poet who recorded much of Greek and Roman mythology, myths were "sheer nonsense" (Hamilton 21).

Enclose the author's name and the page number in parentheses. If several sentences contain information from the same source, then insert the citation at the end of the last sentence.

At the end of your report, include a page that identifies the resources you used in your research. This is called a **bibliography** or a works cited list. Your list must be in alphabetical order.

> Hamilton, Edith. *Mythology*. Boston, MA: Warner Books, 1999.

For each source, list the full information: the author's full name, last name first; the title of the work; location of publisher; publisher; and the date of publication.

Depending on the type of source you use, you must follow certain grammatical rules when listing the title of the work.

Underline or italicize a book, film, work of art, or long musical piece.	Use quotation marks for a short story, play, song, newspaper article, or poem.
A Separate Peace (book) *Citizen Kane* (film)	"Hamadi" (short story) "Macbeth" (play)

while reading your anchor book

Follow these guidelines when citing a source. See the bibliography on page 517 for examples. For more examples, consult a style guide.

Source	Guideline
If the source has one author	Put a period after the author's name, after the title of the work, and at the end of the citation. Use a colon between the place of publication and the publisher. Use a comma between the publisher and year of publication.
If the source has two or more authors	List the authors in the order in which they are credited in the work. Only the name of the first author is listed last name first.
If the author's name is not given	List the citation by its title.
If an organization is credited with the work	Use the name of the organization.

Proofread, Proofread, Proofread!

After spending so much time researching, writing, and revising your report, it would be a shame to have small errors take the reader's attention away from the content of your report.

▶ Prevent this by identifying and correcting any grammatical, spelling, or mechanical mistakes.

▶ Proofreading is a very important step before you publish your work.

Publishing Your Work

Once you've revised, proofread, and polished your work, add a title that sums up your report. Then decide how you want to share it.

Share it with your classmates and family. Share the final product of all your hard work with people around you.

Share your report with a large audience. Find out which organizations might be interested in your topic. Send a copy of your report to one of these groups for publication in a newsletter or on a Web site.

Deliver an impromptu speech. Share your knowledge with your classmates by giving an impromptu (unrehearsed) speech. Describe your topic, including what you wanted to learn, your thesis, and what you discovered as a result of your research.

Sources and Publishing

Directions Study the final draft below of the student model on Alexander the Great. Then, answer the questions.

Student Model: Writing

James Barraclough, Los Alamos, NM
Alexander the Great

Southeastern Europe and western Asia were continually plagued by wars and rebellions in the fourth century B.C. Out of all this turmoil came a boy, Alexander III, a hero and perhaps the greatest military strategist in history. Alexander became King of Macedonia at the young age of twenty and commenced to conquer the Persian Empire and part of modern-day India using brilliant battle strategy and a quickness to act that kept his enemies guessing. He earned his reputation as 'Alexander the Great' by carving an empire of approximately one million square miles out of a land filled with enemies who were often intent on overthrowing him (Walbank 248).

Alexander was born in July 356 B.C. to King Philip II of Macedonia and Olympias, daughter of the King of Epirus. Throughout his life, Alexander was very close with his mother, Olympias, from whom he learned to pray to and to deeply believe in the gods. However, Alexander inherited his military genius and bravery from his father, who conquered all of the Greek city-states and then united them under his rule. Even as a child, Alexander had enough ambition for several men, as shown by his comment after his father had conquered a city: "My father will have everything, and I will have nothing left to conquer" (Wepman 22).

In the spring of 334 B.C., Alexander led a relatively small army of 30,000 infantry, comprised mostly of soldiers called hoplite, who carried 16-foot spears, and 5,000 cavalry, called the Companions, across the Hellespont, a narrow strait. There he met a force of Persian cavalry and Greek mercenaries, sent by Darius III, King of the Persian Empire, which was intended to throw back the invader. However, the Macedonians cut them to shreds by employing Alexander's innovative military strategy (Cartledge 28–29). After that battle, Alexander led his army down along the coast of Asia Minor, taking cities for Greece until he met Darius at Issus. There, Alexander's outnumbered soldiers again routed the Persians, but Darius escaped. As the ancient historian Arrian reports, Darius fled in such a panic, he abandoned his royal chariot. "He even

> James introduces his thesis statement in the first paragraph.

> The paper's organization is chronological, following a clear path from Alexander's birth to his death.

left his bow in the chariot, and mounting a horse continued his flight" (Godolphin 450).

Choosing not to pursue Darius, Alexander continued along the eastern Mediterranean coast into Egypt, liberating the Egyptians from their hated Persian overlords. In exchange for their liberation, the Egyptians named Alexander pharaoh of Egypt.

> Smooth transitions give the paper a sense of flow.

Approximately one year after his return from India, Alexander developed a fever and stomach cramps. These may have been caused by heavy drinking, typhoid, malaria, or poison. The fatal illness kept him in bed until he died on June 11, 323 B.C., at the age of 32. Since Alexander did not appoint a successor to his throne, the mightiest empire of the time, perhaps of all time, fell into disorder and collapsed with his death (Prevas 202–207).

All in all, Alexander—who was just a boy in some people's eyes when he took the throne—rose to the occasion and conquered the world, forging an empire with his heart and sword. Alexander was a complex man who could be harsh, ruthless, and relentless in battle, but he could also be compassionate and sympathetic towards his wounded soldiers. These characteristics inspired loyalty and unity in thousands of soldiers. They followed Alexander wherever he led, even if they had a fierce desire to go home. The man known as Alexander the Great was a king, an emperor, a pharaoh, a conqueror, and most of all, a leader who could charge into battle, knowing his men would follow.

> This conclusion supports and restates the thesis statement of the report.

Bibliography

Alexander, Caroline. "Alexander the Conqueror." *National Geographic*, March 2000: 42–75.

Cartledge, Paul. *Alexander the Great*. New York: Overlook Press, 2004.

Lynch, Kevin. "Aristotle and Alexander." <u>Ancient Greece</u> Oct. 8, 2007. <http://www.posner.org/Lynch243/Greece.htm>

Walbank, Frank W. "Alexander the Great." *Encyclopedia Britannica*. 1990 ed.

Thinking About the Research Process
Final draft: Alexander the Great

1 Identify What type of sources did the student use for this report? How do you know?

_____
_____

2 Apply Proofread and make the necessary changes to this citation.

"Alexander the Great." New York: W.W. Norton, 1967. Ulrich Wilcken.

_____

3 Analyze Read the sentence below from the student's report. Why did the student cite this part of the text?

When Darius fled, the empire was left to Alexander's control (Cartledge 32).

_____

4 Respond What is another title the student could have used for this report?

_____
_____

5 Synthesize Do you think the student succeeded in creating a strong conclusion to his report? Why or why not?

_____
_____
_____

Research

Now, think about your own research paper.

6 Create Review your title. Create a title that does more than just state your topic but instead communicates what is exciting or interesting about your report. Write it in the space below.

_____
_____

7 **Communicate** Does your introduction grab your reader's attention? Make a statement that challenges your readers, ask a question about your topic, or describe your topic using interesting details. Revise it in the space below.

_____
_____
_____
_____
_____
_____

8 **Communicate** Does your conclusion summarize your research and make the reader think about how your topic is important today? Revise it in the space below.

_____
_____
_____
_____
_____
_____

9 **Evaluate** What other revisions did you make in your final draft? Did these changes result in a stronger final draft? Explain your answer.

_____
_____
_____
_____

Write Answer the following question in your Reader's Journal.

10 **Evaluate** Look at the title, introduction paragraph, and conclusion paragraph of your Anchor Book. How are these effective? What techniques could you incorporate in your research report?

6-14 Listening and Speaking Workshop
Analyzing Media Messages

In this activity, your group will compare two contrasting messages appearing in the media. Note that a single advertisement can contain two conflicting messages. For example, a soap commercial says that you should make decisions for yourself, then tells you to use their soap. The second message contradicts the first. Your goal will be to prepare an analysis and then present it to the class. Be sure to identify the purpose for the message—to inform, persuade, or entertain an audience.

Your Task

- Work with a group to select two media messages.
- Evaluate content, strategies, and techniques used to influence an audience.
- Analyze the credibility of the media messages and their impact on public opinion.
- Present your analysis to the class.

Organize and Present Your Panel Discussion

1 Choose two messages. With your group, select two messages from the media. You may choose to use advertisements, news reports or editorials, or political speeches.

2 Research and analyze the messages. Look critically at and respond to the messages, listening to language and analyzing the believability of content. Identify techniques and strategies used to influence an audience, such as technology, lighting, sound effects, graphics, color, motion, and language (for instance, is the tone humorous or ironic or is it serious and straightforward? Does the message use metaphor?). Watch for hidden propaganda or biased information that presents only one point of view, and identify any fallacies of logic that lead to unsupported conclusions. Pay close attention to portrayals of culture, gender, religion, class, and race. Consider how one's background might influence one's interaction with media.

3 Create a visual for your audience. Display your media messages. Use visuals to help you support your analysis.

For example, you might use a compare-and-contrast graphic organizer to explain different techniques used. Include a chart, map, or graph in your presentation.

4 Plan and practice your delivery. Prepare an outline to organize your panel discussion and define your topic with attention to time limit. Narrow your topic as needed. Include primary and secondary sources used to verify research. Modify to include transitions, appropriate grammar, word choice, and pacing as you practice your analysis. Make sure that your presentation has an effective introduction (with a well-defined thesis) and conclusion.

5 Present your panel discussion. All panel members need to be speaking participants, so divide work accordingly. Remember to speak clearly and adjust your tone. Review the rubric to make sure you are meeting all criteria and including relevant evidence to address listener bias.

6 Respond to your audience. Follow up with a question-and-answer session. Be prepared to respond to questions and to provide additional information to clarify points.

Directions Assess your performance. For each question, circle a rating.

SPEAK: Rubric for Oral Interpretation

CRITERIA	RATING SCALE
CONTENT How well did the group analyze the similarities and differences between the two media messages?	NOT VERY VERY 1 2 3 4 5
ORGANIZATION How well did the group respond to questions and audience feedback relevant to the presentation?	1 2 3 4 5
DELIVERY How well did the group explain techniques and common points used in the media to persuade or inform?	1 2 3 4 5

LISTEN: Rubric for Audience Self-Assessment

CRITERIA	RATING SCALE
ACTIVE LISTENING How well did you understand the message given in the speaker's presentation?	NOT VERY VERY 1 2 3 4 5

Be prepared to explain what you learned about the impact that media messages can have on forming an audience's opinion by paraphrasing the speakers' purpose and point of view. Also be prepared to ask further questions concerning the speakers' content, delivery, and purpose.

6-15 Language Coach
Grammar and Spelling

Capitalization

A capital letter is used at the beginning of a sentence and for the first word of a quotation. For example, in the sentence, "Why can't I go to the game?" the *W* is capitalized because it is the beginning of a sentence. A capital letter is also used for the pronoun *I*, and proper nouns, such as geographical names, academic courses, proper adjectives, historical documents, organizations, and titles of people.

Examples	
Algebra I	Dr. Jones
Mount Sinai	University of Michigan
the Declaration of Independence	Thursday
a German shepherd	Rotary Club

Directions Rewrite these sentences. Substitute capital letters or lowercase letters where appropriate.

1. the trucker hauled 2,000 lbs of potatoes from idaho to california.

2. my brother paul runs track for parker school.

3. The bus finally left, and i was relieved that i would not be late for freshman composition.

4. Because he enjoyed walking, mr. smith lived only Three blocks from the Grocery Store.

5. the everglades of florida is one of my favorite places to visit.

6. Paiton yelled, "ouch! that stings!"

Commas, Semicolons, and Colons

A comma (,) is a punctuation mark that signals a brief pause. Use a comma between items in a series, between adjectives in a series, after introductory material, and with parenthetical expressions. Also, use a comma before a conjunction in a compound sentence and to set off appositives, participial phrases, or adjective clauses.

Use a semicolon (;) to join independent clauses that are not already joined by the conjunctions *and, but, or, nor, for, so,* or *yet*. Use a colon (:) before a list of items that follows an independent clause.

Examples
The man had a long, narrow, and sad face.
Sparkling in the light of the sun, the ocean looked beautiful.
Mars, one of the nine planets, can be seen without a telescope.
Dana is six years older than her cousin; she often babysits him.
These cookies contain the following ingredients: flour, brown sugar, butter, eggs, and nuts.
I wanted to buy a new car; however, I had not saved up enough money.

Author's Craft

Look back at the selection "A Visit to Washington, D.C., 1879" on page 483. Combine two independent clauses using a semicolon.

Directions Rewrite these sentences, adding commas, semicolons, and colons where needed.

1. Their new home is beautiful no one would guess it was once a barn.

2. Instead of going shopping they went walking in the park.

3. Four states border Mexico California Arizona New Mexico and Texas.

4. Some cheeses for example American and cheddar are made from cow's milk others are made from goat's milk.

5. Add these things to your list soap bread eggs and milk then come back as soon as you can.

6-16 Writer's Workshop
Research: Multimedia Presentation

A **multimedia presentation** presents information about a topic using a variety of materials, including text, audio, video, and other technology options. This form of presentation may be used to create documentaries, biographies, and news reports. In this workshop, you and a partner will create a multimedia presentation about a topic that interests you.

Purpose to create a multimedia presentation about a topic that interests you

Audience you, your teacher, and your classmates

Your multimedia presentation should include the following elements.

- well-integrated and appropriate audio and visual features from a variety of sources that support your point of view
- visually appealing formatting and presentation
- a focused topic that can be covered in the time and space allotted
- an effective balance between researched information and original ideas
- a presentation tailored to your specific audience
- error-free grammar, including proper format of quotations

Prewriting—Plan It Out

Choose your topic. Select a subject that you know will have a readily available range of multimedia material. Consider current or historical events, musicians or artists whose work you and your partner enjoy, films by your favorite filmmaker, sports teams or athletes, or trends you notice at school or in advertising. Make a list of possible topics, and then choose the one that offers the richest possibilities for multimedia presentation.

Gather multimedia resources. Check your library and the Internet to locate audio and video clips of interviews or speeches, as well as documentaries, photographs, art, and music relating to your topic. Evaluate these primary and secondary sources for their relevance and reliability. Then take notes on what you find, following the note-taking procedures you learned in Lesson 6–5. Be sure to credit your sources. You can use a style guide for additional help with the correct formatting for acknowledging sources. Also be sure to ask your librarian or teacher for information about the latest copyright laws governing the use of material posted on the Internet.

Drafting—Get It on Paper

Create an outline. Like a research report, your multimedia presentation should have a thesis statement that sums up your main idea. Use this thesis statement and your notes to plan your presentation.

Develop an outline that organizes your points in a logical way. Make sure every point and detail relates to your thesis statement. End with an efficient conclusion that restates your thesis and ends with a catchy phrase. Outline two main ideas and supporting details here.

I. Main Point 1 _____

    A. Detail _____

        1. Supporting Detail _____

        2. Supporting Detail _____

    B. Detail _____

        1. Supporting Detail _____

        2. Supporting Detail _____

II. Main Point 2 _____

    A. Detail _____

        1. Supporting Detail _____

        2. Supporting Detail _____

    B. Detail _____

        1. Supporting Detail _____

        2. Supporting Detail _____

Provide elaboration. Use audio and visual aids to enhance your message and provide evidence to support your points.

- Audio and video, such as music or interview clips, can set a mood and provide information.
- Visual aids, such as photographs, slides, charts, graphs, graphic organizers, handouts, spreadsheets, or maps, can organize large amounts of information. If possible, include captions to clarify the images you are presenting.

Use digital tools such as word-processing, Web tools, and presentation software to present additional information. Plan to display text and visuals on posters, onscreen, or as handouts. Remember to credit your sources.

Writer's Workshop continued

Create a script. Use your outline and notes to draft a script and plan your delivery. Write cues in your script to indicate when to use specific media elements. As you write your script, remember to use a variety of media selections evenly throughout your presentation.

Plan your delivery. Even though you and your partner are planning the delivery of a multimedia presentation, your text—whether written or spoken—must function as part of the show. Avoid repeating in words what your other media elements are already communicating. Keep your writing lively, and practice speaking in an engaging style. Vary the pace and volume of your delivery, enunciate clearly, and modulate your voice to create emphasis. You will need to remember to make frequent eye contact with the audience and to respond to their verbal and nonverbal cues.

Revising—Make It Better

Using the following strategies, revise your presentation to make it more coherent, focused, and precise.

Revise to connect media. A seamless delivery is the goal of any multimedia presentation. Look for places where the connection between your script and your multimedia element is unclear. Practice introducing each media element and explaining its connection to your topic by summarizing and/or paraphrasing what is in your script.

Student Model: Revising to Connect Media

> **Visual:** Image of American battleship U.S.S. Arizona
>
> **Sound:** Bugle playing Taps
>
> , including the U.S.S. Arizona shown here,
> **Script:** Eight American battleships ∧ and ten other navy vessels were sunk or badly damaged. Approximately 3,000 naval and other military personnel were killed or wounded.

This additional phrase links the visual to the script.

Revise your word choice. Consider your audience, and define any terms that will be unfamiliar. Look for ways to engage your audience by replacing overused words with more precise and vivid language. Active voice, action verbs, colorful modifiers, and sensory details are some methods you can use to enliven your presentation.

Peer Review Hold a test run of your multimedia presentation with your partner. Give your partner a copy of your script to follow, with instructions to place a check mark next to any points that need clearer transitions or seem out of order. Revise as needed.

Directions Read this student multimedia presentation as a model for your own.

Student Model: Writing

Jessica Leanore Adamson, Boise, ID

The Attack on Pearl Harbor

Slide 1

Visual: Image of Pearl Harbor, ca. 1940

Sound: Airplane/explosion

Script: Pearl Harbor was one of the principal naval bases of WWII. It is located approximately six miles west of Honolulu in Oahu, Hawaii. Early in the morning on December 7, 1941, Japanese submarines and carrier-based planes attacked the U.S. Pacific fleet in Pearl Harbor.

Slide 2

Visual: Image of American battleship U.S.S. Arizona.

Sound: Bugle playing *Taps*

Script: Eight American battleships, including the U.S.S. Arizona shown here, and ten other navy vessels were sunk or badly damaged. Almost 200 American aircraft were destroyed, and approximately 3,000 naval and military personnel were killed or wounded.

> Jessica chose a title that reflects her topic.

> The writer has chosen a topic that can be covered in the brief time allotted to her presentation.

> The sound effects and images are dramatic and appropriate to the topic, audience, and purpose.

Writer's Workshop continued

> **Slide 8**
> **Visual:** Blank screen (black). Words "dereliction of duty" and "errors of judgment" appear letter by letter.
> **Sound:** Typewriter
> **Script:** Shortly after the attack, U.S. President Franklin D. Roosevelt appointed a commission to determine whether negligence had contributed to the raid. The commission found the naval and army commanders of the area guilty of "dereliction of duty" and "errors of judgment."

The writer uses boldfaced heads and other appropriate formatting to present the organization of the presentation clearly.

This model represents the introductory and concluding slides of a multimedia presentation. Slides 3–7 are not shown. In the full report, they present more information, along with supporting audio and visual materials, to develop the presentation's main idea.

Editing—Be Your Own Language Coach

Before you deliver your multimedia presentation, review your script for language convention errors. Pay special attention to sentence structure, in both written and spoken text. Revise any sentence fragments or run-on sentences to create complete sentences. Use a style guide to give proper credit to sources.

Publishing—Share It!

When you publish a work, you produce it for a specific audience. Here are two ways you can share your presentation.

Present to your class or an organization. Deliver your multimedia presentation to your class or contact a local library, club, or elementary school that might be interested in your presentation. Follow your presentation with a question-and-discussion session. Get feedback on the reliability and depth of your research.

Create a web site or web page. Use online tools to post your research on the internet.

Reflecting On Your Writing

Respond to the following questions on the back of your final draft. What new insights did you gain about multimedia presentations by creating one? What did you do well? What do you need to work on? Set a goal you can meet in your next workshop.

Rubric for Self-Assessment Assess your multimedia presentation. For each question, circle a rating.

Planning

CRITERIA	RATING SCALE
	NOT VERY VERY
IDEAS How clearly do you identify your topic?	1 2 3 4 5
RESEARCH How relevant and accurate are your primary and secondary sources?	1 2 3 4 5
ORGANIZATION How well do you employ a clear and logical organization?	1 2 3 4 5
ORGANIZATION Is your presentation a balance of text, audio, and visual elements?	1 2 3 4 5
VOICE Is your writing lively and engaging, drawing the audience in?	1 2 3 4 5
WORD CHOICE How appropriate is the language for your audience?	1 2 3 4 5
SENTENCE FLUENCY How varied is your sentence structure?	1 2 3 4 5
CONVENTIONS How correct is your grammar, especially your use of complete sentences?	1 2 3 4 5

Presentation

VISUALS How well do you organize information using graphic aids such as charts, graphs, diagrams, maps, and illustrations?	1 2 3 4 5
OTHER MEDIA How well do you integrate other media elements, including audio and video components?	1 2 3 4 5
PRESENTATION How well do you deliver your presentation?	1 2 3 4 5

6-17 Connecting to Your Anchor Book
Anchor Book Projects

Now that you have finished reading your Anchor Book, it is time to be creative! Complete one of the following projects.

State Author Project A

Behind every award-winning story, article, or news report is an award-winning author. Authors bring their traditions, beliefs, and experiences into their writing. Identify which state the author of your Anchor Book comes from, and his or her connection to the state. Then, identify two other authors from that same state. One must be an award-winning author, and you should try to include at least one female and one male author.

1. Locate and examine books from your authors representing a mix of genres: from picture books, poetry, and drama to novels and short stories to essays and informational texts. Now, choose one book from each author.

2. Create a visual that shows how the state is reflected in the texts. Use words and pictures to show how traditions, attitudes, beliefs of the authors, and historical or contemporary context are reflected in the texts. Compare the authors' perspectives on characterization, theme, and setting, and also show how they relate to the state.

3. If the authors are from your state, relate your own experience of living in the state to the authors' experience.

Your author project should include the following elements.
- Information about the authors and one of each author's works
- A chart that shows how the state is reflected in the texts

Stage a Press Conference B

Usually, a groundbreaking news story happening in the world is quickly followed by a press conference. This is a media event to which newsmakers invite journalists to give them an update or make a public announcement. Journalists can ask questions they think the public will want answered. The questions are carefully planned before the press conference.

1. Choose one event from your Anchor Book as the topic discussion at a press conference.

2. As a journalist, identify your audience and prepare three questions to ask the speaker.

3. Based on what you know about the event, answer the questions in a way you would expect the speaker to respond.

Your press conference preparation should include the following.
- Choosing an important event from your book
- Understanding who your audience is
- Interview questions and responses relating to the event

It's A Debate

Debating an issue is a great way to learn both sides of a story. Politicians hold debates to inform their constituents. Environmentalists hold debates to discuss issues about our environment. Choose a topic of interest to debate. (Be sure it will interest your audience!) Then, put your ideas together, combine your research notes, and let the debate begin!

1. Organize two teams with students who have researched the same topic, event, or person in their Anchor Books.
2. Review and combine your research notes and sources. Brainstorm ideas and prior knowledge on the topic. Prepare a debate.
3. Stage your debate in front of the class. Can your team persuade the class to believe in your side of the debate?

Your debate preparation and staging should include the following.
- An outline compiling the notes of all your teammates
- A summary of your team's research and viable sources
- An understanding of the two sides of the topic and how to present it to your audience

Free-Choice Book Reflection

You have completed your free-choice book. Before you take your test, read the following instructions to write a brief reflection on your book.

My free-choice book is _____.

The author is _____.

1 Would you recommend this book to a friend? Yes _____ No _____

Why or why not? _____

Write and Discuss Answer the following question in your Reader's Journal. Then, discuss your answer with a partner or your Literature Circle.

 2 **Compare and Contrast** *Are yesterday's heroes and events important today?* Compare and contrast how your Anchor Book and free-choice book answer this question. Use specific details from both books to support your ideas. Then, to extend the discussion, consider whether heroism is important in other subject areas, such as history, science, or current events.

Connecting to Your Anchor Book

Unit Review
Standardized Test Practice

Reading Skills: Setting a Purpose for Reading

Read this selection. Then, answer the questions that follow.

> High school physics... Does everyone need to study it? Well, did you know that the laws of physics lie behind many of our favorite pastimes? Consider music: If you want to understand how instruments or CDs work, you need physics. Artists, who work with color and light, know that physics is the science of light. And the manufacturing of things like plastics, chemicals, and medicines relies on physics, too. So, don't think of physics as the stuff of science nerds. Consider it everyone's tool for understanding many of the important elements of everyday life.

1 Which sentence best helps you set a purpose for reading?

A. High school physics...Does everyone need to study it?

B. If you want to understand how instruments or CDs work, you need physics.

C. Artists, who work with color and light, know that physics is the science of light.

D. So, don't think of physics as the stuff of science nerds.

2 Which of the following states the most valid purpose for reading this passage?

F. to collect evidence that supports arguments against studying physics

G. to understand how artists use physics

H. to discover some persuasive arguments for promoting the study of physics

J. to learn about which items are produced with the help of physics

Reading Skills: Summarizing

3 **Summary** Read this selection. Write a summary in your own words on a separate sheet of paper.

> On Toby's first day helping his uncle as a dog walker, he was given an easy schedule. For four hours, he exercised one dog at a time. Each one was more friendly and obedient than the last. "I think you're ready for something more challenging," his uncle noted the next day. Toby beamed. As the day wore on, his smile faded. He walked two Chihuahuas who snapped at people's ankles. When a stubborn poodle refused to leave the house, he called his uncle for a few tips. Sure, he'd master this job. But it never hurt to ask for a little help.

The Research Process

Read this excerpt from a report about the Mexican artist Frida Kahlo and answer the questions that follow.

> Even in her early life, Frida Kahlo was not free from pain. When she was just 6 years old, Kahlo was nearly immobilized by polio ("Frida Kahlo" 1). To make matters worse, Kahlo was involved in a near fatal crash that changed her life forever. The bus Kahlo was riding one day in Mexico City crashed. Kahlo sustained serious injuries to her abdomen, which made her unable to have children (Woolmer 2). This unfortunate childless reality, so completely out of Kahlo's control, would become a prominent theme in her artwork.
>
> After the bus accident, Kahlo was bed-ridden, undergoing a long period of healing. Kahlo grew so bored in her bed that she decided to paint. Her subject matter was limited to what she found in her room, so she painted her own image (Woolmer 2). Because of her injuries, she was forced to paint while lying on her back.

4 Based on these two paragraphs, the **thesis statement** of the report could be which of the following?

A. Frida Kahlo was in pain for much of her life.

B. Frida Kahlo drew on her lifelong physical pain and misfortune as inspiration for her art.

C. Frida Kahlo never intended to be an artist.

D. Frida Kahlo's inability to have children became a theme in her artwork.

5 The type of organization in the excerpt is _____.

F. compare-and-contrast

G. chronological

H. problem and solution(s)

J. posing and answering questions

6 Why is "Frida Kahlo" in the **internal citation**?

A. It is the subject of the report.

B. The author of the source is Frida Kahlo.

C. The source does not have an author so the title of the source is used.

D. It is the title of an article.

7 If the report were to cite a **primary source,** which of the following might it be?

F. encyclopedia article

G. Frida Kahlo's biography

H. Frida Kahlo's diaries

J. a book about women artists

Unit Review 533

Language Skills: Vocabulary

Choose the best answer.

8 Which of these words has a Hindi origin?

A. Friday

B. kayak

C. leprechaun

D. yoga

9 What is a synonym for the word *jovial*?

F. happy

G. easily upset

H. powerful

J. warlike

10 Which of these sentences contains an English word that comes from another modern language?

A. Sandy treated his sick brother like a leper.

B. Kaya walked her sister to school.

C. Mom cooked gumbo soup for lunch.

D. Nia's moods are mercurial.

11 Which sentence uses a synonym for the word *finale*?

F. The audience applauded loudly.

G. The play came to a dramatic conclusion.

H. Some people like to go to the opera.

J. A sonata is a musical composition that comes from Italy.

Language Skills: Spelling

Circle the letter that contains the correct answer to each question.

12 Which type of word begins with a capital letter?

A. noun

B. proper noun

C. boldfaced term

D. animal

13 Which phrase is capitalized correctly?

F. Dr. Watson

G. my Pet Iguana

H. Mrs. Diaz, a Mother

J. my Street

14 In which sentence are all words capitalized correctly?

A. Tanya likes to play Baseball.

B. Practice is every thursday.

C. Darius is president of our class.

D. My Sister Mia is eight.

15 Read the following sentence.

my Dog likes the Park on Kim street.

Choose the correct revision.

F. My Dog likes the park on Kim street.

G. My dog likes the park on Kim Street.

H. My dog likes The Park on Kim Street.

J. my Dog likes the park on kim street.

Language Skills: Grammar

Choose the best answer.

16 Read the following sentence.

Ben doesn't like hockey it is too rough.

Which punctuation should come after the word *hockey*?

A. a comma
B. a colon
C. a semicolon
D. correct as is

17 Which of the following sentences does not need a comma?

F. Sue turned on her computer to access the Internet.
G. Saul iced his blue swollen ankle.
H. Brenda made the team but Sam did not.
J. Leaping each hurdle Dan won the race.

18 In which of the following items should the period be replaced with a colon?

A. Jen was going camping. She could hardly wait.
B. Jen packed these items. A toothbrush, a comb, and some soap.
C. Jen forgot bug spray. Luckily, Mary had some.
D. It was a moonless night. Thank goodness for flashlights!

19 Which of the following sentences contains the correct number of commas?

F. Mario's cooking teacher is young smart, and daring.
G. This recipe needs eggs cheese and milk.
H. Mom likes making chicken, salad and pudding.
J. Pam likes her food hot, spicy, and full of flavor.

20 Read the following sentence.

That cat whose name is Merlin can play the piano catch mice and say "Mama" he is clever.

Which of these sentences is punctuated correctly?

A. That cat whose name is Merlin can play the piano, catch mice, and say *Mama*, he is clever
B. That cat, whose name is Merlin, can play the piano, catch mice, and say *Mama*; he is clever.
C. That cat, whose name is Merlin, can play the piano catch mice, and say Mama: he is clever.
D. That cat, whose name is Merlin, can play the piano catch mice and say Mama he is clever.

English and Spanish Glossary

A

abash (ə bash′) *v.* embarrass
  avergonzar causar sentimiento penoso.

acute (ə kyōōt′) *adj.* accurate and perceptive
  agudo justo y perceptivo

adapt (ə dapt′) *v.* adjust
  adaptar ajustar

aghast (ə gast′) *adj.* horrified, shocked
  escandalizado horrorizado, indignado

allusion (ə lōō′zhən) *n.* an indirect reference to a well-known person, place, event, literary work, or work of art
  alusión referencia indirecta a una persona, lugar, evento, obra literaria u obra de arte conocida

analyze (an′ə līz′) *v.* examine something in great detail
  analizar examinar en detalle

anticipate (an tis′ə pāt′) *v.* look forward to, expect
  anticipar adelantar un suceso, esperar

apply (ə plī′) *v.* put something to practical or specific use
  aplicar poner en práctica o uso específico

assess (ə ses′) *v.* judge, measure
  evaluar juzgar, medir

august (ô gust′) *adj.* dignified, marked by grandeur
  augusto digno, majestuoso

B

barren (bar′ən) *adj.* empty; unlikely to produce result
  inhóspito desocupado; poco probable que dé resultados

bias (bī′əs) *n.* a personal and sometimes unreasoned judgment or opinion
  tendencia juicio u opinión personal e irrazonable en ciertos casos

billowed (bil′ ōd) *v.* swelled out or bulged
  ondularon se hincharon o inflaron

brazen (brazən) *adj.* brash, forward
  descarado sin pudor; sin vergüenza

C

careen (kə rēn′) *v.* lean to one side while in motion
  inclinar hacerse hacia un lado al estar en movimiento

ceased (sēst) *v.* stopped
  cesó se suspendió

cells (selz) *n.* smallest units of living matter able to function independently
  células las unidades más pequeñas de materia viva que logran funcionar independientemente

cite (sīt) *v.* to refer to or quote by way of example
  citar referirse a algo por medio de un ejemplo

clarify (klar′ə fī′) *v.* to make or become easier to understand
  clarificar hacer o volver más comprensible

classify (klas′ə fī′) *v.* to arrange or group according to some system
  clasificar organizar o agrupar algo de acuerdo con algún sistema

communicate (kə myōō′ni kāt′) *v.* convey information
  comunicar transmitir información

compare (kəm per′) *v.* show how things are alike
  comparar demostrar cómo cosas se asemejan

compliance (kəm plī′əns) *n.* obedience, willingness to yield to someone else's wishes
  conformidad obediencia, la voluntad para complacer los deseos de alguien

conclude (kən klōōd′) *v.* to bring to a close or end
  concluir terminar o cerrar

confirm (kən furm′) *v.* to prove to be true; to verify
  confirmar probar la veracidad de algo; verificar

connect (kə nekt′) *v.* to bring two or more things together to make a different or new whole
  conectar vincular dos o más cosas para formar o completar algo nuevo o diferente

consecrate (kän′si krāt′) *v.* bless
  consagrar bendecir

contact (kän′takt′) *n.* touch or communication
  contacto tacto o comunicación

contrast (kən trast′) *v.* show how things are different
  contrastar demostrar cómo cosas son diferentes

convey (kən vā′) *v.* to make known, give
  transmitir hacer saber, proveer

convince (kən vins′) *v.* to persuade
  convencer persuadir

English and Spanish Glossary

create (krē āt') *v.* make, design
crear hacer, diseñar

critique (kri tēk') *v.* to review or discuss critically
criticar revisar o discutir críticamente

D

database (dāt'əbās') *n.* collection of information organized for speedy search and retrieval
base de datos colección de información organizada para hacer búsquedas de investigación eficientes

decide (dē sīd') *v.* to make a choice or come to a judgment after consideration
decidir hacer una elección o dar un juicio definitivo después de gran consideración

deduce (dē dōōs') *v.* use reasoning to draw something out
deducir razonar para llegar a una conclusión

define (dē fīn') *v.* to identify the meaning of something
definir identificar el significado

depravity (dē prav'ə tē) *n.* lack of morals, corruption
depravación falta de morales, corrupción

derision (di rizh'ən) *n.* mockery, ridicule
irrisión burla, ridiculez

describe (di skrīb') *v.* to give an account of or represent something in words
describir detallar o representar en palabras

determine (dē tur'mən) *v.* to figure out
determinar aclarar o explicarse

differentiate (dif'ər en'shĭ āt') *v.* to show how things are not alike
diferenciar demostrar cómo cosas no se asemejan

diminutive (də min' yōō tiv) *adj.* miniature
diminuto muy pequeño

dingy (din'jē) *v.* unclean, shabby
deslustrado sucio, en mal estado

discuss (di skus') *v.* to consider and argue about something in a deliberative manner
discutir considerar y argumentar un tema de manera deliberada

dispelled (di speld) *v.* driven away, eliminated
disipado expulsada, eliminada

distinctions (di sti[ng]k'shəns) *adj.* discriminations between things as different
distinciones discriminaciones entre cosas diferentes

distinctness (di sti[ng]kt'nis) *n.* clarity
distinción claridad

distinguish (di sti[ng]'gwish) *v.* demonstrate the difference between two or more elements
distinguir demostrar la diferencia entre dos o más elementos

diverged (dī vurjd') *v.* went in different directions
divergieron fueron en direcciones diferentes

diverts (də vurts) *v.* draws one's attention to something else; keeps one agreeably occupied
desvia enfoca la atención hacia otra cosa; mantiene a alguien agradablemente ocupado

E

emblazoned (em blā'zənd) *v.* inscribed
estampado grabado

emphasize (em'fə sīz') *v.* to give special attention; stress
enfatizar dar atención especial; estresar

entertain (ent'ər tān') *v.* to amuse or delight
entretener divertir o deleitar

establish (ə stab'lish) *v.* to create or prove
establecer crear o probar

evaluate (ē val'yōō āt') *v.* judge; determine the worth or strength of something
evaluar juzgar; determinar el valor o fuerza de algo

examine (eg zam'ən) *v.* to study carefully
examinar estudiar detenidamente con cuidado

exasperation (eg zas'pər ā'shən) *n.* irritation; annoyance
exasperación irritación; fastidio

exiles (ek'sīls) *n.* people who have been forced out of their country or home
exiliados personas que han tenido que salir del país u hogar forzosamente

explain (ek splān') *v.* make clear or understandable
explicar aclarar o hacer entendible

F

feinted (fānted) *v.* distracted someone's attention with a trick move
fintó distrajo a alguien por medio de un truco

formulate (fôr'myōō lāt') *v.* to put something in appropriate terms
formular poner algo en términos apropiados

English and Spanish Glossary

frail (frāl) *adj.* thin and weak; delicate
frágil delgado y débil; delicado

G

genetic (jə net′ik) *adj.* relating to biological heredity
genético relacionado a la biología hereditaria

gratified (grat′i fīd′) *adj.* satisfied, pleased
gratificado satisfecho, complacido

H

hallow (hal′ō) *v.* make holy
santificar convertir en santo

hysterical (hi ster′i kəl) *adj.* out of control with emotion
histérico fuera de control emocionalmente

I

identify (ī den′tə fī′) *v.* recognize; to find and name
identificar reconocer; encontrar y nombrar algo

imminent (im′ə nənt) *adj.* likely to occur at any moment
inminente probable que ocurra en cualquier momento

impact (im pakt′) *v.* to have an effect on
impactar que tiene efecto en algo

imply (im plī′) *v.* to mean or suggest without specifically saying
insinuar sugerir algo sin decirlo específicamente

indicate (in′di kāt′) *v.* to show, hint at
indicar mostrar o dar pistas

infer (in fur′) *v.* to draw conclusions based on facts
inferir concluir a base de hechos

influence (in′flōō əns) *v.* to affect something
influir afectar a algo

inform (in fôrm′) *v.* to communicate knowledge
informar comunicar conocimiento

insignia (in sig′nē ə) *n.* badge
insignia emblema

interpret (in tur′prət) *v.* explain the underlying meaning of something by examining all of its elements
interpretar explicar el significado al examinar todos los elementos

J

justify (jus′tə fī′) *v.* to prove or show to be deserved, right, or reasonable
justificar probar o demostrar que se merece, es correcto o razonable

K

kerchiefs (kʉr′chifs) *n.* scarves worn on the head
pañuelos trozos de tela que se llevan en la cabeza

kindled (kin′dəld) *v.* blazing, fiery
prendido encendido; ardiente

L

labyrinth (lab′ə rinth′) *n.* intricate structure or arrangement
laberinto estructura o arreglo complicado

lyric (lir′ik) *n.* words in a song
letra las palabras de una canción

M

melancholy (mel′ən käl′ē) *adj.* gloomy or sad
melancólico triste o sombrío

misinterpretations (mis′in tūr′pritā′shən) *n.* failure to comprehend something correctly
interpretaciónes equivocadas comprensión errónea de algo

modify (mäd′ə fī′) *v.* to change
modificar cambiar

momentary (mō′mən ter′ē) *adj.* lasting only a short time
momentáneo que dura poco tiempo

O

obsession (əb sesh′ən) *n.* something that takes up all of one's thoughts and concerns
obsesión algo que ocupa todos los pensamientos y preocupaciones

organize (ôr′gə nīz′) *v.* arrange in a logical order
organizar arreglar en un orden lógico

P

pensively (pen′siv lē) *adv.* in a contemplative manner
pensativamente de manera contemplativa

perceive (pər sēv′) *v.* to understand; to become aware of
percibir entender; estar consciente de algo

English and Spanish Glossary

persuade (pər swād′) *v.* to convince someone of something by means of argument or entreaty
persuadir convencer a alguien por medio de argumentos

pertinent (purt′'n ənt) *adj.* related to the topic
pertinente relacionado al tema

pervading (pər vād′i[ng]) *v.* saturating, spreading through every layer of something
dominante saturando, extendiéndose por cada nivel

pestering (pes′təri[ng]) *n.* harassment concerning trivial things
fastidio hostigamiento por cosas triviales

pious (pī′əs) *adj.* demonstrating a devotion to God
piadoso quien demuestra una devoción a Dios

plagued (plāgd) *adj.* overrun by a great number of something; afflicted
plagado lleno o cubierto completamente; afligido

pomp (pämp) *n.* display, showiness, splendor
pompa demostración pretenciosa, esplendor

predict (prē dikt′) *v.* make a logical guess about future events
predecir asumir lógicamente acerca de eventos en el futuro

presentable (prē zent′ə bəl) *adj.* clean and neat; ready for inspection
presentable limpio y pulcro; listo para ser inspeccionado

preserves (prē zurvz′) *n.* jams or jellies
confitura mermelada o jalea de fruta

preview (prē′vyōō′) *v.* to look at or show beforehand
adelanto mostrar antes de lo anticipado

propose (prə pōz′) *v.* to present an idea for consideration
proponer presentar una idea para ser considerada

prudence (prōō′dəns) *v.* carefulness, common sense
prudencia cuidado, sentido común

pursuit (pər sōōt′) *n.* chase
persecución seguimiento constante

Q

quake (kwāk) *v.* to tremble
temblar estremecerse

R

recall (ri kôl′) *v.* remember
recordar acordarse

recurring (ri kur′i[ng]) *adj.* occuring over and over again
recurrente que ocurre una y otra vez

reflect (ri flekt′) *v.* to express a thought or opinion resulting from careful consideration
reflexionar expresar un pensamiento u opinión después de extensa consideración

refugees (ref′yōō jēz′) *n.* people who flee their homes for safety
refugiados personas que huyen de sus hogares por razones de seguridad

research (rē′surch′) *v.* search systematically for the facts about something
investigación búsqueda sistematizada de los hechos

respond (ri spänd′) *v.* to say or do something in reply or reaction
responder decir o hacer algo como reacción

restate (rē stāt′) *v.* to state something again, usually in different words
reformular declarar otra vez, usualmente con diferentes palabras

retreat (ri trēt′) *n.* a pulling back from a dangerous situation
retiro apartamiento de una situación peligrosa

review (ri vyōō′) *v.* look at again
repasar ver de nuevo

revise (ri vīz′) *v.* to change something based on new ideas and information
revisar cambiar a base de nuevas ideas o información

S

sacred (sā′krid) *adj.* pertaining to or connected with religion
sagrado ligado o conectado a una religión

savagery (sav′ijrē) *n.* violence
salvajismo violencia

scouted (skouted) *v.* explored an area
exploré reconocí un área minuciosamente

self-sufficiency (self′sə fish′ənsē) *n.* independence, ability to support oneself
autosuficiencia independencia, capacidad de mantenerse por sí mismo

539

English and Spanish Glossary

sentimental (sen′tə ment″l) *adj.* appealing to tender emotions
sentimental que atrae tiernas emociones

sequence (sē′kwəns) *n.* order in which one thing follows another
secuencia orden en el que una cosa sigue a otra

shrivel (shriv′əl) *v.* wither; dry up
marchitarse deslucirse; secarse

signify (sig′nə fī′) *v.* to be a sign of something
significar ser una seña de algo

skim (skim) *v.* to read quickly to note only important information
hojear leer por encima para fijarse sólo en información importante

smoldered (sm ōl′dərd) *v.* burned slowly without flame
ardido quemaron lentamente sin llama

speculate (spek′yə lāt′) *v.* to make a prediction
especular hacer una predicción

suggest (səg jest′) *v.* to mention as something to think over
sugerir mencionar algo para considerar

sullenly (sul′ənlē) *adv.* with irritation, gloom, or ill humor
arisco de manera desagradable, melancólico o de mal humor

summarize (sum′ə rīz′) *v.* make a brief statement of the most important events in a story
resumir reducir a breves términos los eventos más importantes de un cuento

supercilious (sōō′pərsil′ē əs) *adj.* haughty, arrogant
altanero altivo, arrogante

support (sə pôrt′) *v.* to take the side of, uphold, or help; to help prove
apoyo favorecer, defender o ayudar; ayudar a probar

swanky (swa[ng]′kē) *adj.* fancy, ostentatious
opulento lujoso, ostentoso

synthesize (sin′thə sīz′) *v.* put together elements to form a whole
sintetizar juntar elementos para completar algo

T

tantalizing (tan′tə līz′i[ng]) *adj.* something that is a torment because desirable but out of reach
tentador que atormenta porque es deseable pero fuera del alcance

teetered (tēt′ərd) *v.* moved unsteadily
tambaleó movió de manera inestable

tinder (tin′dər) *n.* flammable substance that can be used as kindling
yesca sustancia inflamable que se usa para prender fuego

transaction (tran zak′shən) *n.* an exchange of money or goods; a deal
transacción intercambio de dinero o materiales; un negocio

treaty (trēt′ē) *n.* a formal agreement between countries or peoples
tratado acuerdo formal entre países o personas

truce (trōōs) *n.* a temporary accord with something or between two parties
tregua acuerdo temporal con algo o entre dos grupos

U

usurps (yōō sʉrps′) *v.* takes over, uses up
usurpa que se apodera de algo, usa del todo

V

verify (ver′ əfī′) *v.* to confirm
verificar confirmar

W

wretched (rech′id) *adj.* pitiful, miserable
desdichado lastimoso, miserable

Index of Skills

Literary Analysis

Allusion, 136
Articles, 7, 210
Author's heritage, beliefs, attitudes, 260, 261–265
Author's perspective, 260–265
Author's purpose, 15, 33, 62–65, 183, 214–217, 221, 266–267, 343
Author's style, 7, 87, 266–271
Autobiography, 7, 210, 258–259, 261–265
Biography, 7, 210, 258–259, 261–265
Character, 22, 108, 123–137, 156–157, 158–160, 161–171
   antagonist, 108, 156
   character traits, 158
   dynamic character, 156, 171
   flat characters, 108, 156, 171
   major characters, 108, 156
   minor characters, 108, 156
   protagonist, 108, 156
   round characters, 108, 156, 171
   static character, 156, 171
Characterization, 108, 158–160, 161–171
   indirect characterization, 108, 159
   direct characterization, 108, 158
Character motivation, 373, 386–387, 388–393
Colloquial language, 87
Comedy, 373
Comparing literary works
   author's perspective, 265
   author's style, 266–271, 361
   characters, 393
   character motivation, 393
   compare and contrast, 279
   conflict, 49, 371, 445
   cultural context, 353
   dramatic speeches, 424–433
   expository writing, 227
   figurative language, 312–317
   heroes, 531
   historical perspective, 271, 381, 393, 531
   imagery, 305
   meter, 343
   monologue, 433
   poetic forms/types, 353
   rhyme, 343
   rhythm, 343
   sound devices, 343
   structural organization, 227
   symbolism, 317
   theme, 74–87, 271, 371
   tone, 257
Conflict, 6, 34–35, 36–37, 38–49, 106–107, 109, 112–115, 123, 137, 142–143, 146, 152–155, 161–171, 176–183, 196, 199, 371, 407, 445
   drama, 373, 426–428
   kinds of, 34
Connotation, 219, 231, 238
Context
   cultural, 41, 87, 163, 270, 324–325, 353, 392, 393, 419, 422, 423, 454–455
   historical, 6, 11, 30, 124, 131, 253, 258, 262, 263, 264, 271, 304, 317, 339, 342, 381, 392, 393, 454–455, 481, 501
Critical reviews, 320–323
Denotation, 219, 231, 238
Dialect, 384, 387, 434
Dialogue, 372, 384–393, 417
   dramatic speeches, 424–425, 426–431
Diaries, 7
Diction, 231, 266, 271, 300
Drama, 372–373
   acts, 372
   scenes, 372
   stage directions, 372, 384–385, 388–393, 417
   staging, 372, 416–418, 419–423
   props, 372, 416–418
Dramatization, 372, 417–418, 419–423
Editorials, 210
Essays, 7, 210
Expository writing, 210
Fables, 74
Fiction, 6, 7, 22
   compared to nonfiction, 7, 33
   elements of, 6
   historical fiction, 6
   narrative texts, 22–33
   types of, 6
Figurative language, 266, 268–270, 271, 290, 312–317
   analogy, 237, 238, 274, 312, 313, 317, 383
   direct metaphor, 312
   extended metaphor, 312
   hyperbole, 238, 266, 268, 312
   idioms, 328, 329
   implied metaphor, 312
   metaphor, 55, 266, 268, 312, 317
   oxymorons, 55
   personification, 266, 312, 317
   simile, 266, 268, 312, 317
   understatement, 238
Figures of speech, 312
Flashback, 108, 120, 123–137
Foreshadowing, 108, 121, 123–137, 408
Historical fiction, 6
How-to writing, 210
Informational texts, 7, *see page 547 for complete list*
Irony, 109, 174–175, 176–183, 408
Jargon, 238
Journals, 7, 210
Letters, 7, 210
Media accounts, 210
Memoirs, 7, 92, 210
Mood, 6, 7, 66–73, 343, 353
Narrative texts, 22–33
   fiction, 22
   nonfiction, 22, 210
   personal narrative, 92–95
   short story, 6, 109, 142–145
Narrator, 6, 348
Nonfiction, 7, 22, 210
   compared to fiction, 7, 33
   narrative texts, 22–33, 210
   organization methods for, 211
   purposes of, 210–211
   types, 7, 210
Novellas, 6
Novels, 6, 108–109
Organizational methods, 192, 211, 220–221
Personal voice, 95
Persuasive techniques, 228–229, 233–237, 238, 239
   emotional appeals, 228
   ethical appeals, 228
   repetition, 228, 290
Persuasive writing, 210, 228, 274–277
Plays, 372
Plot, 6, 22, 36–37, 38–49, 108, 373
   climax, 36, 373, 408
   conflict, 6, 34–35, 36–37, 38–49, 106–107, 109, 112–115, 123, 137, 142–143, 146, 152–155, 161–171, 176–183, 196, 199, 371, 407, 445
   drama, 373, 426–428
   falling action, 36, 408
   plot diagram, 36
   resolution, 36
   rising action, 36, 408
   subplots, 108, 109, 146–147
Poetry, 290
   ballad, 346
   compared with prose, 291
   concrete poems, 346
   elegy, 346
   epic, 346
   forms, 346–347, 350–353
   found poems, 291

Index of Skills

free verse, 346
haiku, 347
historical setting, 349
kinds
    dramatic poetry, 346
    lyric poetry, 346
    narrative poetry, 346
line, 291
ode, 361
sonnet, 346
stanza, 334, 344
sound devices, 290, 334–335, 336–337, 340–343, 344
Point of view, 109, 172–173, 176–183
    fiction compared to nonfiction, 6, 7
    first-person point of view, 6, 109, 172
    limited, 172
    omniscient, 172
    third-person point of view, 6, 109, 172
    types, 107
Problem-solution, evaluating, 115
Propaganda, 230
    bandwagon technique, 230
    glittering generalities, 230
    testimonials, 230
Prose, 290
    compared with poetry, 291
Pun, 335
Reflective writing, 210
Rhythm, 290, 336–337, 338–343
Sales brochure, 210
Setting, 6, 7, 22, 66–73
Sound devices, 290, 338–339, *see also* poetry
Sources, 274, 472–473, 480–485, 508, 514–515, 524
    primary sources, 524, 480, 481, 492
    secondary sources, 524, 480, 481
Speaker, 348–349, 350–353
Speeches,
    dramatic, 372, 424–433
    monologue, 424, 424–425
    persuasive, 253, 338–339
    soliloquy, 424, 433
Style, *see author's style*
Suspense, 373, 408–415
Symbolism, 306–311, 317
Text features, 8–14, 20–21, 65, 213, 458, 459, 461
Themes, 6, 18, 74–87, 107, 131
    common/recurring/universal, 74, 371, 415
Tone, 211, 231–237, 266, 271, 343, 353
Topic, 74, 485

Tragedy, 373
Voice, 211, *see also author's style*

Reading Skills and Strategies

Activating prior knowledge, 8, 15, 17, 60, 307, 442, 458, 461
Adjusting reading rate, 17, 458–459, 461
Analyzing text features, 8–14, 20–21, 213, 227, 459, 461, 519
Asking questions, 442–443, 461
    connect to personal experience, 442
    open-ended questions, 467–468
    set a purpose, 461, 467
Author's message, 112–114, 227, 233–237, 254–256
Author's perspective, 260–265
Author's purpose, 15, 62–65, 73, 119, 183, 302–305, 489
Cause and effect, 248–249, 374–381, 400, 513
Classify, 160
Compare and contrast, 150–155
    author's style, 271
    character behavior and motivation, 49, 136, 271
    characters in the same book, 155
    historical perspective, 271
    literary works, 49, 75–87, 97, 199, 227, 257, 266–267, 279, 312–317, 361, 426–433, 445, 531
    poem to nonfiction article, 305
    sociopolitical issues in texts, 265
    theme, 271
Connections
    personal response, 15, 18–19, 136, 150, 217, 404
    to the Big Question, 106–107, 208–209, 288–289, 370–371, 454–455
Context clues, 16–17, 328–333, 407
    idioms, 328–329
Differentiating between fact and opinion, 252–257, 280
Drawing conclusions, 402–407
Evaluating strategies, 463
Foreshadowing, 121, 123–137
Fluency, 232, 337, 338, 353, 344–345, 434–435, 526
Generalizations, 402–407, 498–503
Graphic organizers and charts, 10, 22, 36, 110, 111, 137, 146, 147, 155, 217, 259, 260, 271, 275, 288, 297, 299, 305, 307, 333, 375, 457, 461, 463, 476, 506

Main idea and supporting details, 212–217, 250, 280, 500
    connection between tone and main idea, 232
    using self-stick notes to track supporting details, 9, 118
Main point, 217
Making inferences, 21, 100, 110–115, 148, 157, 217, 259, 348, 385, 393, 415
    using a chart to make inferences, 111
Marking the text, 9–10, 22–23, 26, 37, 38, 68, 74, 75, 78, 123, 161, 176, 222, 233, 261, 268, 302, 308, 310, 314, 338, 340, 350, 375, 388, 410, 419, 426, 429, 481
    using self-stick notes, 118–119
Note taking, 475–480
Paraphrasing, 292–297, 326, 353, 362, 474, 475
Predicting, 8–15, 58, 60, 98, 122
Previewing, 8, 9, 458
Reading aloud, 232, 337, 338, 344–345, 434–435, 526
Setting a purpose for reading, 7, 107, 209, 289, 371, 455, 458–463, 467
Skimming, 458, 461
Speculate, 171, 470
Summarizing, 18, 146, 498–503
    compare summary to original text, 500
    conflict, 157
    determine main idea, 498
    employee agreement, 460
    historical events, 501
    identify sequence, 498
    information about character, 157
    research, 500
    select pertinent information, 498
    writing a summary, 503
Text organization, 112, 115, 152–155, 489
Unknown words, 16, 17
Using a dictionary, 17, 57, 382–383
Using a glossary, 17
Using a grammar handbook, 57
Using online resources, 17, 57
Using a spell checker, 57
Using a style guide, 515, 524, 528
Using a thesaurus, 17, 57, 219, 382
Visualizing, 7, 300–301
Vocabulary building strategies, 16–17, 116–117, 218–219, 298–299, 382–383, 464–465

Vocabulary

Academic vocabulary
    for comparing and contrasting,

Index

examine, differentiate, signify, 150
for discussing author's purpose, *convince, establish, achieve,* 62
for discussing causes and effects, *perceive, impact, influence,* 374
for discussing context clues, *confirm, clarify, restate,* 328
for discussing drawing conclusions, *assume, evaluate, conclude,* 402
for discussing fact and opinion, *cite, justify, bias,* 252
for discussing inferences in literature, *infer, indicate, deduce,* 110
for discussing main ideas and supporting details, *suggest, imply, support,* 212
for discussing paraphrasing, *convey, emphasize, adapt,* 292
for discussing predictions, *anticipate, modify, verify,* 8
for discussing summarizing, *sequence, pertinent, determine,* 498
for setting a purpose for reading, *critique, skim, revise,* 458
Vocabulary building strategies
   Anglo-Saxon word origins, 464–465
   antonyms, 17, 218–219
   borrowed words, 465
   context clues, 16–17, 26, 32, 38, 48, 68, 72, 75, 78, 86, 116–117, 123, 159, 161, 176, 218–219, 230, 233, 258, 261, 268, 298–299, 302, 308, 314, 316, 328, 329, 333, 338, 340, 350, 382–383, 388, 407, 410, 414, 419, 426, 429, 464–465, 481
   dialect, 384
   dictionary, 382–383
   etymology, 382
   Internet, 465
   Greek roots, 116–117
   history of English language, 109, 117
   idiomatic expressions, 383
   Latin roots, 116–117
      mythological word origins, 464–465
   prefixes, 16–17
   roots, 16–17, 116–117, 298–299, 382
   Scandinavian word origins, 464–465
   suffixes, 16–17
   synonyms, 17, 218–219
   unknown words, 16, 17
   using a dictionary, 17, 57, 382–383
   using a glossary, 17
   using a grammar handbook, 57
   using online resources, 17, 57
   using a spell checker, 57
   using a thesaurus, 17, 57, 219
   vocabulary builder, 26, 28, 38, 40, 45, 46, 48, 68, 69, 71, 75, 76, 78, 79, 80, 86, 123, 125, 126, 127, 128, 130, 132, 161, 164, 169, 176, 179, 180, 182, 222, 223, 224, 233, 234, 235, 261, 263, 264, 268, 269, 302, 303, 308, 309, 310, 314, 315, 316, 338, 339, 340, 341, 350, 351, 388, 389, 390, 392, 410, 412, 413, 414, 419, 420, 421, 422, 426, 427, 428, 429, 430, 431, 481, 482, 483
   word map, 299
   word origins, 116–117, 298–299, 464–465

Writing

Writer's workshop
   assessment, writing for, 356–359
   business letter, 438–441
   cause-and-effect essay, 244–247
   compare-and-contrast essay, 190–195
   critical review, 320–323
   descriptive essay, 54–57
   interview report, 492–495
   manual, 396–399
   multimedia presentation, 524–529
   personal narrative, 92–95
   persuasive essay, 274–277
   portfolio, maintaining, 57
   short story, 142–145
Writing process
   prewriting
      assessment, writing for, 356
      business letter, 438–439
      cause-and-effect essay, 244
      compare-and-contrast essay, 190–191
      critical review, 320
      descriptive essay, 54
      interview report, 492
      manual, 396
      multimedia presentation, 524
      note taking, 475, 492
      personal narrative, 92
      persuasive essay, 274
      short story, 142–143
   drafting
      assessment, writing for, 357
      business letter, 439
      cause-and-effect essay, 245
      compare-and-contrast essay, 192–194
      critical review, 321
      descriptive essay, 55–56
      interview report, 493
      manual, 397
      multimedia presentation, 525–526
      personal narrative, 93
      persuasive essay, 275
      short story, 143
   revising
      assessment, writing for, 357–358
      business letter, 439
      cause-and-effect essay, 245
      compare-and-contrast essay, 194
      critical review, 321
      descriptive essay, 57
      interview report, 493
      manual, 397
      multimedia presentation, 526–527
      personal narrative, 95
      persuasive essay, 275–277
      short story, 143–144
   editing
      assessment, writing for, 359
      business letter, 441
      cause-and-effect essay, 247
      compare-and-contrast essay, 195
      critical review, 323
      descriptive essay, 57
      interview report, 495
      manual, 399
      multimedia presentation, 528
      personal narrative, 95
      persuasive essay, 277
      short story, 145
   publishing
      assessment, writing for, 359
      business letter, 441
      cause-and-effect essay, 247
      compare-and-contrast essay, 195
      critical review, 323
      descriptive essay, 57
      interview report, 495
      manual, 399
      multimedia presentation, 528
      personal narrative, 95
      persuasive essay, 277
      short story, 145
   reflecting on your writing and rubric for self-assessment, 57, 95, 145, 195, 247 277, 323, 359, 399, 441, 495, 528–529
Writing strategies
   block method, 192, 321
   brainstorming chart, 438

Index of Skills

BUT chart, 190
cause/effect chart, 245
chain-of-events organizer, 397
comparison chart, 320, 506
character web, 54
detail web, 396
detail charts, 93,
drawing a picture, 142
five senses chart, 142
free-write, 92
idea list, 92
idea web, 356
important event chart, 55,
information organization chart, 493
job qualifications chart, 438
key-word chart, 356
K-W-L chart, 244
outline, 321, 525
plot diagram, 143
point-by-point organization method, 192
question list, 492
quicklist, 190
SEE method, 192
sequence chain, 506
story element chart, 93,
topic list, 54, 274, 396, 524
two-column chart, 275, 492
using transitions to show sequential order, 397
Venn diagram, 191, 506
Models
  Online models and rubrics
    description: descriptive essay, 56
    exposition: cause-and-effect essay, 246
    exposition: compare-and-contrast essay, 193
    exposition: manual, 398
    exposition: writing for assessment, 358
    response to literature: critical review, 322
    narration: personal narrative, 94
    narration: short story, 144
    persuasion: persuasive essay, 276
    research: interview report, 494
    research: multimedia presentation, 527
    workplace writing: business letter, 440
  Professional author models ("Author's Craft")
    conventions
      possessive nouns, 52
      personal pronouns, 88
      quotations, incorporating into writing, 491
      reflexive pronouns, 89
      subject-verb agreement, 141
    detail and imagery
      action verbs, 138
      modifiers, 242
      participial phrases, 394
      prepositional phrases, 243
      present-perfect and past-perfect tenses, 187
      simple tenses, 186
      subordinate clauses, 436
    sentence structure
      basic sentence types, 51
      combining independent clauses, 436
      conjunctions, 272
      simple, compound, and complex sentences, 354
      using a semi-colon, 523
    tone
      active voice, 318, 526
    voice, word choice
      superlative adjectives to persuade, 241
Student models
  assessment, writing for, 358
  business letter, 439, 440
  cause-and-effect essay, 246
  compare-and-contrast essay, 193–194
  conciseness, 439
  connecting media, 526
  critical review, 322
  descriptive essay, 56
  drafting, 93
  interview report, 494
  literary analysis, 74
  manuals, 397–398
  marking text, 9, 23, 74, 111, 118, 312 439
  multimedia report, 527
  note taking, 476
  organization
  SEE method, 193
  personal narrative, 94
  persuasive essay, 276–277
  Reader's Journal, 18
  research report, 516–517
  revising, 439, 493, 511–512, 526
  short story, 144
  summary, 500
  supporting details, 357
  transitions, 397
Peer review
  assessment, writing for, 357
  business letter, 441
  cause-and-effect essay, 245
  compare-and-contrast essay, 194
  critical review, 321
  descriptive essay, 57
  interview report, 493
  manual, 397
  multimedia presentation, 526
  persuasive essay, 275
  short story, 143
Research report
  choosing a topic, 466, 471
  drafting, 504–509
  interview report, 492–495
  multimedia presentation, 524–529
  narrowing a topic, 467–471
  note taking, 475–476
  organization, 505
  outline, 506–507
  plagiarism, 474
  process, 456–457
  proofreading, 515
  publishing, 515
  revising, 510–513
  rough draft, 508
  sources, 472–473, 485, 508, 514–515, 524
Response to literature
  Anchor Book projects, 96–97, 198–199, 278– 279, 360–361, 444–445, 530–531
  exposition, 320–323, 356–359
  free-choice book reflection, 97, 199, 279, 361, 445, 531
  Reader's Journal responses, 15, 18–19, 33, 49, 65, 73, 87, 115, 118–119, 137, 155, 171, 183, 217, 227, 237, 257, 265, 271, 297, 305, 311, 317, 333, 343, 353, 381, 393, 407, 415, 423, 433, 463, 479, 485, 503
  thinking about the selection, 15, 33, 49, 65, 73, 87, 115, 136, 155, 171, 183, 217, 227, 237, 257, 265, 271, 297, 305,311, 317, 333, 343, 353, 381, 393, 407, 415, 423, 433, 463, 479, 485, 489, 503
Technology
  multimedia slides, 528
  presentation software, 525
  spreadsheets, 525
  visual aids, 524–526
  word processing, 525
Timed writing,
  explanation, 61

Index

exposition, 251, 356–159
interpretation, 497
interpretation of literature, 327
response to literature, 149, 401
Writing about your Anchor Book
Reader's Journal responses, 15, 18–19, 33, 49, 65, 73, 87, 115, 118–119, 137, 155, 171, 183, 217, 227, 237, 257, 265, 271, 297, 305, 311, 317, 333, 343, 353, 381, 393, 407, 415, 423, 433, 463, 479, 485, 503
Anchor Book projects
advertisement campaign, 278
author study, 530
body biography, 198
character rewrite, 96
critical review, 444
designing a set, 444
first-person narrative, 199
interview, 279
letter to the editor, 278
mock trial, 360
poetry anthology, 361
press conference, 530
soundtrack, 198
storyboard, 445
time sequence, 97
travel brochure, 96
visual poem, 360

Grammar, Usage, Mechanics

Antecedent, 89–90
Apostrophe, 50
Appositives and appositive phrases, 51
Capitalization, 522
Clauses, 436–437
Commonly confused words, 50
Comparative forms, 241
Double negatives, 50
Gerunds, 395
Homonyms, 219
Homophones, 273
Hyphens, 50
Infinitives, 50
Italics, 514
Modifiers, 242
Number, 90
Online links, 50–53, 88–91, 138–141, 186–189, 240–243, 272–273, 318–319, 354–355, 394–395, 436–437, 490–491, 522–523
Paragraphs, 510
Parallel structure, 359, 510
Parentheses, 487, 514

Parenthetical remarks, 50
Participles and participial phrases, 394–395
Parts of speech
adjectives
articles, 240
proper, 240
compound, 50
articles, 240
adverbs, 240
interjection, 144
conjunctions, 272, 436
coordinating conjunctions, 272
nouns
abstract, 52
appositive, 51
capitalization, 522
common, 51
compound, 50
concrete, 52
plural, 53
possessive, 52
proper, 51, 240, 522
pronouns
agreement, 90
appositive, 51
case, 50, 88
indefinite pronouns, 90
personal, 88
reflexive, 89
prepositions, 243
verbs
action, 138
irregular, 140
linking, 138
participles, 139, 140
principal parts of, 139
regular, 139
subject/verb agreement, 141
tenses, 139, 140, 186–187
Person, 90
Prepositions and prepositional phrases, 243
Professional author models ("Author's Craft")
conventions
possessive nouns, 52
pronoun case, 88
quotations, 491
reflexive pronouns, 89
subject-verb agreement, 141
detail and imagery
action verbs, 138
modifiers, 242
participial phrases, 394
prepositional phrases, 243
present-perfect and past-

perfect tenses, 187
simple tenses, 186
subordinate clauses, 436
sentence structure
basic sentence types, 51
combining independent clauses, 436
conjunctions, 272
simple, compound, complex, and compound-complex sentences, 354
using a semi-colon, 523
tone
active voice, 318, 359
voice, word choice
superlative adjectives to persuade, 241
Punctuation
colons, 523
commas, 50, 523
ellipses, 487
quotation marks, 491, 514
semi-colons, 523
Quotations, 474, 475, 491, 514
Sentences
complex, 354
compound, 354
compound-complex, 354
conjunctions within, 272
declaratory, 51
effectiveness, 511
exclamatory, 51
fragments, 490
imperative, 51
interrogative, 51
run-on, 490
simple, 141, 354
structure, 354–355
subordinating conjunctions, 272
varying patterns of, 355
Spelling
homophones, 273
roots, 116
suffixes, 319
tricky or difficult words, 91
vowel sounds, 188
Subject/verb agreement, 141
Subordinating conjunctions, 272
Superlative forms, 241
Syllables
mispronouncing and misspelling, 91
unstressed, 188
Voice
active, 318, 359
passive, 318, 359
Word choice, 189

545

Index of Skills

Critical Thinking
Adapt, 171
Analyze, 33, 35, 37, 49, 65, 67, 73, 87, 115, 119, 122, 136–137, 147, 155, 157, 160, 171, 173, 175, 183, 197, 213, 221, 230, 237, 253, 259, 265, 267, 271, 297, 305, 311, 313, 317, 333, 335, 337, 343, 353, 381, 387, 393, 409, 415, 418, 423, 425, 433, 471, 473, 479, 507–508, 513, 518
Apply, 65, 67, 173, 217, 221, 259, 297, 313, 329, 333, 349, 353, 385, 407, 418, 423, 463, 466–468, 469, 471, 479, 503, 509, 513, 518
Assess, 15, 229, 301
Classify, 160, 385
Communicate, 519
Compare, 21, 87, 160, 257, 381, 479, 500
Compare and contrast, 49, 97, 136, 155, 199, 227, 265, 267, 271, 279, 305, 353, 361, 433, 445, 479, 531
Conclude, 15
Connect, 15, 217, 301, 317, 393, 404, 415, 423, 433, 479, 485, 489
Contrast, 343, 425
Convey, 297
Create, 21, 393, 416, 518
Deduce, 265, 311, 317
Define, 407
Describe, 49, 67, 227, 232, 317, 474
Determine, 73
Discuss, 58–59, 146–147, 196–197, 248–249, 324–325, 442–443
Distinguish, 343, 485
Draw, 347
Draw conclusions, 404, 407, 472, 479
Emphasize, 297
Establish, 63
Evaluate, 15, 21, 49, 63, 65, 73, 87, 115, 137, 183, 213, 217, 227, 229, 232, 237, 257, 265, 267, 271, 305, 317, 329, 343, 407, 415, 425, 433, 473, 485, 489, 505, 508–509, 513, 519
Examine, 21, 337
Explain, 25, 115, 183, 217, 227, 305, 404, 459, 463, 474, 485, 503, 509
Extend, 197
Identify, 21, 25, 63, 65, 160, 173, 175, 197, 237, 257, 333, 335, 343, 382, 387, 415, 459, 489, 504, 518
Infer, 21, 115, 157, 253, 259, 353, 385, 393, 415, 489
Interpret, 33, 49, 65, 73, 87, 137, 155, 171, 183, 229–230, 232, 237, 271, 307, 311, 313, 329, 333, 343, 349, 353, 382, 387, 393, 415, 423, 433, 500
Justify, 119
Listen, 59
Listen and speak, 232, 293
Locate, 382
Make a judgment, 237
Organize, 471
Paraphrase, 293, 297
Predict, 10, 15, 21, 58, 122, 393
Propose, 197
Question, 59, 442–443, 467
Recall, 33, 136, 183, 333, 393, 407, 489
Reflect, 381, 463
Research, 467, 470, 500
Respond, 25, 73, 136, 230, 305, 415, 518
Restate, 293, 297
Review, 463
Revise, 513
Speculate, 33, 171, 237, 470, 500
Summarize, 217, 460, 503
Support, 115, 257, 463
Synthesize, 147, 307, 433, 468, 471, 504, 507, 513, 518
Verify, 15

Research Skills
Bibliography, 472, 514, 517
Brainstorming, 438, 466
Choosing a topic, 457, 466–471
  key words, 467
  asking questions, 466–467
Citing sources, 474, 514–515
Drafting a research report, 504–509
Encyclopedia, 462–463
Evaluating sources, 472–473
Indexes, 467, 469–471, 472
Internal citations, 514
Internet, 466, 467, 468–469, 471, 473
Interview report, 492–495
Multimedia presentation, 524–529
Narrowing a topic, 467–471
Note taking, 475–476
Organization methods, 456–457, 506–507
Plagiarism, 474
Proofreading, 515
Publishing, 515
Revising, 510–511
Sources, 472–473, 480–485, 508, 514–515
Table of contents, 467, 470
Thesis statement, 504–508
Validity of source, 472–473
Web sites, 472–473

Speaking, Listening, and Media Skills
Active listening, 58–59, 146–147, 184–185, 196–197, 238–239, 248–249, 324–325, 344–345, 434–435, 442–443, 520–521
Analyzing media messages, 520–521
Cartoons and comics, 24–25, 158, 175
Critical viewing, 29, 46, 70, 77, 81, 164, 181, 236, 269, 303, 315, 391, 430, 487
Debate, 531
Dramatic reading, 434–435
Evaluating peers, 57, 185, 239, 245, 275, 345, 435, 441, 521, 526
Group reading
  drama, 434–435
  poetry, 232, 337, 344–345
Group work, 4–5, 58–59, 106–107, 146–147, 196–197, 209, 232, 248–249, 288–289, 324–325, 360, 370, 442–443, 454–455, 531, 524–527
Impromptu speech, 515
Interview report, 492–495
Interviews
  conducting, 279
  transcripts, 486–489
Literature Circles, 58–59, 146–147, 196–197, 248–249, 324–325, 442–443
mock trial, 360
Multimedia presentation, 524–529
Oral interpretation of literature, 184–185
Panel discussion, 520–521
Paraphrasing
  others' comments, 185
  own presentation, 526
Peer review, see Evaluating Peers.
Persuasive speech, 238–239
Poetry reading, 232, 335, 337, 344–345, 346–347, 353
Reading aloud, 232, 335, 336–342, 344–345, 346–347, 434–435, 353
Role-playing 199, 278, 279, 360, 444, 445, 530
Rubrics and self-assessment, 59, 185, 239, 345, 435, 521, 529
Script, 526
Summarizing, 526
Thesis, 238
Using visuals in a presentation, 96, 97, 184, 238, 344, 360, 434, 520, 530

Index of Features

Informational Texts
Advertisements, 208, 267
Bibliography, 517
Book review, 322
Consumer documents
   report, 151,
   warranty, 499
Diagram, 20
E-mail, 63
Encyclopedia entry, 462
Index, 470
Instructions, 459
Internet search page, 468
Interview transcript, 486–488, 494
Interview report, 494–495
Legend, 20
Letters
   letter to the editor, 229
   business letter, 440
Magazine and newspaper articles
   opinion pieces, 233–236, 254–256
   real life, 213, 330–332
      science, 112–114, 152–154,
         214–216, 222–226, 294–296,
         375, 405–406
      social studies, 11–14, 376–380,
         477–478, 481–482, 483, 484,
         501–502
Manuals, 398, 459
Multimedia presentation, 527–528
Online database, 469
Population chart, 9
Preamble to the Constitution of the
   United States, 480
Survey, 473
Table of contents, 470
Warranty, 499
Web site entry, 473
Workplace documents
   memo, 64
   employment agreement, 460

Literature Circles
Asking questions, 442–443
Cause and effect, 248–249
Cultural context, 324–325
Introduction, 58–59
Power and conflict, 196–197
Subplots, 146–147

Reader's Journal
Author's purpose, 65
Author's style, 271
Biography and autobiography, 265
Cause and effect, 381
Character and characterization, 171
Character motivation, 393
Compare and contrast, 155
Conflict, 49
Context clues, 333
Dramatic speeches, 433
Dramatization, 423
Drawing conclusions, 407
Expository writing, 227
Fact and opinion, 257
Figurative language, 317
Finding reliable sources, 479
Flashback and Foreshadowing, 137
Imagery, 305
Interview transcript, 489
Irony, 183
Main ideas and supporting details, 217
Making inferences, 115
Making predictions, 15
Narrative texts, 33
Paraphrasing, 297
Persuasive writing, 237
Plot, 36–37
Poetry, 353
Point of view, 183
Primary and secondary sources, 485
Research process, 519
Revising, 513
Setting a purpose for reading, 463
Setting and mood, 73
Sound devices, 343
Speaker, 353
Staging, 423
Summarizing, 503
Suspense, 415
Symbolism, 311
Theme, 87

Writer's Workshops
Description: Descriptive Essay, 54–57
Exposition: Cause–and–Effect Essay,
   244–247
Exposition: Compare–and–Contrast
   Essay, 190–195
Exposition: Manual, 396–399
Exposition: Writing for Assessment,
   356–359
Narration: Personal Narrative, 92–95
Narration: Short Story, 142–145
Persuasion: Persuasive Essay, 274–277
Research: Interview Report, 492–495
Research: Multimedia Presentation,
   524–529
Response to Literature: Critical Review,
   320–323
Workplace Writing: Business Letter,
   438–441

Assessment
Standardized test practice
   author's purpose, 98
   cause and effect, 400, 446
   compare and contrast, 98, 200
   context clues, 362–363
   drawing conclusions, 446–447
   elements of drama, 401, 447–448
   elements of fiction and nonfiction,
      61, 99–100
   elements of nonfiction, 251,
      281–282
   elements of the novel, 149, 201–202
   elements of poetry and prose, 327,
      363–364
   fact and opinion, 280–281
   grammar, 101, 203, 283, 365, 449,
      535
   inferences, 148, 200
   main ideas and supporting details,
      250, 280
   paraphrasing, 326, 362
   predictions, 60, 98
   research process, 497, 533
   setting a purpose for reading, 496,
      532
   spelling, 100, 203, 283, 364–365,
      448–449, 534
   summarizing, 532
   timed writing
      explanation, 61
      exposition, 251
      interpretation, 497
      interpretation of literature, 327
      response to literature, 149, 401
   vocabulary, 101, 202, 282–283, 364,
      448, 534
Peer review
   assessment, writing for, 357
   cause-and-effect essay, 245
   compare-and-contrast essay, 194
   critical review, 321
   descriptive essay, 57
   interview report, 493
   manual, 397
   multimedia presentation, 526
   persuasive essay, 275
   short Story, 143
Self–Assessment
   assessment, writing for, 359
   business letter, 441
   cause–and–effect essay, 247
   compare–and–contrast essay, 195
   critical review, 323
   descriptive essay, 57
   interview report, 495
   listening and speaking

Index of Features

analyzing media messages, 521
delivering a persuasive speech, 239
oral interpretation of literature, 185
reading drama aloud, 435
reading poetry aloud, 345
manual, 399
multimedia presentation, 529
personal narrative, 95
persuasive essay, 277
portfolio, 95
short story, 145

Author Biographies

In text
Angelou, Maya, 32, Chief Joseph, 481, Cofer, Judith Ortiz, 268, 270, Fleischman, Paul, 308, Douglass, Frederick, 264, Frost, Robert, 310, Gibran, Kahlil, 163, Hansberry, Lorraine, 431, Hughes, Langston, 388, Hurst, James, 123, Komunyakaa, Yusef, 341, Lincoln, Abraham, 338, MacNeil, Robert, 233, Nye, Naomi Shihab, 170, Poe, Edgar Allan, 176, 182, Tennyson, Lord Alfred, 342Thomas, Piri, 48, Zindel, Paul, 68, 72

Online
Angelou, Maya, 33, Anthony, Susan B., 253, Ashabranner, Brent, 15, Bambara, Toni Cade, 157, Bashō, 347, Capote, Truman, 87, Chief Joseph, 485, Chiyojo, 347, Cofer, Judith Ortiz, 173, 271, Dickinson, Emily, 317, Douglass, Frederick, 265, Earley, Tony, 159, Erdoes, Richard, 423, Espada, Martín, 305, Fleischman, Paul, 311, Foote, Horton, 416, Frost, Robert, 307, 311, 346, Garcia, Richard, 317, Goodrich, Frances and Hackett, Albert, 408, Hansberry, Lorraine, 433, Hay, Sara Henderson, 232, Hinton, S. E., 293, Hughes, Langston, 317, 349, 393, 433, Hurst, James, 136, Hwang, David Henry, 424, King, Stephen, 489, Komunyakaa, Yusef, 343, Lazarus, Emma, 353, Lincoln, Abraham, 343, Ling, Amy, 111, Lowry, Lois, 119, MacNeil, Robert, 237, du Maurier, Daphne, 122, Merriam, Eve, 335, Mora, Pat, 353, Myers, Walter Dean, 118, Neruda, Pablo, 313, Nhuong, Huynh Quang, 66, Nye, Naomi Shihab, 171, Ortiz, Alfonso, 423, Paulsen, Gary, 415, Pilkey, Dav, 24, Poe, Edgar Allan, 183, Rooney, Andrew A., 257, Schwartz, Alvin, 37, Shaw, George Bernard, 386, Solt, Mary Ellen, 353, Taylor, Mildred D., 120, Tennyson, Alfred, 343, Thomas, Piri, 49, Uchida, Yoshiko, 35, Walker, Alice, 301, Whitman, Walt, 337, Wilson, August, 433, Yep, Laurence, 87, Zindel, Paul, 73, 384

Index of Authors and Titles

A
A Great and Honorable Leader, 481–482
A Raisin in the Sun, 429–431
A Visit to Washington, D.C., 1879, 483
Achenbach, Joel, 405
Acquainted With the Night, 346–347
Alabanza: In Praise of Local 100, 302–304
Always to Remember: The Vision of Maya Ying Lin, 11–14
America the Not-So-Beautiful, 254–256
Amigo Brothers, 38–48
Angelou, Maya, 26, 32
Animals Among Us, 112–114
Ant and the Dove, The, 74
Ashabranner, Brent, 11
At First, It Is True, I Thought There Were Only Peaches & Wild Grapes, 301
Attic, The, 37

B
Babbitt, Natalie, 149
Bad Boy: A Memoir, 118
Bambara, Toni Cade, 157
Bashō, 347
Beauty Lessons, 173
Birds, The, 122

C
Capote, Truman, 75
Chief Joseph, 481, 483, 484
Child of the Owl, 78–86
Chiyojo, 347
City Is So Big, The, 316
Cofer, Judith Ortiz, 173, 268, 270
Coyote Steals the Sun and Moon, 419–422

D
Dancers, The, 416
Day It Rained Cockroaches, The, 68–72
Dickinson, Emily, 314
Douglass, Frederick, 261, 264
Dreams, 315
du Maurier, Daphne, 122
Dynamo Bicycles warranty, 499

E
Eagle, The, 342
Earley, Tony, 159
E-mail, 63
Employment Agreement, 460
Erdoes, Richard, 419
Espada, Martin, 302
Extreme Weather: Hurricanes and Tornadoes, 152–154

F
Fences, 350
Fire and Ice, 307
Fleischman, Paul, 308
Flying to Fame, 477–478
FOB, 424–425
Foote, Horton, 416
For Some, Pain Is Orange, 294–296
Forsythia, 352
Frost, Robert, 307, 310, 346

G
Garcia, Richard, 316, 324
Gettysburg Address, The, 338–339
Giver, The, 119
Golden Years, 405–406
Goodrich, Frances, 408
Grandma Ling, 111
Grass Harp, The, 75–77

H
Hatchet, 410–414
Hackett, Albert, 408
Hamadi, 161–170
Hansberry, Lorraine, 429, 431
Harlem, 432
Harriet Beecher Stowe, 258–259
Hay, Sara Henderson, 232
Hinton, S. E., 293
"Hope" is the thing with feathers, 314
Hornick, Susan, 294
Hughes, Langston, 315, 324, 349, 388, 432
Hurst, James, 123
Hwang, David Henry, 424–425

I
I, Too, 349
I Hear America Singing, 337
I Know Why the Caged Bird Sings, 26–32
Interview, 232

J
Jim the Boy, 159

K
Kids on the Bus, 501–502
Kim, 308–309
King, Stephen, 458, 486–489
Komunyakaa, Yusef, 340, 341

L
Land, The, 120
Land I Lost, The, 66
Lazarus, Emma, 351
Let Me Hear You Whisper, 384–385
Lincoln, Abraham, 338
Ling, Amy, 111
Local Kids Clean Up Playground, 213
Lowry, Lois, 119

M
MacNeil, Robert, 233
Martín Espada, 302
Memo, 64
Merriam, Eve, 335
Mora, Pat, 350
Moving Plates of Rock, 375
Myers, Walter Dean, 118

N
Neruda, Pablo, 313
New Colossus, The, 351
Nhuong, Huynh Quang, 66
Nye, Naomi Shihab, 161, 170

O
Occupation: Conductorette, 26–32
Ode to Enchanted Light, 313
On Women's Right to Suffrage, 253
Onomatopoeia, 335
Ortiz, Alfonso, 419

P
Paulsen, Gary, 410
Personal Essay: A Beach Diary
Piano Lesson, The, 426–428
Pilkey, Dav, 24
Poe, Edgar Allan, 176, 182
Pygmalion, 386–387

R
Raymond's Run, 157
Recording Your Announcement (instructions), 459
Red Tail Angels, The, 376–380
Rhythms of Rap, The, 330–332
Road Not Taken, The, 310
Rooney, Andrew A., 254
Rumblefish, 293

S
Scarlet Ibis, The, 123–135
Schwartz, Alvin, 37
Shaw, George Bernard, 386
Short-Sided Soccer, 329
Slam, Dunk, and Hook, 340
Sleep, It's Healthy, 246
Solt, Mary Ellen, 350
Surrender in the Bear Paw Mountains, The, 484

Index of Authors and Titles

Tennyson, Lord Alfred, 342
Thank You, M'am, 388–392
The Diary of Anne Frank, 408–409
The Life of Frederick Douglass, 261–264
Thomas, Piri, 38, 48
Tolstoy, Leo, 74
Travel Advertisement: Come to Bermuda, 267
Trouble with Television, The, 233–236

U
Uchida, Yoshiko, 35

V
Volar: To Fly, 268–270

W
Walker, Alice, 301
Water Man Comics, 24–25
Weighing Your Options: Plasma or LCD TV?, 151
What Makes a Car Run?, 214–216
Whitman, Walt, 337
Wilson, August, 426
World Book Encyclopedia entry, 462
World of the Forensic Scientist, The, 222–226

Y
Yep, Laurence, 78

Z
Zindel, Paul, 68, 72, 384

Acknowledgments

Staff Credits

The people who made up *The Reader's Journey* team—representing design, editorial, education technology, manufacturing and inventory planning, market research, marketing services, planning and budgeting, product planning, production services, project office, publishing processes, the business office, and rights and permissions—are listed below. Boldface type denotes the core team members.

Rosalyn Arcilla, **Daniel Bairos,** Suzanne Biron, **Elizabeth Comeau,** Mark Cirillo, Jason Cuoco, Harold Delmonte, Kerry Dunn, Leslie Feierstone Barna, **Shelby Gragg,** Meredith Glassman, Cassandra Heliczer, **Rebecca Higgins,** Sharon Inglis, **Linda Johnson, Angela Kral,** Monisha Kumar, **Margaret LaRaia, Ellen Levinger,** Cynthia Levinson, **Cheryl Mahan, Elise Miley,** Linda Punskovsky, Tracey Randinelli, John Rosta, **Brian Salacki,** Laura Smyth, Ana Sofia Villaveces, **Heather Wright**

Additional Credits

Editorial: Chrysalis Publishing Group, Inc.
Page layout, photo research, art acquisition, production: AARTPACK, Inc.

Text Credits

Arte Publico Press
"Fences" is reprinted with permission from the publisher of *Communion* by Pat Mora. Copyright ©1991 by Pat Mora.

Brent Ashabranner
"Always to Remember: The Vision of Maya Ying Lin" by Brent Ashabranner from *Always To Remember.* Copyright ©1988. Reprinted by permission of Brent Ashabranner.

Atheneum Books for Young Readers, an imprint of Simon & Schuster Children's Publishing Division & Flannery Literary Agency
From "Hatchet" by Gary Paulsen. Reprinted with the permission of Atheneum Books for Young Readers, an imprint of Simon & Schuster Children's Publishing Division from *Hatchet* by Gary Paulsen. Copyright ©1987 Gary Paulsen.

Bancroft Library, University of California, Berkeley
From "Tears of Autumn" by Yoshiko Uchida from *The Forbidden Stitch: An Asian American Women's Anthology.* Copyright ©1989 by Yoshiko Uchida. Reprinted by permission of the Bancroft Library, University of California, Berkeley.

CBS, Inc.
"Stephen King: His books, his life, his wife" by Staff from *60 Minutes Interview With Lesley Stahl (August 2, 1998).* Copyright ©1998 CBS News. Reprinted by permission of CBS News Archives.

Cobblestone Publishing
"Rhythms of Rap" by Kathiann M. Kowalski from Odyssey's March 2002 issue: *Music: Why Do We Love It?,* Copyright ©2002, Cobblestone Publishing, 30 Grove Street, Suite C, Peterborough, NH 03458. All rights reserved. Used by permission of Carus Publishing Company.

Curtis Brown, Ltd.
From "The Day It Rained Cockroaches" by Paul Zindel from *The Pigman and Me.* Copyright ©1992 by Paul Zindel. First appeared in *The Pigman and Me,* published by HarperCollins. Reprinted by permission of Curtis Brown, Ltd.

Copyright Clearance Center
"Kids on the Bus: The Overlooked Role of Teenagers" by Jeffrey Zaslow from *The Wall Street Journal Nov. 10, 2005* http://online.wsj.com/article_print/sb113157886290192848.html. Reprinted by permission of Copyright Clearance Center.

Delacorte Press
"Pinball Machine" by S.E. Hinton from *Rumblefish.* Copyright ©1975 by S.E. Hinton.

Doubleday
"The Birds" by Daphne du Maurier from *Kiss Me Again Stranger.* Copyright ©1952 by Daphne du Maurier.

Dutton Signet, a division of Penguin Group (USA) Inc.
From "The Piano Lesson" by August Wilson from *The Piano Lesson.* Copyright ©1988, 1990 by August Wilson. Reprinted by permission of Dutton Signet, a division of Penguin Group (USA) Inc.

Farrar, Straus & Giroux, LLC.
From *Tuck Everlasting* by Natalie Babbitt. Copyright ©1975 by Natalie Babbitt. All rights reserved. Published by arrangement with Farrar, Straus & Giroux LLC.

Richard Garcia
"The City is So Big" by Richard Garcia from *The City Is So Big.* Reprinted by permission of the author.

HarperCollins Publishers, Inc.
From "The Land I Lost" by Huynh Quang Nhuong from *The Land I Lost.* From "Let Me Hear You Whisper" by Paul Zindel from *Let Me Hear You Whisper.*

HarperCollins Children's Books
From *Child of the Owl* by Laurence Yep. Copyright ©1977 by Laurence Yep. From *Bad Boy: A Memoir* by Walter Dean Myers. Copyright ©1998 by Walter Dean Myers. "Kim" by Paul Fleischman from *Seedfolks.* Copyright ©2002 by Paul Fleischman.

HarperCollins Children's Books & Curtis Brown, Ltd.
"The Attic" by Alvin Schwarz from *Scary Stories to Tell in the Dark.* Text copyright ©1981 by Alvin Schwarz. Used by permission of HarperCollins Publishers.

Ian Henry
"Spin a Pencil Around Your Thumb" by Ian Henry from h*ttp://www.wikihow.com/Spin-a-Pencil-Around-Your-Thumb.* Used by Permission.

Acknowledgments

Hill and Wang, a division of Farrar, Straus & Giroux LLC & Harold Ober Associates
"Thank You, M'am" by Langston Hughes from *Short Stories*. Copyright ©1996 by Ramona Bass and Arnold Rampersad. Reprinted by permission of Farrar, Straus and Giroux, LLC.

The Barbara Hogenson Agency, Inc.
From *The Dancers* by Horton Foote. Copyright 1955, 1983 by Horton Foote.

Henry Holt and Company, LLC
"Acquainted with the Night" from *The Poetry of Robert Frost* edited by Edward Connery Latham, Copyright 1928, ©1969 by Henry Holt and Co., ©1970 by Lesley Frost Ballantine, ©1942, 1956 by Robert Frost. "Fire and Ice" by Robert Frost from *The Poetry Of Robert Frost* edited by Edward Connery Lathem. Copyright ©1923, 1969 by Henry Holt and Company. Copyright ©1951 by Robert Frost. Reprinted by permisson of Henry Holt and Company, LLC.

Susan Hornik
"For Some Pain Is Orange" by Susan Hornik from *Smithsonian, February 2001.* Copyright ©Susan Hornik. Used by permission.

Houghton Mifflin Company
Excerpt from *The Giver* by Lois Lowry. Copyright ©1993 by Lois Lowry. Reprinted by permission of Houghton Mifflin Company. All rights reserved.

James R. Hurst
"The Scarlet Ibis" by James Hurst from *The Atlantic Monthly, July 1960.* Copyright ©1988 by James Hurst. Reprinted by permission of James R. Hurst.

Japan Publications, Inc.
"Temple Bells Die Out" by Basho<macron over the "o">; and "Dragonfly Catcher" by Chiyojo, reprinted by permission from *One Hundred Famous Haiku* by Daniel C. Buchanan, copyright © 1973 by Japan Publications Trading Co., LTD on behalf of Japan Publications, Inc.

Alfred A. Knopf, a division of Random House, Inc. & Harold Ober Associates
"Harlem", copyright 1951 by Langston Hughes from *The Collected Poems of Langston Hughes* by Langston Hughes, edited by Arnold Rampersad with David Roessel, Associate Editor. Copyright ©1994 by The Estate of Langston Hughes. "Dreams" by Langston Hughes, edited by Arnold Rampersad with David Roessel, Associate Editor from *Collected Poems Of Langston Hughes*. Copyright ©1994 by The Estate of Langston Hughes. Used by permission of Alfred A. Knopf, a division of Random House, Inc. "I, Too" by Langston Hughes from *Selected Poems Of Langston Hughes*. Copyright ©1926 by Alfred A. Knopf, Inc. Renewed Copyright ©1954 by Langston Hughes. Used by permission.

Gelston Hinds
"Grandma Ling" by Amy Ling from *Bridge: An Asian American Perspective, Vol. 7, No. 3.* Copyright ©1980 by Amy Ling. Reprinted by permission of Gelston Hinds.

Little, Brown and Company
From *Jim the Boy* by Tony Earley. Copyright ©2000 by Tony Earley. Reprinted by permission. "Ode to Enchanted Light" by Pablo Neruda translated by Ken Krabbenhoft from *Odes To Opposites*. Copyright ©1995 by Pablo Neruda. Reprinted by permission.

Robert MacNeil
"The Trouble with Television" by Robert MacNeil from *The Trouble With Television (Condensed From Speech 11/84 At President Leadership Forum, Suny).* Copyright ©1985 by Reader's Digest and Robert MacNeil. Reprinted by permission of Robert MacNeil.

Eve Merriam c/o Marian Reiner Literary Agency
"Onomatopoeia" by Eve Merriam from *A Sky Full of Poems*. Copyright ©1964, 1970, 1973, 1986 by Eve Merriam. Reprinted by permission of Marian Reiner Literary Agency.

National Geographic Magazine
"Golden Years" by Joel Achenbach from *National Geographic, July 2004.* Copyright ©2004 National Geographic Society. Reprinted by permission of National Geographic Magazine.

Naomi Shihab Nye
"Hamadi" by Naomi Shihab Nye from *America Street*. Reprinted by permission of Naomi Shihab Nye, 2007.

Pantheon Books, a division of Random House Inc.
"Coyote Steals the Sun and Moon" by Retold Richard Erdoes & Alfonso Ortiz from *American Indian Myths And Legends*. Copyright ©1984 by Richard Erdoes and Alfonso Ortiz. Used by permission of Pantheon Books, a division of Random House, Inc.

PARADIGM
From "FOB" by David Henry Hwang from *Trying to Find Chinatown: The Selected Plays.* Copyright ©2000 by David Henry Hwang. Used by permission.

Pearson Education, Inc.
"A Great and Honorable Leader," "What Makes a Car Run?" and "Animals Among Us" by Nila Banton Smith from *Be a Better Reader Eight Edition A.* "Red Tailed Angels" by Nila Banton Smith from *Be a Better Reader Eight Edition B.* "Flying to Fame" by Nila Banton Smith from *Be a Better Reader Eight Edition C.* "World of the Forensic Scientist" by Nila Banton Smith from *Be a Better Reader Eight Edition E.* "Hurricanes and Tornadoes" by Nila Banton Smith from *Be a Better Reader Eight Edition G.* Copyright ©2003 by Pearson Education, Inc., publishing as AGS Globe, an imprint of Pearson Learning Group. All rights reserved. Reprinted by permission of Pearson Education, Inc. From "The Trouble with Television" [with Teaching Materials]" by Robert MacNeil from *Prentice Hall Literature Penguin Edition*. Copyright ©2007 by Pearson Education, Inc., publishing as Pearson Prentice Hall. All rights reserved. "Moving Plates of Rock" from *Prentice Hall World Studies: Asia and the Pacific*. Copyright ©2005 by Pearson Education, Inc., publishing as Pearson Prentice Hall, Upper Saddle River, NJ 07458.

Acknowledgments

Penguin Group (USA) Inc.
"The Land" by Mildred D. Taylor from *The Land*. Copyright ©2001 by Mildred D. Taylor.

Puffin Books
From "Beauty Lessons" by Judith Ortiz Cofer from *An Island Like You*. Copyright ©Judith Ortiz, 1995.

Random House, Inc.
"America the Not-so-Beautiful" by Andrew A. Rooney from *Not That You Asked*.... Copyright ©1989 by Essay Productions, Inc. Used by permission of Random House, Inc. "At First, It Is True, I Thought There Were Only Peaches & Wild Grapes" by Alice Walker from *Absolute Trust In The Goodness Of The Earth: New Poems* by Alice Walker. Copyright ©2002 by Alice Walker. Used by permission of Random House, Inc. "Raymond's Run" by Toni Cade Bambara from *Gorilla, My Love*. Copyright ©1971 by Toni Cade Bambara.

Random House, Inc. & A&C Black Publishers Ltd.
From *A Raisin in the Sun* by Lorraine Hansberry. Copyright ©1958 by Robert Nermiroff, as an unpublished work. Copyright ©1959, 1966, 1984 by Robert Nemiroff. Copyright ©renewed 1986, 1987 by Robert Nemiroff. Used by permission of Random House, Inc.

Random House, Inc. & Flora Roberts, Inc.
From *The Diary of Anne Frank* by Frances Goodrich and Albert Hackett. Copyright ©1956 by Albert Hackett, Frances Goodrich Hackett, and Otto Frank. Used by permission of Random House, Inc. Professionals and amateurs are hereby warned that *The Diary of Anne Frank* by Frances Goodrich and Albert Hackett being fully protected under the copyright Laws of the United States of America, the British Empire, including the Dominion of Canada, and all other countries of the Universal Copyright and Berne Conventions, are subject to royalty. All rights, including professional, amateur, motion picture, recitation, lecturing, public reading, radio and television broadcasting, and the rights of translation into foreign languages, are strictly reserved. Particular emphasis is laid on the question of readings, permission for which must be secured in writing. All inquiries for *The Diary of Anne Frank* should be addressed to Random House, 1745 Broadway, 3rd Floor, New York, N.Y. 10019 and Flora Roberts Inc., 275 Seventh Avenue, New York, N.Y. 10001.

Random House, Inc. & Greenberg Traurig, LLP
"The Grass Harp" by Truman Capote from *The Grass Harp*. Copyright ©1951 by Truman Capote. Used by permission of Random House, Inc.

Random House, Inc. & Virago Press, Ltd.
"Occupation: Conductorette (from *I Know Why The Caged Bird Sings*)" by Maya Angelou from *I Know Why The Caged Bird Sings*. Copyright ©1969 by Maya Angelou. Used by permission of Random House, Inc.

Susan Solt
"Forsythia" by Mary Ellen Solt. Copyright ©1968 by Mary Ellen Solt. Copyright ©1970 by Mary Ellen Solt. Used by permission. All rights reserved.

Society of Authors
From "Pygmalion" by Bernard Shaw from *Pygmalion*. Reprinted by permission of The Society of Authors, on behalf of the Bernard Shaw Estate.

Piri Thomas/Suzanne Dod Thomas
"Amigo Brothers" by Piri Thomas from *Stories from El Barrio* by Piri Thomas. Reprinted by permission of the author.

University of Arkansas Press
"Interview" by Sara Henderson Hay from *Story Hour*. Copyright ©1982 by Sara Henderson Hay. Reprinted by permission of The University of Arkansas Press.

University of Georgia Press
"Volar: To Fly" by Judith Ortiz Cofer from *In Short: A Collection Of Brief Creative Nonfiction*. Reprinted by permission of the author and The University of Georgia Press.

Wesleyan University Press
"Slam, Dunk, & Hook" from *Magic City* by Yusef Komunyakaa. Copyright ©1992 by Yusef Komunyakaa and reprinted by permission of Wesleyan University Press.

World Book Publishing
"Detective Story" by David Geherin, article from *The World Book Encyclopedia* ©2007 World Book, Inc. By permission of the publisher. www.worldbook.com

Writers House, LLC
"Untitled Text" by Dav Pilkey. Copyright ©2003 by Dav Pilkey. "The Adventures of Water Man" Illustration by Dav Pilkey. Copyright ©1978 by Dav Pilkey. Reprinted by permission of Writers House, LLC.

W. W. Norton & Company, Inc.
"Alabanza: In Praise of Local 100" by Martin Espada from *Alabanza*. Copyright ©2003 by Martin Espada. Reprinted by permission of W. W. Norton & Company, Inc.

Note: Every effort has been made to locate the copyright owner of material reproduced in this component. Omissions brought to our attention will be corrected in subsequent editions.

Photo and Art Credits

Cover Design

Judith Krimski

Art Credits

Page 1: Elise Miley & Ted Smykal; **3:** (top) Elise Miley, (bottom) Kerry Cashman; **25:** Dav Pilkey; **38, 40, 43, 45-46, 48:** Alex Williamson; **68-72:** Jonathan Twingly; **75, 77:** Greg Morgan; **103:** Elise Miley; **158:** ©Scott McCloud; **164-166, 168:** Alicia Buelow; **175:** ©2006 guy & rodd Dist. by UFS Inc. guyandrodd.com; **176, 178, 181:** Geoff Granfield; **215-216:** Vincent Corona-Evans; **226:** Alex Williamson; **233-236:** Sarah Jones; **238:** Daniel Guidera; **268-270:** Judith Krimski Illustration; **285:** Elise Miley; **286:** Cyndy Patrick; **315:** Ted Smykal; **316:** Julia Vakser; **368:** Ted Smykal; **391:** Smithsonian American Art Museum, Washington DC/Art Resource, NY; **425:** Nancy Nimony; **426-427:** Jonny Hannah; **429-430:** Chandra Dieppa; **432:** Wendy Wahman; 451: Elise Miley; **453:** Ted Smykal **456:** Daniel Guidera; **464:** Nancy Nimoy; **504:** Daniel Guidera

Photo Credits

UNIT 1
Page xviii: person crossing fingers, Heather Wright; **stack of books,** Heather Wright; **bookcase,** Jamie Kripke/Royalty_Free/Getty Images; **1A quilt,** John Warden/SuperStock; **1B teens,** Superstock; **background,** Atlantide Phototravel/Corbis; **2C athlete,** Philip & Karen Smith/Getty Images; **medal,** Duomo/Corbis; **2D house,** Michel Arnaud/Corbis; **3E metal texture,** istockphoto; **3F field,** Momatiuk- Eastcott/Corbis; **6:** (top) ©Victor Taber/Fotolia; **6:** (bottom) ©Martin Harvey/Corbis; **11:** ©Blaine Harrington III/Corbis; **12:** ©James P. Blair/Corbis; **13:** ©Bettmann/Corbis; **14:** ©James Leynse/Corbis; **20:** ©NASA; **26:** ©Time Life Pictures/Getty Images; **27:** (right) ©Swim Ink 2, LLC/Corbis; **27:** (left) ©Corbis; **29:** (right) used with permission ©Market Street Railway; **29:** (left) ©Charles E. Steinheimer/Time Life Pictures/Getty Images; **31:** ©Visions of American, LLC/Alamy; **32:** ©Mitchell Gerber/Corbis; **48:** ©Chris Lawrence; **58-59:** ©Kristy-Anne Globish/Design Pics/Corbis; **64:** (top) ©iStockphoto.com/Eric Mulherin; **64:** (bottom) ©Ken Chernus/Getty Images; **72:** ©Associated Press; **78:** ©Olaf_Kowalzik/Alamy; **79:** ©Dave G. Houser/Corbis; **81:** ©Bettmann/Corbis; **83:** ©FAN Travelstock/Alamy; **84:** ©Corbis Collection/Alamy; **86:** ©iStockphoto

UNIT 2
Page 102: signs, Superstock; **stack of books,** Heather Wright; **bookcase,** Jamie Kripke/Royalty_Free/Getty Images; **103A, island,** istockphoto; **Al Capone,** AP Photo; **gangster,** Ingram Publishing/AGE footstock; **shirt,** Rubberball/Superstock; **teen girls,** Izabela Habur/istockphoto; **104C Navajo,** Corbis; **coin,** Pearson Learning; **104D young woman,** Getty Royalty Free; **house,** Getty Royalty Free; **trunks,** Royalty Free/Corbis; **105E family,** JP Laffont/Sygma/Corbis; **brick background,** Ablestock /Alamy; flames, Istockphoto; **105F telegram,** istockphoto.com; **letter,** Istockphoto.com; **ration card,** istockphoto; **young woman,** Emely/zefa/Corbis; **handwriting,** Elise Miley; **108:** ©PhotoEuphoria; **111:** ©Wayne Abraham; **112:** (left) ©Steve Taylor/Alamy; **112:** (right) Cal Vornberger/Alamy; **113:** ©imagebroker/Alamy; **114:** (left) ©Alan Schein/Alamy; **114:** (right) ©Papilio/Alamy; **123:** ©Richard Hamilton Smith/Corbis; **124:** (middle) ©Corbis; **124:** (frame) ©Kirsty Pargeter/Fotolia; **127:** ©Joe McDonald/Corbis; **128:** ©James Randklev/Corbis; **130:** ©Maria Brzostowska/Fotolia; **131:** ©The Granger Collection, New York; **133:** (right) ©Norbert Rosing/National Geographic Image Collection; **133:** (left) ©Jeff Skopin/Fotolia; **134:** ©Paul Chesley/Getty Images; **135:** ©OlgaLIS/Fotolia; **151:** (left) ©Judith Collins/Alamy; **151:** (right) ©Judith Collins/Alamy; **151:** ©Nicholas Piccillo; **152:** ©CNP/Corbis; **153:** (right) ©Corbis Collection/Alamy; **153:** (left) Sillycoke/Alamy; **154:** (left) ©Gregg Mayer/Fotolia; **154:** ©Jason Politte/Alamy; **157:** ©Comstock Images/Alamy; **161:** ©Pierre Vauthey/Corbis Sygma; **163:** ©E.O. Hoppé/Corbis; **170:** Handout/KRT/NewsCom; **182:** ©Bettmann/Corbis; **196:** ©Reuters/Corbis

UNIT 3
Page 204: books being carried, INSADCO Photography/Alamy; **stack of books,** Heather Wright; **bookcase,** Jamie Kripke/Royalty_Free/Getty Images; **205A Anne Frank,** Anne Frank Fonds - Basel/Anne Frank House - Amsterdam/Getty Images; **house,** Horacio Villalobos/Corbis; **diary,** Anne Frank House, Amsterdam/Getty Images; **205B airplane,** AP Photo; **marketplace,** Robert Harding Picture Library Ltd/ Alamy; **gas station,** Corbis RF/agefotostock; **subway map,** Hans-Peter Merten/agefotostock; **world map,** Duncan Walker/istockphoto; **206C young woman on left,** Dennis Galante/Corbis; **young woman on right,** Mark Hunt/Superstock; **Flag of Palestine,** istockphoto; **Flag of Israel,** Holger Franke/istockphoto; **stamps,** istockphoto; **206D Frederick Douglas,** Library of Congress; Marcus Garvey, Library of Congress; **Malcolm X,** Michael Ochs Archives/Corbis; **Martin Luther King,** Flip Schulke/Corbis; **stairs,** Brian Rome/istockphoto; **207E Earth,** NASA; **stars background,** istockphoto; **satellite,** NASA; **207F skull,** Doug Mindell Photography; **train tracks,** MedioImages/Getty Images; **sparks,** istockphoto; **208:** (right) ©C Squared Studios; **208:** (left) ©Ken Lucas; **210:** ©Eva Serrabassa/iStockPhoto; **213:** ©Christine Balderas; **213:** (right) ©Stockbyte Platinum/Alamy; **214:** ©Transtock Inc./Alamy; **221:** ©Scala/Art Resource, NY; **222:** ©Chad Baker/Getty Images; **223:** ©Alfred Pasieka/Photo Researchers, Inc.; **224:** ©HannahGal/Photo Researchers, Inc.; **230:** Courtesy of the National Archives and Records Administration; **232:** ©Lori Martin/Fotolia; **248:** ©Matthias Kulka/zefa/Corbis; **252:** Thinkstock; **253:** ©Tetra Images/Alamy; **254:** (top) Bloomberg/Getty Images; **254:** (bottom) Svitlana Kazachek/Shutterstock; **254-256:** ©Photodisc; **255-256:** ©TH-Foto/zefa/Corbis; **256:** (bottom) ©Brand X Pictures/Alamy; **256:** (right) ©Diego Azubel/epa/Corbis; **256:** (middle) ©Chris Rainier/Corbis; **259:** ©The Granger Collection, New York; **261:** (right) ©AP Images/David Duprey; **261:** Courtesy National Park Service, Museum Management Program and Frederick Douglass National Historic Site. Letter to Frederick Douglass from the Department of State, FRDO 3871 http: www.cr.nps.gov/museum/exhibits/douglass/3871.htm; **262:** (top left) ©AP Images/Kathleen Lange; **262:** (middle right) ©Kean Collection/Getty Images; **262:** Courtesy National Park Service, Museum Management Program and Frederick Douglas National Historic Site. Letter from the Department of the Interior, FRDO 3863. http: www.cr.nps.gov/museum/exhibits/douglass/3863.htm; (top right) Columbian Orator, FRDO 650 Photo by Carol Highsmith. http: www.cr.nps.gov/museum/exhibits/douglass/650.htm; (middle left) Letter Authorizing African-American Troops, FRDO 3864. http: www.cr.nps.gov/museum/exhibits/douglass/3864.htm; (bottom right) Letter to Frederick Douglass from the Department of State, FRDO 3871 http: www.cr.nps.gov/museum/exhibits/douglass/3871.htm; (bottom left) Frederick Douglass at desk in Haiti, FRDO 3899 http: www.cr.nps.gov/museum/exhibits/douglass/3899.htm; (bottom middle) Letter to Frederick Douglass from

Photo and Art Credits

the Department of State, FRDO 3871 http: www.cr.nps.gov/museum/exhibits/douglass/3871.htm; **263:** ©Smithsonian American Art Museum, Washington DC/Art Resource, NY; **264:** ©AP Images/Samuel J. Miller; **270:** University of Georgia

UNIT 4
Page 284: cell phone, John Birdsall/agefotostock; **stack of books,** Heather Wright; **284 bookcase,** Jamie Kripke/Royalty_Free/Getty Images; **285B young woman walking through doorway,** Brand X Pictures/Alamy; **286C Art Spiegelman,** Jean-Christian Bourcart/Getty Images; **286D Meriweather Lewis,** Courtesy of The Library of Congress; **William Clark,** Courtesy of The Library of Congress; **compass,** National Museum of American History; Smithsonian Institution; **map,** Corbis; **287E church,** Kevin Fleming/Corbis; **torn piece of paper,** Trevor Hunt/istockphoto.com; **silhouette,** istockphoto; **287F baseball,** istockphoto; **trumpet,** istockphoto; **young woman,** Blend Images/ Superstock; **young man,** Digital Vision Ltd./Superstock; **beach,** istockphoto; **290:** ©Corey Rich/Getty Images; **291:** ©Otto Steininger/Getty Images; **294:** (right) ©Burke/Triolo Productions/Brand X/Corbis; **295:** (bottom) ©EuToch/Fotolia; **295:** (top) ©Khwi/Fotolia; **296:** ©Images.com/Corbis; **301:** ©John Foxx/2005 Getty Images; **302:** ©Purestock/Alamy; **303:** ©Powered by Light/Alan Spencer/Alamy; **304:** ©dbox for the Lower Manhattan Developement Corporation/Corbis; **306:** ©Jan Cobb Photography Ltd/Getty Images; **308:** ©Travis Rowan/Alamy; **309:** (top) ©Martin Shields/Alamy; **309:** (bottom) ©Paul C. Pet/zefa/Corbis; **310:** ©Nick Kirk/Alamy; **313:** ©iStockphoto; **329:** ©Onur Döngel/iStockphoto; **330:** (left) Gareth Byrne/Alamy; **330:** (bottom) 1000 Words/Shutterstock; **331:** ©Mika/zefa/Corbis; **332:** ©James Leynse/Corbis; **335:** ©C Squared Studios/Getty Images; **337:** ©Steve Bly/Alamy; **338:** ©Chuck Pefley/Alamy; **339:** (top) ©Blue Lantern Studio/Corbis; **339:** (bottom) ©Dennie Cody/Getty; **340:** ©Butch Martin/Getty; **341:** Time & Life Pictures/Getty Images; **342:** ©Arthur Morris/Corbis; **344:** ©Workbook Stock/Ejen Chuang/Jupiter; **347:** ©Rebecca Ellis/iStockphoto; **349:** ©E. Simanor/Robert Harding World Imagery/Corbis; **350:** ©Scott Gibson/Corbis; **351:** ©Goodshoot/Corbis; **352:** ©Roger Whitemay/iStockphoto

UNIT 5
Page 366: fingerprints, Elise Miley; **stack of books,** Heather Wright; **bookcase,** Jamie Kripke/Royalty_Free/Getty Images; **367A fence,** Heather Wright; **young man,** Radius Images/Jupiterimages; **367B Marigolds,** Garden World Images Ltd/Alamy; **pavement,** Heather Wright; **368C crowd,** Ryan Mcvay/Getty Images; **Anne Frank,** Anne Frank Fonds - Basel/Anne Frank House -Amsterdam/Getty Images; **368D lockers,** Royalty Free/Corbis; **369E Helen Keller,** Corbis; **sign language chart,** Kean Collection/Getty Images; **handcuffs,** istockphoto; **handwriting,** Christopher Irion/Jupiterimages; **police tape,** istockphoto; **film,** Tetra Images/JupiterImages; **cement wall,** Heather Wright; **outline,** istockphoto; **372:** ©Robbie Jack/Corbis; **373:** ©Boden/Ledingham/Masterfile; **376-377:** ©Bettman/Corbis; **377:** (top) ©Bettmann/Corbis; **378:** ©Corbis; **379:** ©Bettmann/Corbis; **380:** (bottom) ©David Pollack/Corbis; **380:** (top) ©Corbis; **382:** ©Albo/Fotolia; **384:** ©Earl Robbins/Fotolia; **387:** ©Ewa Brozek/Fotolia; **388:** ©Bettmann/Corbis; **392:** ©The Granger Collection, New York; **398:** ©Matteo Natale/Fotolia; **403:** ©Glenda Powers; **405:** ©Dynamic Graphics/Creatas/Alamy; **406:** (top) ©Dynamic Graphics/Creatas/Alamy; **406:** (right) ©Ariel Skelley/Corbis; **406:** (bottom) ©Stocktrek Images; **410:** ©Don Hammond/Design Pics/Corbis; **411:** ©Design Pics Inc./Alamy; **412:** ©Tyler Olson/Fotolia; **414:** ©John Kelly/Alamy; **419:** ©Chuck Place/Alamy; **420:** (bottom middle) ©Bob Rowan; Progressive Image/Corbis; **420-421:** (bottom) ©Matt Brown/Corbis; **421:** (bottom right) ©Bob Rowan; Progressive Image/Corbis; **422:** Lynton Gardiner/Courtesy of The American Museum of Natural History/©DK Images; **431:** ©National Portrait Gallery, Smithsonian Institution/Art Resource NY; **442:** ©Image100/Corbis

UNIT 6
Page 450: Albert Einstein, Underwood Photo Archives/Superstock; **young woman,** stockbyte/Getty Images; **stack of books,** Heather Wright; **bookcase,** Jamie Kripke/Royalty_Free/Getty Images; **451A Felipe Alou,** Stephen Dunn/ Getty Images; **Antonia Novello,** Thais Llorca/epa/Corbis; **Andy Garcia,** AP Photo/Stephen Chernin; **452C baseball players,** AP Photo/Jon Sall; **crowd,** image 100/Corbis; **baseball glove,** Steve Diddle/Istockphoto; **452D iris scan,** Pasieka/Photo Researchers, Inc.; **micrograph,** Dr Jeremy Burgess/Photo Researchers, Inc.; **tennis racket strings,** Christine Gonsalves/istockphoto; **computer motherboard,** Chris Hill/ istockphoto.com; **453E microscope,** istockphoto; **shredded paper,** istockphoto; **security monitor,** istockphoto; **hand, dna,** istockphoto; **hand print,** istockphoto; **459:** ©Stockdisk Classic/Alamy; **462:** (bottom right) ©Vince Mo/Fotolia; **462:** (top) ©Kevin Curry/Getty Images; **462:** (bottom left) UK History/Alamy Images; **462:** (background) ©grivet/Shutterstock; **466:** ©Sean Locke/iStockphoto; **470:** ©Harnett/Hanzon/Getty Images; **472:** ©Chris Collins/Corbis; **473:** (right) ©Eric Isselée; **473:** (left) ©Eric Isselée; **473:** (middle) ©Eric Isselée; **477:** (left) ©Bettmann/Corbis; **477:** (top right) ©Brand X Pictures/Alamy; **477:** (top) ©Photodisc; **477:** (bottom right) ©Getty Images/Hulton Archive; **478:** (left) ©Bettmann/Corbis; **478:** (right) ©Bettmann/Corbis; **481:** (inset) ©Christie's Images/Corbis; **481 & 483-484:** (frame) ©Marcin Pasko/istockphoto; **482:** ©Harald Sund/Getty Images; **483:** ©Stapleton Collection/Corbis; **484:** (inset) ©Corbis; **486:** ©Seth Joel/Corbis; **487:** ©AP Images/Robert F. Bukaty; **488:** ©Time & Life Pictures/Getty Images; **499:** ©John Foxx; **501:** ©Photo by Hank Walker/Time Life Pictures/Getty Images; **502:** (bottom) ©Photo by Hank Walker/Time Life Pictures/Getty Images; **502:** (top) ©Robert Shetterly/Americans Who Tell the Truth, Inc.; **510:** ©Ian Shaw/Getty; **515:** ©PhotoAlto/Alamy; **527:** ©The Mariners' Museum/Corbis

Tips for Improving Reading Fluency

The tips on these pages will help you improve your reading fluency, or your ability to read easily, smoothly, and expressively.

Self-Monitoring for Comprehension

Becoming an active, aware reader will help you get the most from your assignments. Practice using the following strategies to help you monitor your comprehension.

- ▶ Set a purpose for reading beyond just completing the assignment. Then, read actively by pausing to ask yourself questions about the material as you read.

- ▶ Stop reading after a specified period of time (for example, five minutes) and summarize what you have read.

Reading Phrases

Fluent readers read phrases rather than individual words. Use the following ideas to help speed up your reading and improve your comprehension.

- ▶ Rereading increases fluency. Choose a passage of text that is neither too hard nor too easy. Read the same passage aloud several times until you can read it smoothly.

- ▶ Read aloud into a tape recorder. Then, listen to the recording, noting your accuracy, pacing, and expression. You can also read aloud and share feedback with a partner.

Understanding Key Vocabulary

Understanding the vocabulary in a reading can be essential to understanding the concepts that the reading explains. A dictionary is a good resource for finding a word's meaning, but first try these steps.

- ▶ Before you begin reading, scan the text for unfamiliar words or terms and find out what those words mean.

- ▶ While you read, use context – the surrounding words, phrases, and sentences – to help you determine the meanings of unfamiliar words.

Reading is a skill that can be improved with practice. The key to improving your fluency is to read. The more you read, the better your reading will become.